OXFORD ENGLISH NOVELS

General Editor: JAMES KINSLEY

HUGH TREVOR

THOMAS HOLCROFT

The Adventures of
HUGH TREVOR

Edited with an Introduction by
SEAMUS DEANE

LONDON
OXFORD UNIVERSITY PRESS
1973

Oxford University Press, Ely House, London W. 1

GLASGOW NEW YORK TORONTO MELBOURNE WELLINGTON
CAPE TOWN IBADAN NAIROBI DAR ES SALAAM LUSAKA ADDIS ABABA
DELHI BOMBAY CALCUTTA MADRAS KARACHI LAHORE DACCA
KUALA LUMPUR SINGAPORE HONG KONG TOKYO

ISBN 0 19 255355 0

Introduction, Notes, Bibliography, and Chronology
© Oxford University Press 1973

Printed in Great Britain
at the University Press, Oxford
by Vivian Ridler
Printer to the University

CONTENTS

Introduction   vii

Note on the Text   xiv

Select Bibliography   xv

A Chronology of Thomas Holcroft   xvii

THE ADVENTURES OF HUGH TREVOR

Volume I   I

Volume II   97

Volume III   174

Volume IV   266

Volume V   344

Volume VI   423

Explanatory Notes   497

INTRODUCTION

THOMAS HOLCROFT lives on the margins of literary fame. When he is remembered it is usually because Godwin called him one of his 'four principal oral instructors',[1] or because Coleridge regarded him as a likeably energetic if ill-equipped proponent of atheism,[2] or, most of all perhaps, because Hazlitt completed the *Memoirs* in which Holcroft had recorded the picturesque incidents of a chequered career. This merely vicarious fame is by no means undeserved. Holcroft was not, in any sense, a systematic thinker; as a playwright and translator he gained popularity but no fame; and as a novelist, he was, on occasion, a fine preacher. Even as a victim of political repression, he is now almost forgotten when the names of Hardy, Thelwall, and Tooke are remembered. But if he was not sufficiently important to be remembered by posterity, he was sufficiently well known to be made aware of his public's disapproval of the productions of one of the 'acquitted felons'.[3] After his acquittal, his reputation was so damaged that he was forced to publish his plays under an assumed name. But this stratagem failed. Holcroft had to leave England for the Continent. On his return he spent his last seven years in increasing anonymity and poverty. His life thus ended as it had begun. He progressed from obscurity to popularity (as a playwright), to notoriety (as a political radical), and to obscurity again. He has remained there since.

The first three volumes of *The Adventures of Hugh Trevor* were published early in 1794. In October of the same year, on the strength of his participation in the meetings of the Society for Constitutional

---

[1] C. Kegan Paul, *William Godwin, His Friends and Contemporaries* (1876), i. 17.

[2] *The Collected Letters of Samuel Taylor Coleridge*, ed. E. L. Griggs (1956–62), i. 138–9, 215.

[3] The phrase used by William Windham which provoked Holcroft's *Letter to William Windham* (1795).

Information, Holcroft was imprisoned in Newgate on a charge of high treason. His friend William Sharp, the original for the character of Turl in the novel, was questioned by members of the Privy Council on what passed when the Society met. The minutes record: 'He recollects *Holcroft* introduced a philosophical Disquisition about improving the human Mind—This took up a long time, and they did no business.'[1] This evidence might be unkindly taken as an appropriate epigraph for Holcroft's novels and plays. However, his 'Disquisition' yielded little damning evidence to his prosecutors. Released after eight weeks, he set about defending his innocence and trying to regain popularity with the play-going public. It was 1797 before the last three volumes of his interrupted novel were printed and sold. There is no evidence that his experience in prison induced Holcroft to revise radically the last three volumes, although the long attack on the Law in the fourth is hardly fortuitous. But his own principles denied him the luxury of revenge. Instead they imposed upon him the duty of correction. The Law in *Hugh Trevor* is no more corrupt or inhumane than any of the other professions the novel condemns. It is this determined and comprehensive exposure of the moral decay afflicting a whole society that gives the work a particularly heavy flavour of political radicalism.

As in his previous novel, *Anna St. Ives*, Holcroft is concerned with the moral revolution which good example and fortitude can effect in the heart of even a corrupt individual. But the implications of the earlier novel are limited by the fact that it is modelled upon the traditional love triangle with its normal idiom rephrased to allow for the defeat of a Gothic lust by an enlightened reason. The form favours stark oppositions; the virtuous Anna is flanked by a paragon of virtue, Frank Henley, on one side, and by the embodiment of vice, Coke Clifton, on the other. Between them the issue is resolved, amid loud exclamations, and the ideal society emerges at the close. But it is a tiny society of three members. The moulding influence of the large society is hardly felt by the three protagonists who represent subjection to that influence, or freedom from it, in a very crude and programmatic sense. In *Hugh Trevor*, the social context is much denser, and the implications of the action correspondingly wider. It opens with the corrupt society so predominant that the two central characters, Hugh Trevor and Wakefield, are ensnared by its

[1] E. Colby, *The Life of Thomas Holcroft* (1925), ii. 66.

selfish and false values. These two bear an obvious resemblance to Frank Henley and Coke Clifton, but they are more subtly conceived. They avoid becoming blunt gestures representing Virtue and Vice, managing instead to retain a certain presence throughout the novel as men whose natural affinity for one another overcomes the artificial separation created by a corrupt society. This relationship is developed in an arena of moral decision (or perhaps, more precisely, of moral compunction), which is bounded by the virtuous Turl, Olivia, Wilmot, Evelyn, Clarke, and others at one extreme, and by the corrupt Bishop, politicians, tutors, and lawyers at the other. The strong autobiographical element in the novel also helps to give many situations the impress of actuality; and these sporadic scenes are sufficiently related to the theme to subdue in some measure Holcroft's hectoring, moralistic tone. This of itself would be enough to distinguish the work from the bulk of the revolutionary novels of the decade. Not that Holcroft avoids the customary failings of the doctrinaire writer; his work is full of strident rhetoric, exclamation marks, and cautionary tales. The merits of *Hugh Trevor* as a piece of fiction are a good deal less than the book's importance as a document in the development of one strain of radical, Dissenting thought in England.

It is by virtue of his place in this tradition that Holcroft is important. Like Godwin, Paine and, to a lesser degree, Priestley, he exemplifies that radical faith which the related traditions of English Dissent and of the French Enlightenment combined to produce. That faith, well equipped doctrinally by the 1780s, needed a miracle to ignite its missionary sense. In 1789, France supplied the need. After that date, Holcroft could, without exaggeration, be called a fanatic. The torch of Truth had now to be passed to the general public in England and literature was to be its vehicle. Holcroft expounded this Truth with all the garrulity and implacable pedantry of the self-made man. Yet he gave it currency. He repeats his 'message' so often and so vehemently that there is no mistaking it.

Holcroft wanted three things: Sincerity (and not Secrecy), Benevolence (and not Self-Love), and Truth (not Ignorance). Sincerity and Benevolence were qualities to be inculcated, and Truth a goal to be attained. Truth was, at once, a Platonic Idea to be realized upon earth; a Biblical Millennium that was fast approaching; a Utopia that would inevitably be gained; and even, at times, an Eden that would, with equal inevitability, be regained. Richard

Price had already bade this great Abstraction welcome in his famous sermon at the Old Jewry in 1789,[1] but his ecstatic *Nunc dimittis* had been almost obliterated by Burke's *Reflections* and by the rapid and bloody sequence of events in France. Price, obviously no clairvoyant, was, however, a consistent thinker. But Holcroft managed to believe in an Absolute Truth while accepting the materialist epistemology which French thinkers like Helvétius and Holbach had derived from Locke.[2] All Holcroft's writings testify to his conviction that sense impressions are the sole source of ideas; that environment is the controlling influence upon human personality, that error is ignorance, the progress of mind inevitable, freedom of inquiry for all a natural right, and identical conclusions by all a happily inescapable consequence. Further, even while he accepted the Helvétian notion of man as a machine, he leaned towards the Rousseauistic conception of man as an organic being who must be allowed to evolve without artificial interference or restraint. Along with these contradictory views of man and education, Holcroft variously adopted the selfish utilitarianism of Helvétius, and the altruistic utilitarianism of the Dissenting tradition which was based on a conviction of the perennial and cosmic coincidence between Benevolence and Utility. When these contradictions are crossed by a vacillation between primitivism (regaining Eden), and Utopianism (gaining the Millennium), enhanced by a series of ethical judgements based now on emotion (in the predominantly English tradition) and now on reason (in the predominantly French mode),[3] Holcroft's thought may be, with some justice, considered a tissue of contradictions. That, however, is not an entirely damning judgement. He was a propagandist. If he was chaotically eclectic in what he chose to believe, he was fanatically single-minded in what he chose to attack. As a follower of Price, Helvétius, or Rousseau, he could, with consistency, criticize the existing political establishment in England. Its discriminations and illogicalities were to him legion. He believed, with commendable simplicity, that their elimination would automatically introduce the reign of Truth. Like Godwin, and

[1] *Discourse on the Love of Our Country* (1789).
[2] C. A. Helvétius, *De L'Esprit* (Paris, 1758), translated 1759; *De L'Homme* (Londres, 1773), translated 1777. P. T. d'Holbach, *Système de la Nature*, translated 1797; *Système Social* (Londres, 1773). The sale catalogues of Holcroft's library list these works.
[3] On this, see D. D. Raphael, *The Moral Sense* (1947).

unlike Paine, he relied on an internal moral revolution rather than on an external political upheaval to achieve this end. In the meantime, that privileged élite which had seen the light would continue to spread it, firm in the possession of the Truth, unshaken and unembittered by the hostility of those victims of error who opposed the inevitable. Holcroft was again like Godwin and even Paine in this form of secularized Calvinistic thinking.[1]

Burke's *Reflections* and Paine's *Rights of Man* dominated the political debate which raged throughout the decade. The novelists also took part. Robert Bage, Charlotte Smith, Holcroft, and Godwin were outstanding on the radical side; Isaac D'Israeli, Mrs. Elizabeth Hamilton, Charles Lucas, and many others opposed and parodied them. Pamphleteer or novelist, the radical prided himself on the forthright simplicity of his style and on the evident rationality of his arguments in contrast to the emotional (and therefore distorting) rhetoric of Burke and his friends.[2] In *Hugh Trevor*, Holcroft exemplifies this attitude. The style is at its best vigorous, colloquial, without ornament; at worst it is garrulous, exclamatory, pallid. These stylistic variations are produced by a rather hesitant separation of Reason and Passion. The passionately rational character who attacks the corruptions of society so unequivocally is always less impressive than the rationally passionate lover who exhibits all those tender sentiments which society represses. But the opposition between Reason and Passion had to be modified to allow this benevolence its due and domesticity its bliss. However, once that allowance was made, the despotic nature of social institutions could be explained in terms of destructive passion, and the paradisal benevolence of Turl, Olivia, and Evelyn in terms of enlightened reason.

On this basis, the novel mounts a relentless and anarchic attack upon the institutions of late eighteenth-century England. The Law, the Church, the Universities, the aristocracy, and Parliament are all bluntly condemned; so too is the Methodist revival, which is portrayed here as a grotesque display of demagogy and emotionalism. In so far as the novel is a social critique, it eminently achieves

[1] See M. R. Adams, *Studies in the Literary Backgrounds of English Radicalism* (1947), p. 19.
[2] See Joseph Priestley, *Letters to Burke* (1791); F. Stone, *An Examination of Burke's Reflections* (1792); R. Woolsey, *Reflections Upon Reflections* (1790). See also J. T. Boulton, *The Language of Politics in the Age of Wilkes and Burke* (1963).

that moral purpose which Holcroft believed literature should have.[1]
His opponents, of course, thought the purpose to be outrageously
specific and not at all moral.[2]

Nevertheless, *Hugh Trevor* is more than a tract or cautionary tale.
The propagandist intent certainly makes the opposition between a
damned society and a saved élite exorbitantly clear. Even on those
infrequent occasions when Holcroft exploits melodramatic con-
vention to point a moral (as in the mock-Gothic horror of the first
meeting with Mr. Evelyn, or in the emotional extravagance of the
Methodist sermon), the effect is partly spoiled by his laborious
insistence upon the moral import of the incident. Yet there is a
theme in the novel which is not surrendered to propaganda but is
largely embodied in the crucial relationship between Hugh Trevor
and the impostor, Belmont, whose real name is Wakefield. That
theme, typically, is conversion.

The situations of others echo those of Hugh and Wakefield.
The unfortunate Mr. Elford lacks that stern control over his
passions which Hugh won so slowly and Wakefield so late. Wilmot
and Hector Mowbray pallidly re-enact the conversion of the
protagonists. But the force of the book lies in the quality of its
central relationship rather than in any structural refinements, and
certainly not in the hopelessly contrived resolution. Wakefield and
Hugh do not form a simple contrast between right and wrong.
Wakefield marries Hugh's mother, treats her badly, boasts of his
selfishness and success, and yet remains strangely attractive to Hugh.
His conversion is the real triumph for the forces of reason and
goodness. But Holcroft goes to such elaborate lengths to interweave
the fate of these two characters that it becomes gradually apparent
that Wakefield is, in fact, only another aspect of Hugh Trevor, or,
more accurately, another aspect of the problem involved in Hugh's
struggle for integrity and truth. One can accept the moral that
secrecy is bad and leads to difficulty, while open-hearted sincerity
will always win the day. But the almost lavish concern Holcroft
shows for the strangely contorted relationship seems to spring from
a deeper source. Hugh, by nature good, need only be shown the
light to follow it. Wakefield, however, is apparently bad by nature;
he sees the truth and spurns it. Holcroft in fact avoids the severe
implication that human nature might be radically corrupt. Instead

[1] Cf. *Memoirs of Bryan Perdue: a Novel* (1805), Preface, p. iii.
[2] *Critical Review*, xiii (1795), 139–40; *The Anti-Jacobin Review*, i (1798), 52–4.

he poses the problem in this form: given a man like Wakefield, immune to the normal retributory evils of gout and self-reproach, can it be claimed that crime does in fact pay? The problem then demands from Holcroft some form of retribution for an unsocial act which is secret—exactly the same problem Godwin was dealing with in *Caleb Williams*, which was being written at approximately the same time. Holbach had, much earlier, raised the problem in more plainly theoretical form in his *Système Social*. In all three cases, the answer is the same: the secret criminal is punished by the interminable remorse of his own guilty conscience.[1] Holcroft and Godwin both emphasize that this is a much more severe punishment than anything society could inflict. The solution is also acceptable because instinctive remorse implies instinctive goodness. In Wakefield this goodness eventually triumphs, not because he is intellectually awakened to the truth like Hugh, but because he is emotionally awakened to it. The remorse we must believe simply on Wakefield's assertion of it. In contrast to *Caleb Williams*, there is no concentration upon the sufferings of the tortured conscience. Consequently, Wakefield's conversion carries little force; his intellectual defence of selfishness does not compare with Ferdinando Falkland's defence of the feudal conception of honour. Wakefield marries that damp and virtuous female Miss Wilmot; Falkland dies, his reputation in ruins. The resolution in each case is in accord with the intensity with which the respective moral dilemmas are realized. Holcroft failed to see his problem in focus. In bringing back Mr. Elford and setting Hugh comfortably into the society he had been castigating for six volumes, he reduced the conclusion to near-farce. Holcroft himself later regretted the ending.[2] However, even although melodrama, propaganda, and inflated rhetoric rob the novel of a great deal of its potential force, it nevertheless deserves to be remembered along with *Caleb Williams* as a work in which the peculiar moral preoccupations and political fervour of one kind of English Dissenting and utilitarian thought found notable expression.

[1] *Système Social* (1773), i. 157. *Things as They Are; or, the Adventures of Caleb Williams*, ed. D. McCracken (London, 1970), p. 325.
[2] *Colby*, ii. 238. See also *Critical Review*, xxi (1797), 189.

NOTE ON THE TEXT

THE text is printed from the British Museum copy of the first edition (12; 1794–7), collated with the so-called third edition of 1801. The absence of a true second edition is explained by Elbridge Colby in his *Bibliography* (1922). Holcroft was in Paris in 1801 and could not have supervised the edition of that year; he made no alterations, nor does he seem to have envisaged any. A few obvious printer's errors and discrepancies have been corrected. The Preface and the paragraph 'On my return . . . useful to society' (p. 230) were omitted in *1801*.

SELECT BIBLIOGRAPHY

There is no collected edition of Holcroft's work.

BIBLIOGRAPHY. Elbridge Colby, *A Bibliography of Thomas Holcroft* (New York Public Library, 1922). This is not complete.

BIOGRAPHY AND CRITICISM. The primary sources are the *Memoirs of the Late Thomas Holcroft*, completed by Hazlitt from Holcroft's autobiographical writings, 3 vols. (1816), and Kegan Paul's *William Godwin, his Friends and Contemporaries*, 2 vols. (1876). The *Memoirs* were reprinted in 1852 in Longman's Travellers' Library, and in 1926 in the World's Classics series; they also form the third volume of P. P. Howe's edition of Hazlitt's *Complete Works* (1932). There is no modern biography; but there is a greatly expanded edition of the *Memoirs* in Elbridge Colby's *Life of Thomas Holcroft*, 2 vols. (1925). Since then, there have been some close studies of various aspects of Holcroft's career, among them, T. V. Benn, 'Holcroft in France', *Revue de Littérature Comparée*, vi (1926), 331–7; John Hennig, 'Trenck and Britain', *Modern Language Review*, xli (1946), 393–407; S. S. Morgan, 'The Damning of Holcroft's *Knave or Not?*' and O'Keefe's *She's Eloped, Huntington Library Quarterly*, xxii (1958), 51–62.

For early criticism, see the *Monthly Review*, xvi (January 1795); *Critical Review*, xxi (February 1795); *Anti-Jacobin Review and Magazine*, i (July 1798). Among modern studies: Allene Gregory, *The French Revolution and the English Novel* (New York, 1915), pp. 49 ff; Elbridge Colby, 'Thomas Holcroft, Man of Letters', *South Atlantic Quarterly* (January 1923), 53–70; C. B. A. Proper, *Social Elements in English Prose Fiction Between 1700 and 1832* (Amsterdam, 1929), pp. 92–118; J. M. S. Tompkins, *The Popular Novel in England, 1770–1800* (1932), pp. 300–6; Lois Whitney, *Primitivism and the Idea of Progress in English Popular Literature of the Eighteenth Century* (Baltimore, 1934), pp. 248–55; M. R. Adams, *Studies in the Literary Backgrounds of English Radicalism* (Lancaster, Penn., 1947; Franklin and Marshall College Studies, no. 5); V. R. Stallbaumer, 'Thomas Holcroft: a satirist in the stream of sentimentalism', *English Literary History*, iii (1936), 31–62; 'Holcroft's Influence on *Political Justice*', *Modern Language Quarterly*, xiv (1953), 21–30; 'Thomas Holcroft as a Novelist', *English Literary History*, xv (1948), 194–218; R. M. Baine, *Thomas Holcroft and the Revolutionary Novel* (Athens, Georgia, 1965). For the tradition of English Dissenting thought, Sir A. H. Lincoln's *Some Political and Social Ideas of English Dissent, 1763–1800* (1938) is valuable.

A CHRONOLOGY OF
THOMAS HOLCROFT

		Age
1745	Born in Orange Court, Leicester Fields, London; father a shoemaker	
1751–64	Father fails in business, family travels about country, peddling. Holcroft, taught to read by his father, becomes a stable-boy and jockey at Newmarket, an apprentice shoemaker in London	5–18
1764	Taught reading in a school in Liverpool	18
1765–70	Married, returns to London as a shoemaker. Contributions to *The Whitehall Evening Post*. Daughter born. Dismissed from post as secretary to Granville Sharpe for visits to a 'spouting club'	19–24
1770	Acts at the Haymarket; goes as prompter to Dublin with the actor-manager Macklin	24
1771	Returns to England, becomes strolling player, tours England and Scotland with various companies for the following six years	25
1772	First wife dies; marries for second time	26
1773–5	Son, William, and daughter, Sophy, born. Second wife dies	27–9
1777	Returns to London; marries for third time	31
1778	Employed in minor parts by Sheridan at Drury Lane. *Manthorn, the Enthusiast*, a novel, published anonymously in *The Town and Country Magazine*. His first play, *The Crisis, or Love and Fear*, produced once at Drury Lane; badly received	32–3
1780	Daughter, Fanny, born. *Alwyn, or the Gentleman Comedian*, a novel, published; also a pamphlet on the Gordon Riots	34
1781	His play *Duplicity* has some success at Covent Garden. Holcroft forsakes acting for authorship	35
1782–3	In Paris, as correspondent; secretarial duties for English ambassador; collects material for translation; meets leading figures of the salons	36–7
1784	Returns to London; edits *The Wit's Magazine*, which contained illustrations by William Blake. Goes to Paris, and pirates *Le Mariage de Figaro* by Beaumarchais	38

Age

1785–6   Meets William Godwin; becomes friendly with a large group
of radicals, including David Williams, Joel Barlow, Thomas
Paine, Mary Wollstonecraft, James Mackintosh   39–40

1789   Translates *The Life of Baron Frederick Trenck* and Lavater's
Essays on Physiognomy. His son, William, caught by Holcroft
in attempted flight, commits suicide   43

1789–90   Translation of *Posthumous Works of Frederick II, King of
Prussia* (13 vols.)   43–4

1791   A member of the committee which agreed to publish Paine's
Rights of Man. *The Road to Ruin*, his most successful play,
performed; it opens the season in Covent Garden again in
1792   45

1792   *The Road to Ruin*; ten editions in print one year after publica-
tion. *Anna St. Ives*, a novel (7 vols.). Begins contributing to
The Monthly Review; becomes a member of the Society for
Constitutional Information   46

1794   First three volumes of *The Adventures of Hugh Trevor*.
Indicted for High Treason, spends eight weeks in Newgate,
is acquitted without the charge being preferred   48

1795   *A Narrative of Facts Relating to a Prosecution for High Treason*.
Rebukes William Windham in a public letter   49

1797   Last three volumes of *Hugh Trevor*; first three reissued as a
'second edition'. Death of his father   51

1798   His play *Knave or Not?* has a hostile reception   52

1799   Marries for the fourth time; wife Louisa Mercier, niece of the
French Utopian writer and disciple of Rousseau, L.-S. Mercier. Holcroft sells his library and pictures, leaves England
for Hamburg, plagued by debt, ill-luck, and public hostility
toward his work   53

1800   Begins the *European Repertory*, which fails after two numbers.
Moves to Paris for following year   54

1802   Returns to London; piracy from the French, *A Tale of Mystery*, first play in England to be called a 'melodrame'   56

1804   *Travels Through France*   58

1805   *The Memoirs of Bryan Perdue*, a novel (3 vols.). In close contact with Hazlitt   59

1806   Daughter Louisa born   60

1807   Sells library and pictures again   61

1809   Dies on 23 March at his home in London after a long illness,
during which he had dictated a large part of his *Memoirs*   63

1816   *Memoirs of the late Thomas Holcroft* completed by Hazlitt
from material provided by Holcroft's widow (3 vols.)

The Adventures of

HUGH TREVOR

——

——'TIS SO PAT TO ALL THE TRIBE
EACH SWEARS THAT WAS LEVELLED AT ME.[1]

GAY

VOLUME I

PREFACE

EVERY man of determined inquiry, who will ask, without the dread of discovering more than he dares believe, what is divinity? what is law? what is physic? what is war? and what is trade? will have great reason to doubt at some times of the virtue, and at others of the utility, of each of these different employments. What profession should a man of principle, who is anxiously desirous to promote individual and general happiness, chuse for his son? The question has perplexed many parents, and certainly deserves a serious examination. Is a novel a good mode for discussing it, or a proper vehicle for moral truth? Of this some perhaps will be inclined to doubt. Others, whose intellectual powers were indubitably of the first order, have considered the art of novel writing as very essentially connected with moral instruction. Of this opinion was the famous Turgot,[1] who we are told affirmed that more grand moral truths had been promulgated by novel writers than by any other class of men.

But, though I consider the choice of a profession as the interesting question agitated in the following work, I have endeavoured to keep another important inquiry continually in view. This inquiry is, the growth of intellect. Philosophers have lately paid much attention to the progress of mind; the subject is with good reason become a favourite with them, and the more the individual and the general history of man is examined the more proofs do they discover in support of his perfectability.[2] Man is continually impelled, by the vicissitudes of life, to great vicissitudes of opinion and conduct. He is a being necessarily subject to change; and the inquiry of wisdom ought continually to be, how may he change for the better? From individual facts, and from them alone, can general knowledge be obtained.

Two men of different opinions were once conversing. The one

scoffed at innate ideas, instinctive principles, and occult causes: the other was a believer in natural gifts, and an active fabricator of suppositions. Suggest but the slightest hint and he would erect a hypothesis which no argument, at least none that he would listen to, could overthrow. So convinced was he of the force of intuitive powers, and natural propensities, as existing in himself, that, having proposed to write a treatise to prove that apple trees might bear oysters, or something equally true and equally important, he was determined he said to seek for no exterior aid or communication, from books, or things, or men; being convinced that the activity of his own mind would afford intuitive argument, of more worth than all the adulterated and suspicious facts that experience could afford.

To this his antagonist replied, he knew but of one mode of obtaining knowledge; which was by the senses. Whether this knowledge entered at the eye, the ear, the papillary nerves, the olfactory, or by that more general sense which we call feeling, was, he argued, of little consequence; but at some or all of these it must enter, for he had never discovered any other inlet. If however the system of his opponent were true, he could only say that, in all probability, his intended treatise would have been written in the highest perfection had he begun and ended it before he had been born.[1]

If this reasoning be just, I think we may conclude that the man of forty will be somewhat more informed than the infant, who has but just seen the light. Deductions of a like kind will teach us that the collective knowledge of ages is superior to the rude dawning of the savage state; and if this be so, of which I find it difficult to doubt, it surely is not absolutely impossible but that men may continue thus to collect knowledge; and that ten thousand years hence, if this good world should last so long, they may possibly learn their alphabet in something less time than we do even now, in these enlightened days.[2]

For these reasons, I have occasionally called the attention of the reader to the lessons received by the principal character of the following work, to the changes they produced in him, and to the progress of his understanding. I conclude with adding that in my opinion, all well written books, that discuss the actions of men, are in reality so many histories of the progress of mind; and, if what I now suppose be truth, it is highly advantageous to the reader to be aware of this truth.

CHAPTER I

My birth: Family dignity insulted: Resentment of my grandfather: Parental traits of character

THERE are moments in which every man is apt to imagine, that the history of his own life is the most important of all histories. The gloom and sunshine, with which my short existence has been chequered, lead me to suppose that a narrative of these vicissitudes may be interesting to others, as well as to myself.

In the opinion of some people, my misfortunes began before I was born. The rector of * * *, my grandfather, was as vain of his ancestry, as a German baron: and perhaps with no less reason, being convinced that Adam himself was his great progenitor. My mother, not having the fear of her father before her eyes, forgetful of the family dignity, disgraced herself, and contaminated the blood of her offspring, by marrying a farmer's son. Had she married a gentleman, what that very different being, which a gentleman doubtless must have generated, might have been, is more than I, as I now am, can pretend to divine. As it is, however low it may sink me in the reader's opinion, truth obliges me to own, I am but of a mongrel breed.

The delinquency of my mother was aggravated by the daringness of her disobedience; for the rector, having a foresight of what was likely to happen, had laid his express command on her never to see Hugh Trevor, my father, more, on the very night that she eloped. Add to which, she had the example of an elder sister, to terrify her from such dereliction of duty; who, having married a rake, had been left a widow, poor, desolate, and helpless, and obliged to live an unhappy dependent on her offended father. 'I'll please my eye though I break my heart,' said my mother.

She kept her word. Young Hugh was an athletic, well proportioned, handsome man; of a sanguine temper, prone to pleasure, a frequenter of wakes and fairs, and much addicted to speculate; particularly in cards, cocking, and horse-racing.

Discarded by the rector, who was obstinately irreconcileable, my mother went with her husband to reside in the house of her father-in-law. Folly visits all orders of men. Farmers, as well as lords and rectors, can be proud of their families. The match was considered as an acquisition of dignity to the house of Trevor; and my mother, bringing such an addition of honour, was most graciously received.

Here she remained something more than a year; and here, ten months after the marriage, I was born. I had not openly assumed the form which the vanity of man has dignified with divine above a fortnight, before my grandfather, Trevor, died. He had been what is usually called a good father; had lived in reputation, and had brought up a large and expensive family. But as good in this sense usually signifies indulgent, not wise, he had rather afforded his children the means, and taught them the art, of spending money than of saving. His circumstances were suspected, the creditors were hasty to prefer their claims, and it soon appeared that he had died insolvent. The family was consequently dispersed, and I, thus early, was in danger of being turned, a poor, wailing, imbecil wanderer, on a world in which the sacred rights of *meum* and *tuum* daily suffer thousands to perish.

Fortunately, considering the exigence of the moment, my father, who was enterprising, adroit, and loquacious, prevailed on some friends to lend him money to stock the farm, of the lease of which he was now in possession. In this he succeeded the more easily, because he had already acquired the character of an excellent judge of agricultural affairs. He was known to be acute at driving bargains, could value sheep, heifers, steers, and bullocks better than a Leicestershire drover, was an excellent judge of horse flesh, and, during his father's life, had several times proved he knew the exact moment of striking earnest. Had fate sent him to a minister's levee instead of a market for quadrupeds, he would have been a great politician! He would have bought and sold with as much dexterity as any dealer in black cattle the kingdom can boast!

At the first approach of misfortune, my mother had felt great despondency; but when she saw her young husband so active, animated, and fruitful in resource, her hopes presently began to brighten. The parish where the rector resided was four miles from Trevor farm, and the desolate prospect that at first presented itself to the imagination of my mother had induced her to write, with no little contrition, and all the pathos she could collect, to implore pardon for her offence. But in vain. Her humiliation, intreaties, and dread of want, excited sensations of triumph and obduracy, but not of compassion, in the bosom of the man of God. The rector was implacable: his pride was wounded, his prejudices insulted, and his anger rouzed. He had, beside, his own money in his own pocket, and there he was willing it should remain. Now we all know that pride, prejudice, anger, and avarice, are four of the most perverse imps the *dramatis personae* of the passions can afford. The irreparable wrong done to the family dignity, and the proper vengeance it became parental authority to inflict, on such presumption as my father had been guilty of, and such derogatory meanness as that of my mother, were inexhaustible themes.

The severity of her father rendered the fortunate efforts of her husband tenfold delightful. They mutually exulted in that futurity that should enable them to set the unkind rector at defiance; and Hugh often boasted he would prove, though but a farmer, that the blood in his veins was as warm, and perhaps as pure, as that of any proud parson's in the kingdom.

These were pleasant and flourishing but fleeting days. My father, when he went to the fair to purchase his team, happened to see a fine hunter on sale. It was a beautiful beast. Who could forbear to prefer him and his noble form, high blood, and spirited action, to the slouching dull and clumsy cart-horse? Hugh Trevor was not a man so deficient in taste; he therefore, instead of a team of five, brought home three horses for the plough, and this high bred hunter for his pleasure. My mother herself, when she saw the animal, and heard her husband's encomiums, could not but admire; nay she had even some inclination to approve: especially when she listened to what follows.

'My dear Jane,' said my father to her, after alighting from the back of his hunter, which he had walked, trotted, and galloped, to convince her how perfect he was in all his paces, 'My dear Jane, we have an excellent farm; the land is in good condition, the fences sound, and the soil rich: no man in this county understands seeding, cropping, and marketing better than I do: we shall improve our stock and double our rent' (it was a hundred and fifty pounds per annum) 'the first year. I shall soon meet with a smart nag, fit for the side saddle, and shall easily make you a good horse woman; and then, when the seed is in the ground, we may be allowed to take a little pleasure. Perhaps we may ride by the rector's door, and if he should not ask us in we will not break our hearts. Who knows but, in time, we may have cause to be as purse proud as himself?'

My father, as it appears, was sanguine, high spirited, and not without resentment. My mother, though her fancy was not quite so active, did not think his reasoning much amiss; and recollected the jaunts they were to take between seed time and harvest with complacency.

CHAPTER II

Progress of my education, and conjectures on its consequences

Bold in his projects, lucky in his bargains, and fertile in resources, every thing, for a time, which my father undertook, seemed to prosper.

In the interim, I grew apace; and, according to the old phrase, was my father's pride and my mother's joy. His free humour, and the delight she took in exhibiting her boy, had occasioned me, in early infancy, to be handed from arm to arm, and so familiarized to a variety of countenances, as soon to be entirely exempted from the usual fears of children. My father's bargains and sales brought me continually acquainted with strange faces. He was vain of me, fond of having me with him, and, as he called it, of case-hardening me. I became full of prattle, inquisitive, had an incessant flow of spirits, and often put interrogatories so whimsical, or so uncommon, as to make myself remarkably amusing.

From inclination, indeed, and not from plan, my father took some trouble in my education; which I suspect was productive of unforeseen effects. He played with me as a cat does with her kitten, and taught me all the tricks of which he was master. They were chiefly indeed of a bodily kind; such as holding me over his head erect on the palm of his hand; putting me into various postures; making me tumble in as many ways as he could devise; pitching me on the back of his hunter, and accustoming me to sit on full trot; with abundance of other antics, at which he found me apt; yet, being accompanied with laughter and shouts, and now and then a hard knock, they tended, or I am mistaken, not only to give bodily activity, but to awaken some of the powers of mind; among which one of the foremost is fortitude. Insomuch that, since I have had the honour to become a philosopher, I have begun to doubt whether, hereafter, when the world shall be wiser, the art of tumbling may not possibly supercede the art of dancing ? But this by the by.

Nor was my mother, on her part, altogether deficient in activity. Exclusive of providing me with a sister, who from some accident or other was but a puling, wrangling, rickety young lady, she initiated me in the mysteries and pleasures of the alphabet. The rector had taken some trouble to make his daughters good English scholars; and my mother, though she had retained much of his solemn song, could not only read currently, and articulate clearly, but made some attempts to understand what she read. It must be acknowledged, however, that her efforts were but feeble.

I know not how it happened that I very early became in love with this divine art, but such was the fact. I could spell boldly at two years and a half old, and in less than six months more could read the collects, epistles, and gospels, without being stopped by one word in twenty. Soon afterward I attacked the Bible, and in a few months the tenth chapter of Nehemiah[1] himself could not terrify me. My father bought me many tragical ditties; such as Chevy Chace, the Children in the Wood, Death and the Lady, and, which were infinitely the richest gems in my library, Robin Hood's Garland, and the History of Jack the Giant-killer.[2] To render these treasures more captivating, observing the delight it gave me, he used sometimes to sing the adventures of Robin Hood with me; whether to the right tunes, or to music of his own composing, is more than I know.

By accidents of this and the like kind, I became so much my father's play-thing, and toy, that, his affairs then going on prosperously, he put me in breeches before I was four years old, bought me a pony, which he christened Gray Bob, buckled me to the saddle for safety, and with a leading rein used frequently to take me with him to markets, fairs, and races.

But, before I proceed to relate more of my infantine adventures, it will be necessary to introduce a kinsman of mine to the reader's acquaintance; of whom, though the alliance were now of some standing, he has yet never heard.

CHAPTER III

Rational courtship, and prudent views of widowed lovers: A
strange doubt hinted: The husband's code: Laws are quickly
prescribed, and Yes is easily said

I HAVE already mentioned my aunt, her imprudent first marriage,
the rector's resentment, who used to pronounce himself the most
unfortunate of men, in undutiful children, and her irksome
dependence on his bounty. With this aunt Mr. Elford, a man of
much worth, considerable knowledge, and great integrity of
intention, became acquainted, and by a variety of motives was
prompted to pay her his addresses.

No people are so certain of the happiness of a state of wedlock as
a couple courting. Some difference however must be made, between
lovers who have never married, and lovers who, having made the
experiment, find it possible that a drop of gall may now and then
embitter the cup of honey. My aunt's first husband had been a man
of an easy disposition, and readily swayed to good or ill. She had
seldom suffered contradiction from him, or heard reproach. A kind
of good humoured indolence had accustomed him rather to ward off
accusation with banter, or to be silent under it, than to contend.
His extravagance had obliged her to study the strictest economy;
she, therefore, was the ostensible person; she regulated, she
corrected, she complained. She had a tincture of the rector in her
composition, and her husband's follies afforded sufficient opportunities for the exercise of her office.

After his death, which happened early, the wrecks of his originally
small fortune, scarcely afforded her subsistence for a year. By many
humble but grating concessions on her part, and no less proud
upbraidings on the part of her father, she was first allowed a trifling
annuity, almost too scanty to afford the means of life, and, as it were
in resentment to the unpardonable conduct of my mother, was
afterward permitted to return to the parsonage house.

The state of subjection in which she was kept, the dissatisfaction
this evidently created, the gloom that was visible in her countenance,
and that seemed to oppress her heart, added to a disconsolate and
habitual taciturnity, soon occasioned Mr. Elford to consider her
with compassion: and the very question—can I not afford her relief?
gave birth to ideas of a still more tender nature.

These were seconded by a retrospect to his own situation. He had lost a beloved wife, who had left him an infant daughter, in whose future felicity he was strongly interested. He had often considered the subject of education, and had become the determined enemy of boarding-schools, where every thing is taught and nothing understood; where airs, graces, mouth primming, shoulder-setting and elbow-holding are studied, and affectation, formality, hypocrisy, and pride are acquired; and where children the most promising are presently transformed into vain, pert misses, who imagine that to perk up their heads, turn out their toes, and exhibit the ostentatious opulence of their relations, in a tawdry ball night dress, is the summit of perfection.

Determined that his child should be sent to no such academy, he considered a second marriage as necessary. Though an excellent economist, he was utterly a stranger to avarice. My aunt was neither rich, nor handsome, nor young; being, according to the rector's account, on the debtor side of his books, of an adust[1] complection, atrabilarious[2] in look and temper, thirty-four, and two years older than Mr. Elford. But he imagined he could make her happy; or at least could relieve her from a state little less than miserable. He likewise supposed that she was well fitted to promote plans which he held to be wise. Errors in moral calculations frequently escape undetected, even by the most accurate.

But, as he was very sincere and honest in his intentions, he thought proper, while paying his court to her, to explain what his expectations were, and the reasons on which they were grounded. His system was, there must be government; and, if government, there must be governors. This by the by I believe to be a radical mistake in politics; though I likewise believe there is not one man in fifty thousand who would not scoff at me for the supposition. Proceeding in his hypothesis, he concluded that the strongest understanding had a prescriptive and inherent right to govern; and with great candour, thus laying down the law to my aunt, he undisguisedly avowed a conviction that his understanding was the strongest, and that to govern would be his inherent right.

His words were so powerful, his arguments so excellent, his statement of them so clear, and all his deductions so indubitable, that my aunt had not the least objection to offer. 'That must be allowed—that cannot be denied—nothing can be more reasonable' —were her continual answers.

The consequence of all this was a marriage: and my aunt having been noted for her prudence, during the life of her first husband, (though not indeed in having made him her husband) and Mr. Elford's character, for propriety, rectitude and good intention, being still more permanently established, there was not the least doubt entertained, especially by the parties, but that this would be a happy match.

Having thus brought the reader and Mr. Elford together, I must now proceed to relate the manner in which I myself and my good uncle first became acquainted.

CHAPTER IV

My curiosity leads me into danger, but introduces me to a friend, who discovers that he is my uncle

IN the month of August, and the city of *****, a fair is annually held, in which, during those halcyon days of prosperity, my father was an active trafficker. Thither the neighbouring gentry, yeomanry, and dealers in general, repaired, as the best mart in the county, at which to expend their money. It was fifteen miles from Trevor farm.

Curiosity is an incessant impulse to youth. I intreated to go, and my petition was favourably received. When we were there, in consequence of some bargain or sale, it happened that my father had occasion to ride, with a farmer, to a place at some distance from the fair, and in the interim to leave me in the care of the bar-maid of the inn, at which we had put up.

He had not been long gone before I, eager to see what could be seen, broke loose from my keeper, who was too busy to pay much attention to me, and strolled into the throng. I wandered about, without any suspicion of danger, from place to place, I know not how long, to drink in all the knowledge that could enter at my eyes.

How I came there I cannot tell, but at last it appears I had rambled into a coffee-house, put questions to the guests, who found amusement in the novelty of my undaunted air, appearance, and prattle, and, having taken up a newspaper and begun to display my talent, was placed upon a table to read it aloud to the company.

The astonished farmers could scarcely believe their ears, so much was I, a four-year-old child, their superior in learning. Some of them were not certain that I was not an imp of Satan, so utterly did my performance exceed credibility. My beauty too at this age was uncommon; my limbs were straight and strong, my cheeks of the purest red and white, and my full flaxen hair hung in short ringlets down my neck. The mistress and bar-maid kissed me, the men gave me money, and they all eagerly enquired who I was, where I was going, and how I had come there.[1]

In the height of this scene it happened that Mr. Elford came in, who, though two years married to my aunt, till that time had never seen me. Though his understanding prevented any stupid wonder, yet he felt uncommon emotion for a child, unknown to everybody, yet happy and fearless, and so attractive in manners, form, and intelligence. He asked, what was my name? I answered, little Hugh. From whence did I come? From home—Who brought me? Gray Bob.—Where was I going? To see the fair.

In the midst of these interrogatories, a beggar, with a child at her back, and another that she led, came into the coffee-room. In one hand I had a cake, given me by one of the company, which I had begun to eat; and in the other the money, that the kindness and amazement of my auditors had forced upon me. The woman intreated piteously for relief; and the landlord, angry that his guests should be disturbed, advanced to turn her out. She again intreated with great earnestness for charity. That she inspired me with some share of pity, seems certain for I held out my hand with the money to her, and said—Here!

Pleased with my promptness, Mr. Elford bade her take it, and she obeyed. The child at her back, seeing my cake, stretched out its arm; I understood its language, and was going to give it the cake, but checked myself, and said, No; you must not have all; your brother must have a bit; and broke it between them. Seized with one of those emotions, to which some few people are subject, Mr. Elford snatched me in his arms, kissed me, and exclaimed— My good boy, I prophecy thou wilt one day be a brave fellow!

Just as this was passing, the city bellman took his stand opposite the coffee-house door; and, with his *O yes*, gave notice that I was lost; concluding with a description of my age, dress, name, and place of abode.

Mr. Elford immediately conjectured his business, went to listen, was struck when he heard the particulars, and hastily returned to ask me if my name was Hugh Trevor? I answered, yes; little Hugh. He instantly ran after the bellman, told him the boy was found, and I was conducted by Mr. Elford and the bellman, with a crowd in their retinue, back to my terrified father; between whom and my uncle an acquaintance from this time commenced.

CHAPTER V

Benevolent stratagem of my uncle defeated by the unlucky and foolish triumph of my father: The anger and oath of the rector

MR. ELFORD cultivated a small estate of his own, lying about ten miles from Trevor farm, and beyond that village of which my grandfather was the spiritual guide. The daughter for whose sake he had first been prompted to marry again was dead, and this perhaps was one cause that strengthened his affection for me. He frequently rode over to visit us, made himself my play-mate and favourite, encouraged a greater degree of intimacy between the sisters, who were not too cordially inclined toward each other, and soon obtained permission to take me home with him for a fortnight. The disposition he shewed to aid my father, and the possibility that I might one day be his heir, readily induced my parents to comply.

Mr. Elford, as his history will shew, was perhaps liable to greater mistakes than might have been expected from a man of so much understanding, ardour, and goodness of intention; but, though like other men occasionally blind to his own errors, he could not but feel pain at the obduracy of the rector's conduct toward my mother. For this reason, on my first visit to his house, he concerted a plan by which he hoped to effect a reconciliation. From the incidents that occurred, I think it probable that he would have accomplished his purpose, had it not been for a trick that my father played, by which this well meant scheme was rendered abortive.

Squire Mowbray, the lord of the manor in which lay the village where my grandfather lived, kept his coach and his post chariot. The rector, who had a secret enmity to him, or rather to that influence by which his own power was diminished, kept his coach and his post chariot too, lest he should openly avow inferiority, and his dignity be called in question. To add to these honours, he was drawn by a pair of bays.

It happened that one of these animals became unfit for service, was sold, and another was wanting as his successor. A neighbouring horse-breeder had one that was a good match, and for which the rector had bidden money, but not enough. My father, in the mean time, had purchased this and other horses of the owner; and the rector, when it was too late, sent to offer the man his own price.

The breeder made application to my father to have the horse again, with an allowance of profit; to which he consented, till he was accidentally told for whom the horse was designed. Flushed with temporary success and fallacious hopes, Hugh was happy to find an opportunity of shewing that he could resent as well as the rector, and exultingly swore he should not have the horse, if he would purchase him at his weight in gold.

The message, with a due increase of insulting aggravation, was conveyed to the divine; who was so exasperated by this audacious act of insolence and gratuitous rebellion, that he went down on his knees, and took a solemn oath never to forget or forgive the injury.

Whether this became an apostle of peace, or whether divines are all and unexceptionably apostles of peace, are questions which I do not here pretend to analyze.

Ignorant of this event, and glowing with the desire of affording me a grandfather's protection, Mr. Elford pursued his little plot. The rector had always wished for a male heir, the offspring of his own loins; but in this he had not been indulged, by those powers that regulate such matters. A son of his own being therefore past hope, Mr. Elford imagined he might perhaps find consolation in the succedaneum[1] of a grandson.

Accordingly, a few days after my arrival at his house, where I was to stay a fortnight, he invited the rector, who had never yet seen me, to dinner. Without telling him who I was, my uncle made me so diverting, by the art with which he knew how to manage me, that the old gentleman, quite surprized, declared I was a very extra-ordinary child.

So fearless and free was my behaviour, that the rector and I presently became familiar. I shook hands with him, sat on his knee, felt in his pocket, gave him the history of Gray Bob, and asked for a penny to buy me a whip. My request being granted, I wanted immediately to have a horse saddled, that I might ride to market, and make my purchase; and the good humour with which I received the information, that this was a favour not to be obtained, further gained on the old theologian's heart. I asked if he had a horse. He answered, yes, he had many horses; and that if I would go home with him, he would let me ride them all. Come, let us go, said I, taking hold of his hand, and pulling him.

Mr. Elford, waiting for the proper moment, and interrupting me, asked my grandfather—'If you, Sir, had but such a little fellow of your own, what would you do with him?'—'Do!' exclaimed the rector: 'I would make a man of him. Oh that he had been mine twenty years ago!'—'And why not, O that he were mine now?' answered Mr. Elford—'I could be well contented that he were.' As he said this, the rector, strange to tell, sighed—'Your wishes then are gratified,' continued Mr. Elford: 'he is your own.'—'How?'—'Your grandson!'

The reverend pastor was taken by surprise. Certain associations had been set afloat, and the desire of realizing the vision had for a moment obliterated the recollection of revenge. 'Go, Hugh,' said Mr. Elford, 'and kiss your grandfather.' Without asking any questions, or shewing the least token of reluctance, I went up to him, as I was bidden, to give the kiss; but my good-humoured face, stretched out arms, and projecting chin, were presented in vain: the words Hugh and grandfather had conjured up the fiend, and the rector sat motionless.

Not accustomed to meet and therefore not expecting repulse, I climbed up his chair, stayed myself by the breast of his coat, and sat down on his knee. The recollection of his daughter's crime, his contaminated blood, and the insufferable insolence of my father, came strongly upon him. He scowled at me, seized me by the arms, flung me from him with something like violence, and walked hastily out of the house.

The tide of passion ran so high that he would not stay to dine, but departed, muttering anger at the conduct of Mr. Elford, and repeating asseverations of eternal resentment and maledictions against undutiful children.

Mr. Elford felt an emotion something stronger than grief, to see a pastor of the flock of Christ thus cherish the spirit of persecution. On me the scene made but little impression. I had no apprehension that the day was coming, when this inflexible guide of Christians would find his prayers effectual, and his prophecies of vengeance fulfilled. How could I know that there was so hateful a vice as malignity? The holy seer did not indeed indulge his wrath quite so far as Elisha, at least not openly; he did not curse me in the name of the Lord, nor did she-bears come out of the wood to devour me;[1] but I soon enough had my share of misfortune. Preachers of peace, it appears, were always irritable: but to do them justice, I believe they are something less so now than they were of old.

CHAPTER VI

My different preceptors and early propensities: I ride to hunt with my father, which is productive of a strange and terrible adventure

MY father's affairs still continued to wear the appearance of success, and by the aid of Mr. Elford, he extended his speculations. For some few years my time passed merrily away. Under the tuition of my father, I gained health, strength, and intrepidity; and was taught to sip ale, eat hung beef, ride like a hero, climb trees, run, jump, and swim; that, as he said, I might face the world without fear. I grew strong of muscle, and my thews and sinews became alert and elastic in the execution of their office.

To my uncle I was indebted for hints and notions of a more refined and elevated nature. By familiar instances, he endeavoured to make me distinguish between resisting wrongs and revenging them; and to feel the pleasure, not only of aiding the weak, but of pardoning the vanquished.

From the books which I found in his house, I likewise early acquired a religious propensity, which was encouraged by my aunt with all her power, and seconded by my mother. Their education, and the dogmas they had heard from the rector, had given them very high notions of the dignity of the clerical character; in the superior presence of which, temporal things, laymen, and civil magistracy itself, sunk into insignificance. The perusal of Fox's Book of Martyrs,[2] of which I was so fond that I would sit with my aunt for hours, before I was eight years old, and read it to her, aided their efforts: and this childhood bias, as will be seen, greatly influenced my first pursuits in life. We are all the creatures of the necessities under which we exist. The history of man is but the history of these necessities, and of the impulse, emotion, or mind, by them begotten.[1] Of the incidents of my childhood, that which made the deepest impression upon me I am now going to relate.

The daring Hugh, my father, who feared no colours,[2] had long been accustomed, whenever he could find time, and often indeed when he could not, to follow the fox hounds, and hunt with his landlord, the Squire himself. Among his other bargains, he had lately bought one of the Squire's brood mares, Bay Meg, that had been sold because she had twice cast her foal. On the eve of my ninth returning birth-day, being in a gay humour (he was seldom sad) he said to me, 'I shall go out to-morrow morning with Squire Mowbray's hounds, Hugh; will you get up and go with me?' My heart bounded at the proposal. 'Yes,' said I. 'Lord, husband,' exclaimed my mother, 'would you break the child's neck?' 'There is no fear,' retorted I. 'Well said, Hugh', continued my father; 'you shall ride Bay Meg; you are but a feather, she will carry you with ease, and will not run away with you.' 'Never fear that,' replied I, stoutly. My mother at first made some opposition, but my father laughed, and I coaxed, intreated, and teazed, till she complied; for this was by no means the first scene of the kind.

I went to bed with an overjoyed heart, and a head so full of the morrow that I was up dressed and ready the first in the house. The horses were brought out, my father and I mounted, we soon came up with the sportsmen, and away we went in quest of a fox.

We were at first unlucky, and it was late in the day before Reynard was found; but about noon the hounds opened,[3] he started in view, and the sport began.

The chace happened to be long, heavy, and continued for many miles. My father was an eager sportsman. He valued himself both upon his hunter and his horsemanship; and who should be first in at the death was an honour that he would contend with the keenest sportsman in the kingdom, though it were the Squire himself. The running was so severe that Bay Meg became willing to lag. He looked behind, called after me to push on, and I obeyed, and laid on her with whip and heel, as lustily as I could. My father, anxious to keep sight of me yet not lose the hounds, pulled in a little, and the hunted animal, in hopes of finding cover, made toward a wood. Being prevented from entering it, he skirted along its sides, and turning the corner, the hindmost sportsmen followed by a short cut through the wood.

Keeping my eye on my father, I likewise struck into the wood, but, taking a wrong direction, was presently entangled among the trees and brambles, and entirely at a loss. I afterward learned that my father, having lost sight of me for some minutes, stopped, hoping I should come up; and then rode back to seek me, while I was spurring forward in a contrary line.

After many efforts, stoppages, and windings, I at last made my way through the wood, and came to the entrance of an extensive heath. The hounds, though at a great distance, were still in hearing, and Bay Meg, accustomed to the sport, erected her ears and listened after them with great attention. For some time longer she obeyed the whip, and increased her gallop, evidently with a desire to come up with them; but after a while, finding they were out of hearing, she grew sulky, slackened her pace, tired, and at last fairly stood still. I had been so much used to horses that, perceiving her humour, I had the sagacity to turn her head homeward, and she then went on again, though with a sullen and sluggish pace.

On looking round however, and considering, my alarm began. I was in the middle of an extensive heath, or moor, with no living creature, house, or object in sight, except here and there a scattered shrub and a few sheep. It was winter, and the day was far advanced: add to this the wind had risen, and when I turned about, was in my face, and blew a sharp sleet which then began to fall full in my eyes, half blinded me and the mare, and offended her nostrils so much that she once more wheeled about, and refused to proceed either one way or the other.

Not yet quite daunted, while I was making every effort to bring her round, a gust of wind blew off my hat. Forgetting that Bay Meg was tall and I short, and that there was neither gate nor mounting stone to be seen, I alighted to recover my hat. Being down, to get up again was impossible; my foot could not reach the stirrup.

The lowering sky, the approach of darkness, and the utter desert in which I found myself at length conjured up the full distress of the scene, which seized upon my imagination, and I burst into tears.

I continued sobbing, crying, and tugging at Bay Meg, till night had fairly overtaken us. At last I found myself beside some white railing, which was the boundary of a race course within the distance. This at first seemed to promise me relief: with great difficulty I coaxed Bay Meg up to it, climbed upon the railing, and hoped once more to mount. But in vain; the perverse animal set her face to me, nor could any language I was master of prevail on her to approach sideways; and if I lifted my whip, she did but run backward and pull me down.

This contest continued I know not how long, till quite hopeless I gave it up, and again proceeded to lead her, not knowing where or in what direction I was going. After a time the moon appeared, and a very indifferent afternoon was succeeded by a fine night. I continued sobbing, but still proceeded, as fast as I could prevail on Bay Meg to follow me, till propitious fortune brought me to a road, where the wheels had cut deep ruts, and the tread of horses had left the ridges high. Here I once again essayed to mount, and by the help of the stirrup succeeded![1]

Still I knew not where I was, nor what to do; except that my only chance was to go on.

I had not proceeded far before the traces of road began to diminish, and I struck into another path that seemed more beaten. This gradually disappeared, and I soon found myself on the level green-sward, without any marks of footing for my guide. To relieve this new distress I turned to the right, hoping again to recover the track I had lost; instead of which, after riding on I know not how far, I found the heath begin to grow marshy. Again I turned, but so unfortunately that every step the mare set sunk her deeper and deeper in a bog, till at last she could not drag herself out. My danger was extreme; but I rightly conjectured the bog would support me singly, better than it would me and the mare: I therefore jumped off, kept hold of the bridle, which I threw over her head, and by shifting my ground prevented myself from sinking very deep, while I continued my endeavours to relieve the mare. She made a lucky plunge, and I, turning her head in a different direction as much as possible, found myself in part released from this danger: though I was obliged to proceed every step with the utmost precaution.

Once more dismounted, wearied, and despairing, I had no resource but to wander I knew not whither, or lie down perishing with cold on a damp moor, while a severe frost was setting in. Great as my distress was, I had too much courage to sink under it, and I went on, giving some relief to my affliction by sobs and tears.

These various circumstances continued till the night began to be far advanced; but after two or three hours of most tedious and weary wandering I again came to a rising ground, by the help of which with great efforts I once more contrived to mount. I was no sooner in the saddle than I thought I saw a light at a distance, which sometimes seemed to glimmer and as often disappeared. Toward this however I determined to direct my course, and proceeded losing and recovering it till I could catch sight of it no more.

Continuing in the same direction for some time, I came to a barn. Benumbed, fatigued, and ready as I was to drop from the saddle, I entered it as joyfully as a shipwrecked sailor climbs a barren rock. I scarcely could dismount, and it was with great difficulty I could unbuckle and take off the bridle of Bay Meg: but my hands were so frost bitten and my perseverance so exhausted, that the saddle was beyond my ability. I therefore shut the door, and left her to feed on what she could find; while I went and laid myself down among some trusses of straw, that were heaped on one side.

The pain of my thawing hands would not immediately suffer me to go to sleep, and, just as it was beginning to decrease and I to slumber, the door opened and a woman came in. My fears were again alarmed, for as I listened I heard her weep bitterly. In no long time afterward a man leaned forward, through the door, and said—'Mary! Art thou there?'—To which she replied with a sob—'Yea, Tummas; I be here.'

My half frozen blood and my fears again afloat made me tremble through every limb; and there was something in the grief of the woman, and particularly in the voice of the man, which had no tendency to calm my agitation. I could see distinctly, for the moon shone full in at the door. He entered the barn, they sat down together, and after some trifling questions I heard the following dialogue.

'And so, Mary, thou say'st thou beest with child?'

'Yea, Tummas, that I too surely be; the more is my hard hap.'

'And what dost thou mean to do?'

'Nay, Tummas, what doon you mean to do?'

'No matter for that—Thou threatest me, last night, that thou wouldst swear thy bastard to me.'

'For shame, for shame, Tummas, to talk o'that'n! If it mun be a bastard, thou well knowest it is a bastard of thy own begetting.'

'I know better.'

'Oh Christ! Tummas: canst thou look in my face and tell me that?'

'Yea, I can.'

'Thou art a base false man, Tummas!'

'Don't call names.'

'Thou knowest thou art. What canst thou hope for, after swearing so wickedly as thou didst to be true to me and marry me, but that the devil should come for thee alive?'

'No matter for that. If I must go to the devil, it shall not be for nothing. But mayhap thou hadst a better a kept a good tongue in thy head.'

'Thou hadst a better a kept an honest one in thine, Tummas.'

'I'll make thee repent taunting me, as thou hast done, afore folks; and *threaping*[1] and *threating*[2] to lay thy bastard at my door.'

'Do thy worst! Thou hast brought me to shame and misery, and hast sworn thyself to the bottomless pit: what canst thou do more?'

'Thou shalt see.'

As he said this, he deliberately drew a knife from his pocket, and began to whet it upon his shoe—I was breathless: my hair stood on end—The woman exclaimed:

'Jesus God! Tummas; What dost thou mean?'

'Say thy prayers!'

'Merciful Saviour! Why, thou wilt not murder me, Tummas?'

'Thou shalt never go alive out of this place.'

'Christ have mercy upon my sinful soul!'

'I'll do thy business.'

'For the gracious love of the merciful heaven, Tummas, bethink thyself!'

'I'll teach thee to swear thy ugly bastard brat to me!'

'I wunnot, Tummas; I wunnot! For Christ Jesus sake bethink thyself! Dunnot murder me, Tummas! Oh, dunnot murder me! I'll never trouble thee, Tummas, while I have breath; I'll never trouble thee! Indeed, indeed, I wunnot!'

'I know thee better: tomorrow thou would'st tell all; this and all.'

'Never, Tummas: as God shall pardon my sins, never, never, never!'

The poor creature screamed with agony, while the determined fellow kept whetting his knife. At last she made a sudden spring and endeavoured to seize his arm; but, missing her aim, he immediately struck her with his fist and began to stab her.

Unable to contain myself, I shrieked with no less horror and vociferation than the poor mangled creature. The mare herself took fright, and sprang, with the snorting of terror and clattering of hoofs, with her shoulder against the door, endeavouring to get out.

This unexpected noise, aiding his guilt, inspired the murdering wretch with instantaneous dread, and he immediately took to flight; leaving the woman weltering[1] in her blood, groaning, and, as I supposed, expiring.

Impelled by my fears and the horror of the scene, I had no longer any feeling of cold, or sense of debility. I ran to the door, shut it, and finding a fork that stood beside it made as good a cross bar-fastening as I was able. I then resolutely set my own shoulder to it, and there remained, I know not how long, in momentary dread the murderer would return. The woman's groans seemed to diminish, as if she were dying; and I durst neither stir nor speak; for I feared to do any thing but listen.

The energy of my terror was so great that it was very very long before I was weary enough of my situation to be obliged to move. Fatigue, and a dead silence without, at length however induced me first to change my position, and after a time, gradually and with great caution, to open the door and look out. Neither hearing nor seeing any thing, I waited awhile, and then ventured so far as to walk round the barn; though in the utmost trepidation, and possessed by the most horrid fears, which were increased by a great increase of darkness; the moon being then either descending or hidden behind the clouds.

Having made no discoveries, except that every thing was quiet, I once more entered the barn, where all was still as death. The woman had ceased to groan; nor could I, though I listened with the most solicitous attention, hear her breathe. Horror returned in all its force, and I stood immoveable, unknowing what to resolve on or what to attempt. At length I took courage and exclaimed, 'In the name of God, if you are alive, speak!'

The very sound of my own voice inspired unutterable terror; which was augmented by a heavy and long confined groan, proceeding from the woman. She had retained her breath, fearing the return of the assassin. The answer that followed her groan was, 'If you are a Christian soul, get me some help.' I told her I was lost, benighted, and did not know where to go for any. She replied there was a town, not half a mile distant, at the back of the barn; and named the very place at which my aunt and uncle Elford lived.

As soon as surprise and joy would permit, I asked if she knew Mr. Elford. Her answer was, 'I am his servant; and this is his barn.'

Various recollections immediately crouded upon me, and the scene and the voice of poor Mary, to which a moment before I had been so utter a stranger, became familiar to me. 'It is I, Mary; little Hugh,' said I. 'Don't you know me?' A dismal 'Oh!' excited no doubt by the most painful associations, was her answer. I desired her to be quiet and patient, while I ran for aid; assuring her I would soon be back, for that I now knew where I was, and was perfectly acquainted with the road.

Accordingly away I ran, with all the speed I had, to my uncle's house; where, when I arrived, I knocked at the door, pelted the window, and called as vociferously as I could for them to rise. The house-dog barked violently, and my uncle was soon at the window, with my aunt at his back, demanding with surprise and dissatis-faction who I was, and what I wanted? I exclaimed, 'Come down, uncle! A man has been murdering your maid Mary! She will be dead if you do not make haste!' 'Good God!' cried my aunt, pressing forward; 'Child! Hugh Trevor! Nephew! Is it you?' 'Yes, yes, aunt,' answered I: 'make haste and try to save the poor creature's life!'

The astonishment excited by such a messenger, bringing such a message, and at such an hour, may well be imagined. Master, mistress, and servants, were immediately in motion, and the doors opened. Question succeeded question; exclamations were incessant; and my answers quickly communicated much of the terror I myself had felt.

Regulating his proceedings according to my account, Mr. Elford dispatched a servant to the surgeon; and, having prepared a hurdle by way of litter, went with me and two of his men to the barn.

My aunt was very loath I should return; but my spirits, by the various incidents of the night, were much too active to suffer me to feel either hunger, weariness, or want of sleep; and Mr. Elford recollected I might be useful, in preventing the terrors of poor Mary at our approach; for which reason he suffered me to run before, and inform her that help was coming.

When I came to the barn, the moment I set my foot over the threshold, my terrors of murder and of her having expired all returned. After a short pause, I called with a trembling voice, 'Mary! Are you alive?' and my heart bounded with joy to hear her, though dolefully, answer, 'yea.'

Mr. Elford and his attendants soon came up; and the remainder of the story of poor Mary was, that, being removed and put to bed, her wounds though deep and dangerous were found not to be mortal; that she recovered in a few weeks, and by the influence of Mr. Elford was retained in my aunt's service; to the great scandal of the place, where it was affirmed that such hussies and their bastards ought to be whipped from parish to parish, and so, as I suppose, whipped out of the world; that in two months time she was delivered of a fine boy, whom, when my uncle left the country, she maintained by her own hard earnings; and that in the extremity of her distress, when she thought herself at the point of death, she obstinately refused to declare who was her intended murderer; and though, by his having been known to be her *sweetheart*, and his flight from the country where he never more appeared, people were sufficiently convinced who the man was, yet her pertinacious theme was—*she would never be his accuser: if God could pardon him, she could.*

CHAPTER VII

Mistakes and family quarrels of Mr. and Mrs. Elford: His departure, and exile: with the letters he wrote

AND now the period approached when the pleasures of the days of childhood were to terminate, and when I was to experience an abundance of those rude disasters under which the poor, the friendless, and the fatherless, groan.

The first stroke which the malice of fortune aimed at me was the voluntary banishment of my uncle. Though I have forborne to interrupt my narrative by a recapitulation of the unhappy bickerings that took place between Mr. Elford and my aunt, soon after their marriage, yet these bickerings were very frequent, very bitter, and at last very fatal. Instead of the happiness which they and every body had thought so certain, they were completely wretched.

My youth had not prevented me lately from remarking, when at their house, the steady and severe silence which Mr. Elford endeavoured to preserve, and the fixed dissatisfaction and gloom of my aunt. Notwithstanding the efforts they made, especially Mr. Elford, not to suffer their unhappiness to extend beyond themselves, it became frequently painful, even for me, to be in their company. He indeed was often in part successful, in these efforts; but she seldom, or never.

Their mutual discontent was the more easily increased to misery, because it happened between people who each had the character of prudent; and whose partiality individually acquitted them of that disorder, which the want of good temper alone had produced.

In making an estimate of the probable conveniences and inconveniences, agreements and disagreements, that might happen between them, they had reciprocally been deceived.

Mr. Elford had endeavoured to provide against this, by a plain declaration of his sentiments and expectations; which Mrs. Elford had too inconsiderately concluded she should continue to think rational and just. She imagined there was no fear of violent quarrels, between a man of so much understanding as Mr. Elford and a woman so disposed to listen to reason as herself. She was ignorant of the power of habit over her temper. The rector had taught her pride, marriage had taught her misfortune, and pride and misfortune had made her fretful, melancholy and moody. She had suffered no opposition from her first husband; her will had been his law; and she knew not, till she had made the trial, how difficult it is to concede with a good grace. The least thing that offended her threw her into tears. The passions of Mr. Elford and my aunt were mutually too much inflamed for either of them to draw equitable and wise conclusions, and tears he held to be a false, insulting, and odious mode of proclaiming him a tyrant: it was to say, I dare not utter my complaints in words, but my tears I cannot restrain! Too angry to doubt of or examine his reasons, convinced of his own humanity, and his desire to see and make her happy, such an accusation he considered so violently unjust as to be unpardonable.

It must be owned, she did not confine her grief to weeping; she was often seized with fits of hysteric passion, in which the most outrageous and false accusations were indulged. To reply to them, or attempt to disprove what he knew to be so absurd, he thought derogatory to innocence; and the world half suspected him to be the tyrant he had been painted. This increased his sense of injury, and consequently did not diminish the affliction of my aunt.

Of the happiness, indeed, which was to result from this marriage, she had conceived romantic ideas; and when she found herself again involved in the cares of a family, liable to the control of a man who expected the utmost propriety and order, who looked with a strict eye over every department, and whose opinion did not always coincide with her own, she became constantly peevish, and her former gloom grew ten fold more gloomy. She pined after that connubial affection which their reciprocal conduct was calculated to destroy; and from the hasty decisions of passion convinced herself, that no part of the blame was justly her own. Mr. Elford was no less obstinate in the contrary opinion. Taking philosophy such as he found it, he like his neighbours too hastily concluded there were duties and affairs for which men were fitted, but of which women were incapable. Blending much truth with some falsehood, he thus argued:

'The leading features in the character of an amiable and good woman are mildness, complacency, and equanimity of temper. The man, if he be a provident and worthy husband, is immersed in a thousand cares: his mind is agitated, his memory loaded, and his body fatigued. He returns from the bustle of the world chagrined perhaps at disappointments, angry at indolent or perfidious people, and terrified lest his unavoidable connections with such people should make him appear to be indolent or perfidious himself. Is this a time for the wife of his bosom, his dearest most intimate friend, to add to his vexations and increase the fever of an overburthened mind, by a contumelious tongue or a discontented brow? Business, in its most prosperous state, is full of anxiety, labour, and turmoil. Oh! how dear to the memory of man is that wife who clothes her face in smiles; who uses gentle expressions, and who makes her lap soft to receive and hush his cares to rest. There is not in all nature so fascinating an object as a faithful, tender, and affectionate wife!'

Had he wished for a wife who, instead of indulging the caprice of indolence would have awakened him to energy, and have taught him to be just not captious, his desires would have been more rational: but, to a man who had formed a system of obedience to authority, and not to reason, the arguments he used were irrefragable. To a woman who imagined that obedience, in all cases, was the badge of abject slavery, they were absurd. Thus opposite in principle and in practice, their unhappy state of existence finally became so intolerable, to one of them at least, as to occasion the violent measure and the painful sensations described by Mr. Elford in the following letter.

'TO MRS. ELFORD,

'The bitterness of unjust reproach, the invectives of an un-governed tongue, the rancorous accusations of a stubborn heart, these, wretched as they long have made me, to me are now no more. Forgetful man! No more? You I can forsake; but where shall I fly to rid myself of them? You have riveted them upon me, and while I have life they can never die. With you I have travelled through the vale of tears: you, like misery personified, have held the cup of sorrow; have fed me with affliction, strewed thorns beneath my feet by day, and wound adders round my pillow by night. Absence itself cannot afford a cure. Yes, reconcile it to your conscience how you may, you have given my peace a mortal wound.

'You cannot forget, when I first thought of you for a wife, the plainness and sincerity with which I acted. I carefully stated that my family was reputable but not rich, and that I was a younger brother; that my wealth was not great; but that it was sufficient, with industry and the character I had established, to gratify the desires of people whose hearts were not vitiated, and whose wants were bounded. I conscientiously repeated my ideas concerning the regulations and economy of a well governed family; and of the parts which it became the husband and the wife to take. That was the time in which you ought to have made your objections: but then every thing was just, every thing was rational; and from your ready acquiescence to my proposals and the admiration with which you seemed to receive them, I had no doubt of enjoying that serene that delightful state of connubial happiness, so often desired and so seldom obtained.

'On such conditions and with such views, I confidently entered with you into a partnership which unhappily cannot be dissolved. The irrevocable contract was scarcely ratified before it was violated. With a temper habitually gloomy and suspicious, and a mind incapable of bending to those inevitable little anxieties and vexations which occur in the most quiet families, you soon discovered your propensity to repel every thing that your jealous and fanciful temper deemed an infringement of your privileges.

'Let your own heart testify how long and how ardently I endeavoured, by mildness and the most simple and convincing reasons, to bring you back to your duty. But in vain: causes of disagreement became so frequent, and injury succeeded injury so fast, that I was obliged to proceed to those gentle severities which are all that a husband, who preserves a proper respect for himself, can inflict. And gentle they certainly were, when compared to the contumely by which they were provoked. I forbore those tender and endearing epithets, by which former affection should be continually revived. I then avoided and indeed refused to converse with you, except in the company of a third person, or as far as necessity obliged me. Sorry am I to say that, instead of warning you to shun the rocks of mischief, my efforts did but aggravate your folly.

'It is true you had your hours of contrition, in which, with tears and prayers and unbounded acknowledgments of the absurdity of your conduct, together with solemn assurances of reformation, you have for a moment recalled my lost love, and made me hope you would acquire some power over the discordant passions that devoured you. But these promises were so often repeated, and so continually forgotten, that at length they afforded neither hope nor ease: they had only been gleams of sunshine, foreboding that the tempest would soon return with increasing violence. Yes, partial as I know you, and blind to your own errors, you cannot deny that at last you approached the fury, rather than the woman.

'To a man like me, of a delicate temper, quick at discovering errors and eager to redress them, even in cases where they do not personally affect myself but indefatigable where they do, this eternal discord, these quarrels and despicable brawls are become insupportable. I have endured the torture seven miserable years, and surely that is no slight trial: surely that is sufficient to prove I have not wanted patience or fortitude. To be a good husband and a provident father, and to protect those that depend on me from injury and want, are qualities which I believe the whole world will allow me, you alone excepted. *You* upbraid me with faults; *you* accuse me of crimes; *you* proclaim me a tyrant. When I am gone, when your passions have subsided, and when you feel the want of me, you will be more just. You will then lament that nothing, short of this desperate proof, could convince you of the criminality of your conduct.

'Where I shall seek, where find, or where endure existence, or to

what hospitable or inhospitable shore I shall wander, I know not
yet: I only know that in England it cannot, shall not be. We have
lived long enough in misery; which, everlastingly to avoid, seas or
death shall everlastingly divide us.

W. ELFORD.'

This letter, although it contained many marks of that impatience
which had increased his family misfortunes, could only have been
written by a man of virtue, whose very austerity had in it a pre-
ponderance of benevolent intention. Such was my uncle; whose
memory, though but a child, I often had occasion to regret.

By various plausible pretexts, with the hope of forwarding a
fortune that was to descend to me, Mr. Elford had been prevailed on
to lend my father several sums of money, to the amount of seven
hundred pounds. My uncle too had found other occasions for the
exercise of his humanity. His property had been hastily sold, and
therefore disadvantageously, so that the sum with which he went
to seek his fortune on foreign shores was but small. He was enough
acquainted with my father's affairs to know that of the money lent
to him there was little hope.

To me he wrote a letter which will sufficiently shew how kind he
would have been, had he possessed the power. It was inclosed in one
to my father, with directions to suffer me to read it now, and that it
should be preserved and given to me when age should have matured
my understanding. The following were its contents.

'TO HUGH TREVOR.

'My dear boy: young as you are, I have conceived a friendship
and affection for you, which perhaps inflict as severe a pang, at the
present moment, as any one of the distressing circumstances that
occasion my flight. Had I wealth to leave, I would endeavour to
secure you from the baneful effects of poverty; as it is, accept all
that I have to give, my best wishes, my dearest love, and a little good
advice. Though your understanding is greatly above your years, yet
you cannot have experience and knowledge enough of sorrow to
conceive what my feelings are: but if hereafter you should remember
me, and if at that most serious moment when you enter on the
marriage state you should wish for a friend like me to advise with,
let this letter supply my place. The miseries I have endured, by my
mistakes on the subject, are so strongly imprinted on my mind,

that I can think of nothing else; and, inapplicable as it may seem to your present course of thought, I cannot persuade myself but that it is the most interesting of all topics, upon which I could write to you.

'Of the wisdom of entering into the marriage state, and of the virtue of the institution, I have lately begun to entertain the most serious doubts. Whether they are well founded, or are the consequences of my own mistakes of conduct, I dare not at this moment determine: but, while the present forms of society exist, should you arrive at manhood the probability is that you will marry. If then you should ever think of marriage, think of it as a duty; and not merely as the means of self gratification, or the indulgence of some childish and irrational passion, which irrational people dignify with the name of love. Let the affection you conceive for woman be founded on the qualities of her mind.

'But above all things first examine yourself, whether you can endure opposition without anger; and next put the woman you intend to marry to the same test; for, unless you are mutually unshaken in your resolutions on this head, if you marry you are miserable. The task of man and wife is reciprocally arduous. She should be mild, good-humoured, cheerful and tender; he cool, rational, and vigilant; without acrimony, devoid of captiousness, and free from passion. It is mutually their duty to inspect and to expostulate, but to beware how they reprove. Where gentleness and equanimity of temper are wanting, happiness never can be obtained. Believe me, my dear boy, I have never stood so low in my own opinion as when I have caught myself betrayed into petulance, and descending to passion. The combats I have maintained to overcome this weakness are inconceivable.

'Whether it be constitutional in me or habitual I cannot determine'—[Had Mr. Elford been more a philosopher, he would have known that frequent anger is merely a habit.]—'but I suspect that to this I chiefly owe my present misfortunes, as I am half persuaded there is no woman that may not be moulded into what form her husband pleases, provided he possess a superior understanding and an entire command of his temper. But Oh! how severe the task to preserve a perfect equality in despite of the ill humour, caprice, or injustice of a woman for whom you undergo a thousand difficulties, encounter continual labours, and undauntedly expose yourself to every fatigue and danger!—I blush to think I have sunk beneath the trial.—But we have both gone too far to recede: we have mutually said and done what never can be forgotten.

'As good temper is the basis of connubial felicity, means must be taken by which it may be cultivated and preserved. From the first hour of marriage, beware of too much familiarity, and of encouraging or of taking liberties. Be as circumspect in your behaviour as if a stranger were present, and dread deviating from that respect which is due from man to woman, and from woman to man, in a single state. This does not imply coldness, or formality, but the cheerful intercourse of good sense. Behave as you would to a person from whom you are happy to receive a visit, and with whose company you are delighted. Should you indulge those ebullitions of passionate fondness which lose sight of these limits, it is impossible to foretell to what they may lead. A caress neglected, or supposed to be neglected, a kiss not returned with the like warmth, or a fond pressure not answered with equal ardour, may poison a mind which applauds itself for the delicacy of its sensations.

'Do not expect to find your wife all perfection. I know the romance of lovers: they read descriptions in which the imagination has been exhausted, to depict enamoured youth superior to every terrestrial being; and they are convinced that, above all others, the object of their own particular choice has never yet been equalled. Such fanciful and silly people, when time and experience have something allayed their ardour, will often find their dainty taste offended at discovering a mole on the bosom, or a yellow shade in the neck, or any other trifling bodily blemish, which was as visible before marriage as after, had they looked with the same scrutinizing eyes. Be resolute in repelling every emotion of anger or disgust. Never permit a choleric or bitter expression to escape you; for wedded love is but too often of a tender and perishable nature, and such rude potions are its poison.

'I look back at what I have been writing, and am astonished at the subject I have chosen. But the torrent of my thoughts is irresistible: they hurry me away, and persuade me that though young, it is yet possible you may hereafter remember me, and at a time when perhaps you shall have arrived at the exercise of many of those noble virtues which are now only in the bud. I have a great affection for you, my dear nephew, and should be glad that, if you then cannot think kindly, you should at least think justly; and that you should possess some faint picture of the present state of my feelings.

Could you but know all the emotions of my heart, you would bear witness to its honesty; and would own that its efforts have been strenuous, unremitted, and sincere, though unfortunate.

'Years pass quickly away: yet a little while and you will be an actor in this busy world, of which at present your knowledge is small. I am doomed never to see you more; but, while I have life and memory, I shall never forget you.[1]

W. ELFORD.'

CHAPTER VIII

My father becomes a bankrupt: Flies the country: Lists for an East India soldier, and dies on ship-board: Distress of my mother; and the beginning of my misfortunes: I am bound apprentice: Characteristic traits of my master: The dreadful sufferings I undergo; and my narrow escapes with life

YOUNG as I was, I perfectly remember that the strange departure of my uncle Elford produced a very sensible effect upon me. It may well be imagined that, when my understanding was more mature, the perusal of this affectionate letter, and the recollection of his kindness to me in my days of childhood, excited no little emotion.

As for my aunt, prepared as she had been for some violent catastrophe to their quarrelling, she was either so struck by the letter and the remembrance of past follies, or so fearful of the comments and scrutiny of the neighbourhood, that within a month after he was missing she quitted the country, and went to reside at the city of ****, where in less than a year she died. Her departure was private, and the place of her retreat was not known till her last illness; when intelligence was sent to the rector, to whom she bequeathed such property as she possessed.

The absence of my uncle contributed to hasten the approach of that cloudy reverse at which I have already hinted. For some time the ruin of my father's affairs had been prevented by the sums which his eloquence had wrung from the well-meaning Mr. Elford. Hugh was no contemptible orator on these occasions. Hope seldom forsook him, and he built so securely on what he hoped might come to pass as sometimes to assert the thing had already happened. Such convenient mistakes are daily made. If indeed the good graces of fortune would but have kept pace with his expectations, England would not have afforded a more flourishing or gallant yeoman. But, like monopolizers in general, he was apt to speculate a little too deeply. Eager to enjoy, he was impatient to obtain the means of enjoyment. So that, at one time, the turning up of the jack at all fours[1] was to make his fortune; but how provoking! it happened to be the ten: at another it depended on a duck-wing cock, which (who could have foreseen so strange an accident?) disgraced the best feeder in the kingdom, by running away: and it more than once did not want half a neck's length of being realized by a favourite horse; yet was lost, contrary to the most accurate calculations which, as the learned in these matters affirm, had been made from Wheatherby's Racing Calendar.[2]

Thus to repeated disappointments in his bets and his bargains, and to his neglect of his farming affairs, it was owing that, in anno domini —— when I was nine years and a half old, after having expended the property with which he had been supplied, and incurred debts to the amount of little less than a thousand pounds, my father found it prudent to depart by night in the basket of the stage coach for London. And prudent it certainly was, for his effects had not only been seized in execution of a bond and judgment, but the bailiffs from all quarters were at his heels.

My mother at this time was pregnant; the sister I have mentioned was dead; but I had a fine healthy brother about three years old, and it was agreed that we should follow to the great city, as soon as he had found employment; which, according to his notions, was the most easy thing imaginable.

It so happened, however, that he had not been there a full month before the trifling sum he and my mother had collected for his immediate existence was lost, by the turn of a die; contrary to his certain conviction that he had discovered, at a hazard table,[3] the ready way to repair all past mistakes.

To send for wife and children was now out of the question. Destitute of support, without the means of obtaining another shilling, after fasting a day and a half, his courage, that is his appetite, could hold out no longer, and he enlisted for an East-India soldier; having first convinced himself, by the soundest arguments, that he should immediately be made a serjeant; which perhaps was no improbable calculation; that he should then soon get a commission, and that he should undoubtedly return a commanding officer, or general in chief, to the surprise of his friends and the utter confusion of the rector, and all those whom he accounted his persecutors.

That these great events might not actually have happened who shall pretend to say? Miracles of old were plentiful; and even in these unbelieving days strange things have come to pass. But all his unbounded hopes, many of which he had stated in his last letter to my mother, were unexpectedly subverted, by an accident to which it appears men in general are subject. He caught a fever, while the ship in which he was to be a passenger lay waiting in the Downs[1] for a wind; and, in spite of the surgeon and his whole chest of medicines, died: of all which events there was a circumstantial account, transmitted by one of his comrades to my mother.

The ruin of prospects so fair, the desolation of a house and homeless woman, with two orphan children, and pregnant of a third, and the loss of a husband, who at the worst of times had always kept hope alive, were sufficient causes of affliction to my mother. Tears were plentifully shed, and daily and nightly wailings were indulged.

Every resource was soon exhausted, and immediate relief became necessary. To whom could she apply? To whom, but the rector? She wrote to him in terms the most moving, the most humiliating, and indeed the most abject, that her imagination could suggest. But in vain: no prayers, no tears, no terrors, of this world or of the next, could move him. The father, and the divine, were equally inexorable. He pleaded his oath, but he remembered his revenge. After the first letter he would receive no more, and when she wrote again and again, with the direction in a different hand, and using other little stratagems, he returned no answer.

From this extreme distress, and from the intolerable disgrace, as my mother supposed it to be, of coming on the parish,[2] we were relieved, to the best of her ability, by a poor widow woman with four children; who had formerly lived a servant in the Trevor family, and who, after her husband's death, maintained herself and her orphans with incredible industry, and with no other aid but the produce of a cow, that she fed chiefly on the common where her cottage stood. The active good sense with which she did every thing that was entrusted to her, was the cause that she never wanted employment; and she exerted her utmost attention to make her children, as they grew up, as useful as herself.

By this woman's advice and aid, my mother applied herself to spinning; and it was agreed that I should either drive the plough or be put apprentice, as soon as I could find a master.

For my own part, all my sources of pleasure and improvement were at once retrenched. That I had not horses to ride, a father to play with and caress me, and a kind uncle to instruct and delight me, were among the least of my misfortunes. Reading, that great field of enjoyment, which was daily opening more amply upon me, was totally cut off. My curiosity had been awakened, my memory praised, and my acuteness admired: in an instant, as it were, all these joys were vanished.

Previous to my uncle's departure, I had found another mode of obtaining knowledge, and applause. He was musical, and a few persons of the like turn, scattered through the neighbouring hamlets, used occasionally to meet at his house; where they exercised themselves in singing, from the works of Croft,[1] Green, Boyce, Purcell, Handel, and such authors as they possessed.[2] One of them played the bassoon, another the flute, and a third the violin, I had a quick ear, was attracted by their harmony, and began to join in their concerts. A treble voice was a great acquisition; I was apt and they encouraged me, by frequent praise and admiration. My uncle gave me Arnold's Psalmody,[3] in which I eagerly studied the rudiments of the science: but this book, with the rest, was swept away in the general wreck; and I, after having had a glimpse of the enchanted land of knowledge, was cast back, apparently to perish in the gloomy deserts of ignorance. I had no source of information, except my mother; and her stores, at the best, were scanty: at present, labour left her but little leisure, and the little she had was spent in complaint.

The poor widow, indeed, willingly did me every kindness in her power; but that alas was small. With this honest-hearted creature I remained eight months, going out to a day's work whenever I could get one, to weed, drive the plough, set potatoes, or any thing else that they would put me to: till at last a farmer, finding me expert, agreed to take me as an apprentice; on condition that I should serve him till I was one and twenty. The offer was joyfully accepted by my mother, and I had spirit and understanding enough to be happy that I could thus provide for myself.

I had soon reason to repent; my master was the most passionate madman I ever beheld; and, when in a passion, the most mischievous. His cattle, his horses, his servants, his wife, his children, were each of them in turn the objects of his fury.

The accidents that happened from his ungovernable choler were continual, and his cruelty, when in these fits, was incredible; though at other times, strange to tell, he was remarkably compassionate. He one day beat out the eye of a calf, because it would not instantly take the milk he offered. Another time he pursued a goose, that ran away from him when he flung it oats; and was so enraged, by the efforts it made to escape, that he first tore off its wing and then twisted its neck round. On a third occasion he bit off a pig's ear, because it struggled and cried while he was ringing it. One of his children was lamed, and, though nobody knew how it happened, every body gave him credit for the accident. Yet he had his paroxysms of fondness for his children, and for the lame boy in particular. Indeed it was generally remarked that he was the most cruel to those for whom he had the greatest affection. The perception of his own absurdity did but increase his rage, till it was exhausted; after which he has sometimes been seen to burst into tears, at the recollection of his own madness and inhumanity.

One habit arising from his excessive vivacity was that, when he wanted any thing done, he expected the person nearest to him should not only instantly obey, but conceive what he meant from the pointing of his finger, the turn of his head, or the motion of his eye, without speaking a word; while the dread of his anger stupified and rendered the person against whom it was directed motionless.

I continued for an unexampled length of time to be his favourite. The family remarked, at first with surprise, and afterward either with a sense of injustice or of enmity, the restraint he put upon himself, and the great partiality with which he treated me. My superior quickness excited his admiration; he held me up as an example, and laid the flattering unction to his soul[1] that he was no tyrant; on the contrary, when people had but common sense, nobody was more kind.

But old habits, though they may suffer a temporary disguise, are devils incarnate. The tide of passion at length broke loose, and with redoubled violence for having suffered constraint. To add to the misfortune, my thirst after knowledge was the cause, or at least the pretext, of this change. It happened that an old book of arithmetic fell in my way, and, as this was at that time the sole treasure of instruction within my reach, I made it my constant companion, carried it in my bosom, and pored over it whenever I could steal a moment to myself. In the heinous act of reading this book I was twice detected, by my moody master. The first time he cautioned me, with fire in his eyes, never to let him catch me idling my time in that manner again; and the second he snatched hold of my ear and gave me so sudden and violent a pull that he brought me to the ground. He did worse, he took away my book, and locked it up.

Hostilities having thus commenced, they soon grew hot, and were pursued with bitterness, tyranny, and malignity. Proceeding from bad to worse, after a while every thing I did was wrong. In proportion as his frenzy became hateful or rather terrible to his own imagination, his cruelty increased. He seemed, in my instance, to have the dread upon him of committing some injury so violent as perhaps to bring him to the gallows; and several times in his chafing fits declared his fear.

This idea haunted him so much that he adopted a new mode of conduct with me, and, instead of kicking me, knocking me down, or hurling the first thing that came to hand at me, gave himself time enough to take the horsewhip. Yet he could not always be thus cautious; and even when he was, such infernal discipline, though less dangerous, was more intolerable.

The scenes I went through with this man, the sufferings I endured, and the stupifying terrors that seized me if I saw but his shadow, I can never forget. Every thing I did was a motive for chastisement; one day it was for having turned the horses out to graze, and the very next for suffering them to stand in the stable. The cattle of his neighbour, for whom he had a mortal enmity, broke into his field during the night; and for this I was most unmercifully flogged the next morning. The pretence was my not having told him that the fence was defective. Rainy weather made him fret, and then I was sure of a beating. If it were fine, he was all hurry, anxiety, and impatience; and to escape the wicked itching of his fingers was impossible.

One effect that he produced might be thought remarkable, had we not the history of Sparta in its favour; and did we not occasionally observe the like in other boys, under tyrannical treatment. The efforts I was obliged to make, to endure the terrible punishment he inflicted and live, at last rendered me, to a certain degree, insensible of pain. They were powerfully aided indeed by the indignant detestation which I felt, and by the something like defiance with which it enabled me to treat him.

This on one occasion exasperated him so much that, seeing me support the lash without a tear and as if disdaining complaint, he franticly snatched up a pitch-fork, drove it at me, and, I luckily avoiding it, struck the prongs into the barn-door; with the exclamation, 'Damn your soul! I'll make you feel me!' The moment after he was seized with a sense of his own lunacy, turned as pale as death, and stood aghast with horror! My supposed crime was that I had eaten some milk, the last of which I myself had seen the dog lap. Perceiving the terror of his mind, I took courage and told him, 'Jowler eat the milk: I saw him, just as he had done. I would not tell you, because I knew if I had you would have hanged the poor dog.' This short sentence had such an effect upon him that he dropped on his knees, the tears rolling from his eyes, and cried out in an undescribable agony, 'Lord have mercy upon my sinful soul! I shall surely come to be hanged!'

The terror of this lesson remained longer than those who knew him would have expected; but it insensibly wore away.

The efforts I made in the interval to conciliate and avoid wakening the fiend were strenuous, but ineffectual. I shrunk from no labour, and the business with which he intrusted me shewed the confidence he placed in my activity and intelligence. At eleven years old I drove the loaded team, to market or elsewhere, without a superintendant. I was sent in every direction across the country, to bring home sheep, deliver calves to the butcher, fetch cattle, cart coals, or any thing else within my strength.

Various were the distresses in which these duties, and the distempered choler of my master, involved me. On one occasion a wicked boy set his dog at my sheep, and drove them into a turnip field; out of which I could not get them but with great difficulty and loss of time, of which my master demanded a severe account. A calf once broke from me and foolishly tumbled into a water-pit, from which I delivered it at the hazard of my life. Another time, when the roads were heavy, my waggon was set fast in a clay rut, where I was detained above an hour; two drivers refusing to give me a pull because they had both lived with my malicious master; and a third being only prevailed on, for this master of mine was generally hated, by my prayers and tears and the picture I drew of my own distress.

At length the violence of his temper recovered its full elasticity; which was a second time chiefly excited by my earnest longing after knowledge. Notwithstanding that my book was taken from me, my mind was often occupied with the arithmetic I had learned in better days, which had been strongly revived by its contents. At the employment this afforded me I was twice caught by my master; once multiplying and dividing with a nail against the paling, and the second time extracting the square root with chalk on the wall.

These misdemeanours were aggravated by another incident. I one morning happened to find, by good luck as I thought, a half-crown piece that was lying on the high road. The moment I was possessed of this treasure, I began to consider how it ought to be expended. I was in great want of shoes, stockings, and other things; but with those my master was bound to provide me; and, if I attempted to supply myself, the probability was that he would beat me, for not having given him the money.

After pondering again and again on the necessaries I might obtain, the luxuries in which I might indulge, and, what was infinitely more tempting, the stores of learning with which such a sum would furnish me, the recollection of my mother, brother, and sister, for so the young one proved to be, and their distress, with that of the benevolent poor creature who afforded them a shelter, seized me so strongly that I thought it would be wicked not to send my half-crown where it was so much wanted. But how to convey it thither? That was the difficulty. I had no means, no messenger, no soul in whom I durst confide. I therefore resolved for the present to conceal it by pinning it in the lining of my waistcoat; and this was one of those unforeseen events that are generally called lucky chances.

My master's devil was again let loose, and a most uncontrolable devil he was. I had overslept myself, a very uncommon accident with me, and had put him into one of his hateful humours. At breakfast, while eating his bread and cheese, I was set to watch the milk that stood on the fire to boil. By some accident I forgot my office; he saw it rise in the pipkin,[1] looked toward me, could not catch my eye, and, seized with one of his unaccountably hellish fits, sprang forward just as the milk began to boil over, and struck at me with a clasped knife that he held in his hand!

Fortunately for me, the point found resistance, by the saving intervention of my half-crown! The clasp gave way with the violence of the blow, and shutting made a deep gash in his own hand.

Again he turned pale, and, as the blood smeared the floor, knew not I believe whether it was mine or his own. My dame trembling called out, 'Are you hurt, Hugh?' for she too saw the blood, and knew not whose it was. I answered, 'No:' but with a tremulous voice, being in dread of more blows. They soon descended upon me, after he had discovered his mistake, and it was with difficulty that I escaped being thrown behind the fire.

This was not the end of the history of my half-crown. I kept it above three months till I happened to be sent to the market town, with a load of hay. Here, in passing through the street, my eye as usual was attracted by the bookseller's window. I had not forgotten how rich I was, and could not resist. I went in, examined some of the stores the shop contained, and with great difficulty restrained myself to the purchase of the Seven Champions of Christendom,[1] which cost me a shilling. The other eighteen pence I found an opportunity, it being market day, of sending by a neighbour to my mother; with an injunction that six-pence of it should be given to her poor hostess.

With what eagerness I read the valiant deeds of these valiant knights, as I rode home in my empty cart, I will leave the reader to divine: but he will probably pity me when I inform him that I was so deeply engaged in my book as not to perceive the arrival of the cart at my master's yard gate, and that he himself stood at the barn door, contemplating me in the profound negligence of my studies.

Riding in the cart, neglecting the team, having a new book, and reading in it, formed a catalogue of crimes too black to hope for pardon. Not the horse but the cart whip was the instrument of vengeance; and, after having tired himself and left weals of a finger's breadth on my body, arms, legs, and thighs, he completed his malice this time, not by locking up but by burning my book.

I had already lived a year and a half under the tortures of this demon, till they became so intolerable that at last I determined to run away. I was confirmed in this resolution by another dangerous incident, which terrified me more even than any of the preceding, and convinced me that if I stayed any longer with this villainous savage I could not escape death.

I was one day driving the plough for him when a young horse, not half broken in, was the second in the team. I used my utmost endeavours but could not manage him, and the lunatic my master, who was as strong as he was ferocious, caught up a stone and aimed it at the colt (at least so from his manner at the moment I supposed) but struck me with it, and knocked me down immediately in the furrow, where the plough was coming. I saw the plough-share that in an instant was to cut me in two; but the madman, with an incredible effort, started it out of the earth and flung it fairly over me! Unable however to recover his balance, he trod upon my forehead with his hob-nailed shoe, and cut a deep gash just over my eye, and another in my skull: whether with the same foot or in what manner I do not know. My eye was presently closed up, and my hair steeped in the blood that flowed plentifully from both wounds.

There I lay, stunned for a moment, while he was obliged to attend to the frightened colt, which forced the other horses to run, and was become wholly unmanageable. When I recovered I heard him holloa, and saw him struggling with the horses at the farther end of the field; but the impression of the danger I had just escaped was so strong that my resolution of running away came upon me with irresistible force, and, perceiving him so thoroughly engaged, I immediately put it in execution.

I imagine it was some time before he missed me, and he then probably conjectured I was gone home. Be it as it will, I used my legs without molestation; and, committing myself to chance and the wide world, made the best of my way.

CHAPTER IX

My flight: Desponding thoughts: Adventure with a stranger on the road: I am promised relief, but learn a fearful secret that again plunges me in doubt and anxiety: I reveal myself to a near relation: The struggles of passion

THE animation that fear gave me was so great that, though I felt my shirt collar drenched in the blood that flowed from my wounds, I continued to run for at least four miles; and though my pace at length slackened into a walk I still hurried eagerly forward. The dread of again falling into his power, after an attempt so audacious as this, deprived me of any other sense of pain, afforded me strength, and made me forget the completely desolate state to which I had reduced myself. I had no money, no food, no friend in the world. I durst not return to my mother; she was the first person of whom the tyrant would enquire after me. To avoid him was the only plan I yet thought of, and thus impelled I pursued my road.

So long as I was acquainted with the country through which I travelled, I went on without hesitation; but as soon as I found myself entirely beyond my knowledge, I began to look about me. The questions—Where am I? Whither am I going? What am I to do?—inspired a succession of rising fears, which the joy of my deliverance could scarcely counterbalance. I regretted the rash haste with which I had parted with my half-crown. I had not a farthing on earth, I had nothing to sell, nothing to eat, no soul to give me a morsel. It was noon, when I fled from the ploughed field; I had been hard at work from three o'clock in the morning, had since travelled at least twelve or fourteen miles, wounded as I was, and began to feel myself excessively weary, stiff, and craving after food. Where I had got the notion, whether from father, mother, aunt, or uncle, I know not, but I had been taught that to beg was an indelible disgrace; and to steal every body had told me was the road to Tyburn. Starve or hang; that is the law. If I even asked for work, who wanted my service? Who would give me any? Who would not enquire where I came from, and to whom I belonged?

These and many more tormenting ideas were forced upon me by the situation in which I found myself; till at last I was so overcome with fears and fatigue that I sat down to debate whether it were not best, or rather whether I should not be absolutely forced, to turn back.

Still, however, when I came to reflect on the sufferings I had endured, the dangers I had escaped, and the horrible punishment that awaited me if I returned, any expedient seemed better than that terrific project. The distance too, exhausted as I thought myself, was an additional fear, and for a moment I doubted whether I should not lie down and die.

Young minds hold death in peculiar horror, and the very thought inspired returning energy. Among my cogitations I had not forgotten the rector: he was obdurate, hard hearted, and even cruel. But was he so cruel as the fiend from whom I had escaped? From a

latent and undefined kind of feeling, I had made toward that side of
the country where his village lay; and was, as I supposed, within
four or five miles of it. The resolution of making an effort to gain his
protection came upon me, and I rose with some alacrity to put it in
practice. He kept horses, a coachman, and a stable-boy; he had a
garden; he farmed a little, for his amusement. In any of these
capacities I could be useful, and, if he would but give me bread,
I would do whatever he would put me to. He could not surely be so
stony hearted as to refuse. I was inexperienced, and knew not the
force of rancour.

I pursued my way ruminating on these hopes, fears, and disasters,
toward a village that I saw at a distance, where I intended to inquire
the road I meant to take. Descending a hill I came to a bridge, over
a rivulet of some depth, with a carriage way through the water.

Just as I had passed it, I met a post-chariot that drove into the
stream. I was walking forward with my face toward the village, till I
suddenly heard a cry of distress, and looking behind me saw the
carriage overturned in the water. I ran with all speed back to the
brook: the body of the carriage was almost covered, the horses
were both down, and the postillion, entangled between them,
called aloud for help! or his master would be drowned. I plunged
into the water without fear, having, as I have elsewhere noticed,
long ago learned to swim. Perceiving the extreme danger of the
person in the carriage, I struck directly toward the door, which I
opened and relieved him, or confined as he was he must have been
almost instantly suffocated. His terror was exceedingly great, and
as soon as he was fairly on his feet, he exclaimed with prodigious
eagerness, 'God for ever bless you, my good boy; you have saved
my life!'—The pallidness of his countenance expressed very strongly
the danger of perishing in which he had felt himself.

We then both waded out of the water, he sat down on the side of
the bridge, and I called to some men in a neighbouring field to come
and help the postillion. I then returned to the gentleman, who was
shivering as if in an ague fit. I asked if I should run and get him help,
for he seemed very ill? 'You are a compassionate brave little fellow,'
said he; and, looking more earnestly at me, exclaimed, 'I hope you
are not hurt; how came you so bloody?' I knew not what to say,
and returned no answer. 'You do not speak, child?' said he. 'Let
me go and get you some help, Sir,' replied I—'Nay, nay, but are
you hurt?'—'Not more than I was before this accident'—'Where

do you come from?'—I was silent—'Who are you?'—'A poor
friendless boy'—'Have you not a father?'—'No'—'A mother?'
——'Yes: but she is forsaken by her father, and cannot get bread
for herself?'—'How came you in this condition?'—'My master
knocked me down and trod on me'—'Knocked you down and trod
on you?'—'Yes: he was very cruel to me'—'Cruel indeed! Did he
often treat you ill?'—'I do not know what other poor boys suffer,
but he was so passionate that I was never safe.'——'And you have
run away from him?'—'I was afraid he would murder me'——
'Poor creature! Your eye is black, your forehead cut, and your hair
quite clotted with blood'—'I have a bad gash in my head; but I
can bear it. You shake worse and worse; let me go and get you some
help; the village is not far off.'—'I feel I am not well'—'Shall I
call one of the men?'—'Do, my good fellow.'

I ran, and the men came; they had set the carriage on its wheels,
but it was entirely wet, and not fit to ride in. The gentleman therefore leaned on one of them, walked slowly back to the village, and
desired me to follow. I gladly obeyed the order. He had pitied me,
I had saved his life; if I could not make a friend I was in danger of
starving, and I began to hope that I had now found one.

The best accommodations that the only inn in the village
afforded were quickly procured. At first the gentleman ordered a
post-chaise, to return home; but he soon felt himself so ill that he
desired a bed might be got ready, and in the mean time sent to the
nearest medical man, both for himself and to examine my wounds.
What was still better, he ordered the people of the house to give me
whatever I chose to eat and drink, and told them he had certainly
been a dead man at that moment, if it had not been for me. But he
would not forget me; he would take care of me as long as he lived.

This was joyful news indeed; or rather something much more
exquisite than joyful. My heart melted when I heard him; I burst
into tears, and replied, 'I would willingly die to serve him.'

He then went to bed, and as evening came on the fever with which
he was attacked increased. The anxiety I felt was excessive, and I
was so earnest in my intreaties to sit and watch by him, that he was
prevailed on to grant my request. From what I can now recollect,
I imagine the apothecary gave him the common remedy, Dr. James's
powders.[1] When the medicine no longer operated he fell into a sound
sleep, about eleven o'clock, and when he awoke the next morning
found himself much refreshed and free from fever.

In the interim my wounds had been dressed, and to make the truth of my story evident, I took care to shew the bruises, and black and blue marks, with which my body was plentifully covered. Every favourable circumstance, every precaution, every effort was now indeed become necessary; for, late in the evening, I accidentally learned a secret of the most important and hope-inspiring, yet alarming nature. My all was at stake, my very existence seemed to depend on the person who it is true had promised to be my protector, but who, perhaps, when he should hear who I was, might again become my persecutor. The man to whom I had attached myself, whose life I had saved, and who had avowed a sense of the obligation, was no other than my grandfather!

The moment I heard this terrific intelligence, it chilled and animated me alternately; and, as soon as I could recollect myself, I determined not to quit his apartment all night. No persuasions could prevail on me; and when the chambermaid, who sat up with him, attempted to use force, I was so violent in my resistance that she desisted, and suffered me to remain in quiet.

When he awoke in the morning I trembled at the sound of his voice. I remembered the oath he had sworn, which my mother had often affirmed he would never break. He was totally changed, in my idea, from the gentleman whose life I had saved the day before. There had not indeed been any thing particularly winning in his aspect; but then there was a strong sense of danger, and of obligation to the instrument of his escape, who interested him something the more by being unfortunate. But an oath, solemnly taken by a man of so sacred a character? The thought was dreadful!

His curtains were drawn, and my trepidation increased. 'What, my good boy,' said he, 'are you up and here already?' 'He has never been in bed,' answered the chambermaid. 'We could not get him out of the room.' I replied in a faint voice, such as my fears inspired, 'I hoped he was better.' 'Yes, yes,' said he, 'I have had a good sleep, and feel as if I wanted my breakfast; go, my girl, and let it be got ready.'

The chambermaid obeyed his orders, and he continued—'Why did not you go to bed, child?'—'It did not become me to leave you'—'How so?' 'I hope I know my duty better'—'Your duty!' —'Yes, Sir'—'You seem to be an extraordinary boy; you act with great spirit, and talk with more good sense than I should expect from your poverty and education'—'So I ought to do, Sir; though

I am desolate, I have been brought up better than most poor boys'
—'Ay indeed!'

The apothecary entered, and, after having paid all necessary
attention to his patient, informed him of the state in which he had
found me; talked of my wounds and bruises, and the cruelty of the
man that could inflict them; repeated several of the anecdotes of his
tyranny, which I had told him, and concluded with remarks on my
good fortune, in having found so kind a protector.

'The boy has saved my life,' said my grandfather, 'and he shall not
want a friend.' 'Are you quite sure of that, Sir?' answered I, with
emphatical anxiety. 'Never, while I live,' replied the rector. 'Nay,
but are you quite quite positive?' 'Do you doubt my word, boy?'
——'That is very wrong of you indeed, child,' said the apothecary.
—A thought suddenly struck me. If he would but take an oath, said
I to myself? The oath, the oath! that was what I dreaded! An
opposite oath seemed to be my only safe-guard. I continued—'I
swear, Sir, while I have life never to forsake you, but to be dutiful
and true to you'—'Swear boy?'—'Yes, Sir, most solemnly.'—
I spoke with great fervor—'You are an unaccountable boy'—'Oh
that *you* would never forsake *me*'—'I tell you I will not'—'Oh
that you never would!'—'Won't you believe me?'—'Oh that you
never never would!'—'The boy I believe wants me to swear too'
—'Ay; do, Sir; take an oath not to disown me; and indeed indeed
I'll die willingly to deserve your favour'—'Disown you'—'Nay,
Sir, but take an oath. You say I saved your life; I would lay down
my own again and again to save it. Do not deny me, do not turn me
to starve, or send me back to be murdered by my barbarous master'
—'I tell you I will not'—'Nay but'—'Well then I swear, boy, I
will not'—'Do you indeed duly and truly swear?'—'Solemnly,
boy! I take heaven to witness that, if you are not guilty of something
very wicked, while I live I will provide for you.'—I fell on my
knees, caught hold of his hand, burst into tears, and exclaimed with
sobs—'God in heaven bless my dear dear good grandfather! He
has forgiven me! He has forgiven me!' 'Grandfather?' 'I am
Hugh Trevor.'

Never did I behold so sudden a change in the human countenance!
The rector's eyes glared at me! There was something ghastly in the
sunken form of his features! My shirt was still red, and my coat
spotted with blood; the hair had been cut away from the wound on
my head, which was covered with a large plaister. My eye was

black, and swelled up, and my forehead too was plaistered above the eye-brow. My body he had been told was covered with bruises, tears bathed my cheeks, and my face was agitated with something like convulsive emotions. This strange figure was suddenly changed into his grandson! It was an apparition he knew not how to endure. To be claimed by such a wretched creature, to have been himself the author of his wretchedness, to have had an oath extorted from him, in direct violation of an opposite oath, to feel this universal shock to his pride and his prejudices was a complication of jarring sensations that confounded him. To resist was an effort beyond his strength. For a moment he lost his voice: at last he exclaimed, with a hoarse scream—'Take him away'—My heart sunk within me. The apothecary stood petrified with astonishment. The rector again repeated with increasing agony—'Take him away! Begone! Never let me see him more!'

The pang I felt was unutterable. I rose with a feeling of despair that was annihilating, and was going broken hearted out of the room. At that instant the figure of my master started to recollection, and with such terror as to subdue every other fear. I turned back, fell on my knees again, and clasping my hands cried out, 'For God Almighty's sake, do not send me back to my master! I shall never escape with life! He will murder me! He will murder me! I'll be your servant as long as I live. I will go of your errands; take care of your horses; drive your plough; weed your garden; do any thing you bid me; indeed, indeed I will.—Do not send me back to be murdered!'

The excess of my feelings had something of a calming effect on those of the rector. He repeated, 'Go go, boy, go! I feel myself very ill!' The apothecary recovered his tongue and added, 'Ay, my good child, you had better go.'

The altered voice of the rector removed a part of the load that oppressed me, and I left the room, though with no little sensation of despondency. In about half an hour the apothecary came down. He had had a conversation with the rector, who I found could not endure the sight of me again, under my present forlorn or rather accusing form. The remembrance however that I had saved his life was predominant. How his casuistry settled the account between his two oaths I never heard; on that subject he was eternally silent. He was probably ashamed of having taken the first, and of having been tricked out of the second. His orders were that I should go home with the apothecary, with whom he had arranged matters, should be new clothed, wait till my wounds were healed, and then, if he possibly could, he would prevail upon himself to see me.

CHAPTER X

Hopes in behalf of my mother: The arrival of the rector: I gain his favour: Am adopted by him: And effect a family reconciliation. Anecdotes of a school-fellow, and his sister: Grammatical and musical studies: Causes of discontent between the Squire and the rector: Tythes and law produce quarrels: The tragi-comic tale of the rats

SIX weeks had elapsed before my wounds, bruises, and black marks, had totally disappeared; and the scar above my eye still retained a red appearance. The alteration of my person however, aided as it was by dress, was so remarkable as to excite surprise among my village friends. The apothecary prided himself upon the change, persuading himself that the rector would thank him for the present of so fine a grandson. His art and care had wrought miracles, I was quite another creature; the alteration was so prodigious since he had taken me that he was sure there was not so fine a boy in all England.

In the mean time I had written to my mother, whose cottage was about ten miles across the country, from the village where the apothecary lived. He would not permit me to go to her, it might offend the rector; but he agreed that, if she should by chance come to me, there could be no harm in my speaking to my mother. He too understood casuistry. She accordingly came to see me, and was overjoyed at what had happened; it might lead to a general re-conciliation: especially now that my brother and sister were both dead. They had been carried off by the small-pox; and she rightly enough conjectured that the rector would not be the less prone to pardon her for being clear of further incumbrance. She enjoined me to intercede in her behalf, and I very sincerely promised to speak as soon as I dared.

The day at last came on which the rector was to pay his visit, and examine how far I was fit to be his grandson. My terror by this time had considerably abated: he having taken thus much notice of me, I scarcely could believe myself in danger of being rejected. I was not however without trepidation, and when the well known post chariot drove up to the door my heart sunk within me.

The apothecary had two sons, one a year older, and the other some months younger that I was. The eldest was deformed, and his brother squinted abominably. Curiosity had brought them and the whole family into the parlour, to be spectators of the interview. My grandfather entered; I was dressed as genteelly as every effort of the village taylor could contrive; an appearance so different from that of the beaten, bruised, and wounded poor elf he first had seen, with clouted shoes, torn stockings, and coarse coating, dripping with water, and clotted with blood, was so great as scarcely to be credible. The ugliness of my companions did but enhance the superiority of my look; he could not be mistaken in which was his grandson, and the pleasure my pre-eminence inspired excited a smile of no little approbation. For my part I had conceived an affection for him; first I had saved his life, then he had relieved me from distress, and now was come to own me as his grandson. The change of my present situation from that in which I had endured so much misery gave me ineffable pleasure. The entrance of the rector, who had been the cause of this change, and the smile with which he regarded me went to my heart. I kneeled, my eyes flowing in tears, and begged his blessing. He gave it, bade me rise, and thus made me one of the happiest creatures existing.

The rector stayed some time to settle accounts with the apothecary, after which the postillion was called, leave was taken, and I found myself seated beside my grandfather, in that fortunate post chariot from which I had so happily extricated him.

How extreme are the vicissitudes of life! What a reverse of fortune was here! From hard fare, severe labour, and a brutal tyrant, to plenty, ease, and smiling felicity. No longer chained in poverty and ignorance, I now had free access to the precious mines of knowledge. Far from being restrained, I had every encouragement to pursue inquiry; and the happiness of the change was at first so great as almost to be incredible. But the youthful mind easily acquires new habits, and my character varied with the accidents by which it was influenced. Yet, to use my father's language, the case-hardening I had received tempered my future life, and prepared me to endure those misfortunes with fortitude which might otherwise have broken my spirit.

From the day that I arrived at the rectory, I increased so fast in my grandfather's favour that he scarcely knew how to deny me a request. I was soon bold enough to petition for my mother; and though the pill at first was bitter, my repeated importunities at length prevailed, and the rector agreed that, when his daughter should have sufficiently humbled herself, in terms suited to his dignity and her degradation, she should be permitted to kneel at his footstool for pardon, instead of perishing like an out-cast as she deserved.

It was not to be expected that my mother should object to the conditions; the alternative was very simple, submit or starve. Beside she had been too much accustomed to the display of the collective authority, accumulated in the person of the rector, to think of contest. His government was patriarchal, and his powers plenipotentiary. He was the head of his family, the priest of the parish, the justice of peace for the hundred,[1] and the greatest man of miles around. He had no rival, except the before-mentioned Squire Mowbray, whom, if divines can hate, I certainly think he hated.

Of the claims of my late master over me, as his apprentice, I never heard more. Perhaps there was no indenture, for I do not recollect to have signed one; but if there were he certainly was too conscious of his guilt to dare to enforce his right, now that he found me acknowledged and protected by a man so powerful as my grandfather. It is possible indeed that he should never have heard what became of me; though I consider that as very improbable. While I was at Oxford, I was informed that he died raving, with a fever in the brain.

I have mentioned the encouragement I received to pursue inquiry: one of the first things the rector thought of was my education. Now that he had owned I was indeed his grandson, it was fitting that his grandson should be a gentleman. In the parish committed to his pastoral guidance was a grammar school, that had been endowed, not indeed by Squire Mowbray or his ancestors, but, by the family that in times of yore had held the same estate. The pious founder had vested the government not entirely in his own family, and its representatives, but in that family and the rector for the time being. This circumstance, and many others of a parochial nature, conduced to a kind of partition of power, well calculated to excite contempt in the wealthy Squire, who was likewise lord of the manor, and inflame jealousy in heaven's holy vice-gerent, whose very office on earth is to govern, and to detect, reprove, and rectify, the wanderings of us silly sheep.

To this school I was immediately sent; and here, among other competitors was the Squire's eldest son, Hector Mowbray. He was two years older than I, and in the high exercise of that power to which he was the redoubted heir. To insult the boys, seize their marbles, split their tops, cuff them if they muttered, kick them if they complained to the master, get them flogged if they kicked and cuffed in return, and tyrannize over them to the very stretch of his invention, were practices in which he daily made himself more and more expert. He was the young Squire, and that was a receipt in full for all demands.

I soon came to understand that he was the son of a great man! a very great man indeed! and that there was a prodigious difference between flesh and blood of a squire's propagating, and that of ordinary breed. But I heard it so often repeated, and saw it proved in such a variety of instances, that I too was the grandson of a great man, ay so great as openly to declare war against, or at least bid defiance to, the giant power of Magog Mowbray (it was an epithet of my grandfather's giving) I say, I was so fully convinced that I myself was the son of somebody (pshaw! I mean the grandson) that no sooner did young Hector begin to exercise his ingenuity upon me, than I found myself exceedingly disposed to rebel. I had been bred in a hardy school.

At my first admission into this seminary, I did not immediately and fully enter into the spirit and practice of the place; though I soon became tolerably active. At robbing orchards, tying up latches, lifting gates, breaking down hedges, and driving cattle astray, I was by no means so great a proficient as Hector; nor had I any great affection for swimming hedgehogs, hunting cats, or setting dogs at boys and beggars; but at climbing trees, running, leaping, swimming, and such like exercises, I was among the most alert.

My courage too was soon put to the proof, and my opponents found that I entered on action with very tolerable alacrity; so that not to mention sparrings and skirmishes, from which having begun I was never the first to flinch, I had not been a year at school, before I had been declared the conqueror in three set battles. The third was with a butcher's boy, in defence of Hector, who for once instead of giving had suffered insult, but who, though older and stronger than I was, had not the courage to attack his hardy antagonist. My victory was dearly earned, for the boy was considerably my superior in age and strength, and bred to the sport. But this defence of him, and the fear of having me for a foe, induced Hector to court my favour, and often to invite me to Mowbray Hall.

Nor did the whole of my fame end here; the first day I entered the school I was allowed to be the best English scholar, excepting one Turl, a youth noted for his talents, and who while he remained there continually kept his place in every class, as head boy. But this was no triumph over me, for beside having been so long at school, he had three or four years the advantage of me in point of age. Neither did my thirst of inquiry abate, and I had now not only books but instructors; on the contrary, my eagerness increased, and my progress both in Latin and Greek was rapid. The rector was astonished at it, and was often embarrassed by the questions which my desire of learning impelled me to put.

Among my other acquirements, I became a practical musician. The rector could strum the bass tolerably, and his friend the lawyer could play the violin, in which however he was excelled by the clerk of the parish. I retained some remembrance of what I had formerly studied, and felt a great desire to learn; the rector encouraged it, and as the clerk is always the very humble servant and slave of the parson, he was inducted my music master. I loved the art, so that in less than twelve months I had made a sufficient progress to join in Corelli's[1] and even Handel's trios, and thus to strengthen the parsonage-house band.

People who hate each other do yet visit and keep up an intercourse, according to set forms, purposely to conceal their hatred, it being a hideous and degrading vice, of which all men are more or less either ashamed or afraid. To preserve these appearances, or perhaps from the impulse of vanity, the rector admitted of my excursions to Mowbray Hall. For my own part, I found a motive more alluring than the society of Hector, that frequently occasioned me to repeat these visits. His sister, Olivia, two years younger than myself, was usually one of our parlour playmates. Born of the same mother, living in the same family, accustomed to the same manners, it is difficult to account for the very opposite propensities of this brother and sister. Every thing the reverse of what has been recited of Hector was visible in Olivia. He was boisterous, selfish, and brutal; she was compassionate, generous, and gentle: his faculties were sluggish, obtuse, and confined; hers were acute, discriminating, and capacious: his want of feeling made him delight to inflict torture; her extreme sensibility made her fly to administer relief. The company of Olivia soon became very attractive, and the rambles that I have sometimes taken with her, hand in hand over Mowbray Park, afforded no common delight. She too was a musician, and already famous for her fine voice and execution on the harpsichord. I accompanied her on the violin, and sang duets with her so as to surprize and even charm the Squire, and throw the visitors at Mowbray Hall into raptures.

This sweet intercourse however was terminated by the bickerings, back-bitings, and smothered jealousies, between the Squire and my grandfather, which at length burst into a flame. The Squire had succeeded to his estate and manor by the death of a very distant relation, and by this relation the rector had been presented to his living: he therefore considered himself as under no kind of obligation to the Squire; while the latter on the contrary, the advowson[1] being parcel and part of the manor, held the manor, and himself as owner of the manor, to be the actual donor.

To all this was added another very serious cause of discontent, that of tythes; a cause that disturbs half the villages in the kingdom, and that frequently exhibits the man who is sent to preach peace, and afford an example of mild forbearance and christian humility, as a litigious, quarrelsome and odious tyrant; much better qualified to herd with wolves than to be the shepherd of his meek master. It is sufficiently certain that neither Christ nor his apostles ever took tythes; and the esquires, farmers, and landholders, of this christian kingdom, would in general be better satisfied, if their successors were to follow so disinterested and laudable an example.

My grandfather had accepted his rectory at the same commutation[2] that the former incumbent had enjoyed it; and, while the patron to whom he owed the presentation was living, he contented himself with his bargain as well as he could: but, soon after the accession of Squire Mowbray, considering that tie as no longer a clog to his conscience, he began to inquire very seriously into the real value of his first fruits[3] and tythes, personal, predial, and mixed:[4] that is, his great tythes and his small. The calculation inflamed his avarice, and he purchased and read all the books on the subject of tythes he could collect. Being fond of power, and having discovered (as he supposed) that the man who knows the most quirks in law has the greatest quantity of power over his simple and ignorant neighbours, he was a tolerably laborious and successful student of these quirks. I say, tolerably; for it seldom happens that the rector is the most industrious person in the parish.

It was thus that, after having made the whole hundred tremble at his authority, in the exercise of his office of justice of the peace, he next hoped to conquer the Behemoth,[1] Magog[2] Mowbray himself. His own fears of being vanquished and the advice of his friends had indeed, for years, prevented him from proceeding to an open rupture with his parish, and the Squire at its head: but his irritability had been gradually increasing ever since the departure of my uncle Elford. The progress of his avarice at first was slow; but it gained strength as it proceeded, and there was now no one whose opinion had sufficient weight with him to keep it longer quiet. His friend the lawyer, it is true, might have had some such influence over him; but the lawyer had been duly articled to the most famous, that is the most litigious, attorney in the country, and was himself his very famous successor; a practitioner of the first repute.

The Squire, by a trick he thought proper to play, contributed not a little to kindle the smothering embers. My grandfather having announced his intention of demanding a commutation of nearly double the sum, or of being paid his tythes in kind—first his tythes *de jure*, and next his tythes by custom; enumerating them all and each; corn, hay, hops and hemp; fruits, roots, seeds and weeds; wool, milk, chickens, ducklings, and goslings, or eggs; corn rakings and pond drawings; not forgetting agistment[3] and *subbois*,[4] or *sylva caedua*;[5] with many many more of the sweets of our prolific mother earth, which I would enumerate if I did but recollect them, and for which men so often have been and still are impleaded in Court Christian—these particulars, I say, being recapitulated and set forth in terrible array, by the rector, excited in the whole parish so much dread of the rapacious vulture, who was coming with such a swoop upon them, that high and low, young and old, rich and poor, all began to tremble.

The Squire was the only man, at first, who durst bid defiance to the general ravager. The rector's deviation from his original commutation agreement threw him into a rage, and he panted for an opportunity of shewing the contempt in which he held my grandfather and his threats.

Malicious chance favoured his wishes. It happened, while his passions were in full force, that a rat-catcher arrived at Mowbray Hall; which at that time was greatly infested by the large Norway rats.[1] The man had the art of taking them alive, and was accordingly employed by the Squire. While he was preparing to perform his business, the gentle Olivia, very innocently and without any foresight of consequences, chanced to say—'I do not think, papa, that our good rector, who considers all things as tytheable, would be much pleased to have his tythe of rats'—The Squire no sooner heard this sentence uttered than he began to dance and halloo, like a madman; swearing most vociferously—'By G—, wench, he shall ha' um! He shall ha' um! He shall ha' um!'

His boisterous joy at this rare thought, which was indeed far beyond the discovery of his own brain, could not be appeased; nor could Olivia, sorry for what she had done, prevent him from most resolutely determining to put it in practice. The ratcatcher was immediately ordered to entrap as many of his best friends as he possibly could; and a carpenter was set to work to make a covered box, for the rector's tythe-rats, with a lifting door. Hector Mowbray was consulted on the whole progress; and the fancies of father and son were tickled to excess, by the happy prank they were about to play.

The rats were caught, the box was made, and the ratcatcher commanded to select the finest, fattest and largest of them, and enclose them in their cage. In order to heighten and secure their enjoyment, the Squire and Hector chose four of the stoutest servants, gave the cage into their custody, and ordered the ratcatcher to attend. Away they then went in turbulent procession. They even wanted Olivia to go with them to see the sport; and young Hector, probably with malice prepense[2] against me, when she refused, was for using force; but she was a favourite with the Squire, and being very determined was suffered to remain at home.

Arrived at the parsonage-house, they entered the hall. The Squire loudly called for the rector. The noise and vociferation of their approach had rouzed his attention, and he was not long in coming. The servants too were collected, some without the door and others of more authority within it, to hear and see what all this could mean.

I likewise was one of the company.——'Here! here! Mr. Rector,' bawled the Squire, 'we ha' brought you your due. I'll warrant, for once, you sha'n't grumble that we do not pay you your tythes!'

My grandfather, hearing this address, seeing the covered cage, and remarking the malicious grins of the Squire and his whole posse, knew not what to think, and began to suspect there was mischief in the wind—'By the waunds!¹ mister tythe taker,' continued the Squire, 'but you shall ha' your own! Here, lads, lift up the cage: put it on the table; let his reverence see what we ha' brought'n! Come, raise the door!'

The men, with each a broad grin upon his countenance, did as they were bidden: they lifted up the box, raised the door, and out burst above twenty of the largest wildest rats the well stocked barns of Mowbray Hall could afford. Their numbers, their squealing, their ferocity, their attempts to escape, and the bounds they gave from side to side struck the whole parsonage house community with a panic. The women screamed; the rector foamed; the squire hallooed; and the men seized bellows, poker, tongs, and every other weapon or missile that was at hand. The uproar was universal, and the Squire never before or after felt himself so great a hero! The death of the fox itself was unequal to it!

This was but the first act of the farce, the catastrophe of which had something in it of a more tragical cast. Servants partake of the prejudices of their masters, and the whole parsonage-house, young and old, male and female, felt itself insulted. No sooner therefore were the rats discomfited than the rector, summoning all his magisterial and orthodox dignity, commanded the Squire and his troop to depart. Despising the mandate, Magog Mowbray continued his exultations and coarse sarcasms; and, Oh frailty of human nature! the man of God forgot the peaceful precepts of his divine mission, and gave the signal for a general assault. Nay he himself, so unruly are the hands and feet even of a parson in a passion, was one of the most eager combatants. Age itself could not bind his arms.

The battle raged, fierce and dreadful, for sometime in the hall: but heroism soon found it wanted elbow-room, and the two armies by mutual consent sallied forth. Numbers were in our favour, for the very maids, armed with mop-handles, broomsticks, and rolling pins, acted like Amazons. I was far from idle, for I had singled out my foe. Hector, whose courage example had enflamed to a very unruly height, had even dared to begin the attack; and I was no less alert in opposition. But though he was Hector, I as it happened was Achilles, and bestowed my wrath upon him most unsparingly. In fine, valour, victory, and right, were for once united, and we very fairly put the Squire, his heir, his ratcatcher, and his beef-eaters to flight.

The rector, dreading a second attack from the enemy, began to fortify his castle, provide ammunition, and arrange his troops. I acted as his aide-de-camp, burning to be myself commander in chief. But the caution was superfluous: the Squire, like his son, was rather revengeful than valorous, and returned no more to the field.

In the parish however the fortune of the day might be said to wear a very different face, for there was not a farmer who did not triumph at the tythe in kind, which had been paid to the rector; and it became a general threat to sweep the parish of moles, weazles, stoats, polecats and vermin of every species, and tenant the rectory with them, if any thing more was heard on the subject of tythes. Neither did detraction forget to remind the rector of his age, and how shameful it was for a man with one foot in the grave to quarrel with and rob the poor farmers, whom he was hired to guide, console, and love. The poor farmers forgot that, in the eye of the law, the robbery was theirs; and the rector forgot that in the eye of justice and common sense, he had already more than enough. The framers of the law too forgot that to hire a man to love a whole parish is but a blundering kind of a mode. But such mistakes are daily made.

CHAPTER XI

*Different accounts of the battle: Olivia offended: Legal
distinctions, and law-suits commenced*

THE rumours of the village soon made it apparent that the history of the battle royal, as given by the vanquished party, like many other histories, deviated in various particulars from the strict truth. Thus the Squire asserted that he and his myrmidons quitted the field victoriously, drums beating and colours flying; after having driven the enemy back into their citadel and strong holds, out of which they durst not peep: and to the truth of what the Squire asserted his trusty adherents made it a case of conscience to swear.

Encouraged by so good an example, Hector vaunted loudly of his own high feats of arms; and by his narration made it appear, not only how much he had the best of the battle with me, but that it was by kicking him when up, kneeing him when down, striking him when rising, and other such like cowardly foul and malicious acts, that he brought home such a quantity of bruises (of which with all his valour he bitterly complained) together with a pair of black eyes.

Knowing my partiality for his sister, and suspecting that Olivia herself was not without her inclinations, he did not fail to repeat these particulars when she was present; carefully adding such other injurious accusations and epithets as might most effectually lower me in her esteem. His efforts were successful: Olivia was offended, first that her brother should be so cruelly beaten by one of whom she had conceived so kindly, and next that it should be by such base and dishonourable means. Thus one of my chief pleasures, that of visiting at Mowbray Hall, admiring and sometimes mounting the Squire's hunters, and straying through the gardens and grounds with the gentle Olivia, was cut off.

Hector by this time had passed the age of sixteen, and the wrath of the Squire rose so high that he would not suffer him any longer to go to the same school with me: for which reason, it being a part of his plan to send his heir to the university, that he might not only be a Squire but a man of learning, and thus become greater even than his father before him, preparations and arrangements were made something sooner than had been intended, and not long afterward he was entered a gentleman commoner[1] of ****** college, Oxford.

It has been noticed that the farmers thought more of the vexation of their case than of the law; but not so the rector; he thought first of the law, and the law told him that the vexation of the case relative to tythes, was all in his favour. Of the late affray with the Squire indeed he had his doubts. As for the entrance upon his premises, though it might be pleaded it was for a lawful purpose, namely, that of paying tythes, yet, as rats were *feræ naturæ*,[2] and therefore things not tythable, it was very plain that this was a case of trespass *ab initio*, and his action would lie for *a trespass vi et armis*.[3] But unfortunately passion had prevented him from waiting to bring his action, and he had assumed the *vi et armis* to himself in the first instance, not having patience to attend the slow and limping pace of the law. He was not indeed quite certain that, although he and his party gave the first blows, an action of battery brought against Mowbray might not be justified: for did he not come upon him in full force; he, the rector, being in the peace of God and our Lord the King? And did not he, the Squire, by shouting and oaths and blasphemous words, put him, the rector, in bodily fear? And was not the very act of turning ferocious animals, namely, Norway rats, loose in his hall, to the danger of his face, eyes, and throat, a very indubitable and sufficient assault? Was it not likewise clearly in self defence, that the rector and his faithful servants did *molliter manus imponere*[1] on the Squire and his crew?—The *molliter* it is true appeared rather doubtful: but then it was a term of law, and would bear that exact signification which the circumstances of the case required, and lawyers so well know how to give.

Thus, with law in his head, wrath in his heart, and money in his pocket, away went the rector to hold consultations with his now favourite friend the attorney; who has before been mentioned as so thorough bred and far famed a practitioner; the result of which was that an action of *trespass upon the case*,[2] as the safest mode of proceeding, should be brought against the Squire; and that public information should be given that tythes in kind would in six months be demanded from the whole parish; with a formal notice that as malicious threatenings had been uttered against the rector, whom the laws, civil, common, and ecclesiastical, would protect, if any such threatenings should be put in execution actions against the offenders would immediately be instituted.

It was the spring of the year when these resolutions were taken, and before the end of the following November the rector, in consequence of squabbles, insults, and frauds, had brought actions against more than half his parishioners; by which the attorneys, counsellors, and courts were in the end the only gainers, while plaintiff and defendant most ardently concurred and rejoiced in the ruin of each other. But so it is: anger, avarice, and law are terrible things; and malice and selfishness are indefatigable foes.

CHAPTER XII

Progress of my studies: My predilection in favour of theology:
The decay of the rector: His testament, death, and funeral

THREE additional years passed away under the auspices of my
grandfather, during which he pursued his law-suits and I my
studies; though with very different success; he lost the dearest
thing on earth to him, his money; and I gained the dearest thing on
earth to me, knowledge. Among other superfluous appendages,
superfluous to him for he made but little use of it, he had a good
library. Not of his own collecting; he enjoyed it by descent. This
was my daily resort. Its treasures were inexhaustible, and my desire
of information could not be satiated. I spent many happy hours
in it, and it is still remembered by me with that sweet pleasure
which its contents were so well calculated to impart.

I had another accidental advantage. The usher of the school got
preferment, and his successor happened to be well read, both in the
dead and living languages. This person, whose name was Wilmot,
was not only a good scholar and an amiable man but an excellent
poet. He had an affection for me, and I almost worshipped him.
He was assiduous to teach me every thing he knew; and fortunately
I was no less apt and eager to learn. Having already made a tolerable
proficiency in the learned languages, the richness of the French in
authors made me labour to acquire it with avidity. The Italian
poets were equally inviting; so that, by his aid, I mastered the
idioms and attained the spirit of both those languages. The dialects
of the Teutonic were likewise familiar to him, and I made some
progress in the German; being desirous from his recommendation
to read, among others, the works of Lessing,[1] Klopstock, Goethe,
and Schiller. The acquirement of knowledge is an essential and
therefore a pure pleasure; and my time, though laboriously spent,
glided swiftly and happily away.

With respect to amusement, the violin became my favourite. My
now dearest friend, the usher, among his other attainments was a
musician: my affection for him had made him intimate at the
parsonage-house, and his aid greatly promoted our musical parties.

Finding knowledge thus delightful, my zeal to promulgate it was
great. I had as I imagined so much to communicate, that I panted for

an opportunity to address myself to multitudes. At that time I knew no place so well calculated for this purpose as the pulpit; and my inclination to be a preacher was tolerably conformable to the views of the rector. Not but he had his doubts. Few men are satisfied with their own profession; and though he had great veneration for church authority, which he held to be infinitely superior from its very nature to civil government, yet his propensity to dabble in the law had practically and theoretically taught him some of the advantages of its professors. In rank it was true that the Archbishop of Canterbury was the second man in the kingdom, and in the rector's opinion ought to have been indisputably the first. In days of yore, who so potent? But obsolete titles are not equal to actual possessions. The Lord High Chancellor, in this degenerate age, enjoys much more political power. Neither does it in general die with him, like that of the Archbishop. He seldom fails to bequeath an earldom, or a barony at least, to his heir.

On these subjects I had frequent lectures from my grandfather, who perceiving the enterprise of my temper and the progress of my studies, began to entertain hopes that from his loins some future noble family might descend: that is, provided I would follow the advice which he so well knew how to bestow. In support of his argument, he would give me the history of the origin of various Barons, Viscounts, and Earls, which he could trace to some of the lowest departments of the law.

Thus, though he was convinced that the sacerdotal character claimed unlimited authority by right divine, yet, from the perverse and degenerate nature of man, it was most lamentably sinking into decay; while that of the law was rising on its ruins. Had he been a man of the world instead of the rector of a village, he would have heard of another profession, superior to them both for the attainment of what he most coveted, power, rank, and wealth; and would have known that the lawyer only soars to the possession of these supposed blessings by learning a new trade; that is, by making himself a politician.

The effect his maxims produced on me was a conviction that divinity and law were two super-excellent things. But my mind from many circumstances had acquired a moral turn; and, as I at that time supposed morality and religion to be the same, the current of my inclinations was strong in favour of divinity. Whoever imagines the youthful mind cannot easily acquire such moral propensities has never observed it, except when habit and example have already taught it to be perverse. I speak from experience, and well know how much the accounts I had read of Aristides,[1] Epaminondas, Regulus, Cato, and innumerable other great characters among the ancients inflamed my imagination, and gave me a rooted love of virtue; so that even the vulgarly supposed dry precepts of Seneca and Epictetus were perused by me with delight; and with an emulous determination to put them in practice.

My morality however was far from pure: it was such a mixture of truth and error as was communicated to me by conversation, books, and the incidents of life. From the glow of poetry I learnt many noble precepts; but from the same source I derived the pernicious supposition that to conquer countries and exterminate men are the acts of heroes. Further instances would be superfluous: I mean only to remark that, while I was gaining numerous truths, I was likewise confirming myself in various prejudices; many of which it has been the labour of years aided by the lessons of accident to eradicate; and many more no doubt still remain undetected.

And now the period approached when I was to adventure forth into that world of which I had experienced something, had heard so much, and with which I was so impatient to become still better acquainted. The weight of age began to press upon the rector and he had an apoplectic fit, at which he was very seriously alarmed. He then thought it high time to put his temporal affairs into the best order that his own folly would admit; for, in consequence of his lawsuits, they were so much in the hands and power of his friend, the lawyer, that notwithstanding the plausibility and professions of the latter, he trembled when he came to reflect how much they were involved. His former parsimony had led him to hope he should leave great wealth behind him; but, when he came to consult his friend concerning his will, he had the mortification to find how much it had been diminished by his litigious avarice.

The will however was made, but it was under this friend's direction and influence. The lawyer was a lawyer, and, affecting the character of disinterestedness, reminded the rector of the folly of youth, and in how short a period money that had taken a life to acquire was frequently squandered by a thoughtless heir. His advice therefore was that the property should be left to my mother, and that she should have a joint executor. This executor ought to be the most honest of men and the dearest of friends, or he would never perform so very arduous and unprofitable a task with fidelity and effect: a task as thankless as it is laborious, and which nothing should prevail on him to undertake, but the desire to serve some very dear and much esteemed friend.

With respect to my mother and me, I was her darling, and there was no danger that she should marry again; at least infinitely less than that a young man should abuse wealth, of which he had not by experience learned the value. By making me dependent, my assiduity would be increased: but, that all might be safe, it might perhaps be well to set apart a sum, for my maintenance at the university; and, if I should decide for the church when I quitted it, another for the purchase of an advowson; or, if for the law, to place me in the office of some eminent practitioner.

This counsel was so much that of a man of foresight, and knowledge of the world, that my grandfather heard it with pleasure. It was literally followed. One hundred per annum for four years residence at the university was allotted me; and a legacy of a thousand pounds was added, which, though the purchase of an advowson was recommended, was entrusted to my discretion, and when I should come of age left to my own disposal. The will was then copied and signed, and the lawyer, at the request of a dear and dying friend, was prevailed on to be joint executor with my mother. This was the last legal act and deed of the rector, for he died within a month; and with him died his few friendships, his many enmities, and his destructive law-suits. His spiritual flock was right glad that he was gone; and his funeral was only attended by my mother, myself, the lawyer, the master and usher of the grammar school, and a few visiting friends.

When the will was opened, I and my mother were necessarily present. The rector had detailed the arguments which his friend had suggested: he mentioned his fears of youthful folly, but spoke of me with affection and hope, and seriously warned my mother, for my sake, to beware of a second marriage; with which requisition she very solemnly affirmed it was her determination to comply. I was young and high in expectation; for Hugh the second was scarcely less sanguine of temper than Hugh the first. Few people in the world, I was persuaded, were possessed of such extraordinary abilities as myself. I had read, in a thousand places, of the high rewards bestowed on men of learning, wit, and genius; I was therefore eager to sally forth, convinced that I need only be seen to be admired, and known to be employed. These ideas were so familiar to my mind that I intreated my mother to lay no restraint upon her inclinations, for I well knew how to provide for myself: but she was wounded by the request, and begged I would not kill her, by a supposition so cutting, so unaffectionate, and so unamiable. The energy with which she expressed herself somewhat surprized me: a kind of good humoured chearfulness, which resembled indifference rather than sentiment, was the leading feature in my mother's character. She was however on this occasion more sentimental, because as I supposed more in earnest, than usual.

CHAPTER XIII

Preparations for parting: A journey: More of education, or something to be learned in a stage coach

THESE solemn affairs being adjusted, and by the lapse of a few weeks we the mourners more reconciled to our loss, it began to be necessary for me to prepare for my removal to the university: for it was there only, according to the wise laws of our wise fore-fathers (and who will dare to suppose that our forefathers were foolish, or could make foolish laws?) that a regular and incontestible induction can be obtained to the holy ministry, of which I was ambitious.

It was determined I should enter of ****** college, Oxford; the same at which Hector Mowbray had been admitted, and to which all the scholars from the grammar school where I was educated repaired. But there was a warm contest whether I should enter as a commoner,[1] or a gentleman commoner. My mother was eager for the latter, which the lawyer opposed. She could not endure that her dear Hugh should, as it were publicly, confess the superiority of his rival and sworn foe, the insolent Hector. He contended that to affect to rival him in expence were absurd, and might lead to destructive consequences. The lawyer had the best of the argument, yet I was inclined to take part with my mother. Inferiority was what I was little disposed to acknowledge; I therefore consulted my friend the usher. Fortunately he had more wisdom, and alledged some very convincing moral motives, which I too much respected to disobey.

Previous to my departure, I endured much lecturing, which I considered as exceedingly useless, and consequently little less than impertinent. The lawyer reminded me of my youth, and warned me against the knavery of mankind, who he affirmed are universally prone to prey upon one another. This, miracles out of the question, must be the creed of a lawyer. I had a better opinion of my fellow bipeds, of whom I yet knew but little, and heard him with something like contempt. My mother wearied me with intreaties to write to her at least once a week. She should never be easy out of my sight, if she did not hear from me frequently. The omission of a mail would throw her into the utmost terrors: she should conclude I was sick, or dying, nay perhaps dead, and she conjured me to respect her maternal feelings. I did respect them, and promised all she required. She was desirous too that I should continually be with her, during the vacations. The lawyer on the contrary advised me to remain at college, and pursue my studies.

It will seem very unnatural to most mothers, and highly censurable to many moralists, that the person whom I felt the greatest regret at parting with was my instructor and friend, the usher. He was no less affectionate. He too cautioned me against youthful confidence, and hinted that men were not quite so good as they should be. I knew him to be a little inclined to melancholy, and that he considered himself as a neglected man, who had reason to complain of the world's injustice. But, though the belief that this was true moved my compassion, he did not convince me that men were constitutionally inclined to evil. My own feelings loudly spoke the contrary. I had not yet been initiated. I knew but little of those false wants by which the mind of man is perverted. The credulity of youth can only be cured by the experience of age: the prejudices of age can only be eradicated by appealing to the feelings and facts of youth. Man becomes what the mistaken institutions of society inevitably make him: his tendency is to promote his own well being, and the well being of the creatures around him; these can only be promoted by virtue; consequently, when he is vicious it is from mistake, and his original sin is ignorance.

My books, clothes, and effects were forwarded to the next market town, through which the coach that I was to travel in passed. That I might meet it in time on Monday morning, it was necessary to set out the evening before, and sleep at the inn. My mind was by no means free from popular prejudices, when they were of a moral cast, and I was not entirely satisfied at beginning my journey on a Sunday. I struggled against the nonsense of ill omens, for I had read books in which they were ridiculed; but I was not quite certain that the action was in itself right. Things however were thus arranged, and my friends were assembled to take leave of me. The lawyer's reiterated advice teased me; my mother's tears gave me pain; but the pressure of the usher's hand and his cordial 'God be with you!' went to my heart. However, the sun shone, the month was May, the grass was green, the birds were singing, my hopes were mantling, and my cares were soon forgotten. I seemed to look back on my past existence as on a kind of imprisonment; and my spirits fluttered, as if just set free to wander through a world of unknown delights.

Fortune was disposed to favour the delusive vision; for at the inn on the morrow, being roused from a sound sleep to pursue my journey, after stepping into the coach, I found myself seated opposite to the handsomest sweetest young lady I had ever beheld. I except Olivia; but her I had only known as it were a child, and I looked back on those as on childish days. The lovely creature was clothed in a sky-blue riding-habit with embroidered button-holes, and a green hat and feather, with suitable decorations. She had a delicate twisted cane-whip in her hand, a nosegay in her bosom, and a purple cestus[1] round her waist. There were beside two gentlemen in the coach, genteelly dressed; and they all appeared to know each other.

The young lady spoke to every body, without the least reserve or pride, which did but increase the good opinion I had conceived of her. The gentlemen likewise were easy and familiar; and, in spite of my friend the lawyer, I already plainly perceived the world was a very good humoured polite and pleasant world. The young lady was peculiarly attentive and kind to me, and, I being but *a raw traveller*, insisted that the gentleman next her should change places with me, that I might sit with my face toward the horses, lest I should be sick by riding backward. At this however my manly pride revolted, and I obstinately kept my seat, notwithstanding her very obliging intreaties. The phrase *raw traveller* I did not think quite so politely and happily chosen as the rest; but then it fell from such a pair of modest lips, that it was impossible to conceive offence.

After a pleasant ride of three hours, we arrived at the breakfasting place. The coach door was opened, and I, not waiting for the steps, leaped out like a young grey-hound. The lady seemed half inclined to follow me, but was timid. I placed myself properly, promised to catch her, and she sprang into my arms. Suddenly recollecting herself, she exclaimed,—'What a wild creature I am!' and ran away, hiding her face with her hands. I blamed myself for having been too forward, and inwardly applauded her quick sense of propriety. The gentlemen laughed, walked into the breakfasting-room, and invited me to follow them.

In about ten minutes, the young lady entered with apologies, and hoping we knew the rules of travelling too well to wait. She seemed improved in beauty. There was a kind of bloom spread over her countenance, contrasted with a delicate pearl white, such as I had never seen in the finest cherry cheeks of our village maidens. 'It is the blush at the little incident of leaping from the coach', said I to myself, 'that has thus improved her complexion.' She sat down to the table, and, with the kindness that seemed native to her, poured out my tea, sugared and creamed it just to my taste, and handed it to me with sweetness that was quite seducing. I knew not how to return or to merit her favours, and the attempt made me mawkishly sentimental. 'It is delightful', said I, 'when amiable people live together in happy society.' 'It is indeed,' said she, and her bosom appeared gently to heave.

Our feelings seemed to vibrate in unison, but they were disturbed by a sudden burst of coughing of one of the gentlemen, drinking his tea; and were not much harmonized by a fit of laughing with which the other was seized, who told his companion he was *a droll dog*. But what the drollery could be, of a man choked with swallowing too hastily, was more than I could comprehend. The appellation of *droll dog* however was repeated, till the two gentlemen could appease their titillation. I own I thought it a little rude; but they seemed neither of them so well-bred as the lady, and I concluded they could be nothing more than travelling acquaintance. I even supposed I saw them wink at each other, as if there had been something strange or improper in my behaviour.

I then thought it quite necessary to let them know who I was. Accordingly I took an opportunity of succintly telling them whence I came, where I was going, who my relations were, and what my expectations. I let them understand that I had money in my purse, and gave broad hints that I was neither fool nor coward. They were quite civil, but still their looks to each other seemed very significant, and to have more meaning than I knew how to develope. I was a little piqued, but comforted myself with the assurance that I should show them their mistake, if they conjectured any thing to my disadvantage.

Breakfast over, we returned to the coach, and, after handing the young lady, I stepped in as lightly as I had stepped out. She again insisted I should not ride backward, and I for my former reason refused to change my place, till one of those abrupt gentlemen exclaimed.——'What, my young buck, are you afraid of a petticoat?' 'Oh fie!' said the young lady.

Rouzed by this insulting supposition, and despising every kind of cowardice, I immediately crossed over and took my seat by her side. 'Men fellows are very rude horse-godmother kind of creatures,' said the young lady.—The colour flushed in my face.—'Men fellows? Horse-godmother?' It was strange! I was more than half afraid she meant me.—'Not all of them I hope,' said I, as soon as I could recollect myself—'No, not all of them,' answered the young lady, with a gentle smile, and a glance that I thought had meaning.

My flow of spirits being somewhat checked by the behaviour of the gentlemen, I sat silent, and they fell into conversation; by which I learned that one of them was a gentleman of great fortune in Wales, and the other a captain in the army, and that they were well acquainted with London, Dublin, Bath, Brighthelmstone, and all places of fashionable resort. The young lady too had not only been at each of them, but had visited Paris, and mentioned many persons of quality, with whom, as it appeared from her discourse, she was quite familiar. It was evident, from all she said, that she knew how to distinguish the well bred and the polite. She was immensely shocked at any thing that was ungenteel *and low:* it was prodigiously horrid. The whole discourse indeed convinced me that they were all people of consequence; and that my supposition of ill breeding on the part of the gentlemen must have been hasty.

One thing however surprised me, and particularly drew my attention. I valued myself on my knowledge of languages, and the quickness of my ear; yet, though they continually spoke English, they introduced occasional words and phrases which to me were wholly unintelligible. One especially of these phrases seemed so strange that I repeated it to myself again and again. It was—*The kinchin will bite the bubble*—I pondered, and fifty times questioned—'Who is *the kinchin?* What is *bite the bubble?*'[1] But in vain: it was incomprehensible!

We did not stop to dine till between four and five o'clock, and then the young lady at alighting was more circumspect. She having retired, the gentlemen asked me if I would take a turn to the river side, at the back of the inn; and I, to shew that I now understood their characters better, willingly complied. As I was following them, the landlord, who had attended while we were alighting, plucked me by the skirt, and looking significantly after my companions whispered—'Take care of yourself, young gentleman!' then hastily brushed by. The first moment I thought it strange; the second I exclaimed to myself—'Ah, ha! I guessed how it was: I soon found them out! But, if they have any tricks to play, they shall find I am as cunning as they. The landlord need not have cautioned me; I am not so easily caught.'

Thus fortified, I proceeded boldly; and we had not walked two hundred yards before one of them who had stepped forward, stooped and picked up a piece of paper, which he instantly began to read. 'S'death!' exclaimed he, as we approached, 'here is a bill, at three days sight, for fifteen guineas; drawn on Fairlamb and Company, bankers at Oxford. You are acquainted with country bills, captain,' said he, presenting it to his companion: 'do you think it a good one?' His companion took it, examined it, upside and down, to the light and from it, and replied—'As good as the bank! But we must share?' 'To be sure we must,' said the finder. 'Why should you doubt it? 'Tis a trifle; five guineas a piece; but it will serve to pay travelling expences.'

They laughed, and I was staggered at this honourable and generous conduct. I have proceeded too hastily, thought I; and the landlord is own cousin to our lawyer; he thinks every man a rogue. Their liberality is proof sufficient in their favour.—'Come, give us our five guineas a piece,' said the gentleman of Wales to the captain—'I have no ready cash,' answered he. 'I never chuse, when I am travelling, to have more money in my pocket than barely enough for expences.'—'That is exactly my case,' replied the Welsh gentleman. 'But perhaps our young friend may be less cautious, and may have loose cash sufficient.'—'I had twelve guineas,' said I, 'when I left home.'—'Oh, that will just do,' answered the captain. 'We turn off to-morrow morning for Cirencester; you are going to Oxford, otherwise our luck would have been lost upon us, for we would not have gone a mile out of our road for such a trifle.'

My hand was in my pocket, and the guineas were between my

fingers, when my heart smote me. The landlord's significant 'Take care of yourself young gentleman!' my own sagacious conjectures when he gave me this warning, and their strange phrase of *bite the bubble*, all rose to my recollection. They shall not make a tool and a jest of me, said I to myself.

The gentleman of Wales seeing me hesitate, jogged me by the elbow, and said—'Come, come; we must dispatch: dinner is on the table by this time, and the coach will not wait a minute.'—'Those who think me a fool,' replied I, with something of indignation in my countenance, 'will find themselves deceived'—'What do you mean by that, Sir,' retorted the captain—'Strange language, for a gentleman!'

I stopped a moment: my conscience smote me. If I should mistake the character of these gentlemen, thought I, my behaviour will appear contemptible——'Do you mean to insult us?' said the gentleman of Wales.—The captain once more saw my hand in my pocket: I caught his eye; he winked to his companion and said, 'No, no; the young gentleman knows better.'—'Yes,' answered I, instantly fired; 'I know better than to give my money to sharpers' —'Sharpers!' retorted one——'Sharpers!' re-echoed the other, and began mutually to hustle me—My valour was roused: I faced about, with the first blow laid the gentleman of Wales sprawling, and with the second made the captain's eyes strike fire. The attack was infinitely more vigorous and powerful than they could have expected. The Welsh gentleman shook his ears; the captain clapped his white handkerchief to his eyes. They swore a few oaths in concert, but neither of them seemed desirous to continue the combat. Such an attack from a stripling was quite out of all calculation. If however I could guess their motives from their manner, they were rather those of caution than of cowardice. Be that as it will, I could better deal out hard blows than utter coarse expressions, and I left them with a look of contempt.

Entering the dinner room, I found the young lady and told her the story. She was all astonishment! Could not believe her ears! Was never so deceived in her life! Was immensely glad that she now knew her company! She had seen them at Bath, and had imagined them to be, as they professed themselves, gentlemen: but people do not know who and who are together at such public places! She was sorry to ride in the same carriage with them; but dine with them she would not. I asked if I might be permitted that honour; and she readily replied, 'Certainly, Sir: you are a gentleman.'

Proud to be thus distinguished, after dinner, I insisted on paying the bill, and she still more strenuously insisted I should not. She pulled out her purse, which seemed well filled, and put down her quota, which no entreaties could prevail on her to take back. It was her rule.

The horses being ready, we were summoned to our seats, which we took in pairs: the gentleman of Wales and the captain sitting in sullen silence, and the young lady not deigning to address a word to them.

At night we again paired off, and I was admitted to be her companion at supper; she continuing to treat me, since their detection, with a marked partiality.

Supper being over and the lady, unfortunately as she said for her, being to travel the Cirencester road with those odious sharpers, I was again exceedingly desirous to shew some trifling mark of respect, by discharging the bill; which she again peremptorily refused to accept. Unluckily however, going to draw her purse as before, she could not find it!—'It was exceedingly strange!—Infinitely distressing! What could have become of it? Thirty guineas were but a trifle, but to lose them at such a moment was very tormenting!'— She felt again, and having no better success her features assumed a very dismal and tragical cast.

None but a heart of stone could endure, unmoved, the anxiety and distress of so kind, so amiable, and so lovely a creature. I took my eleven guineas, my whole store except a few shillings, told her it was all I had, but intreated she would not put me to the pain of refusing the little supply I had to afford.

She thanked me infinitely; recollected she had left her purse when she retired after dinner to comb up her dishevelled hair, having taken it out with the comb and totally forgotten it; repeated that she was proceeding to London, for which a single guinea would perhaps be sufficient; but unfortunately she was obliged to pass through Cirencester, having a poor relation there, that was sick and in absolute want, and to whom she had promised an immediate relief of ten guineas, with an intention of further support. However she could not think of accepting my offer: it had so strange an appearance! And she would rather suffer any thing than forfeit the good opinion of a gentleman: especially after having conversed with those good for nothing men as if acquainted with them, but of whom she knew nothing, and had therefore supposed no harm.

The debate was long, and managed on both sides with almost equal ardour. At length however I prevailed on her to take ten of the eleven guineas; but not till she had given me a draft on her banker, Signed Harriet Palmer, which she assured me would be honoured the instant it should be presented. I took it to satisfy her scruples, but I had read the old romances, and too well understood the gallantry due from a gentleman to a lady, to think of putting it to the use she intended. I lingered and knew not how to take leave; but the coach would only allow her three hours repose, I therefore reluctantly bade her good night, and we parted with mutual admiration; hoping for some fortunate opportunity of renewing our acquaintance.

CHAPTER XIV

Morning thoughts: Conjectures and expectations. A specimen of Oxford manners, being another new lesson

LEFT by myself on the morrow, and revolving in my mind the events of the preceding day, I had occasional doubts, which had I suffered them to prevail, would have been exceedingly mortifying. The young lady was certainly a beautiful lady: was modest too, and well bred. I had seen nothing to impeach her virtue: on the contrary, it had been the principal topic of our discourse. 'Tis true I had, as became me, been too respectful to put her chastity to any proof. I was not so discourteous a knight.

But then, that she should have been so intimate as she appeared to be with those gentlemen sharpers, that she should be going the same road, that she should lose her purse in so odd a manner, and that she should accept my ten guineas, were circumstances that dwelt irksomely upon my mind. Yet it was totally improbable that so sweet a young creature should be trammeled in vice. What! be the companion of such men, relate a string of falsehoods, give a forged draft on a banker, and even shed tears at distress which, if it were not real, was a most base and odious artifice? That she could act so cunning and so vile a part, and I not detect her, was wholly incredible. I was very unwilling to imagine I could be so imposed upon, so duped. *A raw traveller?* If so, raw indeed! Of all suppositions, that was the most humiliating. I endeavoured but in vain to banish suspicion. In fine, whatever might be the cause, which I could not very well develope, I found the soliloquies of the morning by no means so fascinating as the visions of the preceding evening.

Wearied of this subject, I turned my thoughts into a new channel, and endeavoured to conjecture what Oxford was, and what kind of people were its inhabitants. I had heard it described, and remembered the leading features; its expansive streets, aspiring turrets, noble buildings, and delightful walks. The picture rose to magnificence; but the wisdom learning and virtue of its sages, and their pupils, were still more sublime. High minded and noble youths, thirsting after knowledge, assembled under the auspices of philosophers whose science was profound, and whose morals were pure. The whole fabric rising in beautiful order: under-graduates, bachelors, masters, doctors, professors, presidents, heads of colleges, high stewards, and chancellors, each excelling the other in worth as in dignity! Their manners engaging, their actions unblemished, and their lives spent in the delightful regions of learning and truth. It must be the city of angels, and I was hastening to reside among the blest! A band of seers, living in fraternity, governed by one universal spirit of benevolence, harmonized by one vibrating system of goodness celestial! Among such beings evil and foolish men could find no admittance, for they could find no society.

Theology too would here be seen in all her splendour; active energetic and consolatory; not disturbed by doubt, not disgraced by acrimony, not slumbering in sloth, not bloated with pride, not dogmatical, not intolerant, not rancorous, not persecuting, not inquisitorial; but diffusing her mild yet clear and penetrating beams through the soul, where all could not but be light and life and love! —Oh Oxford, said I, thou art the seat of the muses, thou art the nurse of wisdom, thou art the mother of virtue!—I own my expectations were high.

My reveries concerning my old companion, Hector, were in the same tone. I had heard that he had often been down at Mowbray Hall, during vacation time; but the mutual interdiction of our families had prevented our meeting. He cannot but be greatly altered, said I. It is impossible he should have remained so long in this noble seminary, and continue the same selfish, sensual, and half-brutal Hector Mowbray, whom formerly I knew. I regretted our quarrel: he might now have become an agreeable companion, perhaps a friend. Olivia, too?—She had a sister's partiality for him before; she might now love him infinitely, and justly.

While I sat ruminating, the coach continued rolling onward over hill and dale, passing house, hedge row and heath, till the towers and turrets of Oxford came in view. My heart bounded at the sight, and active fancy industriously continued her fictions. We entered the city and drove clattering along to one of the principal inns.

The moment the coachman pulled up, I stepped out of the carriage and into the street. It was the eve of a new term; the gownsmen were swarming, carriages and horsemen post haste were arriving, the bells were ringing, waiters and footmen were hurrying to and fro, and all was dazzle, all was life. Eager to mingle in the scene, I walked up and down the high street, saw college after college, hall after hall, and church after church. The arches the pillars the quadrangles rose in incessant and astonishing succession. My eyes turned from building to building, gazing with avidity, adding wonder to wonder, and filling the mind with rapture. 'It is all that I had imagined,' said I, 'and much much more! Happy city, happy people, and happy I, that am come to be one among you! Now and now only I begin to live.'

Fearful of bewildering myself in this fairy land, I turned back to the inn, but continued gazing with new amazement at every step. Just as I came to the gate, I heard the galloping of horses behind me, looked round, and there most unexpectedly saw Hector Mowbray, pulling up his horse, with two livery servants, three grey-hounds, and a brace of pointers at his heels! He had new boots, buckskin breeches, a buff waist-coat, a scarlet coat with a green collar, and a gold button and loop, tassel, and hat-band. I was within a yard of him when he alighted. 'Bless me,' said I, 'Mr. Mowbray?'—'G—d —my blood! Trevor! Is it you?'

The apostrophe startled me.

Hector gave three loud cracks with his whip, whistled his dogs, and with a Stentor voice[1] called after one of his servants—'Why holloa! You blind blood of a w—! Why Sam! G— shiver your soul, what are you about? Uncouple Jerry Sneak and Jowler, and give limping Jenny's ear a 'nointing—D— my body, Trevor, I'm glad to see you! When did you arrive? How did you come? In stile; a chaise and four; smoking the road; raising a mist?'—I was ashamed of my stage-coach vehicle and was silent.—'What, my buck, are you to be one of us?'—'I am'—'D—my b— that's right—Jack Singleton! Jack! G— blunder your body! Why don't you answer, you shamble shanked beggar's baby? Go to the Bursar, and tell him to send supper for six and claret for sixteen; served up to a minute. Do you hear?—D— my body, I'm glad to see you! We'll make a night ont! What, are you come to enter at our college?'—'Yes'—'D— my soul, I'm glad ont! D—n me, our college will be the go! D—n me, we are a rare string already! D—n me, we shall beat them all hollow, D—n me, now you're come, d—n me: we shall, d—n me!— Holloa! Sam! Run, you blood of a w—! yonder's Lord Sad-dog turning the corner in his phaeton, four in hand: scamper away and tell him, d—n me, he must sup with me to night. Tell him by G— he must; he and the jolly dog his tutor. Tell him we have a new comer, a friend, a freshman, piping hot, d—n me, from our village; and that we must make him free of Oxford to night, d—n me. Do you hear?'

Astound, breathless, thunder-struck, at this intolerable profaneness, I stood like an idiot, unable to speak or think. Hector took hold of my arm and dragged me along. I obeyed, for I was insensible, soul-less; and even when the return of thought came, it was all confusion. Was this Oxford? Were these its manners? Were such its inhabitants? Oaths twenty in a breath, unmeaning vulgar oaths; ribaldry, such as till that hour I had never heard!

What could I do? I was a stranger. Were they all equally depraved, and equally contemptible?—That, said I to myself, is what I wish to know, and I suffered him to lead me wherever he pleased.

He took me to inns coffee-houses and halls, to call on one companion and *beat up*[1] for another. I saw the buildings; the architecture doubtless was the same, but the scene was changed! The beauties of Oxford were vanished! I was awakened from the most delightful of dreams to a disgusting reality, and would have given kingdoms to have once more renewed my trance. The friends of Hector, though not all of them his equals in turbulence profaneness and folly, were of the same school. Their language, though less coarse, was equally insipid. Their manners, when not so obtrusive, were more bald. They all cursed blustered and behaved with insolence in proportion to the money they spent, or the time they had been at the university. The chief difference was that those who were less rich and less hardened than he had less spirit: that is, had less noise, nonsense and swagger. But, though the scene was not what I expected, it was new, and in a certain sense enlivening, and my flowing spirits were soon at their accustomed height.

The president had been written to and I was expected at college, where, when we came and my arrival was announced, I found an apartment prepared for my reception. Passing through the common room, I saw a face which I thought I recollected. 'Is not that Turl?' said I to Hector—'Pshaw, d—n me, take no notice of such a *raff*,' replied he, and stalked away. I was too ignorant of college cant, at that time, to know that *raff* was the term of contempt for poverty.

As we passed through the quadrangle, the president, entering the gate, saw Hector in his scarlet green and gold, and without his gown and cap, and beckoned to him. Hector, to evade as I afterward learned what he expected, introduced me. The president eyed me for a moment, received me graciously, and desired me to call on him in the morning. He then asked Mowbray why he left his chamber in that dress, and without his gown? Hector answered he had only arrived the day before, had been to take a ride, and had mislaid his cap, which was not to be found; but he had a new one coming home in the morning. The president, after saying—'Well, Sir, I request I may not meet you in this manner again,' passed on. The story of the cap mislaid was a direct falsehood: the old and new cap were both in his chamber, for he had been trying them on and asking me which looked the best. Hector winked his eye, lolled his tongue, and said to me—'That's the way, d—n me, to hum[1] the old ones.'

Supper time presently came, and Hector and his companions were assembled. Beside Lord Sad-dog and his tutor, there was a senior fellow, and a master of arts, all of our college and all of them the prime bucks of the place. My late high expectations of learning and virtue were entirely forgotten. There was novelty in every word they uttered; and I listened to their conversation with the most attentive ardour. Nor did I feel astonishment to hear that dogs, horses, gluttony, drunkenness, and debauchery were the grand blessings of life: Hector had prepared me to hear any thing with but little surprise. The Lord and the Squire gloried in braving and breaking the statutes of the college and the university; the tutor, fellow, and master of arts in eluding them. The history they gave of themselves was, that the former could ride, drive, swear, kick scoundrels, bilk[1] prostitutes, commit adultery, and breed riots: the latter could cant, lie, act the hypocrite, hum the proctors, and protect their companions in debauchery: in gluttony drunkenness and libidinous thoughts they were all avowed rivals.

Hector, descending to trifling vices, vaunted of having been five times in one week *imposed* (that is, reprimanded by set tasks) for having neglected lectures and prayers, and worn scarlet, green and gold; while the more heroic Lord Sad-dog told how he had been twice privately *rusticated*, for an amour with the bar-maid of a coffee-house, whom he dared the vice-chancellor himself to banish the city. Fearful of being surpassed, they exaggerated their own wickedness, and often imputed crimes to themselves which they had neither the opportunity nor the courage to commit.

That I might appear worthy of the choice group among whom I was admitted, Hector, by relating in a distorted manner things that had happened, but attributing to me such motives as he imagined he should have been actuated by had he been the agent, told various falsehoods of my exploits. I had too great a mixture of sheepishness and vanity to contradict him in such honourable society, and therefore accepted praise at which I ought to have blushed.

During supper, while they were all gormandizing and encouraging me to do the same, his lordship, addressing his tutor, asked— 'D—n me, Jack, can you tell me why it was I took you into my pay? What the d-mn-t--n are you good for?'—'Tell you? To be sure I can! You will not pretend that, when you first came under my tuition, you were the man you now are? Who taught you to laugh at doctors, bully proctors, stare the vice chancellor out of countenance, and parade the streets of a Sunday in sermon time but I?'—'You!'—'Yes! I!'—— 'D—n my body, well said, Jack!' roared Hector. 'D—n me you are a good one! Go it! Keep it up! D—n me go it!' The tutor continued—

'Of whom did you learn to scout the gownsmen, cudgel the townsmen, kiss their wives, frighten their daughters, and debauch their maids but I? You were a mere tyro when I took you in hand; you did not so much as know how to throw in a knock down blow!' —'Why you lying son of a——'

I must not repeat his lordship's reply, or the continuation of the dialogue; it was too gross to be read or written. I only intend the above as a short specimen of what lords' private tutors at universities sometimes are, and of the learning which their pupils sometimes acquire.

While at supper, I was continually plied to drink; each pledging me in turn; their intention being, as Hector had declared, to make me free: that is, as drunk as possible. I had not the courage to incur their ridicule by refusing my glass. Beside my spirits were raised, and my appetite, which travelling had increased, was good. My constitution too was strong; for it had been confirmed by exercise and a cheerful mind, and never injured by excess. For these reasons I stood their attacks far beyond their expectation, and my manhood received no little applause.

The night advanced, and they grew riotous. The lord and his tutor were for *sporting the door of a glum*: that is, breaking into the chamber of a gownsman who loves study. Hector vociferously seconded the motion, but the fellow and the master of arts cunningly endeavoured to keep them quiet, first by persuasion, and, when that was ineffectual, by affirming the students they proposed to attack *sported oak*: in plain English, barred up their doors. Had they been without the walls of the college, there would have been a riot; but, having no other ventilator for their magnanimity, they fell with redoubled fury to drinking, and the jolly tutor proposed a rummer[1] round—'D—n me,' said Hector, 'that's a famous thought! But you are a famous deep one, d—n me!'

The rummers were seized, the wine poured out, and his lordship began with—'D-mn-t—n to the flincher.' Who should that be? I, the freshman? Oh, no! For that night, I was too far gone in good fellowship.

This was the finishing blow to three of us. Hector fell on the floor; his lordship sunk in his chair; and I, after a hurrah and a hiccup, began to *cast the cat*: an Oxford phrase for what usually happens to a man after taking an emetic. Happily I had not far to go, and the fellow and the master of arts had just sense enough left to help me to my chamber, where at day light next morning I found myself, on the hearth, with my head resting against the fender, the pain of which awakened me.

CHAPTER XV

*Morning reflections: The advice of a youth and the caution
of a grave senior: Another rencontre*

DISCOVERING myself in this condition, recollecting the scene in which I had so lately been an actor, and feeling my stomach and head disordered and my whole frame burning with the debauch, looking round too and seeing myself in a room where every object reminded me that I was a stranger, and that the eyes of many strangers were upon me and my conduct, I found but little cause of satisfaction, either in myself, the acquaintance I had made, or the place to which I had come.

The more I reflected the more was my mind disturbed. I walked about the chamber unable to rid myself either of my sickly qualms, the feverish distemper of my blood, or the still more fevered distemperature of my mind. It was a violent but I suspect it was a useful lesson. After a while, cold water, washing, cleaning, and shifting my dress, gave me a little relief.

The air I thought would be refreshing; but, as I opened the door to descend the stairs, Turl was passing, and very kindly inquired after my health, said he was happy to see me, and asked if I were come to enter myself at the college. Neglecting, or rather at that moment despising, Hector and his caution, I answered in the same tone and invited him into my room.[1]

Too much ashamed to avow the debauch of which I had been guilty, or the painful feelings that were the result, I endeavoured by questions to gain the information which might best appease my roused curiosity. 'I am but just arrived,' said I: 'will you be kind enough to give me such intelligence as may aid me to regulate my conduct? What I have hitherto seen has rather surprized and even disappointed me. I hoped for perfection which I begin to doubt I shall not find. What are the manners of the place?'—'Such as must be expected from a multitude of youths, who are ashamed to be thought boys, and who do not know how to behave like men.'— 'But are there not people appointed to teach them?—'No.'—'What is the office of the proctors, heads of houses, deans, and other superintendants, of whom I have heard?'——'To watch and regulate the tufts of caps, the tying of bands, the stuff and tassels of which gowns are made: to reprimand those who wear red, or green, and to take care that the gownsmen assemble, at proper hours, to hear prayers gabbled over as fast as tongue can give them utterance, or lectures at which both reader and hearers fall asleep.' 'What are the public rewards for proficiency in learning?'—'Few, or in reality none.'—'Beside numerous offices, are not exhibitions, fellowships, professors' chairs and presentations bestowed?'—'Yes, on those who have municipal or political influence; or who by servility and effrontery can court patronage.'—'Surely you have some men of worth and genius, who meet their due reward?'—'Few; very few, indeed. Sloth, inanity, and bloated pride are here too often the characteristics of office. Fastidiousness is virtue, and to keep the poor and unprotected in awe a duty. The rich indeed are indulged in all the licentious liberties they can desire.'——'Why do so many young men of family resort hither?'—'Some to get what is to be given away; others are sent by their parents, who imagine the place to be the reverse of what it is; and a third set, intended for the church, are obliged to go to a university before they can be admitted into holy orders.'—'That rule I have heard is not absolute.'—'It is supposed here to be little less.'—'Then you would not advise a young person to come to this city to complete his education?'—'If he possess extraordinary fortitude and virtue, yes: if not, I would have him avoid Oxford as he would contagion.'—'What are its advantages, to the former?'—'Leisure, books, and learned men; and the last benefit would be the greatest, were it not publicly dis-countenanced by the arrogant distance which both the statutes of the university and the practice of the graduates and dignitaries prescribe. In my opinion, it has another paradoxical kind of advantage: to a mind properly prepared, the very vice of the place, by shewing how hateful it is, must be healthful. Insolence, haughtiness, sloth, and sensuality, daily exhibited, if truly seen, cannot but excite contempt.'—'You seem to have profited by the lesson.'—'Oh! there is but little merit in my forbearance. I am poor, and have not the means. I am a servitor and despised, or overlooked. Those are most exposed to danger who have most money and most credit; I have neither.' Charmed with his candour, our conversation continued: he directed me in the college modes, and I sent to the Bursar, and prevailed on Turl to breakfast with me. I understood that he had obtained an exhibition, but that, having expressed his thoughts too freely on certain speculative points, he had incurred the disapprobation of his seniors, who considered it as exceedingly impertinent in any man to differ with them in opinion, and especially in such a youth.

It was now time I should visit the president, and we parted. This college magistrate had formerly been acquainted with my grandfather, and I had strong recommendations to him from my native village: he therefore laid aside much of his dignity, and questioned me on various subjects. He took but little notice of the reading and knowledge I was ambitious to display, but gave me much advice and instruction, concerning the college and university discipline, necessary to be observed, which he very seriously admonished me not to neglect.

I endeavoured to find what his opinion concerning Hector Mowbray was, and the lord to whom I had been introduced; but this he evaded, with a caution to me however not to indulge in any imprudent expence.

I then mentioned the name of Turl, at which he seemed instantly alarmed, and replied, 'he should be exceedingly sorry if Mr. Turl were one of my acquaintance. He was a very dangerous young man, and had dared not only to entertain but to make known some very heterodox opinions. He had even proceeded so far as to declare himself an anti-trinitarian, and should therefore certainly never receive his countenance; neither he nor any of his connections. If he escaped expulsion, he would assuredly never obtain his degrees.' I was too orthodox myself not to be startled at this intelligence, and felt a very severe pang that a young man, from whose conversation I had hoped so much, should hold such reprobate doctrines. I had thought he would prove both an instructive and pleasant companion, but I now positively determined to shun his society. Of this I informed the president, and he highly applauded my resolution.

I then proceeded to the ceremony of entering myself of the college, and took the oaths: that is, I subscribed to the thirty-nine articles, took an oath of allegiance and supremacy, an oath to observe the statutes of the university, and another to obey every thing that was contained in a certain huge statute book of the college, brought out on this occasion, which I never saw either before or since. To this hour, what its contents were is a thing to me unknown. What is still more strange, the very persons who oblige you to take these statute-book oaths publickly confess that to obey most of them is impossible. They relate to obsolete customs, the very means of practising which are wanting. Some for example swear to have mass said for the soul of the founder of the college; and others, though men of good estates, swear themselves not worth five pounds per annum. Of these particulars however I was ignorant, and the whole was hurried over so much in the way of form, and without inquiry of any kind, that it seemed like the mere dictate of good manners to do what I was bidden.

Warned by the information which Turl had communicated, and disgusted by what I myself had seen and partaken of, I industriously for sometime avoided Hector Mowbray, who as it happened was too much engaged in his own pursuits to molest me. In about three weeks however he came to me one morning, rallied me in his coarse way, asked if I had entered myself of the glums, and insisted that I should go with him and take a ride to Abingdon. The chaise would be ready in half an hour, and he would introduce me to the finest girl in all England. Thinking his language equivocal and suspecting his intentions, I ventured to ask if she were a modest woman? He burst into a loud laugh and exclaimed (I shall omit his oaths) 'Modest! to be sure! as modest as any of her sex.' This did not satisfy me; I continued to interrogate and he to laugh, but still swearing there was not a modester woman in all England. A strong inclination to take exercise, my own active curiosity, and the boisterous hawling[1] and obstinacy of Hector at length prevailed, and I yielded. I walked with him to the inn, the chaise was ready, and we stepped into it and galloped away.

As we were driving on, the image of the gentle Olivia rose to my recollection. Instantly the thought struck me, 'If it should be! Why not? Who else could it be? Oh, it must! Yes, yes!' I was soon convinced it could be no other than Olivia! the dear the divine Olivia!

In less than forty minutes we were at Abingdon, and the postillion by Hector's direction drove us on the back of the town till we came to a neat newly painted house, at which he was ordered to stop. My heart began to beat. Hector jumped out and thundered at the door. A female threw up the sash, looked through the window, and instantly drew it down again. Alas! it was not Olivia.

There was some delay: the impatient Hector cursed and knocked again, and in a little while the door was opened.

Hector entered swearing, hurried up stairs, bad me follow him, dashed open the door, and a young lady, *in a sky-blue riding-habit*,

*with embroidered button-holes, a nosegay in her bosom, and a purple
cestus round her waist*—leaped into his arms!—I stood in a trance!
It was she herself! That sweet lovely creature, who had lost her
purse, given a draft on her banker, and gone to relieve a poor sick
relation at Cirencester! It was the true and identical Harriet Palmer!
She that had been so attentive to me; had sugared my tea, suffered
me to sup in her company, and been so fearful lest I should be sick
by riding backward! The innocent soul, that had felt her delicacy so
much disturbed by the horse-godmother rudeness of the men-
fellows!—'Bless me!' said I.

She had not time to attend to me. 'What the d-mn-t-n is the
matter?' said Hector. 'Why was not I let in? Who have you here?'
—'Here!' answered the sweet creature. 'How can you suppose I
have any body here?'

There was a watch studded with diamonds lying on the sofa; it
caught the eye of Mowbray; he snatched it up, and with a volley of
oaths asked—'Whose watch is this?'—'Mine!' said Harriet. Hector
looked again. 'Yours? Set with diamonds? A man's gold chain?
Here's the seal of Lord Sad-dog! His arms engraved on it! I
thought I saw one of his fellows, as we turned the corner!'

There was another door, to an inner chamber; to that Hector,
with all his force, applied his foot. A loud laugh was heard within,
the door opened, and out came Lord Sad-dog in *propria persona*.

Miss Palmer, not knowing what better to do, joined his lordship
in the forced laugh. The surly Hector shewed every propensity to
brutal revenge, but had only the courage to bully; in which art the
lord and the lady soon shewed they were as great proficients as
himself.

As for the feelings of the blooming Harriet and me, they were
reciprocal; we were equally averse to acknowledge each other for
acquaintance. I did not wish to be proclaimed the dupe of a
courtezan, nor she to pay back the ten guineas, or be sued for a
fraud. Hector was in no humour to stay, and we soon returned to
Oxford; I ruminating and even laughing, now at myself, now at him;
he in high dudgeon, and finding his choler and his courage increase
in proportion as he was driven farther from danger.

CHAPTER XVI

Education still progressive: A widow's continence: Religious
fervour: A methodist sermon: Olivia in danger: Love dreams:
Fanatic horrors: Present disgrace, and honours delayed

DURING the short period of my absence from my native home,
I had been taught two additional and essential lessons: the first, that
men are not all as good as they might be; and the second, that I was
not quite so wise as I had supposed myself. Having once been
duped, the thought occurred that it was possible I might be duped
again, and I thus acquired some small degree of what is called
worldly caution. At once to display one vice and teach another, to
expose fraud and inspire suspicion, is, to an unadulterated mind, a
severe and odious lesson; and, when repeated too often, is in danger
of inculcating a mistake infinitely more pernicious than that of
credulity; that is, a conviction that man is depraved by nature, and
a total forgetfulness that he is merely the creature of habit and
accident.

Hitherto I had met disappointment; but I had found novelty;
and though it was not the novelty I expected, yet it was invigorating:
it kept me awake. The qualities for which I most valued myself no
one indeed seemed to notice. But the world was before me; I had
seen but little of it; my own feelings assured me genius and virtue
had a real existence, and sometime or another I should find them.

Among consolatory thoughts, the most animating was the
recollection of what Turl had said, that, to the possessor of fortitude
and virtue, Oxford was a place where study might be most
advantageously prosecuted; and, aided by this cheering hope, I
applied myself to books with courage and assiduity.

On the subject of reading however my mind had strong contentions with itself: poetry, and the *belles lettres*, Homer, Horace,
Virgil, Shakespeare, Spenser, Milton, Dryden, Tasso, Ariosto,
Racine, Molière, Congreve, with a long and countless *et cætera*,
were continually tempting me to quit the barren pursuits of divinity
and law, for the study of which I had come to Oxford. Yet a sense of
duty so far prevailed that I went through a course of the fathers,
pored over the canonists, and made many resolute attacks upon the
schoolmen. Not only Aristotle but his doctors, the irrefragable,[1]

the angelic,[1] or eagle-eyed,[1] the subtile,[1] the illuminated,[1] and many more had their peaceful folios vainly disturbed by my researches, and my determination to understand what, alas, in its essence was unintelligible.

In the very beginning as it were of these labours an event took place, which gave a very serious aspect to my future fortunes, though, except the first emotions of regret chagrin and surprise at my mother's conduct, no present uneasiness to me. In despite of his law-suits, my grandfather had left considerable property; which it was supposed would descend to me. It had indeed the disadvantage of being left under the executorship of a lawyer, who represented it to be in a very involved and disorderly state: for, with respect to my mother, though she had immediate possession, she declared that, agreeably to the intention of the rector, her own subsistence excepted, she held it only for my use. Thus, in several of her letters, she had affectionately pressed me not to deprive myself of what was necessary to my situation, to the appearance of a gentleman, or to the support of the family character.

For the first two months we punctually wrote to each other once a week. 'My dear dear Hugh' was the first phrase in all her letters; and 'my kind and good mother' in mine: every maternal anxiety was expressed by her, and by me every return of filial affection and duty.

At length a week came in which I received no letter. I was alarmed, wrote to express my fears, and in a few days was answered, by the lawyer, that my mother was in good health, but was from home on a visit.

A month longer passed away in silence, at the end of which I wrote to my mother, expressing my feelings and fears, and requesting an answer under her own hand; otherwise I should come myself to see what was the matter.

The answer arrived, I hastily opened it, and began to read. It was no longer prefaced with 'my dear dear Hugh:' It was what follows.

'Dear Son,

'You seem impatient to hear from me, and so I sit down to write you an account of something that has happened, which perhaps you will think well of; I hope you will; I am sure you have no reason to think otherwise; though, when one does things all for the best, one is not always best thought of. But I dare say you will not think ill of your mother, for that would not be dutiful, nor at all agreeable to what your poor dear grandfather always taught. Nobody can suppose that I am not come to years of discretion; and you very well know I have always been a good and tender mother to you; and so I always shall be; and I am sure you will not think hardly and improperly of my conduct in any way, for that would be very unkind and unbecoming; and, if I have done all for the best, to be hardly thought of afterwards would be very improper indeed. Mr. Thornby [the lawyer] is a very prudent man, and so I have acted by his advice, which you may well think cannot be wrong; and his nephew, Mr. Wakefield, is a gentleman that nobody need be ashamed of owning; and so, since you must be told, you may as well be told at first as at last—I am married; which I hope and expect you will think was a very prudent thing. I am sure when you come to know Mr. Wakefield you will like him prodigiously. He sends his kind blessing to you, and so I remain your ever loving mother

JANE WAKEFIELD.'

Little as I was attached to personal interest or fearful of being left without a provision, I own this letter electrified me. Was this the tone of affection? Had it vanished so instantly? After such strong and reiterated professions for my sake never to have a second husband, not only to marry but to cool intirely toward me, and to be only anxious, in a poor selfish circumlocutory apology, for a conduct which she herself felt to be highly reprehensible!

The lawyer too! His nephew? Not satisfied with the executorship, he had engulphed the whole in his family, the stipend of a hundred a year while I remained at college, and a thousand pounds for the purchase of an advowson when I should leave it, excepted. I wondered, on reflection, that he should even have advised the rector to this: but it was by affecting disinterestedness that he could most effectually secure the remainder.

But the pain these thoughts occasioned was neither debilitating nor durable. My sanguine self-confidence, though sometimes apalled, has all my life prevented me from being subject to fits of permanent chagrin, or melancholy. The recollection of my mother's passionate promises, the shortness of the time, the suddenness of the change, the family into which she had married, and the instability of a woman that was my mother, drew a few sighs from me, and in these my gloom evaporated. I returned cheerfully to my books and determined to visit home no more, but while a student to make Oxford my home, and not incur the frequently well-merited reproach of being *a term-trotter*.

As for my companion, Hector, whatever the intentions of the Squire his father might be, he considered Oxford only as a place of dissipation, and loved it for nothing but because he was here first let entirely loose, and here first found comrades that were worthy to be his peers. Most of his time was now spent in London, or in parties such as himself and his intimates planned. I suffered little interruption from him: he now and then indeed gave me an indolent call; but, as there was no parity of pursuit, nor unity of sentiment between us, there could be but little intercourse.

Little farther remarkable happened during the three years and ten months of my residence in this city, except the incident that occasioned my removal. By being a constant spectator of the debauchery of the young, and the sensuality of the old, I conceived an increasing dislike of their manners, and sought the company of a few secluded young men, who like myself were severe students. Toward the close of this period I became acquainted with some who were tinged with methodism; and, by frequently listening to their conversation, my thoughts were turned into the same channel. The want of zeal in prayer and every part of religious duty, the tedious and dull sermons heard in the churches, and what methodists call preaching themselves and not their Saviour, were the frequent topics of our animadversion.

This was a doctrine most aptly calculated to inflame an imagination like mine, which was ardent and enthusiastic. Beside it relieved me from a multitude of labours and cares, for, as I proceeded, Thomas Aquinas and his subtilizing competitors were thrown by in contempt. I had learned divinity by inspiration, and soon believed myself fit for a reformer. The philosopher Aristotle with his dialectics and sophisms were exchanged, for those of the philosopher Saint Paul; from whom I learnt that he who had saving faith had every thing, and that he who wanted it was naked of all excellence as the new born babe. This nakedness I had discovered in myself, and in the language of the sect was immediately clothed in the righteousness of Christ Jesus! I, in common with my methodistical brethren, was chosen of the elect! My name was inscribed in the book of life never to be erased! My sins were washed away! Satan had no power over me; and to myself and my new fraternity I applied the text, that 'the gates of hell could not prevail against us!'

To these mysteries, which all the initiated allow are suddenly unfolded, descending like lightening by the inspiration of the spirit and illuminating the darkened soul, to these mysteries no man perhaps was ever a more sudden or a more combustible kind of convert than myself. I beamed with gospel light; it shone through me. I was the beacon of this latter age: a comet, sent to warn the wicked. I mean, I was all this in my own imagination, which swelled and mounted to the very acme of fanaticism.

Under the impulse of these wild dreams, in which my soul delighted, I was sometimes tempted to rise up a prophet, preach salvation to the poor, and confound the wise. Persecution I must expect, but in that I should glory: it was the badge of blessedness, the mark of election, the signing of the covenant. Elevated to these celestial heights, with what contempt did I look down on the doctors, proctors, and preachers of Baal (for such were all the unenlightened) and on their dignities, paraphernalia, and many coloured robes. What were these but the types of Babylon? the ensigns of the scarlet whore? the purple tokens of the beast? In the most extravagant eccentricities of mind it is remarkable what a mixture there is of truth and falsehood, and how nearly and frequently they approach each other.

During the height of this paroxysm, a famous gospel preacher, a divine man, on his way from Shropshire to London, came to hold forth in the vicinity of Oxford: not in churches, they were shut upon him, but in the fields; not to the rich, not to the worldy wise, not to the self righteous, they were deaf, but to the poor in spirit, to the polluted, the hardened reprobate, who wished by faith and repentance, though dyed in sin like scarlet, to be washed white as wool. To hear this teacher of the word, who set up his stool near a village on the Witney road, I repaired: I and many a moaning old woman beside; watchful, with our chorus of amen and our sobs and groans at every divine ejaculation, to aid the heaving motions of the spirit, and take heaven by storm.

The elect were assembled, and with them a greater number of the unconverted; heads were uncovered, a hymn was sung, and a long extempore string of intercessions, praying that the Lord would lay bare his arm and strike the guilty with terror; that Christ crucified would be among them; that they might be washed in the blood of

the immaculate lamb; and that the holy spirit would breathe the
God-man Jesus into all hearts, with many more absurdities, was
uttered.

The preacher then took his text, and chose for his subject the
casting of the buyers and sellers out of the temple. This was an
opportunity not to be lost by me. A gospel minister was indeed a
rara avis, at Oxford. I therefore took out my utensils and very
industriously wrote notes, that the divine breathings of the man of
God might not be lost upon me.——'Buyers and sellers,' said he,
'you must be cast out! The tables of the money changers must be
overthrown; you have defiled the temple of the Saviour! In what do
you trade? In vanity. In gold, silver, iron, brass, houses, corn, cattle,
goods, and chattels. But gold and silver may be stolen; iron will rust;
brass will break; cattle will die; corn will mildew; houses will burn;
they will tumble about your ears! Repent, or you will quickly bring
an old house over your heads! Your goods and chattels will but
kindle the fire in which you are to burn everlastingly! What are
your occupations? Why, to hoard, and sell your souls for gain, that
your heirs may squander and buy a hot place in hell! I am not one
of your fashionable fine spoken mealy mouthed preachers: I tell
you the plain truth. What are your pastimes? Cards and dice,
fiddling and dancing, guzzling and guttling![1] Can you be saved by
dice? No! Will the four knaves give you a passport to heaven?
No! Can you fiddle yourself into a good birth among the sheep?
No! You are goats, and goat like you may dance yourselves to
damnation! You may guzzle wine here, but you shall want a drop of
water to cool your tongue hereafter! You may guttle, while righteous
Lazarus is lying at your gate. But wait a little! He shall soon lie in
Abraham's bosom, while you shall roast on the devil's great
gridiron, and be seasoned just to his tooth!—Will the prophets say,
"Come here gamester, and teach us the long odds?"—'Tis odds if
they do!—Will the martyrs rant, and swear, and shuffle, and cut
with you? No! The martyrs are no shufflers! You will be cut so as
you little expect: you are a field of tares, and Lucifer is your head
farmer. He will come with his reapers and his sickles and his forks,
and you will be cut down and bound and pitched and carted and
housed in hell. I will not oil my lips with lies to please you: I tell
you the plain truth: you will go to hell! Ammon and Mammon and
Moloch[2] are head stoakers; they are making Bethhoron[3] hot for you!
Prophane wretches, you daily wrangle and brawl and tell one

another—"I will see you damned first!"—But I tell you the day
will come when you will pray to Beelzebub to let you escape his
clutches! And what will be his answer?—"I will see you damned
first!"'

To this rhapsody of strange but impressive vulgar eloquence I
listened, with rapture, for nearly an hour; selecting and noting down
the passages that I thought most remarkable, many of which were
too extravagant, if repeated, to be believed. In the height of these
effusions, when the divine man was torturing his lungs to be heard
by the increasing croud, he on his stool, I seated uncapped in a
cart by his side, who should I see approach, in a phæton and pair,
but Hector Mowbray? And by his side——! Yes!—Olivia! The
beauteous Olivia! no longer a child, but tall, straight, perfectly
formed; every limb in the most captivating symmetry, every feature
in the full bloom of youth; intelligence in every look, grace in every
motion, sweetness in every smile! Attracted by curiosity, her
brother arrested his course, drew up, and placed the celestial vision
full in view!

Oh, frailty of the flesh! My new made garb of righteousness
dropped from my shoulders! The old Adam, that had been dead in
me, again revived; the workings of the spirit ceased; I gazed on an
apparition which was indeed heavenly, and forgot the apostles the
prophets and the martyrs! The preacher himself was heard no more;
nor more would have been heard, had he not with all the effrontery
of a fanatic interrupted his discourse, to address himself personally
to Hector and Olivia, by which he excited sensations in me that were
wholly unexpected——'Jehu driveth furiously,'[1] said he; 'but
Jezebel was given to the dogs![2] (My choler instantly began to rise]
Sinners! drive not so fast! The way is broad, and Tophet[3] is gaping,
where is weeping and wailing and gnashing of teeth! You will be
there, poor lost souls, sooner than you expect! The way to heaven
is narrow, much too narrow for your large consciences; and,
though the court is spacious, the gate is too little for you to drive in
with your coaches and six! No, not even your vis a vis,[4] nor your
phætons neither, not so much as a tumbril or a buggie can get past!
But perhaps you think to ride up to the gate, and there to cry,
peccavi![5] and that then it will open, and you will be admitted? But,
no! no! I tell you, no! You shall never be able to utter more than
pec, *pec*, *pec*; and while with your mouths open you are stammering
and stuttering to get out *cavi*, Satan and his blackguards shall come

and peck you, even as crows peck carrion. Yes, Jehu and Jezebel! Remember! I give you warning!'

If I, one of the preacher's disciples, could scarcely refrain from falling upon him for his insolence, what must the choleric and brutal Hector feel, hearing himself repeatedly laughed at by the delighted unmannerly mob, during this impudent harangue? He dropped the reins, jumped from the phæton, sprang through the croud, and began to horse-whip the inspired man in the most furious manner.

And now an accident happened, which of all others that I can remember gave me the most terror. Olivia sat alone in the phæton; the reins were loose, and the fighting shouting and uproar of the divided mob occasioned the horses to take fright. They snorted, kicked, and set off full speed, with the helpless Olivia screaming for aid! The moment Hector left the carriage I saw what was likely to happen, leaped from the cart where I sat, and flew like lightening after the frantic animals. Few men were swifter of foot than I was, but they had the start and were on the full gallop. The danger was imminent. On one side of the road was a gravel pit, on the other the river, and before them was a bridge, the walls of which were not breast high. A cart was passing the bridge, and the mad horses, still on full speed, ran on the wrong side, dashed the phæton against the cart, overturned it, and threw Olivia over the wall into the river!

The freshes[1] had lately come down, and the stream was both deep and strong. I was at the foot of the bridge when she fell, and when I reached the place she was still above water, and had passed the arch on the other side. I instantly stripped off my coat cap and gown, sprang into the eddy, made a few strokes, and, as happy fortune would have it, just caught her as she was sinking!

Loaded with this precious burden, I had the strength of twenty men. I stemmed the current and presently brought her into shallow water, where I could find footing. I then bore her into the nearest house, and every possible aid was immediately administered.

While I was thus employed Hector arrived, his rage boiling over anew, at his lamed horses and broken phæton; for his inquiries concerning his sister were short, as soon as he understood that she was not drowned. I paid as little attention to him as he did to her, and was disturbed only by my fears lest the fright should be productive of fever, or still worse consequences.

Olivia had too much sincerity of heart, and too great a desire to remove the anxiety of those around her, to be guilty of the least affectation. She had received no injury, for the danger being over her mind was too strong not to dispel her fears; and, after reposing an hour and finding herself perfectly well, she insisted on coming down and joining us at dinner. Her thanks to me in words were not profuse, but they were emphatical. 'She was alive, and should never forget that she owed that life to me.' This she three times repeated; once at table, again in the post-chaise in which we returned to Oxford, and once more when we took leave of each other in the evening.

To me this day was indeed a day of tumult. Nothing perhaps more aptly prepares the mind for the passion of love than religious enthusiasm. The subject of my conversation with Olivia was chiefly a revival of former times, which seemed to be remembered by us mutually with glowing regret, as the happiest moments of our existence: times which I inwardly dreaded might never return.

Fanatical reveries excepted, this perhaps was the first desponding thought I had known; at least it was the first I can distinctly remember, and the pang that accompanied it was severe. Olivia was so lovely, her form so enchanting, her manners so captivating, that my eyes were riveted on her, my soul absorbed, and the faculty of thinking arrested. Every look of her beaming eyes penetrated to the heart, every motion of her moist coral lips gave exstacy, and every variation of her features discovered new ineffable and angelic beauties!

Why did the hours fly? Why was the day so short? She had only passed through Oxford in her way to London, and was to depart in the morning. I would gladly have persuaded her to regard her health, and not expose herself so soon after the fright; but in vain. She felt no malady, nor would acknowledge any; and the selfish Hector was rather inclined to hurry her off than invite her to stay. It was years since I had seen her, and to be torn thus suddenly from bliss unutterable? Never had I felt a pang like this before!

In the evening, returned to my chamber and left in solitude, I sat with my arms folded, disconsolate, motionless, and in a profound but yet a most active trance. I remained thus for hours, ardently thinking on Olivia, recollecting every incident of my past life in which she had had the least part, placing all her divine perfections full in view, and unable to detach my mind one moment from the beatific vision.

At length by accident, I cast my eye on two books, that lay on the mantle-piece before me: Baxter's Call to the Unconverted,[1] and the History of Francis Spira:[2] two of the most terrific productions, to such a mind at such a moment, that ever the ravings of fanaticism sent forth. The impulse was irresistible; I opened them, read, and all the horrors of hell came upon me. I was a backslider! Perdition was certain! All the torments that Baxter described were devouring me, and my soul was sinking, like the soul of Francis Spira, into sulphureous flames, there to howl and be eternally tormented by the malignant mocks and mows of inexorable fiends! I have since suffered many evils, or what are called evils, and have known misfortunes such as are supposed to be of the severest kind; but, of all the nights of my life, not one can equal this. I fell on my knees, and attempted to pray, but imagined the ear of mercy shut, and that I beheld the wicked one stand ready to seize and fly away with me! My teeth began to gnash, as if by irresistible impulse; my hair stood on end, and large drops of sweat fell from my face! The eternal damnation, of which I had read and heard so much, seemed inevitable; till at last, in a torrent of phrenzy which I had not the power to controul, I began to blaspheme, believing myself to be already a fiend!

It is by such horrible imagery that so many of the disciples of methodism have become maniacs.

My dereliction of intellect fortunately was but of short duration: overpowered and exhausted, I at length sunk to sleep, my head leaning on the bed and I kneeling by its side. How long I remained thus I cannot tell, but I awoke in a shivering fit from a dream of terror, and found myself in the dark. I hastily undressed myself, got into bed, and shrunk beneath the bed clothes, as if escaping from Satan, whom imagination once more placed at my elbow, in forms inexpressibly horrid.

The visions of the night had left too deep an impression not to be in part revived in the morning. Thoughts however that had lately escaped me were now called to recollection. I remembered having once believed that God was the God of mercy; that for him to delight in the torture of lost souls was impossible; and that I had even doubted of the eternity of future torments. To this relief a more effectual one was added: Olivia could not be forgotten, and my thoughts, by being continually attracted and fixed on her, were relieved from despair, which might otherwise have been fatal.

A week passed away in such kind of convulsive meditations, my attachment to methodism daily declining, and at last changing into something like aversion and horror. At the end of this period, I was sent for in the morning by the president. The incident was alarming! I had broken no college rules, neglected no prayers, nor been guilty of any indecorum. I foreboded that he had heard of my methodistical excursion. The conjecture was true: he told me it was too publicly known to be passed over in silence; that the character of the university had greatly suffered by this kind of heresy; that the vice chancellor, proctors, and heads of houses had been consulted, and that the gentlest punishment they could inflict was rustication for two terms. It would have been much more severe, he said, but for the respect he bore to the memory of my grandfather; who had been a doctor of the university, a worthy pillar of the church, and his good friend.

Though I suspected my opinions, I was not so entirely convinced as openly to renounce them, and I remained silent when he required me to recant. But I requested him to tell me how the event had become public? Not a gownsman was present, except Hector Mowbray; and surely he was above the character of an informer? Especially, thought I, in this instance! The president however was silent; I was suffered to suppose what I pleased, and I left him with the sentence of rustication confirmed, and my long expected academical honours deferred. The only favour granted me was that the punishment should not be made public.

CHAPTER XVII

Disappointment: More marriage accidents: Preparations for a journey

THE delay of two terms was by no means pleasing to me. I had nearly waited the stipulated time, had read *wall lectures*,[1] and had done *juraments*,[2] and *generals*.[3] Aristotle had been laid upon my head, and I had been created *a Soph*.[4] In fine, I had complied with all the forms of the university; forms which once perhaps might have had a meaning, but which are now offensively absurd. I expected the next term to have obtained the degree of bachelor of arts, after which it was my intention to have gone to London, there to have been ordained, and to have sought a flock wanting a pastor, on whom the stores of my theology and the powers of my elocution might have been well bestowed.

Traversed in this design, I determined to repair to the great city immediately, and return to keep my terms at Oxford when the period of rustication should have elapsed. But I had been obliged to furnish myself with books and music, and had found the hundred pounds a year allowed me scarcely sufficient; and, beside the charges of travelling and removal, I was informed that London was an expensive place. It was therefore necessary I should write to the country, for a supply. The correspondence with my mother, though not pursued with all the zeal in which it was begun, had been occasionally continued. At first her letters abounded with eulogiums on her husband, but the subject afterward began to cool with her, and she had lately forborne even to mention his name. In answer to the letters which I wrote, to inform her and lawyer Thornby of my plan and to request a supply, a part of the truth appeared. Her husband was a young man, who, coming sooner into the possession of money than of good sense, had squandered as much of it as he could wrest from his uncle, the lawyer, who affirmed the whole or nearly the whole was wasted; and, when he could obtain no more, had left her to depend on Thornby's bounty and had gone to London.

These disagreeable circumstances were in part communicated by my mother and in part by Thornby, who had written to tell me that, if a small advance were made, it must be deducted from the thousand pounds, bequeathed as before mentioned. To this I willingly agreed, and, giving him all the legal security he required, I received fifty pounds; after which I made the necessary preparations for my intended journey, and obtained letters of recommendation to a clergyman in London, and to the Bishop of —— to whom, when I should have taken my bachelor's degree, I meant to apply for deacon's orders.

END OF VOLUME I

VOLUME II

CHAPTER I

*Retrospect and character: A fore taste of futurity: Entrance
to London, or where does it begin? All alive: A civil
gentleman: Curiosity cooled*

THE period was now approaching in which I must fix on a
profession for life. My choice, as I imagined, was made. There was
no place so worthy of or so fit for the display of great talents as the
pulpit. This opinion I supposed to be too well founded for any
possible arguments to overturn, or even shake. I had heard much of
theology from the rector, but more at Oxford. To promote this
branch of knowledge the university was first established, and by it is
still maintained; consequently it is there the chief object of pursuit,
and topic of discourse. My hour of doubt was not yet arrived, and
of the absolute pre-eminence of the clerical office I was a bold and
resolute asserter.

Nor had my ambition been wholly bounded by the desire of fame:
I was in expectation of my full share of those advantages which the
world thinks more substantial; though this was but a subordinate
consideration. Under all points of view, my constant source of hope
was in the energy of my own mind. Among the numerous examples
which I had seen, of men who had gained preferment, many by the
sole influence of personal interest, and many more by the industry
of intriguing vice, there were some who had attained that end by the
exertion of extraordinary talents and virtue. It is true they were but
few, very few; yet on them my attention had been constantly fixed.
Them I was determined to emulate, exert the same powers, rise by
the same means, and enjoy the same privileges. Every example of
successful genius delighted, animated me, and fired my glowing

imagination. The histories of great men even when persecuted and distressed, a Galileo, a Dryden, or an Otway,[1] did but excite my admiration and my envy. Let me but equal them and I could willingly live with them in poverty and imprisonment, or die with them of misery, malady, and famine.

These were no transient feelings, but the daily emanations of desire. From my infancy, the lessons and incidents of my life had rendered me aspiring; and, however steep and rugged the rock might be described on which the temple of fame stood, I was determined to ascend and enter. I was possessed of that hilarity which, when not regulated by a strong desire to obtain some particular purpose, shews itself in a thousand extravagant forms, and is then called animal spirits; but, when thus turned to the attainment of one great end, assumes the more worthy appellation of activity of mind.

It must be acknowledged I was but little aware how much I had to learn, and unlearn, or of the opposition I should meet from my own prejudices, as well as from those of the world. But dangers never imagined are never feared, and my leading characteristic was the most sanguine hope. Were all the dangers of life to present themselves to the imagination in a body, drawn up in battle array, the prospect would indeed be dreadful; but coming individually they are less formidable, and successively as they occur are conquered. Foreboded, their aspect is terrific; but seen in retrospect, they frequently excite present satisfaction and future fortitude: and this is the way in which they have most frequently been seen by me.

Nor had my time been wholly consumed in gathering the sweets of literature. I had long been exercising myself in writing, improving my style, arranging my thoughts, and enabling myself to communicate the knowledge I might amass. Of sermons I had written some dozens; and the most arduous of the efforts of poetry had been attempted by me; from the elegy to the epic poem, each had suffered my attacks. And, though I myself was not so well satisfied with my performances as to complete these daring labours, yet, I had so far familiarised myself to a selection of words, and phrases, as to be able to compose with much more facility than is usual at such an age.

Possessed, as I was well persuaded, of no common portion of merit, it was a cheering thought that I was now going to bring it immediately to market; at least into view. London I understood to be the great emporium, where talents if exhibited would soon find their true value, and were in no danger of being long over-looked. To London, which was constantly pouring its novelties, its discoveries, and its effusions of genius over the kingdom, I was going.

I did not, as at Oxford, expect to find its inhabitants all saints. No: I had heard much of their vices. The subtle and ingenious arts, by which they trick and prey upon each other, had been pictured to me as highly dangerous; and of these arts, self confident as I was, I stood in some awe. But fore warned, said I, fore armed: and that I was not easily to be circumvented was still a part of my creed.

Such were my qualities, character and expectations, when I entered the carriage that conveyed me toward the great city. It was early in the month of February, the days were short, and evening came on as we reached Hounslow. Brentford I imagined to be London, and was disappointed to find myself again driven out of town. The lighted lamps and respectable buildings of Turnham Green made me conclude that to be the place, or at least the beginning, which Hammersmith did but confirm; and my surprise, at once more finding myself in a noble road, still lighted with lamps and with only here and there a house, was increased.[1]

At Kensington to me London actually began, and I thought myself hurried nearly through it when the coach stopped at the Gloucester Coffee-house, in Piccadilly. I had already for miles been driven through streets, over stones, and never out of sight of houses, and was astonished to be told that I was now only as it were at the entrance of London.

The quantity of carriages we had passed, the incessant clattering of hoofs and rolling of wheels over the pavement, the general buzz around me, the hurry and animation of the people, and the universal illumination of streets, houses, and shops, excited ideas which were new, unexpected, and almost confounding! Imagination conjured up a mass that was all magnificence! The world till now had to me been sleeping; here only men were alive! At Oxford indeed, owing to circumstances, I had felt some similar emotions. But that was a transient scene that quickly declined into stillness and calm: here I was told it was everlastingly the same! The mind delighted to revel in this abundance: it seemed an infinitude, where satiety, its most fatal and hated enemy, could never come.

I had questions innumerable to ask, and made fifty attempts to get intelligence from the waiters, but in vain; they were too busy to attend to me, and treated my interrogatories with impertinent neglect. However, I was overflowing; talk I must, and I attacked various persons, that were coming and going in the coffee-room. Still I could get only short answers, and I wanted volumes.

Thus disappointed, I went and stood at the door, that I might divine as much as I could for myself: for though it was night, in London there is scarcely such a thing as darkness. While I was standing here, a gentleman of a more complaisant temper came up and fell into conversation with me, answered my inquiries, and informed me the king's palace was at no great distance. The king's palace was indeed a tempting object, and he good-naturedly offered to walk and shew it me. This very obliging proposal I readily accepted, and away we went.

As we were going down St. James's-street, as I imagine, the thought occurred 'If this gentleman now should be a sharper? He behaves with great civility; it is very improbable; but who knows? Let him! There is no trick he is master of shall prevail on me to part with the little money I have in my pocket: of that I am determined.'

Scarcely had the idea passed through my mind, before two men ran with such violence against me that they threw me flat on the pavement, and hurt me considerably. My companion and another immediately came to help me up; and the moment I was on my legs my friend and guide requested me to stay there half a minute; he would see that the watch should soon secure the rascals; and off he ran, full speed. The other kind gentleman followed his example.

All this happened in an instant; and, while I was standing in a kind of amazement, a passenger, who had seen the transaction at a distance, came up and asked me—'Are you much bruised, Sir?'—'Not very much.'—'Have you lost nothing?'—'Lost? [The question alarmed me] No: I believe not!'——'Search your pockets.'

Going to do as I was desired and putting my hands down, I found my breeches pockets were both turned inside out, and emptied of their contents. I stood speechless and motionless, while I was informed that it was a common-place trick for gangs of pickpockets to throw unwary passengers down with violence, pretend to pity and give them aid, pick their pockets while helping them up, and then decamp with all possible expedition. But said I, with great simplicity, to my informer, 'Will not the gentleman come back?' ——'What! The man who ran off?'——'Yes.'—'Back! No, no: you will never see his face more, I promise you, Sir; unless you will take the trouble to visit Newgate, or attend the Old Bailey.'

There was no remedy! I stared for a moment, looked foolish, and returned toward the coffee-house; having taken care to mark the way I went. On repeating this story afterward, I learned further that to watch at inns and places where strangers arrive, and to play such tricks as may best succeed with them, is a very frequent practice with sharpers and pickpockets. My only consolation was the sum was small; for I had been cautioned not to travel with much money about me, lest we should meet robbers on the road; and the advice happened to be serviceable. That I had not my watch in my pocket was another lucky circumstance, or it would have disappeared. The fear of highwaymen had induced me to pack it up in my trunk. As for my handkerchief, it was gone, in the company of my purse.

CHAPTER II

A journey in town: Good breeding and morality: A new
order of priests: A clerical character, or the art of pleasing:
Episcopal influence: More gazing: A strange adventure,
and the first sight of a play

As soon as I had breakfasted in the morning, my first care was to change my dress, powder my hair, put my watch in my pocket, inquire my way, and deliver my letters of recommendation. I thought it most prudent to apply first to the clergyman, and take his advice concerning the best manner of appearing before a bishop.

My letters, for I had two, were addressed to the reverend Enoch Ellis, Suffolk-Street, Middlesex Hospital. Which way I went I cannot now tell, but I had so many sights to see, shops to examine, and curiosities to admire, that, by the help of wandering perhaps a mile or much more out of my road, I was at least two hours before I came to my journey's end.

I knocked at the door, and was told by the servant that his master was not at home; but was asked if I had any message? I replied I had letters, which I wished to deliver into his own hand. The reverend Enoch, who as it appeared was listening through an aperture left purposely at the parlour door, put his head out, like a turtle from his shell, and desired the servant to shew the gentleman in; he would be with him in a moment. This was another phenomenon in morals! A clergyman suffer, nay encourage, or, as it must be, command, his servant to tell a lie? It was inconceivable! I knew nothing of fashionable manners, and that being denied to people whom you do not wish to see, instead of being thought insolent or false, was the general practice of the well bred. At that time I understood no single point of good breeding: I had it all to learn! But indeed, so dull am I on such topics, that, to this hour, how it can be a clergyman's or any honest man's duty or interest to teach servants to lie is to me incomprehensible. The difficulty, as I have found it, is to teach both them and all classes of people to tell the truth. What the morality of the practice is cannot be a serious question.

Before I proceed with that part of my story in which the reverend Enoch Ellis takes a share, it is necessary to remark that there has sprung up in modern times a clerical order of men, very distinct in manners and character from the subservient curate, or the lordly parish priest. Houses in London have lately been built much faster than churches. Yet, though the zeal of these times does not equal that of ancient days, when our cities were divided into numerous small parishes, when religion was the universal trade of mankind, and when the temples of superstition reared their proud heads in every alley, still men who know how to turn the penny have found it advantageous, even in these days of infidelity, to build here and there a chapel, and to let each of these chapels out to the best clerical bidder; who in his turn uses all his influence to allure the neighbourhood to hire, in retail, those bits and parcels, called pews, that, for the gratification of pride, are measured off within the consecrated walls which he has hired wholesale.[1] In these undertakings, if the preacher cannot make himself popular, it is at least his interest to make himself pleasing.

Of one of these chapels Enoch Ellis was the farmer general;[2] and this necessary endeavour to please had produced in him a remarkable contrast of character. He was a little man, with thin legs and thighs and a pot belly, but precisely upright: an archbishop could not carry himself more erect: his chest projecting; his neck stiff; his head thrown back; his eyes of the ferret kind, red, tender and much uncovered by the eyelid; his nose flat on the bridge, and at the end of the colour and form of a small round gingerbread nut, but with little nostril; his lips thin; his teeth half black half yellow; his ears large; his beard and whiskers sandy; his hair dark, but kept in buckle, and powdered as white as a miller's hat; his complexion sallow, and his countenance and general aspect jaundiced and mean.

With these requisites, there was a continual struggle, between his efforts to preserve his clerical solemnity and to make himself agreeable. His formal manner of pursing up his face into smiles, for this purpose, had produced a regular set of small wrinkles, folds, and plies, that inevitably reminded those who were not accustomed to him of the grinning of an ape; for he was so fearful of derogating from his dignity that it was impossible for his smile to take the form of meaning.

After waiting about ten minutes this reverend little gentleman, such as I have described, entered, assumed one of these agreeable solemn smiles, and bowed; but instantly recovered his full stature; as if he had been then measuring for a grenadier.

I delivered my letters: one was from the tutor, and the other from a regent master,[1] who was one of the caput.[2] He read them; and, as I was desirous to gain friends in a city of strangers, I anxiously watched his countenance; but I could not perceive that they produced any remarkably favourable effect. Not but he assumed all his civility; was vastly glad to hear his Oxford friends were in good health; should be exceedingly happy to do any thing, that lay in his power, to serve a gentleman of their recommendation. But the duties of his profession were very laborious: they could not be neglected. His calls were incessant: he had not a moment to himself. However, if I could point out any way—that is—he should be prodigiously happy—prodigiously indeed to give me any advice in his power.

I was by no means satisfied with the pauses, hems, and ha's with which he delivered these apologies. However, not knowing what better to do, I mentioned that I had letters to the Bishop of ——, and should be glad if he could tell me which was the properest hour and manner of gaining access to deliver them.

The mention of the bishop was electrical; it produced an immediate and miraculous change in the countenance of the reverend Enoch Ellis. The quantity of emphasis on his favourite epithet, prodigious, was wonderfully increased. He was prodigiously glad to find I was so well recommended! Was prodigiously happy to hear from his friends of ***** college! Should take prodigious satisfaction in serving a gentleman in whose behalf they had written! Nothing could give him such prodigious pleasure! And, that I might be under no difficulty, if I would permit him, he would first make the necessary inquiries, and then attend me in person, to pay my respects to the right reverend dignitary.

This relaxation in his manner flattered and pleased me. He now perceived me to be somebody; my half-offended vanity was appeased, and I accepted his offer with thanks.

To add to these obligations, finding that I was but just come to town, of which I was entirely ignorant, and that I wanted a lodging, he very obligingly told me his servant should inquire in the neighbourhood, and provide me one by the morrow. I endeavoured to make a suitable return to this *prodigious* increase of courtesy by a pedantical, but in my then opinion classical, quotation: *Dii tibi*,[1] —&c. Virgil will tell the rest.

These civilities being all acted and over, I bowed and took my leave, appointing to call again the next morning; and he bowing in return, and waiting on me to the door: I much better pleased with my reception after the mention of the bishop than before; and he no less well satisfied.

I had now nothing to do for the rest of the day but indulge my curiosity, which made very large and imperious demands on all my senses. I walked from street to street, examined object after object, tasted the tarts of the pastry cooks, listened to the barrel organs, bells, tambours de basque,[2] and cymbals of Savoyards, snuffed ten thousand various odours, gazed at the inviting splendour of shop windows innumerable, and with insatiable avidity gazed again! All the delights of novelty and surprise thrilled and tingled through my veins! It was a world of such inexhaustible abundance, wealth, and prosperity as to exceed the wildest of the dreams of fancy! Recollecting what my feelings then were, it seems almost surprizing that I can walk through the same tempting world of wonders, at present, scarcely conscious that such things have any existence.

The sole draw-back I felt to these delights was the fear of sharpers, and thieves; which, owing to my two unlucky adventures, of the lady with the riding-habit and the obliging gentleman who took me to see the king's palace, was so great that I never thought myself in safety.

Under these impressions, I happened in the afternoon to stray through Brydges-street, and saw a croud of people gathered round the play-house doors, who on inquiry I found were waiting to get in. The play bills were pasted in large letters, red and black, against the walls. I read them, and their contents told me it was one of my most favourite tragedies, Rowe's Fair Penitent,[1] and that Mrs. Siddons[2] was to act.

I had never yet seen a play in my life; for so licentious are the manners and behaviour of the youth of Oxford, that the vice chancellor dare not admit players into the city. This was an invitation to enjoyment not to be resisted. I blessed my lucky stars, that had led me by accident that way, and immediately took my stand among the people who surrounded the pit door, and pressed forward to better my situation as much as I could without ill manners.

Here I waited with the hope of pleasure exciting me to patience I know not how long, till the hour of opening the doors approached, about which time the croud was frequently put in motion. I observed that the people around me had several times appeared to be watchful of each other, and presently I heard a voice proclaim aloud—'Take care of your pockets!'

My fears suddenly came upon me! I put my hand down to my fob, and missed my watch! I eagerly looked round as well as I could, hemmed in as I was, and fixed my eyes on!—astonishment!—on my conductor to the palace! The blood mantled in my face. 'You have stolen my watch,' said I. He could not immediately escape, and made no reply, but turned pale, looked at me as if intreating silence and commiseration, and put a watch into my hand. I felt a momentary compassion and he presently made his retreat.

His retiring did but increase the press of the croud, so that it was impossible for me so much as to lift up my arm: I therefore continued, as the safest way, to hold the watch in my hand. Soon afterward the door opened, and I hurried it into my waistcoat pocket; for I was obliged to make the best use of all my limbs, that I might not be thrown down and trodden under foot.

At length, after very uncommon struggles, I made my way to the money door, paid, and entered the pit. After taking breath and gazing around me, I sat down and inquired of my neighbours how soon the play would begin? I was told in an hour. This new delay occasioned me to put my hand in my pocket and take out my watch, which as I supposed had been returned by the thief. But, good heavens! What was my surprize when, in lieu of my own plain watch, in a green chagrin[1] case, the one I was now possessed of was set round with diamonds! And, instead of ordinary steel and brass, its appendages were a weighty gold chain and seals!

My astonishment was great beyond expression! I opened it to examine the work, and found it was capped. I pressed upon the nut[2] and it immediately struck the hour: it was a repeater![3]

Its value could not but be very great; yet I was far from satisfied with the accident. It was no watch of mine; nor must I keep it, if the owner could be found; of which there could be no doubt; and my own was gone past all recovery.

I could not let it rest. I surveyed it again, inspected every part more minutely, and particularly examined the seals. My former amazement was now increased ten fold! They were the very same arms, the identical seals, of the watch on the sopha, that had betrayed the lovely creature in the blue riding habit to Hector Mowbray! The watch too was in every particular just such another; had a gold chain and was studded with diamonds! It must be the property of his lordship.

In vain did I rack invention to endeavour to account for so strange an incident: my conjectures were all unsatisfactory, all improbable. I looked round to see if I could discover his lordship in the house, but without success: the numbers were so great that the people were concealed behind each other. Beside it was long since I had seen his lordship: perhaps his person was changed, as his title had been, by the death of his father. He was now the Earl of Idford. My surmises concerning this uncommon accident kept my mind in continual activity, till the drawing up of the curtain; when they immediately ceded to ideas of a much more captivating and irresistible kind. The delight received by the youthful imagination, the first time of being present at the representation of a play, is not I suspect to be equalled by any other ever yet experienced, or invented. The propriety and richness of the dresses, the deception and variety of the scenery, the natural and energetic delivery of the actors, and the reality of every incidental circumstance were so great as to excite incessant rapture!

To describe the effects produced on me by Mrs. Siddons is wholly impossible. Her bridal apathy of despair contrasted with the tumultuous joy of her father, the mingled emotions of love for her seducer, disdain of his baseness, and abhorrence partly of her own guilt but still more of the tyranny and guilt of prejudice, and the majesty of mind with which she trampled on the world's scorn, defied danger, met death, and lamented little for herself, much for those she had injured, excited emotions in me the remembrance of which ages could not obliterate!

It may here be worthy of remark that the difference between the sensations I then had and those I should now have, were I present at the same exhibition, is in many particulars as great as can well be imagined. Not an iota of the whole performance, at that time, but seemed to me to be perfect; and I should have readily quarrelled with the man who should have happened to express disapprobation. The art of acting I had little considered, and was ignorant of its extent and degree of perfectibility. To read a play was no common pleasure, but to see one was ecstacy. Whereas at present, the knowledge of how much better characters might in general be performed occasions me, with the exception of some very few performers, infinitely to prefer the reading of a good play in the closet to its exhibition on the stage.

The curtain being dropped for the night, I stood for a while gazing at the multitude in motion, unwilling to quit the enchanted spot; but the house beginning to be empty and the lights put out, I thought it was time to retire.

That I might feel no interruption from having so valuable a deposit in my charge, for so I considered it to be, instead of putting the repeater in my fob,[1] I had dropped it securely under my ham; being much rather willing to endure any slight disagreeable sensation it might there excite than run any farther risk.

The precaution as it happened was prudent. As I left the pit, I thought I saw the identical obliging guide and pick-pocket, who had returned me this watch in mistake, for it could be no other way, and, as I ascended the steps, two men who were standing at the door immediately advanced before me, and spread themselves out to prevent my passing; while a third came behind me, put his hand gently round my waist, and felt for the chain. My mind was so alive to dangers of this kind, just then, that I was immediately aware of the attempt, and pushing the men aside with my whole force I sprang up the steps, of which there were not more than half a dozen. I then faced about in the door way, not being acquainted with the passages, nor thinking it safe to run.

The moment I rushed by, one of them asked the other—'Have

you *nabbed* it?' and was answered—'No. *Go it!*' Immediately one of them darted toward me, but I stood above him, was greatly his superior in size and strength, and easily knocked him down. A second made a similar attempt, and met a similar reception.

Hearing the scuffle, one of the house constables who happened to be standing at a little distance under the portico, and some of his assistants, came up; but, before they had time to be informed of the affair, the fellows had taken to their heels.

The constable uttered many exclamations against the rascals, and said, they had become so daring that nobody was safe. They had that very afternoon picked the pocket of the Earl of Idford of a repeater studded with diamonds, under the Piazza,[1] as he was coming out of the Shakespeare,[2] where he had been to attend an election meeting. By this I learned, in five words, what, before the play began, my brain had been ineffectually busied about for a full hour.

Being told that I was a stranger and did not know my road, the constable informed me it would be safest to go home in a coach. I took his advice: a coach was called, and I was once more conveyed to the Gloucester Coffee-house.

CHAPTER III

The advice of Enoch: Complaisance of a peer: A liberal offer and Enoch's sensibility, or the favour doubly returned

MY health, appetite, and spirits suffered no check, from this tide of novelty and tumult of accident. I eat heartily, slept soundly, and rose chearfully. It is true, I came up to London with propensities which, from my education, that is, from the course of former events, would not suffer me to be idle; and in the space of a few hours I had already received several important lessons, that considerably increased my stock of knowledge.

Of these I did not fail to make an active use. They awakened attention, and I began to look about me with quickness and with caution. I had business enough for the day, and my first care was to keep my appointment with the reverend Enoch, whose counsel concerning the Earl of Idford and the repeater I once more thought it prudent to ask.

Thither I repaired, was readily admitted, and told him my story. It related to an Earl, and the ear of Enoch was attentively open. Having heard the whole, he made application immediately to the court calendar, to discover the Earl's town residence, and it was found to be in Bruton street. But how to gain admission? His lordship would not be at home, unless I were known? I replied that I had formerly been acquainted with his lordship, at the university. 'Ay but,' answered Enoch, 'is your face familiar to the servants?' 'No.'—'Then they will not *let you in*. The best way therefore will be to write a note to his lordship, informing him that you have particulars to communicate concerning his repeater. He will then appoint an hour, and you will certainly be admitted. I have enquired concerning my lord, the Bishop: you cannot see him at present, for he is in the country, but will return to town in less than a week, consequently you can wait on the Earl at any hour. It is a lucky event! A prodigiously fine opportunity for an introduction to a nobleman! Be advised by me, and profit by it, Mr. Trevor. If you please, I will attend you to his lordship. You are a young man, and to be accompanied by a clergyman has a respectable look, and gives a sanction. You conceive me, Mr. Trevor?'

I had acuteness enough to conceive the selfishness of his motives, which was more than he intended; but I acceded to the proposal, for I was almost as averse to giving as to receiving pain: beside I was a stranger, and he would be my conductor. The note to his lordship was accordingly written, a messenger dispatched with it, and while he was gone I again repeated the whole story of the watch, which in all its circumstances still appeared to me very surprising, and asked the reverend Enoch if he could account for them?

He replied that the Piazza, where the watch was stolen, was scarcely two hundred yards from the door at which the croud was assembled; that the thief probably thought this croud the best hiding place; that he could not remain idle, and therefore had been busy with the pockets of the people, and among the rest once again with mine; that his terror and confusion, lest he should be detected with a diamond repeater in his possession, might be much greater than usual; that, after having delivered it to me and discovered his mistake, he was very desirous to remedy the blunder, and therefore watched me into the pit; that, seeing me seated, he then went in search of his companions; and that what afterward followed was, first, their usual mode of stealing watches, and, when that failed, a more vigorous attempt to recover a prize of uncommon value.

These suppositions, which Enoch's acquaintance with the town and not the efforts of his imagination had suggested, made the history of the event tolerably probable, and I suppose were very like the truth.

The messenger quickly returned, with a note containing—'His lordship's compliments; he was then at home, and if I should happen to be at leisure would be very glad to see me immediately.'

I told you, said Enoch, that if you meant to play the sure game you must mention the repeater. My vanity would willingly have given another interpretation to his lordship's civility, and have considered it as personal to myself; but the philosophy of my vanity did not in this case appear to be quite so sound as that of the reverend Enoch, and I was mute.

Neither I nor Enoch were desirous of delay, and in a few minutes we were in Bruton street; where the doors opened to us as if the hinges had all been lately oiled. His lordship, who had acquired much more of the man of the world, that is, of bowing and smiling, than when I first saw him at Oxford, instantly knew me, received me and my friend graciously, and easily entered into conversation with us.

The first thing I did was to restore him his watch, and tell him the whole story, with the comments of the constable and of the reverend Enoch. He laughed as much as lords in general laugh, said it was a whimsical accident, and paid me a number of polite compliments and thanks; treated the watch as a trinket which, as he recollected, had not cost him more than three hundred guineas; but the bauble had been often admired, he was partial to it, and was very glad it was thus recovered.

To this succeeded the smiles and contortions of Enoch to make himself agreeable. His endeavours were very assiduous indeed, and to me very ridiculous; but his lordship seemed to receive his cringing and abject flattery as a thing rather of course, and expected, than displeasing or contemptible.

Among other conversation, his lordship did not fail to inquire if I were come to make any stay in town; and what my intentions and plan were? On being informed of these, he professed a great desire to serve me; and added that a thought had struck him, which perhaps might be agreeable to me. If so, it would give him great pleasure. He wished to have a friend, who during an hour of a morning might afford him conversation. Perhaps he might occasionally trouble him to commit a few thoughts to writing; but that might be as it happened. If I would come and reside in his house, and act in this friendly manner with him, he should be gratified and I not injured.

Enoch's open eyes twinkled with joy: sparkle they could not. He foresaw through my means, intercourse with a peer, and perhaps patronage! He was ready to answer for me, and could not restrain his tongue from protesting that it was a prodigiously liberal, friendly and honourable offer.

I had not forgotten his lordship's former jolly tutor, the terms on which they had lived, or the treatment to which this tutor had occasionally submitted. Yet I was not displeased with the proposal. I spurned at the idea of any such submission, but the character of his lordship seemed changed: and changed it certainly was, though I then knew not why, or to what. Nor was it supposed that I was to act as his menial. I therefore expressed my sense of his lordship's civility, and owned the situation would be acceptable to me, as I was not at present encumbered with riches, and living in London I found was likely to prove expensive. I had desired to have a genteel apartment, and Enoch had told me that one had been hired for me at a guinea and a half per week, at which I had been not a little startled. The secret of want of wealth a very cunning man would have concealed: a very wise man, though from other motives, would have told it with the same unaffected simplicity that I did.

Still the transports of Enoch, at his lordship's bounty, were inexhaustible. They put me to the blush: but whether it was at being unable to keep pace with him in owning this load of obligations, or at his impertinent acknowledgment of feelings for me of which I was unconscious, is more than I can tell. For his part, he did but speak on the behalf of his young friend. I had come well recommended to him, and he had already conceived a very singular affection for me. He had no doubt but that I should be prodigiously grateful to his lordship for all favours. His good advice should certainly never be wanting; and patrons like his lordship could not, by any possible efforts, be too humbly and dutifully served.

I did but feebly second this submissive sense of obligation, and these overflowing professions for favours not yet received. Luckily however he talked so fast, and was so anxious to recommend himself, that I had scarcely an opportunity to put in a word. He took all the trouble upon himself.

I ought to have mentioned that, before the proposal was made, his lordship had taken care to inquire if I understood the living languages? He spoke a few sentences in French to me himself, and attempted to do the same in Italian, but succeeded in the latter very indifferently. My answers satisfied him that I was no stranger to these studies.

The fact was, his lordship found it necessary to keep a secretary, to aid him in his politics not only to write but to think; and I afterward learned, from his valet, that he had allowed a hundred a year to one who had left his service that very day. His lordship was doubtless therefore well satisfied with the meeting of this morning, in which he not only recovered his diamond repeater but rewarded the youth who brought it, by suffering him to do the same business gratis for which he had before been obliged to pay.

CHAPTER IV

Memento of an old acquaintance: Gentility alarmed: The family of Enoch: Musical raptures and card-table good breeding

By the order of his lordship, two chairmen with a horse were dispatched for my effects; and possession was given me of the apartment occupied by my predecessor. In this apartment a trunk, which he had not removed, was left; and on it was a direction to Henry Turl. This excited my curiosity: I inquired of the valet, and from his description was confirmed in the conjecture, that my quondam school and college acquaintance, Turl, had been his lordship's late secretary.

Though at college I had considered his opinions as dangerous, yet every thing that I had heard of his behaviour challenged respect. I scarcely knew, at present, whether I wished to have any intercourse with him or not; but the high opinion I had of his understanding made me hope well of his morals, and wish him prosperity.

My good fortune was in danger of being immediately disturbed, by an incident which to me was very unexpected. Instead of being treated as the friend and companion of his lordship, when the dinner hour came an invitation was sent up to me by the house-keeper, from which I understood I was to dine at what is called the second table. At this time I had much pride and little philosophy, and a more effectual way to pique that pride could not have been found. I returned a civil answer, the purport of which was that I should dine out, and immediately wrote a short note to his lordship; informing him that 'I took it for granted his housekeeper had mistaken his intentions, and did not understand the terms on which I presumed I was to live in his lordship's house. His lordship had said he wished me to be his companion, and this distinction would certainly make me unfit to be the companion of his housekeeper.'

The discharging my conscience of thus much vanity gave me immediate relief, and was productive of the effect intended. His lordship took the hint my spirited letter gave, and feigned ignorance of his housekeeper's proceeding. My appearance, person, and understanding he thought would not disgrace his table, at which consequently I was afterward permitted to take my seat.

In the evening, I went by appointment to visit at the house of the reverend Enoch; when I was introduced by him to his wife and daughter, as a very accomplished young gentleman, an under-graduate of Oxford, intended for the church, of prodigious connexions, recommended to a bishop, patronized by an earl, and his very particular good friend.

I bowed and the ladies curtsied. Mrs. Ellis too had studied the art of making herself agreeable, but in a very different way from Enoch. Her mode was by engaging in what are called parties, learning the private history of all her acquaintance, and retailing it in such a manner as might best gratify the humours, prejudices, and passions of her hearers. She had some shrewdness, much cunning, and made great pretensions to musical and theatrical taste, and the belles lettres. She spoke both French and Italian; ill enough, but sufficiently to excite the admiration of those who understood neither. She had lately persuaded Enoch to make a trip with the whole family to Paris, and she returned with a very ample cargo of information; all very much at the disposal of her inquisitive friends.

Her daughter, Eliza, was mamma's own child. She had an *immense deal* of taste, no small share of vanity, and a tongue that could not tire. She had caught the mingled cant of Enoch and her mamma, repeated the names of public people and public places much oftener than her prayers, and was ready to own, with no little self complacency, that all her acquaintance told her *she was prodigious severe*.

In addition to these shining qualities, she was a musical amateur of the first note. She could make the jacks of her harpsichord[1] dance so fast that no understanding ear could keep pace with them: and her master, Signor Gridarini, affirmed every time he came to give her a lesson, that, among all the dilettanti in Europe, there was not so great a singer as herself. The most famous of the public performers scarcely could equal her. In the bravura she astonished! in the cantabile she charmed; her maëstoso[2] was inimitable! and her adagios! Oh! they were ravishing! killing. She indeed openly accused him of flattering her; but Signor Gridarini appealed both to his honour and his friends; the best judges in Europe, who as she well knew all said the same.

Of personal beauty she herself was satisfied that the Gods had kindly granted her a full share. 'Tis true, her stature was dwarfish: but then, she had so genteel an air! Her staymaker was one of the ablest in town. Her complexion could not but be to her mind, for it was of her own making. The only thing that she could not correct to her perfect satisfaction was a something of a cast with her eyes; which especially when she imitated Enoch in making herself agreeable, was very like squinting. Not but that the thought squinting itself a pleasing kind of blemish. Nay there were instances in which she scarcely knew if it could be called a blemish.

By these two ladies I was received with no little distinction. The mother recollected the earl and the bishop; the daughter surveyed my person, with which she was almost as well satisfied as with her own. I heard her tell her female acquaintance, during the evening, that she thought me *immense* well bred; and that in her opinion I was *prodigious* handsome; and, when they smiled, she added that she spoke with perfect *song fro*,[3] and merely as a person of some critical taste.

I could indeed have corrected her English grammar, and her French pronunciation; but I was not at this time so fastidious; as to accuse her of any mistake in judgment, in the opinion she gave of me.

My musical talents gained me additional favour. Miss Eliza was quite in raptures to hear that I could accompany her in a concerto; or take a part in an Italian duet. She vowed and protested again, to her friends, that I was a most accomplished, charming man! She spoke aside, but I was rather remarkably quick of hearing that evening. She proposed a lesson of Kozeluch's[1] immediately. I should play the violin accompaniment, and her papa *as it was very easy* would take the bass.

All voices, for there was *a prodigious large party* by this time, were loud in their assent. Every body was sure, before any body heard, it would be *monstrous fine*; so there was no refusing. The fiddles were tuned, the books were placed, the candles were snuffed, the chord was struck, and off we went, *Allegro con strepito!*[2]

We obeyed the composer's commands, and played with might and main during the first thirty or forty bars, till the *obligato* part came, in which Miss was to exhibit her powers. She then, with all the dignity of a *maëstro di capella* directed two intersecting rays full at Enoch, and called aloud, *piano!*[3] After which casting a gracious smile to me, as much as to say I did not mean you, Sir; she heaved up an attitude with her elbows, gave a short cough to encourage herself, and proceeded.

Her fears give her no embarrassment, thought I, and all will be well. I could not have been more mistaken. The very first difficult passage she came to shewed me she was an ignorant pretender. Time, tune, and recollection were all lost. I was obliged to be silent in the accompaniment, for I knew as little what was become of her as she herself did. Enoch knew no more than either of us, but he kept strumming on. He was used to it, and his ears were not easily offended.

She certainly intended to have been very positive, but was at last obliged to come to a full stop; and, again casting an indignant squint at her father, she exclaimed 'Lord, Sir! I declare, there is no keeping with you!' 'No: nor with you neither!' said Enoch. 'Will you have the goodness to begin again, Mr. Trevor?' continued she. I saw no remedy: she was commander in chief, and I obeyed.

We might have begun again and again to eternity, had we stopped every time she failed: but as I partly perceived my silence in the accompaniment, instead of continuing to make a discordant noise with Enoch and herself, had chiefly disconcerted her, I determined to rattle away. My ears were never more completely flayed! But what could be done? Miss panted for fame, and the company wanted music!

We had the good luck to find one another out at the last bar, and gave a loud stroke to conclude with; which was followed by still louder applause. It was vastly fine! *excessive* charming! Miss was a ravishing performer, and every soul in the room was distractingly fond of music! 'There!' said Enoch, taking off his spectacles. 'There, ladies! Now you hear things done as they should be!'

Not satisfied with this specimen, we must next sing an Italian trio; for Enoch, like Miss, could sing as well as he could play. But it was the old story over again: 'things done as they should be.'

The company by this time were pretty well satisfied; though their praise continued to be extravagant. Miss however would fain have treated them with a little more; and, when she found me obstinate in my negative, she, with a half reprimanding half applauding tap with her fan, for we were by this time very familiar acquaintance, told me that great performers were always tired sooner than their auditors!

While Miss had been thus busied, her mamma had not been idle. She and her friends, who were so fond of music, had frequently in full gabble joined the *con strepito* chorus, and quite completed that kind of harmony in which our concert excelled. Add to which there was the rattling of the card tables, placed ready by her order during the music; for she was too good an economist to lose time. But she professed to have a delicate ear. Enoch had taught her to know when things were done as they should be.

The concert being ended and the cards ready, I was invited to draw for partners. One elderly lady was particularly pressing. I excused myself, and Miss said pouting to her mamma, but looking traverse at the elderly lady, 'Law mamma, you are so teazing! We have made up a little *conversazione* party of our own, and you want to spoil it by taking Mr. Trevor from us! I declare,' continued she, turning her back on the card tables and lowering her voice, 'that old Tabby is never contented but when she is at her honours and her tricks! But let her alone! She never goes away a loser! She has more tricks than honours!'

I presume it was not the first time that she had said this good thing; at least it was not the last, for I heard it every time afterward that the parties met on a like occasion. The old lady however contrived before they broke up to weary me into compliance. I played a single rubber, lost a guinea, and was asked for my half crown to put under the candlestick.[1] I say, asked; for I have before observed that I came up to London ignorant of every point of good breeding. I could not have surmised that the six packs of half dirty cards were to be subscribed for by the company at half a crown a head.

CHAPTER V

Politics and patriotism of a lord: A grand undertaking:
Sublime effusions, or who but I: Politics and taste of Enoch:
The honey changed to gall, or rules for fine writers

THE next day about noon, his lordship sent his compliments, informing me he should be glad of my company. I hastened to him, eager to have an opportunity privately to display, before a lord, my knowledge, wit, and understanding.

After a short introductory dialogue, his lordship turned the conversation on politics, and it so happened that, though my ideas on this subject were but feeble and ill arranged, yet it had not wholly escaped my attention. While I was at Oxford, the want of a parliamentary reform had agitated the whole nation, and was too real and glaring an evil[1] not to be convincing to a young and unprejudiced mind. The extension of the excise laws[2] had likewise produced in me strong feelings of anger; and the enormous and accumulating national debt[3] had been described to me as a source of imminent, absolute, and approaching ruin.

These and similar ideas though all more or less crude I detailed, and concluded my creed with asserting my conviction that government used corrupt and immoral means, and that these were destructive of the end which it meant to obtain.

His lordship was quite in raptures to hear me; and declared he could not have expected such sound doctrine, from so young a man. 'Yes, Mr. Trevor,' continued he, 'government is indeed corrupt! It has opposed me in three elections; one for a county, the others for two popular boroughs. The opposition has cost me fifty thousand pounds, and I lost them all. Time was when the minister might have made me his friend; but I am now his irreconcilable enemy, and I will hang upon his skirts and never quit him, no, not for a moment, till he is turned out of office with disgrace. He ought not to have angered me, for I and my friends kept aloof: he knew I did, and he might——But now I have openly joined the opposition, and nothing less than his ruin shall satisfy me! I am exceedingly happy, Mr. Trevor, to find you reason so justly on these subjects; and to say the truth I shall be very glad of your assistance.'

I answered his lordship that I should be equally glad, if I could contribute to the good government and improvement of mankind by correcting their present errors; and that the vices I had mentioned, and every other vice that I could discover, I should always think it my duty to oppose.

'That,' answered his lordship, 'is right, Mr. Trevor! You speak my own sentiments! Opposition, strong severe and bitter, is what I am determined on! Your principles and mine are the same, and I am resolved he shall repent of having made me his enemy! We will communicate our thoughts to each other, and as you are a young man whose talents were greatly esteemed at **** college, and who know how to place arguments in a striking form, I have no doubt of our success. I will make him shake in his seat!'

His lordship then drew a whole length picture first of his own griefs, and next of the present state of representation, and the known dependence and profligacy of the minister's adherents, which highly excited my indignation. My heart exulted in the correction which I was determined to bestow on them all; and I made not the least doubt but that I should soon be able to write down the minister, load his partizans with contempt, and banish such flagitious proceedings from the face of the earth.

With these all sufficient ideas of myself, and many professions of esteem and friendship from the earl, I retired to begin a series of letters, that were to rout the minister, reform the world, and convey my fame to the latest posterity. I had already perused Junius[1] as a model of style, had been enraptured with his masculine ardor, and had no doubt but that the hour was now come in which he was to be rivaled.

I could not disguise from myself that the motives of his lordship were not of the purest kind: but I had formed no expectations in favour of his morals; and, if the end at which he aimed was a good one, his previous mistakes must be pardoned. He had engaged me in a delightful task, had given me an opportunity of exerting my genius and of publishing my thoughts to the world, and I sat down to my labours with transport and zeal.

So copious was my elocution that in less than four hours I had filled eight pages of paper; two of which at least were Greek and Latin quotations, from Aristotle, Demosthenes, and Cicero. I meant to astonish mankind with my erudition! All shall acknowledge, said I, that a writer of wit, energy, and genius is at last sprung up; one who is profoundly skilled too in classical learning. My whole soul was bent on saying strong things, fine things, learned things, pretty things, good things, wise things, and severe things. Never was there more florid railing. My argument was a kind of pitiful Jonas, and my words were the whale in which it was swallowed up.

I was quite enamoured of my performance, and was impatient for twelve o'clock the next day, that his lordship might admire it! In the mean time, to allay my insatiable thirst of praise, I took it to upright Enoch. When the reverend little man heard that I was employed by his lordship to write on affairs of government, he declared it as a thing decided that my fortune was made: but he dropped his under lip when told that I had attacked the minister—Was prodigiously sorry!—That was the wrong side—Ministers paid well for being praised; but they gave nothing, except fine, imprisonment, and pillory, for blame.

I heard him with contempt, but was too eager in my thirst of approbation to make any reply, except by urging him to read. He put on his spectacles and began, but blundered so wretchedly that I was soon out of patience; and taking the paper from him began to read myself.

No one will doubt but that he was the first to be tired. However, he said it was fine; and was quite surprised to hear me read Greek with such sonorous volubility. For his part it was long since he had read such authors: to which I sarcastically yielded my ready assent. He had partly forgotten them, he said. Indeed! answered I. My tone signified he never knew them—'but you think the composition good do you not?'—'Oh, it is fine! Prodigiously fine!'

Fine was the word, and with fine I was obliged to be satisfied. As for prodigious, it sometimes had meaning and sometimes none: it depended on emphasis and action. I knew indeed that he was no great orator; otherwise I should have expected an eulogium that might have rivaled the French academy,[1] the odes of Boileau,[2] or even my own composition.

I was still hungry: my vanity wanted more food, much more, though I knew not where to seek it. To write down a minister was such a task, and I had begun it in so sublime a style, that rest I could not: though it was with great difficulty, having done with Enoch, that I could escape from Miss and her mamma.

They were dressed to go to a party, and they insisted that I should go with them. It would give their friends such *monstrous* pleasure, and they should all be so *immense* happy, that go I must. But their rhetoric was vain. I was upon thorns; there were no hopes that the party would listen to my manuscript; and as I could not read it to others, I must go home and read it to myself.

As I was going, Miss followed me to the door, called up one of her significant traverse glances, and told me she was sure I was a prodigious rake! But no wonder! All the fine men were rakes!

I returned to my chamber, read again and again, added new flowers, remembered new quotations, and inserted new satire. Enoch had told me it was fine, yet I never could think it was fine enough.

Night came, but with it little inclination in me to sleep: and in the morning I was up and at work, reading, correcting and embellishing my letter before I could well distinguish a word. About nine o'clock, while I was rehearsing aloud in the very heat of oratory, two chairmen knocked at my door and interrupted my revery: they were come to take away the trunk of Turl. The thought struck me and I immediately inquired—'Is the gentleman himself here?' I was answered in the affirmative, and I requested one of the men to go and inform him that an old acquaintance was above, who would be very glad to speak a word with him.

Mr. Turl came, was surprised to see me, and as I received him kindly answered me in the same tone. At college he had acquired the reputation of a scholar, a good critic, and a man of strong powers of mind. The discovery of a diamond mine would not have given me so much pleasure, as the meeting him at this lucky moment! He was the very person I wanted. He was a judge, and I should have praise as much as I could demand! The beauties of my composition would all be as visible to him as they were to myself. They were too numerous, too strong, too striking to escape his notice; they would flash upon him at every line, would create astonishment, inspire rapture, and hold him in one continual state of acclamation and extacy!

I requested him to sit down, apologized, told him I had a favour to ask, took up my manuscript, smiled, put it in his hand, stroked my chin, and begged him to read and tell me its faults. I had a perfect dependence on his good taste, and nobody could be more desirous of hearing the truth and correcting their errors than I was! Nobody!

I was surprised to observe that he felt some reluctance, and attempted to excuse himself: but I was too importunate, and the devil of vanity was too strong in me, to be resisted. I pleaded, with great eloquence and much more truth than I myself suspected, how necessary it was in order to attain excellence that men should communicate with each other, should boldly declare their opinions, and patiently listen to reproof.

Thus urged by arguments which he knew to be excellent, and hoping from my zeal that I knew the same, he complied, took out his pencil, and began his task.

He went patiently through it, without any apparent emotion or delay, except frequently to make crosses with his pencil. Never was mortal more amazed than I was at his incomprehensible coldness! 'Has he no feeling?' said I. 'Is he dead? No token of admiration! no laughter! no single pause of rapture!' It was astonishing beyond all belief!

Having ended, he put down the manuscript, and said not a word!

This was a mortification not to be supported. Speak he must. I endured his silence perhaps half a minute, perhaps a whole one, but it was an age! 'I am afraid, Mr. Turl,' said I, 'you are not very well pleased with what you have read?'

The tone of my voice, the paleness of my lips, and the struggling confusion of my eyes sufficiently declared my state of mind, and he made no answer. My irritability increased. 'What, Sir,' said I, 'is it so contemptible a composition as to be wholly unworthy your notice?'

I communicated much of the torture which I felt, but collecting himself he looked at me with some compassion and much stedfastness, and answered—'I most sincerely wish, Mr. Trevor, that what I have to say, since you require me to speak, were exactly that which you expected I should say. I confess, it gives me some pain to perceive that you mistook your own motives, when you desired me to read and mark what I might think to be faults. You imagined there were no faults! forgetting that no human effort is without them. The longer you write the less you will be liable to the error of that supposition.'—'Perhaps, Sir, you discover nothing but faults?'—'Far the contrary: I have discovered the first great quality of genius.'

This was a drop of reviving cordial, and I eagerly asked—'What is that?'—'Energy. But, like the courage of Don Quixote, it is ill directed; it runs a tilt at sheep and calls them giants.' 'Go on, Sir,' said I: 'continue your allegory.'—'Its beauties are courtezans, its enchanted castles pitiful hovels, and its Mambrino's helmet[1] is no better than a barber's bason.' 'But pray, Sir, be candid, and point out all its defects!—All!'—'I am sorry to observe, Mr. Trevor, that my candour has already been offensive to your feelings. If we would improve our faculties, we must not seek unmerited praise, but resolutely listen to truth.'—'Why, Sir, should you suppose I seek unmerited praise.'

He made no reply, and I repeated my requisition, that he should point out all the defects of my manuscript: once more, all, all! 'The defects, Mr. Trevor,' said he, 'are many of them such as are common to young writers; but some of them are peculiar to writers whose imagination is strong, and whose judgment is unformed. Paradoxical as it may seem, it is a disadvantage to your composition that you have the right side of the question. Diffuse and unconnected arguments, a style loaded with epithets and laborious attempts in the writer to display himself, are blemishes that give less offence when employed to defend error than when accumulated in the cause of truth, which is forgotten and lost under a profusion of ornaments. The difficulties of composition resemble those of geometry: they are the recollection of things so simple and convincing that we imagine we never can forget them; yet they are frequently forgotten at every step, and in every sentence. There is one best and clearest way of stating a proposition, and that alone ought to be chosen: yet how often do we find the same argument repeated and repeated and repeated, with no variety except in the phraseology? In developing any thought, we ought not to encumber it by trivial circumstances: we ought to say all that is necessary, and not a word more. We ought likewise to say one thing at once; and that concluded to begin another. We certainly write to be understood, and should therefore never write in a language that is unknown to a majority of our readers. The rule will apply as well to the living languages as to the dead, and its infringement is but in general a display of the author's vanity. Epithets, unless they increase the strength of thought or elucidate the argument, ought not to be admitted. Of similes, metaphors, and figures of every kind the same may be affirmed: whatever does not enlighten confuses.[1] There are two extremes, against which we ought equally to guard: not to give a dry skeleton, bones without flesh; nor an imbecile embryo, flesh without bones.'

'I understand you, Sir. What you have read is an imbecile embryo?'——'Your importunity, Mr. Trevor, and my desire to do you service have extorted an opinion from me. I must not shrink from the truth: in confirmation of what I have already said, I must add, that your composition is strong in language, but weak in argument.'—'Ha! Much declamation, little thought?'

He was once more silent for a few seconds, and then assuming a less serious tone, endeavoured to turn the conversation by inquiring if I were come to reside in London, and to live with his lordship? I took care to inform him that I considered myself as a visitor in the house; and that I meant to take my degrees, be ordained, and devote myself to the church.

I then attempted to bring him back to the manuscript; but ineffectually: he seemed determined to say no more. This silence was painful to both of us, and after I had inquired where he lived, and made some professions, which formal civility wrung from me, that I should be glad to see him again, we parted. We were neither of us entirely satisfied with the other; and I certainly much the least.

The lesson however did me infinite service. The film was in part removed from my eyes, in my own despite. I read again, but with a very different spirit: his marks in the margin painfully met my eye, with endless repetition. The rules he had been delivering were strong in my memory, and I frequently discovered their application. After the clear statement he had given of them, I could but seldom bring myself to doubt of their justice.

The result was, I immediately went to work; and, disgusted with my first performance, began another. In truth, my too much confidence and haste had made me guilty of many mistakes; which I knew to be such, the moment my vanity had been a little sobered into common sense. I had often written before, and perhaps never so ill.

I now arranged my thoughts, omitted my quotations, discarded many of my metaphors, shortened my periods, simplified my style, reduced the letter to one fourth of its former length, and finished the whole by one o'clock.

His lordship was not so fastidious a critic as I thought Turl had been; he was delighted with my performance. It is true he made some corrections and additions, in places where I had not been so personal and acrimonious, against the minister, as his feelings required; but, as he accompanied them with praise, I readily submitted; and, thus improved, my first political essay was committed to the press.

CHAPTER VI

Further efforts of critical improvement: Doubts of a serious kind suggested: More politics and new acquaintance: A dissertation on rakes

THE critical precepts of Turl were still tingling in my ears; and as I meant to shew the bishop some of the sermons that I had written, or in other words as many as he should be willing to read, they underwent an immediate revisal. Though in general they were less faulty than my post-haste political effort, yet I found quite enough to correct; and was so far reconciled to the benefit I had derived from Turl as to wish to meet him again.

In two or three days therefore, after having expunged, interlined, and polished one of my best performances till I was tolerably well satisfied with it, I visited him at his lodgings. I then owned to him, that I had not received the castigation he gave me quite so patiently as I ought to have done: but I had nevertheless profited by it, and was come to request more favours of the same kind; though I could not but acknowledge I had hopes that my present performance was not quite so defective as the former.

He received me kindly, but took the manuscript I offered him with what I again thought great coldness. He read two or three pages, without as before drawing his pencil upon me, and then paused. 'You have enjoined me a task,' said he, 'Mr. Trevor, which I do not know how to execute to my own satisfaction. You are not aware of the truth, and if I tell it you I shall offend.'—'Nay, Sir; I beg you will not spare me. Speak!'—'You have not explicitly defined to yourself your own motives: you think you are come in search of improvement; in reality, you are come in search of praise.'

—'Not unless praise be my due.'——'Which you are convinced it is.'—'You see deeply into the human heart, Mr. Turl.'—'If I do not, I am ill qualified to criticise literary compositions.'—'And you think my divinity no better than my politics?'—'You do not state the question as I could wish. Divinity I must acknowledge is not a favourite subject with me.'—'I have heard as much.'—'I am too sincere a friend to morality to encourage dissention, quarrels, and enmity, concerning things which whoever may pretend to believe no one can prove that he understands. As a composition, from the little I have read, I believe your sermon to be very superior to your letter; but from the exposition of your subject, I perceive it treats on points of faith, asserts church authority, and stigmatises dissent with reprobation. You tell me you are recommended to a bishop: with him it will do you service! to me it is unintelligible.'

His inclination to heresy, or, which is the same thing, his difference with me in opinion, piqued me on this occasion even more than the unsparing sincerity of his remarks. I answered, I was sorry he did not agree with me, on subjects which I was convinced were so momentous; and owned it was for that reason that, while he remained at the university, I had avoided his society.

He replied, he doubted if it were right to avoid the vicious: and the precaution which he himself thought necessary, on all such occasions, was to inquire whether, in accusing another of vice, he were not himself guilty of error. He considered his own opinions as eternally open to revision; and if any man were to tell him that two and two did not make four, he should have no objection to re-examine the facts, with his opponent, on which his own previous conviction had been founded. We ought to be ardent in the defence of truth; but we ought likewise to be patient and benevolent.

I made some attempts to convince him of the impiety of his scepticism; while he remained cool, but unshaken; and I left him with mingled emotions of pity, for his adherence to doctrines so damnable; and of admiration, at the amenity and philanthropy with which they were delivered.

Thus catechised in criticism and theology, the ardour of my pursuits would perhaps have found some temporary abatement, had it not been rouzed anew. My letter had appeared, signed Themistocles, his lordship's known political cognomen. It was the first in which he had declared openly against the minister. His sentiments in consequence of this letter were become public, and many of the minority, desirous of fixing in their interest one whom they had before considered rather as their opponent than their friend, came to visit and pay him their compliments.

The resolute manner in which I had purposely and uniformly shewn him that I must be treated as his equal had produced its intended effect: I was dismissed with no haughty nod, but came and went as I pleased, and frequently bore a part in their conversation. I had still an open ear for vanity, which was not a little tickled by the frequent terms of applause and admiration with which Themistocles was quoted. His lordship did me the justice to inform his visitors that the letter was written by me. We had indeed conversed together; they were his thoughts, his principles, and it was true he had made such additions and corrections as were necessary. Then, proceeding to invectives against the minister, he there dropped me, and my share of merit.

The mortification of this was the greater because truth and falsehood were so mingled that, however inclined I might be, I knew not which way to do myself justice. But the praise, which they bestowed wholly on his lordship and which his lordship was willing to receive, I very unequivocally took to myself. It gave me animation; the pen was seldom out of my hand, and the exercise was sanative.

Mean while Enoch and his agreeable family, who knew so well when things were as they should be, were not neglected. I was careful to inform them of my rising fame; and my new friends, for so I accounted all those who paid their court to his lordship and his lordship's favourite, were individually named, characterised, and celebrated.

The family heard me with avidity, each desirous of having a share in a lord, and the friends of a lord. Enoch told me I was in high luck, mamma affirmed I was a fine writer, and Miss was sure I must be *a monstrous favourite!* I was a favourite with every body; and, for her part, she did not wonder at it. 'Not but it is a great pity,' added she, aside, 'that you are such a rake, Mr. Trevor.'

This repeated charge very justly alarmed my morality, and I very seriously began a refutation. But in vain. I might say what I would; she could see very plainly I was a prodigious rake, and nothing could convince her to the contrary. Though she had heard that your greatest rakes make the best husbands. Perhaps it might be true, but she did not think she could be persuaded to make the venture. She did not know what might happen, to be sure; though she really did not think she could. She could not conceive how it was, but some how or another she always found something agreeable about rakes. It was a great pity they should be rakes, but she verily believed the women loved them, and encouraged them in their seducing arts. For her part, she would keep her fingers out of the fire as long as she could: but, if it were her destiny to love a rake, what could she do? Nobody could help being in love, and it would be very hard indeed to call what one cannot help a crime.

In this key would she continue, without let or delay, whenever she had me to herself, till some accident came to my relief: for the philosophy of Miss Eliza, on the subjects of love and rakishness, was exhaustless; and though it could not always convince, it could puzzle. I often knew not how to behave, such a warfare did she sometimes kindle between inclination and morality. My resource was in silence; hers in talking. Notwithstanding her very great prudence, I suspect there might have been danger, had I not been guarded by the three fold shield of an unfashionable sense of moral right, strong aspirings after clerical purity, and the unfaded remembrance of the lovely chaste Olivia.

CHAPTER VII

Enoch made acquainted with more of my perfections, which by his advice are brought to market: A bishop's parlour: The bishop himself, or a true pillar of the church: Heretical times and arduous undertakings

NEW honours awaited me. My lord the bishop was come to town, of which Enoch had providently taken care to have instant notice. Among the other good things I had related of myself, I had not forgotten to tell Enoch of the several sermons I had written; nor to shew him that which I had corrected and taken to Turl.

I had another attainment, of which too I did not neglect to inform him; for it was one of which I was not a little proud. Much of my time, during my residence at Oxford, had been devoted to the study of polemical divinity, or the art of abuse, extracted from the scriptures, the fathers, and the different doctors of different faiths.

The points that had most attracted my attention were the disputes concerning the Athanasian creed, and the thirty-nine articles. On both these subjects I had made many extracts, many remarks, and collected many authorities; for I had subscribed the thirty-nine articles, and consequently the Athanasian creed, and what I had done it became me to defend. This is the maxim of all people, who think it more worthy their dignity to be consistent in error than to forget self, revere truth, and retract.

I had beside been well educated for this kind of pertinacity. The rector, when living, was so sternly orthodox as to hold the slightest deviation from church authority in abhorrence. What he meant by church authority, or what any rational man can mean, it might be difficult to define: except that church authority and orthodox opinions are, with each individual, those precise points which that individual makes a part of his creed. But as, unfortunately for church authority, no two individuals ever had or ever can have the same creed, church authority is like a body in motion, no man can tell where it resides. At that time I thought otherwise, and then as now did not refrain from speaking what I thought.

In addition to the other arts of pleasing, which the industrious Enoch had acquired, that of maintaining orthodox doctrines in the presence of orthodox people was one. He was glad to find me so deep a proficient; for to what market could we so profitably carry such ware as to the levee of a bishop?

The little man, scrupulously attentive to whatever might advance me or him in the good graces of the right reverend, advised me to put my corrected sermon in my pocket; which, with or without his advice, I suspect I should have done. 'These particulars,' said the provident Enoch, 'must every one of them be told. But be you under no concern; leave all that to me. Merit you know is always modest.'

Though I had not on this occasion the courage to contradict him, I doubted the truth of his apothegm. The good qualities I could discover in myself I wished to have noticed; and if nobody else would notice them I must. Like other people, I have too frequently been desirous to make my principles bend to my practice.

Though the door was the door of a bishop and we had the text in our favour, 'Knock and it shall be opened,' yet Enoch, no doubt remembering his own good breeding, was too cautious to ask if his lordship were at home. He bade the servant say that a clergyman of the church of England and a young gentleman from Oxford, bringing letters from the president of ****** college and other dignitaries of the university, requested an audience.

The message was delivered, and we were ushered into a parlour, the walls of which were decorated with the heads of the English archbishops, surrounding Hogarth's modern midnight conversation.[1] There was not a book in the room; but there were six or eight newspapers. With these we amused ourselves for some time, till the approach of the bishop was announced by the creaking of his shoes, the rustling of his silk apron, and the repeated hems with which he collected his dignity.

The moment I saw him, his presence reminded me of my old acquaintance, the high-fed brawny doctors of Oxford. His legs were the pillars of Hercules, his body a brewer's butt, his face the sun rising in a red mist. We have been told that magnitude is a powerful cause of the sublime; and if this be true, the dimensions of his lordship certainly had a copious and indisputable claim to sublimity. He seemed born to bear the whole hierarchy. His mighty belly heaved and his cheeks swelled with the spiritual inflations of church power. He fixed his open eyes upon me and surveyed me from top to toe. I too made my remarks. 'He is a true son of the church,' said I.—The libertine sarcasm was instantly repelled, and my train of ideas was purified from such irreverend heresy—'He is an orthodox divine! A pillar of truth! A Christian Bishop!' Thought is swift, and man assents and recants before his eye can twinkle.

I delivered my credentials and he seated himself in a capacious chair, substantially fitted to receive and sustain its burden of divinity, and began to read. My letters were from men high in authority, purple-robed and rotund supporters of our good *Alma Mater*, and met with all due respect. Clearing his sonorous throat of the obstructing phlegm, with which there seemed to be danger that he should sometime or other be suffocated, he welcomed me to London, rejoiced to hear that his good friends of the university were well, and professed a desire to oblige them by serving me.

I briefly explained to him my intention of devoting myself to the church, which he highly commended; and Enoch, who far from being idle all this time had been acting over his agreeable arts, soon found an opportunity of informing the right reverend father in God what powerful connexions I had, how well skilled I was in classical learning, how deeply I was read in theology, how orthodox my opinions were, and to give a climax which most delighted me added that, young as I was, I had already obtained the character of a prodigious fine writer!

He did not indeed say all this in a breath; he took his own time, for his oratory was always hide bound; but he took good care to have it all said. His secret for being eloquent consisted rather in action than in language, and now with the spiritual lord as before with the temporal, he accompanied his speech with those insinuating gesticulations which he had rarely found unsuccessful. He had such a profound reverence for the episcopacy, [bowing to the ground] was so bitter an enemy to caveling innovators, [grinning malignity] had so full a sense of his own inferiority [contorting his countenance, like a monkey begging for gingerbread] and humbled himself so utterly in the presence of the powers that be that, while he spoke, the broad cheeks of the bishop swelled true high church satisfaction; dilating and playing like a pair of forge bellows.

My modesty was his next theme, and with it was coupled the sermons I had written, not omitting the one I had brought in my pocket. But his young friend was so bashful! was so fearful of intruding on his lordship! as indeed every one must be, who had any sense of what is always due to our superiors! Yet as the doctrines of his young friend were so sound, and he was so true a churchman, it might perhaps happen that his lordship would have the condescension to let one of his chaplains read him the sermon of his young friend? He was sure it would do him service with his lordship. Not but he was almost afraid he had taken an unpardonable liberty, in intruding so far on his lordship's invaluable time and patience.

Evil communication corrupts good manners. I could not equal the adulation of Enoch; but, when I afterward came to canvas my own conduct, I found I had followed my leader in his tracks of servility quite far enough.

His lordship, to indicate his approbation of our duplex harangue, graciously accepted the sermon to peruse, informed me of his day and hour of seeing company, and invited me and my friend to become his visitors: with which mark of holy greeting Enoch and I, well pleased, were about to depart.

The retailer of pews recollected himself: no man could be more desirous than Enoch not to neglect an opportunity. After more bows, cringes, and acknowledgments not to be expressed, he requested permission to mention to his lordship that his young friend had made a particular branch of theology his study, of which he thought it his duty to acquaint his lordship. In these days of doubt, rank infidelity, and abominable schism, the danger of the church was felt by every good and pious divine; and her most active defenders were her best friends. His lordship would therefore perhaps be glad to hear that Mr. Trevor had particularly devoted himself to polemics, was intimately acquainted with the writings of the fathers and the known orthodox divines, and was qualified to be a powerful advocate and champion of conformity.

'Indeed!' said his lordship, with open ears and eyes. 'I am very glad to hear it! Have you written any thing, Mr. Trevor, on these subjects?'—'I have made many references, memorandums, and preparatory remarks, my lord.'—'Then you intend to write!'—I saw the satisfaction with which the affirmative was likely to be received and boldly answered, 'I do, my lord.'—'I am very glad to hear it! I am very glad to hear it!'—'Shall I do myself the honour to bring my manuscript, as soon as it is written, and consult your lordship's judgment?'—'By all means, Mr. Trevor! By all means! These are weighty matters. The church was never more virulently and scandalously attacked than she has been lately! The most heretical and damnable doctrines are daily teeming from the press! Not only infidels and atheists, but the vipers which the church has nurtured in her own bosom are rising up to sting her! Her canons are brought into contempt, her tests trampled on, and her dignitaries daily insulted! The hierarchy is in danger! The bishops totter on their bench! We are none of us safe.'

To the reality of this picture I readily assented. 'But,' said I, 'my lord, we have the instruments of defence in our own power: we have the scriptures, the fathers, the doctors of our church and all the authorities for us. The only thing we want is a hero, qualified to bear this cumbrous armour, and to wield these massy weapons.'

The words, 'that hero am I,' quivered on my tongue; and, if my teeth had not resolutely denied them a passage, out they would have bolted.

His lordship agreed that the truth was all on our side: and for his part he wished it to be thundered forth, so as at once to crush and annihilate all heretics, and their damnable doctrines!

'Since I am encouraged by your lordship,' said I, 'this shall be the first labour of my life; and, though I grant it is Herculean, I have little doubt of executing it effectually.' His lordship, though not quite so certain of my success as I was, in the name of the church, again gave his hearty assent; and we, with smiles, thanks, and bows in abundance, took our leave: Enoch with a fine pisgah prospect of the land of promise;[1] and I another Caleb, bearing away the luscious grapes[2] I had been gathering, on which my fancy licentiously banqueted.

CHAPTER VIII

Beatific visions: Irons enough in the fire: Egotism and oratory: Hints on elocution

THIS sudden elevation to fame and fortune, for I had not the smallest doubt that so it was, this double-election of me, who alone perhaps had the power to execute such mighty tasks, was more than even I, sanguine as my expectations had been, could have hoped! To rout politicians and extirpate heresy, to pull down a minister and become the buttress of the church, to reform the state and establish the hierarchy, was indeed a glorious office! Honour and power were suspended over my head: I had but to cut the thread and they would drop and crown me.

But which should I choose; to be the pillar of the state, or the head of the hierarchy? a prime minister, or an archbishop? The question was embarrassing, and it was not quite pleasant that I could not be both.

I did not however forget that I had first some few labours to perform; to which therefore, with all my might, I immediately applied. My busy brain had now fit employment, politics and divinity; but was puzzled with which to begin. The table at which I wrote was richly strewed with invectives, now hurled at state profligacy, now thundered against the non-conforming crew. It was my determination to spare neither friend nor foe. I often remembered the Zoilus[3] Turl, and his heretical opinions; and was ready to exclaim, in the language of the patient Job, .'Oh that his words were now written! Oh that they were printed in a book!'[4] The dictatorial spirit of his reproof, for so I characterised it, had wounded me deeply; and, though I was not depraved enough to feel rancour,

I ardently wished for the means to come, pen in hand, to a fair combat; for I feared no mortal wight: if I had, he perhaps would have been the man. It will hereafter be seen that my wish was gratified.

Some days were wasted in this state of indecision; in which I did little, except write detached thoughts and contemplate the sublime and beautiful[1] of my subjects; till I was rouzed from this lethargy of determination by a hint from his lordship, that it was necessary for Themistocles to appear abroad again; lest his enemies should say he was silenced, and his friends fear he was dead.

A second political letter was then quickly produced; in which, with the fear of Turl before my eyes and carefully conning over his whole lesson, I profited by that advice which I half persuaded myself I despised. I wrote not only with more judgment but with increasing ardour, and the effects were visible: the second composition was much better than the first.

The dish too was seasoned to the palate of him for whom I catered. I peppered salted and deviled the minister, till his lordship was in raptures! It was indeed dressed much more to the taste of the times than I myself was aware. It was better calculated to gall, annoy, and alarm a corrupt system than if I had produced a better composition.

Not only the satellites but the leading men of opposition began now to pay their respects to his lordship. In his company I had the pleasure of meeting several of them, and of being frequently surprised by the readiness of their wit, the acuteness of their remarks, their depth of penetration, comprehensive powers, and fertility of genius. Mr. *** himself came occasionally to visit his lordship, so strenuous and sincere did he appear to be in his political conduct.

During this intercourse, and particularly in these conversations, I had sufficient opportunities of studying his lordship's character. He was selfish, ignorant, positive, and proud: yet he affected generosity, talked on every subject as if it were familiar to him, asserted his claim to the most undeviating candour, and would even affect contempt for dignities and distinctions, when they were not the reward of merit. 'A nobleman might by accident possess talents; but he was free to confess that the dignity of his birth could not confer them. He would rather be Mr. *** (Mr. *** was present) than a prince of the blood. He panted to distinguish himself by qualities that were properly his own, and had little veneration for the false varnish of ancestry. Were that of any worth, he had as much reason to be vain as any man perhaps in the kingdom: his family came in with the Conqueror, at which time it was respectable: it had produced men, through all its branches, whose names were no disgrace to history.' Then summoning an additional quantity of candor he added—'There have been many fools among them, no doubt; and I am afraid some knaves; but what have I to do with their knavery, folly, or wisdom? Society, it is true, has thought fit to recompense me for their virtues: such is the order of things. But I cannot persuade myself that I have received the least tarnish from any of their vices. I am a friend to the philosophy of the times, and would have every man measured by the standard of individual merit.'

These liberal sentiments were delivered on the first visit he received from the leader of the minority. Anger, self interest, and the desire of revenge had induced him to adopt the same political principles: anger, self interest, and the desire of revenge induced him to endeavour after the same elevation of mind. Esop is dead, but his frog and his ox are still to be found.

At this interview, the conversation turned on the last debate in both houses, in which the merits of the speakers were canvassed, and his lordship was severe to virulence against his opponents. He had harangued in the upper house himself; but as his delivery, for it could not be called elocution, was slow, hesitating, and confused, no one ventured to mention his speech.

This was a severe mortification. Among his mistakes, that of believing himself an accomplished orator was not the least conspicuous. Unable any longer to support their silence, he quoted his speech himself: though, with that candor which was continually at the tip of his tongue, he acknowledged it was possible perhaps for him to have delivered his sentiments in a more terse and pointed manner. 'But no man', said he, addressing himself to Mr. *** 'no man knows better than you, how arduous a task it is to speak with eloquence.'

Mr. *** was dumb: but the appellant and the appellee were relieved by the less delicate intervention of one of the company; who declared, perhaps with malicious irony, he never heard his lordship to greater advantage. 'Do you think so,' said the peer, turning to his panegyrist. 'No. I believe you are mistaken. I never can satisfy myself! I am so fastidious in the choice of my phrases! I dislike this word, I reject that, and do not know where to find one that pleases me. I certainly think, for my part, that I spoke vilely. The duke indeed and lord Piper both declared they never heard me greater: but I cannot believe it. Though Sir Francis, who went to the house purposely to hear me, positively swears it was the first speech I ever made: the house had seldom, I believe he said, never heard its equal! Indeed he called it divine; and some affirm he is one of the best judges of elocution in the kingdom. But I am sure he is wrong. I know myself better. I was not quite in the cue; had not absolutely the true feel, as I may say, of my subject. Though I own I was once or twice a little pleased with myself. There might perhaps be something like an approach to good speaking; I dare not imagine it was great. It was not, I believe, indeed I am sure, it was not every thing I could have wished. I am not often satisfied with others, and with myself still seldomer.'

To all this self equity and abstinence, Mr. ***, to whom it was again addressed, made no other answer than that he had not the pleasure to hear his lordship. But the candid peer, in imitation of the poets of the days of Louis XIV and Charles II continued to be the censurer and eulogist of himself.

To change the dull theme, one of the company inquired, what is the reason that many men, who are eloquent in the closet, should stammer themselves into confusion and incapacity, when they attempt to speak in public? To this Mr. *** returned the following acute and philosophical reply.

'A happy choice of words, after we have obtained ideas, is one of the most constant labours of the person who attempts to write, or speak, with energy. This induces a habit in the writer or speaker to be satisfied with difficulty. Desirous of giving the thought he has conceived its full force, he never imagines the terms and epithets he has selected to be sufficiently expressive. If, after having accustomed himself to write, it be his wish to exert his powers as a public speaker, he must counteract this habit; and, instead of being severe in the choice of his words, must resolutely accept the first that present themselves, encourage the flow of thought, and leave epithets and phraseology to chance. Neither will his intrepidity, when once acquired, go unrewarded: the happiest language will frequently rush upon him, if, neglecting words, he do but keep his attention confined to thoughts. Of thoughts too it is rather necessary for him to deliver them boldly, following his immediate conceptions and explaining away inaccuracies as they occur, than to seek severe precision in the first instance. Hesitation is the death of eloquence; and precision, like every other power, will increase by being exercised. It is doubtless understood that I do not speak of orations already written and digested; but of speeches in reply, in which any laboured preparation is impossible.'

His lordship applauded the solution of the difficulty, and some of the company observed the orator had given the history of his own mind.

CHAPTER IX

Literary labours continued: The thermometer of hope still rising: The sermon and the disappointed cravings of vanity

TO carry on two controversies at the same time was certainly favourable to neither; except that abuse, or something very like it, being the key common to both, the subjects were so far in unison. Politics afforded me strong temptations, but theology was still predominant. The thirty-nine articles consequently were not neglected. Memory was taxed, my own manuscripts were examined, and authorities were consulted. His lordship's library abounded in political information, but not in theological, and I had recourse to that of the British Museum.

I did not indeed compose with all the rapidity with which I wrote my first political effusion; for I had not only been rendered more cautious, but, exclusive of the conversations and employment which the peer afforded me, a regular attention was to be paid to the levees of the bishop.

To these the sedulous Enoch carefully accompanied me; for no man pursued his own interest, as far as he understood it, with greater avidity. Circumstances were unfavourable, or he would certainly have been a bishop himself. Learning, talents, and virtue might have been dispensed with, but not these and the total want of patronage.

The bishop, finding us thus continually paired, one day gave me a hint that he should be glad to see me the next time alone. Without suspecting the motive, I was careful to comply with the request; and the ensuing morning, the right reverend dignitary, no other person being present, gave me to understand that he had read my sermon with satisfaction.

After this and various other circumlocutory efforts and hints, he at last spoke more plainly. The subject was a good one, and he had an inclination to deliver it himself, at one of the cathedrals where he intended to preach. But then it must be in consequence of a positive assurance, from me, that I should act with discretion. He did not want sermons; he had enough: but this pleased him: though, if it were known it were a borrowed discourse, especially borrowed from so young a man not yet in orders, it might derogate from episcopal dignity.

Enraptured at the fund of self approbation which I collected from all this, I ardently replied, 'I knew not how to express my sense of the honour his lordship did me; that I could neither be so absurd as to offend his lordship nor so unjust as to be insensible of his favours; that I held the sacerdotal character to be too sacred to suffer any man to trifle with it, much less to be guilty of the crime myself; and that, if his lordship would oblige me by fulfilling his kind intention, my lips should be irrevocably and for ever closed. The honour would be an ample reward, and, whatever my wishes might be, it was more than I could have hoped and greater perhaps than I deserved.'

It might well be expected that at this age I should fall into a mistake common to mankind, and consider secrecy as a virtue; yet I think it strange that I did not soon detect the duplicity of my conduct, nor imagine there was any guilt in being the agent of deceit. But this proves that my morality had not yet taught me rigidly to chastise myself into truth; nor had it been in the least aided by the example of the agreeable Enoch. Perhaps I did not even, at the moment, suspect myself to be guilty of exaggeration.

Notwithstanding the caution given me, no sooner had I quitted the ghostly governor than I hastened to my little upright friend. Tell him indeed I must not: honour, shame, principle, forbade. Yet to keep the good news wholly secret would be to render the severe covenant cruel. What could be done?

Enoch perceived a part of my transport, and reproached me for not having called to take him with me. This was too fair an opportunity to miss. I answered the bishop had desired to see me alone that morning. 'Indeed!' said the suspicious pastor. 'What could be his lordship's reason for that? Have I given offence?' 'No, no,' answered I, with a condescending look to calm his fears; 'but I am not at liberty to tell you the reason. There will be no breach of confidence however in my informing you that his lordship is to preach, next Sunday sevennight, at —— cathedral. Many of the clergy, as I have gathered from him, are to be present; and he intends to make doctrinal points the subject of his discourse. He expects the attendance of his friends, no doubt, and I shall be there.' 'And I too,' said Enoch, 'though I should be obliged to pay a guinea at my chapel for a substitute.'

This point gained and my vanity thus disburthened, I left the divine man, and hastened to Bruton-street, to defend subscription with ten fold vigor. My young laurels were ripening apace: they were already in bud, and were suddenly to bloom. Every new sprig of success burst forth in new arguments, new tropes, and new denunciations. My margin was loaded with the names of High Church heroes, and my manuscript began to swell to a formidable size.

Mean while the day of exultation came, and I and Enoch, with Miss and her Mamma, for I could not be satisfied with less than the whole family, repaired early to the cathedral, bribed the verger, procured ourselves places, and rallied our devout emotions as stedfastly as we could, amid the indecent riot of boys, the monotony of the responses, and the apathy of the whole choir.

In spite of all my efforts and aspirings, never was service more tedious. The blissful minute at length came! His lordship, robed, in solemn procession, moved magnificently toward the pulpit. The lawn expanded, dignity was in every fold, and what had been great before seemed immeasurable! Mamma blessed herself, at the spectacle of power so spiritualized! Miss protested it was immense! Enoch was ready to fall down and worship! I myself did little less than adore: but it was the golden calf of my own creating; it was the divine rhapsody that was immediately to burst upon and astonish the congregation.

The right reverend father in God began, and with him very unexpectedly began my dissatisfaction. His voice was thick, his delivery spiritless, and his candences ridiculous. His soul was so overlaid with brawn and dignity that, though it heaved, panted, and struggled, it could never once get vent. Speaking through his apoplectic organs, I could not understand myself: it was a mumbling hubbub, the

drone of a bagpipe, and the tantalizing strum strum of a hurdy-
gurdy! Never was hearer more impatient to have it begin; never was
hearer better pleased to have it over! Every sentence did but increase
the fever of my mind. Enoch himself perceived it, though he could
not discover the cause. The orator indeed produced no emotion in
him, but that was not wonderful. The effect was quite as good as he
expected! He had never, I believe, been entertained at a sermon in
his life; not even at his own. He went to hear sermons sometimes,
because it was decorous, because he was a parson, and because it
was his trade to preach them; but never with any intention to enlarge his mind or improve his morals.

His lordship however had no sooner descended than he was en-
circled by as many flatterers as thought they had any right to approach: among whom, to my shame be it spoken, I was one. I did
not indeed applaud either his discourse or his delivery; I was not
quite so depraved, nor so wholly forgetful of the feelings he had
excited! but I laboured out an aukward panegyric on the important
duties he had to fulfil, and on the blessing it was to a nation, when
worthy persons were chosen to fill such high offices. Thus endeavouring to quiet my conscience by a quibble, and with a half
faced lie make him believe what it was impossible I could mean.

The discourse too was praised abundantly. It was divine! His
lordship had never delivered more serious and alarming truths! But
though no man could be better convinced that in reality this was all
fact, yet coming from them I knew it to be all falsehood. They could
not characterize what they could not hear; and the maukish adulation curdled even upon my digestive stomach.

The lesson however certainly did me good, though it had yet but
little influence upon my conduct.

CHAPTER X

*The critic once more consulted in vain: The Bishop less
fastidious: The playhouse: Elbows and knees or virtue in
danger: Mrs. Jordan*

IT was possible I found, under the rose be it spoken, even for a
bishop to be a blockhead: but, if that bishop had sense enough to
discern my good qualities, I ought not to be the most unrelenting of

his censurers. My defence of the articles would indeed do its own business: yet to come forth under episcopal auspices was an advantage by which it was perhaps my duty to profit.

Politics necessarily had their interval; but, though this created delay, my manuscript was at length finished, fairly recopied, and impatient to be applauded.

Again the ghost of Turl haunted me. Not with terror! No: I had prepared a charm, that could arrest or exorcise the evil spirit. Let him but fairly meet me on this ground and I would hurl defiance at him.

Refrain I could not, and to him I went. I was surprised to find him at work, engraving! 'Does he,' said I, 'pretend to learning, taste, and genius, yet stoop to this drudgery?'

It was a good prefatory pretext to introduce my main design, and I asked his reason for chusing such an employment? He answered it was to gain a living, by administering as little as he could to the false wants and vices of men, and at the same time to pursue a plan, on which he was intent.

This plan he did not voluntarily mention; and, as my eagerness was all nestling in my manuscript, I made no further inquiry. It was presently produced. 'I have two or three times,' said I, 'Mr. Turl, intruded upon you, and am come to trouble you once more. I have been writing a pamphlet, and should again be glad to have your opinion. I know before you open it you are inimical to its doctrines, although I think them demonstrable. But perhaps you will find arguments in it which you might not expect: and if not, I still should be glad to have your judgment of it, as a composition. It contains a defence of the thirty-nine articles, and indisputable proofs of the duty of religious conformity.'

Turl paused for a moment, and then replied: 'I would most willingly, Mr. Trevor, comply with your desire, were I not convinced of its absolute inutility. The question has long been decided in my mind. No arguments can prove a right, in any man or any body of men, to tyrannize over my conscience. To find a standard to measure space and duration has hitherto baffled all attempts; but to erect a standard to equalize the thoughts of the whole human race is a disposition that is both hateful and absurd. Should you understand the sincerity with which I speak as hostile to yourself, you will do me wrong. Were it in my power to render you service, few men would be more willing; but on this occasion it certainly is not.'

I replied with some pique, 'To condemn any man, any question, or any cause unheard, Sir, is neither the act of a christian nor of a philosopher.'

'Christians, Mr. Trevor,' answered he, 'are so different from each other, that what the act of a Christian may be is more than I know: but, if I may speak as a philosopher, it is an immoral act to waste time in doing any one thing, if there can be any other done that will contribute more to the public good.'

'Do you think, Mr. Turl,' retorted I with indignation, 'that making scratches, with a bit of steel on a bit of copper, is contributing more to the public good than the examination of a question of so much importance ?'—'No, Mr. Trevor: but, I repeat, I have examined the question; and whenever the public good shall make it my duty, am willing to examine it again. I am not I think so called upon at present, and I therefore must decline the task. I could wish you were not to leave me in anger, for I assure you I have an affection for your genius. But it may now be said to be in a state of ferment: when it subsides, if I do not mistake, it will brighten, and contribute I hope to the greatest and best of purposes.

'Upon my honour, Mr. Turl, you are a strange person!'

So saying, I hastily put my manuscript in my pocket and took my leave: offended with his peremptory refusal, but half appeased by the something more than compliment with which it was concluded.

This market always failed me; but I had one that was better calculated for my ware, which was immediately open to me. I hastened to the bishop, displayed my precious cargo, and did not fail to report its value. I stated my principal arguments and boldly affirmed, in conformity with the most approved leaders of our church, that the articles were to be interpreted in an Arminian[1] sense, and that only; that is strictly in regard to the Trinitarian controversy, and liberally in the questions of predestination and grace.[2] Nothing according to my reasoning could be more plain than that they were purposely left ambiguous, in these matters, by the compilers; in favour to men in their public capacity, who I admitted in their private were treated by them as heretics, blasphemers, and antichrists. I allowed no quarter to those who fixed the standard of orthodoxy a hair's breadth higher or lower than I had done; and attacked, with a virulence that shewed I was totally blind to the lameness of my own cause, the socinianizing clergy, who dared subscribe in defiance of the grossness of their heresy, and the Calvinists, who had the impudence to understand the articles in the sense in which their authors wrote them.

Then I had a formidable army of authorities! The fathers: Tertullian, Chrysostom, Austin, Jerome! The famous high church men: archbishops, bishops, deans and doctors; from Whitgift to Waterland, from Rogers to Rutherforth![1] Them I marshalled in dread array, a host invincible! The church thundered by my lips! I created myself the organ of her anathemas, and stood forth her self-elected champion.

All this I detailed to my right reverend patron, who heaved his cumbrous eye-brows, and gazed approbation while I spoke. I was so full of myself and my subject, repeated sounding names and apt quotations with such volubility, and imparted my own firm conviction that this was the death blow to non-conformity with such force, that the rotund man felt some small portion of sympathy, looked forward to happy times, and began to hope he might see the thrones dominions powers and principalities of the church re-established, and flourishing once more! Had this been his only motive, however false his tenets, he would have acted from a virtuous intention; but he had another, with which the reader will in due time be acquainted.

Thus favourably prepossessed, I left my manuscript for his perusal; and he treated me with as much condescension as, for a client so undignified, he could persuade himself to assume.

It must not be forgotten that Enoch was present: this my vanity and his cunning required. He played his part. His congratulations of his young friend, and his amazement at his lordship's most prodigious goodness, would have risen to ecstacy, if ecstacy and Enoch could possibly have been acquainted.

We hied back to Suffolk street, where our good news was as usual related. I had my vanity to feed, and the family had their views.

Miss had been presented with two box tickets, for the benefit of a capital performer. The inimitable Mrs. Jordan[2] was to play the Country Girl,[3] and I was invited by the family and pressed by Miss to accept of one of them, and accompany her to the theatre.

I was not of a saturnine and cold complexion; and, fearful and guarded as Miss was against rakes, I had some latent apprehension that the tempter might be at hand. But the play-house was the region of delight. Mrs. Jordan I had never seen, and to reject a lady's invitation was as cowardly as to refuse a gentleman's challenge.

I had not yet philosophy enough for either, and at the appointed hour a hackney coach was in waiting, and I and Miss Eliza, accompanied by Enoch who had business in the Temple, were driven to Drury Lane Theatre.

Places were kept, we took our seats, and the play began. So intent was I, on plot, incident, character, wit, and humour, that, had I been left unmolested, I fear I should have totally forgotten Miss Eliza. But that was no part of her plan: at least it was no part of her practice. Our knees soon became very intimate, and had frequent meetings of a very sentimental kind: for, she being courageous enough to advance, could I be the poltroon to retreat? They were however very good and loving neighbours, and the language they spoke was peculiarly impressive. The whole subject before us was love, and intrigue, and the way to torment the jealous. Whenever a significant passage occurred, and that was very often, either the feet, or the legs, or the elbows of Miss and me came in contact. Our eyes too might have met, but that I did not understand her traverse sailing. Commentaries, conveyed in a whisper, were continual. Her glances, shot athwart, frequently exclaimed—'Oh la!' and the fan, half concealing their significance, often enough increased the interjection to—'Oh fie!' The remarks of Miss, ocular and oral, were very pointed, and it must be owned that she was a great master of the subject. Whenever the tone of libertine gallantry occurred, she was ready with—'There! That's you! There! There you are again! Well, I protest! Was any thing ever so like? That is you to a T!'

I must tell the truth, and acknowledge she created no little perturbation in my inward man. My thoughts were attracted this way, and hurried that. The divine Mrs. Jordan for one moment made me all her own. Miss insisted on having me to herself the next. Then came theology, a dread of Eve and her apple, supported by a still more redoubtable combatant, virtue, with her fair but inflexible face! And could Olivia, the gentle, the angelic, the beaming Olivia, such as I remembered her in days of early innocence, such as I beheld her reclining in my arms as I bore her from the dangerous waters, could love be the theme and she forgotten? No! There was not a day in which that phenomenon happened; and on such occasions never. Why I thought on her, or what I meant, I seldom staid in inquire; for that was a question that would have given exquisite pain, had I not remembered that the world was soon to be at my command.

But Olivia was absent, and I had entered the lists with a very different heroine. Through play and farce there was no cessation to the combat; and, in spite of the fencing and warding of prudence, before the curtain finally dropped I own I felt myself a little breathed.

The foot-boy was to attend, with a hackney coach. I led my fair Thalestris[1] into the lobby, where Miss Ellis's carriage was vociferated, from mouth to mouth, with as much eclat as if she had been a dutchess.

The foot-boy made his appearance, but no carriage alas was there. Why I was partly sorry and partly glad I leave the reader to divine. It rained violently, and it was with difficulty that I could procure a chair. Into this conveyance Miss Ellis was handed; I was left to provide for myself, and a storm in the heavens fortunately relieved the storm of the passions. The last flash of their lightening exhausted itself in the squeeze of the hand, which I gave Miss before the chairmen shut the door; or rather in that which she gave me in return. Disappointed men often rail at accident, whereas they ought to avow that what they call accident has frequently been the guardian of what they call their honour. I returned home, where, full of the delightful ideas which the fascinating Jordan had inspired, I retraced those discriminating divine touches, by which she communicates such repeated and uncommon pleasure. She is indeed a potent sorceress: but not even her incantations could exclude the august and virgin spirit of Olivia from again rising to view. As for Miss Eliza, keep her but at a hair-breadth distance and she was utterly harmless.

CHAPTER XI

Possibilities are infinite, or great events in embrio: A bishop's dinner and a dean's devotion: A discovery: Clerical conversation: The way to rise in the church

BY this time my political labours began to wear a respectable appearance. A third letter had been published, and a fourth was preparing. I was in high favour. Men of all ranks visited the earl; and dukes, lords, and barons became as familiar to me as gowns and caps had formerly been in the streets of Oxford. I stood on the very pinnacle of fortune; and, proud of my skill, like a rope-dancer that casts away his balancing pole, I took pleasure in standing on tiptoe. Noticed by the leading men, caressed and courted by their dependants, politics encouraging me on this hand, and theology inviting me on that, the whole world seemed to be smiles and sunshine; and I discovered that none but blockheads had any cause to complain of its injuries and its storms.

Having eased myself for the present of my load of divinity, my fourth letter required no long time to finish. I hastened with it to his lordship, my spirits mounting as usual. He took it, but not with his former eagerness; read it, praised it, but with less of that zeal which interested hope supplies.

I remarked the change, and began to inquire what was my fault? 'None,' replied his lordship. 'Your letter is excellent! charming! every thing I could wish!'—'Then I may send it to the press?'—'No: I would wish you not to do that.'—'My lord!'—'Leave it with me. Wait a few days and perhaps you may hear of something that will surprise and please you.'—'Indeed, my lord!'

I stood fixed, with inquiring eyes, hungry after more information. But this was not granted; except that, with a significant smile, he told me he had an engagement of importance for the morning: and with this hint I retired.

It was impossible for me to hear so much, and no more, and to forbear forming conjectures. There was going to be a new ministry! It could not be otherwise!

Mr. *** soon afterward knocked at the door. I looked through the window and saw his carriage. I went to the head of the stairs and heard him received, by the earl, with every expression of welcome!

I had now no doubt but that a place, if I would accept it, would incontinently be bestowed on me; and it was almost painful to think that my future plans were of an opposite kind. Yet, why opposite? Churchmen were not prohibited the circle of politics. My station would be honourable, for they would not think of offering me trifles. And why not step from the treasury bench to the bench of bishops? Let but the love of the state and the love of the church be there, and neither seat would suffer contamination.

A revolution of fortune was certainly at hand: what it was I could not accurately foresee, but that it would be highly favourable no man in his senses could have the least doubt: such was my creed.

The very next day I received a note from the bishop, inviting me to partake of a family dinner, with him and his niece. So it is! And so true is the proverb: it never rains but it pours! Good fortune absolutely persecuted me! Honours fell so thick at my feet that I had not time to stoop and pick them up! In the present humour of things, I knew not whether I might not be invited, before the morrow came, to dine with a party of prime ministers, and be elected their president.

Mean time however I thought proper to accept the bishop's invitation; and, as nothing better did actually intervene, when the hour came I kept my appointment.

Being there, the footman led me up to the drawing-room; in which were a lady, who curtsying told me the bishop would soon be down, and the Dean of ——, another rosy gilled son of the church. I have often asked myself—'Why are butchers, tallow-chandlers, cook-maids, and church dignitaries so inclined to be fat?' but I could never satisfactorily resolve the question.

His lordship soon made his appearance; and, having first paid his obedience to the dean, he took the lady by the hand, and presenting her to me said—'This, Mr. Trevor, is my niece; who I dare say will be glad to be acquainted with you.' Bows, curtsies, and acknowledgments of honours conferred, were things of course.

Miss Wilmot, that was the lady's name, Miss Wilmot and I made attempts to entertain each other. Her person was tall, her shape taper, her complexion delicate, and her demeanour easy. Her remarks were not profound, but they were delivered without pretension. She was more inclined to let the conversation die away than to sustain it by that flux of tongue, which afflicted the ear at the house of the Ellis's. Her countenance was strongly marked with melancholy; and a languid endeavour to please seemed to have been the result of study, and to have grown into habit.

Our attention was soon called to another quarter. 'Dinner! dinner! gentlemen,' exclaimed the right reverend father. 'Come, come; we must not let the dinner get cold! Do any thing rather than spoil my dinner! I cannot forgive that.'

Away we went. When a bishop has the happiness to be ready for his dinner, his dinner is sure to be ready for him. Hunger three times a day is the blessing he would first pray for. No remiss cooks, no delays for politeness sake there. Nor is there any occasion: scandal itself cannot tax the clergy with want of punctuality, at the hour of dinner.

We sat down. The lady carved. There were three of us, for she ate little. But, heaven bless me! she had work enough! It was like boys fighting, one down and the other come on! I might wonder about the fattening of butchers and tallow-chandlers as I pleased, but the last part of my wonder was over. I was no mean demolisher of pudding and pie-crust myself; but lord! I was an infant. 'You don't eat, Mr. Trevor!' said the lady. 'You don't eat, Mr. Trevor!' said the dean. 'You don't eat, Mr. Trevor!' blubbered the bishop. Yet never had I been so gorged since the first night at Oxford; and scarcely then.

I would have held it out to the last; for who would not honour the cloth? But the thing could not be, and I fairly laid down my knife and fork in despair. 'Lord! Mr. Trevor! why you have not done?' was the general chorus. 'There is another course coming!'

It was in vain: man is but man. I fell to at first like the rest, thinking that the engagement though hot would be soon over; but I little knew the doughty heroes, with whom I had entered the lists. The chiefs of Homer, with their chines and goblets and canisters of bread, would have been unequal to the contest. I had time enough to contemplate the bishop; I thought I beheld him quaffing suffocation and stowing in apoplexy; and Homer's simile of the ox and Agamemnon forced itself strongly upon me:

> So while he feeds, luxurious in the stall,
> The sov'reign of the herd is doom'd to fall.[1]

Neither did their eating end with the second course. The table was no sooner cleared of the cloth, and the racy wine with double rows of glasses again placed in array, than almonds, raisins, olives, oranges, Indian conserves, and biscuits deviled, covered the board! To it again they fell, with unabating vigour! I soon found reason to leave them, but I doubt whether for three hours their mouths were once seen motionless! In the act of error its enormity escapes detection. I had momentary intervals, in which I philosophised on the scene before me; but not deeply. I was a partaker of the vice, and my astonishment at it was by no means so great then as it is now.

But there was another circumstance at which it was even extreme, and mingled with high indignation. I was ignorant of the clerical maxim, that the absence of the profane washes the starch out of lawn. Hypocrisy avaunt! They are then at liberty to *unbend!* I was soon better informed. The bishop and the dean, Miss Wilmot being still present, the moment the devil of gluttony would give them leisure, could find no way of amusing themselves so effectually as by attempting to call up the devil of lust. Allusions that were evidently their common-place table talk, and that approached as nearly as they durst venture to obscenity, were their pastime. With these they tickled their fancy till it gurgled in their throats, applied to Miss Wilmot to give it a higher gusto, and, while they hypocritically avoided words which the ear could not endure, they taxed their dull wit to conjure up their corresponding ideas. I must own that, in my mind, poor mother church at that moment made but a pitiful appearance.

Disgusted with their impotent efforts to make their brain the common sewer of Joe Miller, I at last started up, with difficulty bridled my anger, and addressing myself to the lady said, 'Shall we retire to your tea table, Miss Wilmot?' 'Ay, do, do!' replied the father in God. 'Try, Liddy, if you can entertain Mr. Trevor: we will stay by our bottle.'

I led her out; and I leave the initiated to guess with what episcopal reverence All saints and their Mother were introduced, the moment the lady's back was turned.

In the course of conversation with the lady, I thought I remarked many strong traits of resemblance between her and my former friend and instructor, the usher of the grammar school, whose name also was Wilmot. The name perhaps was the circumstance that turned my thoughts into that channel; and the fancied likeness between them soon increased upon me so forcibly, that I could no longer forbear to relate all that I knew concerning him, and to inquire if he were her relation?

While I spoke, she changed colour; and after some hesitation answered, 'he is my brother.'—'And the nephew of his lordship?'—

Her flushings and hesitation were increased. 'I am sorry, madam,' said I, 'if I have been indiscreet.' She answered, in a feeble and inarticulate manner, 'he stands in the same relationship to the bishop that I do.'

The feelings of the lady turned my attention, and prevented me from noticing the ambiguity of the reply. 'I respected and loved your brother, madam,' continued I. 'His stay was but short after I left the school, and I have not heard of him since. Is he in London?' —'I believe so; but I do not know where.'

Every question gave additional pain, and I dropped the subject with saying, that I was happy to be acquainted with the sister of a man who had so essentially aided me in my education, and for whom I had the highest esteem.

I thought I perceived the tears struggling to get vent, and to relieve her I made a short visit to the dignitaries—who were—not drunk! Beware of scandal! Calumny itself could not say that madeira, port, and brandy mingled could make them drunk! Madeira port and brandy mingled were but digestives. No: I found the bishop relating one of the principal incidents of his life; which incident it was his practice to relate every day after dinner.

'And so, Mr. Dean, it was the first day, after I had been consecrated a bishop, that I appeared in my full canonicals. And so you know the young gentlemen [He was speaking of the Westminster boys] had never seen me in them; because, as I was a saying, it was the first day of my putting them on. And so, Mr. Dean, as it was the first day of my putting them on, they had placed themselves all of a row, for to see me pass through them; because, as I say, it was the first day of my putting them on. And you can't think, Mr. Dean, what an alteration it made! Every body told me so! and the young gentlemen as I passed, I assure you, when they saw me with my lawn sleeves and quite in full decoration, being the first day of my putting them on, they all bowed; and I assure you behaved with the greatest respect you can think. For as I tell you it was the first day of my putting them on; so they had never seen me in them before; so, I assure you, they bowed and behaved with the greatest respect. They seemed quite surprized, I made such an appearance! And so, I assure you, they bowed and behaved with the greatest respect; for as I was a saying, it was the first day of my putting them on. Perhaps, Mr. Trevor, you never heard the story of my first appearing in my canonicals? I'll tell it you!'

His lordship then began the story again. He had not a single circumstance to add; yet he would not be stopped in his career by my assuring him that I had heard the whole.

His lordship and the dean then began a discourse concerning the clubs, of which they were both members; with inquiries after and annotations on prebends, archdeacons, and doctors, that had the honour to gluttonize together on these occasions. This, though highly amusing to them, was intolerable dulness to me, and I returned to Miss Wilmot.

At nine o'clock, the dean's carriage was at the door, and he departed. He was a great lover of decorum.

I was preparing to follow his example; but his lordship joined us, and desired me to sit down for half an hour; he had something to say to me. Wondering what it could be, I readily complied.

He then began to ask me, how I liked his niece? and to talk of this and the other young clergymen, who had risen in the church by matrimony. Miss Wilmot I perceived was greatly embarrassed. I listened to him with some surprise; for I had nothing to say. He concluded his remarks with telling me, that we would talk more on these subjects another time.

While the dean had been present, the turn of the conversation was such that, though I made two or three aukward attempts, I could find no opportunity of introducing my defence of the articles. I was now more successful, and his lordship told me it was well written; certainly very well written. He had read it himself, and had consulted two or three very sound divines.

I had no doubt of the fact, yet was glad to hear it confirmed, especially by testimonies that I persuaded myself must be good, and expressed my satisfaction. 'Yes,' said his lordship; 'your defence is very well written, Mr. Trevor; and I have something to say to you about that matter. But I am a little drowsy at present. Ring for my night cap, niece! If you will be with me to-morrow morning at ten o'clock, Mr. Trevor, we'll talk the thing over.'

I then bade the lady and his lordship good night, and returned to Bruton-street, with my brain swimming with cogitations concerning bishops, nieces, deans, articles, sound divines, the church, the sons of the church, sensuality, obscenity, and innumerable associating but discordant ideas, that bred a strange confusion and darkness of intellect.

CHAPTER XII

The killing of the goose with the golden eggs

THE next morning my first business was with the bishop, and I took good care to be punctual. I knew not very well why, but the ardour of my expectations was in some sort abated. The preaching my ser-

mon clandestinely, the niece, and the young clergymen that made
their fortune by matrimony, were none of them in unison with the
open and just dealing which was requisite to my success. The forebodings at which people have so often marvelled are, when they
happen, nothing more than perceptions of incongruity, that disturb
the mind. Of this kind of disturbing I was conscious.

I repaired however to my post, and was ushered up to the prelate.
He began with telling me what an orthodox divine the dean was,
who dined with us the day before; and how sure he was of rising in
the church. I could make no answer. Rise in the church he probably
would; for facts are facts; and I had sufficient proof before me.

My ready compliance with the first act of deceit, that he had
required from me, had not given him reason to suspect he should
find me more scrupulous than many others, whom he had made subservient to his purposes. What measure had he for my conscience,
but the standard that regulated his own? The caution therefore that
he practised with me was only that which the routine of cunning
had made habitual. Introductory topics were soon discarded: he
began to talk of his niece, and again asked if I did not think her an
agreeable handsome young lady? Of her person and manners I had
no unfavourable opinion, and replied in the affirmative. 'I assure
you, Mr. Trevor,' said he, 'she thinks very well of you!'—'Nay, my
lord, she has seen me but once.'—'Oh, no matter for that. Who
knows but you may come to be better acquainted? especially if
something that I have to say to you be taken *right*. You are a likely
young man, Mr. Trevor; and may be a promising young man. I
don't know: that is as things shall happen, and according as you
shall understand things, and be prudent.'

This was a vile preface: it contained more forebodings. But I was
so eager for an explanation that I had scarcely time for augury. He
continued—

'You have been to Oxford, Mr. Trevor, and you have studied.
I was at Oxford, and I studied, and read Greek, and the fathers, and
the schoolmen, and other matters: but all that there won't do alone,
Mr. Trevor. A young man must be prudent. I was prudent, or I
should never have been this day what I am now sitting here, nor
what it may happen I may be. But all that is as things shall happen
to come to pass. We have all of us a right to look forward; and so
I would have you look forward, Mr. Trevor. That is the only prudent way.'

More and more impatient, I answered his lordship, I would be as prudent as I could; and again requested he would explain himself.

'Why yes, Mr. Trevor; that is what I mean. You are a young man. I don't know you, but you come recommended to me, by my very learned friends. You have not the cares of the church to trouble you, and so you fill up your idle time with writing.'—'My lord!'—'Nay, Mr. Trevor, you write very prettily. I could write too, but I have not time. I never had time. I had aways a deal of business on my hands: persons of distinction to visit, when I was young, and to take care not to disoblige. That is a main point of prudence, Mr. Trevor; never disoblige your superiors. But I dare say you have more sense: and so, if that be the case, why you will make friends, as I did. I will be one of them; and I will recommend you, Mr. Trevor, and introduce you, and every thing may be to the satisfaction of all parties.'—

'Well, but how, my lord?'

'Why you have written a defence of the articles: now do you wish to make a friend?'—'I wish for the friendship of all good men, my lord.'—'That is right! To be sure! And you can keep a secret?'—'I have proved that I can, my lord.'—'Why that is right! And perhaps you would be glad to see your defence in print?'—'I should, my lord.'—'Why that is right! And, if it would serve a friend to put another name to the work ——?'—'My lord!' 'Nay, if you have any objection, I shall say no more!' 'I do not comprehend your lordship?'—'A work, Mr. Trevor, would not sell the worse, or be less read, or less famous, for having a dignified name in the title-page.'—'Your lordship's, for example?'—'Nay, I did not say that! But, if you are a prudent young man, and should have no objection?'—'I find I am not the man your lordship has supposed!—'Nay!'—'I will be no participator in falsehood, private or public!'—'Falsehood, Sir! What interpretation are you putting upon my words? I thought you had been a prudent young man, Mr. Trevor! I was willing to have been your friend! But I have done!'——'My lord, I must be free enough to declare, I neither understand the friendship nor the morality of the proposition.'—'Sir! morality! Is that language, Sir? Morality! I am sorry I have been deceived!'—'I have been equally so, my lord, and am equally sorry! I wish your lordship a good morning.'

Away I came, and in my vexation totally forgot to redemand my manuscript. I recollected it however while within sight of the door, and turned back. I knocked, asked for his lordship, and was told he

was not at home! This profligate impudence exceeded belief, and
my choler became ungovernable. 'His lordship,' exclaimed I to the
footman, 'is a disgrace to the bench on which he sits!' The footman
thrust the door in my face, and epithets then burst from me, that
were a disgrace to myself.

I hurried homeward, determined to give vent to my feelings in a
letter, and half determined that it should be publicly addressed to
the rank hypocrite, signed by my own name. My angry imagination
teemed forth the biting taunts that should sting him to madness,
and the broad shame with which he was to be overwhelmed. Active
memory retraced each circumstance, that could blacken the object
of my present contempt and abhorrence; and every trait increased
the bitterness of my gall, and made my boiling blood more hot. Was
this a pastor of the church? a follower of Christ? a Christian bishop?
The question astonished and exasperated me almost to frenzy.

In this temper I arrived in Bruton-street, where another very
unexpected scene awaited me. The earl I was told, had inquired for
me, and desired to see me the moment I should be at home. The
message, by turning my thoughts into a new channel, gave relief to
the impetuous tide of passion. The gloomy scene instantly brightened into prospects the most cheering and opposite. It was good to
have two strings to the bow, especially as this second was of so firm
and inflexible a texture.

All my favourable forebodings were confirmed, when, on entering,
I observed the smiles that played on his lordship's countenance!
He was in a most pleasant humour. 'I hinted to you, Mr. Trevor,'
said he, 'that I should probably have something agreeable soon to
communicate!'

His words gave certainly to expectation! They uttered volumes of
rapture in a breath! The fresh laurels of politics sprouted forth with
tenfold vigour, and the withered fig-tree of theology was totally forgotten!

'There is likely to be a change in affairs then, my lord?' said I,
smiling in rapturous sympathy as I spoke—'There is.'—'Mr. ***
has been with your lordship several times, I think?'—'Yes, yes; I
am courted by all parties, at present'—'Indeed, my lord! Then
Themistocles has become formidable?'—'Yes, yes! I have made
them feel me!'—'I am glad that I have been instrumental.'—
'Certainly, Mr. Trevor; certainly. An architect cannot build
palaces with his own hands. But we will not talk of that:

we must complete the work we have begun'—'And publish our fourth letter?'—'By no means, Mr. Trevor! that would ruin all!' For a moment I was speechless! At last I ejaculated—'My lord!'—'Things at present wear a very different face! we must now write on the other side. You seem surprised?' Well might he say so! I was thunderstruck! 'But I will tell you a secret. The minister and I are friends! I send four members into the house; and if government had not expended five times the sum that it cost me, to carry their elections, I should have sent three more. I have attacked the minister in the house by my votes; I have attacked him in the papers by my writings: so, finding I wielded my two edged sword with such resolution and activity, he has thought proper to beat a parley. He acknowledges that the fifty thousand pounds the election contest cost me were expended in support of our excellent constitution, and that I ought to be rewarded for my patriotism. His offers are liberal, and peace is concluded. We must now vere about, and this was the business for which I wanted you. A good casuist you know, Mr. Trevor, can defend both sides of a question; and I have no doubt but that you will appear with as much brilliancy, as a panegyrist, as you have done, as a satirist.'

How long I remained in that state of painful stupefaction into which I had been thrown, at the very commencement of this harangue, is more than I can say: but, as soon as I could recover some little presence of mind, I replied—'You, my lord, no doubt have your own reasons; which, to you, are a justification of your own conduct. For my part, when I wrote against the minister, it was not against the man. A desire to abash vice, advance the virtuous, and promote the good of mankind, were my motives!'—'Mr. Trevor, I find you are a young man: you do not know the world'——The scene with the bishop was acting over again, and I felt myself bursting once more with indignation. With ineffable contempt in every feature of my face, I answered—'If a knowledge of the world consists in servility, selfishness, and the practice of deceit, I hope I never shall know it.'—'You strangely forget yourself, Mr. Trevor!'— 'I am not of that opinion, my lord. I rather think, it was the man who could suppose me capable of holding the pen of prostitution that strangely forgot himself!'

His lordship hemmed, rang his bell, hummed a tune, and wished me a good morning; and I rushed out of his apartment and hurried up to my own, where I found myself suddenly released from all my labours, and at full leisure to ruminate on all the theological and political honours that were to fall so immediately and profusely upon me.

And here it is worthy of remark that I did not accuse myself; for I did not recollect that I had been in the least guilty. Yet when the earl had asked me to write letters, that were to be supposed by the public the production of his own pen, I had then no qualms of conscience; and when the bishop invited me to favour falsehood, by attributing my best written sermon to him, I concurred in the request with no less facility. When deceit was not to favour but to counteract my plans, its odious immorality then rushed upon me. Men are so much in a hurry, to obtain the end, that they frequently forget to scrutinize the means. As for my own part, far from supposing that I had been a participator in guilt, I felt a consciousness of having acted with self-denying and heroic virtue. This was my only armour, against the severe pangs with which I was so unexpectedly assaulted.

CHAPTER XIII

Gloomy meditations, or pills for the passions: More of Enoch's morality: Turl improves, yet is still unaccountable and almost profane: Consecrated things: Themistocles and vengeance: A love scene: More marriage plots: And a tragi-comic denouement: The fate of Themistocles: The manuscript in danger

I SHUT the door upon myself, as it were to conceal my disgrace, and for a considerable time traversed the room in an agony of contending passions. Rage, amazement, contempt of myself, abhorrence of my insidious patrons, and a thirst of vengeance devoured me. At length I was seized with a bitter sense of disappointment, and a fit of deep despondency. My calculations had been so indubitable, my progress so astonishing, and my future elevation in prospect so immeasurable, that to see myself thus puffed down, as it were, from the very pinnacle not of hope but of certainty, was more than my philosophy had yet learned to support with any shew of equanimity. I sunk on my chair, where I sat motionless, in silence, gloom, and

painful meditation; groaning in spirit, as tormenting fancy conjured up the dazzling scenes, with which she had lately been so
actively familiar.

I was roused from my trance at last by the recollection that I was
in the house of the earl, and starting up, as if to spurn contamination from me, I hurried out, to ease my heart by relating the whole
story in Suffolk street, and to procure myself an apartment.

Enoch, Mamma, and Miss were all at home. I had pre-informed
the family of my engagement to dine with the bishop, and they
began a full chorus of interrogatories. 'Who did I meet?' said
Mamma. 'What did I think of the niece?' asked Miss. 'What did his
lordship say?' inquired the holy man.

I stopped their inquisitive clamours by answering, my eyes
darting rage, 'His lordship said enough to prove himself a scoundrel!'
'Heaven defend me!' exclaimed Enoch. 'Why, Mr. Trevor! are you
in your senses?'—'A pitiful scoundrel! A pandar! A glutton! A
lascivious hypocrite! With less honesty than a highwayman, for he
would not only rob but publicly array himself in the pillage, nay
and impudently pretend to do the person whom he plundered a
favour!'

Enoch stood petrified. He could not have thought that frenzy
itself would have dared to utter language so opprobrious against a
bishop. It was treason against the cloth! The church tottered at the
sounds! But the fury I felt held him in awe—'Lords!' continued I.
'Heaven preserve me from the society of a lord! I have done with
them all. I am come out to seek an apartment. Kingdoms should not
tempt me to remain another hour under the roof of a lord!'

If the eyes of Enoch could have stretched themselves wider, they
would. The females requested me to explain myself. 'A pandar?'
said Mamma. 'Ay,' added Miss; 'what did that mean, Mr. Trevor?'

The question sobered me a little: I recollected my friend the
usher, and the honour of Miss Wilmot, and evaded an answer. It
was repeated again with greater solicitation: scandal stood with
open mouth, waiting for a fresh supply. I answered that for many
reasons, and especially for a dear friend's sake, I should be silent on
that head. 'A dear friend's sake?' exclaimed the suspicious matron.
'Who can that be? Who but Mr. Ellis? Why Mr. —!'

I interrupted her in a positive tone, not without a mixture of
anger, assuring her it was not Mr. Ellis; and then repeated that I
was come in search of a lodging.

At that moment the bishop's servant knocked at the door; I saw him through the window; and a note was received by the foot-boy and brought to Enoch. The instant he had read the contents, he hurried away; telling me that an unexpected affair, which must not be neglected, called him out immediately.

Young as I was, unhackneyed in the ways of men, having so lately left the society of ignorant and inconsistent youth, till that hour I had imagined, though I discovered no qualities in Enoch that greatly endeared him to me, that he was sincerely my friend. His duplicity on this occasion was in my opinion a heinous crime, and I rushed out of the house, with a determination never again to enter the doors.

I precipitately walked through several streets, without asking myself where I was going. At last I happened to think of Turl, and at that moment he appeared to be the man on earth I would soonest meet. I hastened to his lodgings, found him at home, labouring as before, and, instead of feeling the same emotions of contempt for his employment, I was struck with the calm satisfaction visible in his countenance, and envied him.

I remembered his words: 'He worked to gain a living, by administering as little as he could to the false wants and vices of men; and at the same time to pursue a plan, on which he was intent'—A plan of importance no doubt; perhaps of public utility.

It was sometime before I could relate my errand. I hesitated, and struggled, and stammered, but at last said—'Mr. Turl, I yesterday thought myself surrounded by friends: I now come to you; and should you refuse to hear me, I have not a friend in the world to whom I can relate the injustice that has been done me.'—'Pray speak, Mr. Trevor. If I can do you any service, I most sincerely assure you it will add more to my own happiness, than you will easily imagine.'

These words, though few, were uttered with an uncommon glow of benevolence. My heart was full, my passions, like the arrow in the bent bow, were with force restrained, and I snatched his hand and pressed it with great fervour. 'May you never want a friend, Mr. Turl,' said I; 'and may you never find a false one! Your opinions differ from mine, but I see and feel you are a man of virtue.'

I paused a moment, and continued. 'That you are a man of principle is fortunate, because, in what I have to relate, the name and character of a lady is concerned: the sister of a man whom, a very few years since, I loved and revered.'—'You may state the facts without mentioning her name.'—'I have no doubt of your honour.' —'I have no curiosity, and it will be the safest and wisest way.'

I then gave him a succinct history of the whole transactions, between me, Enoch, the bishop and the earl; for I was almost as angry with the first as with the other two. He heard me to the end, and asked such questions for elucidation as he thought necessary.

He then said—'Mr. Trevor, you are already acquainted with the plainness, and what you perhaps have thought the bluntness, of my character. I have but one rule: I speak all that I think worthy of being spoken, and if I offend it is never from intention. What you have related of these lordly men does not in the least astonish me. Their vices are as odious as you have described them. Your great mistake is in supposing yourself blameless. You have chiefly erred in entertaining too high an opinion of your own powers, and in cherishing something like a selfish blindness to the principles of the persons, with whom you have been concerned. Your indiscriminate approbation of all you wrote raised your expectations to extravagance. Your inordinate appetite for applause made you varnish over the picture which the earl gave you of himself; though it must otherwise have been revolting to a virtuous mind: and your expectation of preferment so entirely lulled your moral feelings to sleep, that you could be a spectator of the picture you have drawn of the bishop, the day you dined with him, yet go the next morning to accept, if not to solicit, his patronage. You have committed other mistakes, which I think it best at present to leave unnoticed. In the remarks I have made, I have had no intention to give pain, but to awaken virtue. At present you are angry: and why?'

'Why!' exclaimed I, with mingled astonishment and indignation. 'A peer of the realm to be thus profligate in principle, and not excite my anger!'—'What is a peer of the realm, but a man educated in vice, nurtured in prejudice from his earliest childhood, and daily breathing the same infectious air he first respired! A being to be pitied!'—'Despised!'—'I was but three days in this earl's house. The false colouring given me by his agent first induced me to enter it; but I was soon undeceived.'—

'Well but, a churchman! A divine! A bishop! A man consecrated to one of the highest of earthly dignities!' 'Consecrated? There are many solemn but pernicious pantomimes acted in this world!'— 'Suffer me to say, Mr. Turl, that to speak irreverently of consecrated things does not become a man of your understanding.' 'I can make no answer to such an accusation, Mr. Trevor, except that I must speak and think as that understanding directs me. Enlighten it and I will speak better. But what is it in a bishop that is consecrated? Is it his body, or his mind? What can be understood by his body? Is it the whole mass? Imagine its contents! Holy? "An ounce of civet, good apothecary!"[1] That mass itself is daily changing: is the new body, which the indulgence of gluttonous sensuality supplies, as holy as the old? If it be his mind that is consecrated, what is mind, but a succession of thoughts? By what magic are future thoughts consecrated? Has a bishop no unholy thoughts? Can pride, lust, avarice, and ambition, can all the sins of the decalogue be consecrated? Are some thoughts consecrated and some not? By whom or how is the selection made? What strange farrago of impossibilities have these holy dealers in occult divinity jumbled together? Can the God of reason be the God of lies?'

There was so much unanswerable truth in these arguments, that I listened in speechless amazement. At last I replied, 'I am almost afraid to hear you, Mr. Turl.'—'Yes; it is cowardice that keeps mankind fettered in ignorance.'—'Well but, this bishop? Does he not live in a state of concubinage?'—'The scene of sensuality that you have painted makes the affirmative probable.'——'And my defence of the articles? I will publish it immediately; with a preface stating the whole transaction.'——'You will be to blame.'—'Why so?'—'You may be better employed.'—'What! than in exposing vice?'—'The employment is petty; and what is worse, it is inefficient. The frequent consequence of attacking the errors of individuals is the increase of those errors. Such attacks are apt to deprave both the assailant and the assailed. They begin in anger, continue in falsehood, and end in fury. They harden vice, wound virtue, and poison genius. I repeat, you may be better employed, Mr. Trevor.'——'And is your rule absolute?'—'The exceptions are certainly few. Exhibit pictures of general vice, and the vicious will find themselves there; or, if they will not, their friends will.'—'This Enoch, too!'—'Is I believe a mean and selfish character; though I by no means think the action at which you have taken offence is the strongest proof of his duplicity. To decide justly, we must hear both parties. He saw your passions inflamed. It was probable you would have opposed his going to the bishop; though, if he in any manner interfered, to go was an act of duty.'

The reasonings of Turl in part allayed the fever of my mind, but by no means persuaded me to desist from the design of inflicting exemplary disgrace on the earl and the prelate.

Though a stern opposer of many of my principles, his manners were attentive, winning, and friendly. Being better acquainted with the town than I was, he undertook to procure me a neat and cheap apartment in his own neighbourhood, and in half an hour succeeded.

To this my effects were immediately removed. I was even too angry to comply with the forms of good breeding so far as to leave my compliments for the earl: I departed without ceremony, and retired to my chamber to contemplate my change of situation.

After mature consideration, the plan on which I determined was, immediately to publish the fourth letter of Themistocles, already written; to continue to write under the same signature; and in the continuation to expose the political profligacy of the earl. Themistocles was accordingly sent that very day.

I next intended accurately to revise my defence of the articles, as soon as I should recover the copy from the bishop; to turn the conversation with Turl occasionally on that subject, that I might refute his objections; and then to publish the work. For ordination I would apply elsewhere, being determined never to suffer pollution by the unholy touch of that prelate.

The next morning, my passions being calmed by sleep and I having reflected on what Turl had said, a sense of justice told me that I ought to visit Enoch at least once more; in which decision my curiosity concurred. I went, and found him at home, but dressing.

The mother and daughter were at the same employment: but Miss, imagining it was my knock, sent her attendant to inquire, and immediately huddled on her bed-gown and mob-cap to come down to me. Her tongue was eager to do its office.

'Lord! Mr. Trevor! We have had such doings! Papa and mamma and I have been at it almost ever since! But don't you fear: I am your true friend, and I have made mamma your friend, and she insists upon it that papa shall be your friend too; and so he is forced to comply: though the bishop had convinced him that you are a very imprudent young gentleman; and my papa will have it you don't understand common sense; and that you have ruined yourself, though you had the finest opportunity on earth; and that you will ruin every body that takes your part! You can't think how surprised and how angry he is, that you should oppose your will to an earl,

and a bishop, and lose the means of making your fortune, and perhaps of making your friends' fortunes too: for there it is that the
shoe pinches; because I understand the bishop is very kind to papa
at present; and, if he should take your part, papa says he will never
see him again. But mamma and I argued, what of that? Would the
bishop give papa a good living, said mamma? And what if he would,
says I? Shall we give up those that we love best in the world, because
it is the will and pleasure of a bishop! No, indeed! I don't know that
bishops are better than other people, for my part; and perhaps not
so good as those that are to be given up. So mamma told me to be
silent; but she took my part, and I took yours, and I assure you, for
all what they both said, I did not spare the bishop! So my papa fell
into a passion, and pretended that I was too forward; and I assure
you he accused me of having my likings. I don't know whether he
did not make me blush! But I answered for all that, and said well,
and if I have, who can help having their likings? I have heard you
and my mamma say often enough that you both had had your
likings; and that you did not like one another; and that that was the
reason that you quarrel like cat and dog; and so if people will be
happy they must marry according to their likings. So said my
mamma well but, Eliza, have you any reason to think that Mr.
Trevor has any notions of marriage? So I boldly answered yes, I
had; for you know, Mr. Trevor, what passed between us at the
play-house, and the kind squeeze of the hand you gave me at parting
with me: and so why should I be afraid to speak, and tell the truth?
And so mamma says it shall all be cleared up!'

Her eagerness would admit of no interruption, till it was checked
for a moment by the entrance of Enoch, and the mamma. I suspected
a part of what was to come, and never in my life had I felt so much
embarrassment. 'Well Eliza,' said the matron, 'have you and Mr.
Trevor been talking? Have you come to an explanation?'

I would have answered, but Miss was an age too quick for me.
'Yes, mamma; we have explained every thing to the full and whole.
I have told it all over to him just now, every syllable the same as I
told it to you, and he does not contradict a word of it.'

'Contradict?' interrupted Enoch. 'But does he say the same?'
'No, Sir!' answered I with eagerness; that I might if possible, by
a single word, put an end to the eternal clack and false deductions
of this very loving young lady. 'Lord! Mr. Trevor!' exclaimed Miss,
her passions all flying to her eyes, part fire and part water. 'Sure

you are not in earnest? You don't mean as you say?'—'I am very
serious, Miss Ellis; and am exceedingly sorry to have been so misunderstood!'—'Why will you pretend to deny, Mr. Trevor, that all
that I have been rehearsing here, about the play-house; and about
the kindness with which you paid your addresses to me there, and
indeed elsewhere, often and before time; and about your leading
me to the chair; and then your tenderly taking my hand and squeez-
ing it; and then the look you gave with your eyes; and more than
all the loving manner in which you said good night? Not to mention as before all that you said and did, sitting next to me in the
play-house; enough to win the affections of any poor innocent virgin! You are not such a deceiver as that comes to I am sure, Mr.
Trevor: you have a more generous and noble heart!'

Here Miss burst into a flood of tears, and mamma exclaimed—'I
am very much afraid, Mr. Trevor, there have been some improper
doings!'

Enoch's anger for once made him honest. 'No such a thing!' said
he. 'It is the forward fool's own fault. This is neither the first,
second, nor third time she has played the same pranks.'

The mother and daughter instantly raised their pipes like fifty
ciphered keys in an organ, first against Enoch, then against all the
male kind, and lastly turned so furiously upon me that there seemed
to be danger of their tearing me piece-meal, like as the mad females
of Thrace did the disconsolate Orpheus.[1]

At length I started up in a passion, and exclaimed—'Will you
hear me, ladies?' 'No! no! no!' screamed Miss. 'We won't hear a
word! Don't listen to him, mamma! He is a deceiver! A faithless
man! I did not think there could have been such a one in the whole
world! and I am sure I warned him often enough against it. And
after the true friend that I have been to you, Mr. Trevor! and have
taken your part, tooth and nail! Papa himself knows I have; and
would take your part, through fire and water, against the whole
world! and to be so ungrateful, and so false, and faithless to me in
return! Oh shame, Mr. Trevor! Is that a man? A fine manly part
truly! to win a poor virgin's heart and then to forsake her!'

Finding the sobs and the rhetoric of Miss inexhaustible and every
effort to elucidate fruitless, I rose, told Enoch I would explain myself to him by letter, opened the door to go, was seized by the coat
by the young lady, and could not without violence, or leaving like
Joseph my garment behind me,[2] have torn myself away, if I had not

been aided by Enoch; who, having according to his own story been probably present at such scenes before, had sense enough I suppose to be ashamed of his daughter's conduct.

I hurried home, snatched up my pen, and in an epistle to Enoch instantly detailed, as minutely as I could recollect them, all the circumstances of the heroine's behaviour; acknowledging that I had listened, had suffered the intercourse of knees, legs, and feet, and as she said had once pressed her hand; that for this I feared I might have been to blame; but yet, if this were treachery, I knew not very well how a young man was to conduct himself, so as not to be accused of being either rude, ridiculous, or a traitor.

While I was writing this letter, it occurred to me that perhaps there was no small portion of cunning, in the conduct of Miss; that she and her mamma had remarked my youth, and entire ignorance of the world; that Enoch himself, though more intent on what he thought deeper designs, had entertained similar ideas; that Miss had probably been never before so much delighted with the person of any man, whom she might approach; and that the females had concluded I might have been precipitately entangled in marriage, or marriage promises, by this artful management. Be that as it may: I wrote my letter, eased my conscience, and took my leave of the whole family.

Mean time, Themistocles had lain with the printer several days; while I impatiently looked for its appearance, but in vain. I then began to suspect the paper was under the influence of the earl, wrote to the editor, and read the next day, among the answers to correspondents, that the letter signed Themistocles could not be admitted in their paper: they were friends to proper strictures, but not to libels against government. My teeth gnashed with rage! I was but ill qualified, at this period, to teach the benevolent philosophy which priests of all religions affirm it is their trade to inculcate.

Neither could I procure the manuscript from the bishop. The scene in Suffolk street had occasioned me to delay sending that evening, but the next day I wrote a peremptory demand, for it to be delivered to the bearer; and prevailed on Turl to be my messenger. He returned with information, that the bishop was gone into the country! but that the letter would be sent after him immediately, and an answer might probably be received by the return of post.

I had no alternative, and three days afterward the manuscript was sent, sealed up and labeled on the back—'To be delivered to the author, when called for: his address not being known.'

Thus every new incident was a new lesson; unveiling a system, moral, political and ecclesiastical, which without such experience I could not have supposed to exist. My conversations with Turl came in aid of this experience, and they combined to shake the very high opinion I had conceived of the clerical order: but the finishing blow was yet to come.

CHAPTER XIV

The return to Oxford: A cold reception: Hector and more of his inmates: Olivia and the drive to Woodstock: Symptoms of increasing misfortune: An Oxford scholar brawl: The flight of hope

THE period of my rustication was expired, and the term immediately preceding the summer vacation was on the point of beginning. I resolved therefore to return to Oxford, and according to the claim of rotation take my bachelor's degree. My plans of punishment and my pursuit of fame must indeed lie dormant a few weeks; but I determined they should both be revived with increasing ardour, at my return.

I found no inconsiderable pleasure in revisiting the turrets, groves, and streams of Oxford. Long experience itself could scarcely weed the sentiment from my mind that these were the sacred haunts of the muses. It must be owned that such the fancy could easily make them, and that it is a task in which the fancy delights.

I thought it my duty immediately to visit the president. With respect to any mention of the letters of recommendation, I scarcely knew how to behave. The bishop and the president might have been friends in their youth. The president might have his prejudices. And might there not even be cruelty in rudely tearing away the mask, and showing him what a monster he had formerly taken to his bosom? Should he inquire, I certainly must declare the truth: but should he be silent, what good inducement had I to speak? The morality of this reasoning was more questionable than I at that time suspected.

Silent however he was, on that subject. He received me coldly, asked in a tone that did not wish for information how I liked London, and concluded with saying he hoped I did not return to set the university any more bad examples! Not well satisfied myself with my methodistical paroxysm, I had not a word to offer in its defence. I answered, I hoped I should set no bad examples, either to the university or the world; but that I could only act to the best of my judgment, and if that deceived me I must endure the consequences. 'Exactly so, Mr. Trevor,' said the president, with a formal dismissing inclination of the head; and so we parted.

When I had been at college about a week, Hector Mowbray called on me one morning and told me his father was dead; that Mowbray Hall the manor and its demesnes were all his own; that he had the best pack of fox dogs in the county; hunters that would beat the world; setters as steady as a rifle barrel gun; and coursers that would take the wind in their teeth; and that he was going up to town with his sister, of whom he was glad to be rid, to place her with an aunt. 'She would not let me be quiet,' said Hector, 'but I must come, for she is as obstinate as a mule, and bring our compliments and her special thanks for a signal favour, that is her lingo, which she makes a plaguey rout about; your methodist parson trick, you know, of taking her out of the water; after your damned canting gang had frightened the horses and thrown her into it. She says she should have been in her cold grave, or I don't know what, but for you; but I tell her women and cats are not so easily killed: and so to please her I agreed to come directly and ask you to breakfast with us, and spend the day together. I love Oxford! It was not above thirty miles out of the road, and I never come within a long shot of it without having *a row* with the boys and the bucks. So if you will be one among us, come along. There *is* tall Andrews, spanking Jack as I call him, and three or four more of us, that mean to meet at Woodstock.'

'And take Olivia?'

'To be sure! Andrews is sweet upon her, but she beats off; though he is a fine fellow! a daring dog! all Christ Church can't beat him! and when his father is off the hinges, which he swears will be within these six months, he will make a famous wicked *dash*! I tell her she is a fool for not taking him: but my talking is all spilt porridge! she is as piggish as father himself was! So if you come, why come along.'

This was the first pleasant proposal that had been made to me, since the day of my dining with the bishop! My heart bounded while he spoke! It was with difficulty I could contain my joy; and the effort must have been much greater, had not the brother of Olivia been the dull undiscerning Hector Mowbray.

He would have hurried me away immediately, but I insisted on decorating my person, and fitting it to appear before the angelic Olivia!

Impatience like mine would not admit of languor. I was soon equipped, and flew to feast my senses with rapture ineffable! I staid not to ask whether it were love, or friendship; or what were my intentions, hopes, or fears. I felt a host of desires that were eager, tumultuous, and undecided. The passions were too much in a hurry to institute inquiry or to have any dread of consequences.

I knew indeed that I already had a lover's hatred of Andrews, and even took pleasure to hear him characterised by traits so disgusting. That Olivia should reject such a being was no miracle: and yet it gave me inexpressible gratification!

As I ascended the stairs, strange sensations seized me; such as I had never known before. The elastic bounds with which I had hurried along sunk into debility; aspen leaves never trembled more universally than I did, from head to foot; and as I opened the door my knees, like Belshazzar's,[1] 'smote one against the other.' A sickness of the stomach came over me: I turned pale, and was pushed forward by Hector before I had time to recover myself.

Olivia saw my confusion. In an instant, her sympathetic feelings caught the infection: she feebly pronounced, 'I am glad to see you, Mr. Trevor!' and with the hue of death on her countenance, snatched her handkerchief, turned aside, and uttered two or three hysteric sobs.

Andrews, my rival, Hector's spanking Jack, was present, and burst into a loud laugh! It was a medicine that immediately recovered both of us. The blood hurried back, flushed the cheeks of Olivia, and dyed them with a deep but beautiful scarlet. 'I am a strange fool!' said she. 'You came upon me so suddenly, Mr. Trevor! and I never can see an old friend, after long absence, without these sensations.'

'Long absence!' replied Andrews. 'Why I thought it was only three or four months since the affair of the methodist preacher and the drowning, that you were just now telling me about?' 'Pshaw!'

exclaimed Hector, 'if you pester your pate with her crotchets, you will have enough to do. Come, come, where are the muffins? I begin to cry cupboard.¹ Beside I want to be off.'

While this dialogue passed I recovered sufficient courage to salute Olivia; but affection and awe were so mingled that the burning kiss of love expired in cold blooded constraint and reserve. We then sat down to the tea table, I on one side of Olivia Hector on the other, with his right leg on a vacant chair, his left thrown on Olivia's lap, and Andrews extended sprawling his whole length on a sopha. The two youths began a conversation in their own style, while I endeavoured to entertain Olivia with my remarks on London. I related my principal adventures, expectations, and disappointments, and she appeared to be deeply interested by the narrative. The questions she put, her tone of voice, her countenance, all expressed her feelings; and several times a deep sigh was smothered and with difficulty passed away in a forced hem.

The two youths were so deeply engaged in the pedigree of their pointers, and so warmly contested whose were the best, that I doubt if they knew the subject of our discourse. It was a fleeting but happy hour!

Hector still drove his phaeton, and breakfast being over it was waiting at the door, attended by two grooms with two led saddle horses. 'I will not go, brother,' said Olivia, 'if you drive.' 'He drive?' replied Andrews. 'Never believe it! No, no Miss Mowbray, I will be your Jehu. I will wheel you along, over velvet, every yard smooth as sailing.' 'No Jack,' interrupted Hector, 'that won't do. Trevor is no company, has nothing to say, or nothing that I want to hear. Sister and he will match best. He will tell her what is Greek for a gauze cap, and she will teach him how to make it up. You and I will pair off together on the hunters, and I'll gallop you the last mile into Woodstock for your sum: or, look you, the loser pay the expences of the day.'

To this proposal, seasoned with oaths three at least to a sentence, Andrews continued obstinately averse. As Hector did not drive he would. Nor did he pay any more respect to the opinion of Olivia, who remarked that he was booted and I was not. 'So much the better,' said he; 'that is genteel.' 'Nay but really,' added Olivia, 'I shall not think myself more safe with you, Mr. Andrews, than with my brother.' Mr. Andrews was deaf; he rudely seized her by the wrists, hauled her across the room, and swore if she would not go he would take her in his arms and carry her. My fingers ached to catch him by the collar; but I could not like him cast off all fear of offending Olivia.

Resistance must either have been violent, or in vain. Olivia submitted, and I dared not oppose. We mounted, and Andrews drove, for the first three miles, with some moderation. He then began to play tricks; took a high quarter and a low one,[1] where he could find them, to shew his dexterity; whipped and fretted the horses, increased their rate, and at last put them into a full gallop.

As soon as I perceived what he was doing, I rode full speed after him, and in an authoritative tone called to him to drive with more care. He was obliged to slacken his pace before he could understand what I said. When he had heard me repeat my injunction, which I did with no little vehemence, he looked at me first in astonishment, then with a sneer, and was raising his whip to lash the horses forward with fresh fury. Olivia caught him by the arm, and I immediately called with a voice of thunder, 'By G——, Sir, if you either injure or terrify the lady, I will pull you head long from your seat!'

He made no answer, and the contempt his countenance had exhibited the moment before sunk into sheepishness. I immediately rode forward to the head of the horses, kept a moderate pace, would not suffer him to pass me, unless he meant to stake the horse I rode with the pole, and continued thus for more than a mile, till I was convinced that he had no more inclination to divert himself by terrifying and endangering Olivia.

I rode the rest of the way with the heart burn of anxiety, fearful I had angered Olivia, but not knowing how much. While I kept the lead to oblige Andrews to temperance, he cursed and muttered. 'It was very fine! Mighty proper behaviour to a gentleman! But he should see how it was all to end!' He vented other menaces, which though in too low a key distinctly to reach my ear were loud enough to produce their effect on Olivia.

We arrived at Woodstock, and I dismounted and stood ready to receive Olivia. Andrews followed the example, but she called to her brother and noticed neither of us. He received her as she alighted, and I perceiving her serious look said, 'I hope, Miss Mowbray, I have not offended you?' She made no reply, but stood half a minute, as if to recover being cramped by sitting. Andrews was then on our left, at some distance, and I turned to the same side. She saw me and called, 'Mr. Trevor!' She said no more, but her look was too impressive to be misinterpreted. Hard fate! it could not be obeyed. I pretended indeed to walk away, but the moment she entered the door of the inn I hastened back to Andrews and said, 'If you think yourself insulted, Sir, you have only to inform me of it: I am at your service.'

His answer was—He did not know what I could mean! He had nothing to say to me. I gave him a contemptuous glance, he followed the grooms, and I went to seek Olivia.

I approached with trepidation. 'I perceive, Madam,' said I, 'my conduct is not approved.' She fixed her eye upon me.—'You have been speaking to Mr. Andrews?' I was silent. 'And a duel?' added she, with increasing severity mingled with terror. I hastily interrupted her. 'No, Madam, Mr. Andrews is not a man to fight duels.' —'Mr. Andrews has the more understanding.'

Though the intelligence gave her relief, she spoke in a tone that petrified. 'Surely, Madam,' I replied, 'you cannot be angry with me for protecting you from danger and insult?'—'The danger was trifling, perhaps none; he would not endanger himself; and for insult I must be left to judge in my own case both what it is, and when it deserves notice. Men have little respect for women, when they are so ready to suppose a woman is incapable of being her own protector.'—'Is it then a crime, Miss Mowbray, to tremble for your safety? or to teach manners to a brute?'—'Yes: at least, it is weakness to tremble without cause. You must act as you please, in whatever relates to yourself, but it is inexpressibly criminal to be ready, on every trifling occasion, to take or to throw away life. If this be teaching, we have too many teachers in the world, who have never themselves been to school. I am personally concerned, and you have asked my opinion; otherwise, Mr. Trevor, I should have been cautious of giving it.'

The energy with which this reproof, though severe, was begun denoted what self-flattery might well have construed into affection; for it proved the interest the lovely chider took in the rectitude of my conduct. But the kindness of it seemed to be all killed, in the formality and coldness of the conclusion. I stood speechless. She perceived the effect she had produced, and in a soft and relenting tone added —'I do not seek to wound your feelings, Mr. Trevor. Oh no! Would I could'—The angel checked herself, but soon with returning enthusiasm continued—'Ideas at this instant rush upon my mind that'—Again she paused—'You saved my life—but'—The tears started in her eyes, her voice faltered, she could not proceed. She had rung to inquire for a dressing room, the damned maid entered, Olivia followed, and I remained in speechless stupefaction, with the dreadful *but* reverberating in my ear.

Andrews and Hector came in. Had the former known my thoughts, he would have rejoiced at such ample vengeance. He talked to Mowbray, but took no notice of what had passed. They ordered dinner, and asked if I would stroll with them to Blenheim house ?[1] I excused myself and away they went.

I remained anxiously expecting that Olivia would come down; and, having waited till the approach of dinner time, I sent the maid, with my compliments, to inform her that I should be glad to speak a word to her. The answer I received was that she should see me in half an hour. I sent again, but to no purpose; I could not catch a glimpse of her till the youths had returned, and dinner was on the table.

They brought two gownsmen of Christ Church with them, companions of Andrews, who were quite as talkative and nearly as rude and boisterous as themselves. Olivia had not perhaps all her accustomed vivacity, but she behaved with infinitely more ease and chearfulness than I could have wished, and I felt as if I were the only disconsolate guest.

The players were at Woodstock, and were to exhibit that afternoon. They began at four o'clock, that the gownsmen might have time to return to Oxford; hoping that would be a favourable circumstance for them with the vice chancellor, who, as I have said, is generally inimical to theatrical exhibition, and whose influence extends to Woodstock. The party all voted for the play, except Olivia, who observed their inclination to riot, and ineffectually attempted to persuade them to return. I was glad to find them obstinate; it might afford me an opportunity of speaking with her, for which I would almost have given an eye. A servant was sent to keep places, in one of the six boxes which the theatre, fitted up in a barn, contained.

The youths sat so late to enjoy the folly of their own conversation that the play had begun before we came there, and inquiring for our box we found it in the possession of four gownsmen, who had turned the servant out and seized upon it for themselves. Hector and Andrews began to swear outrageously! Tigers could not have appeared more fierce. They entered the box, and addressed its usurpers in the gross vulgar terms to which they had been accustomed. They were immediately answered in their own language; and tall Andrews and the bulky Hector each laid hold of his man, who were much their inferiors in strength and size, to turn them out.

I was standing to guard Olivia, who seemed pleased that I should be rather so engaged than more actively employed. But my aid was soon necessary: Hector and Andrews each received a blow, which neither of them had the courage to return, though their opponents were little better than boys. Fired at their pusillanimity, I darted by and seized the little gownsmen, one in one hand and the other in the other, pressed my knuckles in their neck, shook them heartily, and dragged them out of the box. The two other collegians of our squadron, seeing this intrepid advance, followed up the victory; Hector and Andrews again blustered and lent their aid, and the box was cleared.

This did not all pass in a moment: the Oxonians, and there were numbers of them in the theatre, crouded to the spot; and it was with difficulty a general riot, to which these youths are always prone, could be prevented.

At last we made way to the box; but no words could persuade Olivia to enter it. She insisted on returning to the inn. I interceded, her brother swore, and Andrews attempted to hold her; but her resolution was not to be shaken. 'I am in a society of mad boys!' said she. 'I hoped to have found one rational being among them, but I was deceived.'

The sentence was short, but every syllable was an arrow that wounded me to the heart. I was the supposed rational being, in whom she had placed her hopes, and by whom she had been deceived. A second time I had disregarded the benevolent wisdom with which she had vainly endeavoured to inspire me, had acted in open defiance of her peaceful morality, and had forfeited all claim to her esteem. I read my doom, not only in her words but in her whole deportment.

While I stood drawing these painful conclusions, motionless, or active only in my fears, a messenger arrived whose coming gave a climax to my ill fortune. He brought a letter, informing Olivia that her aunt, whom she was on her journey to visit, was dangerously ill; and, if Olivia desired to see her alive, she must hasten to London with all possible speed. The news entirely put an end to the endeavours of Hector and his companions to detain her at the play.

A servant was sent forward to prepare a post-chaise for Olivia, in which she insisted on returning to Oxford by herself, and we all immediately proceeded back to the inn.

Just before we reached the inn, Hector and his companions being engaged in noisy disputation, I said to Olivia in a half whisper——'Have I then, Madam, forfeited all claims to your good opinion?'—She paused for a moment and replied—'The incidents of to-day, Mr. Trevor, have but confirmed the character which was long since given me of you, and which I began to hope was not strictly true. The benefit you have conferred on me I shall never forget: it has induced me to be more prompt in my desire to prevent mischief than you perhaps might think became me. Such a trial can scarcely occur again, and if it should I will endeavour to use greater caution. Yet suffer me, for the last time, earnestly to advise you to be less rash. Were I your sister, Mr. Trevor, I should be in continual alarms, and the most unhappy creature existing.'

Andrews heard her voice, and, prompted as I suppose either by jealousy or malice, put an end to our dialogue. I would have given worlds, if I had possessed them, to have continued it only five minutes; but no such blessing could be obtained; Andrews was alert, and Olivia appeared to avoid further parley. In a quarter of an hour the carriage was ready, and Olivia stepped into it and was driven away full speed.

Andrews would have remained, to see the play; and Hector, had not I shamed him into the contrary, would have consented; but in consequence of my remonstrances they mounted, accompanied by the rest of their clamorous comrades on horseback, and I was left to the melancholy office of driving the phaeton, with the seat vacant that had so lately been occupied by Olivia.

We hurried off, helter skelter, no one respecting his neck, and I the least (for Olivia was before) and rode and drove at such a rate that we overtook the chaise a mile before it reached Oxford. What relief was this to me! She sat concealed in the corner of the carriage, and I could catch no glimpse of her. I durst not even drive past, lest I should add to the mortal offence I had already given, and confirm her in the belief that I was no better than a madman: or, in her own emphatic language, a mad boy!

The pain of suspense was quickly over. We all soon arrived at Oxford. A courier had been dispatched from Woodstock by the affectionately impatient niece, with orders to have another chaise in readiness; and, after briefly bidding her brother and the company adieu, she stepped out of the carriage which brought her from Woodstock into the one that was waiting, and again was driven off, while I stood gazing in a trance of painful stupidity.

This was the last glance I had of her! and, rejecting the invitation to supper of Hector and his party with more sullenness than I had ever felt before, I returned to the college, burst into my room, locked the door, and threw myself down on the boards, in a state of the most wretched despondency.

END OF VOLUME II

VOLUME III

CHAPTER I

*Gloomy thoughts: Filial emotions: A journey to the country:
A lawyer's accounts not easily closed: Conscientious scruples:
The legacy received and divided: Return to Oxford: More
disappointment: Treachery suspected: Arrival at London:
Difficulty in choosing a profession*

MY agitation of mind was too violent to be quickly appeased; it did
not end with the day, or with the week; but on the contrary excited
interrogatories that prolonged the paroxysm. Why was I disturbed?
Why angry with myself? Why did I accuse Olivia of being severe,
or what did the accusation mean? What were my views? From the
tumultuous state of my emotions, I could not disguise to myself
that I had an affection for her: but had she ever intimated an affection for me? Was the passion that devoured me rational? She was
of a wealthy family: of the provision her father had made for her I
was ignorant; but I knew that her expectations from the aunt, said
to be now dying, and from others of her kindred, were great. Was
I prepared to accept favours, make myself a dependent, and be subservient to the unfeeling caprice of Hector, or any other proud and
ignorant relation? Did not such people esteem wealth as the test and
the measure of worth? What counterpoise had I, but sanguine
hopes? of the probable fallacy of which I had already received strong
proofs; and which did not, in the pictures that fancy at present drew,
burst upon me with those bright and vivid flashes that had lately
made them so alluring. My passions and propensities all led me to
seek the power of conferring benefits, controlling folly, and of being
the champion of merit, and the rewarder of virtue. Ought I not
either to renounce Olivia, or to render myself in every respect her

equal; and to disdain the degrading insolence with which any pretensions of mine would otherwise be received. Had I no reason to
fear that Olivia herself was a little influenced by personal considerations? Would she have been quite so ready to disapprove, had the
advantages of fortune been on my side? Was this inferiority entirely
disregarded by her? The doubt was grating, but pertinaciously in-
trusive. Would not any proposal from me be treated with the most
sovereign contempt, if not by her, by Hector and her other relations? Why then did I think of her? It was but a very few days since
the wealth and power that should have raised me, far above the
sphere of the Mowbray family, were supposed to be within my
grasp. How painful was the distance at which they now appeared!
My present debility was felt with intolerable impatience. To love
and to be unable to heap happiness on the object beloved, was a
thought that assailed me with excruciating sensations!

At this very period another event happened, that did not contribute to enliven the prospect.

I had lately received intelligence from my mother, the tenor of
which was that she dreaded the approach of poverty; and about a
fortnight after the departure of Olivia, a letter came, by which I
learned that lawyer Thornby had refused all further supplies,
affirming that my grandfather's effects were entirely exhausted;
except the thousand pounds left by the rector at my own disposal.
Of this I had already received fifty pounds; and my mother urgently
declared in her letter that, if I did not apply part of the remainder
for her support, she should be left in the decline of life (the approach
of which she was now very ready to acknowledge) in imminent
danger of want; nay, so as perhaps even to come upon the parish.[1]
My pride revolted at the very thought; and I was angry with her for
having conceived or committed it to paper.

Should I suffer my mother to want? No. To become a pauper?
My heart spurned at the base suggestion. I had been several years
under the tuition of the rector, and had acquired more than was
good of his family dignity. The picture before me was not a pleasing
one, but I would subject myself to any hardships, ay would starve
on a grain a day, rather than abandon my mother. My motives were
mixed; some wrong some right.

This affair made me resolve once more to visit my native country,
and my resolution was immediately put in practice. It was a relief,
though of a painful kind, to the more painful state in which my

undecided thoughts at that moment held me. The man whose contradictory impulses goad him in a thousand different directions,
without permitting him to pursue any one, is happy to be put in
motion.

My arrival was unexpected: my mother, who was but little inclined to accuse herself, received me with much more satisfaction
than embarrassment.

The behaviour of Thornby was not quite so self-complacent. My
questions, concerning the receipt and disbursement of my grandfather's property, were sometimes answered with the affectation of
open honesty; and at others with petulant ambiguity, so that I knew
not whether he meant to shun or to provoke inquiry. 'Executorship
was a very thankless office; it involved a man in continual trouble,
for which he could receive no recompence, and then subjected him
to the suspicions of people, who were unable or unwilling to look
after their own affairs. His very great friendship for the rector had
induced him to take this office upon himself, though he well knew
the trouble and tediousness attending it, and the ingratitude with
which it was always repaid. He had several times in his life played
the fool in the same way, and had always met with the same reward.'

Equivocation is the essence of law, and I believe he spoke truth.

'He should take care, however, not to involve himself in such
officious troubles for the future. As for the accounts, he was ready at
all times, and desirous to have them settled. He had been plagued
enough, and had even paid money out of his own pocket, which he
was sure, whenever a balance came to be struck, he should not be
reimbursed. But there were various affairs that he could not immediately close; law accounts, bad debts, mortgages, and other matters
that required time. He had business of his own to which he must
attend, or be ruined; his clients would have good actions against
him, if it could be proved that their suits were lost by his neglect.
Indeed he was not bound to give me any account; but he always
acted on the square, and therefore defied scrutiny; nay, he wished
it, for what had an honest man to fear?'

He talked so much of his honesty that, if he did not quite persuade
me it was immaculate, he at least led me to doubt.

Beside, as he had reminded me, what claims had I? The property
was bequeathed to my mother; she had married, her husband had
squandered it away, and there was an end of it. Farther inquiry was
but vexation and loss of time. It is true, the supposed wealth of the

rector had quickly disappeared: but if the owner of it, my mother's husband, were satisfied, what could be said?

She indeed hinted to me that Wakefield, finding he could wrest no more from his uncle, unless by filing a bill in Chancery, or some other process at law, for which he had no funds, not to mention the great chance of his being cast in costs of suit, had been obliged to desist; though convinced that the property was not one half expended. He had a better hope. Thornby was old, had no children, and might soon leave him the whole.

With most men this would have been a powerful motive; but the passions of her young husband, my mother owned, were too impetuous to be restrained by the cold considerations of prudence. At first she censured him with reluctance; for to censure him was in reality to adduce mementos of her own folly; but her resentment against him for having deserted her presently overpowered her caution, and the pictures she drew shewed him to be not only dissipated and prodigal but unprincipled. He had even so far offended the law, that it was doubtful whether his life were not in danger; and Thornby, whose plans had been frustrated by his extravagance, had more ways than one of ridding himself of his importunity.

In any case it was necessary to make some provision for my mother; and, embroiled in doubt as I was, the most prudent way that I could imagine was to consult Thornby.

He affected to be very conscientious, and scarcely knew what advice to give. 'My mother was in want, and to desert her would be cruel; yet the money that was devised me was my own: it was bequeathed for a good purpose, and the pious will of the testator ought to be held sacred. I was young, the grandson of a good man, an excellent man, and his dear friend. I had great learning and good sense, and ought not to be deprived of the means that had been left me of establishing myself in life. But then my mother had been tenderly brought up, and a dutiful son to be sure could not desert his parent. It was a difficult point. To purchase a life annuity for her would be the best way of securing her, against the miseries of poverty in old age; but then it would sink deeply into the thousand pounds to make but a very moderate provision of this kind; though he knew no other method in her case that would be so safe.'

While I listened I resolved. To provide for my mother I held to be an indispensable duty; and, notwithstanding my late disappointments, my fears for myself were but few. People of a sanguine temper are subject to temporary doubt and gloom; but the sky soon clears, and though one bright star may shoot and fall, hope soon creates a whole constellation. The earl and the prelate had both been unprincipled; but the failure was in them, not in me. I could not but remember the terror that Themistocles had excited in a prime minister; and the avidity with which a prelate had endeavoured to profit by my theological talents. How certainly and how soon could I bring these talents into notice! How easy the task! I need but mount the rostrum, I need but put pen to paper, and my adversaries would be brought to shame, and mankind taught to do me justice. Incontrovertible facts were in my favour; and to foster doubts and fears would be cowardice, self-desertion, and folly! Such were my conclusions.

I determined therefore, without farther hesitation, to employ the sum of five hundred pounds in the purchase of an annuity for my mother. The remainder would amply supply me, till those rich mines should be explored from the fertile veins of which I had already drawn such dazzling specimens.

I continued in the country almost three weeks; but, as the purchase could not instantly be concluded, I left the stipulated sum in my mother's possession, drew the remainder of the thousand pounds in bills and cash from Thornby, and, with more wealth than I ever bore about me at one time before, returned to Oxford.

Though Olivia was daily and hourly remembered, I had recovered so far by the business in which I had been engaged as to think seriously of pursuing my studies; for by their aid I was to realize those splendid projects on which, as I supposed, the happiness of man depends.

The learning, which the general forms of taking a degree require, is so little that a man of genius is inclined to treat it with contempt: but, if the candidate happen to be obnoxious to the heads of the university, his examination may then be of a very different kind. I had not much doubt; for, from the questions and answers I had so often heard on these occasions, to reject me seemed to be almost impossible. Yet I was not entirely without alarm. The disgrace of rustication that I had suffered, the coldness of the reception I had met from the president on my return to college, and the ambiguity which I conceived I had since remarked in his manner, excited some fear; and my preparatory efforts were so strenuous that I imagined I might defy reproof.

I had been told indeed that malice had a very strange mode of exerting itself, but which was so arbitrary and odious as to be but rarely practised. Any member of convocation, or master of arts, without assigning any cause for his conduct, may object, for two terms, to a person who shall ask leave to take his degree! Nay, these terms ended, another may object, and another! But this was a privilege so disgusting that I had not the least apprehension it would be put in practice against me.

To my utter astonishment, I was mistaken! On the day appointed to ask leave, a master of arts actually did appear, and without supporting his objection by reasoning, charge, or censure, exercised this detestable university veto.

My surprize and indignation, at hearing him pronounce his negative, were so great that I was deprived of utterance. I even doubted the reality of what I heard: I stood gazing, till he was gone, and then exclaimed, as if to a person present—'Me, Sir!—Do you mean me?'

A minute afterward, my interjections were not quite so inoffensive. A torrent of passion burst from me, and he, whose malignity could not justly assert I wanted learning, might, had he stayed, have collected sufficient proofs of my want of philosophy.

My attention had been diverted from the accuser, by my amazement at the accusation; but, as soon as I recovered my recollection, it seemed to me certain that I knew his face. The idea was seized with so much eagerness, and associations occurred so rapidly, that the figure of one of my companions, on the night of the debauch when I first came to Oxford, rose full before me; though he had been absent from the university, so that till this day I had never seen him since. It was the very tutor of the Earl of Idford!

A train of the most tormenting suspicions rushed upon me. I soon learned, from inquiry, that he was intimate likewise with the president. Was not this a combination? What could it be else? This tutor was connected with the earl and the president; so was the latter with the bishop!

The whole plot, in its blackest hues, seemed developed.

My agitation was extreme. I ran from college to college, wherever I had acquaintance, repeating all I knew and much of what I suspected. Nor did I merely confine myself to narrative. I added threats, which, however impotent they might be, were not the less violent. One of my first projects was to seek personal satisfaction of the vile tutor, or if he refused to chastise him with inexorable severity; but this he had taken care to elude, by keeping out of the way.

My denunciations soon reached the ear of the president, and I was given to understand that, if I were not immediately silent, I should be expelled the university; and that a degree would never be granted me, till I had publicly retracted the opprobious words I had uttered. Distant consequences are easily defied. My blood was in a flame, and despising the menace, I publicly declared that my persecutors were as infamous as the tool they had employed; that I should think it a disgrace to be a member of a body which could countenance proceedings so odiously wicked; that I spurned at every honour such a body could confer; and that, with respect to expulsion, I would myself erase my name from the register in which it had unfortunately been entered.

How little is man aware that by intemperance he damns his own cause, and gives the face of seeming honesty to injustice itself! Vicious as the place is, I myself could not abhor such proceedings more than many men in Oxford would have done, had they believed the tale.

Fortune still continued in her wayward mood. On the heel of one perverse imp another often treads. While I remained at Oxford, which was but a few days after this event, the retailing of my wrongs was my chief employment; and in a coffee-room, to which I resorted for this purpose, the following advertisement in a London newspaper met my astonished eye!

THIS DAY IS PUBLISHED:

A DEFENCE OF THE THIRTY NINE ARTICLES

BY THE

RIGHT REVEREND FATHER IN GOD ******

LORD BISHOP OF *****

Injustice had by this time become so familiar to me that, scourged even to frenzy as I was, I sat rather stunned than transfixed by the blow. That this was the very defence of the articles I had written did not, with me, admit of a moment's doubt. Every thing I had heard or remarked, of this wicked but weak church governor, had afforded proof of his incapacity for such a task; yet the injustice, effrontery and vice of the act was what till seen could not have been believed!

Nor did its baseness end here. What could I suppose, but that the bishop had been assiduously tampering with the president; that they and the earl were in a conspiracy against me; that this was the cause of the disgrace and insult put upon me; and that, having robbed me of my writings, there was a concerted and fixed plan to render me contemptible, take away my character, and devote me to ruin?

The longer I thought the more painful were the sensations that assaulted me. I had already been complaining to the whole city. Some few indeed seemed to credit me; but more to suspect; and none heard of my treatment with that glowing detestation which my feelings required. Were I to tell this new tale, incredibly atrocious as it was, what would men think, but that I was a general calumniator, a frantic egotist, and a man dangerous to society? The total inability that I felt in myself, to obtain ample and immediate justice, almost drove me mad.

I had previously determined to quit Oxford, and this new goad did but quicken my departure. My preparations were soon made; and from some vague, and to myself undefined ideas, partly of expedition, and partly of letting the president, the college, and the whole university see that I, Hugh Trevor, was no ordinary person, a chaise and four waited my commands at the gate about noon the next day, behind which my goods and chattels were buckled, and I, after taking leave of the two or three friends who were thoughtless or courageous enough to acknowledge me, threw myself indignantly into it, with more maledictions in my heart than my impatient tongue could find energy to utter.

Arrived in London, it especially became me, as I supposed, to assume that consequence which should teach my enemies respect. I had money in my pocket, anger impelling me, and more pride than prudence. A waiter was dispatched from the Gloucester coffeehouse, and apartments for myself and a valet were hired, in Half Moon Street, at three guineas and a half per week. The valet was a sudden decision, originating in the same false feelings that had lately taken possession of me. When I consulted the mistress of the coffee-house concerning apartments, she said, 'You have a servant to be sure, Sir?' 'Yes, madam;' replied my alarmed vanity. 'No, madam;' instantly retorted my veracity, still more alarmed; 'but I mean to hire one.' 'There,' continued she, pointing to a smart well powdered young fellow that was talking to one of the waiters, 'there stands one out of place, who I dare say will be glad of a good master. Here, Philip!'

I was one of the fools who, right or wrong, imagine it behooves them to be consistent. I was ashamed to retract, had not learned to prevaricate, and Philip, to whom as a footman I could discover no rational objection, was hired.

My effects were presently removed; my useless valet sent to loiter, and improve himself in vice, as valets usually are, and I left to meditate on the plan I had to pursue.

A little reflection induced me to renounce all thoughts of the church; for which indeed the doubts that the conversation of Turl had inspired me with, the inquiries to which these doubts led, and the disgust I had conceived at the character and conduct of the bishop had well prepared me.

For some time I sat perplexed in thought. During the life of the rector, I had often been told that the law was the road to honour; and when at the university, being eager to secure this said honour to myself, I had laboriously read some of the civilians.[1] I say laboriously, for the task was far from inviting. The obscurity of their terms, the contradictions I thought I discovered, and the voluminous perplexity in which the whole was involved, were no alluring pictures.

With what pleasure did the wearied intellect escape from this wilderness of weeds and brambles, to rove through the paradise of poetry. The minstrelsy of genius, sporting with the fancy rouzing the passions and unfolding the secrets of the heart, could fascinate at all times; while nothing could sooner create lassitude and repugnance than the incongruous jargon of law.

But, alas, who ever heard of a poet being made Lord High Chancellor? Appoint him to such a station and he would act like a madman! Instead of employing his journeymen to dig through the rubbish of ignorance for precedents, he would listen to the wants of the injured, and would conceive that by relieving them only he could do justice! Did not the history of the world proclaim that, he who would attain wealth and power must turn the prejudices of mankind to their own harm?

CHAPTER II

The play-house, and an old acquaintance: Satirical
portraits: Reception of a new comedy; or, of how much
worth are praise and blame?

THESE were painful reflections, and, leaving the case undetermined
for the present, I escaped from them by shifting the scene to the
play-house. It happened to be the first night of a new comedy, and
here in the boxes I perceived an acquaintance, whom I had met at
the house of Ellis. His name was Glibly, and the moment he saw me
enter he advanced and accosted me with that familiarity which was
essential to his character.

Glad of company, in a city where I was so little known, I freely
entered into conversation with him; and the amusement he afforded
me well repaid my complaisance. He had long been what is called
upon the town, and was acquainted more or less with all orders of
men. He was intimate with authors, actors, and artists, of every kind
and degree; knew their private and public history, could give anecdotes of each, and enumerate their various performances. Opera
girls and their keepers, musicians and musical dilletanti, connoiseurs
and their jackalls, (picture dealers and auctioneers) collectors, shell
fossil and fiddle fanciers, in short every class of idlers that I have
since found swarming in this miscellaneous town ranked among his
acquaintance.

He had long, as I afterward discovered, been a newspaper critic;
had written prologues, appeared in poet's corner, abounded in sarcastic remarks, and possessed an Athenian loquacity. He had indeed
a copious vocabulary, an uncommon aptitude of phrase, though not
free from affectation, and a tide of tongue that was incessant.

He probably thought my personal appearance creditable, for he
did not quit me during the performance, but amused me with the
satirical portraits of various people, whom he pointed out to me in
the house.

'Do you see that man,' said he, 'who is just entering; three boxes
distant on the right? He is handing two ladies to their seats, and is
followed by a youngster who is all pertness and powder. They make
a great shew, and on a first night give an appearance of good company. That is Mynheer van Hopmeister, a Dutch dancing-master,

with his daughter, son, and a kept mistress. They live all together on very good terms; and his own girl has preserved her character by her ugliness, affectation, and ill breeding. He drives about in his chariot, which passing in the street you would suppose belonged to a Neapolitan Count, or a German Envoy at least. He gives dinners occasionally of several removes,[1] to which he invites all the fools and fiddlers he can find, treats with French wines, and usually makes up a quartet party for the evening, which he spoils by playing a principal part himself. He is nearly two thousand pounds in debt; and, in all things mimicking the great, has been obliged to put his affairs to nurse.[2] Except the booby his son, he is the most prating, forward, ignorant coxcomb of my acquaintance; and that is a bold word. But his impertinence makes him amusing: I will introduce you.'

I thanked my gentleman for his politeness, but declined the offer: and he continued.

'Look at that man in brown, leaning against the pillar! He is a painter, and a man of genius; but the greatest ass existing!'

'How? Of genius, and—!'

'Hear and judge for yourself. No man has studied his art with so much assiduity and zeal, or practised it with greater enthusiasm; but, instead of confining himself to portrait-painting, by which with half the labour and one tenth of the talent he might have made a fortune, he devoted all his youth to poverty and starving, and undertook a series of paintings that would have immortalized a man under the patronage of Leo. X.[3] This task he was years in accomplishing, living all the while on little better than bread and water, and that procured by robbing his nights of the hours of rest; for his pride, which he calls independence, is as great as his ambition, which he dignifies with the title of a love of fame. But the most prominent trait in his character is a jealous——'

Here my commentator, suddenly interrupting himself, pressed my arm, and bade me turn to the left.

'There,' said he pointing, 'is a Mr. Migrate; a famous clerical character, and as strange an original as any this metropolis affords. He is not entitled to make a figure in the world either by his riches, rank, or understanding; but with an effrontery peculiar to himself he will knock at any man's door, though a perfect stranger, ask him questions, give him advice, and tell him he will call again to give him more the first opportunity. By this means he is acquainted with every body, but knows nobody; is always talking, yet never says any thing; is perpetually putting some absurd interrogation, but before it is possible he should understand the answer puts another. His desire to be informed torments himself and every man of his acquaintance, which is almost every man he meets; yet, though he lives inquiring, he will die consummately ignorant. His brain is a kind of rag shop, receiving and returning nothing but rubbish. It is as difficult to affront as to get rid of him; and though you fairly bid him begone to-day, he will knock at your door, march into your house, and if possible keep you answering his unconnected fifty times answered queries tomorrow. He is the friend and the enemy of all theories and of all parties; and tortures you to decide for him which he ought to chuse. As far as he can be said to have opinions, they are crude and contradictory in the extreme; so that in the same breath he will defend and oppose the same system. With all this confusion of intellect, there is no man so wise but he will prescribe to him how he ought to act, and even send him written rules for his conduct. He has been a great traveller, and continually abuses his own countrymen for not adopting the manners and policy of the most ignorant, depraved, and barbarous nations of Europe and Africa. He pretends to be the universal friend of man, a philanthropist on the largest scale, yet is so selfish that he would willingly see the world perish, if he could but secure paradise to himself. Indeed he can think of no other being; and his child, his canary bird, his cookmaid, or his cat, are the most extraordinary of God's creatures. This is the only consistent trait in his character. In the same sentence, he frequently joins the most fulsome flattery and some insidious question; that asks the person, whom he addresses, if he do not confess himself to be both knave and fool. Delicacy of sentiment is one of his pretensions, though his tongue is licentious, his language coarse, and he is occasionally seized with fits of the most vulgar abuse. He declaims against dissimulation, yet will smilingly accost the man whom——'Ha! Migrate! How do you do? Give me leave to introduce you to Mr. Trevor, a friend of mine; a gentleman and a scholar; just come from Oxford. Your range of knowledge and universal intimacy, with men and things, may be useful to him; and his erudite acquisitions, and philosophical research, will be highly gratifying to an inquirer like you. An intercourse between you must be mutually pleasing and beneficial, and I am happy to bring you acquainted.'

This, addressed to the man whom he had been satirizing so unsparingly, was inconceivable! The unabashed facility with which he veered, from calumny to compliment, the very moment too after he had accused the man whom he accosted of dissimulation, struck me dumb. I had perhaps seen something like it before, but nothing half so perfect in its kind. It doubly increased my stock of knowledge; it afforded a new instance of what the world is, and a new incitement to ask how it became so? The inquiry at first was painful, and half convinced me of the truth of manicheism;[1] but deeper research taught me that the errors of man do not originate in the perversity of his nature, but of his ignorance.[2]

These however were most of them after thoughts, for Glibly did not allow us any long pause.

'Yonder, in the green boxes,' said he, 'I perceive Mrs. Fishwife, the actress. She should have played in the comedy we are come to see, but threw up her part from scruples of conscience. It was not sufficiently refined for her exquisite sensibility; it wounded her feelings, offended her morals, and outraged her modesty. Yet in the Green-room, she is never happy unless when the men are relating some lewd tale, or repeating obscene jests; at every one of which she bursts into a horse laugh, and exclaims—'Oh, you devil! But I don't hear you! I don't understand a word you say!' To heighten the jest, her armours are as public as the ladies on Harris's List.'[3]

'But perhaps there is something violently offensive and immoral, in the part she refused?'

'Not a syllable. The writer is too dull even for a *double entendre*, as you will hear. Mere pretence. The author, who happens by some odd accident to have more honesty than wit, and could not in conscience comply with the present vicious mode of bestowing indiscriminate praise on actors, when no small mixture of blame had been merited by many of them, forbore to write a preface to his last piece; from which she had thought herself secure of a large dose of flattery. This is an offence she can never pardon.'

'I have heard,' said Migrate, 'that our actresses are become exceedingly squeamish.'

'Oh ridiculous beyond belief. I have a letter in my pocket from a young friend in a country company, the ladies of which have their sensibility strung up to so fine a tone that he cannot take the tragedy of King Lear for his benefit, because not one of them will play either Regan or Goneril. If their feelings are so exquisite in the country, where our wise laws treat players as vagabonds, what must they be when loaded with all the legal, tragic, and royal dignity of a London theatre ?'

This was so incredible that I expressed my doubts of the fact; but they were ill founded, for Glibly produced the letter.

A moment afterward two more of his acquaintance caught his eye.

'Look to the right,' said he; 'the box next the gallery. There they sit! Mr. and Mrs. Whiffle-Wit! They are now in state! They have really a capacious appearance! Were Rubens or Jordaens[1] but here, we should have them painted in all the riches of oil colours, grinning in company with Silenus and his ass.[2] Let the poor author beware; they are prodigious critics! Madam can write a farce, or even a solution to an enigma, with as little labour as any lady in the land; and her dear Mr. Whiffle-Wit can set them both to music, with no less facility and genius! Nothing can equal them, except his own jigs on the organ! They never fail to attend the first night of a new play; and their taste is so very refined that nothing less than writing it themselves could afford them satisfaction. They never admire any nonsense but their own. The manager and author have always to thank them for exerting their whole stock of little wit, and abundant envy, to put the house into an ill temper. The favour is the more conspicuous because they are *orderly people*. But that perhaps is a phrase you do not understand, Mr. Trevor ? They never pay for their places; yet always occupy a first row for themselves, and in general the rest of the box for their friends; who they take good care shall be as well disposed toward the house and the author as they are. You may be sure to meet them to-morrow, very industriously knocking at every door where they can gain admission, to tell their acquaintance what a vile piece it was; and what a strange blockhead the manager must be, who had refused farces of their writing, and operas of their setting, yet could dare to insult the town with such trash! They have now continued for years in this state of surprise, and there is no knowing when it will end.'

The satire of Glibly was incessant, till the tinkling of the prompter's bell, and the rising of the curtain, put an end to his remarks on persons, and turned them all on the piece. I cannot but own the author opened an ample field for the effluvia of critic gall. I know not whether Glibly might influence the tone of my mind, but I think I never felt such ineffable contempt for any human production as for the thing called a comedy, which I that night saw. Disjointed dialogue, no attempt at plan or fable, each scene a different story, and each story improbable and absurd, quibbles without meaning, puns without point, cant without character, sentiments as dull as they were false, and a continual outrage on manners, morals and common sense, were its leading features. Yet, strange to tell, the audience endured it all; and, by copious retrenchments and plaistering and patching, this very piece had what is called a run![1]

How capricious a thing is public taste! It can regale on garbage, from which Hottentots would turn with loathing, and yet, in the frenzy of idiotism, could reject and condemn Congreve's 'Way of the World!'[2]

Glibly treated the piece with unceasing contempt, yet clapped every scene; and when, on two or three occasions, some few raised their voices and called *off! off!* he more loudly than the rest vociferated, *Go on! go on!* When it was over, he left me; saying it was the most execrable piece he had ever beheld; but he had promised to give it a good character, in the paper with which he was connected, and this he must immediately go and write.

CHAPTER III

Repetition of doubts: A very old acquaintance: Another pleasing rencontre: Perplexity and suspense created

THE adventures of the evening sent me home with no very agreeable reflections. What a world was this! How replete with folly, hypocrisy, and vice! What certainly had the man of virtue that his claims should be heard? Amid the tumultuous pursuits of selfishness, where all were eager to gratify their own passions and appease the capricious cravings of vanity, how might truth and worth ascertain success? The comedy I had seen had convinced me that farce, inanity, and supreme nonsense, might not only pass current but find partisans; yet proofs in abundance were on record that genius itself had no security against faction, envy, and mistaken opposition. I was at present in a state of warfare: and were judges like these to give the meed of victory? How many creatures had the powerful and the proud obedient to their beck; ever ready to affirm, deny, say and unsay; and, by falsehood and defamation, involve in ruin men whose souls were the most pure, and principles the most exalted!

For some days I remained in a state of suspense, continually determining to seek the satisfaction which I supposed my injuries demanded, but undecided with respect to the method.

This delay was still prolonged by another event. My man Philip, one morning when he brought my breakfast, told me that a woman in the house, who lived with a young lady on the second floor, had asked him various questions concerning me; saying she was sure she knew me, that she loved me from her soul, for that I had once saved the life of her and her dear boy, and that she wished very much to see me.

At first this account surprised me. A woman and a boy whose lives I had saved? Where is she, said I? Below in the kitchen, answered Philip. I bade him desire her to come up; and in a few minutes a woman about the age of forty entered, but of whose countenance I had no clear recollection. 'I beg pardon, Sir,' said she, 'for my boldness, but your name I believe is Mr. Trevor?'

'It is.'

'Mr. Hugh Trevor?'

'The same.'

'God in his mercy bless and keep you! Since the night that you saved my life, I never went to bed without praying for you. But you were always a kind, dear, good child; and your uncle, Mr. Elford, was the best of men!'

The epithet, child, and the name of Elford instantly solved the riddle: it was poor Mary; and the boy, whose life I had saved, was the child of which she was delivered, after the adventure of the barn. Her features suddenly became as it were familiar to me. She revived a long train of ideas, inspiring that kind of melancholy pleasure which mind so much delights to encourage. I kissed her with sincere good will: and in sympathy with my feelings the poor creature, yielding to her affections, clasped me round the neck, pressed me to her cheek, exclaimed 'God in heaven for ever bless you!' then, suddenly recollecting herself, with that honest simplicity which was so constitutionally her character, dropped on her knees, and added, 'I humbly beg pardon, Sir, for being so bold!'

After some persuasion, I prevailed on her to sit down: but I could not conquer her timidity and imaginary inferiority so far as to induce her to partake of my breakfast. 'She knew her duty better;

I was a gentleman, once her dear young master, and she should always adore me, and act as was befitting a poor servant, like her.'

We talked over former affairs, and she brought many scenes of my early youth strongly to recollection. On inquiry, she told me she had apprenticed her son to a printer; that till this period she had fed, clothed, and educated him by her own industry; and that he was now likely to be no longer burthensome to her, being an apt and industrious boy, and already capable of supplying himself with clothes by his over-work.

I farther learnt, from her discourse, that she lived with a young lady, whom she affectionately loved; and there was something mysterious occasionally in her phrases, that led me to imagine her mistress had been unfortunate. 'She had been a kind mistress to her; she loved her in her heart. Poor young lady! she did not deserve the mishaps she had met with; and it was a shame that some men should be so base as they were: but, though all the world should turn their back on her, she would not be so wicked. Poor women were born to be misused, by false-hearted men; and, if they had no pity for one another, what must become of them?'

I asked if she had lived with the lady long? She answered, that first and last she had known her ever since she left Mr. Elford's service.

'What! Was she of our county?'

'Yea.'

'Was I acquainted with her?'

Mary hesitated, and my curiosity was rouzed—'What was the lady's name?'

'Miss Lydia Wilmot.'

'Wilmot? Wilmot? Surely, not Miss Wilmot, the niece of the bishop of *****?'

'No, no,' said Mary, ''a's not his niece, 'a has better blood in her veins; thof mayhap 'a may have had her failings. God help us! who is without 'em? A bishop? Lord ha' mercy on us! No Christian soul could have believed there was so much wickedness in the world!'

My impatience increased, and I eagerly demanded—'Did she ever live with the bishop?'

Poor Mary knew not what to answer; I perceived her confusion. 'Go, Mary,' said I, 'and tell Miss Wilmot that Mr. Trevor presents his compliments to her, and will be glad to speak to her the moment she is at leisure.'

After a little hesitation Mary went, continued up stairs some time, and at last returned with—'Miss Wilmot's compliments: she should be glad to see me.'

I hurried to her apartment. My conjectures were too well founded to be false: it was the same Miss Wilmot to whom I had been introduced by the bishop, the sister of the guide of my studies and the friend of my youth. Her embarrassment was considerable, she sunk on the sopha as she curtsied, pointed to a chair, and faintly requested I would sit down.

I exerted myself to assume the tone that should tranquilize her feelings; and by asking and answering my own questions, and endeavouring myself to sustain the conversation, brought her with some little difficulty to join in it.

I was burning to interrogate her concerning the bishop, but was restrained by the fear of wounding her sensibility. I inquired after her brother, but him I found she had not lately seen. I forebore to be minute, but it appeared that they knew not the place of each other's abode. I sat with her an hour; but, notwithstanding my impatience, perceiving she evaded the subject I wished to introduce, and turned the discourse on the common place occurrences of the day. I was too respectful of her delicacy to violate it, and left her with an invitation to drink tea with me the following afternoon, which she accepted.

I saw Mary again in the interim, had some discourse with her, and, by several phrases which she once more let fall, was involved in greater perplexity. A person of my family had *a ruinated* Miss Wilmot of all hope; she never could have justice and right done her now; that was *unpossable*. But mayhap all things *was* for the best. The base man had shewn that he was not worth having. She was sorry, both on her ladyship's account and mine; but there was no help for it. God send him a good end! but she feared it! Such wickedness could never prosper.

This language was totally incomprehensible!—'A person of my family? The base man? Sorry on my account?' What did she mean?

Mary was afraid she had said too much—'I dare not tell you, dear good Sir,' continued she; 'only don't you be *cunsarned*; it is no blame of yours; you will know soon enough.'

In this uncertainty she left me, impatiently hoping some farther explanation from Miss Wilmot; of which I was not disappointed. The afternoon came, Mary announced her mistress, we were left alone, and I could no longer forbear expressing my desire of knowing her history.

At first she felt some reluctance, but, when I informed her how much Mary had already told, she sighed deeply, and said, 'I find, Sir, it is in vain to think of concealment; I will, therefore, since you desire it, relate the few events that are remarkable in my unfortunate life. I fear they are more blameable than extraordinary; for, from what I hear and see in this great city, mine are no uncommon misfortunes. I even fear I am hitherto less wretched and guilty than thousands. God only knows for what I am reserved!'

CHAPTER IV

The story of Miss Wilmot: Family misfortunes: A father's death: A brother's disappointment: Intelligence that astonishes me: Wakefield characterized: The death of Miss Wilmot's mother; and the dread of fatal consequences: Piety and compassion of a bishop: Deep designs of Wakefield: The good faith and affection of a poor adherent

'My father was an officer in the army, in which, though he served all his life, he only attained the rank of major. He was twice married, the second time to my mother at the age of thirty, by whom he had five children, who, except my brother and myself, did not arrive at maturity. Being reduced to the income of half-pay, they retired into their native county, where they lived with such strict œconomy that they contrived to educate us better perhaps than the children of people of much larger fortune.

'My brother was the eldest child, and I the youngest, so that there was an interval of fifteen years between us. My father had been well educated, loved letters, and undertook to be my brother's instructor himself to the age of fourteen. At this period my brother was admitted a chorister at the cathedral of ——, at which city my parents had fixed their residence. They were respected by all the inhabitants, whose wealth, birth, and pride, did not place them at too great a distance; and it was a severe mortification to be unable to provide better for their son; but there was no remedy.

'The disappointments of my father's life had given him a melancholy cast, with an aptitude to be dissatisfied; and this propensity was strongly communicated to my brother. The danger of a war between England and Spain[1] called my father up to town, in the hope of being once more put on actual service. But in this his hopes again were frustrated; and expence without benefit was incurred. Early, however, in the American war, he obtained his wishes; unhappily obtained them, for, having been long unused to the baneful severity of camps, he and many more brave men were carried off, by the damps of the climate to which he was sent. This happened when I was but nine years old; and my mother was left with what little their œconomy had collected, and such scanty provision as is made for officers widows.

'My brother, however, who was truly affectionate, and active in efforts to protect us, afforded my mother some aid. From being a chorister, he had gained admission into the grammar-school; of which, while he remained there, he was the pride and boast. Immediately after our father's death, from the recommendation of his own merit and the misfortunes of the family, he was appointed a Latin usher in the same school; in which station he remained five years. The difference of our age made him consider himself something rather like a father than a brother to me: he loved me tenderly, took every method to improve and provide for me, and expected in return something like parental obedience. The manners of my mother were of the mild and pleasing kind, with which qualities she endeavoured to familiarize me, and the behaviour of the whole family gained general approbation and esteem.

'My brother was deeply smitten with the love of letters: his poetical essays were numerous, many of them were sent up to London and readily admitted into periodical publications.

'Anxious to place his family in that rank which he had been taught to suppose it deserved, for my father and mother were both, though not noble, well born, he did not rest satisfied with these attempts: he wrote a tragedy, and, by the advice of people who pretended to have a knowledge of such affairs, determined to go to London, that he might, if possible, get it on the stage. From this my mother would fain have dissuaded him, but his arguments and importunity at length prevailed. He was then but nine and twenty, and I fourteen.

'I could ill describe to you the state of anxiety and suspence in which his various literary efforts involved him, while he remained in London: but in about two years he returned to the country, despairing of that pleasure, profit, and fame, which hope had delusively taught him to consider as his due. This was the period at which he once more became an usher of the school where you were educated. This too was the period at which my misfortunes began.

'And now, Mr. Trevor, I am coming to events in which you, without any knowledge or interference of your own, may be said to be a partaker.'

She paused a moment: and I, with amazement, doubt, and increasing ardour, requested she would proceed.

'The name of Wakefield must certainly be familiar to you?'

'It is: I am sorry to say it is the name my mother at present bears.'

'If you feel sorrow, Mr. Trevor, what must my feelings be? Mine! who, had there been truth or honour in man, ought to have borne that name myself. Mine! who, when I first heard of your mother's marriage, should not have felt so severe a pang had a dagger been struck to my heart. Mine! who from that moment, or rather from the fatal and guilty moment when I confided in an unprincipled man, have never known that cheerfulness and peace, which once were the inmates of my bosom!'

'You astonish me, madam! Wakefield?'

'Wakefield! Him have I to thank for loss of self-respect, a brother's love, and perhaps a parent's life! I was my mother's companion, consolation, and pride. How can I estimate a mother's grief? She died within a year. Have I not reason to believe her days were shortened by her daughter's guilt?'

The pain of recollection was agonizing. She burst into a flood of tears: nor could every effort she made keep down the deep sobs that for some minutes impeded speech. I used every endeavour to appease and calm her mind: she seemed sensibly touched by that sympathy which intensely pervaded me; and, as soon as she could recover herself, thus continued.

'The kind part you take in my affliction, Mr. Trevor, affords me greater relief than any that perhaps I have felt for years. It is true the faithful Mary, good creature, has almost shed tear for tear: but she herself is the daughter of misfortune, and from her, though grateful, it is something like expected. You are a man; you perhaps have been accustomed to the society of those whose pleasure is the most exquisite when they can most contribute to the miseries of woman: that you should be virtuous enough to contemn such instruction, does more than sooth feelings like mine: and I think we esteem benefits the more the less we expect them.'

'But where, madam, did you first meet with Mr. Wakefield?'

'In the city of —— where he was bred, under his father, to the profession of the law. From what I have seen of you, and from what I have heard of your talents and understanding, I should have expected you to have been the child of extraordinary parents; otherwise, I do not much wonder at your mother's conduct, superior as she was to Mr. Wakefield in years; for, of all the men I ever saw, he is the most deceitful, plausible, and dangerous. Neither man nor woman are safe with him; and his arts are such as to over-reach the most cautious. He has words at will; and his wit and invention, which are extraordinary, are employed to entrap, humiliate, degrade and ruin all with whom he has intercourse. His ambition is to gratify his desires, by triumphing over the credulity of the unsuspecting, whom he contemns for their want of his own vices. It was he that, after having seduced me, placed me in the family of the bishop, laid the plan that I should pass for his lordship's niece, by various falsehoods cajoled me to acquiesce (the chief of which was, that the project was but to save appearances, till he could make me his wife) left me in that unworthy prelate's power, then, returning to the country, plotted the marriage with your mother, and, by his intimate knowledge of the weakness or vice of each character, which he seems to catch instinctively, adapted his scheme with such cunning to the avarice of his uncle as to gain his concurrence and aid.

'It was my clandestine departure at this period, and the rumours and suspicions to which it gave birth, that again drove my brother from the country. For some months neither he nor my mother knew what was become of me.

'At length her decline, and the extreme affliction of dying and never hearing of me more, occasioned her to prevail on my brother to advertise me in all the papers. This he did, by inserting the initials of my name, and such other tokens as he knew must be intelligible to me, should I read the advertisement; informing me at the same time of the dying state of my mother.

'His plan so far succeeded as to come to my knowledge. I read the paper, was seized with horror at the information, and immediately wrote in answer. It was too late! My mother was dead! and I left in that state of distraction to which by a single moment's weakness I had been thus fatally conducted!

'Grief, despondency, and resentment, took firm possession of my brother's mind. He wrote me a dreadful letter of the state of his feelings; and, though he forebore explicitly to accuse me of my mother's death, I could perceive the thought pervaded his mind. After her funeral, he came up to London; but refused all intercourse with me, once excepted. A few days only after that on which the bishop introduced you to me, he came, knocked at the door, inquired if I were at home, and sent up his name.

'Of all the moments of my life, that was the most awful! A death-like coldness seized me! The sound of my brother's name was horror! I know not what I said to the servant, but the feelings of Mr. Wilmot were too racking for delay: he was presently before me, dressed in deep mourning; I motionless and dead; he haggard, the image of despair; so changed in form that, but for the sharp and quick sighted suspicions of guilt, had I met him, I should have passed him without suspecting him to be my brother.

'I can tell you but little of what passed. His sentences were incoherent, but half finished, and bursting with passion that was neither grief nor rage, nor reproach nor pardon, though a mixture of them all. The chief impression that he left upon my mind was, that he should soon be freed from the torment of existence: not by the course of nature; he complained, with agony, that labour, dis-appointment, injustice, and contamination itself could not kill him; but die he would!

'From that day to this, I have never seen or heard word of him more. The deep despair with which he uttered his last resolution has kept me in a state of uninterrupted terror. I daily read all the papers I can buy or borrow with the excruciating dread, every paragraph I come to, of catching his name, and, Oh! insufferable horror! reading an account of his death!

'My state of being seems wholly changed! I am no longer the same creature! My faculties, which formerly compared to those of my brother I thought slow even to stupidity, are now awakened to such keenness of discernment that the world is multiplied upon me a million fold! Sometimes it is all intelligence, though of a dark and terrific hue; at other moments objects swarm so thick that they dance confusion, and give me a foretaste of madness, to which I have now a constant fear that I shall be driven. My own deep shame, the loss of the man whom like an idiot I dearly loved, my mother's death, my brother's letter, and particularly his last visit, have altogether given such an impetuosity to my thoughts as I want the power to repel. Whither they will hurry me God only knows. At one interval I imagine the earth contains nothing but evil! At another, strange to tell! all is good! all is wise! all harmonious! and I reproach my own extreme folly for wanting happiness under so perfect a system!

'Nay, there are times in which I persuade myself I have been guilty of no crime! that there is no such thing as crime! and that the distinctions of men are folly, invented by selfishness and continued by ignorance!

'Indeed, I know not whither my thoughts do not range. At one moment, I seem as if I were actually free to penetrate the bowels of the earth, dive into the deep, transport myself with a wish from planet to planet, or from sun to sun, endure all extremes, overcome them, master all resistance, and be myself omnipotent! The very next instant, perhaps, I doubt if I have really any existence! if waking and dreaming be not the same thing! and whether either of them are definable or intelligible! At this very moment, I know not whither my thoughts are wandering! or whether I ought not to snatch up this or the other weapon of death, and instantly strike you breathless, for having dared to listen to my shame!'

While she spoke, her eyes sparkled, and flashed with that wildness which her tongue with such rapid imagery pictured forth. Had it continued, the tumult might have been dangerous; perhaps fatal; but fortunately the firmness and intrepidity of my mind were equal to the scene. With a cool and collected benevolence of look, and with a determined though not severe tone of voice I said: 'My dear Miss Wilmot, be calm; pause a moment; recollect yourself; I am your friend, I hope you will never find another man your foe.'

The idea suggested an opposite association to her active thoughts; in an instant the fire vanished, her eyes were suffused, her features relaxed, and she again burst into tears and sobs. I was careful not to interrupt the tide of passion; it gave relief; and she presently became more calm. Desirous as I was of hearing particulars concerning the bishop, I gladly listened when, after a sufficient pause, she thus resumed her tale.

'You must not wonder, Mr. Trevor, that I do not tell my story in a connected manner. Whenever I think on the subject, the incidents I have related press upon my mind, produce sensations I cannot command, and for a time obliterate less momentous circumstances.

'The part which the bishop acted in this tragic drama is what I have yet to relate. Mr. Wakefield's father, who let me here remark was an unprincipled man and died insolvent, happened professionally, as a lawyer, to have certain temporalities,[1] in the county where he resided, to manage for the bishop. This brought his son acquainted with the character of the prelate. The relationship in which I stood to him'—I interrupted her.

'To whom, madam?'

'The bishop.'

'I understood he was no relation of yours?'

'He is and is not.'

'Pray explain.'

'He is by marriage, twice removed; not the least by blood. His late lady, a widow when he married her, was the half-sister of my father's first wife; so that by the courtesy of custom he is called my uncle. He is too artful not to have a shelter for his proceedings.—' She continued:

'An adept which as I have before said Mr. Wakefield is, in reading the weak and vicious inclinations of the human heart, he hoped not only to have rid himself of importunity from me, but, by rendering me subservient to this unholy bishop's vile propensities, to have played a deeper game. This is his delight. The pleasure he receives in making other men's follies, passions, and vices, administer to his own, is the greatest he knows. Were he but the cunningest man on earth, he would think himself the greatest.

'His character sympathized with that of the bishop, who was happy to find so artful and so active an agent. It was not till I had been in the prelate's family some time that the whole of their design was explained to me. The bishop frequently used strange, and to me unintelligible expressions; disgusting from any man, but from him inexpressively offensive and odious; yet the full import of them I did not so much as suspect.

'Nor did he omit to make the solemnity of his supposed character an abettor to his hypocrisy. Feelings of compassion, moral affection, and christian forgiveness were assumed. When I first entered his house he gave me to understand that he was acquainted with my crime; this, after mentioning it as a serious sin, affecting pity, he qualified away, and, as people in all such situations must, talked an incoherent jargon; that God hated and loved such sinners; that religion was all powerful, but that man was frail; that Christ died to save us, and therefore though we should fall, as perhaps the best of us were subject to back slidings, his mercy was all sufficient.

'But on this and every occasion, he was careful to say nothing open and direct, by which he should be detected. If ever he ventured so far as to excite serious questions from me, he was ever ready with evasive answers, and had something like reasoning to offer, in defence of his own manners and in ridicule of prudery. He began with caution, but when he had accustomed me to such discourse, and after I had heard it repeated even in the presence of his clerical companions, of which you, Mr. Trevor, were once a witness, my surprize wore away; the pain it gave me was diminished, and he became less and less reserved.

'Still however he did not venture openly to declare himself; and Mr. Wakefield was too busy, in wasting your mother's fortune and gratifying his own desires, to attend to those of the bishop. But his prodigality, which is excessive, after a time brought him to London; and the bishop imagined that, with his help, my scruples would at last be conquered.

'The trial was made; not by the cautious bishop, but by Mr. Wakefield. How such a proposition, coming from the man whom I had dearly loved, and whose wife in justice I considered myself to be, was received, you, who have a sense of the feelings of a highly injured and justly indignant heart, may conceive!

'Yet, impassioned determined and almost frantic as I was, it was with difficulty he could relinquish his plan. Till that hour, I never believed him so utterly devoid of principle; but he then laid bare his heart, hoping to make me a convert to its baseness. He exulted in the power we should obtain over this sensual prelate, and the sums which by these means we might extort. He looked with transport forward, to the opening which this would afford for projects still much deeper. The vices of the great, with which he might thus become intimate, afforded a field ample as his own vice could wish. Nor could all the impatience of indignation, with which I continually interrupted him, impede that flow which the subject inspired.

'At length, disgusted beyond sufferance, I abruptly left him, and sought relief from the racking sensations which he had excited. He then entered into a correspondence with me, till I threatened to shew his letters to the bishop. This induced him to desist, and for some time I heard from him no more. At last he wrote once again, informing me that you, Mr. Trevor, were come to London; characterizing you as ignorant of the world and easily deceived; telling me that you were intimate with the bishop; and advising me to promote a plan of marriage between us, which he had proposed to the prelate as the best way, in his own phrase, of making all things smooth!

'I hope the deep shame I felt, when the bishop introduced you and made the experiment, was sufficiently visible to convince you how repugnant my feelings were to such a crime!

'The bishop finding his first purpose thus defeated, and himself encumbered by a kind of claimant, which his acknowledging me as a niece had brought upon him, was determined at all events to rid himself of me. Immediately before he left town, he wrote me a letter, telling me that my loss of character was become too public for me to receive any further countenance, from a man under the moral and divine obligations which every bishop of the church of Christ must be; that he was going on a visit to his diocese; that he could not think of taking me, it was too flagrantly improper; and that he advised and expected I should immediately return to my relations; further hoping that I should see the enormity of my conduct, and reform.

'Oh! Mr. Trevor, what a world is this! Had he offered me money, I should have rejected it with disdain! but he had not even that much charity. I instantly quitted the house with a few shillings only in my pocket.

'Mary had lived with me and my mother for some years before my elopement: after my mother's death, my residence in the bishop's family being known, I sent for her up to town and hired her. Her artless affection made her my confidante; my situation required it; and, when she heard the bishop's letter read, the kind creature with honest anger instantly went and gave him warning.

'A quarter's wages was all her wealth; for the earnings of her labour she had constantly expended on her boy, for whom she seems to have more than a mother's affection. She has been my constant comforter. Seeing the tears in my eyes, as we left the bishop's house, with a look of mingled pity and indignation she exclaimed—"Do not grieve, dear madam; though I work my fingers to the bone, you shall not want." '

Miss Wilmot was proceeding with her narrative, when she was interrupted by the hasty entrance of Mary. 'Oh madam,' said she, 'the dear young lady and her maid are below. They were coming up stairs, but I told them that you had a gentleman with you! Whereof at which the young lady seemed a little in amaze; till I gave her to know that it was only a friend of your brother's, a person from our own honest country, and she would then a gone away, but as I said I was sure you would be glad to see her, and would go up a purpose to your own room. So do you go, madam, and I'll run down and tell her.'

Miss Wilmot immediately took her leave; and, though my curiosity was a little awakened, a sense of decorum would not suffer me to endeavour to see her visitor. I therefore shut the door, and, as soon as all was silent on the stairs, I took my hat and walked out; that by changing the scene I might dissipate a part of the melancholy which her story had produced.

CHAPTER V

Anger unabated: More news of the bishop: Deliberation on the mode of my revenge: The articles answered; and new assailing doubts: A visit to Turl: Advice given and rejected: And former feelings revived

THE next morning, when I came to reflect on all that I had heard, I was surprised with the degree in which, by my mother's marriage with Wakefield, I appeared to be implicated in the history. The character of Wakefield, his prodigality, and total want of principle, were all of a dangerous cast. Not satisfied with beggaring my mother, he had projected to marry me to his mistress. The recollection of him roused resentment, and cunning and inventive as he was described to be, I wished for an opportunity of punishing his baseness, teaching him his own insignificance, and treating him with the contempt he deserved. If attacked, I had not yet learned the philosophy of forbearance. Though I have been hurried forward too fast to narrate every little incident as it occurred, yet it cannot be imagined that I all this while neglected to peruse the defence of the articles published in the bishop's name. No: it was my very first employment, on my arrival in town; and though considerable trouble had been bestowed to disfigure the work, as written by me, yet in substance I found it to be the same. The wrongs of Miss Wilmot quickened my feelings, and, angry as I was with Wakefield, I felt emotions of ten fold bitterness against the bishop.

Association easily conjured up the earl, the president, the tutor, Themistocles, and the injustice and disgrace I had suffered at Oxford. The fermentation was so great that I was determined, immediately, to expose them to the broad shame that should drive them from human society.

In this benevolent project I was confirmed by another piece of intelligence. One of the rich sees of the kingdom had become vacant. The king's *congè d'elire*[1] was issued, and God's holy vicar the Bishop of ***** himself was translated. What could I conclude, but that the defence which I had written had been the cause? I had been made the stepping stone of vice! I remembered the proceeding of the despot, Frederic of Prussia, with the immortal Voltaire: the orange had been squeezed, and the rind thrown to rot in the highway![2]

My teeth gnashed with the abundance of my wrath, and the impotence of my means. I had hitherto forborne to write from a perplexity of different plans. At one moment I determined to address my foes in the public papers; at another I would concentrate the story, and relate the whole in a pamphlet. Now it should be a history; anon a satirical novel; Asmodeus in London,[3] in which I would draw the characters in such perfection that, without mentioning names, the persons should be visible to every eye. But then this would not be sufficiently serious. Thousands might mistake that for fiction which I wished all the world to know was fact. To give them the least shelter was cowardly to myself, treacherous to society, and encouragement to the criminal.

At last, the pamphlet was the mode on which I determined: and it was begun with all the enthusiasm that the accumulating circumstances could not but inspire, in a being constituted like me. Eager after every species of aggravation, my anger could never be hot enough; the gall of my ink was milk to that of my heart. The bitterness of my feelings was tormenting; words that could burn, contempt that could kill, shame that could annihilate, these and nothing less could satisfy me. Could the serpent revenge fly, how would it dart and sting! Happily for man it can only crawl. That

I had been treated with great injustice was true: but of justice my notions were very inadequate; of revenge I had more than enough for a nation.

While hot in the pursuit of this task, I was diverted from it by the publication of an answer to the articles. The moment I saw it advertised, not sufficiently habituated to the vice of indolence myself to recollect that I had an idle footman below, I hurried to the publisher's, purchased it, and returned with a greyhound speed to devour its contents.

Disgusted as I was with the members of the church, and beginning even to doubt of the perfect orthodoxy of the church itself, I still had too high an opinion of my own arguments to imagine the wit of man could overturn them.

My haste had been so great that I had not taken off the paper, in which the pamphlet was wrapped; and in the shop I had read no more than the title-page. What was my surprise when snatching it from my pocket and opening it, I discovered, at the conclusion of a short preface, the name of Turl! it's author!

My emotions were confused. At one moment an answer from him was what I wished; the next it was something like what I feared. In all argument, I had hitherto found him so cool, so collected, and so clear, that, to my imagination, he perhaps was the only man on earth fit to cope with me. But the grating question, 'Was I fit to cope with him?' would now and then recur. I could not but feel that I had, in a certain manner, been subdued and cowed by his greater extent of knowledge, perspicuity, and masculine genius. By thoughts like these my anxiety, if not my ardour, was increased, and I began to read.

My forebodings were fulfilled. The impotence of my arguments was exposed, their absurdity and self-contradiction ridiculed, their evil tendency demonstrated, their falsehood rendered odious, and the author of them treated like a child. My self respect was wounded at every line, each paragraph was a death stab, and I never before felt myself so completely ridiculous.

As a lesson of philosophy it was the most serious, salutary, and impressive I ever received; for though, while reading, I affirmed to myself that every thing urged against me was weak, or ill founded, inconclusive, or absolutely false, yet the arguments returned with increasing and reiterated force, haunting and oppressing me like a painful dream from which I could not awake.

The evil tendency which he proved against my doctrines was the least to be forgotten. As far as I understood myself, I had a sincere love of truth, and an unfeigned desire to benefit, not mislead and oppress, mankind. As the author of the defence, the heavy charge of immorality was brought against me; not by personal attacks on my substitute, the bishop, but by a detail of the consequences of such doctrines.

This event made me pause and consider, though with but little propensity to candour, concerning the pamphlet on which I was then engaged. Consideration however did but seem to confirm me in my purpose. Let my defence be right or wrong, and I had by no means yet decided in the negative, still the turpitude of the bishop and my persecutors was no less flagitious. These incidents once more turned my thoughts toward Turl, whom I knew not whether to admire, love, or hate. I was not so entirely overwhelmed but that I had arguments, at least I had words, at my command. Beside, I felt a wish to communicate to him my projected attack, and perhaps read a part of my pamphlet, that it might, as it certainly must, meet his approbation. I felt satisfied that what he approved could not be wrong. And how disapprove? On former occasions indeed my hopes, in this respect, had been deceived; but now it was impossible! The case was so clear! In the present instance, there could be but one opinion!

Feelings which were not the most honourable to myself, for their source was egotism, had withheld me from visiting him since my return; but these were now subdued, by others that were more imperious. I was not satisfied with requiring his approbation of my plan of vengeance; my choleric vanity challenged him to the lists, and the combat was resolved upon.

As I was going, I recollected the shortness of the period in which his answer had been composed and published, and this did but remind me of the champion I had to encounter.

I found him, as before, tranquily pursuing his labours; except that now he was writing, engaged as I imagined on the grand work he had projected; though his copper and engraving tools lay dispersed by his side. He received me as usual with calmness, but not without an evident mixture of pleasure. Irritable as my feelings were, I had always experienced something infinitely more dissatisfactory in being angry with him than with any other person. In his countenance there was a sedate undeviating rectitude, that, but for my impetuous disdain of all restraint, would have inspired awe; yet, whenever his eye met the eye of another, there was something so benevolent as almost to disarm ill humour.

Replete with new arguments, as I supposed, but which in reality were only a repetition of those I had already adduced, I burst upon him with a multitude of words; defending my own defence of the articles and attacking his answer. He made various ineffectual attempts to arrest my career, and at last was obliged to suffer me to weary myself; after which he calmly replied.

'The best answer I can give, to all you have urged, is to request you will read the defence of the articles and my answer again, with care. Either I am mistaken or you will find every thing you have said already confuted.'

I endeavoured to divert him from this defence by reference, but he continued to urge that he should only weaken his cause by answering desultory arguments in a desultory way; which in the present case would be folly, because his answer was already given in a clear and as he believed conclusive manner.

Finding his purpose not to be shaken, I asked him if he were aware that I was the author of the defence of the articles? He answered that, seeing the bishop's name to the publication, he could not but suppose the bishop himself had been intimately concerned in the writing of the work: but, from what I had formerly told him, he had suspected me to be a fellow-labourer.

'If so,' said I, 'Mr. Turl, how did it happen that you felt no aversion to the confutation, as you suppose, of a man for whom you had professed a regard?'

He replied, 'You, Mr. Trevor, are well acquainted with my answer: "Socrates is my friend, Plato is my friend, but truth is more my friend." If I myself had written falsehood yesterday, and now knew it to be such, I would answer it to day. Would not you?'

It was a home question, and I was silent.

This subject ended, he made some kind and cordial inquiries concerning my present pursuits, and these furnished the opportunity of unburthening my heart. I related to him, with all the indignation which resentment inspired, my whole history; and ended with informing him of my determination to publish the vice and infamy of all the parties to the world. On this a dialogue began.

'Which way will you publish them?'

'In a narrative, that I am now writing.'

'A sense of duty has obliged me to tell you that, in my opinion you have been guilty of several mistakes already: you are now intent upon another.'

'How so?'

'The excess of your anger perverts your judgment, and you cannot write such a narrative without keeping your passions in a vitiated state. Owing to the prejudices of mankind, you will impeach your own credibility. Moderate men will think you rash, the precise will call you a detractor, and the partisans, who are numerous, of the persons you will attempt to expose will raise a cry against you, that will infinitely overpower the equivocal proofs you can produce. It will become a question of veracity, and yours will be invalidated by the improbability, if not of the guilt, at least of the folly of your persecutor's conduct. You cannot reform them, will do yourself much harm, and the world no good. You will not only misemploy your time for the present, but impede your power for the future.'

'If such be the consequences of honestly speaking the truth, what is the conduct that I am to pursue? Am I to be a hypocrite, and listen with approbation while men boast of their vices, glory in their false principles, and proclaim the destructive projects they mean to pursue?'

'No.'

'Is not silence approbation?'

'Yes.'

'Yet your system will not allow me to speak!'

'You accuse my system unjustly: it is the manner of speaking to which it attends. The precaution of speaking so as to produce good, not bad, consequences is the doctrine I wish to inculcate. He that should sweep the streets of pea-shells, lest old women might break their necks, would doubtless have good intentions; yet his office would only be that of a scavenger. Speak, but speak to the world at large, not to insignificant individuals. Speak in the tone of a benevolent and disinterested heart, and not of an inflamed and revengeful imagination! otherwise you endanger yourself, and injure society.'

'What, shall any cowardly regard to my own safety induce me to the falsehood of silence? For is it not falsehood, of the most contemptible and atrocious kind, to forbear publishing such miscreants to the world? It is this base this selfish prudence, that encourages men like these to proceed from crime to crime. Had they been exposed in their first attempt, their effrontery could never have been so enormous. No! I am determined! Were my life to be the sacrifice, I will hold them up a beacon, alike to the wicked and the unwary! Will paint them in the gross and odious colours that alone can characterize their actions, and drive them from the society of mankind!'

'Do you conceive you are now speaking in the spirit of justice, or of revenge?'

'Of both.'

He who is resolved not to be convinced does not wish to hear his last argument answered. With this short reply, therefore, I rose, took my hat, made some aukward apology, was sorry we were fated to differ so continually in principle, but each man must act from his own judgment; was obliged to him nevertheless for his sincerity and good intention, and once more took my leave, more angry than pleased, much in the same abrupt manner that I had formerly done. The similarity indeed forced itself upon me as I was quitting the door, and I knew not whether to accuse myself of pettishness, obstinacy, and want of candour; or him of singularity, and an inflexible sternness of opposition. At all events, my purpose of publishing my pamphlet as soon as it should be written was fixed; and to that labour I immediately returned.

CHAPTER VI

Story of Miss Wilmot concluded: Olivia not forgotten:
A gaming-table friend characterized: Modern magicians:
Suspicious principles: The friend's absence, and return:
Allegorical wit, and dangerous advice

VARIOUS causes induced me to take the first opportunity of again visiting Miss Wilmot; her story had inspired compassion and respect. She might be in want, and to relieve her would give me pleasure. Beside which I had a number of questions to ask, especially concerning this Wakefield; and some desire to know who and what the young lady, who was so great a favourite with Mary, might be.

In the evening I saw Miss Wilmot; and, in offering her with as much delicacy as possible pecuniary aid, she informed me that fortunately she had found a friend; generous, beneficent, and tender;

not less prudent than kind; and, though very young, possessed of a dignity of understanding such as she had never before met in woman. Miss Wilmot spoke with so much enthusiasm that I, whose imagination readily caught fire, felt a redoubled wish to see this angel.

I hinted it to Miss Wilmot, but with apologies; and she replied that the young lady had expressly requested her visits might be private, and her name concealed. I inquired how they had first become acquainted, and learned that it was in consequence of the friendly zeal of Mary, who had a countrywoman that lived servant in the family of this young lady, and from whom she gained intelligence of the liberal and noble qualities of her mistress. The first retreat of Miss Wilmot, after leaving the house of the bishop, was to a poor lodging provided by Mary. From this she was removed by the friendly young lady to her present asylum, till she could find the means of maintaining herself; and had since been supplied with necessaries through the same channel. 'The favours she confers on me,' said Miss Wilmot, 'are not so properly characterised by delicacy, as by a much higher quality; an open and unaffected sensibility of soul; a benevolent intention of promoting human happiness; and an unfeigned heart felt pleasure which accompanies her in the performance of this delightful duty. The particulars I have now related,' continued she, 'were all that remained to be told when I was interrupted by Mary, at our last meeting; and you are now acquainted with my whole story.'

Every conversation that I had with Miss Wilmot confirmed the truth of her own remark, that her intellect had been greatly awakened by the misfortunes in which her mistakes had involved her; and particularly by the deep despondency of her brother. He, Wakefield, and the young lady were the continual topics of her discourse; but her brother the most and oftenest. I was several times a witness that the papers were daily perused by her, with all those quick emotions of dread which she had so emphatically described. The terror of his parting resolution was almost too much for her, and it was with difficulty she preserved her mind from madness. I saw its tendency, and took every opportunity to sooth and calm her troubled spirit; and my efforts were not wholly ineffectual.

In the mean time I did not forget that I was not possessed of the purse of Fortunatus.[1] On the contrary, I had a mighty task before me. The image of Olivia incessantly haunted me. The ineffable beauty of her form, the sweet and never to be forgotten sensibility that she displayed when I first saw her in the presence of Andrews, at Oxford, and the native unaffected dignity of her mind were my constant themes of meditation. Must I behold her in the arms of another? The thought was horror! Yet how to obtain her? If I studied the law, preliminary forms alone would consume years. From the church I was banished. A military life I from principle abhorred; even my half ripe philosophy could not endure the supposition of being a hireling cut-throat. Literature might afford me fame, but of riches gained from that source there was scarcely an example.

From literary merit however men had obtained civil promotion; it must not therefore be neglected. Of such neglect indeed my passionate love of letters would not admit. With respect to law, though infinitely too slow for the rapidity of my desires, still it was good to be prepared for all events. I therefore entered myself of the Temple, and thus began another snail-pace journey of term keeping.

Youth is a busy season, and, though occupations are forced upon it of a nature too serious for its propensities, it fails not to find time for amusement. In St. James's-street, near the palace, was a billiard-table, to which when an inmate with Lord Idford I had resorted. It was frequented by officers of the Guards, and other persons who were chiefly supposed to be men of some character and fashion. Among them I had met a young gentleman of the name of Belmont, remarkable for the easy familiarity of his address, an excellent billiard player, and who had in a manner attached himself to me, by a degree of attention that was engaging. I thought indeed that I discovered contradictory qualities in him; but the sprightliness of his imagination, and the whimsicality of his remarks, compensated for a looseness of principle, which was too apparent to be entirely overlooked.

He frequently turned the conversation on the county of which I was a native, having, as he informed me, and as his discourse shewed, many acquaintance in that county. Since my return to town I had again met him, and he had sought my company with increasing ardour.

Flattered by this preference, and often delighted with the flights of his fancy, I returned his advances with great cordiality. His appearance was always genteel, but from various circumstances

I collected that he was not at present rich. His expectations, according to his own account, were great; and his familiar habits of treating every man, be his rank or fashion what it might, seemed to signify that he considered himself their equal.

When we first met, after my return to town, he was desirous I should relate to him where I had been, and what had befallen me: and when he heard that I had visited the county of —— he became more pressing to know all that had happened. To encourage me, he gave me the following account of himself.

'For my own part, Mr. Trevor, I am at present under a cloud. I shall sometime or another break forth, and be a gay fellow once again: nor can I tell how soon. I love to see life, and I do not believe there is a man in England of my age, who has seen more of it. Perhaps you will laugh when I tell you that, since we last parted, I have been *vagabondizing*. You do not understand the term? It offends your delicacy? I will explain.'

He saw he had raised my curiosity, and with a loquacity that sat easy on him, and a vivacity of imagery in which as I have said he excelled, he thus continued.

'Perhaps you will think a gentleman degraded, by having subjected himself to the denomination of a vagrant? Though, no; you have wit enough to laugh at gray-beards, and their ridiculous forms and absurd distinctions. Know then, there is a certain set or society of men, frequently to be met in straggling parties about this kingdom, who, by a peculiar kind of magic, will metamorphose an old barn, stable, or out-house, in such a wonderful manner that the said barn, stable, or out-house, shall appear, according as it suits the will or purpose of the said magicians, at one time a prince's palace; at another a peasant's cottage; now the noisy receptacle of drunken clubs and wearied travellers, called an inn; anon the magnificent dome of a Grecian temple. Nay, so vast is their art that, by pronouncing audibly certain sentences which are penned down for them by the head or master magician, they transport the said barn, stable, or out-house, thus metamorphosed, over sea or land, rocks, mountains or deserts, into whatsoever hot, cold, or temperate region the director wills, with as much facility as my lady's squirrel can crack a nut. What is still more wonderful, they carry all their spectators along with them, without the witchery of broomsticks.

'These necromancers, although whenever they please they become princes, kings, and heroes, and reign over all the empires of the vast and peopled earth; though they bestow governments, vice-royalties, and principalities upon their adherents, divide the spoils of nations among their pimps, pages, and parasites, and give a kingdom for a kiss, for they are exceedingly amorous; yet, no sooner do their sorceries cease, though but the moment before they were reveling and banqueting with Marc Antony, or quaffing nectar with Jupiter himself, it is a safe wager of a pound to a penny that half of them go supperless to bed. A set of poor but pleasant rogues! miserable but merry wags! that weep without sorrow, stab without anger, die without dread, and laugh, sing, and dance to inspire mirth in others while surrounded themselves with wretchedness.

'A thing still more remarkable in these enchanters is that they completely effect their purpose, and make those who delight in observing the wonderful effects of their art laugh or cry, condemn or admire, love or hate, just as they please; subjugating the heart with every various passion: more especially when they pronounce the charms and incantations of a certain sorcerer called Shakspeare, whose science was so powerful that he himself thus describes it.

> ——'I have oft be-dimm'd
> The noon-tide sun, call'd forth the mutinous winds,
> And 'twixt the green sea and the azur'd vault
> Set roaring war: to the dread rattling thunder
> Have I given fire, and rifted Jove's stout oak
> With his own bolt: the strong-bas'd promontory
> Have I made shake; and by the spurs pluck'd up
> The pine and cedar: graves, at my command,
> Have wak'd their sleepers; op'd, and let them forth
> By my so potent art.'[1]

'I understand you,' said I; delighted with the picture he had drawn. 'Your necessities have obliged you to turn player?'[2]

'Not altogether my necessities,' answered he: 'it was more from a frolic, and to know the world. That is my study, Mr. Trevor. But can you tell me why players, by following their profession, act in some places contrary to all law, and are called strollers, vagabonds, and vagrants, and in others are protected by the law, and dignified with the high and mighty title of his Majesty's Servants?'—

'Indeed I cannot,' said I.

He continued: 'Mark my words; the day will come, Mr. Trevor, when you will discover that there are greater jugglers in the world than your players, wonderful as their art of transformation is. The world is all a cheat; its pleasures are for him who is most expert in legerdemain and cajolery; and he is a fool indeed who is juggled out of his share of them. But that will not I be.'

He then turned the conversation to me, and what had happened during my visit in the country. I was beginning my short narrative, but we were interrupted by an acquaintance, who joined us; and we two or three times met again in the billiard-room, before any opportunity presented itself.

One evening however he followed me out, and required me to discharge my promise. Accordingly I told him all that had occurred; but not without those feelings of indignation which the subject always awakened. He rather seemed diverted than to sympathize in my angry sensations, and asked me 'whether I thought those men, whom the world call swindlers, black-legs, and other hard names, were not at least as honest as many of their neighbours?'

He paid most attention to my mother's story; and, I having characterized Wakefield according to the traits my mother and Miss Wilmot had given me, he observed that 'this Wakefield must certainly be a cunning fellow, and of no mean abilities.'

'In my opinion,' I replied, 'he is an unprincipled scoundrel; and indeed a greater fool than knave; for, with the same ingenuity that he has exerted to make all mankind his enemies, he might have made them all his friends.'

Belmont's answer was remarkable. 'You have this ingenuity yourself, Mr. Trevor; talents which you have exerted, in your own way. Have you made all men your friends?'

I was silent, and after a moment's pause he added—'Come, come! You have spirit and generosity; I will tell you how you can serve me. I have a relation, from whom I could draw a good supply at this moment, if I had but a small sum for travelling expences. Lend me ten guineas: I will be back in a week and repay you.'

The pleasantness of his humour, and the manner in which he had gained upon me, were sufficient to insure him a compliance with this request. I had the money in my pocket, gave it him, and we bade each other adieu; with a promise on his part that 'he would soon be in town again, new moulted and full of feather.'

I must not omit to notice that, having had occasion to hint at Miss Wilmot, in the story I had told him, but without mentioning her name, which he never indeed seemed desirous to know, he put many questions relating to her. He inquired too concerning her brother; and, though he gave no tokens of deep passion, was evidently interested in the whole narrative. His queries extended even to the bishop, and the earl; and he discovered a great desire to be minutely informed of all that related to me. His interrogatories were answered without reserve, for I understood them as tokens of friendship.

In less than a fortnight, I met him again, at the usual place: for he had always been averse to visit me at my lodgings. This I had attributed to motives of vanity; for example, his not having apartments perhaps, such as he wished, to invite me to in return. His appearance, the moment I saw him, spoke his success. His dress was much improved, he sported his money freely, and being engaged at play more than once betted ten pounds upon the hazard. He was successful in his match, in high spirits, welcomed me heartily, and was full of those flights in which his vigorous imagination was so happy.

'Life,' said he, 'Trevor,' putting on his coat after he had done play, 'life is a game at calculation; and he that plays the best of it is the cleverest fellow. Or, rather, calculation and action are husband and wife; married without a possibility of divorce. The greatest errors of Mrs. Action proceed from a kind of headstrong feminine propensity, which she has to be doing before her husband, Mr. Calculation, has given her proper directions. She often pours a spoonful of scalding soup into his worship's mouth, before the relative heat between the liquid and the papillary nerves has been properly determined; at which, in the aforesaid true feminine spirit, she is apt, while he makes wry faces, to burst into a violent fit of laughter.

'Not but that Mrs. Action herself has sometimes very just cause of complaint against her spouse; as most wives have. For example: If, in coming down stairs, Mr. Calculation have made an occasional error but of a unit, and told her ladyship she had only one step more to descend when she had two, she, coming with an unexpected jerk in the increased ratio of a falling body, is very much alarmed; and when the tip of her rose-coloured tongue has happened, on such occasions, to project a little beyond the boundaries prescribed by those beautiful barriers of ivory called her teeth, it has suffered a sudden incision; nay sometimes amputation itself: a very serious mischief; for this is wounding a lady in a tender part.

'What is error? Defect in calculation. What is ignorance? Defect in calculation. What is poverty, disgrace, and all the misfortunes to which fools are subject? Defect in calculation.'

By this time we were in the street, walking arm in arm toward the park, and he continued his jocular allegory.—

'You tell me you have a mind to turn author; and this makes me suspect you understand but little of the algebra of authorship. Could you but calculate the exact number of impediments, doubts, and disappointments attending the trade, could you but find the sum of the objections which yourself, your friends, and your employers will raise, not only against your book but against the best book that ever was or will be written, the remainder would be a query, the produce of which would be a negative quantity, which would probably prevent both Sir and Madam from reading either the nonsense or the good sense, the poetry or the prose, the simple or the sublime, of the rhapsodical, metaphorical, allegorical genius, Hugh Trevor: for in that case I suspect Hugh Trevor would find a more pleasant and profitable employment than the honourable trade of authorship. I have read books much, but men more, and think I can bring my wit to a better market than the slow and tedious detail of an A, B, C, manufactory.'

I laughed and listened, and he presently broke forth with another simile.

'In what is the maker of a book better than the maker of a coat? Needle and thread, pen and ink; cloth uncut and paper unsoiled; where is the preference? except that the tailor's materials are the more costly. In days of yore, the gentlemen of the thimble gave us plenty of stay-tape and buckram;[1] the gentlemen of the quill still give us a *quantum sufficit*[2] of hard words and parenthesis. The tailor has discovered that a new coat will sit more *degage*,[3] and wear better, the less it is incumbered by trimmings: but though buckram is almost banished from Monmouth-street,[4] it is still on sale in Paternoster-row.[5]

'I once began to write a book myself, and began it in this very style: Fable, said I, is the cloth, and morality the lining; a good diction makes an excellent facing, satire ensures fashion, and humour duration; and for an author to pretend to write without wit and judgment were as senseless as for a tailor to endeavour to work without materials, or shears to cut them. Periods may aptly be compared to buttons; and button holes are like—

'I could find no simile for button holes, and thank heaven! left off in despair and never wrote another line.

'Take my advice, Trevor; quit all thoughts of so joyless and stupifying a trade! Every blockhead can sneer at an author; the title itself is a sarcasm; and Job, who we are told was the most patient of men, uttered the bitterest wish that ever fell from lips: "Oh that mine enemy had written a book!"

'Beside you are a fellow of spirit, fashion, form, and figure; and if you will but keep company with me may learn a little wit. How many fools are there with full purses, which if you be not as great a fool as any of them, you might find the means to empty? He that is bound by rules, which the rich make purposely to rob the poor of their due, is like crows, scared from picking up the scattered corn by rags and a manikin.'

This discourse gave me no surprise; it was what I imagined to be a free loose mode of talking, that did not correspond with his principles of action. I deemed it a love of paradox, a desire to shew his wit and original turn of thought, and was confirmed in the supposition by his ironical and ludicrous replies, whenever I attempted a serious answer. Such was the history of the beginning of an acquaintance of which the reader will hear more.

CHAPTER VII

An important secret betrayed by Mary: Transporting intelligence: The reverse, or rain after sunshine: The reader entrusted with a secret: Strange behaviour of a false friend: Lover's vows

I DID not suffer a day to pass without either seeing or sending to inquire after Miss Wilmot; so that our intercourse was continual. One afternoon, being in my own room, after hearing as I thought footsteps and female voices on the stairs, Mary knocked at my door, and, entering as desired, shewed marks of eagerness on her countenance, the meaning of which a question from me immediately caused her to explain. 'Lord! Sir,' said she, 'you cannot think what a hurry and flurry I be in! And all about you!'

'Me, Mary?'

'You shall hear, Sir. My mistress is gone out to take a walk in the park, as I *avised* her to *divart* her *mellicholy*; and so the dear young lady has *bin* here; Miss—! I had forgotten! I *munna* tell her name. But if ever there *wur* an angel upon *arth* she is one; she says such kind things to my dear mistress, and does not blame her for her fault; for, *thof* she be as innocent herself as the child unborn, she can pity the *misfortins* of her own *sect*, when they a *bin* betrayed by false hearted men; and all that she says is that we *mun* take care to be more be-cautioned for the time to come: and then she says it in so sweet, and yet so *serus* a manner, that I am sure no christian soul if they'd a heard her would dare do other than as she says. And as for a doing a good turn, I do verily believe she would give the morsel out of her mouth afore a poor creature should be driven to sin and shame for want—'

I interrupted her: she had raised some strong surmises, and I was impatient—'But you forget, Mary; you mentioned something concerning me?'

'Oh lord! yea; a mort o' questions a *bin* asked; for she talks as familiarity to me as if she *wur* a poor body herself; which gives me heart, so that I be not *afeard* to speak. Whereof I could not help telling her a great many things about you; as how, when little more but a child, you saved my life; and *consarning* your goodness and kind offers to my dear mistress; and how soft hearted and well spoken you *wur* even to poor me; just for all the world as I said, like her own dear good self. Whereupon it gladdened her heart to hear there *wur* another good creature, as good as herself. And so she asked *ater* your name; which, you know that being no secret, I told her, and then it *wur*, if you had but a seen her! Her face *wur* as pale as my kerchief! and I asked what ailed her ladyship? And she replied in a faint voice, Nothing. So that I thought there must for *sartinly* be a *summut* between you! for she sat down, and seemed to do so! as if a struggling for breath. And I ran for a smelling bottle; whereupon she *wur* better, and said she did not need it. And so she asked how long you had lived in the house, and whether you looked happy? And I answered and said there *wur* not a kinder happier creature breathing. So she asked again if I *wur* quite sure that you *wur* happy? And I said I *wur* mortally *sartin* of it. So then she fetched a deep sigh from the very bottom of her heart, and said she *wur* glad of it, very glad of it indeed. For, said she, my good Mary, for she often calls me good, which I be very sure is her kindness and not my *desarts*, my good Mary, said she, I don't wonder that you do love Mr. Trevor for having a saved your life. He once saved my life; which, says she, I shall remember the longest day I have to breathe: and—'

'It is she!' exclaimed I; for I could hold no longer. 'It is Olivia! Benevolent angel! And does she deign to think of me? Does she inquire after me? Am I still in her thoughts?'

'Anan!' said Mary. 'I hope I a betrayed no secrets? For surely, I ha' not mentioned a word of her name.'

Just as I was continuing to question Mary farther, Miss Wilmot returned. I earnestly requested she would come into my apartment, related the discovery I had made, and spoke with all that enthusiasm which the revival of hope and the ardour of passion could inspire. Miss Wilmot sympathized with my feelings; and, with a fervour that spoke the kindness of her heart, hoped she should one day see a pair so worthy of each other blessed to the full accomplishment of their wishes; but she confessed she had her fears, for she thought that the remark, that lovers best calculated to make each other happy were seldom united, was but too true.

I prevailed on her to take tea with me; Mary waited, and I put a thousand questions to her; for my conversation was all on this subject. I could think of nothing else. O how pure was the delight of this discovery! That Olivia should quit the scenes of tumultuous joy, and seek the forlorn and unfortunate, purposely to mitigate their wants, and administer consolation to their woes, was knowledge inexpressibly sweet to the soul! And that she should still remember me! that my very name should raise such commotions in her bosom! that she should delight to hear my praise, and recollect the fortunate moment when I bore her from death with such affection!—It was rapture unspeakable!

I learned from Mary that she lived with her aunt, a few streets distant; and Miss Wilmot informed me that she constantly visited her twice, and sometimes oftener, each week. How did my bosom burn with the wish that she might return that very evening, or at least the next day! In the impatience and ecstacy of hope, I forgot all impediments. Let me but see her; let me but know that she was in the house, and I supposed the moment of perfect bliss would then be come. Happy evening! Never did seductive fancy paint more delicious dreams, or raise up phantoms more flattering to the heart.

Pains and pleasures dance an eternal round. The very next day brought sensations of an opposite kind. My mother had found no person of whom to purchase an annuity in the country; for, the money being her own by my free gift, she had not thought proper to venture it with Thornby; lest under the pretext of monies advanced, he should make she knew not what deduction. She had therefore written to me, soon after I came to London, to find her a purchaser; and after some delay, which the necessity of consulting persons better informed than myself had occasioned, I had advertised the week before and had entered into a negotiation.

Terms were agreed upon, and the rough copy of a deed for that purpose was brought me the same morning that the following letter arrived.

'SIR,

'In spite of my caution, your mother has played the fool once more. She was too suspicious to trust the money in my hands, though I warned her to beware of accidents. I must say she is a very weak woman. Her husband, Mr. Wakefield, has made his appearance, and has trumped up some tale or another to impose upon her, which I am sorry to find is no difficult thing. He has got the money you gave her; so what is to become of her I do not know. She expects he will fetch her away within a month, and keep her like a lady, on the profits of some place at court, which, according to his account, a friend was to procure for him if he could but raise five hundred pounds. You may think how likely he is to keep his promise. I told her my mind in plain terms, and I believe she begins to be in a panic. She dare not write to you, on which I thought it best to let you know the truth at once; for, as I said before, what is to become of her I do not know.

I am, &c.
NABAL THORNBY.'

The train of ideas which the strange contents of this epistle excited was painful in the extreme. The idiot conduct of my mother tempted me to curse, not her indeed, but, according to the narrow limits of prejudice, God and her excepted, all things else! Yet, who but she was the chief actor in this scene of lunatic folly? Was there a woman on earth beside herself that would have been so grossly gulled?

As for her husband, the bitterness of gall was not so choaking as the recollection of him. The sight or sound of his name excited disgust too intense to be dwelt upon! To suffocate him as a monster, or a sooterkin,[1] seemed the only punishment of which he was worthy.

And here it is necessary I should inform the reader of a secret, of which I was myself at that time and long continued to remain utterly ignorant. Belmont, the man who had purposely thrown himself in my way, industriously made himself my intimate, informed me as I supposed of his private affairs and motives of action, inquired minutely into mine, wormed every intelligence I could give that related to myself out of me, designedly attached me to him by intellectual efforts of no mean or common kind (for he saw they delighted me, and they were familiar to him) Belmont, I say, possessed of a pleasing person, a winning aspect, and an address that, though studied with the deepest art, appeared to be open, unpremeditated, and too daring for disguise, this Belmont was no other than the hated Wakefield! Yes, it was Wakefield himself, that by a stratagem which drove me half mad, while it made every drop of blood in his body tingle with triumph, had thus circumvented me! He it was who borrowed the ten guineas from me, by the aid of which he robbed me of five hundred; and then returned to observe how I endured the goad, laugh at my restive antics, and revel in the plunder which he had purloined with so much facility from foolish Trevor, and his still more foolish mother!

But this was not the only trick he had to play me. Secure in the resources of an invention that might have been occupied in pursuits worthy of his powers, his perverted philosophy taught him to employ these resources only for the gratification of passions which he thought it folly to control, and to exult over men whose sordid selfishness he despised, and whose limited cunning was the subject of his derision. He professed himself the disciple of La Rochefoucault and Mandeville,[2] and his practice did not belie his principles.

From the tenor of his discourse, I am persuaded that, had he found me apt at adopting his maxims, he would have unbosomed himself freely, have initiated me in his own arts, and, by making me the associate of his projects, have induced me to look back on the past rather with merriment than anger. As it was, he reserved himself to act with me as with the rest of mankind; to watch circumstances, and turn them to his own purposes whenever opportunity should offer.

This was the man who was the hero of the letter I had just received! A letter that I could neither read nor recollect without being stung almost to frenzy; yet that I could neither forget nor forbear to peruse!

During two hours I traversed my room, and chafed with something like bursting anguish. A few weeks ago, when I had received my legacy of the lawyer, I seemed to be encumbered with wealth. Reflection and the expence at which I now lived, to the visible and quick consumption of a sum I then thought so ample, had since taught me that I was in imminent danger of being reduced to beggary. I had no profession, nor any means of subsistence till a profession could be secured; at least no adequate means, unless by retiring to some humble garret, and confining myself to the society of the illiterate, the boorish, and the brutal, between whose habits and mine there was no congeniality. The very day before, Olivia, ecstatic vision, had risen in full view of my delighted hopes, and, forgetting the tormenting distance which malignant fate had placed between us, I almost thought her mine. The recollection of her now was misery.

Restless, desponding, agonizing, when this thought occurred, I was hastening to go and communicate the accursed news to Miss Wilmot; but an idea started which, after a moment's reflection, induced me to desist. If I told her, the story of Wakefield must again be revived. Olivia too might be informed of circumstances concerning my silly mother, which, selfishness out of the question, motives of delicacy ought to conceal. Such were my arguments at that time: I had not then the same moral aversion to secrecy[1] that I now possess.

I could not however any longer endure the present scene, and to get rid of it hurried away to the billiard table, where, as usual, I found the then supposed Belmont. He was not himself at play, but was engaged in betting. Impatient to unburthen my heart, for as far as my own affairs were concerned I had now no secrets for him, I hurried him out of the room immediately that the game was ended.

The moment we came into the park, I shewed him my letter, and desired him to read. While he perused it, I saw he was more than once violently tempted to laugh.

'Well!' said he, returning it and restraining his titillation, 'is this all?'

'All!' answered I. 'What more would you have? Could the male-ficent devil himself do more to drive a man mad?'

He looked in my face! I returned the inquisitive gaze! I saw emotions the very reverse of mine struggling to get vent. His opposing efforts were ineffectual; he could contain himself no longer, and burst into a violent fit of laughter!

Astonished at mirth so ill placed and offensive, I asked what it meant? The tone of my interrogatory was rouzing, and recalled his attention. 'Pshaw! Trevor,' replied he, with a glance of half contemptuous pity, 'you are yet young: you are but at the beginning of your troubles. Your over weening fondness for the musty morality of dreaming dotards, or artful knaves who only made rules that they might profit by breaking them, will be your ruin. I tell you again and again, if you do not prey upon the world, the world will prey upon you. There is no alternative. What! be bubbled out of your fortune by a whining old woman? I am ashamed of you!'

'But that woman is my mother!'

'Yes! and a set of very pretty motherly tricks she has played you! Not that in the first instance it was so much your fault, who were but a boy, as that of your old fool of a grandfather. It is now high time however that you should become a man.'

'My grandfather? Say rather it was the scoundrel Wakefield!'

'You seem very angry with this Wakefield! And why? He appears to me to be a fellow of plot, wit, and spirit. Instead of resentment, were I you, I should be glad to become acquainted with the man who so well perceives the stupidity and folly of the animals around him, laughs at their apish antics, and with so much facility turns their absurd whims to his own advantage.'

'Acquainted! Intuitive rascal! I would cut off his ears! Drag him to the pillory with my own hands! He is unworthy a nobler revenge.'

'Pshaw! Ridiculous! What did your mother want but the gratification of her paltry passions? which were but the dregs and lees of goatish inclination; for with her the pervading headlong torrent of desire was passed. Did she think of morality? She would have sacrificed the youth and high spirits of Wakefield to her own salacious doating. Why should not he too have his wishes? Were his the most criminal; or the least fitted for the faculties of enjoyment?'

'You have not heard me defend my mother's conduct: but his

villany to the young lady I formerly mentioned [meaning Miss Wilmot] deserves the execration of every man!'

'That is, as she tells the story. Women, poor simple creatures, are always to be pitied, never blamed! But a little more experience, Trevor, will tell you the devil himself is not half so cunning! Men are universally their dupes; nay their slaves, though called their tyrants. Do not men consume their lives in toils to please them? Who are the chief instigators to what you call vice and folly? Who are the mischief makers of the world? Who incite us to plunder, rob, and cut each other's throats? Who but woman? And is not a little retaliation to be expected? Poor dear souls! Cunning as serpents, Trevor; but, though fond of cooing, not harmless as doves. Crocodiles; that only weep to catch their prey. I once was told of one that died broken hearted; a great beauty, and much bewept by all the maudlin moralizers that knew her. The cause of her grief was a handsome fellow, who of course was a cruel perjured villain. The tale had great pathos, and would have been very tragical, had it but been true. Ages before that in which Jove laughed at them, lover's perjuries were the common topic of scandal, and so continue to be. I have often been reproached in the same way myself, and I once took the trouble to write an apology; for which, as it will suit all true lovers, all true lovers are bound to thank me. Here it is.'

I

Men's vows are false, Annette, I own:
The proofs are but too flagrant grown.
To Love I vow'd eternal scorn;
I saw thee and was straight forsworn!

II

In jealous rage, renouncing bliss,
When Damon stole a rapturous kiss,
I took, with oaths, a long farewell;
How false they were thou best can'st tell.

III

By saints I vow'd, and pow'rs divine,
No love could ever equal mine!
Yet I myself, though thus I swore,
Have daily lov'd thee more and more!

IV

> To perjuries thus I hourly swerve;
> Then treat them as they well deserve:
> Thy own vows break, at length comply,
> And be as deep in guilt as I.

'What think you; was not this a valid plea? Are not women apt to
take the advice here given them? Lovely hypocrites! They delight
in being forced to follow their own inclinations!'

There was no resisting the playfulness of his wit, and the
exhilarating whim of his manner. My ill humour soon evaporated;
and yielding to the sympathetic gaiety he had inspired, I said to
him—'You are a wicked wit, Belmont. But, though I laugh, do not
imagine I am a convert to your mandevilian system: it is false,
pernicious, and destructive of the end which it pretends to secure.'

'Do not abuse my system, or me either', replied he. 'I tell you
I am the only honest man of my acquaintance; and the first effort
of my honesty is, as it ought to be, that of being honest to myself.'

'I hear many men profess the same opinions, but I find them
acting on different principles.'

'You mistake. You are young, I tell you. Every man's actions are
strongly tinged by the principles he professes.'

My countenance became a little more serious—'Surely you do not
avow yourself a rascal?'

'Pshaw! Epithets are odious. I do not know the meaning of the
word; nor do you.'

Our conversation continued; it relieved me from a bitterness of
chagrin from which I was happy to escape. We dined together. His
flow of spirits and raillery were unabating; I combated his opinions,
he laughed at my arguments, rather than answered them, and,
though I even then conceived him to be a very bad moralist, I
thought him a delightful companion.

CHAPTER VIII

Revenge not forgotten: The visit delayed: Wilmot and his poetical powers: Dreadful intelligence: An appalling picture: A fruitless search; followed by a surprising discovery

STIMULATED by the ridicule of Belmont, though I never had a thought of abandoning my mother to want, still I determined, according to the proverb, to let her bite the bridle.[1] Instead of writing, therefore, I waited till she should write to me.

Mean time my pamphlet was the grand object of present pursuit. When I began it, I imagined it would scarcely have been the work of a day, certainly not of a week. I was deceived. To a man who has any sense of justice, who fears to affirm the thing that is not, yet is determined to be inexorable in revenge, no task is so harrassing as that which I had undertaken. Page after page was written, re-written, corrected, interlined, scratched, blotted and thrown in the fire. The work had been three times finished, and three times destroyed. It was a fourth time begun, and still the labour was no less oppressive, irritating, and thorny.

It was in this state at the time that Mary brought me the joyful intelligence relating to Olivia. I had watched with unremitting assiduity during those hours of the day when she had been accustomed to visit Miss Wilmot; but my watchings were fruitless; she came no more.

The fourth day after her last visit, she sent a note to Miss Wilmot, informing her that her aunt was going to Bath for the recovery of her health, to which place it was necessary that she should attend her. The blow was violent, and would have been felt more violently even than it was, had it not been for an event which I must now relate.

The alarms of Miss Wilmot concerning her brother had not been lightly excited: they might rather be called prophetic. She had indeed strongly communicated her terror to me. One morning I was meditating on the subject, and recollecting those early days when gathering the first fruits of genius, I was taught by him to distinguish and enjoy the beauties of its emanations, and the sublimity of its flights. His affection for me, though but a boy, had induced him to give me some short poetical compositions of his own. I was reading them over, with strong feelings, partly of sorrow and partly of indignation, at the folly and injustice of a world that could overlook such merit. One of them in particular, which I had always admired for the simple yet pathetic spirit of poetry in which it was written, I was then perusing. It was the following.

I

Ho! Why dost thou shiver and shake,
    Gaffer-Gray!
And why doth thy nose look so blue?
    ''Tis the weather that's cold;
    'Tis I'm grown very old,
And my doublet is not very new,
    Well-a-day!'

II

Then line thy worn doublet with ale,
    Gaffer-Gray;
And warm thy old heart with a glass.
    'Nay but credit I've none;
    And my money's all gone;
Then say how may that come to pass?
    Well-a-day!'

III

Hie away to the house on the brow,
    Gaffer-Gray;
And knock at the jolly priest's door.
    'The priest often preaches
    Against worldly riches;
But ne'er gives a mite to the poor,
    Well-a-day!'

IV

The lawyer lives under the hill,
    Gaffer-Gray;
Warmly fenc'd both in back and in front.
    'He will fasten his locks,
    And will threaten the stocks,
Should he ever more find me in want,
    Well-a-day!'

V

The squire has fat beeves and brown ale,
    Gaffer-Gray;
And the season will welcome you there.
    'His fat beeves and his beer,
    And his merry new year
Are all for the flush and the fair,
    Well-a-day!'

VI

My keg is but low I confess,
    Gaffer-Gray;
What then? While it lasts man we'll live.
    The poor man alone,
    When he hears the poor moan,
Of his morsel a morsel will give,
    Well-a-day!

In that precise state of mind which associations such as I have described, and a poem like this could excite, when I was alike bewailing the madness and turpitude of mankind, that could be blind to the worth of a man such as Wilmot, while glowing I say and thrilling with these sensations, my breakfast was brought and with it a paper—! What shall I say?—It contained what follows! 'Yesterday a middle aged man, of a genteel and orderly appearance, was seen to walk despondingly beside the Serpentine river. A gentleman, who having met him remarked the agitation of his countenance, suspected his design; and, concealing himself behind some trees at a little distance, watched him, and at last saw him throw himself into the water. The gentleman, who was a good swimmer, jumped in after him; but could not immediately find the body, which after he had brought it out was conveyed to Mary-le-bone watch-house.[1] A few shillings were found in his pocket, but nothing to indicate his name, place of abode, or other information, except a written paper, containing the following melancholy account of himself.

'This body, if ever this body should be found, was once a thing which, by way of reproach among men, was called an author. It moved about the earth, despised and unnoticed; and died indigent and unlamented. It could hear, see, feel, smell and taste with as much quickness, delicacy, and force as other bodies. It had desires and passions like other bodies, but was denied the use of them by such as had the power and the will to engross the good things of this world to themselves. The doors of the great were shut upon it; not because it was infected with disease or contaminated with infamy, but on account of the fashion of the garments with which it was cloathed, and the name it derived from its fore-fathers; and because it had not the habit of bending its knee where its heart owed no respect, nor the power of moving its tongue to gloze the crimes or flatter the follies of men. It was excluded the fellowship of such as heap up gold and silver; not because it did, but for fear it might, ask a small portion of their beloved wealth. It shrunk with pain and pity from the haunts of ignorance which the knowledge it possessed could not enlighten, and guilt that its sensations were obliged to abhor. There was but one class of men with whom it was permitted to associate, and those were such as had feelings and misfortunes like its own; among whom it was its hard fate frequently to suffer imposition, from assumed worth and fictitious distress. Beings of supposed benevolence, capable of perceiving, loving, and promoting merit and virtue, have now and then seemed to flit and glide before it. But the visions were deceitful. Ere they were distinctly seen, the phantoms vanished. Or, if such beings do exist, it has experienced the peculiar hardship of never having met with any, in whom both the purpose and the power were fully united. Therefore, with hands wearied with labour, eyes dim with watchfulness, veins but half nourished, and a mind at length subdued by intense study and a reiteration of unaccomplished hopes, it was driven by irresistible impulse to end at once such a complication of evils. The knowledge was imposed upon it that, amid all these calamities, it had one consolation—Its miseries were not eternal—That itself had the power to end them. This power it has employed, because it found itself incapable of supporting any longer the wretchedness of its own situation, and the blindness and injustice of mankind: and as, while it lived, it lived scorned and neglected, so it now commits itself to the waves; in expectation, after it is dead, of being mangled, belied, and insulted.'

Oh God! what were my feelings while reading this heart appalling story! It contained volumes; and sufficiently spoke the strength of the mind that could thus picture its own sensations. It must be my beloved Wilmot: it could be no one else; or even if it were, the man who thus could feel and thus could write was no less the object of admiration, grief, and a species of regret, of the guilt of which every man partook! It was an act of attainder[1] against the whole world, in the infamy of which each man had his share!

Transfixed with horror as I was, I still had the recollection to conceal the paper from the eye of Miss Wilmot, and that instant to go in quest of the body. The utmost speed and diligence were necessary; she must soon hear of the fatal event, and it was much to be dreaded that this would not be the last act of the tragedy.

According to the indication given in the paper, I went immediately to the watch-house; but was surprised to find that the body was not there. They had heard something of a man throwing himself into the Serpentine river, but could give no farther information.

I then ran to every bone-house and receptacle in the various adjoining parishes; but without success. The only intelligence I could obtain was that the gentleman, who leaped in after the man in order to have saved his life, had taken the body home with him; but no one could direct me where he lived.

The circumstance was distracting! My terrors for Miss Wilmot increased. I knew not what course to pursue. At last I recollected that Turl, from having lived some years in London being acquainted with the manners of the place and possessing great sagacity, might perhaps afford me aid. Personal knowledge of Wilmot he probably had none, for he quitted the grammar school at *** just before Wilmot became its head usher. But I knew not what better to do, and to this, as a kind of last hope, I resorted, and hastened away to his lodgings.

It may well be supposed my tone of mind was gloomy. For a man like Wilmot, with virtues so eminent, sensations so acute, and a mind so elevated, to be thus impelled to seek a refuge in death was a thought that almost made me hate existence myself, and doubt whether I might not hereafter be driven to the same desperate expedient, to escape the odious injustice of mankind. The distraction too which would seize on Miss Wilmot haunted my thoughts; for I was convinced that the intelligence, whenever it should reach her, would prove fatal.

Full of these dismal reflections, I arrived at the door of Turl, knocked, and was desired to come in. Turl rose as I entered, and with him a stranger, who had been seated by his side. A stranger, and yet with features that were not wholly unknown to me. He seemed surprised at the sight of me, examined me, fixed his eyes on me! Memory was very busy! Associating ideas poured upon me! I gazed! I remembered! Heavens and earth! What was my astonishment, what were my transports, when in this very stranger I discovered Mr. Wilmot? Living! Pale, meagre, dejected, and much altered; but living!

Turl was the gentleman in the park, who had observed the deep melancholy visible in his countenance; had fortunately suspected his intention; had brought him out of the water; had discovered favourable symptoms; and, instead of either taking him home or to the watch-house, had conveyed him to St. George's hospital; where he immediately obtained medical aid, that had preserved his life! Turl was the person whose courage, humanity, and wisdom, had prolonged the existence of a man of genius; and who was now exerting all his faculties to render that existence happy to the possessor, and beneficial to the human race! Oh moment of inconceivable rapture! Why are not sensations so exquisite eternal?

CHAPTER IX

I secure Miss Wilmot against the danger of false alarm, and return to hear the history of her brother

EAGER as I was to contribute all in my power to tranquilize the mind of Mr. Wilmot, to renew my friendship with him, and to learn his history from himself, I yet made but a short stay, and hastened home to his sister. Fortunately the tragic tale had not reached her; and, without relating circumstances that if abruptly told might have excited alarm, I informed her that I had that moment parted from him, and that now I had found him I should use my utmost endeavour to reconcile him to her once more.

To hear that he was still in being gave an undescribable relief to her mind. It beamed in her countenance, and called up thoughts that soon made her burst into tears.

Having by this information, secured her against the ill effects which might otherwise have followed, I escaped further question from her for the present, by truly telling her I was impatient to return to her brother.

I found the two friends still conversing for friends and sincere ones they were become. The account given by Wilmot of himself had been taken and sent to the newspaper, without the knowledge of Turl; but he had read it, and it was a sufficient index of the mind of the writer: and the behaviour of Turl through the whole affair, as well as the sentiments he uttered in every breath, were enough to convince Mr. Wilmot of his uncommon worth.

On my return, the latter was defending the right of man to commit suicide; which Turl denied; not on the false and untenable ground of superstition, but from the only true argument, the immoral tendency of the act. He was delicate though decisive in his opposition; and only requested Mr. Wilmot to consider, whether to effect the good of the whole be not the true purpose of virtue? Ought not the good of the whole therefore to be its only rule and guide? If so, can the man, who possesses that degree of activity without which he cannot commit suicide, be incapable of being farther useful to society?

Depressed and gloomy as his state of mind was, Mr. Wilmot testified great satisfaction at our rencontre; and the interest which I unfeignedly took in his welfare soon revived all his former affection for me. My veneration for his virtues, love for his genius, and pity for his misfortunes, tended to calm his still fluttering and agitated spirits. Unfortunate as he himself had been, or at least had thought himself, in his love of literature and poetry, it yet gave him pleasure to find that the same passion was far from having abated in me. He called it a bewitching illusion; Turl affirmed it was a beneficial and noble propensity of soul.

We none of us had a wish to separate, for the imagination of each was teeming with that sedate yet full flow of sentiment which, as Milton has so beautifully described, melancholy can give.[1] Mr. Wilmot had supposed his sister was guilty with the bishop; and when I told her story, with the addition of such probable circumstances as I myself had collected, it afforded him very considerable relief to find that the suspicions to which appearances gave birth had been false.

I did not conceal the desire I had to know by what train of accidents he had been led into a state of such deep despondency; and he thus kindly gratified my wish.

HISTORY OF MR. WILMOT

'The narrative given by my sister, which you, Mr. Trevor, have already repeated, precludes the necessity of any detail concerning my origin. Nor is origin in my opinion of the least moment, except as it displays the habits and growth of mind, and shews how the man became such as we find him to be. At what period of my existence that activity of inquiry, and those energetic aspirings began, which to me were afterward the source of the extremes of joy and sorrow, I cannot tell; but I believe the quality of ardour, though probably not born with us, is either awakened in early infancy or seldom if ever attains strength and maturity. I could not only read with uncommon accuracy and ease, while very young, but can remember I made efforts to reason with my father, the major, on what I read, when I was little more than six years old.

'He, though a man rather of irritable feelings than profound research, was not destitute of literature; and encouraged a propensity in me that was flattering to himself, as the father of a boy remarked for his promising talents; which talents he supposed might lead to distinctions that he had been unsuccessfully ambitious to obtain.

'He considered himself as one of the most unfortunate of men. Imagining personal bravery to be the essence of the military character, he had eagerly cherished that quality; and, having given incontestible proofs that he possessed it in an eminent degree, to be afterward overlooked was, in his judgment, too flagrant an instance of public as well as private ingratitude to be ever pardoned. It was the daily subject of his thoughts, and theme of his discourse; and I have great reason to conjecture that the habitual discontent that preyed upon his mind, and embittered his life, especially the latter part of it, communicated itself to me. I was educated in the belief that the world is blind to merit, continually suffers superior virtue to linger in indigence and neglect, and is therefore an odious, unjust, and despicable world.

'I own I have at some few intervals doubted of this doctrine; and supposed in conformity to your opinion, Mr. Turl, that failure is rather the consequence of our own mistakes, impatience, and efforts ill directed, than of society: but the ill success of my own efforts, aided perhaps by the prejudices which I received from my father, have preponderated; and made me it may be too frequently incline to melancholy, and misanthropy. What can be said? Are not the rich and powerful continually oppressing talents, genius, and virtue? Is the general sense of mankind just in its decisions?

'Beside, an appeal to the general sense of mankind is not always in our power; and that the proceedings of individuals are often flagrantly unjust cannot be denied. In the school where I was educated I was a frequent and painful witness of honours partially bestowed; and prizes and applause awarded to others, that were indubitably due to me. When the rich and the powerful visited the seminary, the sons of the rich and the powerful gained all their attention. Conscious as I could not but be of my own superior claims, I was overlooked!

'Perhaps I felt the repetition of these and similar acts of injustice too severely. Yet, are they not odious? I own the remembrance of them ever has been, and is, intensely painful; and the pain is almost unremittingly prolonged by what every man, who is not wilfully blind, must daily see passing in the world. [Mr. Wilmot sighed deeply] Well well! Would I could forget it!

'After many a bitter struggle in my boyish years to rise into notice, few, very few indeed, of which were effectual, I still continued the combat. In due time, as I was told, my efforts were amply rewarded! But how? Instead of being forwarded in those more noble and beneficial pursuits for which I think I had proved myself fitted, the effusions of genius though known were never once remembered. Oh, no! I obtained, with great difficulty and as an unmerited favour a charitable condescension of power that knew not very well if it ought to be so kind to a being so unprotected, yes, I obtained—— the office of usher! The honour of mechanically hearing declensions, conjugations, and rules of syntax and prosody, repeated by beings who detested the labour to which they were compelled, was conferred upon me! beings who looked on me, not as a benefactor, but as a tyrant! And tyrants all teachers indubitably are, under our present modes of education.

'Humbled and cowed as my genius was, by the drudgery and obscurity to which it was consigned, I yet had the courage to continue those labours by which alone mind is brought to maturity. Alive as I was to a sense of injustice, I recollected that, even if my powers were equal to all that I myself had fondly hoped from them, there were examples of men with at least equal powers, who had been equally ill treated. Equally did I say? Oh Otway! Oh Chatterton![1] What understandings, what hearts, had those men who without an effort, without moving a finger (not to do you justice, of that they were incapable, but) to preserve you from famine, could suffer you to perish? It was needless to repine! I consoled and reconciled myself to my fate as well as I was able. I pursued my studies, read the poets of ancient and modern times with unabating avidity, observed the actions and inquired into the motives of men, and made unceasing attempts to develope the human heart.

'Excluded as it were by the pride, luxury, and caprice of the world from expanding my sensations, and wedding my soul to society, I was constrained to bestow the strong affections that glowed consciously within me upon a few. My mother and sister had a large share of them. To skreen them from the indigence, obscurity, and neglect, to which without my aid they must be doomed, was a hope that encouraged me in the bold project I had conceived.

'I determined to dedicate myself to literature, poetry, and particularly to the stage. Essays of the dramatic kind indeed had been made by me very early. At length, I undertook a tragedy; as a work which, if accomplished with the degree of perfection that I hoped it would be, must at once establish my true rank in society, relieve the wants of my family, and be a passport for me to every man of worth and understanding in the world. How little did I know the world! Fond fool! Over credulous idiot! What cares the world for the toils and struggles, the restless days and sleepless nights of the man of genius! I am ashamed to think I could be so miserably mistaken!

'The ardour with which I began my work, the deep consideration I gave to every character, the strong emotions I felt while composing it, the minute attention I paid to all its parts, and the intense labour I bestowed in planning, writing, correcting, and completing it, were such as I believed must insure success.

'Surely mankind can be but little aware of the uncommon anxieties, pains, and talents that must contribute to the production of such a work; or their reception of it, when completed, would be very different! They would not suffer, surely they would not, as they so frequently do, this or that senseless blockhead to frustrate the labour of years, blast the poet's hopes, and render the birth of genius abortive!

'My tragedy at length was written; and by some small number, whose judgment I consulted, was approved: never indeed with that enthusiasm which I, perhaps the overweening author, imagined it must have excited; but it was approved. "I was a young man of some merit; it was more than they had expected." Nay, I have met with some liberal critics, who have appeared modestly to doubt whether they themselves should have written better!

'Before I made the experiment, I had supposed that every man, whose wealth or power gave him influence in society, would start up, the moment it was known that an obscure individual, the usher of a school, had written a tragedy; not only to protect and produce it to the world, but to applaud and honour the author! Would secure him from the possibility of want, load him with every token of respect, and affectionately clasp him to their bosom! The indifference and foolish half-faced kind of wonder, as destitute of feeling as of understanding, with which it was received, by the persons on whom I had depended for approbation and support, did more than astonish me; it pained, disgusted, and jaundiced my mind!

'The only consolation I could procure was in supposing that the inhabitants of the city were I resided, were deficient in literary taste; and that at a more polished place, where knowledge, literature, and poetry were more diffused, I should meet a very different reception. Experience only can cure the unhackneyed mind of its erroneous estimates!

'London however and its far famed theatres were the objects at which my ambition long had aimed; and thither after various doubts and difficulties it was decreed I should go. The profits of my place I had dedicated to the relief of my family, and my mother's great fear was that, going up to London so ill provided, I should perish there for want. Of this I was persuaded there could be no danger, and at length prevailed.

'The danger however was not quite so imaginary as I in the fervour of hope had affirmed it to be. The plan I proposed was to get another usher's place, in or near town, till I could bring my piece upon the stage. This I attempted, and made various applications, which all failed; some because, though I understood Greek, I could not teach merchant's accounts, or spoil paper by flourishes and foppery, which is called writing a fine hand; and others because, as I suppose, persons offered themselves whose airs, or humility, or other usher-like qualifications, that had no relation to learning, pleased their employers better than mine.

'I soon grew weary of these degrading attempts and turned my thoughts to a more attractive resource. While in the country, I had frequently sent little fugitive pieces, to be inserted in periodical publications; and now, on inquiry, I found there were people who were paid for such productions. I made the experiment; and after a variety of fruitless efforts succeeded in obtaining half a guinea a week from an evening paper; which I supplied with essays, little poetical pieces, and other articles, much faster than they chose to print them.

'In the interim, the grand object for which I had left the country was not neglected. It is a common mistake to imagine that, to get a piece upon the stage, it is necessary to procure a patron, by whom it shall be recommended. To this I was advised; and, in consequence of this advice, wrote letters to three different persons, whose rank in society I imagined would insure a reception at the theatre to the piece which they should protect. I supposed that every such person, who should hear of a poet who had written a tragedy, would rejoice in the opportunity of affording him aid, and instantly stand forth his patron.

'In this spirit I wrote my three letters; and received no answer to any one of them! Amazed at this, I went to the houses of the great people I had addressed; but my face was unknown! Not one of them was at home! I could gain no admission! When now and then suffered to wait in the hall, I saw dancing-masters, buffoons, gamblers, beings of every species that could mislead the head and corrupt the heart, come and go without ceremony; but to a poet all entrance was denied; for such chosen society he was unfit. The very rabble, with which these pillared lounging places swarm, looked on him with a suspicious and half contemptuous eye; that insolently inquired what business had he there? Were the slaves and menials of Mæcenas such? Was it thus at the Augustan court; when the lord of the conquered world sat banqueting with Virgil on his right hand and Horace on his left?

'Why did I read and remember stories so seductive? Why did I foolishly place all my happiness in the approbation of the great vulgar or the small; forgetting that approbation neither adds to virtue nor diminishes? Perhaps, and indeed I fear, my mind was warped. Yet surely the neglect and even odium in which the un-obtruding man of genius is at present overwhelmed, is a damning accusation against the rich and titled great.

'It was long however before I entirely disdained these abject and fruitless efforts. On one occasion I was fortunate enough, as I absurdly thought, to get introduced to a Marquis. It was an awful honour, to which I was unused; and instead of addressing him with the frothy and impertinent levity which characterized his own manners, and which he encouraged in the creatures that were admitted to his familiarity, I stood confounded, expecting he should have read my play, which I had transcribed for his perusal, have understood the value of the poet who could write it, and have been anxious to relieve that acuteness of sensibility which overclouded and hid the man of genius in the timid, abashed, and too cowardly author. He spoke to me indeed, nay condescended to repeat two or three of the newest literary anecdotes that had been retailed to him from the blue-stocking-club,[1] and then civilly dismissed me to give audience to a Dutch bird-fancier, who had brought him a piping bulfinch. But I saw him no more, he was never afterward at home. I was one of a class of animals that a Marquis never admits into his collection. My tragedy when applied for by letter was returned; with "sorrow that indispensible engagements had prevented him from reading it; but requested a copy as soon as it should appear in print." For which, should such a strange event have come to pass, I suppose I should have been insulted with the gift perhaps of one guinea, perhaps of five. And thus a Marquis discharged a duty which his rank and power so well enabled him to perform! But, patience! The word poet shall be remembered with everlasting honour, when the title Marquis shall—Pshaw!

'On another occasion an actress, who, strange to tell, happened very deservedly to be popular, and whom before she arrived at the dignity of a London theatre I had known in the country, recommended me to a dutchess. To this dutchess I went day after day; and day after day was subjected for hours to the prying, unmannered, insolence of her countless lacquies. This time she was not yet stirring, though it was two o'clock in the afternoon; the next she was engaged with an Italian vender of artificial flowers; the day after the prince and the devil does not know who beside were with her; and so on, till patience and spleen were at daggers drawn.

'At last, from the hall I was introduced to the drawing-room, where I was half amazed to find myself. Could it be real? Should I, after all, see a creature so elevated; so unlike the poor compendium of flesh and blood with which I crawled about the earth? Why, it was to be hoped that I should!

'Still she did not come; and I stood fixed, gazing at the objects around me, longer perhaps than I can now well guess. The carpet was so rich that I was afraid my shoes would disgrace it! The chairs were so superb that I should insult them by sitting down! The sofas swelled in such luxurious state that for an author to breathe upon them would be contamination! I made the daring experiment of pressing with a single finger upon the proud cushion, and the moment the pressure was removed it rose again with elastic arrogance; an apt prototype of the dignity it was meant to sustain.— Though alone, I blushed at my own littleness!

'Two or three times, the familiars of the mansion skipped and glided by me; in at this door and out at that; seeing yet not noticing me. It was well they did not, or I should have sunk with the dread of being mistaken for a thief; that had gained a furtive entrance, to load himself with some parcel of the magnificence that to poverty appeared so tempting!

'This time however I was not wholly disappointed: I had a sight of the dutchess, or rather a glimpse. "Her carriage was waiting. She had been so infinitely delayed by my lord and my lady, and his highness, and Signora! Was exceedingly sorry! Would speak to me another time, to-morrow at three o'clock, but had not a moment to spare at present", and so vanished!

'Shall I say she treated me proudly, and made me feel my insignificance? No. The little that she did say was affable; the tone was conciliating, the eye encouraging, and the countenance expressed the habitual desire of conferring kindness. But these were only aggravating circumstances, that shewed the desirableness of that intercourse which to me was unattainable. I say to me, for those who had a less delicate sense of propriety, who were more importunate, more intruding, and whose forehead was proof against repulse, were more successful. By such people she was besieged; on such she lavished her favours, till report said that she impoverished herself; for a tale of distress, whether feigned or real, if obtruded upon her, she knew not how to resist.[1]

'What consolation was this to me? I was not of the begging tribe. I came with a demand at sight upon the understanding, which whoever refused to pay disgraced themselves rather than the drawer.

'She mistook my character, and the next day at three o'clock, instead of seeing me herself, sent me ten guineas in a note, by her French maitre d'hotel; which chinked as they slided from side to side, and proclaimed me a pauper! My heart almost burst with indignation! Yet, coward that I was! I wanted the fortitude to refuse the polluted paper! I thought it would be an affront, and still fed myself with the vain hope of procuring from her that countenance to my own labours which I imagined they deserved, and which therefore I did not think it any disgrace to solicit. The disgrace of reducing men of merit to such humiliating situations was not mine.

'I went twice more; and was both times interrogated in French, by the insolent maitre d'hotel, so as to convince me that he thought my coming again so soon was a proof of no common degree of impudence.

'Oh Euripides! Oh Sophocles! Did not your sublime shades glide wrathful by and menace the wretch in whom your divine art had been so degraded? How did I pray, as I passed the scowling porter, for the death of your great predecessor; that some eagle would drop a tortoise on my head, and instantly crush me to atoms!

'I had been the more anxious after patronage, because I wished the actress whom I have mentioned to play my heroine. There was no tragedian whose powers were in the least comparable to hers. But the difficulty of getting a piece on the stage, at the theatre to which she belonged, all the town told me was incredible. It was a chancery-suit, which no given time could terminate. The manager was the most liberal of men, the best of judges, and the first of writers; as void of envy as he was noble minded, and friendly to merit. Yes, friendly in heart and act, when he could be prevailed on to act. But his rare virtues and gifts were rendered useless, extinguished, by the killing vice of procrastination. He never listened to a story that he did not sympathize with the teller of it. The request must be a wild one indeed which he did not feel an instant desire to grant. He would promise with the most sincere and honest intentions to perform; but, hurried away by new petitioners, or projects of a more grand and important nature, he would with still greater facility forget. All who knew him uniformly affirmed, a soul more expansive, more munificent, could not inhabit a human form; yet, from this one defect, it was frequently his fate where he intended an essential benefit to commit an irreparable injury. He encouraged hopes that were never realized, retarded the merit he meant to promote, and raised up personal enemies who impeded his own utility; conspicuous and grand as this utility was and is, it would otherwise have been unexampled.

'I speak the sentiments of men who I believe were incapable of exaggeration. For my own part I have read his works, and I love him almost to adoring.

'He is I know assaulted by an infinite number of affairs, that all demand his attention. Many of them are totally beneath it, yet are undertaken by him with a too ready compliance; averse as he is to give the solicitor pain, and continually desirous to make every creature happy. He can do but one thing at once. Of the multitude of things to be done, not half are present to the memory at any one time; and, of those that are remembered, what can he do but select the most urgent? The mistake has often been rather in the too ready promise than in the non-performance. If prevented by serious occupation, by love of the chosen companions of his convivial hours, or by habits of forgetful revery, from reading my tragedy and being just to me, I attribute the neglect to its true cause; which certainly was not jealousy of, or indifference to, the man of talents. How can he honour merit, granting it to exist, with which he is unacquainted? Yet let me not be misunderstood; though I love his comprehensive benevolence of soul, I wish it were less undistinguishing:—I cannot applaud or approve the errors into which it leads, both himself and those he means to serve.

'In a word, I could find no mode of securing his attention. I endeavoured to fix it by the intervention of the great; who delighted in his social qualities, did homage to his wit, and were ambitious of his friendship. But in these attempts I likewise failed.

Hopeless therefore of aid from my favourite actress, I sent my play to the other house. How was I relieved, after the delay I had endured and the continual anxiety in which I had been kept, how delighted, by hearing from the manager within a fortnight! He appointed an interview, received me with affability, and immediately proceeded to the business in question.

He began with telling me, he could have wished I had rather turned my thoughts to the comic than the tragic muse; for tragedy was less fashionable, and consequently less profitable both to the house and the author, than comedy or opera. I sighed and answered, it was an ill proof of public taste, when it could receive greater pleasure from the unconnected scenes of an opera than from the fable, pathos, and sublime emotions of tragedy. But I feared the fault was less in the audience than in the poet; and added that the first fortunate writer who should produce a tragedy such as had been written, and such as I hoped it was possible again to write, would find audiences not insensible to his merit.

'He replied, it may be so. I can only answer that each author thinks himself the chosen bard you have described, and that each is disappointed. I am pleased, Sir, continued he, with many parts of your tragedy; but I think it has one great fault; it is too tragical: it rather excites horror than terror. Whether the age be more refined or more captious, more humanized or more effeminate than other ages have been I will not pretend to determine; but you have written some scenes that would not at present be endured. If you think proper to make such alterations as shall soften and adapt them to the present taste, and if I approve them when made, your piece shall then be performed.

'I knew not what to reply. The scenes to which he referred were conceived, as I had imagined, in the bold but true stile of tragedy. I intended them to produce a great effect; and was sorry to be informed, as among other things I had been, that ladies would faint, fall into hysterics, and be taken shrieking out of the boxes at hearing them. I had no remedy but to submit, re-consider, and, by lowering the tone of passion, perhaps spoil my tragedy!

'Oh what a tormenting trade is that of author! He that makes a chair, a table, or any common utensil, brings his work home, is paid for his labour, and there his trouble ends. It was quickly begun, and quickly over; it excited little hope, but it met with no disappointment. The author, on the contrary, has the labour of days, months, and years to encounter. When he begins, his difficulties are immeasurable; and while as he proceeds they seem to disappear, nay at the very moment when he sometimes thinks them all conquered, he discovers that they are but accumulated! Every part, every page, every period, have been considered, and re-considered, with unremitting anxiety. He has revised, re-written, corrected, expunged, again produced, and again erased, with endless iteration. Points and commas themselves have been settled with repeated and jealous solicitude.

'At length, as he thinks, his labour is over! He knows indeed that no work of man was ever perfect; but, circumstanced as he is, the eager prying of his own sleepless eye cannot discover what more to amend. He produces the tedious fruits of incessant fatigue to the world, and hopes the harvest will be in proportion to the unwearied and extreme care he has bestowed. Poor man! Mistaken mortal!

How could he imagine that the sensations of multitudes should all correspond with his own? Educated in schools so various, under circumstances so contradictory and prejudices so different and distinct, how could he suppose his mind was the common measure of man? Faultless? Perfect? Vain supposition! Extravagant hope! The driver of a mill-horse, he who never had the wit to make much less to invent a mouse-trap, will detect and point out his blunders. All satisfied? No; not one! Not a man that reads but will detail, reprove, and ridicule his dull witted errors.

'Well! he finds he is mistaken, he pants after improvement, and listens to advice. He follows it, alters, and again appears. What is his success? Are cavilers less numerous? Absurd expectation! Do critics unite in its praise? Ridiculous hope! If he would escape censure, he must betake himself to a very different trade.

'It was the month of February when my tragedy was returned. The season was far advanced: I had then been nearly twelve months held in suspense; seeking the means of appearing before the public, soliciting patronage, and indulging hope. My mother and sister depended much on my aid. Out of the small pittance which the newspaper essays afforded, I at first made a proportionate deduction; and lived, that is contrived to exist, on the remainder.

'This could not long endure, and I sought other channels of emolument. I wrote a novel, which I hawked about among the booksellers. Some of them printed nothing in that way; others would venture to publish it, and share the profits, but not advance a shilling. One of them offered me five guineas for the two volumes, and told me it was a great price, for he seldom gave more than three.

'At last, I was fortunate enough to obtain double the sum. It was printed; but, being written in haste and in a state of mind entirely adverse to that fine flow which is the token, the test, and the triumph of genius, its success was less than I expected. Still however it more than answered the hopes of the bookseller; and I think I may safely affirm, it had marks of mind sufficient to excite applause, mingled with the censure of just criticism.

'Did it obtain this applause? No—"A vulgar narrative of uninteresting incidents"—was the laconic character given of it in that monthly publication in which, from its reputed impartiality, I most hoped for just and candid inquiry.[1]

'Finding what a terrible animal a critic is, I determined to become one myself. I made the first essay of my talents for censure on such books as I could borrow, and sent my remarks to the magazines; into which they were immediately admitted.

'Thus encouraged, I applied to the publisher of a new review, and informed him of my course of reading, and of the languages and sciences with which I was acquainted. My proposal was graciously received, and I was admitted of that corps which has certainly done much good, and much harm to literature.

'I entered on my new office with great determination; but I soon discovered that, to a man of principle, who dare neither condemn nor approve a book he has not read, it was a very unproductive employment. It is the custom of the trade to pay various kinds of literary labour by the sheet, and this among the rest. Thus it frequently happened that a book, which would demand a day to peruse, was not worthy of five lines of animadversion.

'This is the true source of feeble and false criticism; a task in itself most difficult, and to which the chosen few alone are equal. Deep investigation, scientific acquirement, an acute and comprehensive mind, a correct and invigorating stile, and intelligence superior to prejudice, and an undeviating conscientious spirit of rectitude, are the rare endowments it requires. Its seat should be the summit of mental attainment; for its office is to enlighten. It has to instruct genius itself, and its powers should be equal to the hardy enterprise. In fine, its object ought to be the love of truth; it is the lust of gain. I need not expatiate on the consequences; they are self-evident.

Poor as the trade is, I exercised it with the scrupulous assiduity of which I knew it to be worthy. My labour therefore was as great as my emoluments were trifling; and, though I made no progress toward fame and fortune, my efforts were unremitting. I mention these circumstances to shew that my failure, in my attempts to gain what I believe to be my true rank in society, did not originate either in indolence, want of œconomy, or any other neglect of mine. Day or night, I was scarcely ever without either a book or a pen in my hand. With the most sedulous industry and caution I endeavoured to render justice as well to the works of others as to my own. My uniform study was to increase knowledge, diffuse good taste, and, as I fondly hoped, promote the general pleasure and happiness of mankind.

But, while I was anxiously caring for all, no one seemed to care for me. I and my learning, taste and genius, if I possessed them, wandered through the croud unnoticed; or noticed only to be scorned: insulted by the vulgar, for the something in my manner which pretended to distinguish me from themselves; and contemned by the proud and the prosperous, because of the forlorn poverty of my appearance. Among the fashionable and the fortunate, where I might have hoped to find urbanity and the social polish of a civilized nation, I could gain no admittance; for I had no title, kept no carriage, and was no sycophant. The doors of the learned were shut upon me; for they were doctors or dignitaries, in church, physic, or law. Of science they were all satisfied they had enough: of profit, promotion, and the other good things of which they were in full pursuit, I had none to give. By my presence they would have been retarded, offended at the freedom of my conversation, and by my friendship disgraced. They sought other and far different associates.

'Bowed to the earth as I was by this soul-killing injustice, and wearied by these incessant toils, I still did not neglect my tragedy for an hour. I considered and reconsidered the objections that had been made. I was convinced they were ill founded: but I was not left to the exercise of my own judgment. I had no alternative. To lower the tone of passion was in my opinion to injure my tragedy; but it must be done, or must not be performed. The manager urged arguments that were and perhaps could not but be satisfactory, to any man in his situation: his experience of public taste was long and confirmed: the nightly expences of a theatre made it a most serious concern: the risk of every new piece was great, for the town was capricious. To obtain all possible security against risk, therefore, was a duty.

'The reluctance with which alterations were made occasioned them to be rather slow. At last however I finished them, as much to my own satisfaction as could under such circumstances be expected; and a fair copy, written as all the copies made of it were with my own hand, was again sent to the manager.

'A week longer than in the former instances elapsed, before I heard from him; and, when I did hear, the substance of his letter was that he had a new comedy in preparation; which, it being then the middle of March, would entirely fill up the remainder of the season!

'What could I do? No blame was imputable to him for the delay. It was no fault of his that I was pursued by the malice of poverty; that I was tormented with the desire of effectually relieving the necessities of my family; that I had written to my mother and sister, in the elated moment of hope, an assurance of being able to grant this relief in a very few weeks; and that, buoyed up by these calculations, I had indulged myself in procuring a suit of clothes and other necessaries, of which I was in extreme need, on credit.

'Thou world of vice! thou iron-hearted senseless mass of madness and folly! why did I ever dream that I had the power to arrest thy headlong course, and fix thy bewildered wits, thy garish idiot eye on me? On my weak efforts! my humble wishes! my craving wants! What signs of luxury, what tokens of dissipation, what innumerable marks of extravagant waste did I every where see around me, at the moment that poverty was thus pinching me to the very bone! Here a vain mortal, as insolent as uninstructed, drawn by six ponies; with a postillion before and three idle fellows behind, pampered in vice, that he might thus openly insult common sense, and thus publicly proclaim the folly of his head to be as egregious as the insensibility of his heart was hateful. There trifling and imbecile creatures, who, not satisfied with the appellation woman, call themselves ladies, and expend thousands on their routs, masked-balls, whipped creams, and other froth and frippery, procured from the achs and pains and blood and bones of the poor! Wretches more bent and weighed down by misery than even I was!

'What need I to recall such pictures to your imaginations? Can you look abroad and not behold them? Are not the vices of unequal distribution to be met with in every corner, nook, and alley? Is not the despotism of wealth, that is, of that property which the folly of man so much reveres and worships, every where visible? Does it not varnish vice, generate crime, and trample virtue and the virtuous in the dust? Is the deep sense which I have entertained of the relentless injustice of society all false?

'Impelled as I was by paltry yet pressing wants and debts that would admit of no delay, I sought relief in endeavouring to raise money on the presumptive profits of my tragedy. What can the wretch who is thus besieged, thus hunted do, but yield? I had promised aid to my family; and, depending on that promise which had been much too confidently given, my mother was in danger of having her trifling effects seized; my sister, whom I then tenderly loved, of being turned loose perhaps into the haunts of infamy; and myself of being thrown into a loathsome prison.

'My first attempt was a very wild one, and proved how little I yet knew of mankind. I wrote a letter to a woman of great fame in the literary world; the reputed writer of a work, the praises of which had been often echoed, and whose wealth was immense. To such a person I thought the appeal I had to make must come with resistless force. For a man of literature, a poet, capable of writing a tragedy, that had already been deemed worthy at least of attention from the theatre, and of the merits of which she so well could judge, for such a man she would be all kindness! all sensibility! all soul! What an incurable dolt was I! Thus repeatedly to degrade the character of bard, and thus too in vain. I blush!—No matter!

'I minutely detailed the circumstances of my case, to this female leader of literature; and, assiduously endeavouring to avoid every feature of meanness, requested the loan of one hundred pounds; appealing for the probability of reimbursement to her own conceptions of the rectitude of the mind that could produce the tragedy I sent, and which I requested her first to read. She herself would judge of the danger there might be of its condemnation. If she thought it would fail, I then should be anxious that she should run no risk: but, if not, the loan would be a most essential benefit to me, and perhaps a pleasure to herself.[1]

'Fool that I was, thus to estimate ladies' pleasures! Whether she did or did not read my play I never knew; but this learned lady, this patroness of letters, this be-prosed and be-rhymed dowager, who professed to be the enraptured lover of poetry, wit and genius, returned it with a formal cold apology, that was insulting by its affected pity. "She was *extremely* sorry to be obliged to refuse me! *extremely* sorry indeed! It would have given her *infinite* pleasure to have advanced me the sum I required; but she was then building a *fine* house, which demanded all the money she could *possibly* spare."

'Why ay! She must have a fine house, with fifty fine rooms in it, forty-nine of which were useless; while I, my mother, my sister, and millions more, might perish without a hovel in which to shelter our heads!

'Convinced at last of the futility of applications like these, I sought an opposite resource. If men would not lend money to benefit me, they would perhaps to benefit themselves. One of the actors, with whom I became acquainted, informed me that there was a Jew, who frequented all theatrical haunts, knew I had a play in the manager's hands, and might possibly be induced to lend me the sum I wanted. To this Jew I addressed myself, stated the merits of the case, and, fearful of making too high a demand, requested a loan of seventy pounds.

'His first question was concerning the security I had to give? I had none! The Jew shook his head, and told me it was impossible to lend money without security. I replied, that if making over the profits of my tragedy to the amount of the principal and interest would but satisfy him, to that I should willingly consent. Again he shrugged his shoulders, and repeated it was very dangerous. Jews themselves, kind as they were, could not lend money without security. Beside, money was never so scarce as just at that moment. Indeed he had no such sum himself; but he had an uncle, in Duke's Place, who, if I could but get good *personal* security, would supply me, on paying a premium adequate to the risk.

'I must avoid being too circumstantial. I urged every incitement my imagination could honestly suggest: he pretended to state the matter to his uncle. The affair was kept in suspence, and I was obliged to travel to Duke's Place at least a dozen times: but, at last I gave my bond for a hundred pounds; for which I received fifty, and paid two guineas out of it, on the demand of the nephew, for the trouble he had taken in negociating the business; the uncle being the ostensible person with whom it was transacted.

'Determined to secure my mother from want as far as was in my power, I remitted the whole sum to her, except what was necessary to pay my immediate debts; and blessed the Jew extortioner, as a man who, compared to the learned lady, abounded in the milk of human kindness!

'By the continuance of my literary drudgery, the time passed away to the middle of September; the season at which the winter theatres usually open. I now felt tenfold anxiety concerning my tragedy. The bond I had given at six months would soon become due; failure would send me to prison, perhaps for life; it would disgrace me, would distract my family, would cut short my hopes of fame, and the grand progress which I sometimes fondly imagined I should make. Every way it would be fatal! I trembled at its possibility. Success, which had so lately appeared certain, seemed to become more and more dubious.

'During the summer, I had heard nothing from the manager. I now inquired at the theatre, and was told he was at Bath, and would not be in town in less than a fortnight. I waited with increasing fears, haunted the play-house, and teazed the attendants at it with my inquiries. Of these I soon perceived not only the sneers but the duplicity; for, when the manager was returned to town, and, as I was told by a performer, was actually in the theatre, they affirmed the contrary! He had been, but was gone! I plainly read the lie in their looks to each other. At that time it was new to me, and gave me great pain; but I soon became accustomed though never reconciled to their manners; which were characterized by that low cunning, that supercilious mixture of insolence and meanness, that is always detested by the honest and the open. A set of—Pshaw! They are unworthy my remembrance.

'Finding the manager was now returned, I immediately wrote to him; and a meeting was appointed three days after, at the theatre. He then informed me there were still some few alterations, which he was desirous should be immediately made; after which the tragedy should be put into rehearsal, and performed in about three weeks.

'This was happy news to me. I returned with an elated heart to make the proposed corrections, finished them the same day, and again delivered the piece into the manager's hands. He proceeded with a punctuality that delighted me: the parts were cast, and the performers called to the theatre to hear it read.

'This was a new scene, a new trial of patience, a new degradation. Instead of that steady attention from my small audience which I expected, that deep interest which I supposed the story must inspire, suffusing them in tears or transfixing them in terror, the ladies and gentlemen amused themselves with whispers, winks, jokes, titters, and giggling; which, when they caught my attention and fixed my eye upon the laughers, were turned into an affected gravity that added to the insult. No heart panted! no face turned pale! no eye shed a tear! and, if I were to judge from this experiment, a more uninteresting soul-less piece had never been written. But the manager was not present, and I was not a person of consequence enough to command respect or ceremony, from any party. I complained to him of the total want of effect in my tragedy, over the passions of the actors; but he treated that as a very equivocal sign indeed, and of no worth.

'There was another circumstance, of which he informed me, that to him and as it afterward proved to me was of a much more serious nature. They had not been altogether so inattentive as I had imagined. Amid their monkey tricks and common place foolery, their hearts had been burning with jealousy of each other. Neither men nor women were satisfied with their parts. I had three male and two female characters of great importance in the play, but rising in gradation. Of the first of these all the actors were ambitious; and one of them who knew his own consequence, and that the manager could not carry on the business of the theatre at that time without him, threw up his part.

'In vain did I plead, write, and remonstrate. No reasons, no motives of generosity or of justice, to the manager, the piece, or the public, could prevail; and his aid, though most essential, could not be obtained. Had the part been totally beneath his abilities, his plea would have been good; but it was avowedly, in the manager's opinion and in the opinion of every other performer, superior to half of those he nightly played. That it could have disgraced or injured him partiality itself could not affirm.

'And is the poet, after having spent a life in that deep investigation of the human heart which alone can enable him to write a play, whose efforts must be prodigious, and, if he succeed, his pathos, wit, and genius, rare, is he, after all his struggles, to be at the mercy of an ignorant actor or actress? who, so far from deeply studying the sense, frequently do not remember the words they ought to repeat!

'Every *mister* is discontented with the character allotted him, each envies the other, and mutters accusations against both author and manager. Sir won't speak the prologue, it is not in his way; and Madam will have the epilogue, or she will positively throw up her part. One gentleman thinks his dialogue too long and heavy, and t'other too short and trifling. This fine lady refuses to attend rehearsals: another comes, but has less of the spirit of the author at the fifth repetition than she had at the first. Of their parts individually they know but very little; of the play as a whole they are absolutely ignorant. On the first representation, by which the reputation of a play is decided, they are so confused and imperfect, owing partly to their imbecility but more still to their indolence, that the sense of the author is mutilated, his characters travestied, and his piece rather burlesqued than performed. The reality of the scene depends on the passions excited in the actor listening almost as essentially as in the actor speaking; but at the end of each speech the player supposes his part is over: the arms, attitude, and features, all sink into insignificance, and have no more meaning than the face of Punch when beating Joan.

'Of the reality of this picture I soon had full proof. My tragedy, after a number of rehearsals, during which all these vexatious incidents and many more were experienced by me, was at length performed. To say that the applause it received equalled my expectations would be false: but it greatly exceeded the expectations of others. It was materially injured by the want of the actor who had refused his part. The reigning vice of recitation, which since the death of Garrick[1] has again prevailed, injured it more. The tide of passion, which should have rushed in torrents and burst upon the astonished ear, was sung out in slow and measured syllables, with a monotonous and funeral cadence, painful in its motion, and such as reminded me of the Sloth and his horrid cry: plaintive indeed, but exciting strange disgust!

'My success however was thought extraordinary. The actors when the play was over swarmed into the green-room, to congratulate me. The actresses were ready to kiss me; good natured souls! The green-room[2] loungers, newspaper critics, authors, and pretended friends of the house flocked round me, to wish me joy and stare at that enviable animal a successful poet. One of them, himself an approved writer of comedy, offered me five hundred pounds for the profits of my piece, and as far as money was concerned I thought my fortune was made: doubts and difficulties were fairly over, and the reward of all my toils was at last secure. Sanguine blockhead, thus everlastingly to embitter my own cup of sorrow! Secure? Oh no! The nectar of hope was soon dashed from my lips.

'I must detail the causes of this reverse; they were various and decisive.

'It had been the custom on the appearance of every new play to give it what is called a run, that is to perform it without intermission as many nights as the house should continue to be tolerably filled. The managers of both theatres had at this time deemed the practice prejudicial, and determined to reform it. Of this reform I was the victim. My play was the first that appeared after the resolution had been taken; and, in the bills of the day which announced the performance of my tragedy for the Saturday evening, the public were advertised that another piece would be acted on Monday. Ignorant of the true reason, the town misinterpreted this notice into an avowal that no favourable expectations were formed of my tragedy; and, as the author was an obscure person whose name was totally unknown to the world, none of that public curiosity on which popularity depends was excited.

'This was but one of the damning causes. My play appeared about the middle of October, when the season continued to be fine: the citizens were all at the watering places, the court was at Windsor, the parliament had not met, and the town was empty.[1]

'To add to all this, one of the performers was taken ill on the second night. Another of them thought proper to ride over to Egham races, on the third; where he got drunk and absented himself from the theatre; so that substitutes were obliged to be found for both the parts. In fine though some few, struck as they affirmed with the merits of the play, were just enough to attempt to bring it into public esteem, it gradually sunk into neglect. My third night, after paying the expences of the house, produced me only twenty pounds. On the sixth night, the receipts were less than the charges, and it was played no more. The overplus of the third night was little more than sufficient to defray the deficiences of the sixth; and thus vanished my golden dreams of profit, prosperity, and fame!

'The evil did not rest here. I was in danger of all the misfortunes I had foreseen from the Jew, and the bond. There was not only hardship and severity but injustice in my case, and I determined to remonstrate to the manager. My mind was sore and my appeal was spirited, but proper: it was an appeal to his equity.

'He listened to me, acknowledged I had been unfortunate, and said that, though the theatre could not and ought not to be accountable for my loss, yet some compensation he thought was justly my due. He therefore gave me a draft on his treasurer for one hundred pounds, and wished me better success in future.

'This it is true was of the most essential service to me; it relieved me, not only from imprisonment, but from the degradation of having my honesty questioned. It did not however restore me to the hope that should have rouzed me to greater exertions.

'Some new efforts indeed I was obliged to make; for the time consumed in revising my tragedy, and attending rehearsals, had occasioned me to neglect other pursuits, and I was again some few pounds in debt. No dread of labour, no degree of misery could induce me to leave these debts unpaid. I therefore worked and starved till they were all discharged: after which I returned to the country, and became usher at the school where I first knew you, Mr. Trevor.

'To paint the family distresses that succeeded, the disgrace, the infamy that attended them, the wretchedness that afterward preyed upon me, till I could endure no more, were needless. I was satisfied that I had a right to end a state of suffering, and to be rid of a world that considers itself as burthened not benefited by such creatures as I am. At torments after death, concerning which bigotry and cunning have invented such horrid fables, accusing and blaspheming a God whom they pretend to adore of tyranny the most monstrous, and injustice the most abhorred, at tales like these I laughed.

'You, Mr. Turl, say you can shew me better arguments, moral motives that are indispensable, why I ought to live. These are assertions, of which I must consider. You have restored me to life: prove that you have done me a favour! Of that I doubt! My first sensation, after recovering my faculties, was anger at your officious pity: shew me that it was ill timed and unjust. If you have reduced me to the necessity of again debating the same painful and gloomy question, if you cannot give that elasticity to my mind which will animate it to despise difficulty and steel it against injustice, however good your intentions may have been, I fear you have but imposed misery upon me.'

CHAPTER X

Remarks on the mistakes of Mr. Wilmot, by Turl: Law, or important truths discussed; to which few will attend, fewer will understand, and very few indeed will believe

THE state of mind into which his mistakes had brought him rendered Wilmot an object of compassion. The tone in which he concluded testified the alarming errors into which he was still liable to fall. For this reason, though Turl treated him with all possible humanity and tenderness, he considered it as dangerous to him, and scarcely less so to me, on whom he perceived the strong impression the narrative had made, to be silent. With a voice and countenance therefore of perfect urbanity, he thus replied.

'Do not imagine, Mr. Wilmot, that I have not been deeply penetrated by your sufferings; that I am insensible of your uncommon worth, or that I approve the vices of society, and the injustice and unfeeling neglect with which you have been treated. Thousands are at this moment subject to the same oppression.

'But the province of wisdom is not to lament over our wrongs: it is to find their remedy. Querulous complaint (Pardon me, if my words or expressions have any ill-timed severity: indeed that is far from my intention.) Querulous complaint is worthy only of the infancy of understanding. The world is unjust: and why? Because it is ignorant. Ought that to excite either complaint or anger? Would not the energies of intellect be more worthily employed in removing the cause, by the communication of knowledge?

'You bid me restore the elasticity of your mind. Can you look round on the follies and mistakes of men, which you have the power to detect, expose, and in part reform, and be in want of motive? You demand that I should communicate to you the desire of life. Can you have a perception of the essential duties that you are fitted to perform, and dare you think of dying?

'You have been brooding over your own wrongs, which your distorted fancy has painted as perhaps the most insufferable in the whole circle of existence! How could you be so blind? Look at the mass of evil, by which you are surrounded! What is its origin? Ignorance. Ignorance is the source of all evil; and there is one species of ignorance to which you and men like you have been egregiously subject: ignorance of the true mode of exercising your rare faculties; ignorance of their unbounded power of enjoyment.

'You have been persuaded that this power was destroyed, by the ridiculous distinctions of rich and poor. Oh, mad world! Monstrous absurdity! Incomprehensible blindness! Look at the rich! In what are they happy? In what do they excel the poor? Not in their greater stores of wealth: which is but a source of vice, disease, and death; but in a little superiority of knowledge; a trifling advance toward truth. How may this advantage be made general? Not by the indulgence of the desires you have fostered; the tendency of which was vicious; but by retrenching those false wants, that you panted to gratify; and thus by giving leisure to the poor or rather to all mankind, to make the acquirement of knowledge the grand business of life.

'This is the object on which the attention of every wise man should be turned. He that by precept or example shall prevail on community to relinquish one superfluous dish, one useless and contemptible trapping, will be the general friend of man. He who labours for riches, to countenance by his practice their abuse, is labouring to secure misery to himself, and perpetuate it in society. Who ought to be esteemed the most rich? He whose faculties are the most enlarged. How wealthy were you, had you but known it, at the moment your mind was distracting itself by these dirges of distress.

'He that would riot in luxury, let him wait the hour of appetite; and carry his morsel into the harvest field. There let him seat himself on a bank, eat, and cast his eyes around. Then, while he shall appease the cravings of hunger (not pamper the detestable caprice of gluttony) let him remember how many thousands shall in like manner be fed, by the plenty he every where beholds. How poor and pitiable a creature would he be, were his pleasure destroyed, or narrowed, because the earth on which it was produced was not what he had absurdly been taught to call his own!

'You complain that the titled and the dignified rejected your intercourse. How could you thus mistake your true rank? How exalted was it, compared to the ridiculous arrogance you envied! Were you now visiting Bedlam, would you think yourself miserable because its mad inhabitants despised you, for not being as mighty a monarch as each of themselves? But little depth of penetration is necessary, to perceive that the lunatics around us are no less worthy of our laughter and our pity.

'If I do not mistake, you, Mr. Trevor, are hurrying into the very errors that have misled your noble minded friend and instructor. Your active genius is busying itself how to obtain those riches and distinctions on which you have falsely supposed happiness depends. You are in search of a profession, by which your fortune is to be made. Beware! Notwithstanding that I am frequently assaulted by the same kind of folly myself, I yet never recollect it without astonishment!'

While Turl confined the application of his precepts to Wilmot, I listened and assented with scarcely a doubt: but, the moment he directed them against me, I turned upon him with all the force to which by my passions and fears I was rouzed.

'What,' said I, 'would you persuade me to renounce those pursuits by which alone I can gain distinction and respect in society? Would you have me remain in poverty, and thus relinquish the dearest portion of existence?'

Olivia was full in my thoughts, as I spoke.

'Of what worth would life be, were I so doomed? Rather than accept it on such terms, were there ten thousand Serpentine rivers I would drown in them all!'

Turl glanced significantly first at me and then at Wilmot. 'Do you consider the danger, the possible consequences, of the doctrine you are now inculcating, Mr. Trevor?'

Too much devoured by passion to attend to his reproof, in the sense he meant it, I retorted in a still louder key. 'I can discover no ill consequences in being sincere. I repeat, were there millions of seas, I would sooner drown in them all! You are continually pushing your philosophy to extremes, Mr. Turl.'

'You should rather say, Mr. Trevor, you are pushing your want of philosophy to an extreme.'

'The self denial you require is not in the nature of man.'

'The nature of man is a senseles jargon. Man is that which he is made by the various occurrences to which he is subjected. Those occurrences continually differ; no two men, therefore, were ever alike. But how are you to obtain the wealth and dignity you seek? By honest means?'

'Can you suppose me capable of any other?'

'Alas! How universal, how dangerous, are the mistakes of mankind! Your hopes are childish. The law, I understand, is your present pursuit. Do you suppose it possible to practise the law, in any form, and be honest?'

'Sir!—Mr. Turl?—You amaze me! Where is the dishonesty of pleading for the oppressed?'

'How little have you considered the subject! How ignorant are you of the practice of the law! Oppressed? Do counsel ever ask who is the oppressed? Do they refuse a brief because the justice of the case is doubtful? Do they not always inquire, not what is justice, but, what is law? Do they not triumph most, and acquire most fame, when they can gain a cause in the very teeth of the law they profess to support and revere? Who is the greatest lawyer? Not he who can most enlighten, but he who can most perplex and confound the understanding of his hearers! He who can best brow-beat and confuse witnesses; and embroil and mislead the intellect of judge and jury. Yet the mischiefs I have mentioned are but the sprouts and branches of this tree of evil; its root is much deeper: it is in the law itself; and in the system of property, of which law is the support.'

'Pshaw! These are the distempered dreams of reform run mad.'

'Are they? Consider! Beware of the mischief of deciding rashly! Beware of your passions, that are alarmed lest they should be disappointed.'

'It is you that decide. Prove this rooted evil of law.'

'Suppose me unable to prove it: are its consequences the less real? But I will endeavour.

'He, who is told that, "to do justice is to conduce with all his power to the well being of the whole," has a simple intelligible rule for his conduct.

'He, on the contrary, who is told that, "to do justice is to obey the law," has to inquire, not what is justice! but, what is the law? Now to know the law, (were it practicable!) would be not only to know the statutes at large by rote, but all the precedents, and all the legal discussions and litigations, to which the practitioners of law appeal! Innumerable volumes, filled with innumerable subtleties and incoherencies, and written in a barbarous and unintelligible jargon, must be studied! Memory is utterly inadequate to the task; and reason revolts, spurns at and turns from it with loathing.

'A short statement of facts will, in my opinion, demonstrate that law, in its origin and essence, is absolutely unjust.

'To make a law is to make a rule, by which a certain class of future events shall be judged.

'Future events can only be partially and imperfectly foreseen.

'Consequently, the law must be partial and imperfect.

'Let us take the facts in another point of view—The law never varies.

'The cases never agree.

'The law is general.

'The case is individual.

'The penalty of the law is uniform.

'The justice or injustice of the case is continually different.

'To prejudge any case, that is, to give a decided opinion on it while any of the circumstances remain unknown, is unjust even to a proverb. Yet this is precisely what is done, by making a law.'

'This is strange doctrine, Mr. Turl!'

'Disprove the facts, Mr. Trevor. They are indisputable; and on them the following syllogism may indisputably be formed.

'To make a law is publicly to countenance and promote injustice.

'Publicly to countenance and promote injustice is a most odious and pernicious action.

'Consequently, to make a law is a most odious and pernicious action.

'How unlimited are the moral mischiefs that result! To make positive laws is to turn the mind from the inquiry into what is just, and compel it to inquire what is law!

'To make positive laws is to habituate and reconcile the mind to injustice, by stamping injustice with public approbation!

'To make positive laws is to deaden the mind to that constant and lively sense of what is just and unjust, to which it must otherwise be invariably awake, by not only encouraging but by obliging it to have recourse to rules founded in falsehood!

'Each case is law to itself: that is, each case ought to be decided by the justice, or the injustice arising out of the circumstances of that individual case; and by no other case or law whatever; for the reason I have already given, that there never were nor ever can be two cases that were not different from each other.

'I therefore once more warn you, Mr. Trevor, that law is a pernicious mass of errors; and that the practitioners of it can only thrive by the mischiefs which they themselves produce, the falsehoods they propagate, and the miseries they inflict!'

'This would be dangerous doctrine to the preacher, were it heard in Westminster hall.'

'I am sorry for it! I am sorry that man can be in danger from his fellow men, because he endeavours to do them good!'

CHAPTER XI

Painful meditations: A new project for acquiring wealth: A journey to Bath

THAT the reader may judge of the arguments of Turl, I have been anxious to state them simply; and not perplexed with the digressions, commentaries, cavils, and violent opposition they met with from me. Striking as they did at the very root of all my promised pleasures, how could I listen and not oppose? Destroying as they did all my towering hopes at a breath, what could I do but rave? When my arguments and my anger were exhausted, I sat silent for a while, sunk in melancholy revery. At length I recovered myself so far as to endeavour to console Mr. Wilmot, offer him every assistance in my power, and persuade him to an interview with his sister. Aided by the benevolent arguments of Turl, this purpose was with some little difficulty effected, and I returned home to relate to Miss Wilmot what had happened.

In very bitterness of soul I then began to meditate on the prospect before me. The sensations I experienced were at some moments agonizing! Could I even have renounced fame and fortune, and patiently have resigned myself to live in obscure poverty, yet to live, as in such a case I must do, without Olivia would be misery to which no arguments could induce me to submit. But how obtain her? Where were all my bright visions fled? Poor Wilmot! What an example did he afford of ineffectual struggles, talents neglected, and genius trampled in the dust! Was there more security for me? Turl indeed seemed to resign himself without a murmur, and to be happy in despite of fate. But he had no Olivia to regret! If he had, happiness without her would be impossible!

To attempt to repeat all the tormenting fears that hurried and agitated my mind, on this occasion, were fruitless. Suffice it to say, this was one of those severe conflicts to which by education and accident I was subject; and it was not the least painful part of the present one that I could come to no decision.

I persuaded myself indeed that, with respect to law, Turl's reasoning was much too severe and absolute. It was true I could not but own that law was inclined to debase and corrupt the morals of its practitioners; but surely there were exceptions, and if I pursued the law why should not I be one of them. If therefore the happiness at which I aimed were attainable by this means, I asserted to myself that I had heard no reasons which ought to deter me from practising the law.

In the mean time, I had conceived a project that related to the immediate state of my feelings; the acuteness of which I was obliged to seek some method to appease. Olivia was gone to Bath, with her aunt; and thither I was determined to follow her.

Full of this design, I dispatched Philip with orders that a post chaise should be ready at the door by nine o'clock the next morning; after which, to rid myself as much as possible of the thoughts that haunted me, I once more went in search of the false Belmont.

I found him at the usual place engaged at play. The betting was high, he appeared to be overmatched, and for a few games his antagonist, who like himself was a first rate player, triumphed. My passions were always of the touch-wood kind. Rouzed and tempted by the bets that were so plentifully offered, the thought suddenly occurred how possible it was for a man of penetration, who could keep himself perfectly cool, as I was persuaded I could (What was there indeed that I persuaded myself I could not do?) to make a fortune by gambling! I did not indeed call it by the odious term gambling: it was calculation, foresight, acuteness of discernment. My morality was fast asleep; so intent was I on profiting by this new and surprisingly certain source of wealth! and so avaricious of the means that at a glance seemed to promise the gratification of all my desires!

I had not frequented a billiard table without have exercised my own skill, learned the odds, and obtained a tolerable knowledge of the game itself. So fixed was my cupidity on its object that I began with the caution of a black-leg;[1] made a bet, and the moment the odds turned in my favour secured myself by taking them; hedged again, as the advantage changed; and thus made myself a certain winner. I exulted in my own clearness of perception! and wondered that so palpable a method of winning should escape even an idiot!

The experience however of a few games taught me that my discovery was not quite of so lucrative a nature as I had supposed. The odds did not every game vary, from side to side; people were not always inclined to bet the odds; and, if I would run no great risk, I even found it necessary to bet them sometimes myself. Every man who has made the experiment knows that the thirst of lucre, when thus awakened in a young mind, is insatiable, impetuous, and rash. I was weary of petty gains, and riches by retail. The ardour with which I examined the players, and each circumstance as it occurred, persuaded me that there were tokens by which an acute observer might discover the winning party. I had on former occasions remarked that players but rarely win game and game alternately, even when they leave off equal; but that success has a tide, with a kind of periodical ebb and flow. This said I may be attributed to the temper of the players; the loser is too angry to attend with sufficient caution to his game; he persuades himself that luck is against him, strikes at random, and does mischief every stroke. After a while the winner grows careless, loses a game, and becomes angry and conquered in turn.

Exulting in my prodigious penetration, and fortified in my daring by reasoning so deep, I determined to hedge no more bets. Belmont, whose notice my sudden rage for betting had by no means escaped, was at this time losing, and I was backing his antagonist. To one of the bets I offered, he said, 'Done;' and, though I felt a reluctance to win his money, it seemed ungentlemanlike to refuse. I won the first three bets; and, exulting in my own acuteness and certainty, intreated him in pity to desist. He refused, and I pleaded the pain I felt at winning the money of a friend. Beside, it was not only dishonourable but dishonest; it was absolutely picking his pocket!

My triumph was premature. From this time fortune veered, and he began to win. I was then willing to have taken the other side, but could not procure a bet. He bantering bade me not be afraid of winning my friend's money; it was neither dishonourable, dishonest, nor picking his pocket. Piqued by his sarcasms, I continued till I had lost five and twenty guineas; and then my vexation and pride, which almost foamed at the suspicion of my own folly, made me propose to bet double or quit. I lost again, again resorted to the same desperate remedy, and met with the same ill success. My frenzy was such that I a third time urged him to continue. Fortunately for me his antagonist would play no more, and I was left to reflect that my calculations and avaricious arts to rob fools and outwit knaves were as crude as they were contemptible.

Wrung as I was to the heart, I was ashamed of having it supposed that the loss of my hundred guineas in the least affected me. Belmont insisted that I should sup with him, and when I attempted to decline his invitation bantered me out of my refusal, by asking if I had parted with my hundred guineas to purchase the spleen. During supper I informed him of my intended journey to Bath; and he immediately proposed to accompany me, telling me that he had himself had the same intention. On this we accordingly agreed, and I left him early and retired to bed; but not to rest. The quick decay of my small substance, the helpless state in which I found myself, the impatience with which I desired wealth and power, and the increasing distance at which I seemed to be thrown from Olivia by this last act of folly, kept me not only awake but in a fever of thought.

The next day we set off, and arrived at Bath the same evening; where the first inquiries I made were at the Pump-room, to learn where Olivia and her aunt were lodged. So inconsiderate and eager were my desires, that I endeavoured to obtain apartments in the same house; but ineffectually, they were all let. I was recommended to others however in Milsom-street, in which I fixed my abode. There was not room for Belmont, and he got lodgings on the South Parade.

CHAPTER XII

Desperate measures: Olivia and her aunt: A rash accusation; and its strange consequences: Affairs brought to a crisis

BEFORE I proceed to the history of my Bath adventures, it is necessary to take a brief retrospect of the state of my affairs. The total of my expences, from the time that I received the four hundred and fifty pounds of Thornby, to my arrival at Bath, was about two hundred and forty pounds, including the sum I had lost at billiards, the money I had paid for printing my pamphlet (the last sheet of which I corrected before I left town) thirty pounds that in consequence of a letter from my mother I remitted to her, and twenty for the purchase of a lottery ticket; for, among other absurd and vicious ways of becoming rich, that suggested itself to my eager fancy.

The quick decay of my very small inheritance lay corroding at my heart, and prompted me to a thousand different schemes, without the power of determining me to any. My general propensity however was more to the desperate, which should at once be decisive, than to the slow and lingering plans of timid prudence. In reality both seemed hopeless, and therefore the briefest suffering was the best. At some short intervals the glow of hope, which had lately been so fervid, would return, and those powers of thought that seemed to be struggling within me would promise great and glorious success; but these were only flashes of lightening darting through a midnight sky, the texture of which was deep obscurity; 'darkness visible.'[1]

To one point however I was fixed, that of using every endeavour to learn the true sentiments of Olivia respecting me; and, if any possible opportunity offered, of declaring my own. To effect this I resolved, since I knew not what better method to take, that I would watch the few public places to which all the visitors at Bath resort.

I therefore immediately subscribed to the upper and lower rooms, and traversed the city in every direction.

People, not confined to their chamber, are here sure to be soon met with; and, on the second morning after my arrival, I discovered Olivia, seated at the farther end of the Pump-room. She had an old lady, who proved to be her aunt, by her side; and a circle round her, in which were several handsome fellows, who my jealous eye instantly discovered were all ambitious of her regard.

The moment I had a glimpse of her, I was seized with a trembling that shook my whole frame, and a sickness that I with difficulty subdued. I approached, stopped, turned aside, again advanced, again hesitated, and was once more almost overcome by a rising of the heart that was suffocating, and a swimming of the brain that made my limbs stagger, my eyes roll, and deprived me of sight.

It was sometime before I could make another attempt. At length I caught her eye. With the rapidity of lightening her cheek was suffused with blushes, and as instantaneously changed to a death-like pale. It was my habitual error to interpret every thing in my own favour; and the conviction that she was suffering emotions similar to my own was transport to me.

For some minutes I mingled with the croud, fearful of a relapse on my own part and on hers, but keeping her in sight, and presenting myself to her view, till I was rouzed by an apparent motion of the aunt to rise. I then advanced, but still in an ague fit of apprehension. I attempted to bow, and in a faltering and feeble voice pronounced her name, 'hoped she was well, and'—I could proceed no farther.

My disease was infectious. She sat a moment, severely struggling with her feelings, and then returned a kind of inarticulate complimentary answer.

'What is the matter Olivia?' said the aunt. 'How strangely you look child? Who is the gentleman?'

Olivia made another effort.—'It is Mr. Trevor, Madam; the grandson of the rector of ***.'

'Oh ho! The young Oxonian that my nephew Hector tells the comical story about; of the methodist preacher, and of his throwing you into the water, and then taking you out again.'

The tone, form, and features of the old lady, with this short introductory dialogue, gave me a strong, but no encouraging picture, of her character. Her voice was masculine, her nose short, her mouth wide, her brow bent and bushy, and the corners of her eyes and cheeks deeply wrinkled. I attempted to enter into conversation, but my efforts were aukward; the answers of the aunt were broad, coarse, and discouraging; and Olivia, though embarrassed, I accused of being cold. The manner of the old lady clearly indicated, that she suspected my design; and an endeavour in me to prolong the conversation, by turning it on my native county, drew from her the following animadversions.

'I have heard a great deal about your family, Mr. Trevor; and of the ridiculous opposition which your grandfather pretended to make to my late brother, Mowbray. Your mother, I think, was twice married, and, as I have been told, both times very imprudently; so that the proud hopes which the rector entertained of raising a family were all overthrown. But that is always the case with clandestine matches. Many families, of much greater consequence than ever yours was, Mr. Trevor, have been brought low by such foolish and wicked doings. Young girls that have indulged improper connections, and secret lovers, have involved themselves, and all their relations, in ruin by their guilty proceedings. You are but a petty instance of the base and bad consequences of the crimes of such foolish young hussies. Come, niece!'

They both rose to go. The dialogue that had just passed had no listeners, though of that circumstance the aunt was evidently regardless. The circle round Olivia had presently dispersed, as good manners required, when I a stranger came up. The repugnant and ominous behaviour of the aunt did but increase the impetuous haste that I felt to know the worst, and addressing myself to Olivia, I asked with some eagerness, 'If I might be permitted to pay her my respects while she continued at Bath?'

The aunt fixed her eye on me, 'Look you,' said she, 'Mr. Trevor, you are a handsome young fellow, and I do not want handsome young fellows about my niece. I see too many of them: they have little fortune, and less shame; they give me a deal of trouble; no good can come of their smirking and smiling, their foppery and their forward prate. My niece I believe has much more prudence than is usual with the young minxes of the present day. But no matter for that: I am sure there is no prudence in setting gunpowder too near the fire. I have heard her talk of your taking her out of the water in a manner that, if I did not know her, I should not quite like. So I must plainly tell you, Sir, as I can see no good that can come of your acquaintance, I shall take care to prevent all harm. Not that there is much fear, for she knows her duty, and has always done it. Neither can you have entertained any impertinent notions: it would be too ridiculous! Though what my nephew and Mr. Andrews told me, I own, did seem as if you could strangely forget yourself. But at once to cut matters short, I now tell you plainly, and down right, her choice is made. Yes, Sir, her choice is positively made; and so, though I do not suppose you have taken any foolish crotchets, and improper whims into your head, for that would be too impertinent, yet as you knew one another when children, and so forth, it was best to be plain with you at once, because, though such ridiculous nonsense was quite impossible, I hear on all hands you are a bold and flighty young gentleman, and that you have no little opinion of yourself.'

Dumb founded as I was by this undisguised refusal, this hard, unfeeling reprimand, I made no attempt to reply or follow. The flushings of Olivia's face indeed were continual; but what were they more than indignant repellings of her aunt's broad surmises? Had they been favourable to me why did she not declare them with the openness of which she had so striking an example? She curtsied as she went; but it was a half-souled compliment, that while I attempted to return my heart resented.

They disappeared, and I remained, feeling as if now first made sensible of the extreme folly, the lunacy of all my actions! The dialogue I had just heard vibrated in my brain, burning and wasting it with the frenzy of agonizing recollection. 'I was a forward prating fop, of little fortune, and less shame! Bold and flighty, with no little opinion of myself; again and again I was ridiculous, and impertinent! My crotchets, whims, and nonsense were impossible!'

Nor was this all! There was another piece of intelligence; an additional and dreadful feature of despair; the name of Andrews! Detested sound! Racking idea! 'Her choice is made; positively made!' Excruciating thought! Why then, welcome ruin! sudden and irrevocable ruin!

As soon as I could recover sufficient recollection, I hurried home; where I remained in a trance of torment, and disposed to a thousand acts of madness that were conceived and dismissed with a rapidity of pain that rendered my mind impotent to all, except the inflicting torture on itself.

At last, the agony in which I sat was interrupted by the appearance of Belmont. We had agreed to go to Lansdown races, he told me it was now time, took me by the arm, and hurried me away.

Reckless of where I went, or what I did, I obeyed. The course was at no great distance, a carriage was not to be procured, and we walked. The steepness of the hill, the heat of the day, and above all the anguish of my heart, threw me into a violent heat. The drops rolled down my cheeks, and I put my handkerchief lightly into my hat, to prevent its pressure. Lost in a revery of misery, I acted instinctively, and breathed the dust, heard the hubbub, and saw the confusion around me without perceiving them.

After the first heat there was a battle, toward which I was dragged by Belmont. In the tumult and distraction of my thoughts, I scarcely knew what happened; and feeling in my pocket for my handkerchief I missed it. A croud and a pick-pocket was an immediate suggestion. Neither coolness nor recollection were present to me. I saw a man putting up a red and white handkerchief, which I supposed to be mine, and springing forward, I caught him by the collar, and exclaimed, 'Rascal, you have robbed me!' In an instant the mob flocked round us, and the supposed pick-pocket was seized. 'Duck him! Duck him!' was the general cry; and away the poor fellow was immediately hurried. Half awakened by the unpremeditated danger into which I had brought him, I began to repent. Belmont, who had lost sight of me, came up, and asked what was the matter.

'A fellow has picked my pocket,' said I.

'Of what?'

'Of my handkerchief.'

'Your handkerchief? Is it not under your hat?'

I snatched it off, examined, and there the handkerchief was!—I was struck speechless!

The man whom I had falsely accused made a violent resistance; the mob was dragging him along, rending his clothes off his back, and half-tearing him in pieces. The state of my mind was little short of frenzy. In a tone of command, I bade Belmont follow, made my way into the thickest of the croud, and furiously began to beat the people who were ill-using the prisoner; calling till I was hoarse, 'Let him alone! He is innocent! I am to blame!'

My efforts were vain. A mob has many hands but no ears. My blows were returned fifty fold. I was inveloped by one mob myself, while the poor wretch was hauled along by another. Not all my struggles could save him. I could not get free; and the man, as

Belmost afterward informed me, was half drowned; after which he escaped, and nobody knew what was become of him.

These were but a part of the accidents of the day. My mind was maddening, and I was ripe for mischief. Belmont in the evening went to the hazard table, and I determined to accompany him, to which he encouraged me. The impetus was given, and, as if resolved on destruction, I put all my money, except a ten pound note to pay my Bath debts, in my pocket. Though ignorant of the cause of them, Belmont discovered my inclinations. He took care to be at the place before the company assembled.

An accomplice (as I afterward learned) was present, who displayed guineas and bank notes sufficient to convince me that he was my man, if I could but win them. I was as eager as they could desire, and to increase my ardour was occasionally suffered to win a rich stake. My success was of short duration; I soon began to lose and foam with rage. In the midst of this scene, Hector Mowbray and tall Andrews came in; who unknown to me were at Bath. They saw me close my accounts, and by their looks enjoyed my fury. The whole company, which now began to be numerous, understood that I left off play because I had no more money to lose. The pigeon was completely plucked.

This was the climax of misery, at which I seemed ambitious to arrive. During six hours, I sat in a state of absolute stupor; and echoed the uproar and blasphemy that surrounded me with deep but unconscious groans. I do not know that I so much as moved, till the company was entirely dispersed, and I was awakened from my torpor by the groom porter. I then languidly returned to my lodging, exhausted and unable longer to support the conflicting torture.

END OF VOLUME III

VOLUME IV

CHAPTER I

The pains and penalties of illicit attempts to become rich: The sleep of a gamester: Morning meditations

THE pungency of extreme grief acts as a temporary opiate: for a short time it lulls the sufferer to insensibility, and sleep; but it is only to recruit him and awaken him to new torments.

When I reached my lodgings, I appeared to myself to have sunk into a state of quiescent resignation. The die was cast. My doom was irrevocable; and despair itself seemed to have lost its charm: the animation, the vigour, of misery was gone. I was reduced to an inevitable post-horse kind of endurance;[1] and had only now to be thankful if I might be permitted to exist. From an audacious and arrogant confidence in my own strength, I had suddenly yet by perceptible gradations declined, though with excruciating pangs at every step, till I now at last found myself in a state of sluggish and brute imbecility.

Staggering home in this temper, I undressed myself, went to bed with stupid composure, and felt like a wretch that had been stretched on the rack, and, having just been taken off, was suffered to sink into lifeless languor, because he could endure no more. I was mistaken. My sleeping sensations soon became turbulent, oppressive, fevered, terrific, yet cumbrous, and impossible to awake from and escape.

It was seven in the morning, when I returned to my lodging. When I went to bed, my heaviness was so great that I seemed as if I could have slept for centuries; and, so multifarious and torturing were the images that haunted me, that, the time actually appeared indefinitely protracted: a month, a year, an age: yet it was little more than two hours. The moment struggling nature had cast off her horrible night-mares, and I had once more started into identity, the anguish of the past day and night again seized me. Pains innumerable, and intolerable, rushed upon me. Each new thought was a new serpent. Mine was the head of Medusa:[1] with this difference; my scorpions shed all their venom inward.

Confusion of mind is the source of pain: but confusion is the greatest in minds that are the seldomest subject to it; and with those the pain is proportionably intense. The conflict was too violent to be endured, without an endeavour to get rid of it. I rose, traversed my room I know not how long, and at last rushed into the street; with a sort of feeling that, when in the open air, the atmosphere of misery that enveloped me would be swallowed up, and lost, in the infinite expanse.

The hope was vain: it wrapped me round like a cloak. It was a universal caustic, that would not endure to be touched; much less torn away. I groaned. I gnashed my teeth. I griped my hands. I struck myself violent blows. I ran with fury, in circles, in zigzag, with sudden turns and frantic bounds; and, finding myself on the banks of the Avon, plunged headlong in.

I acted from no plan, or forethought; therefore was far from any intention to drown myself; and, being in the water, I swam as I had run, like a mad or hunted bull.

That unpremeditated sensation which enforces immediate action is what, I suppose, Philosophers mean by instinct: if the word ever had any definite meaning. Thousands of these instinctive experiments are, no doubt, injurious to the animals that make them: but, their number being unlimited, some of them are successful. The benefit is remembered; they are repeated; and a future race profits by the wisdom that becomes habitual. I am well persuaded that my immersion in the stream was assuaging; and gamesters hereafter, or the faculty themselves, may, if they please, profit by the experiment.

I have no distinct recollection of coming out of the water: though I remember walking afterward, two or three hours, till my cloaths were again entirely dry. My feelings, in the interval, were somewhat similar to those of the preceding evening; declining from frantic agitation to stupidity, and torpor.

CHAPTER II

*An unexpected rencontre; and a desperate contest: Victory
dearly bought*

MAN is, or, which is the same thing, his sensations are, continually
changing; and it may be truly affirmed that he is many different
animals in the course of a day. A very unexpected, yet very natural,
incident again rouzed me, to a state of activity.

During my ramble, I had strayed among the new buildings, below
the Crescent.[1] I know not whether I had any latent hope, or wish, of
having a distant sight of Olivia, walking there as is customary for
air and exercise: though I was certainly far too much degraded, in
my own opinion, to intend being seen myself, even by her; much
less by any of those proud beings, those ephemeræ of fortune, with
whom, while I despised their arrogance, not to associate, not to be
familiar, nay not to treat with a sort of conscious superiority, was
misery. We all practise that haughtiness, ourselves, which, in others,
is so irritating to our feelings; and for which we pretend to have so
sovereign a contempt.

As I passed a number of workmen, my moody apathy, though
great, did not prevent me from hearing one of them exclaim, with a
loud and suddenly angry surprize, 'By G— that is he!'

I was at some little distance. I heard the steps of a man running
speedily toward me. I turned round. He looked me full in the face;
and, with no less eagerness, repeated—'Yes! D-mn me if it is not!
Dick! Will! Come here! Run!'

I stood fixed. I did not recollect ever to have seen the exact figure
before me; but I had a strong and instantaneously a painful impression, of the same form in a different garb. It was the man whom
I had accused, the day before, of picking my pocket: the poor fellow
who had been so unmercifully ducked, and ill treated, by the mob.

His impatience of revenge was furious. Without uttering another
word, he made a desperate blow at me. I was unprepared; and it
brought me to the ground. His foot was up, to second it with as
violent a kick; but, fortunately, the generous spirit of my opponent
and the laws of mob honour were mutually my shield. He recollected
the cowardice as well as the opprobrium of kicking a combatant,
when down; and, in the tone of rage, commanded me to get up.

I was not slow in obeying the mandate; nor he in repeating the assault. I warded several of his blows, which were dealt with too much thoughtless fury to be dangerous; but again and again called on him to stop, for a moment, and hear me. I felt I had been the cause of much mischief to the man; and had no alacrity to increase the wrong. My behaviour was not that of fear; and his companions at length got between us, and for a moment prevented the battle.

We were at the bottom of the hill: the beginning of the fray had been seen, and the crowd was collecting in every direction. The beaus descended from the crescent; and left the belles to view us through their opera-glasses, and pocket-telescopes, while they came to collect more circumstantial information. The Mowbray family had just arrived at this public *promenade*. Hector and tall Andrews joined the mob: the aunt and Olivia remained on the walk.

The story of the false accusation, the ducking, and the injuries done to my antagonist, ran, varied and mangled, from mouth to mouth: a general sensation of rage was excited against me; and Hector and Andrews very charitably gave it every assistance in their power. Not satisfied with this, they proposed the *Lex Talionis;*[1] and called—'Duck him!' 'Duck him!' They took care, however, to turn their backs; imagining that, amid the hubbub, I should not distinguish their voices.

My antagonist, though but a journeyman carpenter, had too much of the hero in him to admit of this mean revenge. His anger could only be appeased by chastising me with his own arm; and proving to me, as well as to the crowd, how unworthy he was of that contemptible character which my accusation had endeavoured to fix upon him. He was therefore determined to oblige me to fight.

I never remember to have felt greater repugnance, than I now had, to defend myself, by committing more hurt and injury upon this indignant, but brave, fellow. I tried to expostulate, nay to intreat, but in vain: my remonstrances were construed into cowardice, and fight I must, or suffer such disgrace as my tyro-philosophy was ill calculated to endure.

My antagonist was stripped in form; and, as the diversion of a battle is what an English mob will never willingly forego, I found partisans; who determined to see fair play, encouraged, instructed me, clapped me on the back, and, partly by intreaty partly by violence, stripped off my coat. They were vexed at my obstinate refusal to part with my waistcoat and shirt.

With their usual activity, they soon made a ring; and I stood undetermined, and excessively reluctant; not very willing to receive, but infinitely averse to return the blows he now once more began to deal!

The carpenter was an athletic and powerful man; famous for the battles he had fought, and the victories he had gained. His companions, who evidently had an affection for him, and who knew his prowess, had no supposition that I could withstand him for five minutes: though the hopes of those who were the most eager for the sport had been a little raised, by the alertness with which I rose, after being at first knocked down, and the skill with which I then stood on my defence.

The doubts that pervaded my mind imparted, I suppose, something of that appearance to my countenance which is occasioned by fear; for my adversary approached me with looks of contempt; and, as I retreated, bade me stand forward and face him like a man. The crowd behind seconded him; and, fearing it should be a run-away victory, was rather willing to press upon and push me forward than to recede, and give me any play. Hector and Andrews were all the while very active, as instigators.

My indecision occasioned me to receive several severe blows, without returning one; till, at length, I was again extended on the ground, by a very desperate blow near the ear; which, for a few seconds, deprived me of all sense and recollection.

This was no longer to be endured. As soon as I recovered, I sprang on my feet, condescended to strip, and became in turn the assailant. The joy and vociferation of the mob were immense. They thought it had been all over; and to see me now rise, stand forward, and fight, as I did, with so much determination and effect, was, to them, rapture. They had discovered a hero. Their education had taught them, for such is education, that the man who has the power to endure and to inflict the most misery is the most admirable.

For six successive rounds, I had completely the advantage; during which my brave foe had received five knock-down blows: for that is the phrase. His companions and friends were astonished. The beau pugilists were vociferating their bets; five pounds to a crown in my favour.

The carpenter was as hardy as he was courageous. He collected himself; I had become less circumspect, and he threw in another dangerous blow near my temple, with the left hand, that again felled me insensible to the earth.

I now recovered more slowly, and less effectually. I had been severely breathed, by the violence of exertion. The laws of pugilistic war[1] will not suffer a man to lie, after being knocked down, more than a certain number of seconds. Hector had his stop-watch in his hand; and tall Andrews joined him, to enforce the rule in all its rigour. I was lifted on my feet before I had perfectly recovered my recollection; and was again knocked down, though with less injury. While down, I received a kick in the side; of which my partisans instantly accused Andrews.

Meaning to do me mischief, he did me a favour. The wrangling that took place gave me time to recover; and being again brought in face of my opponent, I once more proposed a reconciliation; and, stretching out my arm, asked him to shake hands. But, no. The ducking was too bitterly remembered. 'He would beat me; or never go alive from the ground.'

For a moment, the generous thought of acknowledging myself vanquished suggested itself: but rising vanity, and false shame, spurned at the proposal, therefore, since he was so desperate, I had no resource but in being equally savage. Accordingly, I bent my whole powers to this detestable purpose, brought him twice more to the ground, and, on the third assault, gave him a blow that verified his own prediction; for he fell dead at my feet, and was taken up lifeless from the place.

Agony to agony! Vice to vice! Such was my fate! Where, when, how, was it to have an end? Were not my own personal sufferings sufficient? Accuse an innocent man of theft; deliver him over to the fury of a mob; and, not contented with that, meet him again to fight, beat, murder him! And without malice; without evil intention! Nay, with the very reverse: abhorring the mischief I had done him; and admiring the intrepidity and fortitude he had displayed!

Nor did it end here: the intelligence that was instantly sent round was horror indeed. He had left a wife and seven children!

CHAPTER III

The kind behaviour of old friends: A joyful recovery: More
misfortunes: Patience per force

NEVER were sensations more truly tragical than mine: yet, as is frequent, they had a dash of the ridiculous; which resulted from the machinations of my good friends, Hector and Andrews. To inspire others with the contempt in which they held, or rather endeavoured to hold, me, and to revenge the insults which they supposed themselves to have received from me, were their incentives. They knew I had been stripped of my money at the gaming-table: they mingled with the partisans of the carpenter; and, informing them that I was a pretended gentleman, advised them to have me taken before a magistrate; for that the law would at least make me provide for the widow and children. Perhaps it would hang me: as I deserved. They farther proposed a subscription, to begin with me; and accordingly they came up to me, as by deputation, with the murdered man's hat.

The mortification they intended me had its full effect. I was pennyless; and the epithets which generous souls like these appropriate, to such upstart intruders upon their rights and privileges as myself, were muttered with as much insolence as they had the courage to assume.

I was not yet tamed. I could not endure this baiting. I hated, almost abhorred, Andrews. He dared to pretend love to Olivia: he had brought me into disgrace with her; nay was soon to rob me of her everlastingly; and, recollecting the kick he had bestowed upon me when down, I called him a scoundrel; and accompanied the coarse expression with a blow.

In a moment, the mob were again in agitation, expected another battle, admired my hardy valour, and called for a ring. Andrews knew better: he saved them the trouble; and shuffled away; followed though scouted[1] even by Hector himself, for his cowardice. Mowbray remembered the battle of the rats; and, by comparison, found himself a very hero.

The moment I was permitted, I enquired to what place the poor carpenter had been taken; and followed with infinite terror, but with a faint degree of hope; some affirming that he was dead, others that he was not. I was attended by several of my admirers.

It would be vain to attempt any picture of what my feelings were, when, coming into his dwelling, I found him alive! sitting surrounded by his wife, children, and companions! I fell on my knees to him. I owned all the mischief I had done him. I conjured him, for God's sake, to forgive me. I was half frantic; and the worthy fellow, in the same free spirit with which he had fought, stretched out his hand, in token of his forgiveness and friendship.

His unaffected magnanimity prompted me instantly to execute a design which I had before formed. 'Stay where you are, my good friends,' said I, to the people that stood round him. 'I will be back in a few minutes. The little reparation that I can make I will make: to shew you that it was from error, and not ill intention, that I have done this brave man so much injury.'

So saying, I ran out of the house, directed my course to my lodgings, and hastened to my trunk; to take out the ten-pound note, which I had reserved to pay my Bath debts. My passions were too much in a hurry to admit of any enquiry how these debts were to be paid, when I should have given the bank-note to the carpenter. I was determined not to enquire; but to appease my feelings, rescue my character, and bestow it on him.

Where were my troubles to end? The persecuting malice of fortune was intolerable. Philip, the footman whom I had hired, but scarcely ever employed, had disappeared: having previously broken open my trunk, and taken, with the ten pounds, such of my linen and effects as he could carry under his cloaths, and in his pockets, without being seen.

This was a stroke little less painful than the worst of the accidents that had befallen me: yet, so harassed was my mind, and so wearied with grieving, that I did not feel it with half the poignancy.

Act however I must. But how? I had left the carpenter and his family in suspense. Must I talk of favours which I could not confer? or mention remuneration that would but seem like mockery? This was painful: but not so painful as falsehood.

I therefore returned, related the story of the robbery, and added that 'my intentions were to have endeavoured to afford some small recompence, for the unintentional injury I had committed. I was sorry that, at present, this accident had deprived me of the power: but I hoped I should not always be so very destitute. I certainly should neither forget the debt I had incurred, nor the noble behaviour of the man who had suffered so much from me. At present I was very unfortunate: but, if ever I should become more prosperous, I should remember my obligation, and in what manner it would become me to see it discharged.'

I was heard with patience, and with no disappointment. My auditors, though poor, were far from selfish. Beside, as I had not previously declared what I had intended, I had excited little expectation. My vanquished opponent, whose name was Clarke, was soothed by the justice I did him, in defending his innocence and praising his courage; and said 'I had given him the satisfaction of a man, and that was all he asked.' He rather sympathized with my loss than felt a loss of his own; and gave various indications of a generous spirit, such as is seldom to be found among persons who would think themselves highly disgraced by any comparison between them and a poor carpenter. I own I quitted him with a degree of esteem, such as neither the lord nor the bishop I had once been so willing, or rather so industrious, to revere had the good fortune to inspire.

Having said every thing I could recollect, to remove the doubts which the whole transaction might have excited against me, I was eager to return to my lodging, and consider what was best to be done.

The probability of tracing my footman and recovering the bank note, a considerable portion of which by the bye was due to him for wages, suggested itself. I recollected that when I rose, after my two hours sleep, he had brought the breakfast; and had manifested some tokens of anxiety, at perceiving the perturbation of my mind. I had hastily devoured the bread and butter that was on the table, and drank a single bason of tea; after which he enquired as I went out, when I should be back? And I had answered, in a wild manner, 'I did not know. Perhaps never.'

From the degree of interest that he had shewn, the robbery appeared the more strange; and the remembrance of his enquiring and compassionate looks made me the less eager to pursue, and have him hanged: though, at that time, I considered hanging as a very excellent thing.

Beside, I had not the means of pursuit: I had no money. He had probably taken the London road; and, profiting by the first stage-coach that passed, was now beyond my reach.

But how was I to act? How discharge my debts? What was to become of me? I could find no solution to these difficulties. I was oppressed by them. I was wearied by the excess of action on my body, as well as mind. I sunk down on the bed, without undressing or covering myself, and fell into a profound sleep.

CHAPTER IV

A fever: Bad men have good qualities: More proofs of compassion: A scandalous tale does not lose in telling: Farewell to Bath

THE emptiness of my stomach (for I had eaten nothing except the bread and butter I mentioned, since the preceding day at dinner) the heats into which my violent exertions had thrown me, and the sudden reverse of cold to which my motionless sleep subjected me, produced consequences that might easily have been foreseen: I awoke, in the dead of the might, and found myself seized with shivering fits, my teeth chattering, a sickness at my stomach, my head intolerably heavy, and my temples bruised with the blows I had received, and having a sensation as if they were ready to burst. To all this was added the stiffness that pervaded the muscles of my arms, and body, from the bruises, falls, and battering they had received.

It was with difficulty I could undress myself, and get into bed; where, after I had lain shaking with increasing violence I know not how long, my agueish sensations left me; and were changed into all the soreness, pains, and burning, that denote a violent fever.

During this paroxysm, I felt consolation from its excess; which persuaded me that I was now on my death bed. I remembered all the wrongs, which I conceived myself to have suffered, with a sort of misanthropical delight; arising from the persuasion that, in my loss, the world would be punished for the vileness of its injustice toward me. Perhaps every human being conceives that, when he is gone, there will be a chasm, which no other mortal can supply; and I am not certain that he does not conceive truly. Young men of active and impetuous talents have this persuasion in a very forcible degree.

All that I can remember of this fit of sickness, till the violence and danger of it were over, is, that the people of the house came to me in the morning, I knew not at what hour, and made some enquiries. A delirium succeeded; which was so violent that, at the beginning of my convalescence, I had absolutely lost my memory; and could not without effort recollect where I was, how I had come there, or what had befallen me. The first objects that forcibly arrested my attention, and excited memory, were the honest carpenter, Clarke, and his wife sitting by my bedside, and endeavouring to console me.

The particulars which I afterward learned were, that Belmont had come, the first day of my illness; had seen me delirious; had heard the account of my having been robbed, and had left a twenty-pound note for my immediate necessities.

So true is it that the licentious, the depraved, and the un-principled are susceptible of virtue; and desirous of communicating happiness. The most ignorant only are the most inveterately brutal: but nothing less than idiotism, or madness, can absolutely deprive man of his propensity to do good.

I was further informed that a sealed paper, addressed to Mr. Trevor, had been received, and opened in the presence of the physician, containing another twenty-pound bank-bill; but the paper that inclosed it was blank: and that Clarke, unable to go immediately to work, and reflecting on what he had heard from me concerning the destitute state in which I, a stranger in Bath, was left by the robbery of my servant, had walked out the next day, had come with fear and diffidence to enquire after me, and that, finding me in a high fever, his wife had been my first nurse.

Her own large family indeed prevented her from watching and continuing always with me; and therefore another attendant was obliged to be hired: but she was by my bed side the greatest part of every day; and her husband the same till he was again able to work; after which he never failed to come in the evening.

He was a generous fellow. I had won his heart, by my desire to do him justice; and my condescension excited a degree of adoration in him, when he found that I was really what the world calls a gentle-man. He had visited me before Belmont had left the money; and, hearing the landlady talk of sending me to the hospital, had proposed to take me to his home; that he and his wife might do a christian part by me, and I not be left to the mercy of strangers.

And here, as they are intimately connected with my own history, it is necessary I should mention such particulars as I have since learned, concerning Olivia.

Hector and Andrews had been busy, in collecting all the particulars they could, relating to me, from the mob; among whom the strangest rumours ran: of which these my fast friends were predisposed to select the most unfavourable, and to believe and report them as true. All of these they carried to Olivia, and her aunt; and the chief of them were, that I had falsely accused a man of theft, had seized him by the collar, dragged him to the water, and had been the principal person in ducking him to death. The brother of this man had discovered who I was; and had followed me, with his comrades, to have me taken before a magistrate: but I had artfully talked to the people round me, had got a part of the mob on my side, and had then begun to beat and ill use the brother. They added that I had stripped like a common bruiser, of which character I was ambitious; that the brother had fought with uncommon bravery; that he had been treated with foul play, by me and my abettors; and that, in conclusion, I had killed him: that, in addition to this, I had prevented a subscription, for the widow and *nine* young children, which had been proposed by them; that I had insulted them, struck at Andrews, and challenged him to box with me, for this their charitable endeavour to relieve the widow and her children; and that, having lost my last guinea at the gaming table the night before in their presence, I should probably run away from my lodgings, or perhaps turn highwayman; for which they thought me quite desperate enough.

It may well be imagined what effect a story like this would produce, on the mind of Olivia: corroborated as it was, though not proved in every incident, by the circumstances which she herself had witnessed from the crescent, by those which she gathered on enquiry from other people, by her own experience of my rash impetuosity, and these all heightened by the conjectures of an active imagination, and a heart not wholly uninterested. She hoped indeed that I had not actually killed two men: but she had the most dreadful doubts.

The impression it made upon her did not escape the penetration of the aunt; and she determined to quit Bath, and take Olivia with her, the very next day. Terrified by the possibility that the predictions of Hector and Andrews should be fulfilled, Olivia ventured secretly to instruct her maid to search the book in the pump room, and find my address, and afterward to send her with the twenty-pound bank-bill: hoping that this temporary resource might have some small chance of preventing the fatal consequences which she feared.

Had they returned to London, by the aid of Miss Wilmot and Mary, she might have made further enquiries: but the cautious aunt directed her course to Scarborough.

I was excessively reduced by the fever. According to the physician and apothecary, my life had been in extreme danger; and eight weeks elapsed before I was able to quit Bath. The expences I had incurred amounted to between eight and nine and twenty pounds. I was fully determined to bestow the ten pounds I had originally intended on Clarke. Thus, after distributing such small gifts among the servants as custom and my notion of the manners of a gentleman demanded, the only choice I had was, either to sell my cloaths, or, with four and sixpence in my pocket, to undertake a journey to London on foot.

I preferred the latter, sent my trunk to the waggon, returned for the last time to my lodging, inclosed a ten pound note in a letter, in which I expressed my sense of the worth of Clarke, and my sorrow for the evil I had done him, and, sending it by the maid-servant, I followed, and watched her to his dwelling.

CHAPTER V

The pain of parting: The prospect before me: Poor men have their affections and friendships

DURING my recovery, I had conversed freely on my own affairs, with Clarke and his wife. They gradually became acquainted with my whole history; and discovered so much interest in the pictures I drew, and entered so sympathetically and with such unaffected marks of passion into all my feelings, that I found not only great ease but considerable delight, in narrating my fears, hopes, and mishaps.

Clarke had a strong understanding; and was not entirely illiterate. His wife was active, cleanly, and kind. Their children were managed with great good sense: the three eldest were put out, two to service, and the other an apprentice; and, large as their family was, they had, by labour and œconomy, advanced a considerable step from the extreme poverty to which such persons are too often subject.

When I went to take leave of them, I could perceive, not only that they were both very much affected, but that Clarke had something more on his imagination. He had a great respect for my gentility, and learning; and was always afraid of being too familiar. At some moments, he felt as it were the insolence of having fought with me: at others a gleam of exultation broke forth, at his having had that honour. He had several times expressed an earnest wish that he might be so happy as to see me again; and, when I assured him that he should hear from me, his feelings were partly doubt, and partly strong delight.

Just as I was prepared to bid them farewell, he gave a deep sigh; and said 'he thought he should soon come to London. He wished he knew where I might be found, and, if he should leave the country, it would be a great favour done him if he might but be allowed to come and ask me how I did. If I would allow him that honour, it would make his heart very light. He had been many years in his present employ; and perhaps his master would be sorry, if he were to leave him; but he had given him fair notice. At one time, he did not believe he ever should have left him; but he thought now he should be much happier in London.'

His tone was serious, there was a dejectedness in his manner, and with it, as was evident, much smothered emotion in his heart. I was affected; and taking his hand, earnestly assured him that, if ever fortune should smile on me, I would not forget what had happened at Bath. His parting reply was, 'God be with you, wherever you go! Perhaps you may see me again sooner than you think for.'

This was the temper in which we took leave, previous to my sending the maid with the ten-pound note: and, as I passed within sight of his door, I felt the regret of quitting a human being whose attachment to me was manifestly so strong and affectionate. But I had no alternative; and I pursued my road.

Winter was advancing: the weather was rainy: the roads were heavy. The cloudy sky sympathised with the gloom of the prospect before me. I had wasted my patrimony, quarrelled with my protectors, renounced the university, had no profession, no immediate resource, and had myself and my mother to provide for: by what means I knew not.

The experience of Wilmot seemed to prove how precarious a subsistence the labours of literature afford; and Wilmot was indisputably a man of genius.

I had not quite concluded against the morality of the practice of the law: but I remembered, in part, the objections of Turl; and they were staggering. Had it been otherwise, where would have been the advantage? I had entered of the Temple: but I had neither the means of keeping my terms nor the patience to look forward, for precarious wealth and fame, to so distant a period.

All this might have been endured: but Olivia?—Where was she? —Perhaps, at that moment, the wife of Andrews!——Or if not, grant she were never to be his, she never could be mine. Yet mine she must be! Mine she should be! I would brave the despotism of her odious enslavers! I would move heaven and earth! I would defy hell itself to separate us!

Such were the continual conflicts to which I was subject: and, while the fogs of despondency rose thick and murky around me, with them continually rose the *ignis fatuus*[1] of hope; dancing before my eyes, and encouraging me step after step to follow on.

Considering how wild and extravagant the desires of youth are, it is happy for them that they calculate so ill; and are so short-sighted. Their despair would else be frequently fatal.

I did not forget, as a supposed immediate means of relief, that my pamphlet against the Earl and the Bishop was printed; and I thought the revenge more than justifiable: it was a necessary vindication of my own honour and claims. I was indeed forty pounds in debt: twenty to Belmont; and twenty more to I knew not whom: though I suspected, and partly hoped partly feared, it was Olivia. I hoped it, because it might be affection. I feared it, lest it should be nothing more than pity; for one whom she had known in her childhood, but whom, now he was a man, she might compassionate; but must contemn. To have been obliged even to Olivia, on these terms, was worse than starving. Such were my meditations through the day; which was a little advanced when I left Bath.

I was eager to perform my journey, and had walked at a great rate. A little before twilight, I heard a distant call, two or three times repeated. At last, I turned round, saw a hat waving, and heard my own name.

I stopped; and the person approached. It was Clarke. I was surprised; and enquired the reason of his following me. He was embarrassed; and began with requesting I would go a little slower, for he had run and walked till he was half tired, and he would tell me.

Clarke was an untaught orator. He had very strong feelings; and a clear head; which are the two grand sources of eloquence. 'You know,' said he, 'how much mischief I have done you; for it cannot be denied. I struck you first, and knocked you down when you *was* off your guard. I set every body against you. I refused to shake hands with you, over and over, when you had the goodness to offer to forgive me. And, last of all, you may thank me for the fever; which brought you to death's door. You forgave me this, as well as the rest. But that was not all. That would not content you. Because I had been used ill, without any malice of yours, nothing would satisfy you but to strip yourself of the little *modicum* that you had, and give it to me. So that, I am sure, you have hardly a shilling to take you up to London. And, when you are there, you are not so well off as I am: you have no trade. I can turn my hand to twenty things: you have never been used to hard work; and how you are to live God Almighty knows! For I am sure I cannot find out; though I have been thinking of nothing else for weeks and weeks past.'

'Why should you suppose I have no money?'

'Because I am sure of it. I asked and found out all that you had to pay. The servants too told me how open-hearted you *was;* so that you had given away all you had. Shame on 'em for taking it, say I! You are not fit to live in this world! And then to send me ten pounds, who have a house and home, and hands to work! But I'll be damned if I keep it!'

'Nay but, indeed you must.'

'I will not! I will not! I would not forswear myself for all the money in the world! And I have sworn it, again and again. So take it! Nay, here, take it!—If you don't, I'll throw it down in the road; and let the first that comes find it; for I'll not forswear myself. So pray now, I beg, for God's sake, you will take it!'

I found it was in vain to contend with him: he was too determined, and had taken this oath in the simplicity of his heart, that it might not be possible for him to recede. I therefore accepted the money: but I endeavoured, having received it to satisfy his oath, to persuade him to take a part of it back again. My efforts were fruitless. 'He had three half crowns,' he told me, 'in his pocket; which would serve his turn, till he could get more: and he had left five guineas at home; so that there was no fear his wife and children should want.'

Happy, enviable, state of independance! When a man and his wife and family, possessed of five guineas, are so wealthy that they are in no fear of want!

Having complied, because I found, though I could equal him in bodily activity, I could not vanquish him in generosity, I requested him to return to the place we just had passed through, and take up his lodging.

He replied, 'To be sure he was a little tired; for he had set out a good hour after me, and I had come at a rare rate. Not but that he could keep his ground, though I was so good a footman; but that it did not become him to make himself my companion.'

'Companion!' said I. 'Why are not you going back to Bath?'

'No: I have taken my leave of it. I shall go and set up my rest in London. I have not been sharking[1] to my master. I thought of it some time since, and gave him fair notice; and more than that, I got him another man in my room; which is all he could demand: and I hope he will serve him as honestly as I have done.'

'What, would you forsake your wife and children?'

'Forsake my wife and children!'

[There was a mixed emotion of indignant sorrow and surprize in his countenance.]

'I did not think, Mr. Trevor, you could have believed me to be such a base villain.'

'I do not believe it! I never could believe it! I spoke thoughtlessly. I saw you were too happy together for that to be possible.'

'Forsake my dear Sally, and our Bill, and Bet, and —— ? No! I'd sooner take up my axe and chop off my hand! There is not another man in England has such a wife! I have seen bad ones enough; and, for the matter of that, bad husbands too. But that's nothing. If you will do me the favour, I should take it kind of you to let me walk with you, and keep you company, now night is coming on, to the next town; and then you may take some rest, and wait for the stage in the morning. I shall make my way; and find you out, I suppose, fast enough in London.'

'Are you then determined to go to town?'

'Yes: it is all settled. I told Sally; and she did cry a little to be sure: but she was soon satisfied. She knows me; and I never in my life found her piggish. God be her holy keeper!'

'Why then, come along. We'll go together. If I ride, you shall ride: if you walk, so will I.'

'Will you? God bless you! You know how to win a man's heart! There is not so good or so brave a fellow, I mean gentleman, upon the face of the earth, damn me if there is! I beg your pardon! Indeed I do! But you force it out of one! One can't remember to keep one's distance, with you. However, I will try to be more becoming.'

The manner of Clarke was more impressive than his words: though they, generally speaking, were not unapt.

We pursued our way together, mutually gratified by what had passed. Perhaps there is no sensation that so cheers, and sooths the soul, as the knowledge that there are other human beings, whose happiness seems knitted and bound up with our own; willing to share our fate, receive our favours, and, whenever occasion offers, to return them ten fold! And the pleasure is infinitely increased, when those who are ambitious of being beloved by us seem to feel, and acknowledge, that we have more amply the power of conferring than even of receiving happiness.

CHAPTER VI

A foolish guide, and a gloomy night: The fears and dangers
of darkness: Casual lights lead to error, and mishap

WHILE we had been discussing the above points, we had sat down; and rose to pursue our journey, as soon as we had brought them to a conclusion. We were on the borders of a forest. As we proceeded, we came up with a countryman; who, enquiring where we were going, told us that, by striking a little out of the road, we might save half a mile. We had nine miles to travel, to the inn at which the stage coaches stopped; and were very willing, Clarke especially, to shorten the way. The countryman said he was going part of the road; and that the remainder was so plain it could not be mistaken. Accordingly, we put ourselves under his guidance.

The sun had been down, by this time, nearly an hour and a half. The moon gave some light; but the wind was rising, she was continually obscured by thick swift-flying clouds, and our conductor advised us to push on, for it was likely to be a very bad night.

In less than a quarter of an hour his prophecy began to be

fulfilled. The rain fell, and at intervals the opposing clouds and currents of air, aided by the impediments of hills and trees, gave us a full variety of that whistling, roaring, and howling, which is heard in high winds.

The darkness thickened upon us, and I was about to request the countryman to lead us to some village, or even barn, for shelter, when he suddenly struck into another path; and, bidding us good night, again told us 'we could not miss our road.' We could not see where he was gone to; and, though we repeatedly called, we called in vain: he was too anxious to get shelter himself to heed our anxiety, and was soon out of hearing.

So long as we could discern, the path we were in appeared to be tolerably beaten: but we now could no longer trace any path; for it was too dark for the ground to have any distinct colour. We had skirted the forest; and our only remaining guide was a hedge on our left.

In this hedge we placed our hopes. We followed its direction, I know not how long, till it suddenly turned off, at an angle; and we found ourselves, as far as we could conjecture, from the intervening lights and the strenuous efforts we made to discover the objects around us, on the edge of some wild place, probably a heath, with hills, and consequently deep vallies, perhaps streams of water, and precipices.

We paused; we knelt down, examined with our eyes, and felt about with our hands, to discover whether we yet were in a path; but could find none.

We continued our consultation, till we had begun to think it advisable to return, once more guided by the hedge. Yet this was not only very uncertain, but the idea of a retrograde motion was by no means pleasant.

While we were in this irresolute dilemma, we thought we saw a light; that glimmered for a moment, and as suddenly disappeared. We watched, I know not how long, and again saw it twinkle, though, as we thought, in something of a different direction. Clarke said it was a Will o'the whisp. I replied, it might be one, but, as it seemed the only chance we had, my advice was to continue our walk in that direction; in hopes that, if it were a light proceeding from any house or village, it would become more visible as we approached.

We walked on, I know not how far; and then paused; but discovered no more of the light. We walked again; again stood still, and looked on every side of us, either for the light or any other object; but we could see nothing distinctly. The obscure forms around us had varied their appearance; and whether they were hills, or clouds, or what they were, we could not possibly discover: though the first we still thought was the most probable.

By this time, we had no certain recollection of which way we had come; or to what point we were directing our course. We were continually in doubt: now pausing; now conjecturing; now proceeding.

We continued to wander, we knew not whither. Sometimes it appeared we went up hill; and sometimes down. We had stepped very cautiously, and therefore very slowly; had warned each other continually to be careful; and had not dared to take twenty steps at a time, without mutually enquiring to know if all were safe.

We continued, environed as it were by the objects that most powerfully inspire fear; by the darkness of night, the tumult of the elements, the utter ignorance of where we were or by what objects surrounded, and the dejectedness which our situation inspired. Thieves and assassins might be at our back, and we could not hear them: gulphs, rocks, or rivers, in our front, or on either side, and we could not see them. The next step might plunge us, headlong, we knew not whither.

These fears were not all imaginary. Finding the ground very uneven on a sudden, and stumbling dangerously myself, I stood still—I did not hear my companion!—I called—I received no answer! I repeated, in a louder tone, 'Clarke! Where are you?' —Still no answer!

I then shouted, with all the fear that I felt, and heard a faint response, that seemed to be beneath me, and at a prodigious distance. It terrified; yet it relieved. We had spoken not three minutes before. I stood silent, in hopes he would speak again: but my fears were too violent to remain so long. I once more called; and he replied, with rather a louder voice which lessened the apparent distance, 'Take care! You'll dash yourself to pieces!'

'Are you hurt?' said I.

'I hope not much,' returned he. 'For God's sake take care of yourself!'

'Can you walk?'

'I shall be able presently, I believe.'

'How can I get to you?'

'I don't know.'

'Stay where you are, and I will try.'

'For God in heaven's sake don't! You'll certainly break your neck! I suppose I am in a chalk pit, or at the bottom of a steep crag.'

'I will crawl to you on my hands and knees.'

'Good God! You will surely kill yourself!'

'Nothing can be more dangerous than to lie here on the wet ground. We must only take care to keep within hearing of each other.'

While I spoke, I began to put my crawling expedient in practice; still calling to Clarke, every half minute, and endeavouring to proceed in the direction of his voice.

I found the rough impediments around me increase; till, presently, I came to one that was ruder than the rest. I crawled upon it, sustained by my knees and right hand, and stretching forward with my left. I groped, but felt nothing. I cautiously laid my belly to the ground and stretched out my other arm. Still it was vacancy. I stretched a little more violently; feeling forward, and on each side; and I seemed to be projected upon a point, my head and shoulders inclining over a dark abyss, which the imagination left unfathomable.

I own I felt terror; and the sensation certainly was not lessened, when, making an attempt to recover my position and go back, my support began to give way. My effort to retreat was as violent as my terror: but it was too late. The ground shook, loosened, and, with the struggle I made carrying me with it, toppled headlong down.

What the height that I fell was I have no means of ascertaining; for the heath on which we were wandering abounds with quarries, and precipices; but either it was, in fact, or my fears made it prodigious.

Had this expedient been proposed under such circumstances, as the only probable one of bringing me and Clarke together again, who would not have shuddered at it? Yet, though it is true I received a violent shock, I know of no injury that it did me.

As soon as I recovered my presence of mind, I replied to Clarke; whose questions were vehement; he having heard me fall. After mutual enquiry, we found we were both once more upon our legs, and had escaped broken bones. Though they had been severely shaken: Clarke's much the most violently.

But where were we now? How should we discover? Perhaps in a

stone quarry; or lime pit. Perhaps at the edge of waters. It might be we had fallen down only on the first bank, or ridge of a quarry; and had a precipice ten fold more dreadful before us.

While we were conjecturing, the stroke of a large clock, brought whizzing in the wind, struck full upon our ear. We listened, with the most anxious ardour. The next stroke was very, very faint: a different current had carried it a different way: and, with all our eager attention, we could not be certain that we heard any more. Yet, though we had lost much time and our progress had been excessively tedious, it could not be two o'clock in the morning. It might indeed very probably be twelve.

The first stroke of the clock made us conjecture it came from some steeple, or hall tower, at no very great distance. The second carried our imaginations we knew not whither. We had not yet recovered courage enough to take more steps than were necessary to come to each other; and, while we were considering, during an intermitting pause of the roaring of the wind, we distinctly heard a cur yelp.

Encouraged by this, we immediately hallooed with all our might. The wind again began to chafe, and swell, and seemed to mock at our distress. Still we repeated our efforts, whenever the wind paused: but, instead of voices intending to answer our calls, we heard shrill whistlings; which certainly were produced by men.

Could it be by good men? By any but night marauders; intent on mischief, but disturbed and alarmed? They were signals indubitably; for we shouted again, they were again given, and were then repeated from another quarter: at least, if they were not, they were miraculously imitated, by the dying away of the wind.

In a little while, we again heard the cur yelp; and immediately afterward a howling, which was so mingled with the blast, that we could not tell whether it were the wind itself, the yelling of a dog, or the agonizing cries of a human voice: but it was a dreadfully dismal sound. We listened with perturbed and deep attention; and it was several times repeated, with increasing uncertainty, confusion and terror.

What was to be done? My patience was exhausted. Danger itself could no longer detain me; and I told Clarke I was determined to make toward the village, or whatever the place was, from whence, dangerous and doubtful as they were, these various sounds proceeded.

Finding me resolute, he was very earnest to have led the way; and, when I would not permit him, he grasped me by the hand, and told me that, if there were pitfalls and gulphs, and if I did go down, unless he should have strength enough to save me, we would go down together.

CHAPTER VII

Difficulties and dangers in succession: A place of horrors and its inmates: A dialogue worthy of the place

As we were cautiously and slowly taking step by step, and, as new conjectures crossed us, stopping to consider, we again saw a dancing light; but more distinctly, though, as we imagined, not very near. We repeated our calls; but, whether they were or were not heard, they were not answered. We ventured, however, to quicken our pace; for we continued, at intervals, to catch the light.

Presently, we saw the light no more; and a considerable time again elapsed, which was spent in wandering as this or that supposition directed us; till at last, suddenly and very unexpectedly, we perceived lines and forms, that convinced us they appertained to some house, or mansion; and, as it appeared to us, a large one. We approached it, examined, shouted, and endeavoured to discover which was the entrance. But all was still, all dark, all closed.

We continued our search on the outside; till, at length, we came to a large gate that was open; which we entered, and proceeded to some distance till we arrived at a door, that evidently belonged to an out-house or detached building. It was shut; and, feeling about, we found that the key was in the lock. We had little hesitation in profiting by the accident. We had been shelterless too long, and the circumstances pleaded too powerfully, for us to indulge any scruples; and accordingly we entered.

We had no sooner put our heads within the door but we found ourselves assaulted with a smell, or rather stench, so intolerable as almost to drive us back: but the fury of the elements, and perhaps the less delicate organs of Clarke, who seemed determined to profit by the shelter we had obtained, induced us to brave an inconvenience which, though excessively offensive at first, became less the longer we continued.

Groping about, we discovered some barrels, and lumber; behind which there was straw. Here we determined to lie down; and rest our bruised and aching bones. Our cloaths had been drenched and dried more than once, in the course of the night; and they were at present neither wet nor dry.

We had scarcely nestled together in our straw, before we again heard the yelping of the cur, and presently afterward the same dismal howls repeated. To these, at no great distance, succeeded the shrill whistling signals. Our imaginations had been so highly wrought up that they were apt at horrible conjectures; and, for my part, my own was at that moment very busily employed in conjuring them up.

In the very midst of this activity, we heard the voices of men, walking round the building. They again whistled, with a piercing shrillness; and, though we heard nothing distinctly, yet we caught tones that were coarse, rude, and savage; and words, that denoted anger and anxiety, for the perpetration of some dark purpose no doubt corresponding to the fierce and threatening sounds we heard.

They approached. One of them had a lanthorn. He came up to the door; and, finding it open, boisterously shut it; with a broad and bitter curse against the carelessness of some man, whose name he pronounced, for leaving it open; and eternally damning others, for being so long in doing their business.

We were now locked in; and we soon heard no more of the voices.

In spite of all these alarms, the moment they ceased our condition, comparing it with the tempest and difficulties without, seemed to be much bettered; and we once more prepared ourselves for sleep, while fear gave place to fatigue.

Our rest was of short duration. We began indeed to slumber; but I was presently disturbed by Clarke, whom I found shaking in the most violent agitation and horror that I ever witnessed in any human being.

I asked 'What is the matter?'

He replied with a groan!

I was awakened from wild slumbers of my own, and strongly partook of his sensations; but endeavoured however to rouze him to speech, and recollection. Again and again I asked 'What have you heard? What ails you?'

It was long before he could utter an articulate sound. At last, shaking more violently as he spoke, and with inexpressible horror in his voice, he gasping said—'A dead hand!'—

'Where?'—

'I felt it!—I had hold of it!—It is now at my neck.'

For a moment I paused: not daring to stretch out my arm, and examine. I trembled in sympathy with him. At length I ventured. Never shall I forget the sensation I experienced, when, to my full conviction, I actually felt a cold, dead, hand, between my fingers!

I was suffocated with horror! I struggled to overcome it: again it seized me; and I sunk half entranced!

At this very instant, the shrill sound of the whistle rung, piercing, through the dismal place in which we were imprisoned. It was answered. The same hoarse voices once more were heard: but in tones fifty fold more dire.

One terror combated the other, and we were recalled to some sense of distinguishing and understanding. We lay silent, not daring to breathe, when we heard the door unlock. Our feelings will not readily be conceived, while the following dialogue passed.

'What a damned while you have kept us waiting, such a night as this!'

'What ails the night? It is a special good night, for our trade.'

'What the devil have you been about?'

'About? Doing our business, to be sure: and doing it to some purpose, I tell you. Is not the night as bad for us as for you? Who had the best of it, do you think? What had you to do, but to keep on the scout?'

'How came you to leave the door open, and be d—mn'd to you?'

'Who left the door open, Jack Dingyface? We left the key in it, indeed; for such lubbers as you to pass in and out: while we had all the work to do, and all the danger to boot.'

'Who do you call lubber, Bull-calf? We have had as much to do as yourselves. There has been an alarm given; for we have heard noises and hallooing all night. For my part, I don't much like it. We shall be smoked:[1] nay it is my belief we are already; and I have a great mind to decamp, and leave the country.'

'You are always in a panic. Who is to smoke us?'

'Well, mark my words, it will come upon us when we least think of it.'

'Think of ——! Hold up the lanthorn. Come, heave in the sack— We were d—mn'd fools, for taking such a hen-hearted fellow among us. Lift the sack an end. Why don't you lend a hand, and keep it steady, while I untie it? Do you think a dead man can stand on his legs? D—mn my body, the fool is afraid he should bite.'

'You are a hardened dog, Randal, bl—st me!'

'Come, tumble the body out. Lay hold! Here! Heave this way. So: that will do. We may leave him. He will not run away. His journey is over. He will travel no farther, to-night. He can't say however but we have provided him with a lodging.'

'D—mn me, where do you expect to go to?'

'To bed. It's high time.'

'I never heard such a dare devil dog in all my life!'

'Don't let that trouble you; for you will never be like me.'

'What is that?'

'What is what?'

'I saw a head.'

'Where?'

'Behind the tub.'

'What then? Is there any wonder in seeing a head, or a body either, in this place?'

'Nay, but, a living head!'

'A living ass!'

'I am sure, I saw the eyes move.'

'Ah! white-livered lout! I wonder what the devil made such a quaking pudding poltroon think of taking to our trade! Come: I am hungry: let us go into the kitchen, and get some grub; and then to bed. Pimping Simon, here, will see his grandmother's ghost, if we stay five minutes longer.'

CHAPTER VIII

The scene continued; and our terrors increased: An interesting dialogue, that unravels the mystery: The beginning of a new acquaintance

HERE to our infinite ease they quitted us, went through an inner door that led to the house, locked it after them, and left us, not only with the dead hand, not only with the dead body, but in the most dismal human slaughterhouse that murder and horror ever constructed, or ever conceived. Such were our impressions: and such, under the same circumstances, they would have been, perhaps, of the bravest man, or man-killer, that ever existed. Alexander and Cæsar themselves would have shook, lying as we lay, hearing what we heard, and seeing what we saw: for, by the light of the lanthorn, we beheld limbs, and bones, and human skeletons, on every side of us. I repeat: horror had nothing to add.

The dancing lights we had seen, the shrill signals and the dreadful howls that we had heard, were now no longer thought mysterious. It was no *ignis fatuus*; but the lanthorn of these assassins: no dog or wolf, baying the moon; but the agonizing yells of murder!

The men were four in number. The idea of attacking them several times suggested itself. Nor was it so much overpowered by the apprehension of the arms with which I concluded such men must be provided, as that my mind was rendered irresolute by the dreadful pictures, real and imaginary, which had passed through my mind.

Clarke, brave as he was, had lost all his intrepidity in this golgotha,[1] this place of skulls; the very scent of which, knowing whence it proceeded, was abhorrent.

No: it was not their arms, nor their numbers, but these fears that induced me, when he that saw my eyes move was in danger of giving the alarm, to close them; and, profiting by the fellow's sympathetic terror, counterfeit the death by which I was environed.

Here then we were. And must we here remain? To sleep was impossible. Must we rise and grapple with the dead; trample on their limbs, and stumble over their unearthed bones, in endeavouring to get out?

Neither could we tell what new horrors were in store for us. Who had not heard of trap doors, sliding wainscots, and other murderous contrivances? And could they be now forgotten? Impossible. All the phantoms memory could revive, or fancy could create, were realized and assembled.

Of the two, I certainly had more the use of my understanding than Clarke; but I was so absorbed, in the terrors which assailed me, on every side, that I was intent on them only; and forgot, while the lanthorn glimmered its partial and dull rays, to consider the geography of the place; or to plan the means of escape, till the moment the men were departing; when I caught a glimpse of what I imagined to be a window facing me.

As soon as our fears would permit us, we began, in low and cautious whispers, to communicate our thoughts. Clarke was pertinaciously averse to rise, and hurtle in the dark with the bones of the dead. By the intervening medium of the straw, he had pushed away the terrific hand; and was determined, he said, to lie still; till day-light should return, and prevent him from treading, at random, on the horrible objects around him; or stumbling over and being stretched upon a corpse.

I had as little inclination to come in contact with dead hands, cadaverous bodies, and dissevered joints, as he could have; yet was too violently tormented to remain quiet, and suffer myself to be preyed on by my imagination. Had I resigned myself to it, without endeavouring to relieve it by action, it would have driven me frantic. I half rose, sat considering, ventured to feel round me and shrunk back with inexpressible terror, from the first object that I touched. Again I ruminated, again ventured to feel, and again and again shivered with horrible apprehensions.

Use will reconcile us to all situations. Experience corrects fear, emboldens ignorance, and renders desire adventurous. The builder will walk without dread on the ridge of a house: while the timid spectator standing below is obliged to turn his eyes away, or tumble headlong down and be dashed to pieces in imagination. Repeated trials had a similar effect on me: they rendered me more hardy; and I proceeded, as nearly as I could guess, toward the window; touching, treading on, and encountering, I knew not what; subject, every moment, to new starts of terror; and my heart now sinking, now leaping, as the sudden freaks and frights of fancy seized upon me.

After the departure of the desperadoes, we had heard various noises, in the adjoining house; among others the occasional ringing of a chamber bell. While I was thus endeavouring to explore my way, arrested by terror at every step, as I have been describing, we again heard sounds that approached more nearly; and presently the inner-door once more opened, and a livery servant, bearing two lighted candles, came in; followed by a man with an apron tied round him, having a kind of bib up to his chin, and linen sleeves drawn over his coat.

The master, for so he evidently was, had a meagre, wan, countenance; and a diminutive form. The servant had evidently some trepidation.

'Do not be afraid, Matthew,' said the master. 'You will soon be accustomed to it; and you will then laugh at your present timidity. Unless you conquer your fears, you will not be able to obey my directions, in assisting me; and consequently will not be fit for your place; and you know you cannot get such good wages in any other.'

'I will do my best, sir,' said the servant: 'but I can't say but, for the first time, it is a little frightful.'

'Mere prejudice, Matthew. I am studying to gain knowledge, which will be serviceable to mankind: and that you must perceive will be doing good.'

'Yes, sir.'

'Reach me those instruments—Now, lift up the body; and turn the head a little this way—Why do you tremble? Are you afraid of the dead?'

'Not much, sir.'

'Lift boldly, then.'

'Yes, sir.'

As the servant turned round, half stupefied with his fears, he beheld me standing with my eyes fixed, watchful and listening with my whole soul, for the interpretation of these enigmas. The man stared, gaped, turned pale, and at last dropped down; overcome with his terrors.

The master was amazed; and, perceiving which way the servant's attention had been directed, looked round. His eye caught mine. He stood motionless. His pale face assumed a death-like hue; and, for a few moments, he seemed to want the power of utterance.

Clarke had remained, astonished and confounded, a silent spectator of the scene. But there was now light; and, though the objects of horror were multiplied in reality, they were less numerous to the imagination. Seeing the fear of the servant, observing his fall, and remarking the gentle and feeble appearance of the master, armed though he was with murderous instruments, Clarke was now rising; determined to come to action. His proceeding disturbed our mutual amazement. He was on his legs; and, as I perceived, advancing with hostile intentions.

The dialogue I had heard, and the objects which I had distinctly seen and examined, had, by this time, unravelled the whole mystery. I discovered that we were in the dissecting-room of an anatomist. Clarke was clenching his fist and preparing to direct a blow at the operator; and I had but just time to step forward, arrest his arm, and impede its progress. 'Be quiet,' said I, 'Clarke; we have been mistaken.'

'For God's sake, who are you, gentlemen?' said the owner of the mansion: recovered in part from his apprehensions, by my pacific interference.

'We are benighted travellers, sir,' answered I; 'who got entrance into this place by accident; and have ourselves been suffering under false, but excessive, fear. Pray, sir, be under no alarm; for we are far from intending you injury.'

He made no immediate reply, and I continued.

'Fear, I find, though she has indeed a most active fancy, has no understanding: otherwise, among the innumerable conjectures with which my brain has been busied within this hour, the truth would certainly have suggested itself. But, instead of supposing I was transported to the benignant regions of science, I thought myself certain of being in the purlieus of the damned; in the very den of murder.'

My language, manner, and tone of voice, relieved him from all alarm; and he said, with a smile, 'This is a very whimsical accident.'

'You would think so, indeed, sir,' replied I, 'if you knew but half of the horrible images on which we have been dreaming. But it was distress that drove us to take shelter here; and if there be any village, or if not, even any barn, in which we could take a little rest till daylight, we should be exceedingly obliged to you for that kind assistance which, from your love of science, and from the remarks I have heard you make to your servant, I am persuaded, you will be very willing to afford.'

By this time, the servant was recovered from his fright; and on his legs. 'Go, Matthew,' said the master, 'and call up one of the maids.' And turning to me he added, 'Be kind enough to follow me, sir, with your companion. I doubt if you could procure either lodging or refreshment, within three miles of the place; and I shall therefore be very happy in supplying you with both.'

We obeyed; I highly delighted with the benevolent and hospitable manner of our host; and Clarke most glad to escape, from a scene which no explanation had yet reconciled to his feelings, or notions of good and evil.

CHAPTER IX

*A review of emotions and mistakes: Repose after fatigue:
Singular thoughts concerning property: Benevolence on a
large scale. A proposal accepted; which greatly alters the face
of affairs: Sketches of war: The hero: The raptures of a
poet: Projects and opinions, relative to law: Thoughts on the
science of surgery*

IN the relation of this adventure, I have given a picture, not of
things as they were afterward discovered to be, but, as they appeared
to us at the time; reflected through the medium of consternation
and terror. We had been powerfully prepared for these, by the
previous circumstances. Our imaginations had been strongly
preyed upon by our distress, by the accidents of falling, and by the
mingled noises we had heard: proceeding from the church-yard
robbers, from the village-dogs and curs disturbed by them and us,
and from the whistling, roaring, and howling which are so common to
high gusts of wind; and so almost distracting to a mind already in a
state of visionary deception and alarm. There was indeed enough
to excite that wild and uncontroulable dread, which rushed upon us
every moment. Mingled as they were with darkness, ignorance, and
confusion, the succeeding objects were actually horrible.

Thus the discourse and dialect, as well as the voices, of the men
employed to furnish dead bodies, were gross and rude; and the
timidity and prejudices of those, who probably were young in the
employment, contrasted with the jokes, vulgar sarcasms, and oaths,
of the boisterous and hardened adepts, though habitual to such
people, gave a colouring to the preceding circumstances, that so
confirmed and realized our fears as not to allow us the leisure to
doubt. To repeat such coarse colloquies and vulgar ribaldry is no
pleasing task; except as a history of the manners of such men, and
of the emotions with which on this occasion they were accompanied.
These indeed made the repetition necessary.

It is likewise true that, in their own opinion, these men were
more or less criminal: and guilt always assumes an audacity, and
fierceness, which it does not feel. They were not intentionally
acting well: but were doing that which they supposed to be a deed
of desperate wickedness, for selfish purposes. Had the consent of

any one of them when dying been asked, to have his body dug up and dissected, he would have heard the proposal with detestation. Consequently, they deceived us the more effectually: for they had the manners of that guilt which, as far as intention was concerned, they actually possessed.

Add to this the spectacle of a dissecting-room; seen indistinctly by the partial glimmerings of a lanthorn. Whoever has been in such a place will recognise the picture. Here preparations of arms, pendent in rows, with the vessels injected. There legs, feet, and other limbs. In this place the intestines: in that membranes, cartilages, muscles, with the bones and all their varieties of clothing, in every imaginary mangled form. These things ought not to be terrible: but to persons of little reflection, and not familiarized to them, they always are.

Escaped from this scene, restored as it were to human intercourse, and encouraged by the kindness of our host, whose name was Evelyn, our pulses began to grow temperate; and our imaginations to relax and gravitate toward common sense. We took the refreshment that was brought us, and conversed during the meal with Mr. Evelyn: partly on the incidents of the night, and partly in answering a few questions; which he put with a feeling that denoted a desire rather to afford us aid than to gratify his own curiosity. After which, as we were weary and he disposed to pursue his nocturnal researches, we immediately retired to rest. Clarke was full to overflowing with cogitation: but, for the present, it was too large, or rather too confused, for utterance; and it soon overpowered and sunk him into sleep.

For my own part, my mind was too much alive to be immediately overcome by fatigue. I lay revolving in thought the incidents of the night; which led me into reveries on the singular character of Mr. Evelyn, on my own forlorn state, on the bleak prospect before me, and on Olivia.

This last train of thinking was not easily dismissed. At length, however, both mind and body were so overwearied that I fell into an unusually profound sleep; from which I did not awake till Clarke, who had risen two hours before, came between nine and ten o'clock and rouzed me, to inform me that breakfast was waiting, and that our host expected my company.

While I was dressing, he told me that Mr. Evelyn had been making many enquiries concerning me; and apologized himself, with marks of apprehension lest he should have done wrong, while he owned that he had answered these interrogatories, by relating such particulars as he knew.

We then went down; and, among other conversation at breakfast, Mr. Evelyn remarked that he understood, from Clarke, we had no urgent business which would make a day sooner or a day later of any material consequence; and he therefore particularly requested we would delay our departure till the next morning. The reason he gave was a kind expression of interest, which what he had heard from my companion had excited; and a desire, not of inquisitive prying but evidently of benevolence, to be as fully informed of my history as I should think proper to make him.

There was something soothing both in the request and in his manner, which induced me to readily comply. Poor Clarke excepted, I seemed as if no human being took any concern in my fate; and to discover that there was yet a man who was capable of sympathizing with me was like filling a painful vacancy of the heart, and afforded something of an incoherent hope of relief.

Not that I was prepared to ask or even to accept favours. I had rather entertained a kind of indignant sense of injury, against any one who should presume to make me his debtor: or to suppose I was incapable of not rather enduring all extremities than so to subject and degrade myself as, in my own apprehension, I should do by any such condescension.

After breakfast, Mr. Evelyn desired me to walk with him; that we might converse the more freely when alone. He then repeated what Clarke had told him, gave a strong and affecting picture of the overflowing kindness and compassion with which my companion had related all he knew, and proceeded afterward to speak of himself in the following terms.

'I am a man, Mr. Trevor, engaged in a trust which I find it very difficult conscientiously to discharge. I have an estate of fifteen hundred a year, and am a creature whose real wants, like those of other human creatures, are few. I live here surrounded by some hundreds of acres; stored with fruits, corn, and cattle; which the laws and customs of nations call mine. But what is it that these laws and customs mean? That I am to devour the whole produce of thus much land? The thing is impossible!'

'Why impossible? You may convert a hundred head of oxen into a service of gold plate. Liveries, laces, equipage, gilding, garnishing, and ten thousand other modes or fashionable wants, which if not gratified render those that have them miserable, would eat up all that ten thousand acres, if you had them, could yield. Are you an Epicure? You may so stew, distill, and titillate your palate with essences that a hecatomb shall be swallowed at every meal. The means of devouring are innumerable, and justified by general usage.'

'General usage may be an apology, but not a justification. Happiness is the end of man: but it cannot be single. On the contrary, the more beings are happy the greater is the individual happiness of each: for each is a being of sympathies, and affections; which are increased by being called into action. It is the miserable mechanism of society which, by giving legal possession of what is called property to the holders, puts it absolutely and unconditionally in their disposal.'

'Why the miserable mechanism? Are you a friend to the Agrarian system?'[1]

'By no means. I was incorrect: The mechanism is defective enough, but I rather meant to have said the miserable moral system of society; which allows every man to exercise his own caprice, and thinks him guilty of no crime though he is in the daily habit of wasting that which might render numbers happy, who are in absolute want.'

'This is an evil of which the world has for ages been complaining: but for which I see no remedy.'

'You mean no remedy which laws or governments, by the inflicting of pains and penalties, can afford: at which, to do them justice, they have been much too often aiming; but have as continually failed.'

'And you imagine, sir, you are possessed of a more effectual prescription?

'I dare not prescribe: it would be an arrogant assumption of wisdom. But I may advise a regimen which has numerous probabilities in its favour. Yet what I must advise has been so many thousand times advised before that it seems impertinence to repeat it; if not mockery. To tell the rich that they seek enjoyment where it is not to be found, that the parade by which they torment themselves to gain distinction renders them supremely ridiculous, that their follies, while they are oppressive and hateful to the poor, are the topics of contempt and scandal even in their own circles, and that the repetition of them inevitably proves that they bring weariness, disgust, ruin, pain, and every human misery, is mere common-place declamation.

'But there is one truth of which they have not been sufficiently reminded. They are not, as they have too long been taught to suppose themselves, placed beyond the censure of the multitude. It is found that the multitude can think, and have discovered that the use the wealthy too often make of what they call their own is unjust, tyrannical, and destructive.

'This memento will come to them with the greater force the oftener they are made to recollect that the spirit of enquiry is abroad, that their voluptuous waste is daily becoming more odious, and that simplicity of manners, a benevolent œconomy, a vigorous munificence, and a comprehensive philanthropy, can alone redeem them; and preserve that social order which every lover of the human race delights to contemplate, but of which they arrogate to themselves the merit of being the sole advocates.

'It is the moral system of society that wants reform. This cannot be suddenly produced, nor by the efforts of any individual: but it may be progressive, and every individual may contribute: though some much more powerfully than others. The rich, in proportion as they shall understand this power and these duties, will become peculiarly instrumental: for poverty, by being subjected to continual labour, is necessarily ignorant; and it is well known how dangerous it is for ignorance to turn reformer.

'Let the rich therefore awake: let them encourage each other to quit their pernicious frivolities, and to enquire, without fear or prejudice, how they may secure tranquillity and promote happiness; and let them thus avert those miseries at which they so loudly and so bitterly rail, but into which by their conduct a majority of them is so ready to plunge.

'The intentions of those among them who think the most are excellent: to assert the contrary is equally false and absurd. But, when they expect to promote peace and order by irritating each other against this or that class of men, however mistaken those men may be, and by disseminating a mutual spirit of acrimony between themselves and their opponents, they act like madmen; and, if they do not grow calm, forgiving, and kind, the increasing fury of the mad many will overtake them.'

'They are like the brethren of Dives.[1] They pay but little regard to Moses and the prophets.'

'Well, Mr. Trevor, you will own at least that, since I can talk with all this seeming wisdom, a small share of the practice will be becoming in me; and what you and all mankind would expect.'

'I may: but not all mankind. There are some who pretend to be so learned, in what they call the depravity of human nature, that, after having heard you speak thus admirably in favour of virtue, they would think it more than an equal chance that you are one of the wickedest of men.'

'Oh, with respect to that, some of my very neighbours do not scruple to affirm that I am so. But, I repeat, I have what I consider as a large estate in trust; and it is a serious and a sacred duty imposed upon me to seek how it may be best employed. I seldom am satisfied with the means which offer themselves; and am therefore always in quest of new.'

'I wonder at that, sir, with your system. Have you no poor in the country?'

'O yes: enough to grieve any penetrable heart. But I know no task more difficult than that of administering to their wants, without encouraging their vices. Of these wants I consider instruction as the greatest; and to that I pay the greatest attention. Food, cloathing, and disease are imperious necessities; and to leave them unprovided would be guilt incredible to speculation, did we not see it in hourly practice. But the poor are so misled, by the opinions they are taught to hold and the oppressions to which they are subject, that, by relieving these most urgent wants we are in danger of teaching them idleness, drunkenness, and servility. I do them the little good that I can, most willingly: but I consider the diffusion of knowledge, by which that which I call the moral system of mankind is to be improved, as the most effectual means of conferring happiness. Are you of that opinion?'

'I certainly am.'

'Then I cannot but think you intend to promote this beneficial plan.'

'I scarcely know my own intentions. They are unsettled, incoherent, and the dreams of delirium; rather than the system of a sage, such as you have imagined.'

'I wish we had been longer acquainted and were intimate enough to induce you to relate your history, and confide your thoughts to me, as to a friend; or, if you please, as to one who holds it a duty to offer aid, whenever he imagines it will answer a good end.'

'To offer aid is kind: but there are very few cases in which he that receives it is not mean and degraded. You however are actuated by a generous spirit; and, as you are inclined to listen, I will very willingly inform you of the chief incidents of a life that has already been considerably checkered, and the future prospects of which are sufficiently gloomy.'

After this preface, I began my narrative; and succinctly related the principal of those events with which the reader already is acquainted. Nor did the state of my feelings and the strong sense of injury which was ever present to my imagination, when I came to recapitulate my adventures since I first left college, suffer me to colour with a negligent or a feeble hand.

Some of the incidents necessarily induced me to mention Olivia, and betray my sentiments in part: which the questions of Mr. Evelyn, put with kindness, delicacy, and interest that was evidently unaffected, induced me at length wholly to reveal, with all the tenderness and the vehemence of passion.

I was encouraged or rather impelled to this confidence by the emotions which Mr. Evelyn betrayed, in his countenance, voice, and manner. His hopes, his fears, and his affections, were so much in unison with my own, his eye so often glistened and his cheek so frequently glowed, that it was impossible for the heart not to open all its recesses, and pour out not only its complaints but its very follies.

Of all the pleasures in which the soul of man most delights that of sympathy is surely the chief. It can unite and mingle not only two but ten millions of spirits as one. Could a world be spectators of the sorrows of Lear, a world would with one consent participate in them: so omnipotent is the power of sympathy. It is the consolation of poverty, it is the cordial of friendship, it is the essence of love. Pride and suspicion are its chief enemies; and they are the vices that engender the most baneful of the miseries of man.

Mr. Evelyn remained, after I had ended, for some time in deep meditation; now and then casting his eyes toward me and then taking them away, as if fearful of offending my sensibility and again falling into thought. At length, fixing them more firmly and with an open benignity of countenance, he thus broke silence.

'I have been devising, my noble young friend, allow me to call you so, by what means I should best make myself understood to you; and how most effectually prevail on you to contribute to my happiness, and to those great ends for which souls of ardour like yours are so highly gifted. I have already sketched my principles, concerning the use and abuse of property. One of those rare occasions on which it may be excellently employed now presents itself. You are in pursuit of science, by which a world is to be improved. To the best of my ability I follow the same track: but I have the means, which you want. You have too little: I have too much. It is my province, and, if you consent, as I hope and trust you will, it will be my supreme pleasure to supply the deficiency. I am acquainted with the delicacy of your sentiments: but I am likewise acquainted with the expansion of your heart, and with its power of rising superior to the false distinctions which at present regulate society. I might assume the severe tone of the moralist, and urge your compliance with my request as a duty: but I would rather indulge what may perhaps be the foible of immature virtue, and follow the affectionate impulse which binds me to you as my friend and brother. Beside these are vibrations with which I am persuaded your warm and kindred heart will more readily harmonize. In youth, we willingly obey impetuous sensations: but reluctantly listen to the slow and frigid deductions of reason, when they are in contradiction to our habits and prejudices. I therefore repeat, you are my friend and brother; and I conjure you, by those generous and magnanimous feelings of which your whole life proves you are so eminently susceptible, not to wound me by refusal. Do not consider me as the acquaintance of a day; for, by hearing your history, I have travelled with you through life, and seem as if I had been the inmate of your bosom even from your years of infancy. No: far from being strangers, we have been imbibing similar principles, similar views, and similar affections. Our souls have communed for years, and rejoice that the time at length is come in which that individual intercourse for which they may most justly be said to have panted is opened. If you object, if you hesitate, if you suspect me, you will annihilate the purest sensations which these souls have mutually cherished: you will wrong both yourself and me.'

There was an emanating fervor in the look, deportment, and the very gestures, of Mr. Evelyn that was irresistible. It surpassed his language. It led me out of myself. It hurried me beyond the narrow limits of prejudices and prepossessions, and transported me wherever it pleased. I was no longer in mortal society; surrounded by selfishness, cunning, and cowardly suspicions. He had borne me on his wings, and seated me among the Gods; whose ministers were wisdom and beneficence. I burst into exclamation.

'I own it, you are my friend! you are my brother! I accept your offers, I will receive your benefits, but I will retaliate.'

I paused. I felt the egotism of my own thoughts, but could not subdue the torrent. I continued inwardly to vow, with the most vehement asseverations, that I would repay every mark of kindness he should bestow fifty fold. The heart of man will not rest satisfied with inferiority, and has recourse to a thousand stratagems, a thousand deceptions, to relieve itself of any such doubts; which it entertains with impatience, and pain.

My own enthusiasm however was soon inclined to subside; and I became ready to tax myself with that meanness and degradation which I had felt, and expressed, at the beginning of the discussion. Of this the quick penetration of Mr. Evelyn seemed to be aware; and he so effectually counteracted these emotions that, at length, I abandoned all thoughts of resistance; or of betraying those jealousies which would now have appeared almost insulting, to a man who had displayed a spirit so disinterested.

This subject being as it were dismissed, our conversation recurred to my present affairs, and future prospects; and, while we discoursed on these, that which might well at this period be called the malady of my mind exhibited itself. Though I had as it were lost sight of Olivia, though I knew not but she might at that time be a wife, and though, whatever her condition might be, I had sufficient reason to fear that if she thought of me it was with pain, not with love, still that she must and should be mine was a kind of frantic conclusion with which I always consoled myself. But for this purpose riches presented themselves as of the first necessity; and riches themselves would be useless, unless obtained with the rapidity rather of enchantment than by the ordinary progress of human events.

I did not conceal this weakness from my friend, and ventured to propose a plan on which I had previously been ruminating; though I had foreseen no means of putting it in practice. Every man had heard of the fortunes acquired in the east, and of the wealth which had been poured from the lap of India. The army there was at all times open to men like myself; youthful, healthy, and of education. 'Tis true I had been of opinion that there were strong moral objections to this profession: but these my more prevalent passions had lulled me into a forgetfulness of, and I stated this as the most probable scheme for the accomplishment of my dearest hopes.

Mr. Evelyn, anxious not to wound me where I was most vulnerable, began by soothing my ruling passion; and then proceeded to detail the physical chances of a ruined constitution, of death, and of failure; and afterward to represent, with unassuming but with stedfast energy, the moral turpitude first of subjecting myself to the physical evils he had recited, and next of hiring myself to enmity against nations I had never known, and of becoming the assassin of people whom I had never seen, and who had not had any possible opportunity of doing me an injury, or even of giving me an offence.

The objections I started, partly to defend the opinions I had begun with, and partly because I felt myself loth to relinquish a plan by which my imagination had been flattered, soon became very feeble: but the interesting nature of the subject prolonged the discussion till it was nearly dinner time.

In the course of this enquiry, Mr. Evelyn delineated the contemptible yet ridiculous arts which are employed to entrap men into the military service; pourtrayed the inevitable depravity of their morals, and gave a history of the feelings worthy of fiends which are engendered, while they are trained to fix their bayonets, load their pieces, level them, discharge them at men they had never seen before, strike off the heads of these strangers with furious dexterity, stab the ground in full gallop on which they are supposed to have fallen and to lie helpless, and commit habitual and innumerable murders in imagination, that they may be hardened for actual slaughter.

He afterward gave an enlightened and animated sketch of the abject condition of those who command these men, of the total resignation which each makes of his understanding to that of the next in rank above him, and of the arrogant, the ignorant, the turbulent, the dangerous and the slavish spirit which this begets. He finished the picture with a recapitulation of the innumerable and horrid miseries which everlastingly mark the progress of war; which he painted with such force and truth that I recoiled from the contemplation of it with abhorrence.

My feelings had been so agitated by this discourse that my imagination was thoroughly rouzed. My former ideas, concerning the enormous vices of war, had not only been revived but increased;

and, though I began with debating the question, I soon ceased to oppose: so that my thoughts were rather busied in filling up the picture, and collecting all its horrors, than in apologizing for or denying their existence. This was the temper of mind in which Mr. Evelyn, attending to his own concerns, left me for a short time; and my heart was so agonized by the recollection that this was a system to which men were still devoted, and of which they were still in the headlong and hot pursuit, that I then immediately, and perhaps with less effort than I ever made on a similar occasion, produced the following poem:

THE HERO

ALL hail to the hero whom victory leads,
　　Triumphant, from fields of renown!
From kingdoms left barren! from plains drench'd in blood!
　　And the sacking of many a fair town!

His gore-dripping sword shall hang high in the hall;
　　Revered for the havoc it spread!
For the deaths it has dealt! for the terrors it struck!
　　And the torrents of blood it has shed!

His banners in haughty procession shall ride,
　　On Jehovah's proud altars unfurl'd!
While anthems and priests waft to heaven his praise,
　　For the slaughter and wreck of a world!

Though widows and orphans together shall crowd,
　　To gaze as at heaven's dread rod,
And mutter their curses, and mingle their tears,
　　Invoking the vengeance of God:

Though, while bloated Revelry roars at his board,
　　Where surfeiting hecatombs fume,
Desolation and Famine shall howl, and old Earth
　　Her skeleton hordes shall intomb:

All ghastly and mangled, from fields where they fell,
　　With horrible groanings and cries,
What though, when he slumbers, the dead from their graves
　　In dread visitation shall rise:

Yet he among heroes exalted shall sit;
  And slaves to his splendor shall bend;
And senates shall echo his virtues; and kings
  Shall own him their saviour, and friend!

Then hail to the hero whom victory leads,
  Triumphant, from fields of renown!
From kingdoms left barren! from plains drench'd in blood!
  And the sacking of many a fair town!

I was too full of my subject, and poet like too much delighted with
the verses I had so suddenly produced, not to shew them immediately to Mr. Evelyn.

He seemed to do them even more than justice: he read them again
and again, and each time with a feeling now of compassion, now of
amazement, and now of horror, that shewed how strongly the
picture had seized upon his soul. The associations of misery which
his imagination added were so forcible that tears repeatedly rolled
down his cheeks. To this more soothing trains of thought succeeded.
The pain of the past and the present was alleviated by a prospect of
futurity. Our minds rose to a state of mutual rapture, excited by a
foresight that the time was at length come in which men were
awakening to a comprehensive view of their own mad and
destructive systems; that their vices began to be on the decline and
no longer to be mistaken for the most splendid virtues, as they had
formerly been; and that truth was breaking forth upon the world
with most animating force and vigour.

There have been few moments of my life in which I have
experienced intellectual enjoyment with a pleasure so exquisite.
Clarke himself, unused as his thoughts had been to explore the
future and wrest happiness to themselves by anticipation, partook of
our emotions; and seemed in a state similar to those religious
converts who imagine they feel that a new light is broke in upon
them. It was a happy afternoon! It was a type of those which shall
hereafter be the substitutes of the wretched resources of drinking,
obscene conversation, and games of chance, to which men have had
recourse that they might rouze their minds: being rather willing to
suffer the extremes of misery than that dullness, and inanity, which
they find still more insupportable.

This incident united me and Mr. Evelyn more intimately, and
powerfully, than all that had passed. The warmth with which he

spoke, of the benefits that society must receive from talents like mine, dilated my heart. Every man is better acquainted with his own powers and virtues than any other can possibly be; and, when they are discovered, acknowledged, and applauded, instead of being denied or overlooked as is more generally the case, the pleasure he receives is as great as it is unusual.

Our conversation after dinner reverted to the plans I was to pursue. The law necessarily came under consideration; and Mr. Evelyn, not having considered the subject under the same points of view as Turl had done, was strongly in favour of that profession. He foresaw in me a future Judge, whose integrity should benefit and whose wisdom should enlighten mankind. He conceived there could be no function more honourable, more sacred, or more beneficial. An upright judge, with his own passions and prejudices subdued, attentive to the principles of justice by which alone the happiness of the world can be promoted, and by the rectitude of his decisions affording precedent and example to future generations, he considered as a character that must command the reverence and love of the human race.

My imagination while he spoke was not idle. I helped to fill up the picture. It placed me on the judgment seat. It gave me the penetration of Solomon, the benevolence of Zaleucus,[1] and the legislative soul of Alfred. As usual, it overstepped the probable with wonderful ease and celerity. Not only the objections of Turl disappeared, but the jargon of the law, its voluminous lumber with which I had been disgusted when reading the civilians at college, and all my other doubts and disgusts, vanished.

Our inquiries accordingly ended with a determination that I should continue my journey to town, should keep my terms at the Temple, and should place myself, as is customary, under one of the most eminent barristers.

This necessarily brought me to consider the expence; and the moment that subject recurred I felt all the pain which could not but assault a mind like mine. I had nurtured, not only the haughtiness of independance, but the supposition that, in my own extraordinary powers and gifts, I possessed innumerable resources; and, at moments, had encouraged those many extravagant flights with which the reader is already well acquainted.

However, after all that had passed, and for the reasons that had been sufficiently urged, I found it necessary to submit: though by the concession my soul seemed to be subdued, and its faculties to be shrunk and half withered. It was an oppressive sensation that could not be shaken off, yet that must be endured. Such at least was my present conclusion.

In the course of the evening, Mr. Evelyn at my request stated his reasons for pursuing his own course of studies; and instanced a variety of facts which convinced me of the benefits to be derived from the science of surgery, of the rash conclusions to which modern theorists and enquirers have been led, and of the necessity there is that some practitioner, equally well informed with themselves but aware of the evil of false deductions, should demonstrate the mischief of hasty assertion, and that things which are only conjectural ought not to be given as indubitable.

Of this nature he considered their hypotheses relating to the brain, the nervous system, the lymphatic fluid, and other subjects; concerning which many curious but hitherto equivocal facts have been the discovery of modern research.

Mr. Evelyn not only read all the best authors, but went to London, every winter, and assiduously maintained an intercourse with the most able men, attended their lectures, was present at their operations, and fully informed himself of their differences both in opinion and practice.

But his frame was delicate, a too long abode in London always occasioned pulmonary symptoms, and experience taught him that his native air was more healthful and animating than any other. The difficulties attending his studies were greatly increased by his residence in the country; but they were surmounted by his precaution, and by the general favour which his benevolence secured to him among the neighbouring people. Though there were not wanting some who considered him as a very strange, if not a dangerous and a wicked, man.

It is curious yet an astonishing and an afflicting speculation that men should be most prone to suspect, and hate, those who are most unwearied in endeavouring to remove their evils. That a surgeon must be acquainted with the direction, site, and properties, of the muscles, arteries, ligaments, nerves, and other parts, before he can cut the living body with the least possible injury, and that this knowledge can only be acquired by experience, is a very plain proposition. It is equally self-evident that a dead body is no longer subject to pain; and that it certainly cannot be more disgraced by the knife of a surgeon than by the gnawing of worms. When will men shake off their infantine terrors, and their idiot-like pre-possessions?

CHAPTER X

The departure: Ejaculations: Present pleasures and future hopes: A strange dialogue in the dark; and a generous and beautiful defender

THE pleasure I this day received in the company of Mr. Evelyn was uncommon, the friendship with which he had inspired me was pure, and the respect that my heart paid to his virtues was profound. But eagerness of pursuit was my characteristic. My plan being formed, every moment of delay would have been torment; and he, entering into all my thoughts and sympathising with all my wishes, prompted me to follow my bent. It was therefore agreed that I and my companion should depart by one of the coaches which would pass an inn at some distance in the morning. A messenger was accordingly dispatched to take places in the first vacant coach, arrangements for money-matters were made with every possible delicacy by my friend, the night passed away, day returned, and we departed.

I will leave the reader to image to himself the crowding sensations that pressed upon my heart on this occasion, the tumult of thought which incidents so sudden and unexpected produced, and the feelings which mutually passed between me and my noble bene-factor. I shall live, said I, to acknowledge this in my old age. I shall have a story to tell, a man to describe, and a friend to revere, that will astonish and render common hearers incredulous. But this was the language of my heart: not of my tongue. That was dumb. A pressure of the hand, with eyes averted, was all the utterance I had.

A child and its mother were the only passengers beside ourselves. The coach, which was to be in London at ten that night, rolled along, they were asleep, I was silent, and poor Clarke was full of ejaculation.

'If there be a good man on God's earth, that gentleman is one! He will find his road to heaven safe enough! He will be among the sheep, and sit on the right hand of God! I hope I shall be in his company! Though that can't be. I am unworthy. I may think myself happy to sit far enough lower down. Not that I can say; for I find the best people have the least pride. Perhaps as it is in earth so it may be in heaven. God send us all safe there together! For my part, I think that within these few weeks I am a different kind of a creature. But what can a poor carpenter do? He must not speak to gentlefolk, unless in the way of his work: so he can have no sociability, but with his poor neighbours. And though some of them to be sure be as good-meaning people as any on earth, they are no better learned than himself: so they can teach him nothing. But I have happened on good luck, so I have no right to complain. And I am very sure, in my own mind, that there is good luck in store for us all: for providence else would not have brought us and guided us where it did, by such marvellous means; so that, while we thought we were breaking our necks and falling into the hands of murderers, and being frightened out of our senses by the most shocking sights I must say that ever were seen, we were all the while going straight on as fast as we could to good fortune! So that it is true enough that man is blind, but that God can see.'

What pleasure does the mind of man take in solving all its difficulties! How impatient is it that any thing should remain unexplained; and how ready to elevate its own ingorance into mystery and miracle!

To have remained longer silent, while the honest heart of my companion was thus overflowing with kindness, would have been no proof of the same excellent and winning quality in myself. I encouraged his hopes, in which I was very ready to participate. My own pleasing dreams revived in full force; and I presently ranged my cloud-constructed castles, which I built, pulled down and rebuilt with admirable facilty, and lorded it over my airy domains at will. 'Tis a folly to rail at these domains: for there are no earthly abodes that are half so captivating.

Nothing worth mentioning happened on the road till we came to the last stage but one, where we changed horses; at which time it was quite dark. Our female companion and her child had been set down at Hungerford; and two new passengers, both ladies, as soon as the horses were put to, were shewn to the carriage.

They had a footman, who mounted the box; and we soon learned from their discourse that they had been waiting for the nephew of the elder lady, who was to have taken them in his phaeton, but that they had been disappointed. They had been on a visit, and had been brought to Salt-hill in a gentleman's carriage; which they had sent back. While the coach had stopped, I had fallen into a doze; but awoke when it began to move again, and when I heard the voices of females conversing.

The old lady spoke most, and complained of the rudeness of her nephew in subjecting them to the inconvenience of a stage-coach, or of waiting they knew not how long till post-horses should come in, which as they were informed would be tired and unfit for more work: it happening that there was a great run at that time on the Bath road.

The reader will presently understand that they were people of real fashion; and the eldest lady spoke of persons and things which denoted that high life was familiar to her. This gave Clarke a new opportunity of wondering how he, a poor carpenter, came into such company: which he directly expressed to me, with the simplicity and undisguise that are common to such characters.

The old lady, who had before signified her chagrin at the expedient to which her nephew had reduced her, did not find her pride soothed when she learned that she was in company with carpenters: for it soon appeared that she considered me and my companion as familiar acquaintances of the same rank.

Her young friend was likewise led into this error; and, when the former began to express her disgust too freely to accord with the feelings of the latter, she interrupted her with saying '*Ayez la bonté, madame, de parler François.*' 'Be kind enough, madam, to speak French.'

The old lady complied; and a conversation ensued which certainly will neither surprise nor move the reader so much as it did me. Should he ask how I, as a man of honor, could suffer them to remain in the deception of imagining I did not understand them, let him wait till he knows enough to surmise what the emotions were that were in a moment kindled in my bosom. At first, indeed, they were but dark and improbable conjectures: but, dark as they were, they shook my whole frame.

The dialogue that ensued soon testified that the old lady was in no very complacent temper of mind. Her beginning sentences expressed dissatisfaction, were sarcastic, and evidently glanced at her young companion, whose replies were mild and conciliating.

But, not satisfied with indirect reproach, her assailant, still speaking French, continued her interrogatories to the following effect.

'And are you still determined, Miss, to persist in your obstinate refusal of his lordship?'

'Let me intreat you, dear madam, not to enter on that subject again.'

'Oh, to be sure! You very kindly intreat me to torment myself as much as I please, so that I do not trouble you!'

'How can you, madam, accuse me of such cruelty? Is it just? Am I indeed of such a nature?'

'Yes, indeed are you, Miss: however you may flatter yourself. It is nothing but perversity that can make you trifle with the honor and happiness of your family—Now you are silent! Your fine spirit no doubt disdains to reply!'

'What can I say?'

'Say that you are a headstrong girl; acknowledge your fault, and consent to be the wife of a peer—Silent again!'

'I could wish, madam, not to make you more angry.'

'No, indeed; there is no occasion for that! You have been doing nothing else for many weeks past. For my part, I cannot conceive what your objection can be! Had that desperado been living, for whom since his death you have acknowledged what you call your weak prepossession, I should have known very well to what cause to attribute your stubbornness: but, as it is, I cannot conceive either your motives or your meaning. Nothing however is to be wondered at, in a young lady of your character. No prudent person would have dared to indulge a thought in favour of a mad adventurer, whose actions were as rash as they were insolent, whose family was mean yet had dared to oppose and even make ridiculous attempts to rival that from which you are descended, and who yet was himself an outcast of that family.'

'It is cruel, madam, to disturb the ashes of the dead!'

This was the first word of retort that had escaped the chidden sufferer; and this was uttered in a voice half suffocated with passion.

'Cruel, indeed! Every thing is cruel that contradicts the wishes of young ladies, whose melting tenderness is ruinous to themselves and to every body that ought to be most dear to them.'

'You must pardon me, madam, for again and again repeating, in my own defence, that there is no part of my conduct which can justify such an accusation.'

'How, Miss! Is an avowed partiality for a fortune-hunter no proof? Is it no stain on the character of a modern young lady? Is it no insult to her family?'

'It was a partiality which had never been avowed, till death had put an end to hope. It was produced and counteracted by very extraordinary circumstances: but, however strong it might be at some moments, which I acknowledge it was, for I disdain falsehood, it was not indulged. I needed no monitor to shew me there were too many reasons why it ought not to be.'

'I have not patience. A runagate! A vagabond! A gambler! A prize fighter! One of the lowest and most contemptible of adventurers! who had betrayed his patrons, who had flown in the face of his benefactors, who was capable of every kind of malice and mischief, and who had not a single virtue!'

'Madam, I cannot listen to such an assertion as that, however I may offend you, without continually protesting it is unfounded; and that you have been greatly misinformed. I scorn to apologise for his mistakes: but I know that he had virtues which those who have given you this character of him are never likely to possess. How he could be guilty of the crimes of which he has been accused I cannot conceive. Even when a boy, I have heard him express sentiments which I shall never forget; and which have since been confirmed by his actions. You were acquainted with none of them. You speak from report; and from report which I am sure was false, and wicked. His heart I know to have been compassionate, his principles such as no mean mind could have conceived, and his courage blameably great; though it saved my life. [Tears half choked her utterance.] But for him I should have been where he now is: a different train of events might have taken place, and he perhaps might have been living. I owe him my life, and you must forgive me if I cannot sit patiently and hear his memory traduced without the least occasion: for, [Her sobbing could not be stifled.] since he is dead, you can no longer think him dangerous.'

Oh Olivia!

Gracious God! What were the throbs the thrillings, the love, the indignation, the transports, of my soul! How did a few moments raise and allay in me the whirlwind of the passions! How did my frame tremble, and madden, and shiver, and burn! How were my lips at once bursting with frenzy and locked in silence! It was my guardian angel that protected me, that pleaded for me, that awed me to patience, and that repaid by her seraphic praise the virtue she had inspired!

Oh, yes, it was Olivia! It was she herself that had the justice, the fortitude, and the affection, to assert the dignity of truth, to controvert an overbearing aunt whom she revered, for this aunt had her virtues, and to speak in defiance of that hypocrisy which inculcates the silence that intends to deceive, and which teaches females that sincerity is an unpardonable vice.

CHAPTER XI

False conclusions rectified: A lover's reveries: The dangers of a stage-coach, in a dark night and a fog: The discovery of more old acquaintances, and the journey pursued

IT has been truly remarked that the most serious and even the most dignified emotions are sometimes mingled with the most ludicrous. When the divine Olivia had ended, there was a momentary pause; and Clarke, meditating no doubt on the advantages of which he had been deprived, and to the enjoyment of which every man feels he has a right, directing his remark to me, suddenly exclaimed—'What would I give now if I understood all that these ladies were saying as well as you do!'

'*Est-ce donc que Monsieur sçait parler François?*—What, sir! Can you speak French?' said the aunt with a burst of surprise.

'Yes, madam,' answered I; in a low and tremulous voice.

'*Gesù Maria! Chi l'avrebbe pensato! Parliamo Italiano, Signora.* Good God! who could have thought it! Let us speak Italian, Miss,' continued she: but, suddenly recollecting herself, added—'Perhaps, sir, you speak that language, too?'

'Yes, madam.'

A dead silence ensued; which was only once or twice interrupted by an exclamation of discontent from the aunt. Each became busied with their own thoughts: mine were distracted by doubts and apprehensions, concerning the manner in which I ought to act. I could come to no determination. To be seen by the aunt would not only have wounded her pride, and if possible have rendered her more implacably my mortal enemy than she had been, but it would have subjected Olivia, toward whom my heart was bursting with affection, to a series of new assaults and persecutions. Nay the sudden sight of me might overpower her, and even have dangerous effects. Such at least were the whisperings either of my tenderness or my vanity. And yet to miss this opportunity, to acquaint her with none of those overwhelming sensations that were all thankfulness, love, and adoration, and not so much as to inform her that I was still living, still perhaps capable of all the good that she had ever supposed of me, was in every view of it tormenting. How had she struggled to conceal her emotions when she mentioned my death, and that I had saved her life! Should I deserve this tenderness, if I could leave her to grieve a moment longer? Such unkindness were not only unworthy of me, but might be dangerous: it might even risk her compliance to the proposed match.

And here a torrent of painful anxieties and surmises rushed upon me. The hateful subject was brought fully to my recollection. Andrews was no longer the rival I had to dread. A lord had entered the lists: a peer of the realm had sued for Olivia. Who could he be? Was it likely that she should long withstand the solicitations of her aunt, endure her bitter upbraidings, and suffer the rude taunts of her brother, while rank and splendor were courting her acceptance, while coronets were crouching at her feet and supplicating her compassion? Which of our ancient barons could he be? How should I learn? Was he young, handsome, courteous, engaging? Had he the virtues and the high qualities which imagination is so apt to attach to the word noble?

Another train of conjecture seized upon my thoughts. How did it happen that they should believe me dead? Who were the authors of this false report? It must surely be intentional deceit; perhaps of the aunt, perhaps of Hector; invented to induce her to comply with their wishes, and ally them to the peerage. I must not suffer it to continue. The aunt appeared to believe it; and that Olivia had no doubt of it was certain. My fears confirmed me in the suspicion that it was a family artifice.

I was at length awakened from these reveries by the aunt; who expressed her surprise and impatience at the slow driving of the coachman. It seems it had continued for some time, though not remarked by me; and it was not long before the coach stopped, when I perceived that we were in an uncommonly thick fog. Olivia was still silent, but the aunt was alarmed by the voices of men;

and, as the darkness and mist prevented all danger of my being known, I opened the coach-door and jumped out; and Clarke followed my example.

I found on enquiry we were passing Cranford-bridge at the beginning of Hounslow-heath, that a broad-wheeled waggon had approached, and that the coachman unable to distinguish the road had alighted to lead his horses, lest we should be overturned. He had trusted the reins to the footman who remained on the box.

By the caution of the coachman, the waggon was safely passed, and he thought proper to mount his box again: but he durst not venture to drive fast; and, as I was alarmed for the safety of Olivia, I and Clarke continued beside the horses.

We had not gone fifty yards before we were again entangled with a timber carriage; the driver of which, embarrassed by the fog, had turned it across the road.

The waters, which lie in the hollows on the Hounslow-side of the bridge, had been greatly increased by the late tempests, and heavy rains. The coach horses began to snort with more vehemence; for they had for some time been disturbed with fright; and one of them, running against the projecting timber, plunged, and terrified the rest: so that the two fore-horses, quitting the road, dashed into the water, dragged the coach after them in despite of the driver, and the near-wheels were hurried down the bank.

It fortunately happened that the declivity was not steep enough immediately to overturn the coach; otherwise Olivia and her aunt would probably have lost their lives.

Bewildered by the fog, neither I nor Clarke could act with that promptitude which we desired. I however got to the horses' heads, myself above the knees in water, and stopped them just in time. I called to Clarke to come to me; and, as I knew him to be both strong and determined, I committed the horses to him and ran to support the carriage, lest it should overturn.

The coachman sensible of his danger, took care to alight on the off-side. The footman did the same; and I, with an air of authority which the circumstances inspired, ordered them to come to me and support the coach. They obeyed. I hastened round to the other side, opened the door, first took out the aunt, and then accomplished the wish of my heart: I held the lovely Olivia once more in my arms, and once more pressed her to my bosom, without the least alarm to her delicacy.

For how many rapturous moments are lovers indebted to accident! Mine indeed would have been a single bliss, and therefore unworthy the name, had not the tenderness and the truth of Olivia so lately been manifested. But this addition made the transport undescribable! To be in my arms yet not to know me, but to suppose me dead, to feel my embrace and to have no suspicion that it was the embrace of love, to be once more safe and I myself once more her protector, oh Imagination! Strong as thou art, thy power is insufficient for the repetition of such a scene, for the complete revival of such ecstacy!

I was unwilling to part with my precious burthen, which I had no longer any pretence to retain. 'Pray, sir, put me down,' said the angel; with a sweet, a gentle, and a thankful voice. 'We are very safe now: for which both I and my aunt are infinitely indebted to you.'

I could make no reply: but I pressed her hand with something of that too ardent rashness of which the aunt had accused me.

The old lady too did not forget her acknowledgments. She had no doubt now that I was a gentleman. My behaviour proved it. She should be very proud to thank me, in a more proper place, for my civilities; and would endeavour to repay the obligation if I would do her the favour to call in Hertford-street.

Olivia was not one of those who think only of themselves. 'Having been so good, sir,' said she, 'as to take us out of danger, perhaps you could be serviceable to the poor coachman.'

'Let me first see you back to the inn, ladies.'

'Some accident may happen in the mean time. The horses are unruly. We will stay here till all is safe.'

The advice was just, and it came from Olivia. I obeyed and hastened to the coachman; who was busied in loosing the traces, and relieving the horses from the carriage. This was presently done; and the coach was left, till proper aid and more light could be obtained.

I then returned to Olivia; and, when the coachman came up, the aunt enquired if their danger had been great?

'I don't know, madam, what you may call great,' answered he; 'but, if that gentleman had not stopped the cattle, and if the near wheels had gone one yard nay two feet farther I should have had an overturn; and then how either you or I could have got out of that gravel pit is more than I can tell. For my own part, I know, I thank him with all my heart; and the other gentleman too: for it is not often that your gentleman are so handy. Instead of helping, they generally want somebody to help them. I hope they'll be civil enough to take a glass with me. By G— they shall go to the depth of my pocket, and welcome.'

'If that be the case,' replied the aunt, 'we are all very much obliged to them indeed! But I will take care never to travel in a fog again.'

Just as this was passing, we heard at a distance, and as if coming from the inn, a shouting of 'Hollo! Hoix! Coachee! Coach! where are you all?'

'I declare,' said the aunt, 'that is my nephew's voice! This is very lucky! He will now take us in his phaeton.'

'Surely, madam,' exclaimed I, 'you would not trust yourself and this young lady in a phaeton such a night as this; when you see the most experienced drivers are liable to such accidents?'

'If the lady does,' continued the coachman as he was going, 'why I shall suppose she does not value a broken neck of a farthing.'

We then proceeded back to the inn, and were presently joined by Hector; whom the aunt immediately began to rate.

While she was thus employed, I, endeavouring to disguise my voice, as I had before done in the few sentences I had uttered, and addressing myself to Olivia, said, 'I should be exceedingly concerned, madam, if I thought you would suffer Mr. Mowbray to drive you home till day light shall appear.'

'I certainly shall not, sir;' answered she. 'But do you know my brother?'

'Madam!'

'You are acquainted with his name; and I don't recollect that it has been mentioned.'

I hesitated, Hector turned upon us, we were approaching the light, and, with a suddenness which fear and passion inspired, knowing that Mowbray did not understand Italian, I said in an under voice—'*Il Signor Hugo Trevor non é morto, bellissima Signora;* Mr. Trevor is not dead, dearest lady'——At the same instant I snatched her hand, pressed it, was about to raise it to my lips, but recollecting myself, turned short round, and added, '*Addio!*'

Clarke was at my back; and I plucked him by the coat, and whispered—'Come with me.'

But what of Olivia? Was she dead to feeling at this strange mysterious moment? Did no rushing torrent of ideas suddenly overwhelm her? The man whose loss she had lamented not in his grave; that man again her saviour, her guardian genius in the dark hour of dread and danger; acquainted in a way the most extraordinary with her thoughts, and favourable wishes; or, as she was too severely inclined to term it, her passion and its folly; a witness that she did not credit all which malice could urge against him, nor listen in base silence when her perhaps too partial heart pleaded in his behalf; nay more, that man the protector of her aunt, by whom he had been so often and so bitterly reviled; that man travelling in obscurity; in familiar society with a carpenter, yet braving peril in her behalf, and shunning the thanks which the uncommon services he had rendered might boldly make him claim; avoiding them most certainly because of the mean condition to which he was reduced; faithful in his affection; for such his behaviour spoke him; but unfortunate, depressed, despised; sinking under poverty; languishing away his youth; or crushed by accumulating disasters!—Did no such fears, no such tender recollections, assail her bosom?—I have described her ill indeed if that could be supposed. I must pursue my narrative: for how can I picture what most indubitably must have passed in her heart, since I feel myself so very incapable of delineating my own!

This adventure did not entirely end here. I wished to have gone forward on foot to Hounslow without delay: but Clarke interceded, for a glass of brandy. He said the water had chilled him; and he was still more importunate with me to take the same preventative. I had no fear for myself; for I had no such feeling: but, as I did not think I had any right to trifle with his health, I returned with him; taking the precaution to go through the passage to the kitchen door.

Here, just as we came to the threshold, who should be coming in face of us, carrying a pair of candles, but my quondam servant, Philip!

The instant he beheld me, he turned pale, trembled, set down the lights, stood aghast for a moment, and then took to his heels.

Though not so terrified, I was almost as much surprised as he; and suffered him to escape before I had the presence of mind to know how to act. As however it was my plan to avoid being known myself for the present, I thought proper to make no other enquiry than to ask whose servant he was? and was answered that he came with the ladies, who had just returned from the coach.

Various conjectures instantly crossed my imagination; all of which were associated with the sudden flight from Bath, the robbery he had committed, the seeming honesty and even affection of his character previous to that event, his now being in the service of Olivia, for I understood him to be her own valet, and the story of my death. But, though my curiosity was greatly excited, the present was not the time in which these mysteries could be unravelled. We therefore took Clarke's prescription against cold; and, leaving Cranford bridge, pursued our road to Hounslow: where we arrived about eleven o'clock, and put up at an inferior inn lest any accident should bring us again in company with the aunt and the nephew.

CHAPTER XII

Meditations on what had passed: The condolence of Clarke:
Arrival at London: The meeting of former friends: Law
arrangements

IT may be well supposed that the incidents of this night were not easily driven from my imagination. While we were walking, the care we were obliged to take, and the gloom around us, prevented any thing from escaping me sufficiently marked to attract the notice of my companion. But, when we were seated in a room with lights, and my mind was no longer diverted by other objects, the reveries into which I fell, the interjections that broke from me, the hasty and interrupted manner in which I ate and drank, the expressions of extreme joy which altered my countenance at one moment, and the solemn seriousness which it assumed the next, with my eyes fixed, while the tears rolled down my cheeks, at last so agitated poor Clarke that he exclaimed—'For God's sake, Mr. Trevor, what is the matter with you?'

My silence, for I was unable to speak, did but increase his alarm——'Are you taken ill? What has befallen you? Won't you open your mind to me? If I could do you any good, I hope you don't think I should be backward? Are you unhappy?'

'No, no.'

'I am very glad of that. But something uncommon I am sure has happened to you: though it may not be fit perhaps that I should hear

what. And I don't want to be a busy body; though I must say I
should be more at ease, if I was quite sure that all was right. That's
all. I have no other curiosity.'

'All is not right: but yet I hope it will be. I know not by what
means. It seems indeed impossible! And perhaps it is; and yet I
hope! I hope! I hope!'

'Well, well: I am glad of that. We should all hope. We are bid to
hope. God help us if we did not. Perhaps I can't give you any help?
I suppose that is beyond me. I am sorry for it. But what can a poor
carpenter do, in the way of befriending a gentleman?'

'A poor carpenter can have a kind heart; and I do not know
whether that is not the most blessed thing on earth! Did you ever
hear me repeat the name of Olivia?'

'Yes; when you were light-headed, I heard the name many a time
and often. And the nurse said you raved of nobody else. But we
could none of us find out who she was. Though, I must say, I have
often enough wished to ask: but that I did not think it became me
to seem to be at all prying.'

'That is the lady you have been in company with to-night. It is
she whom you have helped me to save. I was sufficiently indebted to
you before: but what am I then at present?'

'Well, that to be sure is accidental enough! I could not have
thought it! How oddly things do fall out! But I am glad of it with
all my heart!'

'I could not see much of her, to be sure; though I looked with all
the eyes I had: but I thought somehow she seemed as fine a young
creature as I had ever beheld since the hour I was born; which the
mildness of her voice did but make the more likely. I thought to
myself, I never in my days heard any living soul so sweet-spoken.
So that I must say things have fallen out very strangely.

'I always said to my Sally, there must be something between you
and the gentlewoman the name of *which* was on your tongue's end
so often, while you were down in the fever; and I am glad to the
heart that you have happened on her again so unexpectedly: though
I can see no good reason, now you have found her, why you should
be in such a hurry to get away.'

The unaffected participation of Clarke in all my joys and
sorrows, the questions which his feelings impelled him to put,
and the fidelity of his nature, as well as the impulse which
passion gave me to disburthen my mind, were all of them induce-

ments to speak; and I informed him of many of those particulars which have already been recited.

The more intimately he became acquainted with my history, the more powerfully he seemed imbued with my hopes and fears; and the better satisfied I was with the confidence I had reposed in him. I am unable to paint the honest indignation of his feelings and phraseology at the injustice which he as well as I supposed had been done me, the depression of his countenance when I dwelt on the despair and wretchedness which the almost impossibility of my obtaining Olivia inspired, and the animation with which he seemed as it were to set his shoulders to the wheel, when my returning fervor led me to the opposite extreme, and gave me confidence in my own powers and the strenuous exertions on which I was resolved.

The conversation continued long after we retired to rest; so that our sleep was short: for we were up again very early, before it was light, and continued our journey to London; where we arrived a little after nine in the morning.

I immediately proceeded to the lodging of Miss Wilmot; whom I found where I had left her, and who was truly rejoiced to see me. Clarke had never been in London: I therefore took him with me, gave a proper account of him to Miss Wilmot, and we all breakfasted together, while Mary waited; whose features as well as her words sufficiently testified the unexpected pleasure of the meeting, and who artlessly related the apprehensions of herself and my few friends, at not hearing from me.

My first enquiries were concerning Wilmot and Turl; and I was delighted to learn that Wilmot, whom I left in a sickly state of mind that was seriously alarming, had been awakened by Turl to a more just sense of human affairs; and had recovered much of the former vigour and elasticity of his talents.

His sister told me that he was at present engaged in a periodical publication; and had beside composed a considerable part of a comedy: of which Turl, as well as herself, conceived the greatest hopes.

The reader scarcely need be told that this intelligence gave me great pleasure. It led me to revolve mighty matters in my own mind, created emulation, and inspired me with increasing confidence and alacrity. Yes, said I, exultingly, genius may safely encounter and dare difficulties. Let it but confide in itself and it will conquer them all.

While we were conversing Wilmot came in.

I must leave the imagination to paint the welcome we gave each other.

I was surprised at the change which had taken place in his form and physiognomy; and at the different aspect they had assumed. Not that the marks of melancholy were quite eradicated: but, when I considered his whole appearance, he was scarcely the same person.

I produced surprise in him of a contrary kind. There was neither the wonted freshness of my complexion nor the fashionable ease of my air and dress, which he had remarked but a few months before; and he took the first private opportunity that offered to enquire, with great earnestness, if there were any means by which he could be of service?

Under the general selfishness which our present institutions inspire, such questions are wonderfully endearing. I answered him that I had found a friend, whose principles were as liberal and enlarged as they were uncommon; and that I would take an early occasion to give him an account of my present designs, and the posture of my affairs.

He informed me that the severe application of Turl had enfeebled his health, and had induced him to reside for a few weeks at a small place by the sea-side, that he might enjoy the benefits of bathing and the fresh breezes; for which purpose he had left London the week before: that neither Wilmot nor Turl himself considered his case at present as the least dangerous, but that they had both agreed this was a prudent step; and that he had received a letter from Turl, informing him of his safe arrival; and that he thought he had already derived benefit and animation from the journey.

Turl was not a man to be known and to be thought of with apathy. The intelligence Wilmot gave me, softened as it was by the circumstances attending it, produced a very unpleasant feeling. The possibility of the loss of such a man, so wise, so benevolent, and so undaunted in the cause of truth, was a sensation for which I have no epithet. Wilmot perceived what passed in my mind, and again assured me of his thorough persuasion that there was not any danger.

We passed as much of the morning together as Wilmot could spare from his occupations; after which we parted, and each proceeded on his own concerns: I to enquire after a dwelling-place;

and he to his literary engagements: while Clarke, instructed by Mary, went in search of a lodging for himself through those streets that were most likely to afford him one at a reasonable rate.

Mr. Evelyn had a relation of a younger branch of the family in the law, whose name was Hilary, to whom I was recommended; and from whom I received the utmost attention, in consequence of the letters I brought. This gentleman was an attorney of repute, a practitioner of uncommon honesty, assiduous and capable as a professional man, a firm defender of freedom even to his own risk and detriment, a sincere speaker, a valuable friend, and in every sense a man of worth and principle.

Happy at all times to oblige, he willingly undertook the task assigned to him by Mr. Evelyn's recommendation; and, in pursuance of his advice, I hired an apartment in the neighbourhood of Queen's-square Bloomsbury: that I might be within a convenient distance of the inns of Court, yet not entirely buried in the noise and smoke of the disagreeable part of the town.

I likewise informed Mr. Hilary of my determination not to be a dumb barrister; and having, from my appearance and mode of enunciation as well as from the letters of Mr. Evelyn, conceived rather a high opinion of my talents, he applauded my plan: in pursuance of which he recommended me to place myself with Counsellor Ventilate; a man of high situation in the law. I readily consented; and it was agreed that he should speak to that gentleman immediately on the subject, and appoint a meeting.

CHAPTER XIII

More meditations relating to Olivia; concluding with a love-letter: Doubts concerning its conveyance

IT cannot be supposed that Olivia was out of my thoughts. Knowing her kindness toward Miss Wilmot, I carefully took the first opportunity to inform the latter of the chief incidents that had passed; and to concert with her some means, if possible, of obtaining an interview.

Miss Wilmot no longer received any pecuniary aid from Olivia. Wilmot considered it as a duty to provide for his sister; and had too lofty a sense of independance to admit the repetition of these favours. Yet how far that pride of heart, which teaches us, not only that we should not submit to receive pecuniary assistance from any human being except from our relations, but that these relations can accept of no relief, however much they may be in need of it, without tarnishing our honor, is a question which deserves to be seriously examined. Not but, at that time, it squared very aptly with my opinions. It may be further remarked of relations that, as they sometimes think they ought only to receive aid from each other, so, they most of them imagine that, from each other, they may un-blushingly extort all they can. The generous Wilmot indeed was in no danger of this last mistake.

But though money was no longer a motive for intercourse, between the gentle Olivia and Miss Wilmot, there was no danger that either of the friends would forget the other; and the latter was too sincerely interested in the happiness both of me and Olivia not to be willing to promote that happiness, by every means in her power.

What these means should be was the difficulty we had to solve. To use any kind of stratagem would offend the delicate and justly-feeling Olivia. To come upon her by surprise, even if the opportunity should offer itself, would not be a manly and dignified proceeding.

I had always thought highly of that courage which, mild as her manners were, she never failed to exert on trying occasions. Her defence of me in the coach was a proof that I had not over-estimated her fortitude. It likewise shewed that she was under mistakes concerning me that were dangerous, should they remain unexplained; and that, whenever I thought of them, which was but too often, excited my utmost indignation.

Bold however as she was in my defence when she supposed me dead, very different sensations might assail her when she should be convinced (if she still doubted) that I was living. Her submission to her aunt seemed to be unlimited, as long as she supposed that to comply would be less productive of harm than to resist: but I had witnessed that she would not consent to actions of great moment, which her heart disapproved.

These facts made it improbable that she would grant me an interview, without her aunt's knowledge. What then was to be done? A letter, that should fully explain my thoughts, my plans, my determination, and my hopes and fears, appeared to be the most eligible mode. Were I to prompt her to a clandestine correspondence, I was well aware that I should highly and justly offend her. She would consider it as little less than an insult. Her conduct was open, her mind superior to deceit; and to be ignorant of this would be to shew myself unworthy of her. The lover should disdain to excite his mistress to any action which he would disapprove in a wife; and this was a rule not to be infringed, by him who should aspire to the noble-minded Olivia.

To write then I resolved; and in such a manner as to open my whole soul to her, awaken her affections, call forth her admiration, agitate her with pity and love, and ensure her perseverance.

Alas! I took the pen in hand, but was miserably deceived. I had undertaken an impossible task. Thought was too rapid, too multifarious, too complicate; and the tracing of letters and words infinitely too slow, and frigid. At last however, after repeated attempts, I determined on sending the following: with which when written I was very far from satisfied; but of that I despaired.

'To the woman whom my soul adores how shall I address myself? Tumultuous thoughts, hopes that vanish, and fears that distract, are ill fitted for such a talk. Governed by feelings which will admit of no controul, I can only claim your pardon on the plea of inability to preserve that silence which it is temerity, or something worse, to break. My thoughts will have passage, will rush into your presence, will expose themselves to the worst of calamities, your reproof and anger. Distracted as I am by a dread of the dangers that may result from my silence, I persuade myself that these dangers are more immediate and threatening, though scarcely more painful, than your disapprobation.

'You have supposed me dead; though by what strange accident I cannot divine. Under that supposition, it was my miraculous fortune, my ecstatic bliss, to hear you, with a purity of heart and a dignity of sentiment such as none but a heart like yours could conceive or express, avow a former partiality in favour of one who, whatever may be his other faults, would gladly resign his life to secure your happiness: of one who, in his over-weening affection has fondly and foolishly cherished the persuasion that this happiness is inseparable from his own: nay who partly hopes and partly believes, so blind is his egotism, that he is the only man on earth who fully comprehends your wonderful worth and matchless virtues; and who is pursuing the fixed purpose of his soul, that of finally deserving you, from the conviction that he through life will be invariable in that admiration, that tenderness, and that unceasing love without which the life of Olivia might perhaps be miserable. These may be the dreams of vanity, and folly: yet, if I do not mistake, they are the dreams of all lovers. They are indeed the aliment or rather the very essence of love. What delight can equal that of revelling, in imagination, on the happiness we can bestow on those who have bliss so ineffable to bestow upon us?

'What then if I were to see this Olivia mated with a man so dull of faculty as soon to lose all sense of the wondrous treasure in his possession: who never perhaps had any discriminating knowledge of its worth; and who shall be willing to barter it for any vile and contemptible gewgaw that may allure his depraved taste, or sickly appetite? Is there no such man? Are these fears wholly groundless?

'At what an immeasurable distance do I seem cast from the enjoyment of that supreme bliss to which, perhaps, the frenzy only of imagination could make me aspire! There is but one means by which I can be happy. Either I am to be the most favoured of mankind, or I am nothing. Either I rise into godlike existence, or I sink unknown and never to be remembered. Either we are made for each other, or—I dare not think on the reverse. It is too distracting.

'Yet I have no hope! What I now write is presumption, is madness! And why? It is not your beauty, your virtues, or the supreme qualities of your mind that would raise this gulph of misery between us. No. Avarice, vanity, and prejudice are my enemies. It is they that would sacrifice you at their altars. That you will persevere in your refusal is my only hope.

'How shall I palliate, what I cannot defend, my behaviour while I overheard you and your aunt? In vain do I plead that I was asleep, when you came into the coach; and that I first discovered you by the sound of your voice and the turn of the conversation; that I dreaded exciting any sudden alarm in you: perhaps it was a vain dread: and that, when I ought most to have spoken, when I became the subject of the discourse, I was then chained in silence by un-conquerable emotions. Yet to be a listener? Indeed, indeed, it is a thing that my soul disdains! But I have done many such things; not knowing, while they passed, what it was that I did.

'My destiny now is to study the law; and to this my days and nights shall be devoted: but the distance at which I see myself from the goal is a thought which I am obliged, by every possible effort, to shut out of my memory.

'I am in want of consolation; but since your society is denied me, I know not where it may be found. I own, there are moments in which I am fearfully agitated. Yet I do not solicit an answer. Let me rather perish than prompt you to an action of the propriety of which even I am obliged to doubt; since it cannot I suppose be done without concealment. Oh that you knew every thought of my heart! You would then perceive the burning desire I have to make myself every way worthy of that unutterable bliss to which I aspire.

'Madman! I aspire?

'With what contempt would such daring be treated, by those whom custom and ties of blood have taught you to revere! I confess this is a thought which I cannot endure. Yet I can less endure to relinquish my impossible hopes. Could you conceive what these contradictory and tormenting sensations are, you would perhaps be induced to pardon some of the extravagant acts which I heard you so mildly, yet so justly, censure.

'To be yours then is the end for which I live; and yet my pride and every other feeling revolts, to think I should entreat you to accept a pauper, either in wealth or principle. Well, then, I will not waste my time, in complaint. Let me become worthy of you, or let me perish! Fool! That is impossible. But if fall I must, I will endeavour to make my ruin respectable.

'Suffer me to inform you that I have lately acquired a friend whose virtues are beyond my praise, and who has urged me to accept his aid, in forwarding my studies and pursuits, as an act of duty incumbent on us both. Our acquaintance has been short; and so, considering the serious nature of the subject, was the debate that led to this conclusion: yet his arguments seemed unanswerable, and I hope I have not yielded too lightly. Oh that it was allowed me to consult your exquisite sense of right and wrong! But wishes are vain.

'Thus far I have intruded, yet know not how to end. My only hope that you will take no offence at what I have written is in the conscious respect that my heart feels for you; which I think cannot have misguided my pen; and the knowledge that you are too just lightly to attribute mean or ill motives to me.

'How languid is all that I have written! Am I so impotent that I can present none of the images that so eternally haunt me, that wing me into your presence, furnish me with innumerable arguments which seem so all-persuasive, melt me in tenderness at one moment, supply me with the most irresistible elocution the next, and convince you while they inspire me with raptures inexpressible? Are they all flown, all faded, all extinct? Where is the fervor that devours me?

'I would pray for your happiness! I would supplicate heaven that no moment of your bliss should be abridged! Shall it then be disturbed by me? Oh no. Unless authorised by hopes, as different as they are wild and improbable, pardon but this, and you shall never more be subject to the like importunity from

HUGH TREVOR.'

Having written my letter, I had to devise the means of having it delivered. If it were addressed directly to her, what certainty had I that it would not be opened by the aunt? Nay was not that indeed the most probable? And would it in that case ever be seen by Olivia? In my apprehension certainly not.

I had then to chuse whether I would send a messenger, who should wait about the house and take some opportunity to deliver it clandestinely; or commit it to the care either of Mary or Miss Wilmot.

The messenger was a very objectionable expedient: it was mean, and liable to detection. The medium of Mary was something of the same kind; and the friendship and intelligence of Miss Wilmot rendered her intervention much the most desirable.

It was a delicate office to require of her. But she could speak the truth: she could say that it was to relate some facts which Olivia might even desire to know, that it contained nothing which I myself should wish her to conceal, if she thought fit to shew it; that it did not invite her to any improper correspondence; and that it was the only one which, under the present circumstances, I meant to obtrude upon her.

That Miss Wilmot might be convinced I had neither deceived myself nor her in this account, which I should instruct her to give of it, I hastened with it to her lodgings, and requested her to read it before it was sealed. Having ended, she was so well satisfied with the propriety both of writing and delivering it that she readily undertook the latter office; and, with her I left it, hoping that Olivia would soon call, would read it in her presence, and that I should quickly learn what might be the sensations it should produce.

CHAPTER XIV

Counsellor Ventilate and the law: Raptures excited by the panegyric of Blackstone: Dialogues legal and political, with characteristic traits

MEANTIME the appointed interview between me and Counsellor Ventilate took place. This gentleman was characterized by those manners, and opinions, which the profession of the law is so eminently calculated to produce. He had a broad brazen stare, a curl of contempt on his upper-lip, and a somewhat short supercilious nose. His head was habitually turned upward, his eye in the contrary direction, as if on the watch in expectation to detect something which his cunning might turn to advantage, and his half-opened mouth and dropping jaw seemed to say, 'What an immense fool is every man I meet!'

His whole manner and aspect appeared to denote that he was in a continual revery; and that he imagined himself in a court of law; brow-beating a witness, interrogating an idiot, or detailing cases and precedents, to shew the subtlety with which he could mislead and confound his hearers. A split-hair distinction without a difference gave him rapture; and whenever it happened to puzzle, which was but too often, he raised his left shoulder and gave a hem of congratulation to himself: denoting his conviction that he was indisputably the greatest lawyer in the world! And, if the greatest lawyer, he was as certainly, according to his own creed, the greatest man! For the rest of mankind, if put in competition with lawyers, what were they? What but poor, silly, imbecile creatures?

One standard, by which he delighted to measure his own talents, was the length to which he could drawl out a reply. Was there a man to be found who could speak eight hours unceasingly? He would surpass him. When his turn came, nine should not suffice. He would be more dull, contradictory, and intolerable, than his rival by an hour, at least. He would repeat precedents, twist sentences, misconstrue maxims, and so perplex and entangle his own intellect that his hearers had no way of getting rid of the pain he excited; except by falling a-sleep, or determining not to listen. It must be owned however he had some charity for them; for to sleep he gave them a very sufficient provocative.

Being one of the retainers of government, he had a seat in the House of Commons: where he used to rise in his place and address the Speaker, with no less logic, love of justice, and legislative wisdom, than he was wont to display when pleading in the courts.

It was in vain that he exposed himself to the ridicule of this most discerning body, not less witty than virtuous. Of shame he was incapable. He would again and again rise in his place, totally forgetful of past flagellation, and again and again convince Mr. Speaker and the honorable members: persisting to labour, in the hope of making them all as profound reasoners as himself. No matter that the thing was impracticable: he would get up and do his duty, and sit down and receive his own applause.

To mention shame in this case was indeed absurd. How should a man blush at reproof which he cannot comprehend? His skull was so admirably fortified, by nature, that it was equally impenetrable to the heavy batteries of argument or the skirmishing artillery of wit. Let the cannon roar: he heard it not. He was abstractedly contemplating those obscure depths in which he remained for ever seated; and where he had visions innumerable, though he saw nothing.

One favourite and never-failing object, on these occasions, was to instruct the house in law. And here the devil, who is himself a kind of lawyer, for he devours his best friends, the devil I say chose these opportunities to vent his choicest malice. He did not set a lawyer to confound a lawyer: that were but a stale device. He humbled him out of the mouths of men who had occasionally read law-books, it is true: but who had read them without a lawyers' obliquity; and had enquired what was the simple unadulterated intention of their authors. Now law, which in all its stages has a quibble in either eye, that may mean good or may mean ill, is every where, except in a Court of Justice, capable of a good interpretation. This is not a rule without an exception: but in many cases at least, law has something intentionally beneficial in its principle.

For this beneficent vital-spark every body, but a lawyer, is in search; and it is what every body, but a lawyer, is delighted to find. No wonder therefore that a lawyer should meet discomfiture, and confusion, when he pretends to discuss the abstract nature of justice, in any place except in these aforesaid Courts of Justice.

Thus it happened that Mr. Ventilate was, on all such occasions, confounded in that honorable house, of which he was an honorable member: which indeed, when we remember who were his opponents, was less miraculous than the immaculate conception— Pshaw! I mean the transmigrations—of Vishnoo.[1]

Much of the conceit and ridicule of the character of Mr. Ventilate was apparent, even to my eye, at our first meeting. But he was a person of great practice, and had the reputation of a sound lawyer: which signifies a man who has patience to read reports, and a facility at quoting them. Beside, I was in haste; and rather inclined to leap over an obstacle than to go round it.

Accordingly our arrangements were made, and the next day I attended at his chambers; with a firm and as I supposed not to be shaken determination to become one of the greatest lawyers the world ever beheld.

The first book I was advised to read, as a historical introduction to and compendium of law, was Blackstone's Commentaries.[2] This author had acquired too much celebrity for any man of liberal education to be ignorant of his fame. I therefore began and continued to read him with all the prepossession that an author himself could wish in his favour. The panegyric he makes on English laws, and the Constitution of Britain, gave me delight and animation. The reproof he bestows, on gentlemen who are ignorant of this branch of learning, and on the perplexities introduced into our statute-law by such 'ill-judging and unlearned legislators,'[3] and his praise of the capacity they would acquire for administering justice, to which sacred function they are so often called, were this ignorance removed, gave dignity to the study I was about to pursue.

Then the account given of Servius Sulpicius![4] who, according to my learned author, 'left behind him about a hundred and four-score volumes of his own compiling!' How wonderfully did it move my admiration! I previously knew that in most countries, which are denominated civilized, law was voluminous: but I had never till then imagined that one man could himself compile a hundred and four-score volumes! And, as it seems, could compile them at his leisure too: for his chief business was that of oratory! Beside which it lives on record that, being a firm patriot, he was a wise and indefatigable senator! But it appears that Sulpicius could devour law with greater ease than Milo,[1] or perhaps even than Cacus[2] himself, could oxen.

Neither was it recorded that this prodigy of legal learning began young. And should I then despair of equalling him? No, no: get me into one of my trances and, had he compiled as many thousands of volumes, I should scarcely have suspected that I could not compile as fast as he.

As I read on, how did I deplore the quarrel between Vicarius[3] and his opponents: or, in other words, between the pandects[4] and the common law of England: with the ignorance that had nearly been the result! How rejoice in the institution of those renowned hot-beds of law, the Inns of Court: by the aid of which, had not the rage for enacting laws kept pace with the rage for studying them, there were hopes that the whole kingdom would in time have been so learned in the science that every man might indeed have become his own lawyer.

How did I regret that I had not studied common-law while at college! How sympathetic with my author, when he exclaims— 'That a science, which distinguishes the criterions of right and wrong; which teaches to establish the one, and prevent, punish, or redress the other; which employs in its theory the noblest faculties of the soul, and exerts in its practice the cardinal virtues of the heart: a science, which is universal in its use and extent, accommodated to each individual, yet comprehending the whole community; that a science like this should ever have been deemed unnecessary to be studied in a university, is a matter of astonishment and concern!'[5]

How did I bless the memory of Mr. Viner,[6] who had found a remedy for this evil, by establishing an Oxford professorship; and how promise to make myself master of his abridgment, till I had every case it contained at my tongue's end! What were four and twenty volumes in folio? Compared to Sulpicius, it was a trifle!

The eulogium that I next came to on a university education, how grateful was that to my heart! I was not, as my oracle described, though one of the 'gentlemen of bright imaginations, to be wearied; however unpromising the search.'[7] Neither was I to be numbered among those 'many persons of moderate capacity, who confuse themselves at first setting out; and continue ever dark and puzzled during the remainder of their lives.'[8] The law being itself so luminous, there was no fear of that with me.

I met indeed with one overwhelming assertion. 'Such knowledge
as is necessary for a judge is hardly to be acquired by the lucubra-
tions of twenty years!'[1]

But this to be sure must be meant of dull fellows. As to the limits
of genius, they were unknown.

My pleasure revived in full force, when I arrived at my author's
definition of law: which he states to be—'a rule of civil conduct,
prescribed by the supreme power in a state; commanding what is
right, and prohibiting what is wrong.'[2] What will you say to that,
friend Turl? exclaimed I: putting down the book, and pausing. Can
any thing be more provident, more wise, more desirable?

In short, I found the writer so clearly understood and satisfactorily explained the nature of law, and the benefits arising from it,
that, for my own part, I began to be ashamed of my former
stupidity. It was all so self-evident that it seemed disgraceful not to
know it as it were by intuition. I was in that precise temper of mind
which renders conviction an easy task: for I was in haste to be rich,
and famous; and the desire of wealth and fame are two of the
strongest provocatives to faith that the sagacity of selfishness has
ever yet discovered.

While I was in the midst of all these admirings, my attention was
roused by a dialogue that passed between two of my senior fellow-
pupils, whose names were Rudge and Trottman, which the former
thus began.

'That was a d— rascally cause we were concerned in yesterday.'

'Rascally enough. But we got it.'

'I can't say but I was sorry for the poor farmer.'

'Sorry! Ha, ha, ha! You remind me of an unfleshed-recruit: or a
young surgeon, who has just begun to walk the hospitals. Frequent
the Courts, and you will soon learn to forget commiseration, and
attend to nothing but law. Docking of entails[3] gives the lawyer as
little concern as the amputation of limbs does the surgeon: they are
both of them curious only about the manner, and dexterity of the
operation.'

'I suppose it will ruin the man.'

'He was a fool for making it a criminal prosecution. He should
have brought an action for damages.'

'It is an aggravating thing for a man to have his daughter
seduced, be beaten himself because he was angry at the injury, and,
when he sues for redress, not only be unable to obtain it, but find

his fortune destroyed, as well as his daughter's character, and his own peace.'

'The law knows nothing concerning him, or his fortune, character, peace, or daughter. It is and ought to be dead to private feeling. It must consider nothing but the public benefit: nor must it ever condescend to vary from its own plain and literal construction.'

'That is strange: for its origin seems to have been in those very feelings, to which it is so dead.'

'Undoubtedly. But it provides for such feelings each under its individual class; and if a man, seeking redress, shall seek it under a wrong head, that is his fault; and not the fault of the law.'

'It is a fault, however, that is daily committed.'

'Ay to be sure: or there would be but few lawyers.'

'How so?'

'Why, if a man doing wrong was certain, or almost certain, of being detected and exposed, the chances would be so much against offenders that offences would of course diminish.'

'Then the prosperity of lawyers seems to result from the blunders which they themselves commit?'

'No doubt it does; and, as the blunders are innumerable, their prosperity must be in proportion.'

'There seems to be something wrong in this; though I cannot tell what or why.'

'Ha, ha, ha! You have no cause to complain: you are a lawyer, and your own interest must teach you that every thing is right. Except indeed that the classes or heads I mentioned, and consequently the blunders, are not numerous enough. But, thank heaven, we have a remedy for that: for our statute-books are daily swelling.'

'Why, yes! Some people say they are pregnant with mischief: of which it is further asserted that they are daily delivered.'

'Ay, certainly; and to the great joy of the parents.'

'Who are they?'

'Enquire for the father at St. Stephen's;[1] and for the mother at Westminster-hall.[2] I assure you they are both enraptured at their own offspring. The old lady sits in state, and daily praises her babes with the most doating loquacity. And she does this with so grave a face that it is impossible to forbear laughing, when you hear her. She is so serious, so solemn, so convinced that every thing she utters is oracular, and so irascible if she does but so much as smell a doubt concerning the beauty and perfection of her brats, that there is no scene in the world which tickles my imagination so irresistibly as to watch her maternal visage during her eulogiums, while the big-wigs are nodding approbation; or the contortions of her physiognomy, when any cross incident happens to impede the torrent of her fondness. With all due respect to her motherly functions, she is a very freakish and laughable old lady.'

'You have a turn for ridicule: but I confess, if I thought your picture were true, I do not believe my sensations would be so pleasant as yours appear to be.'

'And why, in the name of common sense?'

'How can one laugh at the mistakes and miseries of mankind?'

'For a very simple reason: because it is the only way that can render them endurable. None but a fool would cry at what cannot be corrected.'

The colloquy between my companions here took another direction, less interesting to me, and left me to pause and ruminate. This picture, said I, is satirical I own: but surely it is unjust. Blackstone, beyond all doubt, understood the science profoundly; and his account of it is very different indeed.

I turned back to the passage I have quoted.

'It distinguishes the criterions of right and wrong; teaches us to establish the one and prevent punish or redress the other; employs in its theory the noblest faculties of the soul, and exerts in its practice the cardinal virtues of the heart: it is universal in its use and extent, is accommodated to each individual, and yet comprehends the whole community.'

How just, how ennobling, how sublime is this praise! To compare it to the doatings of an old woman is extremely false: nay is pernicious; for, by exciting laughter, it misleads the judgment.

My companions being silent, I was impelled to address myself to Trottman. 'I wonder, sir,' said I, 'that you should be such an enemy to law.'

'I an enemy! You totally mistake. I am its fast friend. And with good reason: I find it a very certain source of ease and affluence even to the most stupid blockheads, if they will but drudge on; and of riches, honours, and hereditary fame, to men of but very moderate talents. I may surely expect to come in for my share; and therefore should be a rank fool indeed were I its enemy. I leave that to innovating fanatics. Let them dream, and rave, and write: while I mind my own affairs, take men as they are and ever must be, profit by supporting present establishments, and look down with contempt on the puppies who prate philosophy, and bawl for reform.'

I was stung. Conscious of the turn my own thoughts had taken, I suspected that he had divined this from some words which I might have dropped, and that his attack was personal: I therefore eagerly replied—'Your language, sir, is unqualified.'

'I meant no offence. If you are a reformer, I beg your pardon. I never quarrel about what I have heard certain pompous gentlemen call principles.'

'Then all those persons, who differ in opinion from you, are puppies; and pompous gentlemen?'

'Oh dear, no, sir! Only all those that are absent. The company, you know, according to the received rule, is excepted.'

There was something impudently humble and satirical in his look, while he uttered this: yet so contrived as to make the man appear a pettish angry blockhead, who should take offence at it; and I certainly was not inclined to quarrel with my new comrades, the first day of our acquaintance.

Beside, Trottman was a little insignificant man, in appearance; pot-bellied, of a swarthy complexion, but with keenness, cunning, and mockery in his eye; and whose form and figure, as well as his turn of mind, must have made it ridiculous to have quarrelled with him. I therefore waited for some more fortunate opportunity, to repay him in his own coin: for I was as unwilling to be vanquished by wit, and satire, as by force of argument, or of arms.

Rudge, whose temper was more placid but who had an enquiring mind, said, 'You do not know my friend Trottman yet, Mr. Trevor. He cares but little who has the most reason, so that he may have the most laughter.'

'Life is a journey,' added Trottman; 'and, if I can travel on terra firma, with a clear sky, and a smiling landscape, let those that please put to sea in a butcher's tray, and sail in quest of foul weather.'

'Yes, sir, but the search of ease is the loss of happiness; and to fly from danger is the likeliest way to meet it: that is, when you either seek or fly without a guide.'

'And who is this guide to safety?'

'It is, what you appear to hold in contempt, Principle.'

'Ha, ha, ha! Right! The blind leading the blind. Conjure up one phantom to seek for another. How prodigiously we improve!'

'From what you have said, I am not surprised that you should consider principle as a phantom. But you only quarrel with the word: for, as principle can mean nothing more than a rule of action, deduced from past experience and influencing our present conduct, you, certainly, like other men, act from principle. It is a moral duty to shun pain, and keep your fingers out of the fire.'

'Not if I want to sear up a wound.'

'You are excellent at a shifting blow. But why would you apply the cautery? Because principle, guided by experience, has previously told you that to cauterize is in some cases the way to heal.'

'But empirics, who cauterize without healing, are daily multiplying upon us.'

'Were that granted, it is but empiric opposed to empiric. Men have been groaning under their sufferings for ages; and, since ages have proved that the old prescriptions were insufficient, I can neither see the danger nor the blame of following new.'

'Zeal may be purblind, and perhaps could not see a guillotine: but her neck might chance to feel it.'

'Then you think a guillotine a more terrible thing than a halter, an axe, or perhaps even a rack?'

'It will do more work in less time.'

'And you suppose it to be principle, or if you please innovation, that has given this machine its momentum?'

'Suppose! Is there any doubt?'

'Infinite. I imagine it to be given, if we may be allowed to personify, neither by Innovation nor Establishment; but by the rashness and ill temper with which these heroines have mutually maintained their positions. Innovation struck the ball at first too impetuously: but Establishment took it at the rebound, and returned it with triple violence. Brunswickian manifestoes,[1] and exterminating wars, were not ill adapted to raise the diabolical spirit of revenge. An endeavour to starve a nation, which it was found difficult to exterminate by fire and sword, was not a very charitable act in Madam Establishment. Her swindling forgeries were little better; and that her turn should come, to be starved and swindled, is not miraculous: though it is deplorable. Heaven avert her claims to the guillotine!'

My antagonist had no immediate reply; and Rudge exclaimed, with some satisfaction, 'Why, Trottman, you have met with your match!'

'Not I, indeed,' answered he, peevishly. 'I am only lost in a labyrinth of words; and am waiting for Principle to come and be my guide. But I am afraid she carries a dark lanthorn, which will but blind those that look.'

'I suspect, sir,' said I, 'you are less at loss for a joke than an argument; and that you prefer bush-fighting. For my own part, I love the fair and open field of enquiry.'

'As this is a field that has no limits, nor any end to its cross roads, I am content, as you say, to sit down under my hedge and be quiet.'

'No, no; I did not say that: for I see you love to draw a sly bow at passengers.'

'I have now and then brought down a gull, or an owl.'

'Have you shot any of those birds to-day?'

I felt no compunction in making this triumphant retort to his sneer. And here our dialogue ended. Though it was a kind of declaration of war; I mean a war of words; which, as we became more acquainted, was occasionally waged with some asperity.

But, in one respect, Trottman was my superior. To sneer was habitual to him: but it was always done in a manner which seemed to indicate that he himself had no suspicion of any such intent. So that he continually appeared to keep his temper; and never triumphed so effectually as when he could provoke me to lose mine. On which occasions his additional conciliatory sarcasms, accompanied with smiles denoting the enjoyment of his victory, never failed to make me feel my own littleness. And this is a lesson for which I consider myself as very highly in his debt.

I now pursued my reading; and employed the rest of the day in beginning to copy the manuscript precedents, that were to capacitate me for the practice of law: for the number of which, that were in his possession, Mr. Ventilate was famed.

My ardour however had felt some trifling abatement, by the very different picture and panegyric of the law as given by Trottman, opposed to that I had been contemplating. But I had this very powerful consolation: that, as Trottman knew very little of what I supposed to be the true principles of politics, it was highly probable he was no better acquainted with those of law.

CHAPTER XV

*Former resentments revised: Doubts protracted: Conjectures
on the sincerity of a delicate yet firm mind*

ABOVE a fortnight passed away, during which I received no word of
intelligence concerning Olivia. At some moments I felt great
affliction from this suspense: at others I collected myself and
determined to pursue my plan with all the vigour in which it had
been conceived.

In the interval, I wrote several times to Mr. Evelyn. To this I was
prompted from the very nature of my engagements and situation.
Beside which I had not forgotten my pamphlet against the Earl and
the Bishop, that lay ready for publication; though the acrimony of
my feelings was much abated. The propriety of making the world
acquainted with this affair was one of the subjects of my correspondence with Mr. Evelyn: to whom I had the candour to state my
own opinions and sensations, on one part; and, on the other, the
objections that had been urged by Turl.

In the history I had given Mr. Evelyn of myself, I was impelled,
as well by inclination as necessity, to delineate the character of Turl,
with which he could not but be charmed; and with his arguments
and dissuasions on this subject. With these the ideas of Mr.
Evelyn entirely coincided. He wrote delightful letters; full of
animation, feeling, and friendship; and his persuasion therefore had
the greater effect.

Wilmot concurred in the opinion of both; and, being thus pressed
by the men whom I most loved and revered, I endeavoured to
consign my resentment and its effusions to oblivion, and to dismiss
the subject entirely from my mind.

At length, my suspense concerning Olivia found some, though
far from a satisfactory, relief.

As she had paid no visit to Miss Wilmot, the latter of course had
found no opportunity to deliver my letter. One evening, however,
as I was sitting after tea with Miss Wilmot and her brother, a note
came of which the following were the contents.

'Miss Mowbray presents her kind and tenderest respects to Miss
Wilmot, and informs her that she has been in town for some short

time. Assures her that her not having called is far indeed from any decline of former friendship, the sincerity of which is invariable: but that there are motives which prevent her, for the present, from the enjoyment of that satisfaction. She would have been most happy to have communicated her thoughts to Miss Wilmot in person: but she is the slave of circumstances which, for family reasons and indeed from other motives; she is forbidden to explain; and to which she is obliged to submit. She confides in the goodness and friendship of Miss Wilmot, who she is well assured will not misinterpret that which is unavoidable; and, cherishing the hope of a more favourable opportunity, wishes her all possible happiness: requesting that, if by any means in her power it can be increased, Miss Wilmot will acquaint her with those means: that she may have the wished-for occasion of proving the ardour and sincerity of her affections.

'Hertford-street, Nov. 17th.'

Miss Wilmot gave me this note to read; and the commentary I immediately made was that, finding I was alive, the fear of a rencontre with me was the obstacle to her visits.

They agreed that this was a very probable supposition: but how far the aunt was any way concerned in it was matter of more uncertain conjecture. Miss Wilmot knew that Olivia had informed her aunt of the visits she was before accustomed to make; and, as her ideas concerning sincerity were delicately strict, it was more than probable that she had disdained to conceal any of the circumstances with which she herself was acquainted. I therefore thought it almost indubitable that she had been no less frank on the present occasion than was habitual to her on others; and time afterward discovered that my conclusions were right.

'With what unequal weapons,' exclaimed I, 'do the lovers of truth and the adherents of hypocrisy contend!'

'They do indeed,' replied Wilmot. 'But, contrary I believe to your supposition, the former have infinitely the advantage: for the latter systematically deceive themselves.'

What was to be done? Was I to pursue some covert mode of conveying my letter? Should I send it openly? Or ought I to let it remain, and patiently wait the course of events, which, by endeavouring to forward, I might but retard? Wilmot, who, though he had too much sympathy to communicate all his fears, had but little expectation, judging from the failure of his own plans of the success of mine, advised me to the latter; and, perplexed as I was with doubt and apprehension, I followed this advice.

END OF VOLUME IV

VOLUME V

CHAPTER I

*A cursory glance at law fictions: Legal suppositions endless:
The professional jargon of an attorney: An enquiry into the
integrity of barristers and the equity of decisions at law:
A. and B. or a case stated: A digression from law to
philosophy*

IN the mean time, my application to the law was incessant; and consequently my intercourse with lawyers daily increased. I endeavoured to load my brain with technical terms and phrases, to understand technical distinctions, and to acquaint myself with the history of law fictions, and the reasons on which they had been founded.

To these subjects my attention had been turned by Mr. Hilary; who, being a Solicitor, was well acquainted with the value of them, to the man who meant to make himself a thorough lawyer.

The consideration of this branch of law staggered my judgment. Trottman and Hilary were intimate. The latter had invited us and other friends to dinner; and, as I found the acuteness of Trottman useful to me in my pursuits, I took this and every occasion to put questions: which he was very ready to answer. As it happened, my enquiry on the subject of law fictions brought on the following dialogue: which was supported by Trottman entirely in his own style.

'According to your account then,' said I, in answer to a previous remark, 'in *Banco Regis*[1] the King is always *supposed* to be present.'

'No doubt, what question can there be of that? One invisible kind of being can as easily be supposed as another. And I hope you will not dispute the actual presence of that pleasant gentleman called the devil, in any one of our courts?'

'By no means!'

'As for his majesty, he, God bless him! by the nature of his office is *hic et ubique:*[1] here, there, and every where. He is borne in state before each Corporation Mayor, whether Mr. or My Lord; and reposes peacefully in front of Mr. Speaker, or the Lord High Chancellor: investing them by his sacred presence with all their power.'

'How so?'

'How so! Do you forget the mace upon the table?'

'Authority then has that virtue that, like grace divine into a wafer, it can be transfused into wood.'

'Yes. A lord's white wand, a general's baton; a constable's staff. It is thought necessary, I grant, in some of these cases that the block should be carved and gilded.'

'Well, the position is that, in *Banco Regis*, the King is always present.'

'So says the law.'

'But the law, it appears, tells a lie; and, from all that I have heard, I wish it were the only one that it told.'

'Could the law hear, sir, it would take very grave offence at your language. It only assumes a fiction.'

'John Doe and Richard Roe, who are the pledges of prosecution, are two more of its *supposes*, or lies. I beg pardon. I should have said fictions.'

'Why, yes: considering that John Doe and Richard Roe never made their personal appearance in any court in the kingdom, were never once met, in house, street, or field, in public, or in private, nay had never yet the good luck to be born, they have really done a deal of business.'

'They resemble Legion, entering the swine: they plunge whole herds into the depths of destruction.'[2]

'Or, if you will, they are a kind of real yet invisible hob-goblins: by whom every human being is liable to be haunted. It must however be allowed of them that they are a pair of very active and convenient persons.'

'To lawyers. But God help the rest of mankind! Are there many of these fictions?'

'More than I or any man, I believe, can at one time remember.'

'From the little I have read, this appears to be a very puzzling part of the profession.'

'Not at all; if we will take things as we find them, and neither be more curious nor squeamish than wise. I will state the process of a suit to you; and you will then perceive how plain and straight-forward it is. We will suppose A the plaintiff: B the defendant. A brings his action by bill. Action you know means this: '*Actio nihil aliud est quam jus prosequendi in judicium quod sibi debetur:*' or, 'a right of prosecuting to judgment, for what is due to one's self.' B is and was *supposed* to be in the custody of the Marshal. Observe, *supposed to be:* for very likely B is walking unmolested in his garden; or what not. B we will say happens to live in Surrey, Kent, or any other county, except Middlesex; and is *supposed* to have made his escape, though perhaps he may have broken his leg, and never have been out of his own door. And then the latitat[1] *supposes* that a bill had issued, and further *supposes* that it has been returned *non est inventus,*[2] and moreover *supposes* it to have been filed. B lives in Kent, you know; and this latitat is addressed, in *supposition*, to the Sheriff of the county, greeting; though as to the Sheriff he neither sees, hears, nor knows any thing concerning it; and informs him that B (not-withstanding he is confined to his bed by a broken leg) runs up and down, in *supposition*, and secretes himself in the Sheriff's county of Kent: on which ——'

'I beg your pardon: I cannot follow you through all this labyrinth of *supposes.*'

'No! Then you will never do for a lawyer: for I have but just begun. I should carry you along an endless chain of them; every link of which is connected.'

'And which chain is frequently strong enough to bind and imprison both plaintiff and defendant.'

'Certainly: or the law would be as dead in its spirit as it is in its letter.'

'I fear I shall never get all the phrases and forms of law by rote.'

'Why, no. If you did, heaven help you! it would breed a fine confusion in your brain. You would become as litigious and as unintelligible as our friend Stradling.'

'Mr. Stradling,' said Hilary, 'is one of my clients: an unfortunate man who, being a law-printer, has in the way of trade read so many law-books, and accustomed himself to such a peculiar jargon, as to imagine that he is a better lawyer than any of us; so that he has half-ruined himself by litigation. He is to dine with us, and will soon be here.'

'I will provoke him,' continued Trottman, 'to afford you a sample of his gibberish; you may then examine what degree of instruction you suppose may be obtained from a heterogeneous topsy-turvy mass of law phrases.'

'But why irritate your friend?'

'You mistake. He has it so eternally on his tongue that, instead of giving him pain to shew the various methods in which he supposes he could torment an antagonist at law, it affords him the highest gratification.'

'Our friend Hilary here is better qualified for the task of instruction; but he feels some of your qualms; and is now and then inclined to doubt that there is vice in the glorious system which regulates all our actions.'

'I deny that it regulates them,' said Hilary. 'If people in general had no more knowledge of right and wrong than they have of law, their actions would indeed be wretchedly regulated!'

This was a sagacious remark. It made an impression upon me that was not forgotten. It suggested the important truth that the pretensions of law to govern are ridiculous; and that men act, as Hilary justly affirmed, well or ill according to their sense of right and wrong.

Mr. Stradling soon after came; and Trottman very artfully led him into a dispute on a supposed case, which Trottman pretended to defend, and aggravated him, by contradiction, till Stradling roundly affirmed his opponent knew nothing of conducting a suit at law.

The volubility of this gentleman was extraordinary; and the trouble I thought myself obliged to bestow, at that time, on the subject could alone have enabled me to remember any part of the jargon he uttered, in opposition to Trottman: which in substance was as follows.

'Give me leave to tell you, friend Trottman, you know nothing of the matter; and I should be very glad I could provoke you to meet me in Westminster-hall. If I had you but in the Courts, damn me if you should easily get out!'

'I tell you once more I would not leave you a coat to your back.'

'You! Lord help you! I would *traverse* your indictment, *demur* to your plea, bring my *writ of error*, *nonsuit* you. Sir, I would *ca sa fi fa* you. I would *bar* you. I would *latitat* you, *replevin* you, *refalo* you. I would have my *non est inventus*, my *alias*, and *pluries*,[1] and *pluries*, and *pluries*, *ad infinitum*. I would have you in *trover*; in *detinue*; I would send your loving friend Richard Roe to you. I would *eject* you. I would make you *confess lease entry and ouster*. I would file my *bill of Middlesex*; or my *latitat* with an *ac etiam*. Nay, I would be a worse plague to you still: I would have my bill filed in B. R. I would furnish you with a special original for C. P. You talk! I would sue out my *capias*,[1] *alias*, and *pluries*, at once; and outlaw you before you should hear one word of the proceeding.'

Bless me, thought I, what innumerable ways there are of reducing a man to beggary and destruction according to law!

Trottman thus provokingly continued.

'My dear Mr. Stradling, your brain is bewildered. You go backward and forward, from one supposition to another, and from process to process, till you really don't know what you say. If I were your opponent, in any Court in the kingdom, I should certainly make the law provide you a lodging for the rest of your life.'

'Bring your action! That's all! Bring your action, and observe how finely I will *nonpros* you: or reduce you to a *nolle prosequi*.[2] You think yourself knowing? Pshaw. I have nonsuited fifty more cunning fellows, in my time; and shall do fifty more.'

God help them! thought I.

'I have laid many a pert put[3] by the heels. You pretend to carry an action through the Courts with me! Why, sir, I have helped to ruin three men of a thousand a year; and am in a fair way, at this very hour, of doing as much for a Baronet of five times the property.'

I listened in astonishment.

'And do you take a pleasure in remembering this?' said Hilary.

'Pleasure!' answered Stradling; staring. 'Why, do you think, Mr. Hilary, I should have taken a pleasure in ruining myself? What did I do but act according to the laws of my country? And, if men will oppose me, and pretend to understand those laws better than I do, let them pay for their ignorance and their presumption. Let them respect the law, or let their brats go beg.'

'The law I find, sir,' said I, 'has no compassion.'

'Compassion, indeed! No, sir. Compassion is a fool; and the law is wise.'

'In itself I hope it is: but I own I doubt the wisdom of its practice.'

'But this practice, you must know,' said Trottman, with a wink to Stradling, 'Mr. Trevor means to reform.'

'Oh,' replied Stradling, 'then I suppose, when the gentleman is at the bar, he will never accept a brief, till he has first examined the equity of the case.'

'That, sir,' I replied, 'is my firm intention.'

'Ha, ha, ha! Mr. Trevor, you are a young man! You will know better in time.'

'And do you imagine, sir, that I will ever hire myself to chicanery, and be the willing promoter of fraud? If I do, may I live hated, and die despised!'

'Ay, ay! Very true! I don't remember that I ever met with a youth, who had just begun to keep his terms, who did not profess much the same. And, which is well worthy of remark, those that have been most vehement in these professions have been most famous, when they came to the bar, for undertaking and gaining the rottenest causes.'

'You shall find however, sir, that I shall be an exception to this rule.'

'Excuse me, Mr. Trevor, for not too hastily crediting hasty assertions. I know mankind as well as I know the law. However, I can only tell you that if your practice keep pace with your professions, you will never be Lord Chief Justice.'

'Do the judges then encourage barristers, who undertake the defence of bad and base actions?'

'To be sure they do. They sometimes shake their heads and look grave: but we know very well they defended such themselves: or, as I tell you, they would never have been judges. If two men have a dispute, one of them must be in the wrong. And who is able to pronounce which, except the law?'

'My dear Mr. Stradling,' said Trottman, 'you are again out of your depth. When two men dispute, it almost always happens that they are both in the wrong. And this is the glorious resource of law; and the refuge of its counsellors, and its judges.'

Trottman and Stradling were accustomed to each other's manner; and, notwithstanding the language they used, nothing more was meant than a kind of jocular sparring: which would now and then forget itself for a moment, and become waspish; but would recollect and recover its temper the next sentence.

I replied to Trottman—'It is true that, when two men dispute, it generally happens they are both in the wrong. But one is always more in the wrong than the other; and it should be the business of lawyers to examine, and of the law to decide upon, their different degrees of error.'

'What, sir!' exclaimed Stradling. 'If you were counsel in a cause for plaintiff A, instead of exposing the blunders and wrongs of defendant B, would you enquire into those of your own client?'

'I would enquire impartially into both.'

'And if you knew any circumstance which would infallibly insure plaintiff a nonsuit, you would declare it to the Court?'

'I would declare the truth, and the whole truth.'

'Here's doctrine! Here's law!'

'No,' said Trottman; 'it is not law. It is reform.'

'It ought to be law. As an advocate, I am a man who hire out my knowledge and talents for the avowed purpose of doing justice; and am to consider neither plaintiff nor defendant, but justice only. Otherwise, I should certainly be the vilest of rascals!'

'Heyday!' thundered Stradling: and, after a pause, added—'It is my opinion, those words are liable to a prosecution, Mr. Trevor; and, by G—, if you were to be cast in any one of our Courts for them, it would be no fault either of the bench or the bar if the sentence of the law, which you are defaming, did not shut you up for life!'

'My friend Trevor mistakes the nature of the profession he is studying,' added Trottman. 'He forgets that the question before a Court is not, what is this, that, or the other; which he may think proper to call justice; but, what is the law?'

'To be sure, sir;' continued Stradling. 'It is that which, as a lawyer, you must attend to; and that only.'

'I will cite you an example,' said Trottman.

'A was a gentleman of great landed property. B was an impertinent beggarly kind of sturdy fellow, his neighbour. A had an estate in the county of —— that lay in a ring-fence: a meadow of nine acres excepted, which belonged to B. This meadow it was convenient for A to purchase; and he sent his steward, who was an attorney, to make proposals. B rejected them. The steward advised A to buy the estate that belonged to C, but that was farmed by B. The advice was followed. The lease of B expired the following year; and a new one was denied by A, unless B would sell his meadow. B consented. A bought the meadow, but determined to have his revenge. For this purpose A refused payment, and provoked B to commence an action. The law he knew very well was on the side of B: but that was of little consequence. Plaintiff B brought his action in Trinity Term. Defendant A pleaded a sham plea: asserted plaintiff had been paid for his meadow, by a firkin of butter: [All a lie, you know.] long vacation was thus got over, and next term defendant files a bill in Chancery, to stay proceedings at law. Plaintiff B files his answer, and gets the injunction dissolved: but A had his writ ready and became plaintiff in error, carried it through all the Courts: from K. B. to the Exchequer-chamber; and from the Exchequer-chamber, as A very well knew that B had no more money, A brought error into Parliament:[1] by which B was obliged to drop proceedings. His attorney, of course, would not stir a step further; and the fool was ruined. He was afterward arrested by his attorney for payment of bill in arrear; and he now lies in prison, on the debtors'-side of Newgate.'

'How you stare, Mr. Trevor!' added Stradling. 'Every word true. We all know a great lord who has carried I cannot tell how many such causes.'

'And were the judges,' said I, 'acquainted with the whole of these proceedings?'

'How could they be ignorant of them? Judgment had passed against defendant A in all the Courts.'

'And did they afford the plaintiff no protection?'

'They protect! Why, Mr. Trevor, you imagine yourself in Turkey, telling your tale to a Cady,[2] who decides according to his notions of right and wrong; and not pleading in the presence of a bench of English judges, who have twice ten thousand volumes to consult as their guides which leave them no opinion of their own. It is their duty to pronounce sentence as the statute-books direct: or, as in the case I have cited, according to precedent, time immemorial.'

'And this is what you call law?'

'Ay! and sound law too.'

'Why then, damn the ——'

'You do right to stop short, sir.'

'It appears to me that I am travelling in a cursed dirty as well as thorny road,' said I, with a sigh.

'Why, to own the truth,' added Trottman, 'you must meet with a little splashing: and, unless you can turn back and look at it with unconcern, I should scarcely advise you to proceed.'

'I shall certainly reconsider the subject!'

'A pair of lawyers, like a pair of legs, are apt to bespatter each other: but they nevertheless remain good friends and brothers. If you send your spaniel into a muddy pool, you ought to take care, when he comes out, that he does not shake the filth he has collected over his master.'

'I wonder, sir, that you should continue one of a profession which you treat with such unsparing severity.'

'And I, sir, do not wonder at your wonderings. Life is a long road; and he must have travelled a very little way indeed who expects that it should be all a bowling-green. Pursue your route in which direction you will, law, trade, physic, or divinity, and prove to me that you will never have occasion to shake off the dust from your feet in testimony against it, and I will then pause and consider. You are of the sect of the Perfectibles.'

'And you of the cast of the Stand-stills.'

'Oh no. I conceive myself to be among children at a fair, riding in a round-about. Like the globe they inhabit, men are continually in motion: but they can never pass their circle.'

'And do you suppose you know the limits of your circle?'

'Within a trifle. The experience of states, empires, and ages has decided that question with tolerable accuracy.'

'But, what if a power should have arisen, of which you have not had the experience of states, empires and ages; except of a very small number? And what if this partial experience, as far as it goes, should entirely overthrow your hypothesis?'

'I know that, in argument, your *if* is a very renowned potentate. If the moon should happen to be a cheese, it may some time or another chance to fall about our ears in a shower of maggots. But what is this mighty power, that has done so much in so short a time; and from which you expect so many more miracles?'

'It is the art of printing. When knowledge was locked up in Egyptian temples, or secreted by Indian Bramins for their own selfish traffic, it was indeed difficult to increase this imaginary circle of yours: but no sooner was it diffused among mankind, by the discovery of the alphabet, than, in a short period, it was succeeded by the wonders of Greece and Rome. And now, that its circulation is facilitated in so incalculable a degree, who shall be daring enough to assert his puny standard is the measure of all possible futurity? I am amazed, sir, that a man of your acuteness, your readiness of wit, and your strength of imagination, can persist in such an affirmative!'

'The *argumentum ad hominem*. Very sweet and delectable. Thank you, sir.'

'Every thing is subject to change: why not therefore to improvement? That change is inevitable there are proofs look where you will: that which is called innovation must consequently be indispensible. Examine the history of your own science. When England was infested with wolves, we are told that King Edgar imposed an annual tribute of thirty wolves' heads on the Welsh Princes; that the breed might be extirpated. Had this tribute been levied, after the race was partly destroyed, the law would have counteracted its own intention: for, in order to pay the tax, the tributary Princes must have encouraged the breed; and once more have stocked the country with wolves.'

Stradling was little better than infected with what have been lately stigmatised by the appellation of Jacobinical principles,¹ and exclaimed, with great exultation—'Your remark is very true, sir; and it is an example that will serve admirably well to illustrate another point. Placemen and pensioners, a race more ravenous and infinitely more destructive than wolves, have been propagated for the support of the Executive Government; and the breed increases so rapidly that it will very soon devour its feeders.'

'And next itself.'

'With all my heart! Let me but see that vermin extirpated, and I shall die in peace!'

'Very right, Mr. Stradling;' said Trottman, with great gravity. 'Placemen, and pensioners are vile vermin! And so will remain, till your party comes into office.'

'If ever I could be brought to accept of place, or pension, may I ——!'

'I believe you: for I am well persuaded your virtue will never be put to the trial. Otherwise, I should imagine, it would find as many good arguments, I mean precedents, in favour of the regular practice in politics as in law.'

Here our dialogue paused. Dinner was announced, and law, politics, and patriotism were for a while forgotten, by all except myself, in the enjoyments of venison and old port.

CHAPTER II

More painful doubts, and further enquiries: Unexpected
encouragement and warm affections from a character before
supposed to be too cold: Hope strengthened and confirmed

DESULTORY as the conversation I have recited had been, it left a
very deep impression upon my mind. It was roundly asserted, by
every lawyer to whom I put the question, that the whole and sole
business of a counsellor was the defence of his client. Right or
wrong, it was his duty to gain his cause; and, with respect to the
justice of it, into that, generally speaking, it was impossible that he
should enquire. Briefs were frequently put into his hand as he
entered the Court; which he was to follow as instructed.

It did now and then happen that a cause was so infamous as to put
even the hacknied brow of a barrister to the blush: but it must be a
vile one indeed! And even then, when he threw up his brief, though
paid before he began to plead, it was matter of admiration to meet so
disinterested an example of virtue, in an advocate.

It was in the practice of the law that I hoped to have taken
refuge, against the arguments of Turl: which, averse as I had been
to listen, proved even to me that, in principle, it was not to be
defended.

The train of thinking that followed these deductions was so very
painful that I was obliged to fly from them; and seek advice and
confirmation in the friendship of Wilmot, before I should write on
the subject to Mr. Evelyn. For the latter task indeed my mind was
not yet sufficiently calm, collected, and determined.

My chief consolation was that the subject had thus been strongly
brought to the test of enquiry, before the expiration of the month
which, according to agreement, I was to be with Counsellor
Ventilate, previous to the payment of my admission-fee; of which,
as it was a heavy one, thus to have robbed the charities of Mr.
Evelyn would have given me excessive anguish.

I know not whether I was sorry or glad when I came to Wilmot's
lodging, to find Turl there. He had returned from his bathing
excursion; having been called back sooner than he expected by his
affairs.

He was cheerful, and in excellent spirits. His complexion was clear, his health improved, and his joy at our meeting was evident and unaffected. He even owned that, hearing I had devoted myself to the law, he had returned thus soon the more willingly once again to argue the question with me: for that he felt himself very highly interested in the future employment of talents of which he had conceived extraordinary hopes; and that he thought it impossible they should be devoted to such a confusing study, were there no other objection to it, as that of the law, without being, not only perverted and abused, but, in a great degree, stifled.

After an avowal like this, it required an effort in me to summon up my resolution, and honestly state the doubts and difficulties that had arisen in my own mind. It was happy for me that my friends were men whose habitual sincerity prompted me to a similar conduct. I therefore took courage, opened my heart, and, while describing my own sensations, was impelled to confess that the practice of the law could with great difficulty indeed be reconciled to the principles of undeviating honesty.

'I most sincerely rejoice,' said Turl, 'that these doubts have been suggested to you by other people, rather than by me: for I am very desirous you should not continue to think me too prone to censure. And, in addition to them, I would have you take a retrospect of your plan. To induce you to despond is a thing which I would most sedulously avoid: but to suffer you to delude yourself with the hopes of sudden wealth (and when I say sudden, I would give you a term of ten years) from the practice of the law, unless you should plunge into that practice with the most unqualified disregard to all that rectitude demands, would be to act the cowardly disingenuous hypocrite; and entirely to forget the first and best duties of friendship.

'Should you ask—"What path then am I to pursue?" I own I am totally at a loss for an answer. The choice must be left to yourself. You are not ignorant that it is infinitely more easy to point out mistakes, which have been and still continue to be committed daily, than to teach how they may be entirely avoided. Of this I am well assured, if you will confide in and exert those powers of mind that you possess, they must lead you to a degree of happiness of the enjoyment of which, I am sorry to say, but few are capable.

'From my own experience and from that of all the young men I meet, who are thrown upon the world, I find that the period which is most critical and full of danger, is the one during which they are obliged unsupported to seek a grateful and worthy way of employing their talents.

'My own resource has been that of cheerfully submitting to what are called the hardships of obscure poverty; and of consoling myself, not only with a firm persuasion that by this course in time I shall infallibly change the scene, but that, till this time shall come, I am employing myself on the subjects which can best afford me present satisfaction. That is, in endeavours, however narrow and feeble, to enlarge the boundaries of human happiness; and by means like these to find a sufficiency for my own support.

'I know not that I ought to advise you to pursue a similar plan: though I can truly say I am unacquainted with any other, which is equally promising.

'How to answer or appease the imperious demands of your present ruling passion I cannot devise. Neither can I say that I am convinced it is blameable except in its excess. That you should desire to obtain so rare and inestimable a treasure as that of a woman who, not to insist upon her peculiar beauty, is possessed of the high faculties with which she whom you love is affirmed to be endowed, is an ambition which my heart knows not how to condemn as unworthy. There is something in it so congenial to all my own feelings that to see you united to her would give me inexpressible pleasure.

'You will perhaps be surprised to hear me own that, notwithstanding the obstacles are so numerous that I have no perception of the manner in which they are to be overcome, I yet rejoice with you that you have discovered such a woman; that she has assuredly a rooted affection for you; and that you have thus obtained one advantage over all your friends, a strong and unconquerable motive to outstrip them in your efforts.

'Shall I add that, desperate as your case seems to be, I participate in your sanguine hopes? I do not deem them entirely romantic, but share in that which the phlegmatic would call the frenzy of your mind; and half-persuade myself that you will finally be victorious.

'Then summon up your fortitude. Do not suffer the failure of ill-concerted plans either to lessen your ardour or give it a rash and dangerous direction. Be cool in decision, warm in pursuit, and unwearied in perseverance. Time is a never failing friend, to those who have the discernment to profit by the opportunities he offers. Let your eye be on the alert, and your hand active and firm, as circumstances shall occur, and I shall then say I scarcely know what it is that you may not hope to achieve!'

Wilmot stood with his head resting on his arm, leaning against the mantle-piece. When Turl began, his eye was cast down, a compassionate melancholy overspread his countenance, and a deep sigh broke from him unperceived by himself. As our mutual friend proceeded, his attitude altered, his head was raised, his eye brightened, his features glowed, his soul was wrapt in the visions which were raised by Turl, and, unconscious of his own existence or that he spoke, his interrupting ejaculations now and then involuntarily burst forth——'That is true!—Well argued!—Do you think so?—Indeed!—I am glad of that!—Don't despond, Trevor! Don't despond!—'Tis folly to despond!'

Just as he repeated the last sentence, ' 'Tis folly to despond,' so full a remembrance of his former trains of thought came over him, and there was so divine a mixture of hope and melancholy in his face, which seemed so to reproach himself and to encourage me, that, divided as my feelings were between the generous emanations of Turl and these torrents of affection from a man who had suffered so deeply, I seized the hand of each, pressed them both to my heart, instantly dropped them again, covered my face, fell against the wall, and sobbed with something like hysteric passion.

Of all the pleasures of which the soul is capable, those of friendship for man and love for woman are the most exquisite. They may be described as—'the comprehensive principle of benevolence, which binds the whole human race to aid and love each other, individualized; and put into its utmost state of activity.'[1] Selfishness may deride them; and there may be some so haunted by suspicion, or so hardened in vice as to doubt or deny their existence. But he that has felt them in their fullest force has the best as well as the grandest standard of human nature; and the purest foretaste of the joys that are in store, for the generations that are to come.

This is the spirit that is to harmonize the world; and give reality to those ideal gardens of paradise, and ages of gold, the possibility of which, as the records of fable shew, could scarcely escape even savage ignorance.

What clue shall I give the reader to my heart, that shall lead him into its recesses; and enable him to conceive its entire sensations? That Turl, from whom I imagined I had met so much discouragement, whose scrutinizing eye led him to examine with such severity, and whose firm understanding possessed such powers of right decision, that he should not only sympathize with me but partake in my best hopes, and countenance me in my soul's dearest pursuit, that Turl should feel and act thus, was a joy inconceivably great, and unexpected!

He now no longer appeared to me as one to whom, though I could not but revere him, I durst not confess myself; but as a generous, anxious, and tender friend. My former flashes of hope had usually been succeeded by a gloomy despair, that made me half suspect myself to be frantic: but, after this concession and encouragement from Turl, they seemed instantly to spring into consistency, probability, and system.

Turl highly approved my forbearance, and caution, respecting the letter I had written and was so anxious to convey to Olivia.

This farther coincidence of opinion not only induced me to persevere in my plan, but afforded me a degree of grateful satisfaction, and self-respect, that was exceedingly consolatory.

CHAPTER III

More traits of the character of Mr. Evelyn: A new project of a very flattering nature: Borough interest and a patriotic Baronet

IT may well be supposed that Turl was induced to enquire, and I to explain, the means by which I should have been enabled to pursue the study of the law: for he had heard of my misfortunes, and the dissipation of my finances.

This brought the behaviour and character of Mr. Evelyn in review: and the admiration of Turl, with the terms of affection and respect in which he spoke of that gentleman, was additional delight. He had never entertained any serious doubt, he said, but that such men existed: perhaps many of them: yet to discover a single one was an unexpected and, to say the truth, a very uncommon pleasure.

But Mr. Evelyn was to be made acquainted with my change of sentiment; and of my being once more destitute of any plan for my future guidance. It was necessary that he should not deem me a man of unsettled principles; frivolous in propensity, and fantastic in conduct. For, though perhaps my pride would have felt gratification at no longer considering myself a dependent on the favourable opinion or calculations which another might form concerning me, and my good or ill qualities, yet I could not endure to sink in his esteem.

I therefore applied myself, immediately, in the most assiduous manner, to collect and state such facts as I had gathered, relative to the practice of the law: and, that the argument might be placed in the clearest light possible, I begged of Turl to take that part of the subject which related to its principles upon himself.

Thus provided, I wrote to Mr. Evelyn; and my letter was fortunate enough to produce its desired effect.

Nor was he satisfied with mere approbation. His anxious and generous friendship would not suffer him to rest; and he immediately made a journey to town, to consult with me, since this project was rejected, what should be my new pursuit.

His behaviour verified all the assertions of his former discourse, concerning the hopes that he had conceived of my talents. He considered nothing within the scope of his fortune as too great a sacrifice, if it could but promote the end he desired. For this purpose he not only consulted with Wilmot, and Turl, but led me into such conversations as might best display the bent of my genius; and afford him hints, on which to act.

And now he was induced to form a design such as I little expected; and which required of me the acceptance of obligations so great as well might stagger me, and render it difficult for me to consent.

He had remarked that my enunciation was clear and articulate, my language flowing, my voice powerful, and my manner prepossessing. Such were the terms which he used, in describing these qualities in me. The youthful manliness of my figure, he said, added to the properties I have mentioned, was admirably adapted for parliamentary oratory. My elocution and deportment were commanding; and principles such as mine might awe corruption itself into respect, and aid to rouse a nation, and enlighten a world. Mr. Evelyn, like myself, was very much of an enthusiast.

He did not immediately communicate the project to me: which was indeed first suggested to him by accidental circumstances: but previously examined whether it was, as he supposed it to be, possible to be carried into effect.

Sir Barnard Bray had the nomination of two borough members: one of which he personated himself, and disposed of the other seat, as is the custom, to a candidate who should be of his party; and consequently vote according to his opinion.

He had long been the loud and fast friend of Opposition. No man was more determined in detecting error, more hot in his zeal, or more vociferous in accusation, than Sir Barnard: his dear and intimate friend, the right honourable Mr. Abstract, excepted; who was indeed pepper, or rather gunpowder itself.

Mr. Evelyn was the cousin of this patriotic baronet.

It happened just then to be the eve of a general election; and, as the last member of Sir Barnard had been so profligate, or so patriotic, as the worthy member himself repeatedly and solemnly declared he was, as to vote with the Minister, who had previously given him a place and promised to secure his return for a Treasury borough, Mr. Evelyn, knowing these circumstances, was persuaded that the Baronet would be happy to find a representative for *his* constituents, whose eloquence added to his own should avenge him on the Minister; if not tumble him from the throne he had usurped.

Mr. Evelyn and the Baronet were on intimate terms: for Sir Barnard took a particular pleasure in every man who perfectly agreed with him in opinion; and, though this definition would not accurately apply to Mr. Evelyn, yet, on the great leading points in politics they seldom differed.

As to morals, as a science, Sir Barnard on many occasions would affect to treat it with that common-place contempt which always accompanies the supposition of the original and unconquerable depravity of man; of the verity of which the Baronet had a rooted conviction. In this hypothesis he was but confirmed by his burgage-tenure voters,[1] by the conduct of the members he had himself returned, and by certain propensities which he felt in his own breast, and which he seriously believed to be instinctive in man.

Beside, if Mr. Evelyn differed at any time in opinion with a disputant, the suavity of his manners was so conciliatory that opposition, from him, was sometimes better received than agreement, and coincidence, from other poeple. This suavity, by the by, is a delightful art. Would it were better understood, and more practised!

CHAPTER IV

*Sage remarks on the seduction of young orators, the influence
of the crown, and the corruption of our glorious constitution:
Old and new nobility: Poor old England: Necessary
precautions: The man with an impenetrable face*

FULL of the project he had conceived, Mr. Evelyn visited the
Baronet, who happened to be in town, and proposed it to him in
the manner which he thought might most prepossess him in my
favour.

Sir Barnard listened attentively, and paused.

It happened that he had lately been meditating on the danger of
introducing young orators into parliament: for he had found, by
experience, that they are so marketable a commodity as to be
almost certain of being bought up. The trick he had himself been
played was bitterly remembered; and he had known and heard of
several instances, during his parliamentary career, of a similar kind.

Yet he could not but recollect that, when he and his former
spokesman had entered the house, arm in arm, there was a sort of
buzz, and a degree of respect paid to him, which had instantly
diminished as soon as this support was gone.

There is something of dignity in the use of crutches; and he that
cannot walk alone commands attention, from his imbecility.

'I do not know what to think of this plan,' said the Baronet.
'I find your flowery speakers are no more to be depended upon, in
the present day, than the oldest drudges in corruption!

'You know, cousin, how I hate corruption. It is undoing us all,
It will undo the nation! The influence of the crown is monstrous. The
aristocracy is degraded by annual batches of mundungus and
parchment lords;[1] and the constitution is tumbling about our ears.
The old English spirit is dead. The nation has lost all sense and
feeling. The people are so vile and selfish that they are bought and
sold like swine; to which, for my part, I think they have been very
properly compared. There is no such thing now as public virtue.
No, no! That happy time is gone by! Every man is for all he can get;
and as for the means, he cares nothing about them. There is
absolutely no such thing as patriotism existing; and, to own the
truth, damn me if I believe there is a man in the kingdom that cares

one farthing for those rights and liberties, about which so many people that you and I know pretend to bawl!'

'This is a severe supposition indeed. It implicates your dearest and most intimate friends. Only recollect, Sir Barnard, what would your feelings be, if the same thing should be asserted of you?'

'Of me, truly! No, no, cousin Evelyn; I think I have been pretty tolerably tried! The Minister knows very well he could move the Monument sooner than me. I love the people; and am half mad to see that they have no love for themselves. Why do not they meet? Why do not they petition? Why do not they besiege the throne with their clamors? They are no better than beasts of burthen! If they were any thing else, the whole kingdom would rise, as one man, and drive this arrogant upstart from the helm. I say, Mr. Evelyn, I love the people; I love my country; I love the constitution; and I hate the swarms of mushroom peers, and petty traders, that are daily pouring in upon us, to overturn it.'

Was it weakness of memory? Was it the blindness of egotism? Or was it inordinate stupidity, that Sir Barnard should forget, as he constantly did, that his father had been a common porter in a warehouse, had raised an immense fortune by trade, had purchased the boroughs which descended to his son, and had himself been bought with the title of Baronet by a former minister? Was it so very long ago, that Sir Barnard, with such a swell of conscious superiority, should begin to talk of the antiquity of his family? But, above all, how did he happen not to recollect that the disappointment which now preyed upon and cankered his heart was the refusal of a peerage?

I really can give no satisfactory answer to these questions. I can only state a fact: which daily occurs in a thousand other instances.

Mr. Evelyn brought the Baronet back to the point; and remarked to him that, at the present period, when the Minister was so powerful in numbers, to bring in a mere yes and no member with himself would be a certain mode of not serving the country, the constitution, and the people, whom he so dearly loved; that the safety which is derived from a man's insignificance is but a bad pledge; and that he thought himself very certain I was as dear, nay and as incorruptible, a lover of old England, or at least of the welfare of mankind, as Sir Barnard himself.

'Shew me such a man, cousin,' exclaimed the Baronet, 'and I will worship him! I will worship him, Mr. Evelyn! I will worship him!

But I am persuaded he is not to be found. I have learned, from too fatal experience, that I am certain of nobody but myself! Small as the number in Opposition is, if they were but all as sound-hearted as I am, and would set their shoulders to the wheel and lay themselves out for the good of their country as I do, I say it, Mr. Evelyn, and take my word for it I say true, we should overturn the Minister and his corrupt gang in six months! Nay, in half the time! However, as you are so strongly persuaded of the soundness of the gentleman's principles whom you recommend, let me see him, and talk to him; and then I will tell you more of my opinion.'

'There is one point, Sir Barnard, on which I suppose I need not insist; it is so obvious.'

'What is that, cousin?'

'You being as you state a man of principle, and incapable of being biassed to act against what you conceive to be the good of the nation, you must expect that every man, who resembles you in patriotism and fortitude, will act from himself, and will resist any attempt to control him.'

'Oh, as to that, we need say nothing about it. Those things are never mentioned, now-a-days: they are perfectly understood. But who is your young friend? Is he a man of property?'

'No.'

He will be the more manageable, thought Sir Barnard.

'Where will he get a qualification?'

'I will provide him with one.'

'You say he is a gentleman.'

'As I understand the term, he certainly is: for, in addition to those manners and accomplishments which are most pleasing to the world, he not only possesses a good education but a sense of justice which makes him regard every man as his brother; and which will neither suffer him to crouch to the haughty nor trample on the poor.'

'Why, that is very good. Very right. I myself will crouch to no man. And, as for modesty and humility, in the youth of the present day, why they are very rarely found: and so I shall be happy to meet with them.'

'Nay, but Mr. Trevor delivers his sentiments with rather an unguarded freedom, and with peculiar energy, or indeed he would be ill qualified to rise in the assembly of which I wish to see him a member, and undauntedly oppose the arrogant assertions that are there daily made.'

'Arrogant! G— confound me, Mr. Evelyn, if I am not sometimes struck dumb, with what I hear in that house! There is that Scotch-man[1] in particular, who will get up, after our allies have been defeated, our troops driven like sheep from swamp to swamp, where they die of the rot, and our ships carried by hundreds into the enemy's ports, and will roundly assert, notwithstanding these facts are as notorious as his own political profligacy, that our victories are splendid, our armies undiminished, and our trade protected and flourishing beyond all former example! He makes my hair stand on end to hear him! And when I look in his face, and see the broad familiar easy impudence with which he laughs at me and all of us, for our astonishment, why, as I tell you, damn me if I am not dumb-founded! I am struck all of a heap! I have not a word! I am choked with rage, and amazement! Compared to him your brothel-keeper is a modest person! Were but our fortresses as impenetrable as his forehead, curse me if they would ever be taken. He is bomb-proof. The returns that lie on the table can make no impression upon him; and you may see him sneer and laugh if they are pointed to in the course of an argument.

'In short, cousin Evelyn, the nation is ruined. I see that clear enough. Our constitution will soon be changed to a pure despotism. Barracks are building; soldiers line our streets: our commission of the peace is filled with the creatures of a corrupt administration; constables are only called out to keep up the farce; and we are at present under little better than a military government.'[2]

Though Mr. Evelyn would have been better satisfied, had Sir Barnard's sense of national grievances been equally strong but less acrimonious, yet he was pleased to find that these grievances were now more than ever become a kind of common-place bead roll of repetitions: of which their being so familiarly run over by the Baronet was sufficient proof: for a people that are continually talking of the evils that afflict them are not, as Sir Barnard and others have supposed, dead to these evils. The nation that remarks, discusses, and complains of its wrongs, will finally have them redressed.

CHAPTER V

Serious doubts on serious subjects: Personal qualms, and
considerations: An interview with Sir Barnard: Fears and
precautions, or a burnt child dreads the fire

WHAT farther passed in the conversation I have recited was of little moment: except that an appointment was made, on the following day, for me to be introduced to the Baronet.

Thus far successful, Mr. Evelyn returned; and, as he was a man of a firm and ingenuous mind, he thought it adviseable to hold a consultation with me and my friends, on the prosecution of his plan.

That personal considerations might in no degree influence the enquiry, he first proposed the question, without intimating to what it might lead, of—'how far it became a virtuous man to accept a seat, on those conditions under which a seat only can be obtained, among the representatives of the people ?'

Without wearying the reader with the arguments that were adduced, let it suffice to inform him that we all agreed it was a very doubtful case; that, in this as in numerous other instances, manners, customs, and laws, obliged us to conform to many things which were odiously vicious; and that to live in society and rigidly observe those rules of justice which would best promote the general happiness was, speaking absolutely, a thing impossible.

Whether the greatest political characters would best fulfil their duties by refusing to submit to the corrupt influence of elections, to test-oaths, and to the mischiefs of ministerial management within the walls, or whether they ought to comply with them, and exert their utmost faculties in pointing out these evils and endeavouring to have them redressed, was a point on which we all seemed to think the wisest men might suspend their judgment.

In one thing we appeared to be entirely agreed: which was that such pernicious practices were in all probability more frequently exposed, and brought into public discussion, through the medium of an assembly like this, than they would be did no such assembly exist.

Neither must I detail what afterward passed, before I was brought to accept the proposal of Mr. Evelyn. It would be tedious.

This proposal did not confine itself to the single act of giving me a seat in parliament; and of furnishing me with a qualification. It insisted that the qualification should be a real and not a fictitious deed.

To accept the actual possession of three hundred a-year as a bounty, for which I could make no return, was I own humiliating to my pride. It made the question continually recur—'Whether it did not give me the air of an impostor? A kind of swindler of sentiment? A pretender to superior virtue, for the purpose of gratifying vice?'

It seemed at a blow to rob me of all independence; and leave me a manacled slave to the opinions, not only of Mr. Evelyn, but, by a kind of consignment, of his relation the Baronet; and even to both their humours.

In fine, it was a most painful sacrifice; and required all the amenity and active friendship of Mr. Evelyn to bring to my mind, not only my duties, but, the power that I should have at any time of resigning my seat, returning the deeds, and sheltering myself in my primitive poverty.

To this I added a condition, without which my refusal would have been absolute. It was that I should give a deed of mortgage, bearing interest, to the full value of the lands assigned.

I shall forbear to dwell on sensations that were very active at the moment; which, on one hand, related to all that concerned Mr. Evelyn, my obligations, and something like dependence; and, on the other, to my sudden promised elevation toward the sphere in which my ambition was so eagerly desirous to move. Neither will I insist on that which caused my heart to beat yet more high, the approach that I thus made to the lovely object of all my wishes.

Leaving this endless train of meditation, I proceed to relate events as they occurred.

I attended Mr. Evelyn, according to appointment; and paid my respects to his cousin, Sir Barnard. Having engaged myself thus far, I own I was sufficiently piqued to desire to make a favourable impression: in which I was almost as successful as I myself had hoped.

At the first sight of me the Baronet was prepossessed; and when we entered into conversation and he gave me an opportunity of uttering my sentiments concerning men and measures, I painted so forcibly that he was almost in raptures.

The only circumstance in which I failed was my frequent interruption, and impatience, when he in turn began to declaim. I had the vice of orators: I heard no man's arguments, or language, that pleased me so well as my own. I could not listen without an irritating anxiety, that was for ever prompting me to supply a word, suggest a thought, or detect a blunder. And, to a man who loves to make a speech, it is intolerably mortifying to hear himself corrected, and cut short, in the middle of a sentence.

However I was sufficiently guarded not to give any offence that was strong enough to be remembered; and Sir Barnard was so thoroughly engrossed, by the idea of the conspicuous figure which he and his new member should make in the house, that he was absolutely impatient to secure me: being fully persuaded that he had discovered a treasure; of which now, at a general election, he was in considerable danger of being robbed.

The only precaution he took was to draw from me repeated asseverations that I would not desert the cause of the people: by which, as I afterward found, he understood his own private opinions; and not that which he had literally expressed. On this head he seemed never satisfied; and the terms in which he spoke, both of the member who had deserted him and of all political tergiversation whatever, were the bitterest that his memory could supply.

CHAPTER VI

A dinner party, and fortune in good humour: The opera
house, and small talk: Sagacious female discoveries: Olivia,
and the art of fascinating: An old acquaintance suddenly seen
and dreaded, though despised: Timely recollection: The opera
great room, and more discoveries

THESE points settled, the Baronet proposed to introduce me to his friends and connections, particularly of the political kind. For this purpose he began with inviting me and Mr. Evelyn to dine with him on the Friday following, when he was to have a mixed party of ladies and gentlemen, but chiefly of such as agreed with him on public affairs.

When the day came, I was presented to the company by the Baronet with encomiums, and seated on the left of Lady Bray.

A Scotch lord was on her right: it being her ladyship's custom to divide the ladies and gentlemen.

A young fellow properly introduced, if he be new in the circles of fashion and possessed of a tolerable figure, is in no danger of being ill received. I had not indeed learned to be an adept at small talk: a qualification which, contemptible as it is, will supply the want of every superior requisite, whether of mind or person: but I had an aptitude to oblige, be attentive, and speak the moment I found I had any thing to say.

I had laid no plan on this occasion: not having then read, or not remembering, I know not which, Lord Chesterfield's sage reflections,[1] on the necessity of a statesman's being well with the ladies. It happened however that, on this occasion, I was received with distinguished marks of approbation by the dear angels: from several of whom I received visiting-invitations.

Music and the opera were among the topics on which they conversed. I was found to be an amateur; and Lady Bray was one of the dilettanti, had concerts at her own house, and a box at the opera: to both of which she said I should at all times have free admission.

This was too pleasing an offer to be refused; and I willingly agreed to attend her ladyship the following evening, and hear the charming music of *I Zingari in Fiera* by Paisiello.[2]

The opera season began rather early that year, many families were not yet come to town, we had little delay from the string of coaches, and, had her ladyship not provided against the misfortune by taking care to go more late than usual, we should have been so unfashionable as to have heard the first act. As it was, we arrived before it was over.

The thing on which her ladyship bestowed her immediate attention was to examine, by the aid of her opera-glass, which of the subscribers were in their boxes; and how many of her particular friends were among them. Politeness induced me to accompany her in this excursion of the eye: for not to have listened to the names, titles, and ages, of her friends, with the births, deaths, marriages, creations, and presentations at court of them and their families, of which materials small talk is chiefly if not wholly composed, would have been the very highest defect in good breeding.

Why yes. Listen I did, as long as I was able: till my eyes, tongue, and faculties were all riveted to one spot!

Her ladyship's box was near the centre. She had carried my eye from box to box completely along one side, and had proceeded to about three of the opposite, when she directed her glass to one, with the owners of which she had no acquaintance: but she knew the names of all; for she had them engraved on her fan.

That name was Mowbray! And the persons in it were Hector, his aunt, and Olivia!

I was silent, gazing, entranced! Her ladyship had talked I know not how long; and I had neither answered nor heard one word.

'Bless me,' said she, 'Mr. Trevor! why you are *absolutely* in a revery all of a sudden! That Miss Mowbray I find is a very dangerous young lady: for I am told that all the men are *positively* mad after her; and here are you *absolutely* struck speechless! What! Not a word yet?'

'I beg ten thousand pardons.'

'Why this seems like love at first sight! You are not acquainted, I suppose, with the Mowbrays.'

'Yes, my lady: from my infancy.'

'Oh, oh! Why, then to be sure you are intimate with this beauty; who *absolutely* eclipses us all. I assure you she is *positively* the belle of the day. I hear she has the very first offers. But you are not silly enough to act the dying swain? What, no answer? Well, well: I see how it is! But, as we never read in any of the morning papers of gentle youths who break their hearts for love, in the present ungallant age, you are in no great danger. Though I think I never saw any creature look more like what I should suppose one of your true lovers to be than you did just now: for, beside your speechless attitude, which was *absolutely* picturesque and significant, you were *positively* pale and red, and red and pale, almost as fast as the ticking of my watch. And even yet you are *absolutely* provoking. I cannot get a word from you!'

'Your ladyship's raillery quite overpowers me.'

'I declare I am *positively* surprised at what I have seen. Had a stranger been all of a sudden struck, the wonder would not have been *absolutely* so great: but it is *positively* unaccountable in you who are a familiar acquaintance of the family.'

'I cannot boast of that honor.'

'No, indeed! Why, do not you visit the Mowbrays?'

'I do not.'

'What, you are a dangerous man; and are forbidden the house? Well, I declare, I shall *absolutely* know your whole history in five minutes without your having *positively* told me a word.'

'Your ladyship has a lively imagination.'

'I have heard that the aunt is a very cautious *chaperon*. But, I tell you what: I will be your friend. The Mowbrays are lately become intimate with two families where I visit. And I will *absolutely* take you with me, on one of their public nights. I will *positively*.'

This proposition was so grateful, and my thanks were so much more prompt than my recollection, that her ladyship was quite confirmed in her surmises; and not a little pleased with her own talent at discovery.

Her accusation however was very true. All she could *positively* say could not *absolutely* draw my attention from the box of Olivia, whose turns and motions I was anxiously watching; hoping that some lucky accident would guide her eye toward me.

Nay I partly hoped and partly feared the same of the aunt: my emotions being now influenced by the respectable station which I at present seemed to occupy; and now by the remembrance that even this might turn to my disadvantage, in the jealous apprehensions of the old lady.

Busied as my thoughts were and absorbed in anxious attention, this anxiety was soon overcome by a much more powerful feeling.

A gentleman entered Olivia's box! My eyes were instantly turned on him. Recollection was roused. My heart beat. It surely was he! I could not be mistaken! My opera-glass was applied, and my fears confirmed. It was, indeed, the Earl of Idford.

Here then, in a moment, the enigma was solved. The peer who had aspired to the hand of Olivia, and who tempted her with all his opulence and all his dignity, could be no other than Lord Idford. He had long been intimate with Hector, and now comes without ceremony and joins the family. See how the aunt smiles on him! Nay, mark! Olivia is attentive to him! Her lips move! Her eyes are directed to his! She is conversing with him, and at her ease, while I am racked by all the terrors that jealousy can raise! What, can she not cast one look this way? Is she fascinated by a reptile? Is there no instinctive sympathy, that should make her tremble to betray the dearest interests of love in the very presence of the lover! Does she act complacency, and sit calm and unruffled! Has she no foreboding that I will dart upon that insect; that thing; which, being less than man, presumes because it is called Lord! Thinks she that I will not crush, tear, tread, him to dust? He, the defrauder of my fair fame, who plundered me of the first fruits of genius by infamous falsehood, who joined in plotting my destruction by arts which the basest cowards blush at! Is he the fiend that comes to snatch me from bliss; and plunge me into pangs and horrors unutterable?

From these ravings of the mind I was a little recovered, by the very serious alarm which the wild changes of my countenance produced in Lady Bray. I apologised, pleaded indisposition, but presently was lost again in revery. Fortunately, a gentleman of her ladyship's acquaintance came into the box, and left me to continue my embittered meditations.

Olivia was now attentive to the music; and the lord had only her aunt and Hector, apparently, to bestow his conversation upon.

This was some relief; and so far allayed the fever of my mind as to call me back to self examination, and to question my own conduct.

For the earl I could not but have the most rooted contempt. I could not compare myself with him, and entertain a doubt, concerning who ought to be preferred.

But what reason had I to accuse Olivia? What did these angry emotions of my soul forebode? Perhaps that my habitual irritability, were she mine, would make her miserable!

What was the end of existence? Happiness. Had I not a right then to be happy? Yes. But so had she. So had her aunt. Nay so had that rival, odious and despicable as he was, whose appearance had raised this tempest in my soul.

But was constraint, was force, justifiable in this aunt; or in this insignificant, this selfish lord?

Force it is said is the law of nature; and it is that law which impels the ravenous tiger to spring upon the lamb, and suck its blood, to appease his craving appetite. But, if so, if self-gratification were a defensible motive, the detestable Norman robber, the monster who inhabited a cave and seized on every stray virgin, to deflower, murder her and prey on her remains, was justifiable.

In the agitated mind, dreams like these are endless. While they were passing, I stared with fixed attention toward Olivia; and, had she not been almost motionless, my passive trances could not have continued.

The first dance was over, the second act had begun, more visitors came to pay their respects to Lady Bray, and I endeavoured to recollect myself and shake off a behaviour that might well be construed inattention, if not ill manners; and might injure me even in that point on which I was then so deeply intent. I uttered two or three sentences; and her ladyship complimented me on being once more awake.

The persevering attention of Olivia to the scene, for it was impossible to forbear glancing at her every moment, contributed to calm my fears.

It did more: it was a most beneficial lesson to me. It called me again to the consideration of that impetuosity of temper which was so dangerous in me. Into what acts of frenzy and desperation might not these fevers of the soul hurry me? What in the present instance could I urge to justify such excess? Had I not heard the reproaches of her aunt for her having refused the hand of this Lord: if this Lord it should happen to be? When he entered the box, what had she done, that should excite such frantic ecstacies in me? What, except return those civilities without which it is impossible for man or woman to be amiable? Did she now coquet, prattle, and display her power; tempted as she was by such a public scene of triumph? Was not her demeanour as chastely cautious as my own exigent heart could desire?

Every question that the facts before me suggested was an aggravating reproof of my headlong passions; and, luckily for me, my thoughts took that train which was most corrective and healthful. They led me too to dwell, with a melting and mild rapture, on the endearing virtues of Olivia: dignified, yet not austere; firm, yet not repulsive; circumspect, yet capable of all those flowing affections without which circumspection is but meanness.

Nor were these visionary attributes: such as the disordered imagination of a lover falsely bestows. They were as real as those personal beauties by which they were embellished.

To aspire to the possession of a woman so gifted, and to be the lunatic which my own reproaches at this moment pictured me, was to demand that which I did not deserve. To be worthy of her, it was fit I should resemble her.

I endeavoured to obey these admonitions. I schooled myself, concerning my remissness to Lady Bray. I recovered my temper, became attentive, talked rather pleasantly, and re-established myself in her good graces: in which I could perceive I had somewhat declined, by the folly of my behaviour. To remind the reader on every occasion of the progress of intellect, and the benefits derived from experience, would be to weary his patience, insult his understanding, and counteract my own intentions. It would suppose in him a total absence of observation, and reasoning. Yet to be entirely silent might lead the young, and the inattentive, to imagine I had in the beginning proposed a mode of instruction which, as I proceeded, I had either forgotten, abandoned, or had not the power to execute. If such will attend to the alteration in my conduct, they will perceive that I, like every other human being, could not but reflect more or less on the motives that actuated me; and profit by the lessons I received: though rooted habits and violent passions were the most difficult to cure.

After the curtain dropped, I accompanied Lady Bray into the great room; and perceived among the throng, at some little distance, Olivia, and her aunt, attended by the peer.

I had foreseen the possibility of this; and had reasoned that there might be more danger in an abrupt rencontre, of this kind, than in meeting Olivia and her terrible aunt at the house of Lady Bray's friend, as her ladyship had promised me; where I should receive her countenance, and that of the family to which I should be introduced. I therefore endeavoured to direct her ladyship's attention from the place where the Mowbray party was, and succeeded in my endeavours.

Soon afterward, I saw Hector, with a knot of fashionable youths; among whom I was rather surprised to discover my at that time unknown father-in-law, Belmont.

I had no inclination to be noticed by this groupe; and, as Lady Bray's carriage was presently afterward *stopping the way*, I had the good fortune to escape unperceived, or at least unaccosted, by both parties.

CHAPTER VII

A debt discharged: A tavern dinner and a dissertation: The man of the world ridiculing the man of virtue: or, is honesty the best policy? Fools pay for being flattered: Security essential to happiness: A triumphant retort, and difficult to be answered: Vice inevitable, under a vitiated system: A dangerous attack: or an exhibition of one of the principal arts of a gambler: A few cant phrases

To the friendship of Mr. Evelyn I had so far subjected myself and the spirit of independence which I was very properly ambitious to cherish as, for the present, to accept the aid he was so desirous to bestow. I was something like compelled to be his debtor, but was unwilling to be the debtor of any other man on earth; and, as he had enabled me to appear in the style I have described, and furnished me with money, I was determined to seek out Belmont, and discharge the debt which his bounty had conferred; after he had previously plundered me, at Bath. He had sunk in my esteem: I now considered him as a professed gambler: but I remembered this action as that which it really was; an effort of benevolence, to aid a human being in distress.

Thus actuated, I went the next day to the billiard-table which he had been accustomed to frequent; where I once more found him at play. He met me not only unabashed, but with something like cordiality. He had so accustomed himself to his own hypothesis, that 'self-gratification is the law of nature,' and had so confused a sense of what true self-gratification is, with such an active faculty of perverting facts and exhibiting pictures of general turpitude, that he had very little sense of the vice of his own conduct; and was therefore very little subject to self-reproof. He behaved to me with the utmost ease and good humour; and, when his match was over, proposed that we should dine together at the Thatched-house.

For a moment, I questioned the propriety of assenting: but, seeing him now as before familiar with the officers of the guards, and people of whose company no one was ashamed, and recollecting where and how I had seen him the evening before, I did not long hesitate. Beside which, I was prompted, not only by the pleasure which his conversation gave, but by an increase of curiosity to be better acquainted with who and what he really was.

As soon as we were alone, I discharged my conscience by repaying him the twenty pounds. This gave occasion to the following dialogue.

'I perceive, Trevor, you are still the same. You pique yourself on paying your borrowings. Had it been a debt of honour indeed, I should not have been surprised: for those are debts that must be discharged. Otherwise, it would introduce a very inconvenient practice indeed.'

'I believe, as you say, it would be inconvenient beyond description to you—What do you call yourselves?—Oh! I recollect: "sporting gentlemen" is the phrase. It would be inconvenient I say, to you sporting gentlemen.'

'Whom, when we sporting gentlemen are absent, you call blacklegs, rooks, Grecians, and other pleasant epithets. Some such word, I could perceive, was quivering on your tongue. You remember the plucking you had at Bath; and, though you are too much ashamed of having been duped to mention it, yet it remains on your mind with a feeling of resentment. That is natural: but it is foolish.'

'Is it foolish to have a sense of right and wrong?'

'Where is that sense to be found? Who has it? I have continually a sense, if so you please to call it, that there is something which I want; and by that I am impelled to act.'

'True. But Locke, I think, tells us that crime consists in not taking sufficient time to consider, before we act.'[1]

'And, begging his pardon, wise as in a certain sense I allow you this Locke was, in the instance you have cited, he was an ass. If I do not mistake, he has before proved to me that I cannot act without a motive; and then he bids me stop when I am in such a hurry that no motive occurs to my memory.'

'According to this, an actual murderer is not a more guilty man than he who only dreams that he commits murder?'

'Make what you will of the inference, but it is accurate. They are both dead asleep, to any ideas except those that hurry them forward.'

'That is, in plain English, there is no such thing as vice.'

'Might you not as well have said as virtue?'

'Speaking absolutely, I do not pretend to deny what you assert. But you will not tell me that the man who robs me, and leaves me bound to a tree in danger of starving, has not done me an injury?'

'Will you be kind enough to shew me who it is, among those who have any thing to lose, that does not rob? Men who enjoy the pleasures of life rob those who are deprived of them of their due; and, according to my apprehension, the latter have a right to make reprisals.'

'Upon my soul, Belmont, you have a most inveterate habit of confounding every thing that should guide and regulate mankind. You shift the question, confound terms, and are the most desperate gladiator of vice I ever encountered. Your dangerous genius is a mine; where the ore is rich indeed, but the poisonous vapour that envelopes it deadly.'

'Each to his system. We have both the voyage of life to make. You place that very sober and discreet person called Honesty at the helm; by the single direction of whom you expect to attain happiness: which is just as rational as to hope to circumnavigate the globe with one wind. I take a different course: it is my maxim to shift my sails, and steer as pleasure and interest bid.'

'Acting as you do, I cannot wonder that you should make a jest of honesty.'

'Upon my honour I treated Sir Honesty with every possible decorum, till I found that the insidious rascal was making a jest of me. Not that I am quite certain I am not more truly the friend of this very respectable person than those who pretend they are always in his company; for I neither cant with Madam Morality nor pray with Dame Methodism: though I cannot but think I am almost as religious, as moral, ay and as charitable too, as your devotees and sabbath-keepers; who go to church to pray and be saved, and leave their servants to stay at home, roast the meat and be damned.'

'I must again repeat, you have the most active fertility at embroiling all order and system I have any where met with.'

'Ha, ha, ha! Order and system are very pretty words. But you make a small mistake. It is not I that embroil. I find confusion already established; and, since I cannot correct it, give me a reason why I ought not to profit by the chaotic hubbub?'

'But I say you can correct it. You are one of the men who might have been best fitted for the task.'

'I know not what I might have been: but I feel that I am not. The first right of man, ay and, to talk in your own idiom, the first moral duty too, is to be happy; and he is an idiot that, having a banquet spread before him, forbears to taste because he himself is not the purveyor. What matters it to me how it came there? Why am I to be excluded? Have I not as exquisite a relish as he that provided for the bill of fare?

'Let dull fools puzzle their brain concerning moral fitness, which they have not elevation enough of mind to understand; give me enjoyment.

'Let me eat the pine apple while they are discussing the moral fitness of feasting on such luxuries.'

'This doctrine would subject the world to your appetites and pleasures.'

'And is not that a noble doctrine? It is the wish and passion of the world to be gulled; and gulled let it be. Let it have its enjoyments; give me mine.

'One man is my banker, and is assiduously careful to keep cash at my command; which he transfers to me in the most gentleman-like and honourable manner imaginable: namely, by a box and dice.

'Another is my steward; and he lays out my grounds, stocks my park with deer, builds me palaces, erects me hot-houses, and torments heaven and earth to furnish my table with delicacies; for all of which I pay him in the current coin of flattery. It is true I permit him to call these things his own: but the real enjoyment of them is notoriously mine. He, poor egotist, talks bombast and nonsense by wholesale. I applaud and smile at his folly; while he imagines it is at his wit. The poor man is amused with fine speeches, unsubstantial flatteries, cringes, bows, and hypocritical tokens of servility; which are so many jests upon him.

'Thus is he mocked with the shadow, while I banquet upon the substance. I bask in arbours and groves, without once having given myself a thought concerning planting or pruning. I feast on the fish, without so much as the trouble of catching them; and still less of constructing the pond. By the provision he makes, that is, by avarice and extortion, he nurtures a brood of sycophants and slaves. Wife, children, friends, servants, all have the same character, only differently shaded: except that, if any of them can become his tyrants and tormentors, they all are ready for the task. I have studied the noble arts both of tickling and tormenting: by which I have subjected this very self-important race to my will and pleasure.'

'For a man whose acuteness has carried him so very far, I am amazed that it did not impel him to advance one step farther. Happiness is what I and all men desire, as certainly as you do: but that happiness is of a strange kind, and held by a frail and feeble tenure, that is agitated by innumerable fears: that, if the means on which it depends be detected, is wholly destroyed; and that, when lost, finds infamy and misery its certain substitutes.

'Mark what I say; and mark it deeply. There can be no happiness without security; and there can be no security without sincerity. Therefore, hypocrites, of every class, are acting contrary to their own intentions. They are providing misery for themselves, as well as for others: instead of the substantial pleasures of which they are in search.'

'Indeed? The Lord have mercy then upon all establishments: legal, political, and ecclesiastic!'

'Let me farther observe to you that the system of general enjoyment, which you propose, is something, if I may so call it, more than rational: it is dignified; it is sublime. I feel with you that he is a poor circumscribed egotist, who can enjoy nothing but that which he calls his own. Let me taste every blessing which the hand of nature presents: let me banquet with you on her bounties: but let me not embitter the delicious repast by fraud, that enslaves me to an eternal watchfulness; depredation, that puts even my life in jeopardy; and a system founded in lies, and everlastingly haunted by the spectres of self-contempt.'

Our dialogue was interrupted, by the entrance of the waiters.

When we had dined, Belmont began to enquire concerning my prospects and affairs.

'I expect,' said he, 'you will be less communicative and open hearted, now, than you formerly were. You have discovered, what I never attempted to conceal, that my present dependence is on the exercise of talents which your gravity despises: especially since they have laid you under contribution. This misfortune however, had you possessed them, despicable as they are, you would have escaped.'

'Yes: just as the man, who hanged himself last night, escaped a head-ach this morning. I will own to you I cannot take the pleasure in your company, or think of you with that friendship, which I formerly felt: for, though I find your conversation no less animating, like strong liquors, it leaves an unwholesome heat behind.

'However, I have no objection to inform you that fortune has given me a momentary respite from persecution. How soon she may think proper to stretch me on the rack again is more than I can foresee: though I greatly suspect her of cruelty and caprice. She seems at present to be in one of her best humours; and has given me a kind of promise to make me one of the sage legislators of this happy land.'

'What do you mean?'

'That I shall be a member of the new parliament.'

Belmont burst into a violent fit of laughter. At first, I was at a loss to conjecture why; and especially why it should be so long, and so unaffected: but I soon learned it was a burst of triumph, which he could not restrain.

'I congratulate you, Mr. Trevor,' said he, with a momentary gravity, 'on your noble and moral pursuits!—The lecture you have been reading, as well as those I have formerly heard you read, now come upon me with invincible force!—There is no resisting precept thus exemplified by practice!—How loud, how lofty, how sovereign, is the contempt in which you hold hypocrisy!—How severe will the laws be that you will enact, against petty depredators!—I foresee you will hang, not only those that handle a card, or a dice-box, but, those that make them.—Then what honours, what rewards, what triumphs, will you decree to your own wholesale marauders! your great captains; chosen, empowered and paid by yourself and sages no less moral and disinterested!—With what gusto will you send him to swing who commits a single robbery: and with what sublime oratory will you exalt the prowess of the man who has plundered, starved, and exterminated nations—"A Daniel come to judgment! Oh wise young judge, how do I honor thee!"[1]

I remained speechless, a few moments; and entirely disconcerted. I was irritated; though I knew not precisely at what. I attempted to answer; but was so confused that I talked absolute nonsense.

After some time, however, I recollected that my purpose in going into parliament was to counteract all these abuses. I then recovered my faculties, and urged this plea very emphatically.

Still the moral dignity, and virtue, of the honourable house I was about to enter, dwelt with such force on the imagination of Belmont that I could get no reply from him: except sarcasms, such as those I have repeated, with the same intervening fits of laughter as the images suggested themselves to his mind.

And here, lest the reader himself should be misled like Belmont, I must remark that no mistake is more common, and I believe none more pernicious, than that of imagining that, because man has not attained absolute and perfect virtue, the very existence of virtue is doubtful.

Hence it happens that he, who in any manner participates in the vices of a nation, or a body of men, is reproached as if loaded with the whole guilt.

Hence likewise, because men without exception are more or less tainted with error, all pretensions to superior moral principles are laughed at, as false and ridiculous.

This is the doctrine at least which the people who most offend these principles are the most zealous in propagating. Belmont had no refuge against self-reproach, but in cherishing such trains of thought.

That the vices which are the most despised in society instead of being the most despicable are virtues, if compared to actions that find honor and reward, is a truth too glaring to be denied. That the cant with which these master crimes are glossed over, and painted as just, expedient, ay and heroic actions, that this diabolical cant should be and is adopted by men even of the highest powers, is a fact that astonishes and confounds. It impels us continually to ask —Are they cowards? Are they hypocrites? Or is the world inhabited by none but lunatics? And that men even of such uncommon genius as Belmont should be entangled, and bewildered, by the destructive incongruity of those who assume to themselves the highest wisdom, because they possess the highest stations in society, is a proof how incumbent it is on such as are convinced of these melancholy truths to declare them openly, undauntedly, and with a perseverance that no threats or terrors can shake.

When we had taken as much wine as Belmont could prevail on me to drink, and he was very urgent, he asked if I played Piquet?[1]

I answered in the affirmative.

'You no doubt then play it well.'

'I do not think it a game of much difficulty.'

'It is my opinion I am your master at it.'

'That may be.'

'Though you do not think it is. Will you try?'

'What, with a man who avows he does not scruple to take every advantage?'

'Have you not eyes? Are you, a metaphysician, a wit, and a senator, so easily deceived?'

'A man may lose his temper; and with it his caution.'

'So you think yourself able to instruct the world, but not to keep your mind calm and circumspect for half an hour?'

'Had I a sufficient motive, I should suppose I have strength enough for such an exertion.'

'Then try. The exercise will be wholesome. Shew your skill and acuteness. Here is your twenty-pound bill: win and take it; or own that you have no confidence in yourself.'

'I have that confidence which assures me I shall, one day or other, convince you that I understand the road to happiness better than yourself.'

'Yet you are cursedly afraid of me. You scarcely can sit still. You blame your own rashness, in venturing to spend the afternoon with me: and now you would as soon handle burning coals as a pack of cards in my company.'

'And what is it you find so omnipotent in yourself, that it should induce you to all this vapouring?'

'I tell you again, you dare not oppose your penetration to mine. You pretend to despise me, yet own I am your master. A child is not in more fear of the rod than you are of me.'

He saw he had sufficiently piqued me, and rang the bell for cards. They were brought: he shuffled, cut them, and continued to banter me.

'What card do you chuse?—The knave of hearts?—There it is!' [He shewed it, with a flirt of the cards, at the bottom of the pack.] His brother of diamonds?—Look! You have it!—Of spades? —Presto! It is here! You have three knaves on your side, you see. I will keep the fourth, and drive you out of the field—Come, for twenty?'

'I see your aim, and am devilishly tempted to shew you that you are not half so cunning as you think yourself.'

'I know you are: but you dare not. You cannot shake off your fears. The wit, the metaphysician, the young senator suspects he is only a half-fledged bird.'

'Cut for deal, sir.'

'Why, will you venture?—The nine.'

The sudden recollection of Mr. Evelyn, the money I had received from him, the generous confidence he had reposed in me, and the guilt of daring to abuse that confidence, fortunately seized me with a kind of horror. I snatched up the cards, dashed them in the fire, and in a moment recovering myself said—'You shall find, sir, that, whether I can or cannot master you, I can master myself.'

'Come, you do not go out of this room without the *chance* of losing twenty guineas for twenty.'

'Done!' answered I, impetuously: which he in an instant echoed with Done! Done! and, again bursting into laughter, held out his hand and bade me pay my losings.

I immediately discovered, without his explanation, that he had entrapped me, by the equivocal sense of the word *chance;* and I drew out my purse to pay him, with a strong feeling of indignation that I should be so caught.

However, as it was not his intention to profit by so bald and bare-faced a quirk, he only laughed; and exclaimed—'How much the young gentleman is his own master! But I will not pick your pocket. If at any time I should want twenty pounds, I shall have a fair claim to ask it as a loan.'

'Would you but really act like a man of honour, there would be no need of such an artifice.'

'Perhaps not, for the first time. But if my poor honor were starving, and could not repay its borrowings, I am afraid my honor would irrevocably be lost. I therefore prefer, since in either case lose it I must, to lose it and eat. But the birds are now beginning to flock together; and I must begone, to the pigeon-house: the rookery.'

'I do not understand the terms.'

'The plucking office: the crab and nick nest: the pip and bone quarry: the rafflearium: the trumpery: the blaspheming box: the elbow shaking shop: the wholesale ague and fever warehouse.'[1]

'In plain English, to an assembly of gamblers.'

'Where I shall meet with much the same degree of honesty, virtue, wisdom, and all that, as is to be found in certain other assemblies.'

CHAPTER VIII

Bad company painful, as well as dangerous: A short note, exciting much expectation: A question that shocks and surprises: Clarke and Olivia, or the overflowing of a full and friendly heart: Various mistakes rectified: The reading of the letter and the emotions it produces: Resolutions worthy of virtuous love

I LEFT the tavern in no very pleasant temper of mind: impatient that I should be unable to convince, and reform, a man of such extraordinary acuteness as Belmont: vexed that he, on the contrary, should persuade himself that he was my master; and should actually irritate me to a dangerous excess of vanity: and disgusted that vice and virtue should be so confused, in the minds of men, as to render their boundaries almost undiscoverable.

Such I mean was the impression that Belmont had left upon my mind, by repeating the stale but dangerous maxim that—men are vicious by nature; and, therefore, that to profit by their vices is no more than just.

When I arrived at my lodgings, which were now in Albemarle-street, for I had changed them, I found the following note from Miss Wilmot.

'Come to me immediately. I have something to tell you which you little expect.'

Belmont and my chagrin were forgotten in an instant; and away I hurried, brim full of agitation, conjecture, and impatience.

I found Miss Wilmot alone; and her first words were—'Oh, Mr. Trevor! you are a happy man!'

I stood panting, or rather gasping, with hope; and made no reply. She thus continued.

'Miss Mowbray has been here.'

'Good heavens!'

'She has acted like herself. I know not how I shall tell you the story, so as to do her justice.'

'For the love of God, proceed!'

'As nearly as I can recollect her words, she began in this manner.

' "I cannot tell, my dear friend," addressing herself to me, "what you will think of my conduct. At one moment I suspect it to be wrong; and at the next blame myself for not having taken my present step sooner. I have surely been grossly misled. This indeed I have long suspected; and it cannot but be my duty to enquire. Have you lately seen Mr. Trevor?"

' "I never fail to see him every day. I have a letter from him, for you; which he has disdained to take any clandestine means of conveying to you. Here it is."

' "Before I date think about his letter, answer me one question. Is he a murderer?"

' "A murderer! In the name of God! what can induce you to make such an enquiry?"

' "I have been assured that he has caused the death of two men: one of whom he killed himself."

' "Where? When? How?"

' "At Bath. By delivering one over to the fury of the mob; and by afterward provoking, insulting, and fighting with the other."

' "Heavens and earth! It is false! wickedly false!'

' "Nay but do you know his story?"

' "Perfectly. I have heard it, not only from himself, but, from the man whom I suppose you have been told he has murdered."

' "What man?"

' "Nay you shall hear and see. You shall have the whole history from the person's own mouth."

' "Is he alive? Is he in London?"

' "I will send for him. He will be here in a few minutes. You will then hear what this man has to say. He almost adores Mr. Trevor."

'I immediately dispatched Mary for Mr. Clarke, who works not far off, as I suppose you know, and who came running the moment he heard that the lady you are in love with enquired for him.

'Mary informs me that his heart leaped to his eyes (it was her own phrase) when he was told she wanted to question him concerning you; that he sprang up, clapped his hands, and exclaimed— "I am glad of it! I am glad of it! The time is come! All shall be known! He shall be righted! I will take care of that! He shall be righted!"

'He entered the room breathless; and, the moment he saw Miss Mowbray, he could not forbear to gaze at her: though bashfulness made him continually turn his eyes away.

'She addressed him, with that mildness of manner which is so winning in her, and said—"I have taken the liberty, sir, to send for you; to ask a few questions."

'He replied, with a burst of zeal—"I am glad of it, madam! I am glad of it, from my heart and soul! I wish you knew all I could tell you about Mr. Trevor: but it is quite *un*possible that I should remember it one half. Only this I will say, and dare the best man in England to deny it, there is not such another brave and kind-hearted gentleman walks the earth. I have had proof enough of it. He knows, for all he is a gentleman, ay and a true gentleman too, for he has parts, and learning, and a christian soul, which does not teach him to scorn and make a scoff of the poor: he knows that a man is a man; even though he should only happen to be a poor carpenter, like myself. God in heaven bless him! say I."

'The enthusiasm of your generous humble friend overpowered Miss Mowbray; she burst into tears, and hid her face. Her passion was catching, and I followed her example. Clarke continued.

' "On that night that he had the good hap to save your life, and the life of that old cankered lady, which as I find from all that passed she must be, though he talks of her too kindly by half, why the stopping of the frightened horses, just do you see in the jaws of destruction, and propping the coach was all his doing. He knew better what he was about than the coachman himself. And then, if you had seen him, as I did, after all was over! I thought I had loved my Sally dearly. And so I do! But what am I? I thought too I durst have stood up to the boldest man that ever stood on shoe leather! And perhaps I durst: but I find I am nothing in any case to *he*. For which he never despises me: but insists upon it that I am as good a man as he, in any way. And as for you, madam, he would jump into burning lakes rather than a hair of your head should be singed. I know it: for I have seen it."

'"I know it too," said Miss Mowbray; sobbing. Then, with an effort to quell her passion, she asked in a firmer tone: "Pray, sir, tell me: did not you work at Bath?"

'"Yes, madam: the greatest part of my life."

'"You appear to know of a battle, that Mr. Trevor fought?"

'"Yes, yes, madam. I know it pretty well. I shall remember it as long as I live, for more reasons than one."

'"Was there a man killed?"

'"No, madam: God be praised! I should have died in my sins, unprepared and wicked as I was: being possessed with passion. He, God bless him! for all he is a gentleman, begged my pardon like a man; and held out his hand, and prayed over and over that I would forget and forgive. But, as I tell you, I was possessed. I could be nothing else: because, in the way of hard fighting, I despised a gentleman. But he gave me to know better, as obstinate as I was: for, even after he had beaten me once, why, he begged and prayed, as he had done at first, to make it all up. But, as I said before, the Evil One had taken hold of me; and I refused to give in, till I was carried as dead as a stock off of the place."

'"Then it was you that was reported to have been killed?"

'"Why, yes, madam: because it could be nobody else."

'"Nay, but was not there a poor man ducked to death?"

'"No: God be thanked, once again! It was not quite so bad as that. Though the hot-headed fools and rabble, that got hold of me, did use me ill enough, I must say: for which I was so angry with Mr. Trevor; and it was therefore that Old Nick put it into my head that I would beat him. For I cannot deny but the ducking did dwell upon my memory."

' "Were you then the same person that was so ill treated at Lansdown races?"

' "Yes, madam: for which, though I used to be angry enough before time at pick-pockets, I will take special care never to have a hand in ducking any body, as long as I live."

' "And is there no truth whatever in the story that two men were killed, by the ungovernable passion and malice of Mr. Trevor?"

' "Killed by Mr. Trevor, madam! No, no! He is not that sort of man. He would rather be killed himself than be the death of any christian soul: 'specially if he was a poor body. I can say that for him. Why he fought like a mad man, to save me from the mob; when they were hustling me, and dragging me along. But, while one part of them gathered round him, the other had got far enough off with me. It being all a mistake about a handkerchief: which he told them. And, though I heard him and saw him beat about just as if he had been a lion to save me, I could not forget how I had been used, when I met him the next day. But I hope God will forgive me! which I do believe he will, for Mr. Trevor has shewn him the example. I beg pardon! God forgive me! I only mean that, though Mr. Trevor is a good gentleman, the Lord of heaven must be a better; and even more charitable and melting in his heart. Which, to be sure, is very strange: because I do not altogether understand how it can be."

' "Then it seems your brother is still living?"

' "Brother, madam? I never had any brother! nor any thing of that kind: except my wife's sisters, *which* I love because I love *she*."

' "What strange tales I have been told!"

' "That I dare be sworn you have, madam, from what I have heard. Because there was the sham-Abraham[1] friends of Mr. Trevor: one of *which* kicked him, when he was down!"

' "Is it possible?"

' "It is as true as God is in heaven, madam!"

' "Do you know his name?"

' "He was as tall as a Maypole. And then after he had done this cowardly trick, why he durst not stand up to Mr. Trevor, like a man. And so, madam, finding as you have been told a parcel of trumpery tales, I hope in God you will be kind enough not to believe one of them; now that you see they are all false. For if there be a gentleman on the face of the earth that loves a lady to desperation, why, Mr.

Trevor is he; as you would have been satisfied, if you had *set* by his bedside when as he was down in the fever; like as I and my Sally did; and had heard him rave of nobody but you. And then if you had seen him too the night after he took you out of the coach! and then went on to Hounslow. Which, as he said, seeing it was parting with you, was worse than tearing his heart out of his body! But he was so afraid of doing you harm! and of setting that cross old lady to scold you! For he would suffer death rather than anger you. So that, while I have breath to draw, I shall never forget, when we came to the inn, how he looked! and stood quite lost and changing colour! and while his face was as set as stone, the tears kept trickling down his cheeks! At which I was put into a panic: for I did not at that time know what it was about, nor who we had been in company with. Which was the more surprising, when I came to hear! For which, as he knows you to be so good a lady, I am sure you must see all these particulars just in the same light."

'Miss Mowbray had heard sufficient. Her heart was bursting. It was with difficulty she could check her feelings, and she made no reply. Your unassuming but intelligent friend understood her silence as an intimation to him to withdraw. Zealous as you hear he was in your behalf, this thought put an end to his loquacity. But, as he was retiring, Miss Mowbray drew out her purse, and said to him—"Let me beg you, sir, to accept this; as a recompense, for—for having aided in saving the lives of me and my aunt."

'As she stretched out her hand, he looked up at her, as long as he durst; and then, turning his eyes away, said—"Why, as for money, madam, I thank you as much as if I had it: but, if I was to take it, what would that seem? but as if I had been telling a tale only to please you: when I declare, in the face of my Maker, it is every word truth! And a great deal more! And as for saving your lives, I was as willing I own as another: but I was not half so quick in thought as Mr. Trevor. Because, as the coachman said, if he had not catched hold of the horses in that very instant nick of the moment, it would have been all over! So I hope, madam, you will not take it amiss that I am not one of the sort *which* tell tales to gain their own ends."

'Here he instantly left the room: by which he intended to shew that he was determined.

'Clarke was no sooner gone than Miss Mowbray burst into the most passionate, and I really believe the most rapturous, flood of tears that the heart of woman ever shed! And how melting, how overflowing with affection, the heart of woman is, Mr. Trevor, I think you know.

'Good God! How pure, how expressive, how beaming, was the pleasure in her eyes! though she sobbed so violently that she had lost all utterance. How did she press my hand, gaze at me, then bury her face in my bosom, and struggle with the pleasure that was becoming dangerous in its excess!

'After some time, her thoughts took another turn. She instantly recovered the use of speech and exclaimed—"Oh, my friend! I almost hate myself, for the injustice which I, as well as others, have done Mr. Trevor—I, who had heard from his lips a thousand sentiments that ought to have assured me of the generous and elevated virtues by which his actions were directed! He has twice saved my life; and yet, because on some occasions he has happened to act differently from what I have supposed he ought to have acted, I have taken upon me to treat him with coldness that was affected, with reproof when I owed him thanks, and with rudeness such as I supposed became my sex.

' "For me he has risked his life again and again, without hesitation: while I have sat in timid silence, and countenanced calumnies which it was impossible I could believe; though I seem as if I had endeavoured to believe them, from the disgrace which I knew would justly light on me, should these calumnies prove false. False I could not but think them, false they have proved, and I am unworthy of him. I have presumed upon the prejudices which I knew would protect me, in the opinions of the foolish, and gain me their applause, and have treated him with a haughtiness which he ought to despise. Has he deserved it? Has he been guilty of one mean or seductive art, that might induce me to betray a duty, and gratify him at the expence of myself and others? Has he entered into that base warfare of the sexes by which each in turn endeavours to deceive?"

'The thought suddenly struck her, and interrupting herself she hastily asked—"Where is the letter you mentioned? I will read it. I know I shall read my own condemnation: but I will read it."

'I presented the letter, and replied, "Mr. Trevor instructed me to tell you, when I delivered it, that it contains nothing which he wishes you to conceal, should you think fit to shew it; that it does not invite you to any improper correspondence; and that it is the only one which, under his present circumstances, he means to obtrude upon you."

'Evidently overcome by the generous rectitude of your conduct, and more dissatisfied with her own, she broke the seal and began to read.

'She hurried it once over with great eagerness, and trepidation. She then paused; debating whether she should unburthen her mind immediately of a crowd of thoughts: but, finding they crossed and disturbed each other, she began again and read aloud; interrupting herself by remarks, as she proceeded.

' "*My reproof and anger*"—Yes, yes, I have taught him to treat me like a Sultana. He punishes me justly without intending it.

' "*You have supposed me dead*"—Here, addressing herself to me, she added—"It was his servant, Philip, who being hired by a gentleman that came to Scarborough brought us this false intelligence. His story was that he saw Mr. Trevor's distraction, on the morning after he had lost his money at a gaming-table; to which rashness as it should seem he was driven by despair; that Mr. Trevor ran into the fields, in a fit of frenzy, and threw himself into the Avon: that he, Philip, who had followed as fast as he could, hastened to the place but never saw him more; and that consequently and beyond all doubt he was there drowned.

' "Philip, according to his own account, hurried into the water, and used every means in his power to find the body: but, not being successful, he returned to his master's lodgings, took some trifles that had been given him, and left Bath by the morning coach for London; having nobody in Bath to give him a character, and being less likely there to meet with another place."

'I informed Miss Mowbray that this was part of it true, and part false: for that Philip had taken a ten-pound note, which more than paid him his wages; and that the other things, which he carried away, had not been given him.'

' "Indeed!" exclaimed Miss Mowbray, "I am exceedingly sorry to hear it: for, after his second master left Scarborough and he was hired by my aunt to wait on me, he behaved with great diligence and honesty.

' "Yet this accounts in part for his running away: which he did that very night after I suppose he had discovered it was Mr. Trevor, at Cranford-bridge; and I have never seen or heard of him since.

' "I am persuaded he thought Mr. Trevor dead: for, after I had heard my brother's account of the battle, I thought the time and the circumstances contradictory, and repeatedly questioned Philip; who persisted in declaring he saw Mr. Trevor jump into the river and drown himself.

' "Philip's account was that he had himself been out on errands early in the morning, at which time he supposed the battle must have been fought; and, though there were many contradictory circumstances, the positiveness with which the two tales were told led me to believe that the chief incidents of both were true. And, as I say, the flight of Philip from Cranford-bridge persuades me that he actually had believed Mr. Trevor dead.

' "I am sorry the poor fellow has done this wrong thing, and been frightened away: for I never before heard a servant speak with so much warmth and affection of a master, as he did of Mr. Trevor."

'She then continued to read; and made many observations, which expressed dissatisfaction with herself and were favourable to you, till she came to where you inform her that you had begun to study the law.'

' "By this I find," said she, "the story I have just heard is false."

'I asked, "What story is that, pray?"

'She replied, "I was last night at the opera; where I saw Mr. Trevor, with Lady Bray. Having so lately met with him under circumstances so different, and apparently disadvantageous, you may imagine that the joy I felt and the hope I conceived were not trifling.

' "My aunt saw him, likewise: but, as she was not so familiar with his person as to have no doubt, she first watched and then questioned me: though, as she upbraidingly told me, she needed only to have enquired of my looks.

' "I ought perhaps first to have informed you that I had thought it my duty to use the utmost sincerity, undeceive her, and declare all that I knew of what had passed at Cranford-bridge.

' "I performed this task on that very night, while her heart was alive to the danger she had escaped, and when she expressed a lively regret that the person from whom she had received such signal aid had disappeared. Except his silence in the coach, she said every thing bespoke him to be a gentleman: well bred, well educated, courageous, and as active as he was bold.

' "When she was told that the gentleman, of whom she had been speaking with so much warmth, had a peculiar motive for being silent, and that this gentleman was no other than Mr. Trevor, she was very much moved. The recollection of the manner in which she had been treating his character, and of the alacrity with which he had afterward saved her life, was exceedingly strong; and far from unmixed with pain. Before she was aware of herself, she exclaimed, "This Mr. Trevor is a very extraordinary young man!"

' "Unfortunately for Mr. Trevor, our servant, Philip, had absconded; and a train of suspicions immediately arose in her mind. It might be a conspiracy among them; a desperate and unprincipled contrivance, to effect a desperate and unprincipled purpose.

' "In this supposition she confirmed herself by every possible surmise: each and all resting upon the assumed league between Philip and Mr. Trevor.

' "I vainly urged that the sudden disappearing of both entirely contradicted such a conjecture; that Mr. Trevor, if he were capable of an action like this, must be as wicked as he was mad; and that I had every reason to believe him a man of the most generous and elevated principles. As you may suppose, these arguments from me only subjected me to reproof, sarcasm, and even suspicion.

' "My aunt fortified herself in her opinion; and behaved with a more jealous watchfulness than ever. She even terrified me with the dread of that which I could not credit: the possibility that what she affirmed might be true.

' "But, that I might do every thing in my power to prove that one part of her surmises was false, I determined cautiously to avoid, for the present, seeing or even hearing any thing concerning Mr. Trevor. And this was my inducement for writing the note, which you received.

' "My mind however suffered a continual conflict. I debated on the propriety of listening to the daily defamation of Mr. Trevor, when there were so many presumptive facts in his favour, and not endeavouring to prove that it was false; and I accused my conduct of apparent hypocrisy: of assuming a calm unconcern which my heart belied.

' "The sight of him at the Opera renewed my self-reproaches, in full force; and, likewise, fortunately awakened my aunt's curiosity.

' "Accordingly, one of our morning visits, to-day, has been to a friend of Lady Bray's; and there we learned that Mr. Trevor had been introduced, by Sir Barnard, to his lady and their common friends; as a young gentleman coming into parliament, and supposed to be possessed of extraordinary talents.

' "This I find by his letter is untrue; and there still appears to be some mystery which perhaps, as you see him so often, you may be able to unravel."

'I immediately requested her to look at the date of the letter; by which she saw it had been written several weeks: and afterward made her acquainted with all the particulars I knew, concerning your beginning and renouncing the study of the law, and your new political plans: most carefully remembering to give your noble minded friend, Mr. Evelyn, his due share of what I had to relate.

'Oh! how did her eyes swim, and her features glow, while I stated what I had heard of his sentiments and proceedings! Yes! She has a heart! a heart to match your own, Mr. Trevor.

'She then read the remainder of the letter; but with numerous interruptions, all of them expressing her admiration of your conduct by criminating her own.

'When she had ended, she spoke to me nearly as follows.

'"I am now, my dear friend, determined on the conduct I mean to pursue. Oh! How it delights my heart that Mr. Trevor accords with me in opinion, and advises me to that open sincerity after which I have long been struggling, and which I am at length resolved to adopt! I mean to inform my aunt of all that I know, as well as of all that I intend. I will tell her where I have been, shew her this letter, repeat every thing I have heard, and add my fixed purpose not to admit the addresses of any man on earth; till my family shall authorise those of Mr. Trevor. For that, or for the time when I shall be unconditionally my own mistress, however distant it may be, I will wait.

'"Tell Mr. Trevor that my heart is overwhelmed by the sense it feels of his generous and noble conduct; and it exults in his manly forbearance, which so cautiously guards my rectitude rather than his own gratification; that I will obey his injunction, and that we will have no clandestine correspondence; but that our souls shall commune: they shall daily sympathise, and mutually excite us to that perseverance in fidelity and virtue which will be their own reward, and the consolation and joy of our lives.

'"If my aunt, my brother, or any of their acquaintance, should again calumniate Mr. Trevor, I will forewarn them of my further determination to inform him, and enquire into the facts. But I hope they will neither be so unjust nor so ungenerous. At least, I think my aunt will not; when she hears the truth, knows my resolution, and remembers Cranford-bridge.

' "Of misinterpretation from Mr. Trevor I am in no fear. Had he one sinister design, he never could have imagined the conduct he has so nobly pursued. But to suppose the possibility of such a thing in him would be a most unpardonable injustice. The man who should teach me to distrust him, as a lover, could never inspire me with admiration and confidence, as a husband. But different indeed has been the lesson I have learned from Mr. Trevor.

' "Oh that Mr. Evelyn! What a godlike morality has he adopted! How rational! How full of benefit to others, and of happiness to himself!

' "But Mr. Trevor's friends are all of this uncommon stamp; and I own that to look into futurity, and to suppose myself excluded by prejudice and pride from the enjoyment of such society, is perhaps the most painful idea that can afflict the mind. I am almost afraid of owning even to you, my kind and sympathising friend, the torrent of emotions I feel at the thought of the pure pleasures I hope for hereafter; from a life spent with a partner like Mr. Trevor, heightened by the intercourse of the generous, benevolent, and strong-minded men who share his heart."

To detail all that farther passed, between Olivia and Miss Wilmot, with the particulars which the latter related to me, would but be to repeat sensations and incidents that are already familiar to the reader. And, with respect to my own feelings, those he will doubtless have anticipated. What could they be but rapture? What could they inspire but resolution: the power to endure, and the will to persevere?

CHAPTER IX

The study of oratory: Remarks on fashionable manners and
their consequences: A public dinner: Emotions at the meeting
of quondam acquaintance: Amenity without doors and anger
within compatible: A discovery made by the Baronet: The
contending passions of surprise, resentment, and pity: Ravages
committed by vice: An awful scene, or a warning to gluttony

PREVIOUS to this event, I should have imagined it impossible to have increased my affection: yet, if admiration be the basis of love, as I am persuaded it is, my love was certainly increased. I now seemed to be setting forward on a journey, of the length of which I was indeed wholly ignorant; but the road was made plain, and the end was inexpressible happiness. I should therefore travel with unwearied alacrity.

But, that I might shorten this unmeasured length of way, it was necessary I should be as active in pursuit as I was ardent in my passion: and the stimulus was a strong one. Oratory accordingly, Olivia excepted, became the object that seemed the dearest to my heart. Demosthenes and Cicero were my great masters. They and their modern competitors were my study, day and night. No means were neglected that precept or example, as far as they came within my knowledge, could afford: and the additional intercourse which I thus acquired with man, his motives, actions, and heart, was a school of the highest order.

I did not however entirely confine myself to the society of the dead: the living likewise constituted a seminary, in which I found frequent opportunities of gaining instruction. Impelled by curiosity and ambition, I was not remiss in cultivating an acquaintance among those people of fashion to whom I gained access.

But, as the tribe that bestow on themselves this titillating epithet have a light and versatile character, as they abound in praises that are void of discrimination, and promises that are unmeaning, and affect at one moment the most winning urbanity, and at the next the most supercilious arrogance, though they gave me much pleasure, they likewise gave me exquisite pain.

The more I became acquainted with them, the more I was amazed, that the man who had been talking to me in the evening on terms of the utmost apparent equality, if I met him the next morning, did not know me.

Some of them would even gaze full in my face, as if to enquire—'Who are you, sir?' but in reality to insult me. The looks of these most courteous and polished people seem to say 'In the name of all that is high-bred, how does it happen that persons of fashion do not unite to stare every such impertinent upstart out of their company?'

Of all the insolence that disturbs society, and puts it in a state of internal warfare, the insolence of fashion wounds and imbitters the most. It instantly provokes the offended person to enquire—'What kind of being is it, that takes upon him to brave, insult, and despise me? Has he more strength, more activity, more understanding than myself?' In numerous instances, he is imbecile in body, more imbecile still in mind, and contemptible in person. Nay he is often little better than a driveller.

He, whom the *hauteur* of fashion has compelled to reason thus, will soon be led to further and more serious inferences.

Nothing can reconcile men, so as to induce them to remain peaceable spectators of enjoyments beyond their attainment, except that unaffected benevolence which shall continually actuate the heart to communicate all the happiness it has the power to bestow. This only can so temper oppression as to render gradual and orderly reform practicable.

But I am talking to the winds.

This wavering between extreme civility and rudeness was conspicuous in the behaviour of the Bray family toward me. Her Ladyship, at one moment, would overlook me, I being present, as if no such person had been in existence: or as if he were not half so worthy of attention as her lap-dog; for, as a proof, on the lap-dog it was lavished: yet, at another, I was *absolutely* the most charming man on earth. I had *positively* the most refined taste, good breeding, and all that that she had ever known.

With Sir Barnard I was sometimes an oracle. To me his discourse was directed, to my judgment his appeals were made, and my opinions were decisive. In other fits he would not condescend to notice me. If I interfered with a sentence, he would pursue the conversation as if an objection made by me were unworthy of an answer; and perhaps, if I asked him a question, he would affect to be deaf, and make no reply.

These are arts which render the condition of a supposed inferior truly hateful: and, as they were severely felt, they were severely remembered, and now and then retaliated in a spirit which I cannot applaud.

If the history of such emotions were traced through all their consequences, and if men were aware how much the principal events of their lives are the result of the petty ebullitions of passion, that branch of morals which should regulate the temper of mind, tone of voice, and expression of the countenance, would become a very serious study.

This remark is as old as Adam: and yet it relates to a science that is only in its infancy.

How fatal the want of such a necessary command of temper had been to me the reader already knows: and, though at moments I was painfully conscious of the defect, and it was become less obtrusive, it was far from cured. It still hovered over and influenced my fate: as will be seen.

The old parliament was not yet dissolved: it had met, and was sitting. But the defection of Sir Barnard's member was of late date; and, as the Baronet had his motives for not wishing to provoke the honorable member whom he had made too violently, there was a kind of compromise; and the apostate was suffered to keep his seat, during the short remainder of the term.

Sir Barnard however, as I have said, delighted in his prop. It was as necessary to him as his cane; and I generally accompanied him, when he visited any kind of political assemblies.

It happened that there was an annual dinner of the gentlemen who had been educated at *******; of which dinner Sir Barnard was appointed one of the stewards. That he might acquit himself of this arduous task with eclat, I was of course presented with a ticket; and attended as his aid de camp.

The company was numerous, and the stewards and the chairman met something more early than the rest, to regulate the important business of the day.

When I entered the committee room, with the Baronet, the first person that caught my eye was the Earl of Idford.

I shrunk back. I had a momentary hesitation whether I should insult him or instantly quit the company; and disdain to enter an apartment polluted by his presence.

I had however just good sense enough to recollect that a quarrel, in such a place, nobody knew why, would be equally ridiculous and rash: and that to avoid any man was cowardly.

The thought awakened me; and, collecting myself, I advanced with a firm and cool air.

Habit and perversity of system had done that for his lordship to which his fortitude was inadequate. He was at least as cool, and as intrepid, as myself; and bowed to me with the utmost ease and civility. To return his bow was infinitely more repulsive than taking a toad in my hand: yet to forbear would have been a violation of the first principles of the behaviour of a gentleman. I therefore reluctantly and formally complied. I hope the reader remembers how earnestly I condemn this want of temper in myself.

His lordship took not the least notice of the coldness of my manner; but, with simpering complacency, 'hoped I had been well, since he had had the pleasure of seeing me.'

My reply was another slight inclination of the head, tinctured with disdain: on which his lordship turned his back, with a kind of open-mouthed nonchalance that was truly epigrammatic; and fell into conversation with Sir Barnard, who had advanced toward the fire, with all the apparent ease of the most intimate friendship: though, since his lordship had changed sides, they had become, in politics at least, the most outrageous enemies.

This brought a train of reflections into my mind, on the behaviour of political partisans toward each other; and on the efforts they make, after they have been venting the most cutting sarcasms in their mutual parliamentary attacks, to behave out of doors as if they had totally forgotten what had passed within: or were incapable, if not of feeling, of remembering insult.

What is most remarkable, the men of greatest talent exert this amenity with the greatest effect: for they utter and receive the most biting reproaches, yet meet each other as if no such bickerings had ever passed.

It is not then, in characters like these, hypocrisy?

No. It is an effort to live in harmony with mankind: yet to speak the truth and tell them of their mistakes unsparingly, and regardless of personal danger. In other words, it is an attempt to perform the most sacred of duties: but the manner of performing it effectually has hitherto been ill understood.

Sir Barnard had witnessed the short scene between me and his lordship; and presently took occasion to ask me in a whisper, 'How and where we had become acquainted?'

I replied 'I had resided in the house of his lordship.'

'Ay, indeed!' said the Baronet. 'In what capacity?'

My pride was piqued, and I answered, 'As his companion; and, as I was taught to suppose myself, his friend. But I was soon cured of my mistake.'

'By what means?'

'By his lordship's patriotism. By the purity of his politics.'

I spoke with a sneer, and the Baronet burst into a malicious laugh of triumph: but, unwilling that the cause of it should be suspected, it was instantly restrained.

'What concern had you,' continued he, 'in his lordship's politics?'

'I have reason to believe I helped to reconcile him to the Minister.'

'You, Mr. Trevor! How came you to do so unprincipled, so profligate, a thing?'

'It was wholly unintentional.'

'I do not understand you.'

'I wrote certain letters that were printed in the ——'

'What, Mr. Trevor! were you the author of the three last letters of Themistocles?'

'I was.'

The Baronet's face glowed with exultation. 'I knew,' said he with a vehement but under voice, 'he never wrote them himself! I have said it a thousand times; and I am not easily deceived. Every body said the same.'

There is no calculating how much the knowledge of this circumstance raised me in Sir Barnard's opinion; and consequently elevated himself, in the idea he conceived of his own power. 'Had he indeed got hold of the author of Themistocles? Why then he was a great man! A prodigious senator! The wish of his heart was accomplished! He could now wreak vengeance where he most wished it to fall; and fall it should, without mercy or remission.' His little soul was on tip-toe, and he overlooked the world.

Though we had retired to the farthest corner of the room, and his lordship pretended to be engaged in chit chat with persons who were proud of his condescension, I could perceive his suspicions were awakened. His eye repeatedly gave enquiring glances; and, while it endeavoured to counterfeit indifference by a stare, it was disturbed and contracted by apprehension.

Malignity, hatred, and revenge, are closely related; and of these passions men of but little mental powers are very susceptible. It is happy for society that their impotence impedes the execution of their desires. I was odious in the sight of Lord Idford in every point of view: for he had first injured me; which, as has been often remarked, too frequently renders him who commits the injury implacable; and he had since encountered a rival in me; which was an insult that his vanity and pride could ill indeed digest.

Still however he was a courtier; a man of fashion; a person of the best breeding; and therefore could smile.

A smile is a delightful thing, when it is the genuine offspring of the heart: but heaven defend me from the jaundiced eye, the simpering lip, and the wrinkled cheek; that turn smiles to grimace, and give the lie to open and undisguised pleasure.

It was a smile such as this that his lordship bestowed upon me, when I and the Baronet joined his group. Addressing himself to me, with a simper that anticipated the pain he intended to give, he said—'Do you know, Mr. Trevor, that your friend the bishop of * * * * is to dine with us? You will be glad to meet each other.'

I instantly replied, with fire in my eyes, 'I shall be as glad to meet that most pious and right reverend pastor as I was to meet your lordship.'

Agreeably to rule, he bowed; and gave the company to understand he took this as a polite acknowledgment of respect. But his gesture was accompanied with a disconcerted leer of smothered malice, which I could not misinterpret. It was sardonic; and, to me, who knew what was passing in his heart, disgusting, and painful.

I had scarcely spoken before my lord the bishop entered; and with him, as two supporters—Heavens! Who?—The president of the college where I had been educated; and the tutor, whose veto had prevented me from taking my degrees!

In the life of every man of enterprise there are moments of extreme peril. In an instant, and as it were by enchantment, I saw myself surrounded by the cowardly, servile, dwarf-demons, for so my imagination painted them, who had been my chief tormentors. Or rather by reptiles the most envenomed; with which I was shut up, as if I had been thrown into their den; and by which, if I did not exterminate them, I must expect to be devoured.

But these feelings were of short duration. My heart found an immediate repellent, both to fear and revenge, in my eyes. Good God! What were the figures now before me? Such as to excite pity, in every bosom that was not shut to commiseration for the vices into which mankind are mistakenly hurried; and for their deplorable consequences. What a fearful alteration had a few months produced! In the bishop especially!

He had been struck by the palsy, and dragged one side along with extreme difficulty. His bloated cheeks and body had fallen into deep pits; and the swelling massy parts were of a black-red hue, so that the skin appeared a bag of morbid contents. His mouth was drawn awry, his speech entirely inarticulate, his eye obscured by thick rheum, and his clothes were stained by the saliva that occasionally driveled from his lips. His legs were wasted, his breast was sunk, and his protuberant paunch looked like the receptacle of dropsy, atrophy, catarrh, and every imaginable malady.

My heart sunk within me. Poor creature! What would I have given to have possessed the power of restoring thee to something human! Resentment to thee? Alas! Had I not felt compassion, such as never can be forgotten, I surely should have despised, should have almost hated, myself.

The president was evidently travelling the same road. His legs, which had been extremely muscular, instead of being as round and smooth in their surface as they formerly were, each appeared to be covered with innumerable nodes; that formed irregular figures, and angles. What they were swathed with I cannot imagine: but I conjecture there must have been stiff brown paper next to the smooth silk stocking, which produced the irregularities of the surface. The dullness of his eyes, the slowness of their motions, his drooping eyelids, his flaccid cheeks, his hanging chin, and the bagging of his cloaths, all denoted waste, want of animation, lethargy, debility and decline.

The condition of the tutor was no less pitiable. He was gasping with an asthma; and was obliged incessantly to struggle with suffocation. It was what physicians call a confirmed case: while he lived, he was doomed to live in pain. Where is the tyrant that can invent tortures, equal to those which men invent for themselves?

These were the guests who were come to feast: to indulge appetites they had never been able to subdue, though their appetites were vipers that were eating away their vitals.

How strongly did this scene bring to my recollection Pope on the ruling passion! I could almost fancy I heard the poor bishop quoting

> 'Mercy! cries Helluo, mercy on my soul!
> 'Is there no hope?—Alas!—Then bring the jowl.'[1]

The present man is but the slave of the past. What induced the president and the tutor, when the bishop's more able-bodied footmen had rather carried than conducted him up stairs, officially to become his supporters as he entered the room? Was it unmixed humanity? Or was it those servile habits to which their cunning had subjected them? and by which they supposed not only that preferment but that happiness was attainable.

Humanity doubtless had its share; for it is a sensation that never utterly abandons the breast of man: and, as it is often strengthened by a consciousness that we ourselves are in need of aid, let us suppose that the president and the tutor were become humane.

Though feelings of acrimony towards these persons were entirely deadened in me by the spectacle I beheld, yet I knew not well how to behave. I was prompted to shew them how placable I was become, by accosting them first: but this might be misconstrued into that servility for which I had thought of them with so much contempt. Beside, the bishop and the president, if not the tutor, were in the phraseology of the world my superiors; and etiquette had established the rule that, if they thought proper to notice me, they would be the first to salute.

His lordship however eased me of farther trouble on this head, by asking the bishop—'Have you forgotten your old acquaintance Mr. Trevor, my lord?'

What answer this consecrated right reverend father returned I could not hear. He muttered something: but the sounds were as unintelligible as the features of his face; or the drooping deadness of his eyes. The president, however, hearing this, thought proper to bow: though very slightly, till the earl added, with a significant emphasis on the two last words—'Sir Barnard is become Mr. Trevor's particular friend;' which was no sooner pronounced than the countenances of both the bishop's supporters changed, to something which might be called exceedingly civil, in the tutor, and prodigiously condescending, in the president.

This was a memorable day: and, if the event which I have now to relate should be offensive to the feelings of any man, or any class of men, I can only say that I share the common fate of historians: who, though they should relate nothing but facts, never fail to excite displeasure, if not resentment and persecution, in the partisans of this or that particular opinion, faction, or establishment.

The dinner was served. It was sumptuous: or rather such as gluttony delights in. The persons assembled, I am sorry to say it, were several of them gluttons; and encouraged and countenanced each other in the vice to which they were addicted.

Dish succeeded to dish: and one plateful was but devoured that another and another might be gorged.

Fatal insensibility to the warning voice of experience! Incomprehensible blindness!

The poor bishop was unable to resist his destiny.

I had a foreboding of the mischief that might result from a stomach at once so debilitated and so overloaded. I wished to have spoken: I was tempted to exclaim—'Rash man, beware!' I could not keep my eyes away from him: till at length I suddenly remarked a strange appearance, that came over his face; and, almost at the same instant, he dropped from his chair in an apoplectic fit.

The description of his foaming mouth, distorted features, dead eyes, the whites of which only were to be seen, his writhings, his——

No! I must forbear. The picture I witnessed could give nothing but pain; mingled with disgust, and horror. If I suggest that poor oppressed nature made the most violent struggles, to empty and relieve herself, there will perhaps be more than sufficient of the scene of which I was a spectator conjured up in the imagination.

The bishop had been a muscular man, with a frame of uncommon strength; and the paroxysm, though extreme, did not end in death. Medical assistance was obtained, and he was borne away as soon as the crisis was over: but the festivity for which the company had met was disturbed. Many of them were struck with terror; dreading lest they had only been present at horrors that, soon or late, were to light upon themselves. They departed appalled by the scene they had witnessed, and haunted by images of a foreboding, black, and distracted kind.

From these Sir Barnard himself was not wholly free: though he had been less guilty of gormandizing than many of his associates: and, for my own part, this incident left an impression upon me which I am persuaded will be salutary through life.

CHAPTER X

A few reflections: A word concerning friends, and the duties of friendship: News of Thornby; or the equity of the dying: The decease of my mother: A curious letter on the obsequies of the dead: The real and the ideal being unlike to each other

HOW different is the same man, at different periods of his existence! How very unlike were the bowing well bred Earl of Idford, and the asthmatic tutor, of this day, to the Lord Sad-dog and his Jack; whom, but a few years before, I first met at college!

The president too at that time was, quite as much in form as in office, one of the pillars of the university. And the bishop! What a lamentable change had a short period produced!

Happy would it be for men did they recollect that change they must; and that, if they will but be sufficiently attentive to circumstances, they may change for the better.

Time kept rolling on; and I had variety of occupation. Neither my studies, my fashionable acquaintances, nor those whom I justly loved as my friends, were neglected. Mr. Evelyn continued for some time in town; attending to his anatomical and chymical studies. Wilmot had completed his comedy. It had been favourably received by the manager; and was to be the second new piece brought forward. Turl, with equal perseverance, was pursuing his own plans: and, though I heard nothing more from Olivia, my heart was at ease. I knew the motives on which she acted; and had her assurance that, if I should be again defamed, I should now be heard in my own defence.

I was careful not to forget honest Clarke; nor was the kindhearted Mary neglected. The good carpenter had sent for his wife and family up to town; and Mary was happy in the friendly attentions of Miss Wilmot, and in the orderly conduct and quick improvement of her son.

One of my pleasures, and duties as I conceived it to be, was to introduce Turl and Wilmot to such of my higher order of acquaintance as might afford both parties gratification. There is much frivolity among people of rank and fashion: but there is likewise some enquiry and sound understanding; and, where these qualities exist in any eminent degree, the friends I have named could not but be welcome.

It is the interest of men of all orders to converse with each other, to listen to their mutual pretensions with patience, to be slow to condemn, and to be liberal in the construction of what they at first suppose to be dangerous novelty.

Turl was peculiarly fitted to promote these principles: and Wilmot, in addition to the charms of an imagination finely stored, was possessed, as the reader may remember, of musical talents; and those of no inferior order. Days and weeks passed not unpleasantly away: for hope and Olivia were ever present to my imagination, and of the ills which fortune had in reserve I was little aware.

While business and pleasure thus appeared to promote each other, it came to my knowledge that an advertisement had appeared in the papers: stating that, if Hugh Trevor, the grandson of the reverend **** rector of ***, were alive, by application at a place there named, he might hear of something very much to his advantage.

I cannot enumerate the conjectures that this intelligence immediately excited; for they were endless. I searched the papers, found the advertisement, and hastened to the place to which it directed me.

The information I there received was not precisely what my elevated hopes had taught me to expect: but it was of considerable moment. I learned that my grandfather's executor, Mr. Thornby, was dead; that his nephew, Wakefield, had taken possession of the property he had left; but that he had done this illegally: for the person who caused the advertisement to be put into the paper was an attorney, who had drawn and witnessed the will of Thornby, which will was in my favour; and which moreover stated that the property bequeathed to me was mine in right of a will of my grandfather's; which will Thornby had till that time kept concealed. Whether the testament he had produced, immediately after the death of the rector, were one that Thornby had forged, or one that my grandfather had actually made but had ordered his executor to destroy, did not at present appear. The account I gave of it in a preceding volume, and of the manner in which it was procured, was the substance of what I learned from the conversation of my mother and Thornby at the time.

A death-bed compunction had wrested from the deceased an avowal of his guilt; and the facts were explicitly stated, in the preamble of his will, in order to prevent the contest which he foresaw might probably take place, between me and his nephew. He seemed to have been painfully anxious to do justice at last; and save his soul, when he found it must take flight.

The business was urgent; and, if I meant to profit by that which was legally mine, it was necessary, as I was advised, immediately to go down and examine into all the circumstances on the spot.

I was the more surprised at what I had heard because it was but very lately that I had sent a remittance to my mother; which she had acknowledged, and which must have been received after her husband had taken possession of his uncle's effects. But, when I recollected the character that had been given me of Wakefield, as far as the transaction related to him, my surprise was of short duration.

With respect to my mother, I heard with no small degree of astonishment that she had been applied to, in order to discover where I might be found; and that she had returned evasive answers: which as it was supposed had been dictated by her husband; under whose control, partly from fear and partly from an old woman's doating, she was completely held.

To say that I grieved at such weakness, in one whom I had so earnestly desired to love and honor with more than filial affection, would be superfluous: but my surprise would have instantly ceased, had I known who this Wakefield was; with whom my mother had to contend.

Reproach from me however, in word or look, had I been so inclined, she was destined never to receive. The career of pain and pleasure with her was nearly over. On the same day that I made the enquiries I have been repeating, a letter arrived; written not by her, but at her request; which informed me that, if I meant to see her alive, I must use all possible speed: for that she had been suddenly seized with dangerous and intolerable pains; which according to the description given in the letter, were such as I found from enquiry belong to the iliac passion;[1] and that she was then lying at the last extremity.

Two such imperious mandates, requiring my presence in my native county, were not to be disobeyed; and I departed with the utmost diligence. At the last stage, after a journey of unremitted expedition, I ordered the chaise to drive to the house of the late Thornby; where on enquiry I was informed that my mother lay.

I found her in a truly pitiable condition. Quicksilver[2] had been administered, but in vain; and she was so thoroughly exhausted that the sight of me produced but very little emotion. Her medical attendant pronounced she could not survive four-and-twenty hours; and advised that, if there were any business to be settled between us, it should be proceeded upon immediately.

Had this advice been given to persons of certain habits, assuredly, it would not have been neglected; and, perhaps it ought not to have been by me: but, whether I was right or wrong, I could not endure to perplex and disturb the mind of a mother in her last agonies. The consequence was, she expired without hearing a word from me, concerning her husband, Thornby, or the property to which I was heir; and without making any mention whatever herself of the disposal of this property.

I was indeed ignorant of what degree of information she could afford me. Her conduct had been so weak that to remind her of it, at such a moment, would, as I supposed, have been to inflict a severe degree of torment.

This, as the reader will learn in time, was not the only shaft by which my tranquillity was to be assaulted. My mother though she was, there was yet another death infinitely more heart-rending hanging over my head. The recollection is anguish that cannot end! Cannot did I say? Absurd mortal. Live for the living; and grieve not for the dead: unless grief could bid them rise from their graves.

I must proceed; and not suffer my feelings thus to anticipate my tale.

Knowing that Wakefield was no other than Belmont, the reader will not be surprised that he should think proper to elude, under these circumstances, the discovery which a meeting must have produced. My mother, actuated by a conviction that death was inevitable, had sent for me without his privity: so that I afterward learned he was in the house, when I drove up to the door: and, seeing me put my head out of the chaise, immediately made his escape through the garden.

A man less fertile in expedients would have found it difficult to forge a plausible pretext, to evade being present and meeting me at the funeral: but he, by pursuing what wore the face of being, and what I believe actually was, very rational conduct, dexterously shunned the rencontre. The following letter, which he wrote to me, will explain by what means.

'Sir,

'Persons of understanding have discovered that the obsequies of the dead may be performed with all due decorum, and the pain, as well as the very frequent hypocrisy, of a funeral procession, which is attended by friends and relations, avoided. They therefore with great good sense hire people to mourn; or send their empty carriages, with the blinds up: which perhaps is quite as wise, and no doubt as agreeable to the dead.

'He that would not render the duties of humanity, while they can succour those that are afflicted, may justly be called brutal; but, those duties being paid, what remains is more properly the business of carpenters, grave-diggers, and undertakers, than of men whose happiness is disturbed by useless but gloomy associations; and who may find better employment for their time.

'I, for example, have business, at present, that calls me another way. I therefore request you will give such orders, concerning the funeral, as you shall think proper: and, as I have no doubt you will agree with me that decency, and not unnecessary pomp, which cannot honor the dead, and does but satirise the living, will be most creditable to Mrs. Wakefield's memory, the expence, as it ought, will be defrayed by me.

I am, sir,

Your very obedient humble servant,

F. WAKEFIELD.'

Had such a letter been written by a man who had pretended fondness for his wife, it might perhaps have been construed unfeeling: if not insulting to her memory. But, as the case was notoriously the reverse, the honest contempt of all affectation, which it displayed, I could not but consider as an unexpected trait in the character of such a man as I supposed Wakefield to be.

There is a strange propensity in the imagination to make up ideal beings; and annex them to names that, when mentioned, have been usually followed with certain degrees of praise, or blame. These fanciful portraits are generally in the extreme: they are all virtue, or all vice: all perfection, or all deformity: though it is well known that no such unmixed mortals exist.

My mind having acquired the habit rather to doubt than to conclude that every thing which is customary must be right, funeral follies had not escaped my censure: but the thing which excited my surprise was that a man like Wakefield, who I concluded must have thought very little indeed, since he both thought and acted on other occasions so differently from me, should in any instance reason like myself; and some few others, whom I most admired.

Convinced however as I was that he now reasoned rightly, I wanted in this case the courage to act after his example. It would be a scandal to the country for a son, pretending to filial duty, to be absent from his mother's funeral. The reader will doubtless remember that town and country are two exceedingly distinct regions.

CHAPTER XI

*More alarming intelligence: An honest youth, with a printer's
notions concerning secrecy: The weak parts of law form the
strongest shield for villany: A journey back to town: Enoch
Ellis and Glibly again appear on the scene of action: A few
of the artifices of a man of uncommon cunning delineated:
A momentary glance at a mountain of political rubbish: By
artful deductions, a man may be made to say any thing that
an orator pleases*

THIS scandal I was, notwithstanding my discretion, destined to
afford. In addition to the arguments of Wakefield, accident supplied
a motive too powerful to be resisted.

I have mentioned my intention to suppress the pamphlet which
I had written, in the fever of my resentment, against the Earl, the
Bishop, and their associates. The edition which had been printed
for publishing had lain in the printer's warehouse, till the time that
I had determined against its appearance.

The child of the fancy is often as dear to us as any of our children
whatever; and I was unwilling that this offspring of mine should
perish, beyond all power of revival. I therefore had the edition
removed to my lodgings, and stowed in a garret.

A copy however had been purloined; and probably before the
removal. This copy came into the possession of an unprincipled
bookseller; who, regardless of every consideration except profit, and
perceiving it to be written with vehemence on a subject which
never fails to attract the attention of the public, namely personal
defamation, had once more committed it to the press.

As it happened, it was sent to be reprinted by the person with
whom the son of Mary was bound apprentice; and the whole was
worked off except the title-page, which fell into the hands of the
youth.

Desirous of shewing kindness to Mary, it may well be supposed
I had not overlooked her son. His mother had taught him to consider me as the saviour of both their lives; and as such he held me in
great veneration. These favourable feelings were increased by the

praise I bestowed on him, for his good conduct; and the encouragement I gave him to persevere.

Richard, for that was his name, suspected it could be no intention
of mine to publish the pamphlet: because he had been employed
to stow it in the garret: and, as he was an intelligent lad, and acquainted with the tricks of the publisher for whom he knew his
master was at work, he hastened in great alarm to communicate his
fears; first to his mother, and then by her advice to Miss Wilmot.

The latter immediately informed her brother. He saw the
danger, wrote to me to return without delay, doubting whether even
I should have the power to prevent the publication, and proceeded
himself immediately to the printer to warn him of the nature of the
transaction.

The man was no sooner informed of Mr. Wilmot's business than
he became violently enraged with his apprentice, Richard; accused
him of betraying his master's interest, and the secrets of the
printing-house, which ought to be held sacred, and affirmed that
he had endangered the loss of his business.

Richard was present, was aware of the charge which would be
brought against him, and was prepared to endure it with considerable firmness: though he had been taught to believe that such complaints were founded in justice.

Wilmot could obtain no unequivocal answer from the master:
either that he would or would not proceed. He consequently supposed the affirmative was the most probable; and therefore, that he
might neglect nothing in an affair which he considered as so serious,
he hastened from the printer to the publisher.

Here, in addition to the rage of what he likewise called having
been betrayed, he met with open defiance, vulgar insolence, and
vociferous assertions, from this worthy bookseller, that the laws of
his country would be his shield.

The fellow had been frequently concerned in such rascalities,
and knew his ground. He was one of the sagacious persons who had
found a cover for them. Where law pretends to regulate and define
every right, the wrong which it cannot reach it protects.

This is a branch of knowledge on which a vast body of men in the
kingdom, and especially in the metropolis, depend for their subsistence. And a very tempting trade it is: for our streets, our public
places, and our courts of justice, as well as other courts, swarm with
its followers; at which places they appear in as high a style of

fashion, that is of effrontery, as even the fools by whom they are aped, or the lawyers and statesmen themselves by whom they are defended. This I own is a bold assertion; and is perhaps a hyperbole! Yes, yes: it is comparing mole hills to mountains. But let it pass.

Wilmot, in his letter to me, did not confine himself to a bare recital of facts. Fearful lest they should escape my recollection, he urged those strong arguments which were best calculated to shew, not only what my enemies might allege, but what just men might impute to me, should this intemperate pamphlet appear: which, in addition to its original mistakes, would attack the character of the Bishop, a man whose office, in the eye of the world, implied every virtue. And how immoderately would its intemperance and imputed malignity be exaggerated, should it appear precisely at the moment when I knew disease had deprived him of his faculties! had rendered him unable to defend himself, and to produce facts which I might have concealed; or give another face to truth, which I might have discoloured!

These arguments alarmed me in a very painful degree. I was averse to quit the place before my mother was interred: especially as my reasons for such an abrupt departure could not be made public: but I was still more averse to an action which, in appearance, would involve me in such a cowardly species of infamy.

Accordingly, I made the best arrangements in my power: leaving orders that the funeral should be conducted with every decency; and, after a very short conversation with the attorney, who had witnessed the will of Thornby and given me the information I have already mentioned, I travelled back to London with no less speed than I had hurried into the country.

I arrived in town on Thursday night; and the pamphlet was advertised for publication on the following Monday. The advertisement, being purposely written to excite curiosity, repeated the subject of the pamphlet: which asserted my claims to the letters of Themistocles, and to the defence of the thirty-nine articles; the acrimony of which charge was increased by a personal attack on the Earl of Idford, the Bishop, and their associates.

When I came to my lodgings, I found two notes: one from a person stiling himself a gentleman employed by the Earl; and another from Mr. Ellis, on the part of the Bishop: each requesting an interview. Answers not having been returned, these agents had come themselves; and, being informed that I was in the country, but was expected in town before the end of the week, they left a pressing message; desiring an answer the moment of my arrival.

Eager as I was to ward off the danger that threatened me, I considered the application that was made, especially on the part of the Earl, as fortunate. I understood that the only means of suppressing the pamphlet would be by an injunction from the Lord Chancellor; and this I imagined the influence of the Earl might essentially promote: for which reason I immediately wrote, in reply to these agents, and appointed an interview early the next morning.

The place of meeting was a private room in a coffee-house; and, though my eagerness in the business brought me there a few minutes before the time named, Ellis and his coadjutor had arrived before me. They acted in concert, and had met to compare notes.

I found the purveyor of pews and paradise still the same: always inclined to make himself agreeable.

The other agent was seated in a dark corner of the room, with his back to the light, so that I did not recognise him as I entered. How much was I surprised when, as he turned to the window, I discovered him to be the loquacious Mr. Glibly; the man whose principles were so accommodating, whose tongue was glossy, but whose praise was much more sickening and dangerous than his satire.

The civilities that were poured upon me, by these well-paired gentlemen, were overwhelming. It was like taking leave of a Frenchman, under the ancient *régime*: there was no niche or chink for me to throw in a word; so copious was the volubility of Glibly, and so eager was the zeal of Ellis.

From the picture I before gave of the first, the reader will have perceived that he was a man of considerable intellect: though not of sufficient to make him honest. His usual mode, in conversation, was to render the person to whom he addressed himself ridiculous by excessive praise; and to mingle up sarcasm and panegyric in such a manner as to produce confusion in the mind of the object of it, who never knew when to be angry or when to be pleased, and laughter in every body else.

At first the most witty and acute would find amusement in his florid irony: but they could not but soon be wearied, by its methodical and undeviating mechanism; which denoted great barrenness of invention.

In the present instance, he had a case that required management: a patron to oblige, and an opponent to circumvent. He had therefore the art to assume a tone as much divested of sneering as habit would permit; and began by insinuations that were too flattering to fail of their effect, yet not quite gross enough to offend. My person, my appearance, my parliamentary prospects, my understanding, my friends and connections, all passed in review: while his praise was carefully tempered; and as I imagined very passably appropriate.

Hence, it certainly promoted the end for which it was given: it opened my heart, and prepared me for that generous effusion which rather inclines to criminate itself than to insist on every trifle that may be urged in its favour.

Apt however as he was at detecting vanity in others, he was as open to it himself, I might almost say, as any man on earth. He began with a profession of his friendship for the Earl of Idford: in which he assumed the tone of having conferred a favour on that noble lord; and I will not deny that he was right. All his acquaintance were friends; and perhaps he had the longest list of any man in London: for the effrontery of his familiar claims upon every man he met, from whom he had any thing to hope or fear, was so extraordinary as to render an escape from him impossible. He had parroted the phraseology of the *haut ton*, and its arrogant apathy, till the manner was so habitual to him that he was unconscious of his own impudence.

Thus, in conversing on this occasion of the Earl who had deputed him, the only appellation he had for his patron was Idford. 'I told Idford what I thought on the subject. For I always speak the truth, and never deceive people: unless it be to give them pleasure; and then you know they are the more obliged to me. Glibly, said Idford to me, I know you will act in this business without partiality. For I must do him justice, Trevor, and assure you that Idford is a good fellow. I do not pretend that he is not sensible of the privileges which rank and fashion give him. He is vain, thinks himself a great orator, a fine writer, a wise senator, and all that. I grant it. How should it be otherwise? It is very natural. He would have been a devilish sensible fellow, if he had not been a lord. But that is not to be helped. You and I, in his place, should think and act the same. We should be as much deceived, as silly, and as ridiculous. It is all right. Things must be so. But Idford is a very good fellow. He is, upon my honor.'

The surgeon that has a difficult case will not only make preparations and adjustments before he begins to probe, lacerate, or
cauterize, but will sometimes administer an opiate; to stupefy that
sensibility which he apprehends is too keen. Glibly pursued much
the same method; and, having exhausted nearly all his art, till he
found he had produced as great a propensity to compliance and
conciliation as he could reasonably hope, he proceeded to the
business in question.

'You no doubt guess, my dear Trevor, why my friend Ellis here
and I desired to meet you?'

'I do.'

'To say the truth, knowing as I do the soundness of your understanding, the quickness of your conception, and the consequences
that must follow, which, acute as you are, you could not but foresee,
I was amazed when I read your advertisement!'

'It is prodigiously surprising, indeed!' added Ellis: eager at every
opportunity to throw in such touches as he thought would give
effect to the colouring of his friend, and leader.

'Why,' said I, 'do you call it my advertisement?'

'I mean of a pamphlet which it seems has been written by you.'

'But is going to be published without my consent.'

'Are you serious?' said Glibly: staring!

'It is not my custom to deceive people, Mr. Glibly; *not even to
give them pleasure.*'

'I am prodigious glad of that!' exclaimed the holy Enoch. 'Prodigious glad, indeed!'

'But you have owned it was written by you?' continued Glibly.

'I know no good that can result from disowning the truth; and
especially in the present instance.'

'My dear fellow, truth is a very pretty thing on some occasions:
but to be continually telling truth, as you call it, oh Lord! oh Lord!
we should set the whole world to cutting of throats!'

'To be sure we should!' cried Ellis. 'To be sure we should! That
is my morality exactly.'

'Men are men, my dear fellow. A lord is a lord: a bishop is
a bishop. Each in his station. Things could not go on if we did not
make allowances. To tell truth would be to overturn all order.'

'I am willing to make allowances: for all men are liable to be
mistaken.'

'I approve that sentiment very much, Mr. Trevor,' interrupted

Enoch. 'It is prodigious fine. It is my own. All men are liable to be mistaken. I have said it a thousand times. It is prodigious fine!'

'But I cannot conceive,' added I, 'that to overturn systems which are founded in vice and folly would be to overturn all order. You may call systematic selfishness, systematic hypocrisy, and systematic oppression order: but I assert they are disorder.'

'My dear fellow, nothing is so easy as to assert. But we will leave this to another time. I dare say that in the main there is no great difference between us. You wish for all the good things you can get; and so do I. One of us may take a more round about way to obtain them than the other: but we both intend to travel to the same goal. I own, when I heard of your *brouillerie* with my friend Idford, I thought you had missed the road. But I find you have more wit than I supposed: you are now guided by another finger-post. Perhaps it might have been as well not to have changed. The treasury bench is a strong hold, and never was so well fortified. It is become impregnable. It includes the whole power of England, Scotland, and Ireland; both the Indies; countless islands, and boundless continents: with all the grand out-works of lords, spiritual and temporal; governors; generals; admirals; custos rotulorum,[1] and magistracy; bodies corporate, and chartered companies; excise, and taxation; board and bankruptcy commissioners; contractors; agents; jobbers; money-lenders, and spies; with all the gradations of these and many more distinct classes: understrappers innumerable; an endless swarm; a monstrous mass. Can it be conjured away by angry breath? No, no. It is no house of cards: for an individual to attempt to puff it down would be ridiculous insanity.'

'A mass indeed! "Making Ossa like a wart."[2] Yet the rubbish must be removed; and it is mine and every man's duty to handle the spade and besom. But men want to work miracles; and, because the mountain does not vanish at a word, they rashly conclude it cannot be diminished. They are mistaken. Political error is a pestilential cloud; dense with mephitic[3] and deadly vapours: but a wind has arisen in the south, that will drive it over states, kingdoms, and empires; till at last it shall be swept from the face of the earth.'

'My dear fellow, you have an admirable genius: but you have mistaken its bent. Depend upon it, you are no politician: though you are a very great poet. Fine phrases, grand metaphors, beautiful images, all very admirable! and you have them at command. You

are born to be an ornament to your country. You have a very pretty
turn. Very pretty indeed! And so, which is the point that I was
coming to, concerning this pamphlet. It relates I think to certain
letters that appeared, signed Themistocles.'

'And to a defence, by my lord the bishop, of the thirty nine
articles,' added Ellis: eager that he and his patron should not be
omitted.

'You, my dear fellow, had some part in both of these publications.'

'I do not know what you mean by some part. The substance of
them both was my own.'

'Ay, ay; you had a share: a considerable share. You and Idford
were friends. You conversed together, and communicated your
thoughts to each other. Did not you?'

'I grant we did.'

'I knew you would grant whatever was true. You are the advocate
of truth; and I commend you. Idford mixed with political men,
knew the temper of the times, was acquainted with various anecdotes, and gave you every information in his power. I know you are
too candid to conceal or disguise the least fact. You would be as
ready to condemn yourself as another. You have real dignity of
mind. It gives you a certain superiority; a kind of grandeur; of real
grandeur. It is your principle.'

'It ought to be.'

'No doubt. And I am sure you will own that I have stated the case
fairly. I told you, Mr. Ellis, that I knew my friend Trevor. He has
too much integrity to disown any thing I have said. I dare believe,
were he to read the letters of Themistocles over at this instant, he
would find it difficult to affirm, of any one sentence, that the
thought *might not possibly* have been suggested in conversation by
my friend Idford. I say *might not possibly*: for you both perceive
I am very desirous on this occasion to be guarded.'

'It certainly is a difficult thing,' answered I, 'for any man
positively to affirm he can trace the origin of any one thought; and
recollect the moment when it first entered his mind.'

My lips were opening to proceed: but Glibly with great eagerness
prevented me.

'I knew, my dear fellow, that your candor was equal to your
understanding. Mr. Ellis, who hears all that passes, will do me the
justice to say that I declared before you came what turn the affair
would take.'

I was again going to speak, but he was determined I should not, and proceeded with his unconquerable volubility; purposely leading my mind to another train of thought.

'I am very glad indeed that the advertisement which appeared was not with your approbation. On recollection, I cannot conceive how I could for a moment suppose it was your own act. A man of the soundest understanding may be surprised into passion, and may write in a passion: but he will think again and again, and will be careful not to publish in a passion. And the delay which has taken place might have proved to me that you had thought; and had determined not to publish. Your countenance, when you disowned the advertisement just now, convinces me that I do you no more than justice, by supposing this of you.'

Here the artful orator thought proper to pause for a reply, and I answered, 'I own that I wrote in a spirit which I do not at present quite approve.'

'I know it. What you have said and what you have allowed have so much of liberality, cool recollection, and dispassionate honesty, that they are, as I knew they would be, very honourable to you.'

'Prodigiously, indeed!' said Enoch.

Glibly continued: 'Your behaviour, in this business, entirely confirms my good opinion of you; and I give myself some credit for understanding a man's true character: especially the character of a man like you. My good friend Ellis and I are entirely satisfied. What has passed has removed all doubts, and difficulties. We are with you; and shall report every thing to your advantage.'

'I wish you to report nothing but the truth.'

'I know it, my dear fellow. That is what we intend. So, without saying a word more on that subject, we will now consider what is best to be done. I understand that the edition about to be published is pirated; and I suppose you will join us in an application to the Lord Chancellor for an injunction.'

'Most eagerly. That was my reason for wishing to see you, so immediately after my arrival in town; imagining that an application from Lord Idford, and the bishop, would be more readily attended to than if it came from a private and unknown individual.'

'To be sure it would, Mr. Trevor!' said Enoch. 'An application from an earl and a bishop, is not likely to be overlooked. They are privileged persons. They are the higher powers. Every thing that concerns them must be treated with tenderness, and reverence, and humbleness, and every thing of that kind.'

The spirit moved me to begin an enquiry into privileges; and the tenderness and humility due to earls and bishops: particularly to such as the noble and reverend lords in question: but Glibly guessed my thoughts, and took care to prevent me!

'As to those subjects, my dear Ellis,' said he, 'Trevor thinks and acts on a different system from you and me and the rest of the world. We must not dispute these points, now; but away, as fast as we can, and put the business for which we met in a train. The publication must be stopped. It would injure all parties; and, as you, my dear friend [Turning to me] justly think at present, would be disgraceful to its author.'

After what had been urged by Turl and Wilmot, and the reasoning that had followed in my own mind, I knew not how to deny this assertion: though it was painfully grating. But the reader will easily perceive that this and other strong affirmations, such as I have related, were designedly made by Glibly. He artfully gabbled on, that he might lead my mind from attending to them too strictly; and that he might afterward, if occasion should require, state them, with the colouring that he should give, as things uttered or allowed by me.

It ought not to be thought strange that I was deceived by Glibly, barefaced as his cunning would have appeared to a man more versed in the arts which over-reaching selfishness daily puts in practice. He confessedly came in behalf of a party concerned; and, as such, a liberal mind would be prepared to expect a bias from him rather in favour of his client. His face was smiling; his tones were soft and smooth; the words candor, honesty, and integrity, were continually on his tongue. He affected to be a disinterested arbitrator; and allowed that his friend Idford, as he called him, might or rather must be tainted with the vices of his station, and class. Could a youth, unhacknied in the world, feeling that treachery was not native to the heart of man, not suspecting on ordinary occasions that it could exist, could such a tyro in hypocrisy be a fit antagonist for such an adept?

Deceit will frequently escape immediate detection: but it seldom leaves the person, upon whom it is practised, with that clearness of thought which communicates calm to the mind; producing unruffled satisfaction, and cheerful good temper.

CHAPTER XII

A lawyer and his poetical wife and daughters, or the family
of the Quisques: Praise may give pain: A babbler may bite:
More of the colouring of cunning: A trader's ideas of honesty,
and the small sum for which it may be sold

WE quitted the coffee-house; Glibly in high spirits, and Enoch
concluding things had been done as they should be: but, for my
own part, I experienced a confusion of intellect that did not suffer
me to be so much at my ease. I had an indistinct sense of being as
passive as a blind man with his dog. Instead of taking the lead, as
I was entitled to have done, I was led: hurried away, like a man
down a mountain with a high wind at his back: or traversing dark
alleys, holding by the coat-flap of a guide of whose good intentions
I was very far from having any certainty.

We proceeded however to the house of a solicitor in chancery;
who transacted business for the Earl.

Here Glibly, attentive to the plan he had pursued, began by
informing Mr. Quisque, the lawyer, that he had come *at the request*
of his dear friend, Trevor, to entreat his aid in an affair of some
moment. 'Mr. Trevor is a young gentleman, my dear Quisque, that
you will be proud to be acquainted with; a man of talents; a poet;
an orator; an author; a great genius; an excellent scholar; a fine
writer; turns a sentence or a rhyme with exquisite neatness; very
prettily I assure you. I mention these circumstances, my dear
Quisque, because I know you have a taste for such things: and so
has Mrs. Quisque, and the two Miss Quisques, and all the family.
I now and then see very pretty things of their writing in the
Lady's Magazine.[1] An elegy on a robin red-breast. The drooping
violet, a sonnet. And others equally ecstatic. Quite charming!
rapturous! elegant! flowery! sentimental! Some of them very smart,
and epigrammatic. It is a family, my dear Trevor, that you must
become intimate with. Your merit entitles you to the distinction.
You will communicate your mutual productions. You will polish
and suggest charming little delicate emendations, to each other,
before you favour the world with a sight of them.'

The broadest and coarsest satire was never half so insulting, to
the feelings, as the common-place praise of Glibly.

The barren-pated Ellis caught one of the favourite diminutives of Glibly; and finished my panegyric by adding that, 'he must say, his friend, Mr. Trevor, was a prodigious pretty genius.'

Who but must have been proud of such an introduction to the family of the Quisques; by such orators, such eulogists, and such friends?

Acquainted with Glibly, and accustomed to hear him prate, Mr. Quisque seemed to listen to him without surprise, pleasure, or pain. It was what he expected. It was the man. A machine that had no more meaning than a Dutch clock; repeating cuckoo, as it strikes.

Among Glibly's acquaintance, or, as he called them, his dear friends, this was a common but a very false conclusion. He had not adopted his customary cant without a motive. The man, who can persuade others that he gabbles in a pleasant but ridiculous and undesigning manner, will lead them to suppose that his actions are equally incongruous, and void of intention. He will pass upon the world for an agreeable harmless fellow, till his malignities are too numerous to escape notice; and then, where he was before welcomed with the hope of a laugh, he will continue to be admitted from the dread of a bite.

A lawyer however feels less of this panic than the rest of mankind: because he can bite again. The cat o' mountain will not attack the tiger.

Glibly returned to the business in hand; and again repeated that he was come *at the request* of his dear friend, Trevor, to procure an injunction: that should prevent the publication of a pamphlet, which had been written against his friend, Idford.

'And my lord the Bishop of ****,' added Enoch.

'Who is the author of it?' demanded Quisque.

'I am, sir;' answered I.

'For which my friend Trevor is very sorry;' added Glibly.

I instantly retorted a denial. 'I never said any thing of the kind, Mr. Glibly. But I should be very sorry indeed if it were published.'

'Nay, my dear fellow, according to your own principles, if I do not mistake them, that which ought not to be published ought not to be written.'

The remark was acute: it puzzled me, and I was silent. He proceeded.

'It is a business that admits of no delay. I should be extremely chagrined, extremely, upon my honor, that my dear friend Trevor should commit himself to the public, in this affair. He that wantonly attacks the characters of others does but strike at his own.'

I again eagerly replied 'The attack from me, sir, was not wanton. It was provoked by acts of the most flagrant injustice.'

Glibly as eagerly interrupted me.

'My dear fellow, why are you so warm? I was only delivering a general maxim. I made no application of it; and I am surprised that you should.'

The traps of Glibly were numberless; and not to be escaped. Words are too equivocal, and phrases too indefinite, for men like him not to profit by their ambiguity. To them a quirk in the sense is as profitable as a pun or a quibble in the sound. They snap at them, as dogs do at flies. It is no less worthy of observation that, though some of his actions seemed to laugh severity of moral principle out of countenance, he continually repeated others which, had his conduct been regulated by them, would have ranked him among the most worthy of mankind.

After farther explanation from Quisque, it was admitted that the interest of all parties made it necessary for him to act with great diligence, speed, and caution.

Through the whole of this scene, Glibly was consistent with himself; in giving it such a turn and complexion as to make it requisite, for the preservation of my character above the rest, to prevent the pamphlet from being published. If, whenever I detected his drift, I urged the true motives by which I was actuated, he always immediately admitted them, praised them, and allowed them to be superlatively excellent: but never failed to give them such an air as should suit the project he had conceived; and allow of such an interpretation, in future, as would exculpate my opponents and criminate myself. But he effected this with such fluency, and so glossed over and coloured his intention that, like profound darkness, it was every where present, but neither could be felt nor seen.

My own activity in this affair, which if I meant to render my interference effectual was inevitable, contributed to the same end. I accompanied the whole party, Quisque being one, to the shop of the publisher.

Here I detailed the consequences, as well to myself as to the Earl and the Bishop; and vehemently denounced threats, if the villany that was begun should be carried into execution. Not all the quieting hints of my assistants could keep my anger under. I lost all patience, at every word. My utmost indignation was excited by so black a business.

The situation was not a new one to the dealer in the alphabet. He was an old depredator; and had before encountered angry authors, and artful lawyers. He was cool, collected, and unabashed. Not indeed entirely: but sufficiently so to excite astonishment.

He affirmed the copy-right to be his own: would prove he had obtained it legally; and would face any prosecution that we could bring. He knew what he was about; and was not to be frightened. He had printed one edition; and had no doubt that several would be sold. He was an honest tradesman; and must not be robbed of his profits. What would the country be if it were not for trade? It ought to be protected: ay and would be too. The law was as open to an industrious fair trader as to any lord in the land. Let him too be no loser and then it would be a different thing: but, as for big words, they broke no bones; and he knew his ground.

The hints of the honest trader were too broad to be misunderstood; and Quisque replied—'I think you mean, sir, that you wish to be repaid the expence you have sustained?'

The fellow answered, with the utmost effrontery, 'I have a right, sir, to be indemnified for the loss of my profits on the sale of the work.'

Anger and argument were equally vain. There were two ways of proceeding. Silence and safety might be purchased: or the law might be let loose on a knave, who set it at defiance. The one was secure: the other problematical; and replete with the danger which we wished to avert.

Quisque asked him what was the sum that he demanded? His reply was more moderate than from appearances we had reason to expect: it was one hundred pounds.

Glibly desired he would permit us to consult five minutes among ourselves. He withdrew; and the fluent agent remarked the sum was a trifle: but, trifling as it was, he had no doubt but feelings of delicacy and honor would dictate that it ought to be jointly paid, by the three parties principally concerned.

He had urged a motive which I knew not how to resist, and I gave my assent. By this manœuvre he gained the point which he intended. He implicated me, as paying to suppress a pamphlet which, according to his interpretation, I at present allowed to be defamatory, and unjust.

The money however was paid, and the copies of the pamphlet were delivered: and, being determined if possible to avoid such another accident, those that I had caused to be printed were dislodged from their garret; both editions, a single copy of each excepted, were taken into the fields by night, and burned; and thus expired a production which had aided to drain my pocket, waste my time, and inflame my passions.

END OF VOLUME V

VOLUME VI

CHAPTER I

*A new and bold project conceived and executed by Wakefield:
The difficulty of making principles agree with practice
discussed: Fair promises on the part of an old offender, the
hopes they excite and the fears that accompany them*

THE affair of the pamphlet being removed from my mind, I had
leisure to attend to the other difficulty that had lately crossed me;
by the possession which Wakefield had illegally taken of effects
which he asserted to be his, in the double right of being heir to his
uncle and the husband of my mother, but which, if my information
were true, appertained to me.

It may well be supposed I communicated all my thoughts to
friends like Evelyn, Wilmot, and Turl; and endeavoured to profit
by their advice.

Law had lately undergone a serious examination from us all; and
it was then the general opinion among us that, though it was impossible to avoid appealing to it on some occasions, yet nothing
but the most urgent cases could justify such appeals. Enquiries that
were to be regulated, not by a spirit of justice but by the disputa-
tious temper of men whose trade it was to deceive, and by statutes
and precedents which they might or might not remember, and
which, though they might equivocally and partially apply in some
points, in others had no resemblance, such enquiries ought not
lightly to be instituted. Neither ought the habitual vices which they
engender, both in lawyer and client, nor the miseries they inflict,
upon the latter in particular, and by their consequences upon all
society, to be promoted.

In the course of the conversation at the tavern, when I dined and spent the afternoon with the false Belmont, this subject among others had occurred. Having told him that I had quitted all thoughts of the law, he enquired into my motives; and, being full of the subject and zealous to detail its whole iniquity, I not only urged the reasons that most militate against it both in principle and practice, but, in the warmth of argument, declared that I doubted whether any man could bring an action against another without being guilty of injustice. I considered crime and error as the same. The structure of law I argued was erroneous, therefore criminal; and I protested against the attempting to redress a wrong, already committed, by the commission of more wrong.

The death of Thornby happened immediately after this conversation took place; and it is not to be supposed that a man like my young but inventive father-in-law could forget, or fail in endeavouring to profit by, such an incident.

One morning while at breakfast, I received a note from him, signed Belmont; in which he requested me again to dine and spend the afternoon with him: alleging that an event had taken place in which he was deeply interested: adding that he had been lately led to reflect on many of the remarks I had made; and that he hoped the period was come when he should be able to change the system to which I was so inimical, for one that better agreed with my own sentiments: but that my advice was particularly necessary, on the present occasion.

The note gave me pleasure. That a man with such powers of mind, and charms of conversation, should have only a chance of changing, from what he was to what I hoped, was delightful. And that he should call upon me for advice, at such a juncture, was flattering.

I answered that an engagement already formed prevented me from meeting him, on that day: but I appointed the next morning for an interview. Dining I declined; as a hint that I disapproved the attempt he had made to entrap me.

The engagement I had was to accompany Lady Bray, to one of the families acquainted with the Mowbrays; and where it was expected we should meet Olivia, and her aunt. This expectation, which kept my spirits in a flutter the whole day and increased to alarm and dread in the evening, was disappointed. Whether from any real or a pretended accident on the part of the aunt, who sent an apology, was more than I had an opportunity to know.

I kept my appointment, on the following morning; and was rather surprised, when we met, at perceiving that the still pretended Belmont, like myself, was in deep mourning. I began to make enquiries, to which he gave short answers; and, turning the interrogatories upon me, asked which of my relations was dead?

'My mother.'

'Oh: I remember. Mrs. Wakefield. Are you still as angry with her husband as ever?'

'I really cannot tell. Though I have what most people would think much greater cause.'

'Indeed! What has he done more?'

'Taken possession of property which is mine.'

'By what right is it yours?'

'It was bequeathed me by my grandfather; and since that by his executor.'

'The uncle of this Wakefield, I think you told me?'

'Yes. A lawyer. One Thornby; who was induced by death-bed terrors to restore what he had robbed me of while living.'

'That is, he lived a knave, and died a fool and a fanatic.'

'I suspect that he died as he had lived. Knavery and fanaticism are frequently coupled.'

'And how do you intend to proceed?'

'I do not know. I have not yet consulted a lawyer.'

'Consulted a lawyer? You surprise me! When last I saw you, I was half convinced by you that a man cannot justly seek redress at law. Its sources you proved to be corrupt, its powers inadequate, and its decisions never accurate; therefore never just. This was your language. You reprobated those accommodating rules by which I endeavoured to obtain happiness; and urged arguments that made a deep impression upon me. Now that self-interest gives you an impulse, are your principles become as pliant as mine; which you so seriously reproved?'

I paused, and then replied—'I imagine you take some delight in having found an opportunity of retorting upon me; and of laughing at what you still consider as folly.'

'Indeed you mistake. I hope by reminding you of your own doctrine to induce you to put it in practice. The virtue that consists only in words is but a vapour.'

'Surely you will allow this is an extreme if not a doubtful case. I do not mean to commence an action, till I have considered it very seriously: but I presume you do not require infallibility of me? Or, if you do, it is what I cannot expect from myself. I have frequently been led to doubt whether principles the most indubitable must not bend to the mistakes and institutions of society. This doubt is to me the most painful that can cross the mind: but it is one from which I cannot wholly escape.'

'Your tone I find is greatly altered. How strenuous, how firm, how founded, were all your maxims; when last we met.'

'And so, I am persuaded, the maxims of truth will always remain.'

'Then why depart from them? Another of them, which I likewise recollect to have heard from you, is that the laws which pretend to regulate property, whether by will, entail, or any other descent, are all unjust: for that effects of all kinds should be so appropriated as to produce the greatest good.'

'I do not see how that can be denied. But this is strongly to the point in my favour, as I suppose: for the institutes of society render the application of the principle impracticable; and therefore I think the property may have a greater chance of being applied to a good purpose, if allotted to me, than if retained by this Wakefield; whose vices are extraordinary.'

'You believe him to be a man of some talent?'

'All that know him affirm his understanding would be of the first order, were it worthily employed.'

'Then would it not be a good application of the property in contest, if it should both enable and induce him so to employ his understanding?'

'Oh, of that there is no hope.'

'How do you know? I believe you have thought the same of me: but you may chance to be mistaken. And now I will tell you a secret. I am in the very predicament of this Wakefield. A relation is dead, who has left his property away from me: by what right is more than I can discover; at least in the spirit of those laws which pretend to regulate such matters: for their spirit is force. Lands wrested from the helpless they consign to the robber. I am in possession; and doubt whether, even according to your code, I ought to resign. I certainly ought not according to my own. I will acknowledge to you that I think well of the man who claims the property I withhold. But I cannot think so well of him as of myself: for I cannot be so well acquainted with his thoughts as with my own. I know my

own wants, my own powers, and my own plans. I should be glad
to do him good, but I should be sorry to do myself ill. You accuse
me of having fallen into erroneous habits, of making false calculations, and of tasting pleasures that are dangerous and of short
duration. I have ridiculed your arguments: but I have not forgotten
them. Neither has the enquiring spirit that is abroad been unknown
to or unnoticed by me. Early powers of mind gave me the early
means of indulgence. I revelled in pleasure, squandered all I could
procure, and was led by one successful artifice to another, till I
became what I can certainly no otherwise justify than by the selfish
spirit of the world. In this I find the rule is for each to seize on all
that he can, with safety; and to swallow, hoard, or waste it at will.
I have attempted to profit by vice which I knew not how to avoid.
But, if there be a safer road to happiness, I am no idiot: I am as
desirous of pursuing it as you can be. The respect of the world, the
security from pains and penalties, and the approbation of my own
heart, are all of them as dear to me as to you. I have thought much,
have had much experience, and have the power of comparing facts
and sensations as largely perhaps as another.

'I will not deny that to trick selfishness by its own arts, to laugh
at its stupidity, and to outwit its contemptible cunning, are practices
that have tickled my vanity; and have perhaps formed one of my
chief sources of pleasure. But habit and pleasure led me to extend
such projects; and to prey upon the well-meaning, and the kind,
with almost as much avidity as on those of an opposite character.

'However, though I did not want plausible arguments in my own
justification, I cannot affirm that my heart was wholly at ease. New
thoughts have occurred, other prospects have been contemplated,
and my dissatisfaction has increased. You cannot but have remarked
that, in the course of human life, most men undergo more than
one remarkable change. The sober man becomes a drunkard, the
drunkard sober, and the spendthrift sometimes a rational economist:
though perhaps more frequently a miser.

'Yet, though I am disposed to alter my conduct, supposing me to
possess the means of bidding defiance to mankind, I have no
inclination to subject myself to their neglect, their pity, or their
scorn. Be it want of courage or want of wisdom, I have not an intention to shut myself out from society. If I may be admitted on fair
and liberal terms, I am content: but, I honestly tell you, admitted
I will be. I have shut the door of dependency upon myself, were

I so inclined. Offices of trust would not be committed to me. And to live rejected, in poverty and wretchedness, pointed at and pretended to be despised by the knaves and fools with whom the world is filled, is a condition to which I will never submit.

'Consequently, the property of which I have possessed myself I am in either case determined to use every effort to keep. If I am suffered to keep it quietly, my present inclinations are what I have been describing. If contention must come, we must then have a trial of skill upon the opposite system.'

I listened to this discourse, attentive to every sentence, anxious for the next, and agitated by various contradictory emotions. I saw the difficulties of the supposed case; and knew not what to answer, or what to advise. That a man like this should become what he seemed half to promise was a thought that consoled and expanded the heart. But that it should depend upon so improbable an event as that of another renouncing a claim, which the law gave him, to property in dispute, was a most painful alternative. My sensations were of hope suddenly kindled, and as suddenly killed.

After waiting some time without any reply from me, he added 'Let us suppose, Mr. Trevor, a whimsical, or if you please a strange, coincidence between the man with whom you have been so angry and myself. I mean Wakefield. What if he felt some of the sober propensities toward which I find a kind of a call in myself?'

'He is not to be trusted. In him it would be artifice: or at least nobody would believe it could be any thing else.'

'Mark now what chance there is, in a world like this, for a man whom it has once deemed criminal to reform. Oppressed, insulted, and pursued by the good, what resource has he but to associate with the wicked?'

'He that, with the fairest seeming and the most specious pretences, affirming time after time that, though he had deceived before, he now was honest, he that shall yet again and again repeat his acts of infamy cannot complain, if no man should be willing to trust his happiness to such keeping.'

'I find what I am to expect from you. The very same will be said of me.'

'No: you have not been equally unprincipled, and vile.'

'These are coarse or at least harsh terms. However, I take them to myself; and affirm that I have.'

'How can you make such an affirmation? How do you know?'

'A man may calculate on probabilities; and this is a moment in which I do not wish to conceal the full estimate which I make of my own conduct from you. Being therefore, seriously and speaking to the best of my judgment, as culpable as Wakefield, let my course of life hereafter be what it will, I find I am to expect no credit for sincerity from you?'

'You do not know Wakefield.'

'Neither it seems do you.'

'There is something in your countenance, in your conversation, and in the free and undisguised honesty even of your vices, that a man like Wakefield cannot possess.'

'Have you forgotten that, though I can be open and honest, I can be artful? Do you not remember billiards, hazard, and Bath?'

'Yes: but Wakefield would be incapable of the qualities of mind which you are now displaying. With you I feel myself in the company of a man of a perverted but a magnanimous spirit. With all your faults, I could hug you to my heart. But Wakefield! who made women and men alike his prey; to whose devilish arts the virtue and happiness of an amiable, I may say a charming, woman were sacrificed; and the life of one of the first of mankind was endangered; that he should resemble you, and especially that he should resemble you with your present inclinations, oh! would that were possible!'

'There is generosity in the wish. It denotes a power in you of allaying one of the most active fiends that torment mankind: the spirit of revenge.'

'It is a spirit I own to which I have been too subject; and which I could wish to exorcise for ever.'

'Put it to the test. Let us suppose you should discover as much of promise in Wakefield as you imagine you do in me.'

'I should then put *him* to the test. I should demand of him to repair the wrongs he has done Miss Wilmot!'

'What if you should find him already so disposed?'

'Impossible. Or if he were, it would be with some design!'

'Ay: perhaps a proposition that you should leave him quietly possessed of the disputed property.'

'And, having obtained that, he would desert his second wife as he had done his first.'

'There is some difference between a young woman and an old one. Beside, if your account be true, Mrs. Wakefield, though she was your mother, was very inferior to Miss Wilmot.'

'You forget that he seduced this lady, and deserted her.'

'I have heard or read of a man who, after being divorced even from a wife, became more passionately in love with her than ever.'

'Wakefield is incapable of love.'

'You frame to yourself a most black and deformed being of this Wakefield.'

'And you suppose a degree of sympathy, between yourself and him, which cannot exist.'

'Why not? His wit, person, and manners, I have heard you describe as winning.'

'I only gave the picture which I had from an affectionate though a most injured woman.'

'I recollect the story perfectly. When you repeated it, notwithstanding my raillery, I was more moved than you had reason to imagine. I am persuaded that Wakefield himself, had he listened to it, would have felt a few uneasy sensations.'

'I fear not.'

'Why so? Is he made of materials totally different from other men? Dissect him, and I imagine you will find he has a heart.'

'But of what quality?'

'Better than you at present seem to give him credit for.'

'What grounds have you for thinking so favourably of him?'

'Very excellent. Don't be surprised. I know the man.'

'Is it possible?'

'Where is the wonder? Knaves of other classes associate, and why should not gamblers?'

'It may be, then, you are deputed to speak in his behalf?'

'I wrote to you, and introduced this conversation, for that very purpose. I know him as intimately as I can know any man. I would speak of him as of myself, of his defects as of my own, and I declare it as my opinion that, if he might be permitted to enjoy his uncle's property in peace, he would change his system. To this property he supposes he has the best claim. He is Thornby's heir at law; and, as to the manner in which the wealth he left was acquired, if a general inquisition were made into the original right to every species of property, he is persuaded that ninety-nine rich men in a hundred would be turned into the streets to beg.'

'What you have related has greatly surprised me. You have pleaded and continue to plead his cause very powerfully: but have you no consideration for me? Granting all you have supposed in his favour possible, am I so situated as to justify a romantic renunciation of claims which, if asserted, may aid me to accomplish my dearest hopes?'

'To a man like you perhaps I could be contented to resign these claims. I need not say "perhaps": I am certain I could, were I thoroughly persuaded you would forsake a life of artifice and plunder, and were I myself only concerned.

'But that is not the case. I have an object to accomplish so dear to my heart that it swallows up lesser considerations, and will not allow me to neglect any honest means by which it may be promoted. Wealth to me is indispensible; wealth that shall place me on a level with a rich and proud family with which I have to contend. I have an impulse such perhaps as you have never felt. There is a woman in the world, endowed with such qualities that to say I passionately love her is a most impotent expression of what I feel: for to tenderness and ardour of affection must be added all that simplicity, purity, and grandeur of soul can inspire. To think of life without her is to think of a world sterile, desolate, and joyless: of a night to which day shall never succeed: and of existence arrested and chained in motionless despondency.'

'Which might be very pitiful; or very sublime: just as you please: but which would be very absurd.'

'Granted: but this is the fever of my mind; the disease to which, should my hopes be disappointed, I feel myself dangerously impelled.'

'The interpretation of all which is, that, though you have discovered principles, which if pursued would secure to yourself and mankind in general certain happiness, and that though you can deal forth their dogmas and point out the path which others indubitably ought to take, yet, when your own passions are concerned, you act like the rest of the world. And you do this, not blindly, as they do, but, with your eyes open; at the moment that you are reminded of your maxims, and acknowledge their truth.'

'Your accusation is premature. I have hitherto done nothing more than express my feelings and my doubts.'

'But these doubts, spurred on by these feelings, assure me that you will proceed against Wakefield.'

'You may think yourself assured: I conceive myself to be uncertain. I would willingly condemn myself to great punishment, were it to promote any plan of the goodness of which there should be a conviction. I can even suppose cases in which I would not only devote my life, for that in comparison appears to be a trifle, but would resign the woman whom my soul adores. Sacrifices like these however cannot be expected on light occasions. The good to be obtained ought to be evidently greater than the evil to be endured.'

He paused a moment to collect his ideas, and then replied.

'If, Mr. Trevor, you are the man of that eminent virtue which I have sometimes thought you, and to which by your discourse to me you have certainly made very lofty pretensions, I would advise you to reflect on what I shall once more state. I know that this Wakefield, of whom you think so ill, and who has been quite as guilty as you have supposed, is now inclined to be a different man. I would have you consider, first, to whom does the property in justice belong? I think you will find that to be doubtful. Next, supposing it to be legally yours, may you not nevertheless be defrauded of it by law? And, lastly, appeal to your own principles, and ask yourself whether it be not better that you should have a chance of doing the good which you conceive would be done, by recovering such a man as Wakefield to that respect in society by which his talents might be well employed; or whether it can be consistent with your own sense of right to take methods which you acknowledge to be precarious, and unjust, in order to dispossess him and to appropriate that to yourself to which, if you are impartial, you will perhaps find it difficult to prove, even to your own satisfaction, that you have a clear and undoubted claim?'

Through this whole scene, instead of diverting my attention from the argument by gay raillery, witty allusions, or a recurrence to the depravity of man, and the practice of the world, he kept closely to the question, preserved the tone of earnest discussion, and, having uttered what I have last repeated, took his leave with that serious air which he had thus unexpectedly assumed, and maintained.

CHAPTER II

The plan of Wakefield pursued, and the hopes and fears of an affectionate woman: News of Philip: An artless exculpatory tale

QUITTING the place, meditating on the scene that had passed, surprised at every part of it, at the interested manner of the man, at the intimate knowledge which he professed to have of Wakefield, at the promises and the threats which he appeared to make in his name, at the coincidence not only of their characters, if his account were true, but at their similar incidents of fortune and corresponding inclinations to reform, astonished while I recollected these various particulars, instead of returning immediately to my lodgings I called on Miss Wilmot.

When I came to the door, I had scarcely decided with myself whether it were advisable to relate what had passed to her, which as she was personally in question I thought myself bound to do whenever it could be done with safety; or whether, if related at present, it might not excite hopes that would be disappointed, and anxieties prejudicial to her peace.

She no sooner saw me than she exclaimed—'I am very glad you are come, Mr. Trevor! I have two unexpected affairs, on which I wish to consult you. One of them relates to myself; and I will begin with that because you are not only concerned in it but are appealed to in a very remarkable manner. I have received two extraordinary letters; by both of which I have been not a little affected. Pray read this first. It is from Mr. Wakefield. The promises it contains, the style it assumes, and the appeal it makes, are so strange as to appear either like miracle or romance.'

She then gave me a letter, and I read as follows.

'Should you imagine, Lydia, that because I have long forborn all intercourse with you I have forgotten you, be assured you are mistaken. I have treated you so shamefully, and deceived you so often, that I have little right to expect you should believe my professions, be moved by my intreaties, or remember me with any other feelings than those of hatred. Yet, to deal sincerely with you, this is what I do not expect. I have had such proofs of the kindness of your heart, and the strength of your affection, that my confidence is still entire.

'It is the more unshaken because my own intentions are direct: of which the plainness with which I shall deliver my thoughts will I imagine be some proof.

'I once more repeat, I have behaved to you like a —— Spare me the word. It is enough to recollect that I have been the thing. I could plead the extreme vivacity of my youth, my ungovernable passions, and the dangerous temptation of critical moments; but that I will not exhibit any feature of pitiful apology, or endeavour to extenuate what I cannot defend.

'You are intimate with Mr. Trevor. You know that his mother, my late wife, is dead; and you have heard of a will, said to have been left by my uncle. I feel but little scruple in affirming that I imbibed many of the vices of my early youth from being placed under this uncle's care. That such a man should die like a coward, and endeavour to disinherit a relation to save his soul, supposing this disinheritance to be true, would be no miracle. It would only be an act of contemptible stupidity.

'I will not here enter into any enquiries of a legal kind: for I will be open enough to own that, being in possession both in right of my wife and as the heir of my uncle of the property he left, and determined as I am to assert my claims, which I think paramount to those of any other person, I will not commit myself even to you. On the contrary, I write this letter purposely that you may shew it to Mr. Trevor.

'You will ask my motive for this, and perhaps will be surprised at my answer.

'By certain whimsical accidents, I have become acquainted with Mr. Trevor's principles. I believe, or I rather know, him to be possessed of a heart and understanding equally excellent. I wish to appeal to them both. When he shall read this, he will have had a conversation relating to me; which may have led him to expect the language I am about to use. In an argument concerning property he cannot forget that he lately delivered himself thus:

"If I strictly adhere to the principle of justice, I must not singly consider my own wishes; which may create innumerable false wants, and crave to have them gratified. I must ask is there no being, within my knowledge, who may be more benefited by the enjoyment of that which I am desirous to appropriate to myself than I can? If so, what right have I to prefer self gratification to superior utility?"

'Mine is a case in point.

'Again: property is left for which he may be induced to contend; and which, should he do so, will probably be dissipated in law. If not, it may with no less probability be decided by law to be mine. He affirms that to contend at law is immoral.

'Do you and he listen to what I have now to say.

'I am desirous of totally changing my conduct. I have a heart more capable of affection than you, Lydia, have reason to suppose; and I love you. My ambition at present is to do you much more good than I have ever done you harm. I am once more at my own disposal; and, unless that ardent love which you formerly bore me be entirely changed, which I do not believe it is, I am now sincerely desirous to make you my wife.

'But I will not deceive you. I can only be such a husband as you desire on condition of being left in quiet possession of that which I believe to be my own. I have ruined my character. Offices of emolument are not easily obtained; but, if they were, I am not a man to be trusted. I will not live a beggar; deprived of all the blessings in which the fools around me wallow, till they turn them into curses. I wish to live happily: unmolesting, and unmolested: but, if I must either prey or be preyed upon, I am still resolved rather to act the fox than the goose.

'I know you will condemn this determination; but I am speaking openly; and telling you what my intentions are, without entering into their defence.

'Supposing Mr. Trevor to be convinced that the law will decide the property contested in his favour, the sacrifice demanded of him is perhaps too great to be expected from any man. Yet, from what I have heard and what I know, this is the sacrifice that I do expect. I expect it from his abhorrence of pretending to seek justice by the aid of law. I expect it from that principle which decides in favour of the greatest good. And I expect it from the earnest desire I have heard him express that you might be restored to that happiness which, for a time, you have lost.

'Should he or you conclude that the motives I now urge originate in that artifice of which I have been very justly accused, I ought perhaps to feel no surprise, and shall certainly make no complaint. But, believe me or believe me not, I have spoken with a sincerity of heart for which I am likely to gain but little credit. Such I feel, at this moment, are the misfortunes to which cunning subjects itself. I am a man but little subject to fear: yet, I own, the fear of being thought still to possess nothing better than this cunning assaults me, obliges me to omit the tender epithets that are in my thoughts, and without addition to sign myself

F. WAKEFIELD.'

While I read, the eyes of Miss Wilmot were fixed upon my countenance. Whenever I looked toward her, I could perceive the strong emotions, of hope and fear, by which she was agitated.

When I had ended, I said—'Mr. Wakefield is indeed an extraordinary man! Be his intentions honest or base, the strength and clearness of his mind and his knowledge of the human heart, when we recollect how these faculties have been employed, are truly astonishing. If this be a plan of artifice, it is little less than miraculous. Yet who can believe it to be any thing else?'

Miss Wilmot heaved a deep sigh, and attempted to speak: but she only stammered. Her utterance failed; and her eyes were cast on the floor. Hope and despair were combating; and the latter was the strongest. She wished to confide, she wished to plead for the possibility of his being sincere: but the mischief he had inflicted, the deceit he had practised, and a remembrance of the picture she had formerly given me of him, rushed upon her mind; and her spirits sunk.

'Look up, lovely Lydia,' said I, taking her hand, 'and revive. There is, there must be hope. The man who could write this letter cannot be all villain.'

The struggle of the passions was violent. A momentary wildness, such as I had formerly witnessed, flashed in her eyes; she started from her seat, griped my hand, then bursting into tears exclaimed— 'Oh Mr. Trevor!' and dropped down again upon the chair.

Eager to relieve a heart so overcharged, I again addressed her. 'If,' said I, 'the property left by Mr. Wakefield's uncle can really be employed to so noble a purpose as that of reclaiming him and making you happy, let me perish rather than endeavour to counteract such blessings. Let me be the thing he so much dreads, a beggar: but let me obey the purest passions of the heart, when they are sanctioned by the best principles of the understanding.'

Till this instant she had forgotten that, if I consented to enrich him, I must rob myself. But the thought no sooner occurred than she cried, 'No! It must not be! It cannot be! To require it of you is infamous. It debases him, and would make me hate myself; were I to participate in such an action.'

'You judge too severely,' I replied. 'I am not so unfortunately circumstanced as he is. My character is not lost. I am not shut out of society. I have friends, plans, and prospects; and, granting him to be sincere, his arguments, as far as they relate to him and me, are I suspect unanswerable. Of that sincerity I would fain not doubt: but it is our mutual duty to be wary. Here therefore at present the matter shall rest. I am determined to bring no action, till time and future events shall teach me the course I ought to pursue.'

Overwhelmed by a sense of obligation, and by the thronging emotions of every kind that assailed her, she was again half suffocated with passion. As she recovered her eyes sufficiently spoke her feelings.

When she grew calm, she was led to ask what conversation I had had, and with whom, relative to Mr. Wakefield? I gave her the history of my acquaintance with the supposed Belmont, and of the scene that had passed that very day: which she thought altogether surprising, and seemed to shrink with the fear that it was an artful plan, contrived by artful men. She was in some sort appeased, however, when I once more reminded her of my determination to wait and hope for the best.

I then enquired concerning the second letter she had mentioned? To which she answered—'It is addressed to me, as a mediator: but relates entirely to you, and the person who wrote it; your poor penitent servant, Philip.'

She gave it me; and these were its contents.

'Honoured madam,

'I make bold to lay my case before you; which as it is very grievous I hope it may move you to pity me. I am the young man that lived with my honoured master Mr. Trevor; in the same house, madam, that you are pleased to live. My name is Philip. I have been guilty of a very great fault; for which my conscience worries me night and day. So that I am sure I shall never forgive myself: though I take my holy saviour to witness it was more a mistake than a thought of committing so wicked a crime. I was in a flurry, so that I did not know what I was about; for to think of having robbed a master that was so kind to me is such a sin and a shame as never was. But I had no notion but that my poor dear master had drowned himself in the river; and so, as he had told me the day before to make up my account and he would pay me the next morning, I thought it was hard that I should lose my wages and the money beside which I had laid out for washing, and newspapers, and tea, and sugar, and other materials of that kind: which, though my wages *was* only eight pounds eight shillings, made up the whole to twelve pounds five and threepence three farthings. Which was the reason to make me do so base a thing as it would else have been as to break open the box, and take out a ten pound note, and four pair of stockings, and two waistcoats: because I knew very well my master's kindness so that it is ten to one if he had lived to make his will he would have given me them and more. After which I hurried away: being as I was told of a place, with an old master that I was sure would take me again. But I had no more thought that Mr. Trevor was living than the child unborn: which since I discovered I have never been at rest; being out of place, and having nobody now to ask for a character, which is the greatest misfor*tin* that can behappen a poor servant that never was guilty of such an action as breaking open his master's box, and running away with his money and things, in all my life before, or since. So that I was tempted to list for a soldier; but that I happened, honoured madam, to meet your maid Mary, and she persuaded me to write to Mr. Trevor: which I durst not do, though I know his goodness. So she said your honoured ladyship would be so kind and tender hearted as to lay my case before Mr. Trevor, and my dear and honoured mistress, Miss Mowbray, both of *which* I would run to the world's end to serve. On which she said she was sure they would take my case into merciful consideration, and grant me their gracious forgiveness.

'Which is the humble petition of your distressed servant to command, honoured madam.

PHILIP FRANKS.'

Poor fellow! Forgive thee? What is thy crime? An inaccuracy. A mistake of judgment. A desire to do thyself right, without intentional wrong to me or any one. Yet for this mistake, differently circumstanced, thou mightest have lost thy life, and have been hanged like a dog!

I too accused thee of robbery, of taking more than thy due, when thou tookest less. Hadst thou offered thy old waistcoats and stockings to a street hawker, he would not have given thee half the surplus that was thy due.

Such were the reflections that broke from me, after perusing his simple but affecting defence.

Mary was called up, and questioned. She knew where he lived: for the poor, little inclined to suspicion, confide in each other. It is the rich only that tempt them to be treacherous.

After consulting with Miss Wilmot, it was determined that she should write to Olivia; enclosing Philip's letter, and requesting her to give him a character. I knew she would take care to see him paid the wages that were his due; and, as I had been the cause of his want of employment since the fright he took at Cranford-bridge, I left money to reimburse him for the loss of his time from that period.

The people I mixed with, and the prejudices of the world, required that I should keep a servant: but, though the man that was with me was by no means so great a favourite as Philip had been, I did not think I had sufficient cause to discharge him for another. There was an additional motive for not wishing Philip to be my servant again; at least not under my present circumstances. Olivia's aunt had imagined we were in league, at Cranford-bridge; and, should she see him once more in my service, that suspicion might either be revived or strengthened.

CHAPTER III

The period of contention approaches, and the unabated patriotism of the Baronet: Hector and the Earl become enemies, and I am made the subject of newspaper calumny: Threatening appearances: A journey projected: A tragical event, giving occasion to the practice of some small portion of humanity

THE dissolution of parliament was hourly expected. Flying reports fixed it to happen on different days; but none of them very distant. The zeal of Sir Barnard, in behalf of his country and its constitution, was unabated. The measures of ministry were wicked beyond example; and the servility of parliament was unequalled, since the time of the Tudors. Such was the Baronet's continual theme.

From him, and the political circles I frequented, I heard news in which I might be said to be personally concerned. In consequence of the firm refusal of Olivia, a rupture had taken place between Lord Idford and the family: much at first to the regret of the Mowbrays; till the turn that the quarrel took enflamed the latter.

Hector Mowbray had great property, and influence, in the county of which he and I were both natives. Of this county the Earl was the Lord Lieutenant; and here he likewise had his dependents, and partisans. The Mowbrays were wealthy; and Hector was ambitious of being elected knight of the shire. When it was first proposed, the aunt forwarded the project: for there was no probability that any other candidate so powerful should start. The joint interest of the Earl and the Mowbrays would defy opposition.

The Earl however understood traffic; and, finding himself so positively refused by Olivia, he thought proper to inform the family that she must either be induced to consent, or, instead of aiding to bring Hector into parliament, he should himself propose and support another candidate with the whole weight of his interest.

The threat was galling. It was insinuated first to the aunt; and, when Hector was informed of it, he affected to vapour and treat it with defiance; but, on better consideration, he and the aunt thought proper to importune Olivia, hoping they should oblige her to comply. Threats and intreaties alike were vain. Her resolution was not to be shaken; and the Earl more openly declared that, if she should think proper to persist, he would beggar himself rather than Hector should carry his election.

Hector had been canvassing the county, had subscribed to races, been present at the assizes, given public dinners, and taken various means to increase his popularity; of which he had become inordinately vain. Inflated therefore with a certainty of victory, he threw down the gauntlet, and dared the Earl to the field.

In the mean time, paragraphs appeared in a morning and an evening paper, both of them sold to Government, and the echoes of each other, that were evidently aimed at me, and my connections. At first I could not have conceived how I should have attracted the attention of those worthy gentlemen, who earn their bread by the daily manufactory of lampoons: but I was soon informed that this is become a regular branch of business; and that the motives to carry it on are many. These motives originate in paymasters, of various descriptions: of whom the treasury is supposed to be the chief.[1]

The libels, of which I was the subject, aimed to be satirical; but were too dull of wing to hit their mark: they were only malignant. They could neither tickle the fancy nor gall the heart; but they proved that I had lurking enemies, who wished to wound, did they but know when and where to strike.

It was well known that my professedly dear friend, Glibly, was principally concerned in the morning paper where these libels generally appeared. When I first became acquainted with him, he affected indifference to parties; and was ready to praise or laugh at either, as circumstances should happen to direct him: but, when the temper of the times became intolerant and acrimonious, he thought it prudent to take a decided part. That such a man should declare in favour of the weakest was not to be expected; and he now associated with the known hirelings of ministry, of whom I was a still more open and undisguised opponent.

By these attacks on me, Glibly therefore, for they were undoubtedly a part of his handy-work, Glibly, I say, had a three-fold motive. He indulged a propensity, which strange to say he had acquired, of wounding in the dark, that he might smile and shake hands with the insulted person in broad day; he answered the end for which ministry retained him, that of decrying all its antagonists; and he particularly forwarded the views of another of his dear friends, the Earl.

The general complexion of paragraphs like these is falsehood; which is sometimes direct, though it is more commonly a perversion of existing facts. The pamphlet I had written, which had been partially made known to the public by the advertisement that had appeared, the patronage of Sir Barnard, my ambitious views on the Mowbray family, with such other particulars as the indefatigable Glibly could collect, sometimes delivered in obscure allusions and at others more openly, were the topics of calumny. How many of these ingenious devices to irritate and injure were framed I never knew: for I seldom read them myself, though I heard of them sufficiently often to be assured that they were numerous.

There were various means by which they might have been stopped; and of which, in ordinary cases bribing is chiefly practised: but in this instance fighting, or the law, would have been more effectual. Of these however I totally disapproved. Defamation is an evil: but death is generally and perhaps always a greater; and to prevent enquiry is among the worst of evils. I was not yet sufficiently acquainted, however, with the mistakes to which men are subject, or rather impelled by the institutions they admire, not to feel great surprise and some indignation at the obstacles which I found were continually to impede my career. He who has never travelled into the country of Mosquitoes is not aware how slight a net-work covering will preserve him from their sting.

These were trifles, and would have been unworthy of notice had they not resembled the small cloudy speck, which, though scarcely visible in the distant horizon, approaches, and swells, and bursts over the head in a storm. The beginning contest between the Earl and the Mowbray family, the interest which the worthy Mr. Glibly had thought proper to take in me and my affairs, the patriotism of Sir Barnard, nay the friendship of Mr. Evelyn himself, that best of men, were but so many links in the chain of that fate which was impending.

At present, however, with respect to the Baronet, I daily increased in favour. He frequently requested me to accompany him when he went down to the house; and paraded with me, arm in arm, through the avenues: catching every man he knew by the button, and introducing me; then descanting on the news of the day, the victories of the minister among his creatures and in the house, and the defeats of his projects every where else.

At length it was generally affirmed and believed that parliament would be dissolved in a fortnight; and, as Sir Barnard wished to keep well with his borough, he proposed that we should go down and visit the worthy and independent electors: among whom he observed we might spend a few days in a pleasant manner, and advantageously to his interest, till the writ of election should be issued. This was on the Wednesday: but, as there was to be a debate and probably a division of the house on Friday, his sense of public duty would not permit him to be absent on such an occasion, and we agreed to defer our journey till Saturday morning.

During this short interval an incident occurred, which it is necessary I should relate. It happened on the Thursday that, after spending the day near Richmond, where I had been invited to dine, I was returning home on horseback, followed by my servant: for I thought myself obliged to practise some part of that aristocracy which I nevertheless very sincerely condemned.

The night was starlight; and, as we were cantering down a lane at the entrance of Barnes common, we heard distant cries and the report of a pistol, in the direction as we believed in which we were proceeding. I immediately stopped, and listened very attentively: but all was soon silent. Being convinced as well by the cries as the firing of the pistol that a robbery, if not something worse, had been committed, and not certainly knowing from what point the sound came, I rode gently forward and continued to listen with the utmost attention: desiring my servant to do the same.

We rode on, still walking our horses and looking cautiously round for some time, without any sight or sound of man approaching us, till we came to a gate at the edge of the common. Here I saw a horse standing patiently, without his rider; and stopping once more to look and listen, I presently perceived an indistinct object: which I discovered to be a man; wounded and weltering in his blood.

I spoke to him: but no answer was returned, nor any sound. I then raised the body in my arms, and it appeared to be lifeless.

What was to be done? A human being, who might be dead or might not, in either case, must not be left in such a situation.

The neighbourhood is populous, and I could distinguish lights at no very great distance. Fearing lest, if I sent my servant he should blunder, or that the persons he might address himself to would be less likely to pay attention to him than to me, I bade him remain by the dead or wounded man; and, mounting my horse, I rode away immediately to procure aid.

My direction was across the common; and fortunately I met with a carriage, which proved to be a hackney coach returning to town with two passengers. I ordered the coachman to stop, and he immediately supposed I was a highwayman: but, being undeceived, he refused to go out of his way for the purpose I required.

The persons within, hearing a kind of squabble, and understanding when they listened the nature of it, spoke to me; and enquired into the particulars. By good luck, they happened to feel properly, and joined me against the coachman; who, though unwillingly, was obliged to submit; and, when he came to the point where the roads join, to turn back and receive the wounded man into the carriage. The passengers alighted, I ordered my man to take the horse of the stranger in charge, and we proceeded slowly to the first inn.

Here I immediately enquired for surgical and medical assistance;

and, as the people of these villages are many of them opulent, good practitioners were presently procured.

While the messengers were dispatched, I had leisure to examine the stranger; whose appearance, figure, and countenance, were altogether extremely interesting. His hair was abundant, but milk white, his features were serene, and his form in despite of age was still manly. The benevolence of his countenance was heightened by the blood with which his locks were in part clotted, and that had streamed over his face upon his clothes and linen.

The medical gentlemen arrived nearly at the same time, the stranger was examined, the pulsation of the heart was perceptible, and, though the contusions on the head and the temple were violent, and he had been shot in the shoulder, so that the ball had passed through behind, they were of opinion, as there was no fracture of the skull, that the wounds were not mortal. The appearance of the stranger, and the condition in which I found him, had made a lively impression upon me. I was fearful of leaving him, in an unknown place, amidst the casualties and hurry of an inn, to the care of waiters, and the neglect of persons who had scarcely leisure to be humane. I therefore determined to send my servant to town, and stay with him that night. I had an appointment and other business in the morning; but I could be at London in less than an hour: that was therefore no obstacle.

Hoping to have discovered his place of abode, I desired his pockets to be searched before the people present: but they were entirely emptied; and contained no paper, or memorandum, that could afford information.

After some time, by the aid which was procured, his pulse began to quicken, and his lungs to do their office; and, that nothing might be omitted, I prevailed on the physician to remain with me at his bed-side, and attend to every symptom, above half the night. With this he the more willingly complied because he was apprehensive of fever, when the circulation should recover all its elasticity.

In the morning, though very unwillingly, I was obliged to forsake my charge: but not till I had left money with the physician, who made himself accountable to the innkeeper for all expences. Being a humane person, I believe he would have done this without my interference. But in addition to that every mark about the stranger, his look, his dress and the horse on which he was mounted, denoted him to be a gentleman; and when I left him, though the physician thought it was probable he might not recover the use of his understanding and the power of speech for a day or two, he yet was persuaded that he would not die.

CHAPTER IV

An incident in the park, or the danger of unruly dogs and horses: The fortitude and affection of Olivia: A visit to the wounded stranger

KNOWING the habits of Sir Barnard to be precise, and pettish, so that if I counteracted the arrangement he had made it would put him into a disagreeable temper, I resolved, as we were to depart early the next morning, to return as soon as possible to the stranger. About two in the afternoon, I was riding through the park for this purpose: and here another incident occurred; which, though it excited extreme terror, it afterward afforded uncommon delight.

A few days before, I had witnessed a lady on a run-away horse, who was seized with fright, dropped from the saddle, and bruised herself exceedingly. She would have been in no danger, if she had behaved but with the ordinary resolution of a man; and the accident led me to reflect on the ill education to which women are subjected. They seem to be esteemed by men in proportion as they are help-less, timid, and dependent. It is supposed they cannot be affectionate unless their leading feature be imbecility.

Just as I had crossed the bridge over the Serpentine river, two ladies and a gentleman with their grooms, all on horseback, were turning round; and went off in a hand gallop toward Kensington gardens. I was riding fast, at no great distance; and perceived it to be Olivia, her aunt, and some person whom I did not know. Olivia was mounted on a fine blood horse; and a large dog rushed by him in pursuit of me, being tempted by my fast galloping.

The horse of Olivia had previously been put upon his mettle. I saw the danger, and instantly pulled up: but he began to plunge, and kick, in a manner that would have unhorsed most men. The dog then turned from me, and attacked the animal that was highest in motion; and the horse immediately set off full speed. The foolish servant, being frightened, began to gallop after her. I was obliged to do the same, and stop him: for the clattering of feet behind did but increase the fury of the runaway horse.

Terrified however as I was, when I first noticed the vicious propensities of the horse, the courage of Olivia was such, her seat was so firm, and she kept so steady a hold of the strong curb rein, that I felt a confidence she would overpower the horse; if the fear and folly of some other person should do no mischief. I therefore followed at a proper distance; and, when I saw several horsemen who attempted to cross her, I shouted and waved my hat for them to keep off.

My hopes were justified. She avoided every danger, by her management and presence of mind; and, by her use of the curb and the aid of the wall at the end of the ride, arrested the course of the intemperate animal.

Having kept the grooms back, I was the first that came up with her; and, leaping from my saddle, I seized the reins and held them till the servant arrived. I then enjoyed one more rapturous moment, such as I had indeed but little foreseen: I received her in my arms.

Not a minute before, how firm and collected had her mind and actions been: but no sooner did she feel my embrace than her frame was suffused. A thousand ideas, that had no relation to the danger which her own fortitude had escaped, immediately rushed upon her; she sunk upon my shoulder, and burst into a flood of tears. They were the heart easings of ten thousand of the foregone anxieties of love.

How could I have hated the broad day, and the prying eyes that were upon us! How welcome would the fogs and darkness of Cranford-bridge have been! My adventurous spirit would then have surely imprinted the first kiss of love! as chaste as it would have been ecstatic.

This bliss, alas, was not to be. The crowd approached. I pressed her hand, and, as an assurance of fidelity, she gently returned the token of kindness. Such mute signs being all that were permitted.

Perceiving I must leave her, I again requested she would not mount the unruly horse; and she replied, with a heavenly smile, 'Have no fear for me. I will be careful of myself;' to which she added in a low whisper: 'for my preserver's sake!'

Oh moments of unutterable bliss! Who can estimate your worth? One of you will outweigh a life, such as the dull round of common place nothings can yield.

Did not my eyes thank her? Did not the strong workings of my colour and countenance inform her of what was passing within? Oh yes! And in the same language she involuntarily replied. He who shall suppose there was one emotion which celestial purity might not approve cannot comprehend Olivia. They were emanations such as those only who have souls, as well as bodies, are acquainted with.

The tide of ecstacy must turn. The aunt came up, I bowed, she returned my salute in a manner that shewed her mind was affected by contradictory emotions, and I mounted my horse and guided his head toward the Park gate; through which I passed; feeling, at the moment, that I was passing the gate of paradise.

I had not however left all my heaven behind me. No: I bore with me ample stores for delicious revery. The fortitude of Olivia, the firm and easy grace with which she kept her seat, her admirable management and quick presence of mind, her unabating courage at one moment, and her melting tenderness at the next, were not the food but the feast of love.

In this revelry of the imagination I indulged, till I arrived at the inn; where I found the physician, agreeable to appointment; and was informed by him that the stranger still continued insensible: but that the symptoms appeared to be rather more than less favourable.

I remained with the patient during some hours, till the necessary preparation for my journey obliged me to depart. I then left a sufficient sum with the physician; and, after most earnestly recommending the stranger to his care, reluctantly returned to town.

Though I had obtained a promise, from the physician, that the patient should be removed to his own home, as soon as it should be discovered, or to the house of the physician, whenever it might be done without danger, I yet could not help questioning whether to leave him to the mercy of persons, with whom I was unacquainted, that I might take a journey to visit the free and independent electors of an English borough, were faithfully to fulfill the duties of humanity. Add to which the venerable and benevolent appearance of the stranger was so uncommonly interesting that it made a strong impression upon my imagination.

But it was necessary to decide, and I acted as mortals are obliged to do on such occasions: not knowing what was best, I adopted that which appeared to be the most urgent.

CHAPTER V

*The journey to the borough of the Baronet: Independent
electors, and their motives satisfactorily explained: Evil
communication corrupts good manners: Electors eager to make
hay while the sun shines, and being once bought wish again
to be bribed*

THE following morning at the hour appointed, Sir Barnard and
I set off for the borough of ****: at which we arrived without delay
or accident.

The number of voters was little more than thirty; and the first
business, after our arrival, was to invite them to a dinner.

It has long been remarked that men in a body will be guilty of
actions of which individually they would each be ashamed. In an
assembly, however, the purpose of which is conscious iniquity, few,
who have not witnessed such scenes, will be aware of the efforts
that each man will make to argue himself into a belief of his own
upright intentions: or of the eager assent with which his endeavours
will be seconded by his associates.

In the present instance, for example, what were the motives of the
worthy electors? Sir Barnard explained them, to the perfect satisfaction of all parties.

But what were they? The love of the constitution: the honest
struggles that honest men were making to displace a corrupt
minister: their very eager and laudable attempts to free an oppressed
and ruined country, relieve it of its taxes, recover its trade, and
revive the glory of old England: to effect these great and good
purposes was the whole and sole end at which they aimed. Were all
the electors through all the boroughs, cities, and counties of Great
Britain but as virtuous as those of the borough of ****, it would
indeed be a happy land.

Yet, strange to say, what different masks does self-assuming
virtue wear! State the per contra. Imagine only how many free and
independent electors were at this period exulting, in a similar
manner, at the purity of their own conduct; while giving their votes
for the support of government, the maintenance of order, and to
preserve the immaculate statesman, the saviour of the nation, the

great financier, the first of orators, the admiration of Europe, and the wonder of the world, in power!

Who will deny that a general election is the season when all the disinterested virtues, all the pure patriotism, all the most generous and best qualities of the soul are called into action? How are the morals of the people improved! To what a height of grandeur does human nature rise; and how captivating is the point of view in which it is seen! Æra of incomprehensible excellence!

Can it be supposed that I, who was to be the representative of such free and noble souls, through whose lips their patriotic spirits were to breathe, I, in whom one five-hundredth part of the virtue of the whole island was to be compressed, and bottled up ready for use, being as I was in company with sages whose office it was to choose one still more sage than themselves, thus circumstanced, was it possible that I should not imbibe some portion of their sublime wisdom? Had I no sympathy? Were all my affections and passions and patriotism extinct?

Oh no! Mocking, says the proverb, is catching: and, however in my sober moments, among sober people, reasoning on objects at a distance, I might systematise and legislate for the conduct of myself and others, being an actor in the scene, whether its atmosphere were healthy or contagious, I never yet found that I could wholly escape imbibing a part of the effluvia. I gave toasts, made speeches, sung songs, ay and wrote them too, and became so incorporated with my constituents, lovers as they were of liberty, that, the cut of our cloaths and countenances excepted, I might in this moment of overflowing sapience have been taken for one of themselves.

I was little aware, however, when I consented to make this journey, of its consequences. Disinterested as these worthy voters were, and purchased by wholesale as they had been when the family of the Brays bought the borough, they yet had wives and daughters; who wore watches, and rings, and gowns; and who would each of them think themselves so flattered, by a genteel present from me, that there was no describing the pleasure it would give them! Every *particular* about me told them I was very much of a gentleman.

Beside which, one lady had a great affection for a few pounds of the best green tea, bought in London. Another discovered that the loaf sugar in the country was abominable. A third could not but think that a few jars of India pickles, and preserved ginger, would be a very pretty present. It would always remind her of the giver. A fourth could not but say she *did* long for a complete suit of lace; cap, handkerchief, and ruffles: and so on through the whole list.

The men too were troubled with their longings. With one it was London porter: with another it was Cheshire cheese and bottled beer. They would both drink to the donor. Their neighbour longed very vehemently indeed for the horse I rode: and, finding that the animal was too great a favourite to be parted with, he compounded for twelve dozen of old port.

When these hints, which looked very like demands, were first given me, I applied to Sir Barnard; doubting much whether any of them ought to be complied with: but he let me understand that such things were politic, and customary; and that a seat in parliament, even when bestowed, was not to be had free of expence.

What could be done? To have required him to pay these disbursements would have had so much the appearance of meanness, that it was what I could not propose. To request a loan in advance of Mr. Evelyn was sufficiently grating to the feelings: but he had a liberal spirit, it was the least painful of the two, and I had no other resource. Fortune was whetting the darts she soon intended to hurl.

CHAPTER VI

News from Mowbray petitioning for aid: The period of universal uproar arrives, and the Baronet pursues his patriotic purposes: A few sketches of a county contest at a general election: Hector loving in his liquor: Qualms of conscience, which are thought very unseasonable and very ridiculous: The incomprehensible defection of Sir Barnard, and the suspicion that lights on me

WHILE we were spending our time in this 'pleasant manner, and advantageously to the Baronet's interest,' we received intelligence of our quondam friends, the Earl and young Mowbray; who were canvassing the county, in which they had vowed opposition to each other, with indefatigable zeal: so that a ruinous contest, probably to both parties, was predicted.

In this county Sir Barnard himself had some interest: for he had some lands there: and Hector prevailed on a common friend to write in a very urgent style to the Baronet, requesting his aid. How could so great a lover of his country as Sir Barnard, indignant too as he felt himself at the apostacy of the Earl, refuse a request by which his own patriotic purposes might be forwarded?

At length parliament was dissolved; and the whole kingdom was immediately in a tumult. Driving, rioting, and uproar began. God help the poor post-horses, hostlers, and chambermaids!

The writ for the Baronet's borough was made out, his agents were ready, and, as there could be no opposition, our business was soon over. It was high time: for my pocket was tolerably drained. And as the worthy electors very industriously compared notes, when any one of them discovered that the present made to his neighbour was of greater value than the *compliment* which he had received, I had immediate intimation of my own injustice: which it was expected I should correct.

This serious business settled, and these accounts closed, the Baronet now had leisure to think of his friends; and he turned his thoughts to the annoying of Lord Idford. He had purchased me as well as his borough: for he had made me his own member, and meant to profit by me in all possible ways. He had discovered my electioneering talents. I was very engaging among the women: a matter of no small moment in such affairs: and 'though I was rather shy of my glass, yet I could sing an excellent song, which I could likewise make, quite suitable to the occasion.' He therefore proposed that we should both journey into my native county, and there exercise all our wit and ingenuity, to aid in bringing in my old school-fellow, Hector.

It cannot be supposed that, in an affair where the family and the brother of Olivia were so seriously implicated, I could be totally unconcerned. With respect to the question of who was the most virtuous, or the most wise, who the greatest orator, the best patriot, or the properest person to take a seat among the grand national council of sages, the Earl or the 'Squire, that was not easily determined. It was a point therefore that did not disquiet my conscience. My compliance was consequently given with a hearty good will; and we both prepared for the holy work.

How it happened that the vice which inevitably attaches itself to such conduct, self-evident, gross, and glaring as it is, fatal to private morals and public virtue, odious in its practice and hellish in its consequences, how the baneful complexion of this monster vice should at first so totally escape me is more than I can declare. Hurry of thought, confusion of intellect, and eagerness of passion are the only probable conjectures I can make. My mind was so intent on the manner in which I could best prove my respect for Olivia, and all that related to her, that this appears to have been a gulph vast enough for all recollection, sense, and idea!

A post-chaise and four soon brought us to the field of battle; and then I own my blood began to circulate, and my feelings to awaken. Still it was but gradually that my spirits mounted to the proper tone.

Before we entered the place where the election was to be held, we heard the jangling of bells and the shouts of men. The postillions spared neither whip nor spur; and, as we galloped furiously along the streets, the people came swarming out: the women and children saluting us with their shrill trebles; and, it being dark, the men crowding to follow with torches and more sonorous hubbub. Every inn was a scene of confusion. When we drove up to that which was the head-quarters of Hector, his partisans immediately flocked round us, and, a courier having previously announced our arrival, saluted Sir Barnard with all the force of lungs they could heave: elated in proportion to the uproar they made.

The 'Squire and his friends, vociferous though they were, and heated with anticipated triumphs, wine and wassail, heard the glorious din, learned its cause, and came reeling forth to embrace their puissant ally. Quitting as they did the fumes of buttocks and sirloins, gammons and hams, turkies and geese, wines, brandies, beers and tobacco, they all came reeking; each involved in his own atmosphere.

Their joy was boisterous, and not to be repulsed. Hector was as drunk as the animal that brought the royal David his sucking pigs;[1] and as loving as the monster in the Tempest.[2] He could not indeed curse so poetically: but what he wanted in variety he supplied by repetition; and his oaths and his raptures were countless.

He bestowed a part of them upon me; for, not only did feasting make him fond, but, he had just memory enough left to recollect that I was now become an M.P. and he was not quite sure whether, till he had gained his election, I might not at present be almost as great a man as himself. I was moreover his electioneering friend: which virtue would, for a fortnight to come, be inestimable.

I had been disgusted with the eating and drinking required at the ready-bought borough of ****: but that was abstinence itself, compared to the scene in which I had consented to become an actor. Away the Baronet and I were dragged, by the most jovial crew: Hector our leader, and seating himself in state at our head.

'Clean glasses!' bellowed the hero; and, seizing his own, smashed it against the wall: commanding us to follow his noble example. Midway drunkenness disdains to think: all arms were raised, and destruction was impending. Fortunately, there were two sober men in company; and, seeing what had happened, we both loudly called —'Forbear!' 'You have cut one of the waiters,' added I; addressing myself to Hector, and pointing to a man whose face was smeared with blood. 'Damn him!' retorted the brave Hector. 'Put him down in the bill.' The mighty man was pleased at his own second-hand wit; and, as an old joke is the soonest understood, they all joined in the laugh.

Eager to make the new comers welcome, that is as drunk as himself, Hector insisted that the Baronet and I should drink three bumpers each; and, as the fatigue of travelling had rendered this no difficult task, we complied.

He then swore we would *set to* for the night; but I perceived that his night would not be a long one. Toasts were called for, however, and liquor was swallowed, till its vapours half deprived the redoubted Hector of the faculty of speech. At this period, he began to mutter nonsense, on a subject on which I should have been better pleased with his silence than his praise. He made the lovely Olivia his theme; and in the fulness, not of his heart, but, of his stomach, told me how dearly she loved me—'Yes, my boy, she does, by G—! And she's right! Damn me, she's right! I say it; by G—, my boy, she's right! You are my friend!—You are my friend, and she's right. And as for Lord kiss —— damn me, he's a sneaking scoundrel! I say it, a sneaking ——! So she's right! Damn me, she's right!'

He continued to repeat his oaths, and 'She's right,' till, entirely overpowered, he sunk; and would have dropped from his chair, if the waiter whom he had cut with the glass had not caught him. Some of the guests had withdrawn, some were sleeping, and some were senseless: but the few who could open their eyes, and see to such a distance, triumphed in the defeat of their leader: which they considered as victory to themselves.

Riot now paused per force. The Baronet pleaded fatigue, and retired. I followed his example, and once more found myself alone; left to ruminate on the methods which men take to make each other happy; on their different modes of happiness, in their different stations: and on waiters who, being maimed or killed, are to be charged in the bill.

Though these thoughts were not of the most delightful kind, they did not prevent me from sleeping. The new day brought new cares; and presented projects, in which I was required to take my part, that led me to very serious meditations indeed. The poll was to begin that day week; and Hector and his friends, roused from the torpor of overloaded revelry by the importance of the business, assembled to consider how they should best collect and marshal the voters of whom they supposed themselves to be certain, and cajole and bring over such as they imagined might be gained.

Of this labour each man was to take his allotted share; and direct bribery was openly proposed as the general medium by which the great end in question was to be promoted.

This was what I had not foreseen. I was not only young but, as I have before remarked, I had thought but little on the affair: except as it continually presented the image of Olivia to my mind. I now found myself most painfully situated. I had discovered principles of human conduct in which I had gloried. I had asserted them unsparingly; and had promised myself that from them I would never depart. In doubtful cases, I might decide and act erroneously: but, when the way was clear, my conduct should be the same.

These principles I was required to abandon; and the shock was severe. The transactions which had lately passed in the Baronet's borough increased the difficulty. In what light could the presents that I had made be considered? In what were they different from and how much better than bribes? To these I had submitted when my own interest was in question. Again: for what purpose had I consented to accompany Sir Barnard, if not to exert myself in favour of his friend? And not only his friend but the brother of Olivia; though this was a silent grief, known only to myself. However I stated my scruples: which, as soon as they were heard, were the subject of laughter. I repeated them in a still more serious tone, and was reminded of the facts, and motives which I have just been mentioning.

The struggle was violent. The arguments I had to urge were

something like insults, on every body present that heard me; and I was answered sometimes with ridicule, at others with anger, and not unfrequently with something very like contempt.

The Baronet in particular augured very unfavourably, concerning the subserviency which he expected from me; and once or twice spoke in a very dictatorial tone: but, finding himself answered with no little indignation, he had no remedy but to chew the cud in silence.

Assailed on all sides, as it happened I had the good sense, in despite of every mockery and insinuation, to remain firm; and the only part I could be prevailed upon to take determinately was that of aiding in a fair and open canvas, leaving those who were less conscientious to distribute bribes. As it was imagined however that I possessed some abilities, my services were accepted on my own conditions.

Meanwhile the waste that was committed, the bribes that were paid, and the money that was squandered in every way, as well in London, where voters were eagerly purchased and sent down by coach loads, as in distant parts of the county and kingdom, convinced me that the sums which this election would cost must be enormous. I even thought it my duty to take an opportunity, in one of Hector's half sober moments, to remonstrate with all the arguments and energy I could collect; and endeavoured to persuade him to decline the poll. But my efforts were useless. He was equally vain of his wealth and his influence. His purse perhaps was as deep as that of the proud peer; his friends as numerous; and he would carry his election though he were to mortgage every foot of land he possessed.

Finding him resolved, I became anxious in his behalf, strained every nerve, rode in all directions night and day, and so effectually exerted myself in enquiring who were the independent men likely to be influenced by honest motives, that I procured him above fifty votes.

With respect to himself, the continual drinking, vociferating, and riot of the scene had made him so hoarse that, previous to the day of election, his husky whispers were not audible.

The evening before the poll opened, an incident occurred for which, at that time, I knew not how to account. It was no less amazing than incomprehensible. I had returned very much fatigued, after hard riding, and found a message had been left for me by Sir Barnard; who desired to speak with me immediately.

I obeyed the summons, and found him alone. He opened the conversation in a strange blustering tone: complaining of having been neglected, or insulted; he did not seem to know which; and, to my astonishment, declared his satisfaction at the scruples which I had professed. He knew not what to say to such corrupt proceedings. Perhaps an honest man ought to have no concern in them; and, for his own part, he certainly should trouble himself no farther on the present occasion. He had met with but little thanks for what he had already done; and he had come to a resolution not to bring up his voters.

Acquainted with the corrupt arts by which the promises of these voters, generally speaking, had been gained, I knew not what to reply: though I felt no little chagrin. With the aid of Sir Barnard, it was supposed that Mowbray's election would certainly have been carried: but without that aid I was persuaded it would as certainly be lost.

This opinion I forcibly repeated: adding that, though elections like these were destructive beyond description to the general happiness, and though I could not defend having taken any part whatever in one of them, yet the mischief in the present instance had already been done. If Sir Barnard had received any insult, or even suffered any neglect, I intreated that he would permit me to be the mediator, and state his griefs: being persuaded, from all I had seen, that nothing injurious to his person or his interest had been intended.

His answers were evasive. He acted as men frequently do, who have some secret purpose which they dare not avow: he affected that waspish irritation of temper to which he was subject on many occasions; but on none so frequently as when he suspected himself to be wrong.

While we were in the heat of this discourse, a chaise and four drove up to the door. It was for the Baronet. His trunk and mine were both prepared, by his orders. The men were buckling the former behind the carriage; and he requested me to accompany him to town.

I was thunderstruck! I could neither account for such sullen intemperance nor the secrecy of this haste. I again urgently intreated I might acquaint Mr. Mowbray, and his committee: but he peremptorily refused, and repeated his desire that I would accompany him immediately. No arguments, no prayers, could move him: so that, at last, I hastily left the room, in search of Hector and his friends.

He guessed my intention, and as soon as I was gone stepped into the chaise and ordered the boys to drive away full speed: leaving me behind to act as I should think proper; but with a message that, if I wished to oblige him, I must mount my horse and ride after him with all expedition. I might overtake him at the next inn; and our servants and horses would then follow at leisure.

It was some time before I could find Mowbray, or any of his party. They were at another inn, promoting the good cause; and, when I informed them of the intentions of Sir Barnard, they scarcely could believe me: but, when they heard the chaise was at the door, they hurried with me; full of anxiety and dismay. We were too late. Sir Barnard was gone: long out of hearing, and out of sight.

The consternation was extreme. Stupefied as his faculties were, for a moment Hector was roused. Conjectures were formed, but none presented themselves that could account for such extraordinary conduct. No one knew of any offence that had been given the Baronet. It was remarked indeed, on recollection, that the last day or two he had not testified the same alacrity and zeal: but no man could guess his motive.

At length the indignation of Hector took vent in a volley of curses, which were plentifully and emphatically bestowed. And so keenly was the stroke felt, that he put a very unusual quantity, small though it was, of variety in his oaths. Not only the body and blood of Sir Barnard, but his liver, eyes, and heart, were consigned over to Satan.

Even I, though I had procured votes distinct from the interest of the Baronet, and had refused to follow him to town, in which refusal I persisted, still I did not escape suspicion. No direct allegation was made: but the questions that were put to me were sufficiently expressive of doubt.

The irritated mind is apt at error; and I disdained to make a personal application of the guilt by which I knew myself uncontaminated.

CHAPTER VII

*The opening of the poll: My first essay at public oratory:
The general feelings of men in favour of virtue, though
contradicted by their practice: The hateful spectacle of a
corrupt election, and more cause of complaint against the
Baronet: A false accusation resented*

PASSION dispels passion, and care combats care. Sir Barnard was
gone, diligence was the more necessary, and preparations for the
approaching day would not admit of neglect. It may well be said
that circumstances and situation make the man. Hector, who had
no habitual capacity for business or intellect for order, was inspired
by the occasion with a degree of talent of which at other times he
was incapable. The fatigue he underwent was excessive; and, impossible as it was that he should create any strong sympathy, I still
felt some interest in his behalf; and some alarm at the fixed hoarse-
ness by which his lungs were threatened, and the alteration which
incessant drinking and unusual efforts had produced in his
appearance.

The night was passed with more than ordinary tumult. It was late
before the riotous guests departed; and our rest was short. The
day of beginning contest soon broke upon us, the word of command was given to muster, and all was in action. The friends of the
opposing parties collected, each round their respective leaders:
favours for the hat and bosom were lavishly distributed: the flags
were flying: a band of music preceded each of the processions: and,
when the parties approached the hustings, each band continued to
play its own favourite air with increasing violence: as if war were
to be declared by the most jarring discord, and harmony driven
from the haunts of men.

The grating sounds were increased by balladsingers, marrowbones and cleavers,[1] and the vociferous throats of men who seemed
to imagine that, if they were but sufficiently noisy, they could not
fail of being victorious.

The scaffolding was mounted, the candidates appeared, and
mouths, ears, and eyes were open; for the reception of all the wisdom and patriotism, with all the *comicality* and *fun*, which the

orators were expected to bestow. A mob delights in being harangued; and is thrown into raptures by every kind of mountebank.

Jealous perhaps of his own honor, the god of eloquence decreed that neither the wit nor the wisdom of Hector should that day be heard. He was too hoarse for any effort to make him audible: but, as stirring and ambitious spirits on such occasions are always abroad, tongues were not wanting to trumpet forth his high deserts.

The candidates for oratorical fame were several, I was of the number: and, as the gloss of my newly acquired dignity dazzled other eyes as well as my own, I was permitted to take the lead. It was my first essay; and I felt a momentary alarm: but, full of youthful spirits and high in blood, I dashed forward; and uttered what first occurred.

My voice was powerful, my nonsense was applauded, my fears vanished, and I became more collected. The real grievances of mankind, under the best government that ever yet existed, have at all times been so numerous that an orator, who makes them his theme, is never in want of facts and arguments.

Could I then feel this deficiency at an epocha like the one in question: when means so despotic were daily adopted to curb the growing spirit of enquiry that despot ministers might pursue measures so tragical; so subversive of the order which they pretended to maintain, and so destructive to the happiness they were appointed to guard? Alas! the topics were so numerous, so melancholy, so almost maddening, that the man who would paint them truly must temper and rein-in his feelings with an iron arm: otherwise, imagination will so hurry him away that, while describing evils past, evils present, and evils impending, there is danger of his being deemed an incendiary.

I spoke ill. When I remembered what I had said, and what I might and ought to have said, I was indignant at my own want of recollection. The applause that I received nevertheless was prodigious: the acclamations of the mob were even awful. They displayed a feeling of justice so acute, so prompt, and so powerful, that I was borne out of myself; and imagined for a moment, not merely that the day of reform was at hand, but that it was come.

Men are rendered selfish, and corrupt, by the baneful influence of the systems under which they live: but it is well worthy the attention of those who believe mankind to be generally capable of great happiness, and who are desirous to promote it, that, however the wants of the wretched may tempt them to accept the immediate relief that is within their reach, they never collectively fail to bestow the most unbounded applause, on those principles by which their own proceedings are condemned. They are not in love with baseness: it is forced upon them.

The reader is doubtless aware that Hector and his friends assumed to themselves the merit of what is called the independent interest; and that his opponent was supported by the whole influence of the court party. The numerous groans and hisses, and the few plaudits, bestowed upon the orators of this party, were additional proofs of what is the general sense of mankind; and that on the subject of corrupt influence at least they judge rightly. In this general sense I own that my soul triumphed: and the pangs which I felt, after the poll began, to perceive that, whatever men might think, they could forget their duty and vote only as their interest directed, were undescribable.

However, the party of Hector was strong. The struggle was violent. Every scandalous art of election was resorted to, by both sides. A spirit of rancour daily and hourly increased. The opponents came to frequent blows. Beastly drunkenness, bloated insolence, and profligacy of principle, met the eye on every side; and I almost hated myself, not only for being present at and participating in it, but, to find that I belonged to a race of animals capable of such foul and detestable vice.

From this distress I was relieved by an event which in itself was very far from satisfactory. The poll had proceeded for some days with tolerable equality; and Hector had rather the advantage: though the voters in the interest of Sir Barnard had not given him their assistance; to which they had frequently been urged. At length, they appeared. And how great was the surprise and indignation of our whole party, to see them marshalled on the opposite side, with the favours of the Idford candidate in their hats, and uniformly come up and poll against us!

On the same day, twelve of the votes which had been promised to me were likewise brought over to the opposite interest; and ten more of them refused to poll for either party.

The coincidence of this desertion revived the suspicions of Hector and his party, concerning me. This sudden turn of the poll against him rendered his temper ungovernable; and, in the frenzy of passion, he made no scruple of openly affirming that I was no less guilty than the Baronet.

It was not merely the consciousness of innocence that I felt. I had been so indefatigable in every possible way, I had ridden and walked and talked, I had been his defender, his eulogist, his orator, his slave, and had as it were so fouled my conscience in his cause that indignation closed my lips. I disdained reply, or self vindication; and, casting a glance such as irresistible feeling dictated, left the committee room in which the accusation was made without answering a word.

CHAPTER VIII

The return to town: A visit to Sir Barnard: Admission denied:
Enquiries after the wounded stranger, who had disappeared:
An endeavour to guard against misrepresentation: The fears
and feelings of friends

MY determination was taken, my servant was called, my horses ordered, and I immediately departed for London. My thoughts were far from being clear, or of a pleasant kind. The scene I had left was the most odious that I had ever beheld. Hector I was convinced would lose his election; and, what was more valuable, his health. I saw prognostics which I thought could not be mistaken; and which afterward proved as baleful as I then imagined them to be. Whether the contest might not ruin the family was more than I knew; and what the effect might be on Olivia, and even on our hoped for union, I could not foresee.

The enigmatical conduct of Sir Barnard was no less perplexing. His sudden desertion of Hector, and of the cause which he had so loudly defended, were alarming. For what other interpretation could be put upon the voters in the Baronet's interest, who not only refused to poll according to their promise, but were all of them brought up in support of the Idford candidate? Yet I was loth to conclude that an event so fatal to all my hopes, as well to my private affections as to my public duties, had taken place.

My horses were excellent, and carried us seventy miles in less time than it would have taken to go post. I intended to have ordered a chaise for the remainder of the way: but a mail coach was to pass in half an hour, and I waited. There happened to be a vacancy in which I seated myself; and by these means I arrived in town early in the morning.

As soon as the day was far enough advanced, my first care was to visit Sir Barnard; and I own I approached the street and the house with a foreboding heart. What had happened could not be unintentional. It was too decided, too abrupt, and had too many marks of unprincipled treachery. I knocked, made my enquiries, and was informed the Baronet was not at home. I asked for Lady Bray; and not at home was again the answer.

As this was what I apprehended, it excited but little surprise, though much vexation. However I left my card; and departed more full of meditation even than I came. Not at home I had no doubt signified that my visits were no longer welcome.

Still it was necessary I should know the truth; and, as I had been too intimate with the family to be ignorant of the haunts of Sir Barnard, I went to the Cocoa tree, a place to which he daily resorted, and there lounged away between two and three hours over the papers; hoping he would come.

I was again disappointed. The Baronet did not make his appearance; and I began to conjecture that perhaps the servant had told me truly: he might be out early; on business, or I knew not what.

As it was past his hour at the Cocoa tree, perhaps I should now find him at home. I therefore went back; and again made my enquiries, and again received the same dry laconic answer. It had an ill face: but I had no immediate remedy.

My next most pressing object of attention was the wounded stranger; whom I had left under the care of the physician, and whom I immediately determined to enquire after: not without some silent reproaches to myself, for having so long been absent on schemes such as those in which I had been concerned, to the neglect of perhaps a more serious duty. For duty seemed to require that men should rather abstain from elections, such as they are at present, than become aiders and abettors of them.

My horses not being arrived, and disliking the vehicle of a hackney coach, I walked forward to the inn at which the stranger had been left; musing much on the prospect before me, which was once more beginning to be heavily overcast.

Being come to my journey's end, I found the stranger had been removed two days after I left him to London: but the people of the inn could give me no farther intelligence, concerning him or the place of his residence.

I then asked them to direct me to the house of the physician: which they did, but told me that he had left the kingdom.

Determined however to make every possible enquiry, I went to the house; where I found only a person who was left in charge of the premises, and who knew nothing more than that the physician was gone with a patient to Lisbon.

These little incidents, trifling as they appeared, afforded me an excellent proof of the absurdity of false modesty: which induces men, from the egoistical fear of being thought vain, to conceal or disguise the truth. The physician had bestowed high eulogiums on my humanity: after which, he had hinted a desire, but with well-bred reserve, to know who I was; and I, catching the apparent delicacy of his feelings and thinking but very little on the subject, imagined there would be ostentation in personally taking to myself his praises, by giving him my name and place of abode. I therefore told him I would answer that question when we became better acquainted; if he should then find he had no reason to alter his good opinion of me.

Thus do men by affecting not to be vain, indulge a kind of double refined vanity; and lead themselves and others into error.

Being disappointed in all my enquiries of this day, my next care was to see Miss Wilmot. Surrounded as I was by persons who thought me inimical to them, and therefore were probably my inveterate enemies, I knew not what false reports might be spread; nor how to guard against them in the public opinion. But I had one consolation. Olivia had declared she was resolved to enquire, before she again gave the least credit to calumny. It was therefore essentially necessary that I should acquaint Miss Wilmot with all that had passed.

It was now evening; and, when I came to her lodgings, I found her brother and Turl both there. Though my absence had been short, the meeting gave me no little pleasure. It would likewise save me the trouble of a thrice told tale: for to friends like these my heart was always open; and I had something like an abhorrence of concealment, and secret transactions. I wished them to share in all my joys; and, as to my griefs, they not only excited their sympathy but produced remarks and counsel, by which they had often been cured.

I told my story; and it may well be imagined my hearers were neither inattentive nor unmoved. The selfishness and depravity into which men are driven, and the vices of which being thus impelled they are capable, exemplified as these vices were in my narration, drew heavy sighs from the gentle and kind hearted Lydia, made her much oppressed brother groan in spirit, and excited in Turl those comprehensive powers that trace the history of facts through a long succession, and teach, by miseries that are past, how miseries in future are to be avoided.

The general feeling however was that danger was hovering over me. The indignation of Wilmot, at the treatment of men who most endeavoured to deserve well of their age and country, was very strong.

Neither was Turl less moved. His manner was placid, yet his feelings were acute. But, though they might vibrate for a moment toward discord, they touched the true harmony at last. He who has fixed principles of action is soon called to a recollection of his duties, and the manner in which he ought to act.

Roused by his friendship for me, I should rather say by his affection, he collected his faculties; and presented to the imagination so sublime a picture of fortitude, and of the virtue of enduring injuries and oppression with dignity, that he prepared my mind most admirably for the trials that were to succeed.

CHAPTER IX

A second and more successful attempt to obtain an interview with the Baronet: An enigmatical dialogue: The meaning of which however may be guessed

IT was not only the wish of my heart but it was quite necessary for me to see Mr. Evelyn. However, it was exceedingly desirable that I should previously meet the Baronet: lest, in what I should say, my surmises might be false; and I might produce a family disagreement between persons who would both have conferred essential benefits on me, if the supposed defection of Sir Barnard should not be true. I determined therefore once more to go to the Cocoa tree and wait.

As it happened, waiting was not necessary. The Baronet was there; and, though there was something of coldness in his manner, it was by no means what my fears had taught me to expect. Salutation having passed, I requested to speak with him. We retired into a private room; and he began by telling me he was glad to see me again in town; and no longer continuing to support a person whom he no longer esteemed his friend.

At hearing this remark, and the significance with which it was delivered, my evil augury returned upon me in full force. I answered that I had quitted Mr. Mowbray not because I had deserted his interest, but because I had been unjustly accused.

'Accused of what, Mr. Trevor?'

'Of having been influenced by you to betray a party which I had pretended to espouse.'

'And were you not influenced by me, Mr. Trevor?'

'I never can be influenced by any man, Sir Barnard, to commit an action which my heart condemns.'

'Do you mean, Mr. Trevor, that your heart condemns me?'

'The question is very direct; and I am not desirous of wounding your feelings, Sir Barnard: but I must not be guilty of falsehood. I certainly wish you had acted otherwise.'

'Then you pretend to set up for yourself, Mr. Trevor; and to have no deference whatever for me, and my opinions.'

'Personally, as a gentleman who meant to do me service, I wish to preserve every respect for you, Sir Barnard. But I hope you do not expect of me any deference that should, on any occasion whatever, induce me to abandon either my public or my private duties.'

'Very well, Mr. Trevor. Very well. I dare say you are so perfectly acquainted with your duties that no man on earth, not even he who had been your greatest friend, could induce you to alter any of your notions.'

'I should hope, Sir Barnard, that either friend or enemy might so induce me: provided he had truth and reason on his side.'

'Very well, Mr. Trevor. All that is very fine. I dare say you understand your own interest, and will take your own road: even though you might if you pleased travel more at your ease, and in better company, by going another way.'

'Will you be kind enough to explain yourself, Sir Barnard?'

'No, Mr. Trevor. I shall give no explanations, till I am sure I am talking to my friend: my fast friend, Mr. Trevor: that will think and act with me. If you will give me your word and honor as a gentleman to that, why then we will talk together.'

'If by thinking and acting together, Sir Barnard, you mean that you expect I should blindly and implicitly conform to any tergiversation—I mean to any change——'

'You need explain yourself no farther, Mr. Trevor. I very well understand your meaning. My friend is my friend, Mr. Trevor; and he is no other man's friend, Mr. Trevor. I could not but suppose you understood all that perfectly at first; and I am very sorry to be so much deceived. But it is my misfortune to be always deceived, and entrapped; and——'

'Entrapped, Sir Barnard! I hope you do not apply that word to me?'

'Nay, nay, Mr. Trevor, I want no quarrelling.'

'Nor do I, Sir Barnard. But, if you suppose me capable of taking any advantage of what you may now think an ill-placed confidence in me, you egregiously mistake both my intentions and my character.'

'I hope I do, Mr. Trevor. You have a great fluency: but I hope I do.'

I saw him preparing to go; and, being exceedingly anxious to have a determinate answer, I added—'Let me intreat you, Sir Barnard, to give me an explicit declaration of what you expect from me.'

'You must excuse me, Mr. Trevor. I shall say no more, at present. You say I mistake your intentions. I hope I do. Time will tell. When you are my friend, I shall be very glad to see you; and so will Lady Bray. Good morning to you, Mr. Trevor.'

CHAPTER X

Reflections on the mutability of fortune, on money expended, and on the duties of love and friendship: A strange incident, shewing the propensity of man to superstitious terrors: A lamentable and unexpected event

WELL might I forebode the approach of evil: and, except that complaint is of no avail, is waste of time, is unhappiness and therefore is immoral, well might I complain of those sudden strokes of fate by which, whenever my prospects began to be flattering, they were suddenly obscured in darkness and despair. But, if I had not supposed myself marked in an extraordinary manner as the child of fortune, to whose smiles and frowns I seemed to be capriciously subjected, I know not what should have induced me to have written my history; or rather the history of my youth; for of what is yet reserved for me I am still ignorant.

Not that I pretend to consider the hypocrisy, selfishness and profligacy of titled folly, and church pride, as things in themselves extraordinary. It was the coincidence and the number and manner of them, by which in the crisis of my fate I seemed to be so repeatedly and so peculiarly affected, that occasioned surprise and pain.

Yet what was all that I had hitherto felt from persons like these, when I remember that which I was now immediately doomed to feel? The perverted and the vicious it is true can excite emotion, and excite it strongly. But how comparatively feeble does their utmost malice seem, as far as it affects only ourselves, when brought in competition with the thunder-bolt that strikes the virtuous; that shuts the gate of hope; and that robs us of those unspeakable pleasures which imagination has fondly stored, as a grand resource against evil, fall when and how it may?

Parting from the Baronet, expecting what was almost certain some change of political sentiment, no matter how brought about, by which my flattering expectations were at once to be rooted up, my thoughts inevitably flowed into that train which was bitterness little short of anguish. Mr. Evelyn was a man of such peculiar virtue and disinterested benevolence, of a heart so generous and so little capable of accusing me in consequence of the baseness of others, that to have suspected him of such a mistake would have been the height of injustice. But I could not forget the sums that he had advanced, in all four hundred pounds, the more than probable failure of all the plans for which they had been advanced, and the incapacity I had and should have to repay these sums.

Neither could I forbear to take a retrospective view of the manner in which they had been expended. Could I approve of that manner? Could I forget how short a time it was, though I had squandered my own money, since I had forfeited no atom of my independence by accepting the earnings of others? Suppose this parliamentary plan to fail, and fail it must, for there were no hopes that I could honestly retain my seat, to what other means could I resort? While

I continued to indulge in wild and extravagant schemes of enriching myself, by which I did but impoverish others, ought I to require of Olivia to partake of my folly, and its consequences? Had I nothing but the cup of wretchedness to offer, and must I still urge her to drink? Was it not my duty rather to tear myself at once away from her; and place some insurmountable barrier between us, that should relieve her from such an ill-fated predilection?

Full of these thoughts, I proceeded toward the residence of Mr. Evelyn. It was necessary that I should see him immediately: for silence would have been the meanest deceit. I went with an afflicted heart. But how did I return? Why do I say afflicted? No! Anguish, real anguish, since I had known him, had not yet reached me. But it was coming. It was rushing forward, like a torrent; to bear away inferior cares and sorrows, and engulph them wholly.

Unexpected events are sometimes peculiarly marked, by certain uncommon incidental circumstances. As I was walking hastily forward, anxious to meet Mr. Evelyn at home, I saw a coffin borne before me by four men at some distance. Their pace was brisk. I had several streets to pass, before I arrived at the house where Mr. Evelyn had apartments; and still the coffin turned the way that I was to go.

I overtook and went before it: but the gloomy object had excited my attention, and I presently looked behind me. Still it took the same route. I looked again, and again; and it was continually at my heels.

It is strange how imagination will work, and how ideas will suggest themselves. I wished it any where else; but it seemed to pursue me.

At length I came to my journey's end; and, having knocked at the door, looked round with a kind of infatuated fear. The coffin was following, and I stood with an absurd and fanciful trepidation, waiting that I might once see it fairly past the door. Yet I was no bigot, no believer in omens, and was almost ashamed of an idea which the coffin itself and the gloomy state of my mind had suggested: but which was in reality superstitious. The servant came, and the door was opened: but the coffin approached, and I would not stir till it should pass me.

Pass it did. But where? Into the passage.

I stood speechless. The men asked where it was to go? 'Into the first floor,' was the answer.

It was the apartment of Mr. Evelyn.

Heavens! What was the pang that shot across my brain? I gasped for utterance: but still was dumb. A dread so terrible had seized me that there I stood; motionless and stupefied.

The woman who opened the door and directed the men belonged to the house; and, just as the bearers were proceeding with the coffin up stairs, Matthew, the country servant, who had attended Mr. Evelyn in the dissecting room the first night of our meeting, came in.

The moment he saw me, the poor fellow burst into tears; and exclaimed—'Oh sir!'

His look and the tone of his voice were sufficient. There was but one event that could have produced them, in such an extraordinary and unfeigned degree of grief. My horrible fears were fulfilled.

He paused a moment, sobbed, and again cried in a most piercing and lamentable tone, 'My poor master!'

I must draw the curtain over feelings that I cannot pretend to paint. How long I stood, what I first said, or what my looks were, are things of which I know nothing. I only recollect that my eyes were stone, and had not a tear to shed.

CHAPTER XI

A proof of the danger of not attending to trifles: A feeble attempt to characterise a man of uncommon virtue: The dying anxieties of Mr. Evelyn

THE melancholy particulars of this strange tragedy were that, three days before, Mr. Evelyn, being then in perfect health, had been dissecting a limb in a high state of putrescence. During the operation, the instrument had slipped, and made what he considered only as a scratch of the skin; and so slight that he did not immediately deem it worthy of notice: though, when he had ended, he felt a tingling; and then thought it prudent to wash with vinegar, and bind it up to keep out the air.

He was so busily engaged, during the day, that he paid no more attention to it; though he once or twice felt a throbbing that was unusual. Being fatigued, and finding his spirits rather agitated, he took a gentle opiate at going to rest: but was waked in the middle of the night, by symptoms of a very alarming kind. The morbid humour that was introduced into the system, small as it probably was in quantity, was so active that Mr. Evelyn was seized with a violent inflammatory fever: so that he was delirious when he woke, and died in less than eight and forty hours after he received this slight wound.

Such is the uncertain fate of man, in this state of ignorance. To such sudden accidents of sickness and death are the good and the bad, the foolish and the wise, continually subject; and such at present is the frail tenure of life that the man in whose hall we feasted on Monday, or the blooming beauty with whom we sung and danced, ere the week passes away, are descended to the grave.

What tribute can friendship or affection pay, to the memory of a man like this? There is only one that is worthy of his virtues; and that is to record them: that, he being gone, his example may inspire the benevolence he practised; and teach others to communicate the blessings he conferred.

Oh that I had the power to pourtray those virtues in all their lustre! Ages unborn would then rejoice, that such a man had lived; and feel the benefits he would have bestowed. But it is a task that cannot be accomplished in a few pages. His life was a vast volume of the best of actions, which originated in the best of principles. Peace, love, and reverence, be with his memory.

For my own part, if, in addition to that uncommon public worth which he possessed, and that noble scale of morality by which he regulated his life, the personal kindness which he heaped on me be remembered, I must have less of affection than savage brutality, did no portion of his spirit inspire me while I speak of these events.

Nor did his friendship end while understanding had the least remaining power. His last act of benevolence was a strenuous but incoherent effort to prevent the mischief which, disturbed as his functions were, he still had recollection enough to apprehend would fall on me.

The reader is informed of the mortgage I gave Mr. Evelyn, when I received not merely a qualification but the possession of an estate; and I imagine he will not think I was too scrupulously careful, to guard and prove the honesty of my intentions, when I further tell him that, for the sums of money which Mr. Evelyn advanced, I insisted on giving my promissory notes for repayment. I was pertinacious, and would accept such favours on no other terms.

This mortgage and these notes were lying in the possession of Mr. Evelyn, at the time of his death. He had apprehended no danger, till the fever and the delirium seized him: at the beginning of which he called his servant, Matthew (I tell the story as the poor fellow told it to me), and, giving him a key, bade him go down to his bureau, and search among his papers for a parchment and some notes, that were tied together with red tape.

Having uttered this, he began to talk in a wild and wandering manner; of fetters, and prisons; and asked Matthew if he knew why such places were built? 'So make haste, Matthew,' said he, 'and burn the parchment, and burn the notes, and burn the bureau. After which, you know, all will be safe, Matthew; and they can never harm Mr. Trevor. You love Mr. Trevor, Matthew: do not you?'

His recollection then seemed to return; and he asked, 'Of what have I been talking? Go, Matthew; seek the parchment and the notes: tied with red tape. Observe: there is no other parchment tied with red tape. Bring them to me directly.'

Matthew had taken the key; but just as he was going the Doctor, who had been sent for, arrived.

Matthew went, however, as he was directed; and, applying the key to the lock, found it was a wrong one.

The Doctor, alarmed for the state in which he saw Mr. Evelyn, immediately wrote a prescription, and rang for the servant to run and have it prepared at the shop of the next apothecary. Matthew answered the bell; and Mr. Evelyn seeing him eagerly demanded— 'Where is the parchment? Have you brought me the parchment? Why do not you bring me the parchment?' 'For,' said Matthew, 'I held out the key; and he saw I had nothing else in my hands.'

The Doctor asked Matthew what parchment his master wanted? And Matthew replied, he could not tell: except that his master said it was in the bureau, and tied with red tape. 'Why do not you bring it?' said Mr. Evelyn. Then turning to the Doctor, added—'It is a bundle of misery; and you know, sir, we ought to drive all misery from the face of the earth. I cannot tell how it came in my possession. Why do you not go and bring it me, Matthew? And pray, sir, do you see it destroyed. Promise me that; I beg you will! Because Mr. Trevor is in the country. I am afraid elections are but bad things. What, sir, is your opinion? For I think I shall die; and he will then have no friend on earth to secure him the poll.'

'Seeing my poor master was so disturbed in his mind,' said Matthew, 'the doctor *bid* me run as fast as I could for the stuff he had ordered: which I did. But I was obliged to wait till it was made up; and when I *come* back my poor dear master was more distracting light-headed than ever. But still he kept raving about the parchment; and his cousin, Sir Barnard; and you, Mr. Trevor: all which the Doctor said we must not heed, because he did not know what he said. Though, for all that, I could not but mightily fear there was something hung heavy on his mind: for, as long as ever he could be heard to speak, he kept calling every now and then for the parchment. And after that, when he lay heaving for breath and rattling in the throat and nobody could tell a word that he said, he kept moving his lips just in the same manner as when he could make himself heard. I do believe he was calling for it almost as the breath left his body. And I cannot but say that I wish I had found it, and brought it to him; for the ease and quiet of his soul.'

CHAPTER XII

Doubts concerning the justice of wills and testaments: The provident care of the Baronet: A demonstration of his ardent love for his country: Hector loses his election: My determination to accept the Chiltern Hundreds

WHEN a man discovers that the pathos of his story, and the virtues which he has in contemplation, are entirely beyond the power of language, what method can he take but that of leaving off abruptly: that he may suffer the imagination to perform an office to which any other effort is inadequate? As Mr. Evelyn lived so he died. To prevent evil and to do unbounded good was his ruling passion. It never left him, till life departed.

It is a phenomenon which has frequently been remarked that, in a state of delirium, the mind has its luminous moments: during which it seems to have a more clear and comprehensive view of consequences than in its more sober periods of health. The evil that excited so strong and painful an alarm in the mind of my dying friend was no idle dream. The Baronet was his heir at law. Mr. Evelyn had made no will: for not only was his death premature but,

knowing the mischiefs that have arisen from disputes concerning
testamentary bequests, he strongly doubted of the morality of
making any. It was never his intention to hoard; and, hoping or
I might rather say expecting to have a clear prospect of the approach
of death, his plan was to distribute all the personal property in his
possession before he died, in the manner that he should suppose
would be most useful.

However, whether it were a just sense of rectitude or an improper pride of heart, I own that I felt pleased, as far as myself was
concerned, that the intentions of Mr. Evelyn, when he called for the
parchment, were not executed. I did not indeed foresee all that was
to happen: but I felt an abhorrence of being liable to be suspected
of I know not what imputed arts, or crimes; by the aid of which
malice or selfishness might assert I had come into the possession of
so large a part of Mr. Evelyn's property.

Not that, if the deeds and notes had been destroyed, I should
have thought it just to have retained the estate that I held. But my
virtue was not fated to be put to this trial. When I met Sir Barnard
at the Cocoa tree, he not only knew of the decease of Mr. Evelyn
but had ordered seals to be placed on all the locks; under which
it was imagined that papers or effects might be secured. Having
heard the story of Matthew, I could have no doubt but that the
mortgage deeds, and the notes for sums received, would now fall
into the Baronet's power.

It is true I might, if I pleased, bid him defiance. No: I ought
not to have said, if I pleased; but, if I could condescend to acknowledge myself a scoundrel. He had made me his own member, and
had himself impowered me to avoid the punishment which is
assigned by law to unfortunate debtors: for, under this best of
governments, such as a representative of the people was now my
privilege. This immaculate constitution, to which all the homage
that man can pay is insufficient worship, vaunted as it is and revered
by all parties, or all parties are broad day liars, for all and each
strive to be most loud and extravagant in praise of it, this constitution in its very essence decrees that things which are vile and unjust,
in one man, are right and lawful, in another.

Well then: by the aid of this constitution, which I too must
praise if I would escape whipping, I might seat myself as Sir
Barnard's member, and aid to countenance and make laws, to which
I and the other wise law-makers my coadjutors should not be

subject. I might, however offensive the term may be to certain
delicate ears, I might become a privileged swindler; and rob every
man who should do me the injustice to think me honest.

It cannot be supposed that so dear a lover and so ardent an
admirer of the constitution, as Sir Barnard was, should once
suspect that I would not benefit myself by all its blessings: that is,
that I would not cheat him to the very best of my ability. This
supposition had induced him, during our conversation at the Cocoa
tree, to struggle with and keep down those indignant risings with
which, notwithstanding the modulated tone of his voice, I could
see he was more than half choaked.

After what I had heard and situated as I was at present, I had very
little doubt either of the purity of his patriotism or the manner in
which it would affect me. Still however I had some. There might
be a change in his politics; but it might neither be of the nature nor
of the extent that I feared.

But these doubts did not distress me long. They were entirely
removed, by that most authentic source of intelligence the Gazette;
in which, about a fortnight after the death of Mr. Evelyn, I read
the following unequivocal proof of the Baronet's inordinate love of
his country.

'The King has been pleased to grant the dignity of a Baron of the
kingdom of Great Britain to Sir Barnard Bray, Baronet; by the
name stile and title of Baron Bray, of Bray hall in the county of
Somerset; and to the heirs male of his body, lawfully begotten.'

I was now no longer at a loss for the reason of the Baronet's late
sudden departure, and the desertion of his political friends at the
election. What are friends? What are elections? What is our country,
compared to the smiles of a prime minister; and the titles he can
bestow? Nothing now was wanting to the honor of the house of
Bray! It might in time I own pant after a Dukedom; and a Duke
of Bray might as justly be stiled princely and most puissant as many
another Duke. But at present it was full with satisfaction.

This court document, brief though it was, spoke volumes. It was
a flash of lightning, that gave me a distinct view of the black and
dreadful abyss that was immediately before me; and into which
I foresaw I must be plunged.

On the same day, I read that the Idford candidate had been
returned for the county of ****; and that consequently Hector had
lost his election.

This was not all. Heated by the illiberal practices which always attend such contentions, knowing the bribery that he had used himself, and convinced that he could prove the same corrupt means to have been resorted to by his opponent, he was not satisfied with the devastation he had already committed upon his fortune; but was determined to demand a *scrutiny*: and if he should be foiled in that effort, he was resolved to try the merits of the election before a committee of the house of commons. Such was the report that was immediately propagated; and which was afterward verified by facts.

With respect to myself, convinced as I was of its danger, I had made my choice. My fixed purpose was to vacate my seat in parliament. It might perhaps be questioned, since the pretended voters had in reality no voice, and their imaginary representative was no more than a person nominated by the new Lord Bray, whether I ought to resign an office which, as I supposed, I should fill for the good of mankind; and give place to some person who, obedient to his leader, would do the reverse?

But one act of baseness cannot authorize another. To bear about me a sense of self-degradation, a certainty that I was sheltering myself from the power of my late patron by a privilege which I considered as highly vicious, a subterfuge such as every man who deserves the name ought to despise and spurn at, this was insufferable. I had lost much: for I had lost hopes that had been extravagant and unbounded in promise: but I had not lost a conscious rectitude of heart, without which existence was not to be endured.

CHAPTER XIII

The comedy of Wilmot successful: The wounded stranger seen at a distance: Oratory abandoned with regret: The dangers that attend being honest: A new invitation from Hector: A journey deferred by an arrest, and another accidental sight of the stranger

I T is happy for man that there is scarcely any state of suffering, whether of mind or body, in which pain is unremitting; and wholly unmixed with pleasure. If he be unhappy himself, it will be strange should there be no one more fortunate for whom he has an affection: no friend that is more prosperous, and in whose prosperity he takes delight.

The season of the year had arrived when the comedy of Wilmot had been put into rehearsal, and was to be performed. It was a trying occasion; and those who knew him loved him too well to be absent; though the few intimate friends who had read the piece had no doubt of its success. The partial failure of his tragedy had produced no jealousy of rivalship: though, as its merits had been publicly acknowledged, it had incurred no disgrace. In private life, he was beloved; and, as a public man, his merits had not yet created him enemies. He has since, indeed, in that respect, not been so fortunate. But he has never thought it just to complain: being convinced that mistake, though it should be rectified, should not be resented.

The evening of representation arrived, the house was crowded, the company brilliant, and the plaudits with which the author was honoured established his reputation, and confirmed the judgment of his friends.

During the performance, I sat in the boxes; and, among the spectators in the pit, I discovered a man whose hair was white, whose locks were venerable, and who I was well convinced was the stranger whom I had found wounded at the entrance of Barnes common. I was in a side-box, and he was near the opposite pit door; so that the distance made it rather doubtful: yet the more I looked the more I was convinced it was the same person. The comedy was nearly ended when I first saw him; and I determined, as soon as I had heard the epilogue, to go and satisfy myself how far my persuasion was true.

I went round to the door; but the pit was so crowded that it was with difficulty I could make my way to the seat. When I was there my labour was lost: I could not find him; and, enquiring for him by description of the persons near where he sat, they told me that such a gentleman had been there; but that he complained of the heat, and had left the house immediately after the curtain dropped.

This incident gave me considerable chagrin. However, as his person was very remarkable, and being persuaded he was actually the wounded stranger, I conceived hopes that I should again meet him; in some place where the danger of losing sight of him would not be so great.

There being no expectation of his return, I went in search of my friends: in company with whom, rejoicing in the success of Wilmot and glorying in the acquisition of poetry and the stage, I wholly forgot myself and my own affairs, and spent one more very delightful evening.

These affairs however were not long to be forgotten. The returns of the elections throughout Great Britain had all been made, and the new parliament summoned to assemble. It was with infinite and deep regret that I found myself excluded by my own sense of rectitude. I would willingly have taken my seat, had it been only for one night: for I was eagerly desirous of an opportunity to deliver my thoughts, and urge some of those useful truths which may be uttered with more safety there than in less privileged places.

But I was too well acquainted with the customs and forms of the house to hope that this opportunity could now be found. I had no parliamentary friends; no supporters; and there was not the least probability that a youth so wholly unknown should *catch the speaker's eye*, whose notice so many were ready to solicit.

These things having been duly weighed, I had already applied for the chiltern hundreds[1] and my seat was declared vacated: to the great joy of Lord Bray; and his now bosom friend, the Earl of Idford. This joy was the greater because it was an event of which they had not the least expectation. The due forms of law had been observed, the seals had been removed from the locks of my late inestimable friend, his cousin the new peer was in possession of the mortgage and the notes for money received, and he had no conception of any motives that could induce me to an act which must leave me entirely at his mercy.

It cannot however be supposed, as I have already said, that I had any intention to retain the estate; which I had received from Mr. Evelyn as a qualification, and a support. It was now the property of Lord Bray; and obligation to him was a thing that would not admit of a question. I did not therefore wait for any notice from his lordship, or his attorney, but desired Mr. Hilary to inform him that I was ready at any time to give up the deeds, and receive back the mortgage.

This would have been a trifle. It was not a sacrifice; but a riddance: by which, could it have ended here, I should have regained something of that elasticity of heart which independence only can feel. Here, however, it could not end. I was obliged to instruct Mr.

Hilary to add that I was willing to give my own personal security, by bond or in any manner my creditor should please, for money received and interest due: but to acknowledge that I had no immediate means of payment. In other words, that my person was entirely at the disposal of himself and the law. I might have reminded him that more than half of my debt was incurred by *genteel presents* to his craving electors; and that he had informed me that it was a necessary expence: but to this I could not condescend.

The little business which, during his life, Mr. Evelyn had in law Mr. Hilary had always transacted. He had a sincere regard for me, and a reverence for the memory of his late kinsman; whose earnest recommendation of me he did not forget. Being well acquainted with the character of Lord Bray, he foresaw and warned me of my danger. While a baronet, to behold himself a peer had been his lordship's darling passion: but that was now gratified; and, as he was proud, he was likewise revengeful. In this case, however, to warn was useless. I had no alternative, except by means that were dishonorable.

Nor was the resentment of Lord Bray single, or so much to be apprehended as that of the Earl, with whom he had entered into strict alliance. My behaviour to Lord Idford had uniformly been what he deemed so very insolent that his antipathy may be said to have taken birth at my first act of disobedience: my refusal to dine at the second table. Since then, as he conceived, it had been progressive in aggravation. My scorn of his selfish politics, my attempt to continue the Letters of Themistocles, and write him who was the supposed author of them into disgrace, the pamphlet of which I was the author, the activity with which I had canvassed in favour of Mowbray, and to sum up all my daring to rival him with the woman on whom he would have conferred his person, his dignity, and his other great qualities, were all of them injuries that rankled at his heart. When these things are remembered, few will feel surprised that the Earl should indulge a passion which is in itself so active: or that he should induce Lord Bray to pursue that kind of conduct to which he was already so much disposed.

The danger however must be faced; and Mr. Hilary wrote, as my attorney, to state the circumstances above recited. A week elapsed before he received an answer: but at the end of that time his lordship's attorney replied, that personal security for so large a sum could not be accepted: my bond would be no better than the notes I had given: and that I was required immediately to pay what was due, to the estate and heirs of the late Mr. Evelyn.

The spirit in which this note was written proved the temper of my creditor; and an incident soon occurred by which his propensity to persecute was called into action. The scrutiny which Hector had demanded was over, and decided against him: but, understanding that there was an absolute breach between me and Lord Bray, Mowbray was convinced that he had accused me falsely. As he was almost certain that he could prove bribery and corruption to have been practised by his opponent, he persisted in determining to bring it before the house of commons. This business kept him still in the country, where he and his partisans were busily collecting information.

He had experienced my utility in the course of the election, he wished to enjoy the same advantage at present, and he and his committee likewise discovered that my evidence was essentially necessary. He therefore wrote me an apology, spoke in the handsomest terms he could recollect of the services I had done him, requested me to come down once more to aid him in his present attempt, and stated the points on which my future testimony would be useful. He further informed me that a gentleman of the law, whom he named, was to set off the morning after I should receive the letter, at ten o'clock, and come post; and that he should be much obliged to me if I would take a seat in the same chaise.

The letter was read in the committee room, as a matter of business; and in this committee room Lord Idford had a secret agent, from whom he gained intelligence of all their proceedings that deserved notice.

Desirous as I was of obliging the brother of Olivia, I made no hesitation to comply. The evening before I was to go down into *****, I went to Mr. Hilary; to acquaint him with the place of my destination, and the manner in which he might direct to me, if any thing new should occur. The agents of Lord Bray, or to speak more truly of the Earl, had been exceedingly industrious; and a writ was already procured. It was intended to take me as I stepped into the chaise, or that evening if possible, and accordingly the door where I lived was watched, and I was seen to come out. My usual pace was brisk, but I happened now to be in haste; and, as they told me themselves, the setters lost sight of me for some time, were afterward cautious of coming up to me in any public street where a rescue was probable, and followed me till I came almost to the door of Mr. Hilary.

Here there was a carriage standing; and, to my great surprise and joy, I saw Mr. Hilary with a light, conducting out the very person whom I had some time before discovered in the pit, and whom I now knew to be the wounded stranger.

I hesitated whether I ought to spring forward, and intrude my enquiries immediately upon him, or make them of Mr. Hilary, with whom it appeared he was acquainted; and, at this instant, the bailiff and his two men came up with me, and told me I was their prisoner.

While I stood astonished at this sudden and at that precise time unexpected event, the carriage with the stranger in it drove away; and Mr. Hilary shut the door without seeing me.

There is a sense of indignity and disgrace in being arrested, at which all those who have not been frequently subjected to it revolt. I was wholly ignorant of the manners of the people who had laid their hands upon me. I had heard of giving bail: but I had likewise heard that it was a thing of danger, to which men were generally averse; and I had a bitter repugnance to ask any thing which I thought it was likely should be refused. Neither had I any probable person to ask: for my little law reading had taught me that the sureties of a debtor must be house-keepers.

Unwilling therefore to trouble Mr. Hilary, and finding myself without resource, I desired the bailiff to take me wherever he pleased, or wherever the law directed. 'I suppose, Sir, you do not mean we should take you to jail?' said the bailiff.

Ignorant as I was and surprised at the question, I asked where else they meant to take me? He replied 'To my house, Sir: or to any other lock up house[1] that you choose.'

'A lock up house, Sir!' said I. 'Pray what is that?'

The bailiff knew not how to give a direct answer; but replied 'There *is* some lock up houses at which a gentleman may be treated like a gentleman: though I cannot say but there *is* others that *is* shabby enough. I see very well, Sir, you are a young gentleman, and do not know the trim[2] of such things: so, if you please to go to my house, you will find very civil usage. I can tell by your cut, Sir, that you are no scrub;[3] so my wife will take care to furnish you with every thing that is genteel and polite.'

The man smelled excessively of brandy and tobacco; which, corresponding with his gait, looks, and language, seemed an introduction to the purgatory to which I was doomed. I thought proper however to accept his offer, and go to the house where I was to be treated with so much politeness and gentility.

CHAPTER XIV

The good breeding of a bailiff: A period of dejection: A visit from Mr. Hilary: The hopes he conceives

THE bailiff and one of his followers walked beside me, cautiously keeping in advance; and the other marched behind till we came to a stand of coaches, and I was asked whether one of them should be called? I was thoroughly ashamed of my company: but a deep sense of indignity confuses thought; and, till it was proposed by the bailiff, I had forgotten that there was such a thing as a coach. His proposal was immediately accepted; and we were driven through Lincoln's-inn-fields into Carey-street, where we were obliged to alight and pass through several narrow allies.

I had no great expectations of the gentility of the bailiff's abode: but, slender as they were, the few I had were disappointed. I was wholly unused to such places: this I suspect was one of the meanest of them; and the approach to the house, as well as all that was in it, bespoke wretchedness, and inspired disgust.

As soon as we entered the doors, the bailiff called aloud for Charlotte (the name of his wife) and desired her to bring light into the drawing room. 'Why what do you talk of, George?' replied Charlotte. 'Are you drunk? Don't you know the gentleman is there that you brought in this morning?'

'Do you think I don't know what I am about?' answered George. 'I have brought another gentleman: so that there gentleman must come down, and *hoik*¹ into the best parlour.'

'I am sure,' retorted Charlotte with great vivacity and significance, 'he has behaved vastly proper, since he came into my house. He has had friends with him all afternoon; and dined, and called for wine, and done every thing that was genteel.'

Though half in a trance, I was sufficiently awake to understand her meaning. I therefore interrupted the bailiff, who had begun to reply with passion. 'You are very right, Madam;' said I. 'The gentleman must not be disturbed. I have no friends that drink wine; and I drink none myself.'

This hint was quite sufficient. Neither the drawing room nor the best parlour were now to be had; and I was shewn into a dirty back place, which was little more than a closet, decorated with a wooden cut of Lord Lovat[1] over the mantle piece, and corresponding pictures of the king and queen on each side.

Before she shut the door, Charlotte demanded 'if I chose to have some more coals on the fire? And whether I would have two candles or one?' 'Whatever you please madam,' I replied. 'Nay, sir,' said she pertly, 'that is just as you please.' I made no answer, and she shut the door with a dissatisfied air; which she locked on the outside.

At any other time, this George and Charlotte, with their drawing-room, would have presented many whimsical associations to my mind: but at present my attention was called to the iron bars of the one window of my prison hole; and to the recollection that, in all probability, I was now shut up for life. The weight of evil was so oppressive that I sat motionless, in sullen stupefaction, for a considerable time.

Hearing no sound whatever, the bailiff I suppose was alarmed: for he unlocked the door, and coming in abruptly exclaimed 'Oh! I thought it could not be!' Meaning probably that I could not possibly have escaped through the window. Recollecting himself, he asked 'if I did not think proper to send to some friends?' To which I laconically answered, 'No.'

'But I suppose you mean to give bail, sir?'

'I have none to give.'

'I perceive how it is, sir. You are not used to the business; and so you are cast down. You must bethink yourself: for I dare say a young gentleman like you will find bail fast enough; *becase* why, the sum is not quite four hundred and forty pounds. We have people enough *which* will go of any message for you; so I would advise you to send, though it is late; *becase*, as you *says* you don't drink, there will be no good much in your staying here. Not but what we have as good beds, and as good wines and all sorts of liquors, and can get any thing else as good as a gentleman needs lick his lips to. There *is* never *no* complaints at our house. So you had better take my advice, and cheer up your spirits; and get a little something good in your belly, in the way of eating and drinking; and send to let your friends know as how you are *nabbed: becase* nothing can come of it otherwise, neither to you nor *no*body else.'

His discourse awakened me enough to remind me of the necessity of sending to the gentleman, with whom I had intended to travel the next day, and inform him of the impossibility of my taking the journey. This led me to reflect further. The remark of the bailiff was just: delay was prejudicial. What had happened could not be kept secret, secrecy was in itself vicious, and to increase evil by procrastination was cowardly. Thus far roused, I presently conceived and determined on my plan. I saw no probability of avoiding a prison: but, being in this house, I was resolved first to see my friends. I had already sold my horses, and discharged my servant. Clarke, I knew, would reproach me, if I did not accept his goods offices in my distress; when such good offices as he could perform would be most necessary. I intended therefore to request him the next morning to go round and inform such of my friends as I wished to see: but, as the bailiff told me it would be proper to send for my attorney immediately, I thought proper to dispatch a messenger; with one note to him, and another to the gentleman with whom I was to have travelled.

Mr. Hilary was at home and came instantly on the receipt of my billet. When he saw me, he endeavoured to smile; and not appear in the least surprised, or affected. But his feelings betrayed him; the tears started into his eyes, and he was obliged to turn away his face. He made an effort, however, and recovered himself: after which, he rather endeavoured to enter into easy conversation than to talk of business. By this I suspected that he neither durst trust himself nor me; till a little time should have reconciled us to the scene.

This was a proper opportunity for enquiries which my sudden misfortune had not made me forget. I questioned him concerning the stranger, whose person I described; and mentioned my having seen Mr. Hilary light him out of the house, the moment before I was arrested.

'What do you know of him?' said Mr. Hilary, with an eager air. 'Have you ever seen him before?'

'Yes; if I am not very much mistaken.'

'Nay but tell me, what do you know?'

'First answer me concerning who and what he is?'

'A gentleman of large fortune, the last of his family, and a great traveller.'

'Has he met with any accident lately?'

'Yes. But why do you ask?'

'And why do you seem so much awakened by the question?'

'Because he is excessively desirous of discovering some gentleman, who found him after he had been robbed, and left, supposed to be dead; that he may if possible reward his preserver. Now there are some circumstances, as related by the people of an inn to which he was taken, that have suggested a thought to me which, should it prove true, would give me inexpressible pleasure.'

'What are they?'

'That the good Samaritan, who performed this act of humanity, was a young gentleman with a servant out of livery; that he and his man rode two blood horses, both bright bays; that the servant's name was Samuel; and that the master was in person very like you. All which correspond; and I really believe, by your smiling, that it actually was you.'

'Suppose it: what then?'

'Why then I am sure you have gained a friend, who will never suffer you to go to prison.'

The word friend conjured up a train of ideas, which almost overcame me. 'I have lost a friend,' said I, 'who would not have suffered me to go to prison. But he is gone. I accepted even *his* favours with an aching and unwilling heart; and prison itself will not, I suspect, be so painful to me as more obligations of the same kind, and conferred by a person who, though I am strongly prepossessed in his favour, I scarcely can hope should equal Mr. Evelyn. And, if he even did, an extravagant supposition, I should still hesitate: I doubt if a prison itself be so hateful as a knowledge that I am only out of one on sufferance; and that, when any caprice shall seize my creditor, I may be hunted like a ferocious beast; and commanded to my den, like a crouching cur.

Mr. Hilary endeavoured to combat this train of thinking: but it was not to be conquered. The short period of trial since the death of Mr. Evelyn had afforded me too many proofs of the painful sensations which such a knowledge can excite; and of the propensity which I had to give them encouragement. To be as I have said the slave of any man's temper, not as an effort of duty but from a sense of fear, was insufferable. A prison, locks, bolts, and bread and water, were to be preferred.

Mr. Hilary sat with me till bed time; and, not only to put the bailiff in good humour, but to cheer my heart and his own, ordered supper, and drank more plentifully of wine than was his custom: urging me to follow his example. I did not refuse: for I had a contempt for any thing that had the appearance of an incapacity to endure whatever the tyranny of rancorous men and unjust laws could inflict. The stranger, he told me, was gone down into the country; from whence he would return within a week: but he forbore to mention his name, as he had been instructed; the stranger having enquiries to make, which induced him to keep it secret.

Before he left me, Mr. Hilary received instructions from me to be given to Clarke: after which we quitted the best parlour, into which we had been introduced with great ceremony to sup; and I retired to try how soundly I could sleep, in one of the good beds of a lock-up house.

CHAPTER XV

Morning visitors: A generous proposal rejected: The affectionate friendship of Miss Wilmot: A very unexpected visitor: His extraordinary conduct, and a scene of reconciliation: A letter which excites delightful sensations

THE morning came, the diligence of Mr. Hilary was that of a friend, and the best parlour was soon filled: the reader will easily guess by whom. There is an undescribable pleasure, when we are persecuted by one set of human beings, to receive marks of affection from another. It is a strong consolation to know that kindness and justice have not wholly forsaken the earth.

Wilmot, Clarke, and Turl were with me. I called for breakfast; and felt a gratification at enjoying another social meal, before being immured in I knew not what kind of dungeon. Charlotte and her maid, Pol, were very alert; and I believe she almost repented that I was not in the drawing-room, since she found I had so many friends.

Clarke was asked to partake; but answered with a 'no thank you, Mr. Trevor.' I supposed it was awkward bashfulness. I did him wrong. He had a more refined and feeling motive: for, when I pressed him very earnestly, he replied—'At another time, Mr. Trevor, such a favour would make me happy; and you know I have not refused: but, just now, why it would look as if, because you are under misfortunes, I might take liberties.'

Honest-hearted generous fellow! He was still the same. But he breakfasted with us. Be assured, good reader, he breakfasted with us.

And now I had a contest to undergo, which was maintained with so much obstinacy that it became truly painful. Wilmot, in consequence of the success of his comedy, had the power to discharge my debt; and on this at first he peremptorily insisted. But it was what I could not accept. He was, I knew, an Evelyn in soul: but I too panted to be something. I could not endure to rob him of the labour of a life, and walk at large oppressed by the consciousness of impotence: of a depressed and sunken spirit; of which groveling meanness would be the chief feature. Such at least were my sensations: and they were too impetuous to be overcome.

In the ardour we mutually felt, Turl was appealed to by both. At first he strongly inclined to the side of Wilmot: but, hearing my reasons and perceiving the anguish which the proposal gave, he at length said—'Let us pause awhile. We are friends. Imprisonment is a detestable thing; and there is no danger that, as friends, we should suffer each other to endure it long, if there should be any possible and honest means of imparting freedom. We need make no professions. In one part of his argument, Mr. Trevor is undoubtedly right. If he can relieve himself, by his abilities and industry, which he is persuaded he can, it is his duty. For it will not only increase his immediate happiness, but it will give confidence to his efforts, and strength to his mind: qualities that are inestimable. Impediments serve but to rouse the man of genius. To reject aid from a sentiment of haughtiness is a vice: but to despair of our own resources is the death of all true greatness of character. In any case, suspend your contest; in which, though from the best of motives, you are both too warm. Examine your arguments at leisure. If Mr. Trevor can be rendered most happy and useful by accepting your offer, it will then be just in him to cede: but remember once more we are friends, that know each other's worth; and it will be just that I should partake in his release. To this I know you will both joyfully consent. If good can be done, you will not deny me my share!'

It was characteristic of Turl never to speak on serious occasions without leaving a deep impression on his hearers. Wilmot heaved a profound sigh, but was silent.

Having thus far prevailed, I was desirous of being immediately removed to prison: but to this they both vehemently objected. It had an air of ostentation: of affecting to love misery for misery's sake. Time ought to be taken for consideration; and evil should not be sported with, though when unavoidable it ought to be endured with fortitude.

While these debates took place, it was no uninteresting spectacle to contemplate the changes in the countenance of Clarke. Before the adventure of Bath, he had risen much above the level of his companions: but now, when he saw a man willing to part with all he possessed to rescue another from prison, and heard strong reasons why it was probable the offer ought not to be accepted, his feelings were all in arms. His passions, while Wilmot pleaded, were ready to break their bounds; and, when he listened to the answers that were returned, his mind was filled and expanded. He discovered that there is a disinterested grandeur in morality, of which he had no previous conception. He was in a new world; and a dark room, with barred windows, was heaven in all its splendor.

Having agreed to follow their advice, Wilmot and Turl left me; with a promise to return early in the evening: but poor Clarke said 'he had no heart for work that day; and he could not abide to leave me shut up by myself. He saw plainly enough I had true friends; such as would never forsake me: and no more would he, though he could do me no good.' When however I represented to him my wish to be alone, that I might consider on my situation, and requested he would dine with his family, and bring some books from my lodgings in the evening, he complied.

The morning of the day was chiefly consumed; and I was not suffered long to remain alone. I had scarcely dined before a coach stopped at the door, and Charlotte came in with demure significance in her face. 'There is a young lady, sir,' said she, '*which* says her name is Wilmot, *which* wants to see you.'

At this moment, she was the most agreeable visitor that could have arrived. Her heart was full, her eyes were swollen, and red with weeping, and, as soon as she entered the room, she again burst into tears.

It has often been asked why sorrows like these should excite so much gratification? The answer is evident. They are not only tokens of personal respect and affection, but they are proofs that injustice cannot be committed without being perceptibly and often deeply felt by others, as well as by those on whom it is exercised.

When she had appeased her feelings sufficiently to be able to speak, I found that, like her brother, she was come with a disinterested plan for my relief. She began by blaming herself for not having strenuously enough opposed my forbearance with respect to Wakefield; and pleaded with great energy of feeling to persuade me immediately to do myself right. I took the first favourable opportunity to interrupt her; and enquired if she had seen or heard any thing of Wakefield since the letter he wrote? She answered, he had been with her above an hour that very morning.

'In what temper of mind was he?'

'Extremely exasperated.'

'Not at you?'

'Oh no: at Lord Bray: at your persecutors: at the world in general. He says you are not fit to live in it: you are no match for it. You have been persuading him, contrary to all history and experience, that men are capable of virtue and happiness. In short, he owns that he was more than half convinced: but that he believes he shall be obliged to relapse into his former opinions.'

'I have persuaded him?'

'So he says.'

'When? Where?'

'I cannot tell. I thought from his discourse that he had met with you.'

While we were engaged in this conversation, Charlotte again entered; and told me there was a gentleman of the name of Wakefield, who desired to see me. 'Is it possible?' exclaimed Miss Wilmot.

The door opened, and he appeared. 'Belmont!' cried I, with surprise. 'Why did you announce yourself by the name of Wakefield?'

He stretched out his hand to me, and turned his face aside: then recovering himself replied 'The farce is over.'

'What do you mean?'

'That I suppose you will despise me. But do, if you please: for, though I love you, I too despise to fear you. I have done you various wrongs. My name is Wakefield. I have been one of the infernal instruments to bring you here: but I am come to make you all the atonement in my power, and take you out. Forgive me only so far as not to insult me, by repeating your contempt of that villain Wakefield. It is a damned undigestible term: but I deserved it; and you applied it to me without intending an affront. I know you are as brave as you are generous. Till I met with you, I thought myself the first man in the world: but, notwithstanding my evasive raillery, I felt your hand upon me. I sunk under you. There was something in you that excited my envy, at first; and afterward, perhaps, a better passion. What damned accidents they were that made me what I have been I cannot tell. I know not what I shall be: but I know what I am. I disdain penitential promises. If you will be my friend, here is my hand. Good fortune or bad, we will share it together.'

Thus invited, could I refrain? Oh no. I cannot describe the scene that passed. We did not embrace, for we were no actors; and, as our passions for a time were too big for utterance, we were silent.

Miss Wilmot at length looked up; and, while the tears were streaming down her cheeks, her countenance assumed an expression infinitely beyond smiling, though something like it, while she exclaimed—'This is a happy day!'

Her eye first met mine, and then Wakefield's. He instantly hung his head, and said—'Lydia! When we were alone, I could just endure to look at you: but now I cannot. Yet I am an ass. What is done is done. The affections that I have are yours: but I must not, no nor I will not be afraid, even of my own thoughts. I know I have nothing to fear from you. Man is a strange animal; and may be many things in the course of a short life.'

Wakefield then rang the bell, and desired the bailiff would send immediately to Lord Bray's attorney; that my debts might be settled, and I released; and to call, as he knew they must for form's sake, and see that there were no more detainers.

Hearing him give these directions, I could not but ask his meaning? 'What,' replied he, with generous indignation, 'do you suppose that I am come to cant about virtue? That, at least, is a vice of which you have never yet found me guilty. I am here to pay your debts, with money in my possession. Whether, in a court of law, it would be proved to be yours or mine I neither know nor care. But there is something better that I do know: which is that, if I were in your place and you in mine, you would not long let me remain in a house like this. With respect to the future, I am partly persuaded we shall neither of us act the miser.'

Miss Wilmot again exclaimed—'This is a happy day!'

Wakefield was impatient to see me released; and was well acquainted with bailiffs. 'If you are expeditious,' said he to George, 'you will have a guinea for your industry. If you are dilatory, not a farthing more than your fees.'

The promised guinea gave the messenger wings; and in less than an hour the debt was discharged, and a receipt in full delivered.

Just as this account was closed, another messenger came from a different quarter. The anxiety of Miss Wilmot had induced her to take a bold step. In the first emotions of grief, she wrote to Olivia; and informed her of every circumstance, as well as of the place of my detention. This information produced the following letter, and the bills inclosed; as mentioned in its contents.

'I have no words to speak my feelings. I have never yet had an opportunity, since I thought the love I bear you justifiable, to declare them. This is the time. To be silent now would argue a distrust of you, which would degrade me; and render me unworthy both of you and the dignified virtues by which your conduct is guided. Every new fact that I hear of you does but increase that affection; which I find ennobled by being so worthily placed. After the proofs you have so repeatedly given, it would be cowardice and hypocrisy to say less.

'I inclose you five hundred pounds. They are my own. I would sooner even see you suffer than be guilty of an action which I know you could not approve. They are what I have reserved, from money allowed me, to be employed on any urgent occasion. Surely there can be few more urgent than the present. Your refusal of them would wound me to the soul. It would break my heart. I need not add any thing more.

OLIVIA MOWBRAY.'

Who will tell me that virtue is not its own reward? Who will affirm that to conquer selfish desires, to render the passions subservient to reason, and to make those principles we commend in others rules for ourselves, is not the way to be happy? The tide of joy was full to overflowing! And yet, when I recollected that, though no longer a prisoner it was denied me to obey the yearnings of my heart and pass the threshold of Olivia, how suddenly did it ebb!

CHAPTER XVI

A journey to aid Hector once more projected: An interview
with the wounded stranger: A discovery of great importance

I SHALL forbear to repeat the joy and congratulations of friends,
with other less events; and hasten to one which gave a more surprising turn to my affairs than even any that I had yet experienced.
The morning after my release, it was my intention to go down into
the county of ****: agreeable to the desire of Hector. Of this
I informed Mr. Hilary, the evening before: but, as I was become
very cautious in money matters, I meant to go by the coach.

When he heard this, Mr. Hilary smiled: and told me, if I would
go post, he believed he could find me a companion, who would
willingly bear half the expence.

I enquired who? and found it was no other than the stranger. He
had been down into Cambridgeshire, to settle some affairs; and was
now preparing for a journey into my native county, for purposes
which he will himself presently explain. A proposal more agreeable
than this could not have been made to me; and it was agreed that
we should meet and breakfast with Mr. Hilary. When I made the
appointment, Mr. Hilary pressed me with unusual earnestness not
to be induced to break it, by any accident whatever.

The morning came, I was punctual, and the stranger was there.
He had slept at the house of Mr. Hilary. 'This, sir,' said the latter,
presenting me, 'is the young gentleman of whose acquaintance you
are so very desirous.'

The stranger regarded me earnestly; and, with great emotion in
his countenance, asked—'Are you, sir, the humane person, who
found me almost expiring; and by whose care I am now among the
living?'

'I hope, sir, you do not think there was any thing extraordinary
in what I did?'

'I wish I had not reason so to think. How many there are who,
from mean and selfish motives, would have passed me I cannot say:
but there are few indeed that would have discharged the office you
undertook with so much unaffected and generous benevolence.
I am in your debt, sir, not only for my recovery, for which I can
never repay you, but literally for money expended. I shall forbear

thanks, for I have none that are adequate; but suffer me to rid myself of petty obligations.'

'I understand, sir, that you are rich, and I am not. I therefore inform you, without hesitation, I left twenty pounds with the physician.'

'You may well suppose that I returned, after my recovery, to enquire for my preserver. I was then informed of your whole proceedings; and of the anxiety with which, after your journey, you came to complete the charitable office you had begun. And I own, sir, that I was so desirous of seeing a person who, in the very fervour of youth, could act and feel as you have done that, one excepted, you are the man on earth I am most happy to meet.'

'Mr. Hilary tells me that we are to be travelling companions.'

'Most willingly. I have long been a wanderer, and am lately returned to end my days in my native land. During my absence, the elder branches of my family are all deceased. I brought back with me more than sufficient for my own wants: but their property has descended to me, and I now very unexpectedly find myself wealthy.'

'And have you no descendants, sir?'

'None. I am at present in search of a distant relation: whom if I should find, and find him such as my present hopes and past knowledge have pictured him, I shall be one of the happiest of men. To make this and another enquiry is the purpose of the journey I now mean to take. When I left England, I had no intention ever to return: I therefore resolved to hold no correspondence with the persons whom I have left; that I might not revive the memory of scenes and events which had been full of anguish. By accident, about eighteen months ago, being then at Grand Cairo I was informed that a person of my family had long been dead. This determined me to settle my concerns abroad, and revisit my native country. As however my informer spoke only from report, I am desirous, before I make myself known, to verify this fact. I have my reasons; which, from what I have said, you may suspect to be those of resentment. But not so; they are only what I conceive to be necessary precautions. Acrimony and anger have long since died away; and I have but too much cause to condemn those actions of my life in which they were indulged. The relation, whom I hope to find, I may unfortunately discover to be more likely to misuse the wealth, that has devolved to me by the death of the elder branches of my family, than to make it a blessing to himself and others. It is true he is not my heir at law. I have no heir: what I possess is at my own disposal. But he was once my greatest favourite: and I would avoid any action that should excite hopes which it might be weakness and vice in me to gratify.'

This short narrative was not merely delivered with a serious air; but it was accompanied with somewhat of a plaintive tone, that rendered the venerable stranger unusually interesting. It likewise excited various wild yet not impossible conjectures in my mind, which made me very eager to pursue the discourse. Mr. Hilary, whose mind had been full of conjectures mingled with doubt, had not informed him of my name.

'Is the person,' said I, 'in search of whom you mean to take this journey young, or old?'

'About four and twenty. He was the son of my wife's sister; therefore my relation only by marriage. He was certainly the most extraordinary child I ever beheld. I cannot recollect him but with inconceivable emotions of affection. Of all the sportive little creatures I ever met with, he was the most active, the most undaunted, and the most winning. Heaven bless the sweet boy! He was my delight. My eyes overflow whenever I recall to mind the feats of his childhood, which can never be long forgotten by me. My wife and her sister had been at variance, and the first time I saw him was at a fair; when he was not five years old. I found him placed on a table, where he stood reading the newspaper to country farmers; who were collected round him, and hearing him with astonishment. They seemed to doubt if he could possibly be a child, born of a woman; and were more inclined to think him a supernatural being. His flaxen curly hair, his intelligent eyes, his rosy cheeks, his strong and proportioned limbs, and his cheerful animated countenance, rendered him the most beautiful and most endearing of human creatures. The discriminating sensibility which he displayed was enchanting. Oh should he be living, should I find him, and should he be at present all that his infancy promised, God of heaven and earth! I should expire. The pleasure would be too mighty for my years. But, should I survive it, I should once again before I die feel the animating fervor of youth.'

I listened in amazement. I was not then acquainted with all the incidents of my childhood so perfectly as, by hearing them repeated, I since have been: but I knew enough of them to be persuaded the discourse that I had heard could relate only to me.

I paused. I gazed. My eyes were riveted upon the narrator. At length I exclaimed—'What I have just heard, sir, has excited very strange ideas. They seem almost impossible: and yet I am persuaded they are true. Pardon a question which I cannot refrain to ask. Surely I cannot be mistaken! Your name is Elford?'

'Sir!'

'You are my ——'

'Speak! Go on! What am I?'

'My uncle!'

'Heavens! Mr. Trevor! Is that your name?'

'It is.'

'Oh! God! Oh! God! Oh! God!—Hugh! Little Hugh! My boy! My sweet boy!'

Mr. Elford was almost overcome. In a moment he again cried—'My saviour too! Still the same! Courageous, humane, generous! All that my soul could desire! Oh shield me, deliver me from this excess of joy!'

CHAPTER XVII

The conclusion

ONE event only excepted, little remains to be told of my story; and that one is doubtless anticipated by the imagination of the reader. To describe the enquiries that passed between me and my uncle, the various fortunes we had encountered, and the feelings they excited, would be to write his history and tediously repeat my own. My difficulties now disappeared. I was the acknowledged heir of a man of great wealth: therefore, I myself am become a great man. Heaven preserve me from becoming indolent, proud, and oppressive! I have not yet forgotten that oppression exists, that pride is its chief counsellor, that activity and usefulness are the sacred duties of both rich and poor, that the wealth entrusted to my distribution is the property of those whom most it can benefit, that I am a creature of very few wants, but that those few in others as well as in myself are imperious, and that I have felt them in all their rigour. Neither have I yet shut my doors on one of my former friends. But I am comparatively young in prosperity. How long I shall be able to persevere in this eccentric conduct time must tell. At present

I must proceed, and mention the few remaining circumstances with which the reader may wish to be acquainted.

After my uncle had heard me describe Olivia, and mention the motives which induced me to wish to aid her brother, he immediately determined on taking the journey we had before proposed. We neither of us wished to separate. Robust in 'a green old age,'[1] he had no fear of fatigue from travelling this distance; and it would be a pleasure to revisit, in my company, scenes which would bring my former sports and pranks to his recollection. He heard from me a confirmation of the death of Mrs. Elford; and heard it with the same tokens of melancholy in his face which he had betrayed, when he spoke of her himself.

That I should have wished before I took this journey, short as it was, to have seen Olivia, related all my good fortune and partaken in the pleasure it would excite in her, may well be imagined: but forms, and delicacies, and I know not what habitual feelings, forbad me the enjoyment of this premature bliss. I wrote however, and not only to her but to those tried and invaluable friends who were not to be neglected.

We found Hector in a lamentable state. Instead of the bluff robust form, which but shortly before he had worn, his limbs were shrunk, his cheeks formerly of a high red were wan and hollow, his voice was gone, his lungs were affected, and his cough was incessant. He had himself at last begun to think his life in danger; and was preparing to return to town for advice: consequently our stay was short. His reception of me however was friendly. The increasing debility which he felt softened his manners; and, when he understood the good fortune that had befallen me, he seemed sincerely to rejoice.

And now let me request the reader to call to mind, not only my first emotions of love for Olivia, and the violence of the passion that preyed upon me while struggling between hope and despair, but those late testimonies of affection, such as a mind so dignified as hers could bestow; and then let him imagine what our meeting must be. Should he expect me to describe her, such as she was and is, in all her attractions, all her beauties, and all her various excellence, he expects an impossible task. To be beloved by her, to be found worthy of her, and to call her mine, are blessings that infinitely exceed momentary rapture: they are lasting and indubitable happiness.

†κ k

I know not if it will give him pleasure to be told that, could I have delighted in revenge, I might have satiated myself with that unworthy and destructive passion. The committee, appointed to decide on the election, voted the Idford candidate guilty of bribery and corruption. The fortune of the Earl, like that of Hector, has suffered depredations which half a century will probably not repair. The new-made peer and his party daily became so obnoxious to the nation, by the destructive tendency of their measures, that they were and continue to be haunted by terrors that deprive them of the faculties common to man. My heart bears witness for me that I do not speak this in triumph. I should be no less vicious than unworthy, could I triumph in the misfortunes of any human being: but I were a wretch indeed, were I to make mistakes that are the scourge of mankind a subject of exultation.

Must I repeat more names? Is it necessary to say the virtues of Turl and Wilmot are too splendid to need my praise: or that my social hours are most beneficially and delightfully spent in their society? That I have amply provided for the generous-minded Clarke? That Philip is once more the good and faithful servant of a kind mistress? That Mary and her son are equally objects of my attention? And that I do not mean to boast of these things as acts of munificence: but as the performance of duties?

This were unnecessary. Neither shall I be required to particularize the present happiness of Lydia, now Mrs. Wakefield; and of that man of brilliant and astonishing faculties who is her affectionate companion and friend, and from whose exertions, if I am not strangely mistaken, the world has so much to profit and so much to expect. Like me, he is in the enjoyment of affluence; and he enjoys it with a liberal and munificent spirit. Are there any who hate him, because he once was guilty of hateful crimes? I hope not. It is a spirit that would sweep away half the inhabitants of the 'peopled earth.' For my own part, I delight in his conversation, am enlivened by his wit, and prompted to enquiry by the acuteness of his remarks. He is a man whom I am proud to say I love.

I have told my tale. If it should afford instruction, if it should inspire a love of virtue, briefly, if it should contribute to the happiness of mankind, I shall have gained my purpose. My labours will be most richly rewarded.

THE END

EXPLANATORY NOTES

ABBREVIATIONS

Colby   *The Life of Thomas Holcroft*, ed. Elbridge Colby, 2 vols., 1925.

Commentaries   Sir William Blackstone, *Commentaries on the Laws of England*, 4 vols., 1821 edn.

Grose   *Grose's Classical Dictionary of the Vulgar Tongue*, ed. Eric Partridge, 1963.

Johnson   Samuel Johnson, *A Dictionary of the English Language*, 2 vols., 1755.

Page 1. The epigraph is a misquotation from Gay, *The Beggar's Opera*, ii. x, Air xxx.

Page 3. (1) *Turgot*: Anne-Robert Jacques Turgot (1727–81), a Physiocrat and Controller-General of France 1774–6. The remark is from Condorcet's *The Life of M. Turgot* (1787), p. 62.

(2) *perfectability*: The theme of Condorcet's *Esquisse d'un tableau historique des progrès de l'esprit humain* (1795) and of Godwin's *Political Justice* (1793 and 1796).

Page 4. (1) *Whether this . . . been born*: a standard argument of the empirical tradition.

(2) *it surely . . . enlightened days*: this passage is quoted for satiric effect in Isaac D'Israeli's *Vaurien: or, Sketches of the Times*, 2 vols. (1797), i. 36. The Mr. Glib of this novel is a caricature of Holcroft.

VOLUME I

Page 9. (1) *tenth chapter of Nehemiah*: contained the points of the Covenant and the names of those who sealed it; hence, a difficult reading exercise.

(2) *Chevy Chace . . . Jack the Giant-killer*: Chapbooks. Holcroft's own reading was similar. See Colby, i. 89, and John Ashton, *Chapbooks of the Eighteenth Century* (1882).

Page 11. (1) *adust*: burnt-up, hot as with fire, scorched (Johnson).

(2) *atrabilarious*: melancholick (Johnson).

Page 13. This is adapted from an experience of Holcroft's son, William. (See Colby, i. 302.)

Page 15. *succedaneum*: a substitute.

Page 17. (1) *The holy . . . devour me*: cf. 2 Kings 2: 24.

(2) *Fox's Book of Martyrs*: the popular title of John Foxe's *Acts and Monuments of matters happening in the Church* first published in English in 1563. It extolled the heroism of the Protestant martyrs of Mary's reign.

Page 18. (1) *We are all . . . begotten*: a stock belief of the materialist school, especially in France.

(2) *feared no colours*: feared no foe.

(3) *opened*: began to cry in pursuit.

Page 20. *. . . succeeded*: an autobiographical incident. (See Colby, i. 11–13.)

Page 22. (1) *threaping*: arguing loudly.

(2) *threating*: rebuking.

Page 23. *weltering*: rolling in agony.

Page 34. (1) *the jack at all fours*: a card game played by two.

(2) *Wheatherby's Racing Calendar*: James Wheatherby's official *Racing Calendar* first appeared in 1727.

(3) *hazard table*: a gaming table, hazard being a game at dice.

Page 35. (1) *waiting in the Downs*: a famous roadstead and favourable anchorage in the English Channel.

(2) *coming on the parish*: reduced to dependence on parish funds for the relief of the poor.

Page 36. (1) *Croft*, etc.: William Croft (1678–1727), English organist and composer; probably Maurice Greene (1695–1755), English organist and composer and a founder of the Society of Musicians; William Boyce (c. 1710–79), the leading English-born composer of the eighteenth century; Henry Purcell (1659–95), one of the greatest of English composers.

(2) This scene is referred to by A. R. Humphreys, *The Augustan World* (1964), p. 38.

(3) *Arnold's Psalmody*: John Arnold (1720–92) published *The Compleat Psalmodist*, a widely popular work, in 1741.

Page 37. *the flattering unction to his soul*: *Hamlet*, III. iv. 145.

Page 40. *Pipkin*: a small earthen boiler (Johnson).

Page 41. *Seven Champions of Christendom*: a romance by R. Johnson, printed about 1597; a chapbook favourite in the eighteenth century.

Page 45. Dr. James's powders: Robert James, an English physician (1705–76), gave his name to these powders which caused a prompt and heavy perspiration. He compiled the *Medical Dictionary* (1743–5).

Page 51. hundred: subdivision of a county or shire having its own court; applied sometimes (as here) to the court itself.

Page 53. Corelli's Arcangelo Corelli (1653–1713), Italian violinist and composer.

Page 54. (1) *advowson*: right of presentation of a clergyman to a church or ecclesiastical benefice.

(2) *commutation*: substitution of one kind of tithe payment for another.

(3) *his first fruits*: not less than one-sixtieth and not more than one-fortieth of the crop.

(4) *tythes, personal, predial, and mixed*: tithes which were respectively paid in the products of manual labour or manufacture, which were products of the soil, and which consisted of natural products which had been nurtured and preserved in part by the care of man, e.g. wool, milk, eggs.

Page 55. (1) *Behemoth*: cf. Job 40: 15–34.

(2) *Magog*: cf. Gen. 10: 2. and Rev. 20: 7–9.

(3) *agistment*: in this case a tithe paid to the vicar by the occupier of pasture land.

(4) *subbois*: wooded land.

(5) *sylva caedua*: wood or timber preserved for annual cutting.

Page 56. (1) *Norway rats*: *rattus norvegicus*, the brown rat, believed to have first reached Great Britain from the East about 1730.

(2) *malice prepense*: malice aforethought.

Page 57. By the waunds!: a common pronunciation of 'wounds', especially when used as an oath.

Page 59. (1) *gentleman commoner*: a student rank at Oxford, distinguished by certain privileges and immunities.

(2) *feræ naturæ*: by legal definition, such animals as are of a wild nature or disposition and so require to be made tame by art or to be kept in confinement.

(3) *vi et armis*: by force of arms.

Page 60. (1) *molliter manus imponere*: lit. to lay hands upon gently; legally, the phrase defines the furthest extent to which an officer of the law may go when making an arrest under any normal circumstances.

(2) *trespass upon the case*: referring to writs which had to be specially drafted so as to include a good deal of narrative matter in which particular circumstances were set out in unusual detail.

Page 61. Lessing etc. Gotthold Ephraim Lessing (1729–81), German essayist, critic, and dramatist; Friedrich Gottlieb Klopstock (1724–1803),

German poet (Holcroft met Klopstock in 1799; see Colby ii. 286); Holcroft had used hints from Goethe's *Clavigo* for his comedy *He's Much to Blame* (1798) and translated *Hermann und Dorothea* (see Colby ii. 287). (Hugh Trevor's reading is Holcroft's.)

Page 63. Aristides &c.: Athenian statesman, surnamed the Just (*c.* 530–468 B.C.); Theban general and statesman (*c.* 418–362 B.C.); Marcus Atilius *Regulus* (d. *c.* 250 B.C.), Roman general who exemplified the Roman qualities of endurance and severity; Marcus Porcius Cato (234–149 B.C.), Roman statesman, general, and writer who sought to restore the integrity and simplicity of manners typical of the early days of the Republic; Lucius Annaeus Seneca (*c.* 4 B.C.–A.D. 65), Nero's tutor (ordered to commit suicide he left, instead of a will, the pattern of his life); and the Greek Stoic philosopher active about A.D. 100 who taught that evil is only apparent, happiness a matter of will. This would have charmed Holcroft.

Page 65. a commoner: an Oxford student who pays for his meals and is not 'on the foundation'.

Page 67. cestus: a band or girdle.

Page 69. the kinchin . . . bubble: a slang phrase meaning that the dupe will be deceived (Grose).

Page 75. a Stentor voice: an extremely loud voice.

Page 76. beat up: search around.

Page 77. hum: to impose upon, hoax (Grose).

Page 78. bilk: to cheat, to defraud, by running in debt and avoiding payment (Johnson).

Page 79. rummer: a large drinking glass.

Page 80: William Sharp (1749–1824), engraver, republican, and enthusiast was the model for the character of Turl (see Colby, ii. 64).

Page 83. hawling: probably means a coarse kind of railing.

Page 85. the irrefragable: Alexander of Hales (d. 1245).

Page 86. angelic: St. Thomas Aquinas (1226–74); *eagle-eyed*: could refer to John Faber of Bordeaux (d. 1340), or to Gregory of Rimini (d. 1358), *subtile*: Duns Scotus (*c.* 1265–1308); and *illuminated*: a name applied to Raymond Lull and to Ruysbroek.

Page 90. (1) guttling: to guttle, to feed luxuriously: to gormandize; a low word (Johnson).

(2) *Ammon and Mammon and Moloch*: all demon gods associated with riches and with child sacrifice.

(3) *Bethhoron*: the combined name of two neighbouring towns where

Joshua and Judas Maccabeus won two historic Jewish victories; cf.
Joshua 10; 1 Mac. 3; Joshua 16: 3, 5; 18: 13, 14; 21: 22.

Page 91. (1) *Jehu . . . furiously*: cf. 2 Kings 9: 20.

(2) *Jezebel . . . dogs*: cf. 2 Kings 9: 10, 36.

(3) *Tophet*: or Topheth, the valley (of Hinnom, probably), where the
Jews performed the rites of human sacrifice. Cf. Jer. 7: 31–2.

(4) *vis a vis*: a carriage, which holds only two persons, who sit face to
face, and not side by side, as in a coach or chariot (Johnson).

(5) *cry peccavi*: admit guilt.

Page 92. *freshes*: floods from mountain streams.

Page 94. (1) *Baxter's Call to the Unconverted*: Holcroft is again remembering his youthful reading (see Colby, i. 92–3). Richard Baxter (1615–91),
the famous Puritan minister at Kidderminster, showed his concern for
conversion in his *A Call to the Unconverted to Turn and Live and Accept
of Mercy* (1657).

(2) *History of Francis Spira*: a chapbook relating the sad fate of a
convert to Catholicism.

Page 95. (1) *wall lectures*: at Oxford, lectures delivered according to
statute by a regent-master (see note to p. 103) to empty benches.

(2) *done juraments*: Oxford slang, used of a student who had reached
the rank of Senior Soph.

(3) *generals*: disputations, examination later known as Responsions.

(4) *Soph*: colloquial form for sophister, a student one year below a
bachelor.

VOLUME II

Page 98. *Otway*: Thomas Otway (1652–85), whose plays were especially
popular in the eighteenth century.

Page 102. (1) *hired wholesale*: a common practice by this date. See
Esther de Waal, 'New Churches in East London in the Early Eighteenth
Century', *Renaissance and Modern Studies* ix (1965), 98–114.

(2) *farmer general*: under the Ancien Régime in France, the agent who
collected moneys for the government from the district under his control.
The office was abolished in 1789.

Page 103. (1) *regent master*: at Oxford and Cambridge, a Master of Arts
of not more than five years' standing.

(2) *caput*: Holcroft is confused here. The caput was the ruling body of
the University of Cambridge, not of Oxford.

Page 104. (1) *Dii tibi*: Virgil, *Aen.* i. 603.

(2) *tambours de basque*: tambourines.

Page 105. (1) *Fair Penitent*: Nicholas Rowe (1674–1718), poet laureate and dramatist, completed this highly sentimental tragedy in 1703. Its main roles of Calista and Lothario were widely sought after by actors and actresses. Holcroft's audition for the theatre indicates Rowe's and Otway's popularity. (See Colby, i. 129.)

(2) *Mrs. Siddons*: Sarah Siddons (1755–1831), a famous actress. She played the part of Calista in Rowe's play fourteen times in the season of 1783.

Page 106. (1) *chagrin*: a kind of skin or leather with a rough surface.

(2) *the nut*: a small spur-wheel.

(3) *a repeater*: repeating watches and clocks were first made about 1676; the name 'repeater' became current around 1770.

Page 107. *fob*: a small pocket (Johnson).

Page 108. (1) *the Piazza*: Piazza Coffee-House, Covent Garden.

(2) *the Shakespeare*: Shakespeare's Head Tavern, Covent Garden.

Page 114. (1) *the jacks of her harpsichord*: upright pieces of wood fixed to the backs of the key levers and fitted with quills which plucked the strings as the jacks rose on the keys being pressed down.

(2) *bravura . . . cantabile . . . maëstoso*: passages requiring respectively a brilliant, a smooth, and a majestic rendering.

(3) *song fro*: phonetic rendering of Miss Eliza's pronunciation of *sang froid*.

Page 115. (1) *Kozeluch*: Leopold Kozeluch (1752–1818), Bohemian musician. At first a popular composer of ballets, later Court Composer at Prague.

(2) *Allegro con strepito*: quick, with vivacity.

(3) *obligato*: the obligatory or essential part in a score; *maestro di capella*: chief musician, musical director; *piano*: soft.

Page 116. *my half crown . . . candlestick*: as a contribution to pay for the purchase of the cards.

Page 117. (1) *parliamentary reform . . . an evil*: in 1785 Pitt tried to introduce a measure of parliamentary reform but was defeated; so too was Earl Grey's motion for reform in 1793. With the Revolution and the war with France, reform ceased to be a political possibility.

(2) *extension of the excise laws*: taxes imposed by Pitt in the late eighties on male and female servants, hair powder, dogs, clocks, watches.

(3) *national debt*: this had doubled as a consequence of the Seven Years War.

Page 118. *Junius*: the pseudonymous author of a series of letters attacking the administrations of Grafton and North and the personal government of George III. They appeared in the *Public Advertiser* between 1769 and 1772.

Page 119. (1) *eulogium* . . . *French Academy*: an *éloge*, or discourse in honour of a man newly received into the Academy or delivered on the death of one of its members.

(2) *Boileau*: Nicolas Boileau-Despréaux, French poet and critic, the most influential exponent of classical standards.

Page 122. *Mambrino's helmet*: in *Orlando Furioso* a magic helmet acquired by Rinaldo from the pagan king Mambrino. In *Don Quixote*, a barber's brass basin seized by the hero.

Page 123. *There is one best . . . confuses*: a manifesto for the kind of prose written by Godwin, Bage, Paine, Holcroft, and others. See J. T. Boulton, *The Language of Politics in the Age of Wilkes and Burke* (1963).

Page 129. *Hogarth's modern midnight conversation*: a famous painting in which Hogarth (1697–1764) displays a group passing into total drunkenness. Prints from the painting became popular.

Page 132. (1) *Enoch . . . land of promise*: cf. Jude 14.

(2) *another Caleb . . . grapes*: cf. Num. 13: 23–30.

(3) *Zoilus*: a grammarian who attacked Homer; identified with captious malignant criticism.

(4) *'Oh that his words . . . book!'*: Job 19: 23.

Page 133. *the sublime and beautiful*: a sneer at Burke's *A Philosophical Enquiry into the sublime and beautiful* (1757).

Page 141. (1) *Arminian*: after Jacobus Arminius (1560–1609), Dutch Reformed theologian.

(2) *Trinitarian controversy . . . and grace*: Socinianism and, later, Unitarianism, both of which denied the Trinity, had influential followings in the eighteenth century. Arminianism opposed the deterministic logic of Calvinism and insisted on the existence of free will, rejecting thereby the notion of the elect. Methodism, which Holcroft portrays so satirically in this novel, embraces both Arminian and Calvinistic attitudes.

Page 142. (1) *Whitgift . . . Rutherford*: John Whitgift (*c.* 1530–1604), Archbishop of Canterbury, defender of the Church of England against the Papacy and against the Puritans; Daniel Waterland (1683–1740), Anglican theologian; John Rogers (*c.* 1500–55), editor of Matthews Bible and the first British Protestant martyr under Mary; and Samuel Rutherford (*c.* 1600–61), Scottish Presbyterian divine.

(2) *Mrs. Jordan*: Dorothea or Dorothy Jordan, Irish actress, famous for her comic roles. She played in two of Holcroft's dramas.

(3) *the Country Girl*: Wycherley's play *The Country Wife* (1675) was

adapted by Garrick in 1766 as *The Country Girl*, with its 'indecencies' removed.

Page 144. Thalestris: Queen of the Amazons.

Page 147. So while . . . doom'd to fall: Pope, *Odyssey*, iv. 719–20.

Page 159. An ounce . . . apothecary: *King Lear*, IV. iii. 133–4.

Page 162. (1) *Orpheus*: his grief for the loss of Eurydice led him to treat with contempt the Thracian women, who in revenge tore him to pieces in the course of their Bacchanalian orgies.

   (2) *leaving like Joseph my garment behind me*: Gen. 39: 12.

Page 166. like Belshazzar's: Dan. 2: 5, 6.

Page 167. cry cupboard: crave for food, feel hungry.

Page 168. a high quarter and a low one: the parts into which the road was divided by the horse-track and the wheel-ruts.

Page 170. Blenheim house: Blenheim Palace, Oxfordshire, built by Sir John Vanbrugh between 1705 and 1720, the most baroque and monumental mansion in England.

VOLUME III

Page 175. to come upon the parish: see note (2) to p. 35.

Page 182. civilians: authorities on Civil Law.

Page 184. (1) *of several removes*: of several courses.

   (2) *put his affairs to nurse*: put his affairs in the hands of economic managers to avoid bankruptcy.

   (3) *Leo X*: Pope 1513–21; famous for his promotion of literature, science, and art.

Page 186. (1) *manicheism*: a form of religious dualism preaching two eternal principles of Good and Evil. Holcroft believed that evil was contingent and would disappear.

   (2) *the errors . . . ignorance*: cf. Helvétius, *De l'esprit* (1759), ch. iv; 'L'erreur n'est donc pas essentiellement attachée à la nature de l'esprit humaine.'

   (3) *Harris's List*: John Harris (1756–1846), publisher. He employed authoresses like Mrs. Trimmer, Mrs. Lovechild, Mrs. Hofland, to write books for the nursery.

Page 187. (1) *Jordaens*: Jakob Jordaens (1593–1678), Flemish painter who studied under Rubens and followed him as leader of the Antwerp school.

   (2) *Silenus and his ass*: Greek forest-god, part man, part horse, often depicted riding on an ass; figure of drunkenness.

Page 188. (1) *I never felt such ineffable contempt . . . what is called a run*: cf. Holcroft's preface to his play *Seduction* (1787): 'The theatre is a subject of such consequence to virtue, happiness, and man, that I cannot forbear speaking of it with a sense of feeling which, I fear, I cannot impart.'

(2) *Congreve's 'Way of the World!'*: it was coldly received when played at Lincolns Inn Fields in 1700.

Page 193. *a war between England and Spain*: probably a reference to Pitt's attempt to insist upon such a war in 1761.

Page 198. *temporalities*: material possessions of the church or clergy.

Page 202. (1) *congè d'elire*: in common law, the king's permission royal granted to a dean and chapter, in time of vacation, to choose a bishop.

(2) *Frederic of Prussia . . . highway*: the remark, attributed to La Mettrie, appears in Condorcet's *Life of Voltaire* (1789), p. 69. It was widely quoted in the scurrilous literature of the decade.

(3) *Asmodeus in London*: Asmodée, the devil in Le Sage's famous novel *Le Diable boiteux* (1707), became a chapbook hero in the eighteenth century. The novel was frequently translated and widely imitated. Hugh Trevor's ambition was realized in 1808 when Sir Charles Sedley published *Asmodeus: or, the Devil in London*.

Page 208. *the purse of Fortunatus*: unlimited wealth. Thomas Dekker's play *The Pleasant Comedie of Old Fortunatus* (1600) had been popularized in the chapbooks also.

Page 211. (1) *'I have . . . art'*: *The Tempest*, v. i. 41.

(2) *player*: cf. Colby, i. 172–83.

Page 214. (1) *stay-tape and buckram*: binding lace and strong linen cloth stiffened with gum. Tailors were colloquially known as staytapes (see Grose).

(2) *quantum sufficit*: enough.

(3) *degage*: casually.

(4) *Monmouth-street*: traditionally the street for tailors.

(5) *Paternoster-row*: publishers' street, 'that fountain of learning from which the perennial stream of literature for ever flows' (Mrs. Elizabeth Hamilton, *Memoirs of Modern Philosophers* (1800), p.) v.

Page 219. (1) *sooterkin*: an imaginary afterbirth attributed to Dutch-women: 'supposing that by their constant use of stoves, which they place under their petticoats, they breed a kind of small animal in their bodies, called a sooterkin, of the size of a mouse, which when mature slips out' (Grose).

(2) *La Rochefoucault and Mandeville*: both François, 6th duc de la Rochefoucauld (1613–80) and Bernard Mandeville (1670–1733) argued that every form of virtue is at bottom self-love.

Page 220. *aversion to secrecy*: shared by Holcroft and Godwin. In the Advertisement to his play *Knave or Not?* (1798), Holcroft mentions the play's continental sources because he considered 'the least concealment . . . as derogatory to that veracity which it is the peculiar duty of moral writers to inculcate'.

Page 224. *bite the bridle*: 'to be pinched or reduced to difficulties' (Grose).

Page 226. *watch-house*: used as a station for municipal night-watchmen.

Page 228. *act of attainder*: by which a traitor is deprived of all his civil rights and capacities.

Page 230. *Milton . . . can give*: Il Pensoroso.

Page 232. *Oh Otway! Oh Chatterton!* Thomas Otway, the dramatist (1652–85), died in misery; Thomas Chatterton, the poet (1752–70), committed suicide.

Page 236. *blue-stocking-club*: a term, common by 1790, used to designate evening salons, self-consciously intellectual, and presided over by hostesses like Mrs. Montague.

Page 237. . . . *how to resist*: passage quoted in Colby, i. 253–5.

Page 241. . . . *and candid inquiry*: this is a version of Holcroft's difficulties in having *Alwyn* published. Cf. Colby, i. 219–20.

Page 245. . . . *a pleasure to herself*: related in Colby, i. 206.

Page 249. (1) *death of Garrick*: in 1779.

(2) *the green-room*: room provided for actors and actresses when they are not required on the stage.

Page 250. *the town was empty*; this episode relates to Holcroft's play, *Duplicity*. Cf. Colby, ii. 242.

Page 258. *black-leg*: 'a gambler or sharper on the turf or in the cock-pit: so-called, perhaps, from their appearing generally in boots; or else from gamecocks, whose legs are always black' (Grose).

Page 260. *'darkness visible'*: Paradise Lost, i. 63.

VOLUME IV

Page 266. *post-horse kind of endurance*: exhaustion after sharp strenuous effort, like that of a post-horse which was galloped at full speed between posts with the mail.

Page 267. *Medusa*: one of the three Gorgons. She had serpent hair and a stone-inducing glance.

Page 268. *the Crescent*: the Royal Crescent, an ellipse containing thirty houses, part of the architectural scheme designed by John Wood (1705–59), and chiefly executed by his son John in 1767–9.

Page 269. Lex Talionis: law of retaliation.

Page 271. The laws of pugilistic war: a set of rules devised by Jack Broughton (1704–89), champion prize fighter of England between *c.* 1740 and 1750.

Page 272. scouted: scorned, derided.

Page 280. ignis fatuus: will o'the wisp.

Page 282. sharking: cheating or having 'an eager desire to cheat or defraud another' (Grose).

Page 290. smoked: hunted out.

Page 292. golgotha: field of skulls; Matt. 27: 23.

Page 299. the Agrarian system: the period between 1770 and 1810 saw the most rapid growth in the enclosure system.

Page 300. Dives: Luke 16.

Page 308. Zaleucus: celebrated Greek lawgiver. He was not, as the reference here seems to imply, distinguished for his benevolence. His code was severe, and he killed himself to uphold it.

Page 333. (1) *Vishnoo*: has second place in the sacred Hindu triad and embodies the preserving principle.

(2) *Blackstone's Commentaries: on the Laws of England*, 4 vols., 1765–9.

(3) *ill-judging . . . legislators*: a phrase from the *Commentaries*, i. 10 (1821 edn.).

(4) *Servius Sulpicius*: eminent Roman jurisconsul, friend of Cicero. He did in fact leave about 180 treatises or fragments of treatises. Cf. *Commentaries*, i. 12.

Page 334. (1) *Milo*: Greek athlete, famous for his strength.

(2) *Cacus*: in Roman mythology, the half-human son of Vulcan. He stole Geryon's cattle.

(3) *Vicarius*: Vacarius, according to the *Commentaries*, i. 17–20.

(4) *pandects*: otherwise called the Digests; a compilation of the Roman Law under Justinian.

(5) *that a science. . . . astonishment and concern*: *Commentaries*, i. 27.

(6) *Mr. Viner*: Charles Viner (1678–1756), jurist, referred to in the *Commentaries*, i. 27–30. His encyclopaedic if ill-arranged *General Abridgement of Law and Equity* (1742–53) was published in twenty-three volumes folio; in 1791–4 the second edition came out with an index in twenty-four volumes octavo. Holcroft confuses these editions here.

(7) *gentlemen . . . the search*: slightly misquoted from *Commentaries*, i. 31.

(8) *many persons . . . their lives*: *Commentaries*, i. 31.

Page 335. (1) *Such knowledge . . . of twenty years*: *Commentaries*, i. 37.

(2) *a rule . . . is wrong*, *Commentaries*, i. 46. This is in fact Blackstone's definition of municipal law.

(3) *Docking of entails*: putting an end to a settlement which has been made on a number of persons in succession.

Page 336. (1) *St. Stephen's*: St. Stephen's Chapel, part of Westminster Palace, used from 1547 until 1840 for the meetings of the House of Commons.

(2) *Westminster-hall*: the seat of the chief law-court of England.

Page 339. *Brunswickian manifestoes*: the Duke of Brunswick issued a manifesto in July 1792 threatening the French revolutionaries in dire terms.

VOLUME V

Page 344. *Banco Regis*: the court of King's Bench.

Page 345. (1) *hic et ubique*: here and everywhere.

(2) *Legion . . . destruction*: cf. Mark 5: 9; Luke 8: 30.

Page 346. (1) *latitat*: literally, 'he lies hidden'; in legal language, a writ running outside a county to summon one who lay concealed there to the King's Bench.

(2) *non est inventus*: he was not found.

Page 347. *traverse*: pleading which denies allegations contained in the pleading or accusation of an adverse party; *demur to your plea*: in criminal action, a pleading by the prosecution admitting the facts alleged in the plea, but denying their sufficiency to obtain the defendant's discharge; *writ of error*: usually, a writ issued out of the superior court employed to review the judgements of the courts of common law; *nonsuit*: a judgement given against the plaintiff when he is unable to prove a case, or when he refuses or neglects to proceed to trial once an issue has been brought to a point where it must be determined; *ca sa*: short form of *capias ad satisfaciendum*; an old form of a writ of execution for the arrest and imprisonment of the defendant until the claim against him should be satisfied; *fi fa*: short form of *fieri facias*, an ordinary writ of execution whereby the officer is commanded to levy and seel and to make up, if he can, the amount of the judgement creditor's demand; *bar*: a plea or objection of force sufficient to arrest entirely an action or claim at law; *replevin*: a proceeding by which the owner recovers possession of his goods; *refalo*: an abbreviation of *recordari facias loquelam*, i.e. that you cause the plaint to be recorded; *alias, and pluries*: at common law, if after taking out one writ of execution, the plaintiff took out a second, it was called an alias writ; if he took out more, all further writs were called pluries writs.

Page 348. (1) *trover*: a common law action for the recovery of damages involving the conversion of private property; *detinue*: a common law action wherein a party claims the specific recovery of goods and chattels or of deeds and writings unlawfully detained from him; *confess lease*: to admit the claim in the plaintiff's writ; *entry and ouster*: taking actual possession of land and wrongful dispossession from real property of a party who is entitled to it; *bill of Middlesex*: an old form of civil process used in the King's Bench, by which civil actions were commenced; *ac etiam*: to circumvent a statute, an *ac etiam* clause was added to the bill of Middlesex commanding the defendant to be brought in to answer the plaintiff's charge of trespass 'and also' to a bill of debt; *B.R.*: B(*ancus*) R(*egis*), King's Bench; *C.P.*: c(*uria*) P(*alatii*), the palace court; *sue out*: as applied to process, to issue to and deliver to a person qualified and also authorized to serve it; *capias*: a writ issued for the purpose of securing the person or property of a defendant in a civil action.

(2) *nonpros*: *non prosequitur*, same as 'nonsuited'; *nolle prosequi*: an agreement not to proceed further in a particular suit.

(3) *put*: 'country put; an ignorant awkward clown' (Grose).

Page 351. (1) *brought error into Parliament*: never a very frequent proceeding. A petition to the king was a necessary preliminary. Litigants were discouraged from appealing to parliament.

(2) *Cady*: a Turkish Civil Judge.

Page 353. *Jacobinical principles*: for which, of course, Holcroft had been indicted for high treason.

Page 357. *the comprehensive . . . state of activity*: seems to be Holcroft's own declaration, although it could have come from a number of other writers such as Godwin, Hartley, or Priestley.

Page 360. *burgage-tenure voters*: 'Tenure in burgage . . . is where the king or other person is lord of an antient borough, in which the tenements are held by a rent certain' (*Commentaries*, ii. 82).

Page 361. *mundungus and parchment lords*: the number of Lords under Pitt rose from 193 in 1784 to 268 in 1797. See A. S. Turberville, *The House of Lords in the Eighteenth Century* (1927), p. 492.

Page 364. (1) *that Scotchman*: Henry Dundas, first Viscount Melville (1742–1811), who profoundly and disastrously influenced Pitt's war strategy. He was Secretary for War in the bleak year 1797.

(2) *Our constitution. . . . military government*: a somewhat melodramatic account of Pitt's repressive rule in that decade.

Page 368. (1) *Lord Chesterfield's sage reflections*: the celebrated *Letters written by the late right honourable Philip Dormer Stanhope, Earl of Chesterfield, to his son, Philip Stanhope, Esq.* (1774).

(2) *Paisiello*: Giovanni (1740–1816), Italian composer of the comic opera *I Zingari in Fiera* (1789). Paisiello's *Il Barbiere di Siviglia* (1782) was based on the play by Beaumarchais which Holcroft later pirated.

Page 375. Locke . . . tells us . . . act: he does not. I have been unable to trace the quotation. It sounds suspiciously like Holcroft himself.

Page 379. '*A Daniel . . . honour thee*': *Merchant of Venice*, IV. ii. 23–4.

Page 380. Piquet: a card game played by two, with a point scoring system.

Page 382. rookery . . . fever warehouse: a rook was a gambler or, as Belmont prefers, a sporting gentleman (cf. pp. 374–5). A rookery, like all the other slang terms collected here, is a gambling den.

Page 386. sham-Abraham: or shamabram, a cheat or treacherous person. The Abraham man or bedlam beggar is described in Audeley's *Fraternitye of Vagabondes* (1565): 'An Abraham man is he that walketh bare armed, and bare legged, and fayneth himself mad, and caryeth a pack of wool, or a stycke with baken on it, or suche lyke toy, and nameth himself poore Tom.'

Page 400. '*Mercy . . . jowl*'; Pope, *Epistles to Several Persons*, i. 240–1.

Page 405. (1) *iliac passion*: an intestinal obstruction.

(2) *Quicksilver*: '. . . under proper regulation, it is a most excellent medicine' (Johnson).

Page 414. (1) *custos rotulorum*: Master of the Rolls.

(2) '*Making Ossa like a wart*': *Hamlet*, v. i. 306.

(3) *mephitic*: offensive to the smell.

Page 418. the Lady's Magazine: subtitled *Or, Polite Companion for the Fair Sex*, it was edited by Oliver Goldsmith between September 1759 and December 1763.

VOLUME VI

Page 441. regular branch . . . the chief: on the payment of writers of lampoons and treasury influence, particularly on the newspapers, during Pitt's period of office see Lucyle Werkmeister, *The London Daily Press 1772–1792* (Lincoln, Nebraska, 1963), p. 344.

Page 452. (1) *the animal . . . sucking pigs*: a sow. Cf. 'as drunk as David's sow'.

(2) *monster in the Tempest*: Caliban.

Page 458. marrowbones and cleavers: principal instruments in a band of rough music played by butchers on public occasions.

Page 477. the chiltern hundreds: the stewardships of the Chiltern hundreds, an ancient paid office in the gift of the crown, used as a pretext for enabling a member to resign his seat; first used in 1750.

Page 480. (1) *lock up house*: a house for the temporary detention of offenders.

(2) *trim*: state, situation.

(3) *scrub*: 'a low mean fellow, employed in all sorts of dirty work' (Grose).

Page 481. *hoik*: move quickly; a hunting term used to incite the hounds.

Page 482. *Lord Lovat*: Simon Fraser, twelfth Baron Lovat, notorious Jacobite intriguer, executed in 1747.

Page 495. '*a green old age*': in Dryden, *Oedipus*, iii. 1; Pope, *Iliad*, xxiii. 925.